Dites Oui

Say Yes

B. P. Manning

ISBN: 0615757413

ISBN 13: 9780615757414

Printed in the United States of America

For Beatrice,

Thanks for doing so well with the little you had

Chapter One

Low, wispy clouds crowned the crest of their dazzling heads. Ebony festoons of night thickened, dribbled aloft the tall, majestic throngs that so eerily cluttered a murky black sky. Algid thickness easily stifled the night's spangle. Snuffed like the wicks of a million tapers all shrouded at once, the heavens showed no semblance of light.

Varnished across the foundations below, frost skimmed the crust of inlets and fields, smearing what it could in a dazzling speckle of silvery white. It glazed the surface like enclave mist in adjunct of the sun. A frigid gust swirled raptly through the expanse in-between. Snaking rashly through taut crevices and unprotected husks, it frolicked with the frenzied innocence of kids; yet carved with the virulent edge of a blade. Slashing with ease through the defensive armor of their bodies, vagrants and matriarchs alike bore full evidence of its numbing.

Though hardly unseen, its sting reared with a stealth-like strike. Drilling deeper the longer the warring endured. Its intent seemed hardly virtuous but instinctively malign. Spelt thus with the mew of its sardonic dance, as limbs, in compliance with such operose force, bowed low in a torturous sway. Icy breath nipped harshly at shivering bones, making warmth the hunted trove for one and all. Though only a few now braved the unleashed vengeance, the ornery weather seemed so determined to bestow.

The streets of uptown Charlotte and its surroundings sat tranquil. Birthing evidence of the hour, though, in truth, it exposed, more fixedly, the arrogance of winter's frosted embrace in the severity of its smite. With thermostats proudly displaying their ever descending figures, "fourteen degrees" their faces seemed to sneer. Yet night had barely rested its weary head.

Julia Berwick stepped from the incubated warmth of her vehicle and sighed, cringing as a seemly pugnacious chill sliced beneath the tense layers of her flesh. In retaliatory guise, a shiver promptly rattled her tautening frame. Shuddering through her core as blast of glacial air pelted the exposed walls of her garage, gluttonously imbibing the meager warmth it once held. The wintry gust swallowed the exposed space in less than the honing of a trice. With coat drawn tight against her body, Julia hurried from the drafty room. Eager to feel the warmth of her house, tired feet showed no waver in their hurry. Thus, the coil of her vapored breath plumed softly in her hustle, published fixedly like a mutinous trail around her face with the slightest weight yielded in each pant. Gingerly swinging the large portal shut, she bolted the barrier masterfully without discord or sound, though she could not say the same for what seemed the reverberated grouse of an eruption. Yowling puckishly in its laborious plunge, each inch felt like a brazen heckle from the distinctive yawn of an ominous garage door. Calming visibly with the release of an audible breath, weary shoulders promptly fell as the raucous chorus died. In follow, night again offered no disrupting jangles to be feared, but spoke of its mysteries in the welcomed assonance of a whisper. Julia savored for a moment the essential swaddling of heat. Almost purring in acquiesce of the pleasure such luxury provided and the simplicity of the need.

With a quiet draught of the balmy air, she slowed the expulsion of her breath, alleviating with that the raised hammering in her chest. Languidly, a lazy sigh followed the slow doffing of black, leather boots, tucked firmly beneath her arm. Julia again gave what seemed a timid sigh, discomfited by the hour. She tacked a meek moil to her deed, as if she now feared the sound of her breathing would somehow alert the sleeping occupants of the house.

The mute polish of the wood floor bred startlingly cool underfoot. Cooler than the vacated warmth of her boots, mildly dampened socks declared such observation a factual plight, chilling her toes aptly as she gingerly plotted the placement of each step.

To the casual observer, such peculiar action might be considered an enigmatic display. But to the depleted mother of two, it was a paramount right. Cognizant of her children's uncanny ability to hear her breathe, Julia lightened the volume of each breath. Dimming the potency of her trudge, the dynamic of her passage grew stealthy, for their talent at proving the certitude of that, came frequently at the most inopportune time. A skill well-honed that, at times, had tested the frazzled boundaries of her nerves, one she preferred not to encounter in her present caste of fatigue.

Drenched in darkness, profiles of familiar shadows crouched disconcertingly low. Drifting eerily from blackened corners of the rooms, they gaped questioningly at her cautious progression through the house. A distant street lamp offered its scant light to the slumbering abode, permitting her deft maneuvering of the space with the absence of injury or damage. Julia yawned with inaudible force amidst the glut of her shuffle. Dithering of a sudden in what seemed a swift discard of her strength, now feeling rapidly drained. Warmth cloaked her tired body like a quilt to malleable clay.

With cynicism pasted to its small, rectangular face, the microwave publicized the waning hour in a glare of yellowy-green. *Twelve fifty-one AM*. It shrilled through the muted space. *You're too late to assume your task. Too late to tuck your children in bed and too late to kiss them good night*. This, the infallible appliance maintained in an equally grating scream. And the mocking strongly echoed the cacophonous chants already active in her cognitive sense.

Dragging her fingers through the long, curly mass of her hair, Julia sighed, sheepishly appraising the inflicted reproach, though perceptive that guilt was the embedded shrine on which she now stood. Irrespective of the act, or how unavoidable the task, there was no easing the berating voice. However, with their grandmother attending affably to their every desire, she was at least certain they were seen lovingly off to bed, a fact that had lessened the whirring of her guilt a mere pinch.

Grumbling muscles sang in extol like a choir newly primed. Affirming the assurance of said malaise as she staggered past the mountainous ascension so cruelly branded as stairs. Grateful the promise of reprieve sat strongly within hand, since her bed now summoned from the secluded shadows postured so lordly at the back of the house. A soft glow brushed along the open edges of her bedroom door, spilling faintly to the floor. Warmth bid her welcome like the curling of a hand. Julia walked tentatively across the room to the consoles flanking her bed, gazing happily at the occupant now sprawled in the large, luxurious cot. Her eyes fed greedily on the nourishment acquainted with the splendorous sight. As if guarding the dainty figure so gloriously displayed, the warm radiance illuminated the youthful camber of Rachel's beautiful face, washing what it could of her twelve year old body. It highlighted the still form of what rested beneath the plushness of her covers. Tiny, brown ringlets clung sparsely to her small temple, anchored in place by veil pimples of sweat. Her breath sailed soundless and soft, yet it soothe like an aged requiem once cherished in some distant land.

"At least I get to tuck one of you in." Julia gurgled on the tail of a sigh, pinning the blanket high beneath the hollow of Rachel's small chin. The whispered words floated unheard above the doll-like bundle in the oversized bed, ascending through the quiet at a crawl. A near deific vision to behold in her place of rest, yet the angelic purity of her daughter's slumber seemed surely to belie the wreckage in her wake, and although angels they were, in truth. The pair, most assuredly, had their non-angelic moments for sure. With love frolicking gladly within the dark depths of her eyes, Julia kissed the moistened beads on her daughter's forehead in concurrence of the thought. Adjusting the gleam of the small lantern on the stand, she left it to hold watch over the room. Thus, pointing its dim warmth in every direction at once. Elated, in her edging, for the sumptuousness promised in the torrents of a hot shower, her body spontaneously smiled in anticipation of such treat.

Neither titled nor hampered by the meaning ascribed to such chore, her bed had grown to be an adopted heaven for her children. Together their family had spent endless hours nestled in the warmth of its cozy spread, for it was truly the heart of their family den, though with the wealth of her absence of late. Her bed had become more of a waiting station than anything else. A modest gesture to some, but to her it was greatly applauded for the happiness it granted, as the sight was a profoundly comforting one. Bequeathing much peace on the dregs of each day, it sated, some, her longing for the monotony of a once treasured chore. Hence, the scarcity of her presence was at least palatable with having such end. Yet, at times, some more prominent than others, the spectacle they yielded was almost amusing to observe. With two so small spread so amply over the large surface of her bed, they usually left her no more than a sliver for her rest.

The oddity of the hour furnished little, in proof, in that of the normalcy of her everyday life. For at any other period in time, excluding of late, she would have long since been secured in her bed, or at the very least, bundled within the heated confines of her home. She would have had the added pleasure of enjoying the animated faces of her children, as the three would have since voiced stories with passion while snuggling in bed. She would have heard endless chatter regarding the exploits of their day. Answered curious questions about tomorrow, and laughed as the scratched emergence of their guiltless humor unfolded itself. She would have had the thrill of enjoying dinner as they always had. Playtime, conflicts and time snuggled with them in their own beds, all this had she been where she should. They would've said goodnight without a hitch of bias staining their affection, granting her the pleasure of a warm, melting hug, each sweet enough for you to hang your dreams on, though it was not so in their household of late. Tonight again she slunk home well past the proper hour to enjoy her kids. Yet eons too early to make amends for what's already done, unusual though it is.

For the past three weeks, work had been the dominant impetus in her world, leaving little time for anything but. The adaptation of her book to the big screen, dithered wholly between exhilaration and exhaustion in little more than a flash. Spliced quite affably with everything in-between, the toilsome process left her with naught but to see to its end.

Brain-storming with Phillip Brevard and Michael Dunhill had her mind jutting to its max. Yet for her, the experience had been pure paradise to endure. Frustration was but a scuff she would simply tolerate without ever voicing real words. She would say naught on the strain these long hours had entailed. Since creative sparring was now a favorite pastime of hers. Between them, the contribution had been an immeasurable well, accrued with inputs that can later be colligated into something inspiring. It's a new side to the progression of her work.

The hours just seemed to whisk by faster than their mouths had time to realign in a simulant of rush-hour. Only now the congestion was due to a shepherding of speech. At those times when their babble overrun the best of intent, and time fraught excruciatingly late, as it often does, she has had the option of taking a room at the Ritz Carlton hotel. The lavish lodging had been chicly labeled their workplace for the past few weeks, providing them with a sumptuous space with which to thrive creatively. But sleeping in her own bed and being home for her children had her politely refusing their gift.

The men were as different in their disposition as the palm was to the knuckled tips of the same hand. Phillip Brevard was tall, handsome, smart and a complete pleasure to converse with regardless of topic. Whether the subject remained anchored on work, or waded through the many tiers of life. The result was the same. The married father of two had made working on their project more fun than she once thought she had a right to expect.

His partner, Michael Dunhill seemed strangely, the quieter of the two. Quieter than she expected a man with a reputation as his would be, though he looked as good in person as every coerced photo you find splashed across the pages of magazines.

Michael, the younger of two boys, was born to father, Paul William Dunhill, a famous architect known for his sleek, artfully ingenious designs, exhibited well in the body of his work, and venerated in buildings like the Schaumburg Research Center in Washington D.C. His mother, Hyacinth Carr-Dunhill, was a famous actress from the sixties that dominated her time. Two academy awards pillared Hyacinth's illustrious career, sprinkled throughout with three nominations to complement the auspicious table attesting to the extensive body of her work. His lineage was a well revered colloquy for the majority to explore.

Both parents were known for their stable generosity to numerous charities. Mutually compelled, their outspoken humanitarian voices were as punctual as the unfailing music of one's heart. Diligent in their fight to aid and empower those less formidable in their efforts. Their tireless work was a well-known verity that stretched well beyond the circle in which they resided.

Once Michael was born, Hyacinth slowly dropped from the spotlight, dedicating herself, instead, to her children. She worked quietly behind the scenes, while her husband barreled forward in their unending fight. Submersing herself in the throes of parenting, none could have predicted her devotion having the morose results that it had—the least of all her.

The boys grew up wild and fast. Faster than they should have. And both ran, without reluctance, to the opposite of their parent's prestigious career, as each masterfully commanded the spotlight for all the wrong things.

William Paul Dunhill, the eldest of the two, did not thrive as fortunate as the cohorts that he led, for the handsome part-time model-slash-actor, never lived to see the momentous stature of twenty-eight. His motorcycle collided with a support column—three months prior to the occasion at hand—on the Sunshine Skyway Bridge in Tampa Bay, Florida. With no skid mark and hardly any traffic on the road, a conclusion was easily drawn by an adjudicating public, and varied speculation went rampant all at once. The autopsy report was never released to the public at large, but supposed experts implied well to the gargantuan extent of his imbibing. Supposedly, there were enough opiates and alcohol in his system to have killed him either way.

Fifteen years had somehow flown by since that unfortunate night, and the brother left behind had grown, in his own time, into a respected man. Moving comfortably from drug rehabs to charity benefits and movie premieres, having since niched out a successful career for himself. Yes, the well confirmed bachelor still gets his face plastered across the tabloid pages from time to time, sighting his supposed tiffs with a supermodel or two. But nothing that would dare raise the brows of even the most priggish spectators he had.

With his brother gone and his father following eight years subsequent of that, all that remained conspicuous of the once dynamic Dunhill family was a mother and her son. Yet Michael seemed not in the least interested in changing the bleak status of their family's plight, nor in slowing down the ferocious extent of his amorous drive.

The man of today resembled nothing in the way of his youth. Conferring with the head now fastened on his shoulders, his insight and astuteness won him an Academy

Award nomination for his directorial debut, winning said award three years later for a stirring film depicting spousal abuse. His body of work had slowly grown to a remarkable stack, provoking his best critics to sit up and take notice of the man and the opulence of his work, earning him a wealth of respect from those that now considered him a peer.

In those rare interviews he allowed, he now made certain the reflection states little about the man and his life, and more about his charities and the lengthening scroll of his work. The attention he seemed to once crave in his youth, he charmingly eludes now in his prime. Satisfied, it would seem, to meld softly in the background of everything else.

His evolution seemed, in some sense, a captivating fact that had since dawdled in her head consequent of their introduction, making the matter a worthy irritant to her thoughts. Perhaps the loitering was linked to the tension in her creative pondering, a side of her that vestiges of the man have held notably in hand. Or was it just that she empathized with the tempestuous effort of his strife? Understanding that struggles were a natural bluff in the exigent of each emergent life, knowing for sure, the toll that such climb can sometimes take. It was a process that, at times, seemed unremitting in the agony it gave. Whatever the reason at hand, Julia knew well what the pain of a loss can do to one's mind, her own pain staying fresh heedless of time. It festered and boiled at intervals, as if it had only been a day since that dreadful morning. Yet, in truth, it was not. Three years had since passed, and still only the harshest phrase was used when describing the shattering loss to her world.

The death of her father, George Kenneth Waltham, did not come to them as a shock, but festered like the anticipated crack in a crash. Taken prematurely from his family in the wee hours on a Friday in late July. His loss had been a debilitating strain, feeling much like boulders pressing their wide bodies across the width of her chest. Even the smallest breath, at times, came labored with pain.

Her father was, by far, the revered beacon in the structure that was their family. He could breathe life into any situation with just the gift of his presence. Without him; that light no longer brightened, nor shine, as nothing glowed with quite the same sheen as it once did.

His death came quick, or so they were told by many. Only eleven months after his cancer diagnosis, and although she was unsure how one could measure the appropriateness in the time it took to lose a loved one. She was somehow glad about the shortened length of his suffering. She was glad they did not have to spend years watching him dim in agony, deteriorating from the man they simply adored. No. It was good how he went in the end. He was weakened by the poison that invaded his body, but he still seemed big and strong to her. The man who lingered stubbornly between awareness and death was, in every way, the dissidence of her dad. Unable to grant them the clarity of speech in the end, he was the person from whom her personality was drawn. Ever her valiant protector, his well-worn armor still burnished with the radiance it had always held. Only now, the fit seemed somehow weighty for his gaunt frame.

Delia, her distraught mother, instantly took to her bed, falling into a dark pit of depression. She refused all involvement, including the partaking of food. Julia's fear soared to astounding heights with this new dilemma. Her own sorrow adopting a backseat to what, most certainly, lied ahead should such problem not be addressed. It tortured the already rent regions of her mind. Yet, she knew, somehow, she had to withstand to persevere in the struggle she now had. She did not intend, however strenuous, to lose both parents within a short assemblage of weeks. She'd be damned if she'd allow such tragic sequel without a monumental fight.

Bodily removing her mother from her home, Julia acquired the proper help that she needed; anything to stem the rapid descent of her mother's mind. It took weeks turning into months, and countless hours at her mother's side to reap the full benefit of such a pitiless decision. Talking to her, to nurture the cause, about any and everything, she even enlisted the virtuous help of her children to assist in the attainment of her wish. Together they embroiled her in a sundry of activities, all aimed in aiding her return to them.

Their small family had always been closely knit as a functioning unit emboldened by love, so staying faithful to that was not at all a hard feat. Being an only child abets much in the way of reaction, even when the reaction is considered a strain.

Coercing her now improved mother to give up her home became her most obdurate task. A domicile with a rich thirty-year-plus retention, every portion of their lives was well documented inside each room. More than the premise of a mere inorganic structure, the perception itself had been a notable anchor between them. A choice made by her parents once they transplanted from the north, making the Carolinas their home, birth place was an irrelevant point. It was the only structure engraved in the crux of her memories. The only home she had ever known. All her fond recollections were stashed within the cheery walls of each room. This, she was quite sure, would not be easily done. Since the task would again be a rending to her mother's already beleaguered heart, though the need to ensure her continuous health made the matter, most adamantly, a must.

With angst determination, Julia needled her point home, accomplishing the deed within the vicinity of a year. Though she suspected it was mostly the benefits of having limitless access to her grandkids that finally made her infinite resolve buckle and give. Perhaps in the end it became too painful to endure the stay, living in a house with a lifetime of memories. A house daubed with reminders everywhere of the life she once lived and a love that was no more. Whatever the reason, it hardly changed the result that they now had, and she was just too grateful to care or question deeply the whys. Grateful she no longer had to worry about the peril of her mother's health, at least not with the same terror attached to her frets.

The benefit of a live in grandparent was a priceless indulgence. And with it, she got to witness the resemblance of life returned to a once spunky, enlivened face. Her new zest for life did not come with nearly the same spirited sprawl that it once had. The woman of prior years seemed, in most part, to be gone. Still, Julia's expectations had neither floor nor ceiling written within its lines. She dared not mar the prospect with foolish belief of what was to be. Not when it came to her mother. Not with the kind of love her parents shared. That passion lasted them for the better part of forty years. Expectations or boundaries would have been an insult to the love that they shared.

Her own marriage to David lasted not even a third of that subsistence, only seven years in maximum. A mere pittance in comparison to all that they had. Married immediately out of college, they were both so young. Yet, they were much the same age as her parents when they tied the knot. Her love for him was unending, or so she thought. He, the handsome art student, and she, an aspiring journalist filled with wild dreams, both poised to take the world on by storm. But time drifted and something changed within her and what she once thought was her wants.

Babies controlled her mind, instead of bylines, deadlines or the securing of her source. The passion she once had to conquer the world somehow dwindled and died. All the plans they made together. All their plotted goals, she threw then all out the window in a flash for the want of something else. Her share of the pie in a hectic metropolis no longer bore the flavor it once had. Instead, her heaven came with a white picket fence, wrapped around a small house. Two cars and three-point-five kids was all that she wanted, supplanting all likeness of the woman she once was. Outside of that hypnotic farce, there was just nothing left that she considered a need. In time, David adjusted to her unceasing pleas, and together they made new plans that changed the focus of their path, bringing family from the backburner to the front. He did all that just for the appeasing. Just for her.

Julia worked as a freelance writer while he became the struggling artist with odd jobs to his name. And, at least for a while, they were happy with the undertaking of their prospective part, or so she thought. Or was it just that having her wish rendered her fully blind? She was still irresolute on that, though the complexity of the question had troubled her dearly, enduring, even with time, as a steady fix in her memory and her life. Seven years and two children later, friends, instead of lovers, rested next to each other in bed. It did not seem a logical objective to stay fixed on this road. Hence, supplemental adjustment was made once again, constructing between them new plans. They each took separate paths to the furtherance of self, veering thus as individuals, but not as parents in the crux of their children's life.

Five years have come and gone since that dark, wintry day, and as parents, they still share every-part of each other's lives. That involvement grows ever prominent with the well-being of their children. From homework to teachers' conferences, they equally split everything throughout the year, which included a joint family vacation with David's new wife and their two year old son as a longstanding part of their pack. The friendship they once had was no longer as bulbous as it once was, but conversation between them still came without strain.

With the rending of their wilted world, time seemed to have hung apprehensively in a sphere, and her new status took some adjusting to. Eventually, she did master the wavering of her qualms enough so to start a successful career for the betterment of herself. Subsequent years then grew to be exceptional, with the current year trouncing all others bracing its back. It topped an outstanding pinnacle in her career. The year's existence came with the successful publication of her tenth book, "Early Night" and has walked her felicitously to her present artistic under-takings.

Professionally, her accomplishments have been truly impressive. Interpreted as such, if only in her eyes, for her boundless rewards. Although, in trueness, the matter warranted no further arbiter than herself, for outside of a few things, her complaints on life remained a limited feature. Content in her skin, she strived to bypass grievance or talks of exhaustion for something else, but savor instead, the merits that came with her work. Reminding herself daily of the fortunes she's had, seemed a miniscule deed to dispense, and was inherently thankful for the benefits that accompanied that fact.

Chapter Two

Trees large and unyielding, strewn abundant across the matting of a dormant lawn, with bare knotted limbs sprawled obtrusively through a foggy chill. They fashioned the turf like platoons awaiting some vital command to dispatch an attack. Beautifully roused, the softening atmosphere stirred from its cherished interlude of rest. Straddling the magnificent splendor, the spectacle made it no longer night, though logically, such marvel veered as not yet morning for most. Not so, when time floundered remarkably sweet at the week's end.

Richard's body twitched sharply in retort to the newly refulgent change, stiffening under the bulky blue blanket as if from a stretch. The long edges of the thick coverlet dropped in part to drape the far side of his bed. Shifting under the heavy wrapping, he again jerked with the impulsive haste attributed to a tic, settling in time like a latent rug. Brown eyes opened slowly beneath tightly woven brows, fringed thickly with dark, uncannily long lashes. The thick margins thence fluttered in adjustment to the meager light, quivering quickly in their touch. They worked feverishly to dispose of the dithering tentacles yet bloated with sleep. Drowsy orbs meekly tallied the dense shadows yet swathing the room, chipping at the receding dark as they toil.

The stiff, hazy hue of oblivion gradually lessened. Consciousness slowly sobered his wakening mind, bringing with it realization clipped to an impending spree, his small body jounce sharply with the potency of the excitement he had. "*Yes!*" Richard crooned to none but the somber space, though his exulted hiss leapt through the darkened room like the whistling kiss of a steam engine. *It's Saturday*! His mind averred in a squawk, the enlivened shriek almost breaking the loosened barrier of his lips. In remedy, his back slapped the dense padding of his bed in rejoinder of that. A rare day, though well sought for its rewards. It's the day when the appointed ruler reels off a list of their desired decree, and today's strict governing belonged solely to *him*!

A smile favoring the taunt of an impish sneer, ripened in the corners of his mouth, as the thought of having his way left him ecstatic. Outside the protective cordon of his window, morning had barely developed. Hence, darkness stood more apparent than light, and of that, very little touched the shuttered confines of his room. The hockey mural on his wall still stood shrouded in the shadowy space, as if haloed by a sinister drift of fog tinged with magma. Its artistic details prevailed far from apparent to the eyes. But no-one, advocating caution of such chance, had bothered to establish a rule pertaining to time, so technically, there could be no fault found with his choice. The first light of morning was as good as the midday sun, and since they were fated to do his bidding. He bids that the day begins, *now*!

With a quick flip, Richard sprang from the sheltered warmth of his bed, bounding to his feet. Wiry arms flew widespread with the austerity of his stretch, choking back the haughtiness of his smile. His small body tensed with the force of a fastidious yawn. In a silent dash, Richard winged through the cloak, stillness of the house, rounding each corner on a single leg. He blazed determinedly down the stairs like a plummeting spark, his heels barely landing in their hurry, though they thudded through the reticence of dawn with the efficacy of a mallet being dropped. Trudging a path on his mother's bed, he announced his presence stridently, strangely enough, to two sleeping heads.

"It's time to wake up!" Richard proclaimed in what sounded like a shriek.

"Hmm, urgh, you're up already?" Julia grumbled groggily, her voice pealing muffled from below the cloud of a down spread.

"It's morning!" Richard replied in a shrill boast, almost singing the words as he trounced the padding between them, plopping his body in its new nesting spot. The heavy covering tipped to the left of his hip, slanting as if something alive scuttled beneath the distended ball of his weight. The bedding shifted roughly for a trice, bubbling this way and that until his mother's face emerged from its shallow depths before long. Quietly, she peered at him through a tight frown, a simple question publicized well on the set mien of her face, and he needed no translation to understand the gist of what was implied. In that same soundless question, her attention walked over the dim room, eyeing her window in appraisal from below the set awning of her brows. She cringed as if spotlights were parked in the sleepy hollow of her eyes. In the grayness, the soft gleam of her mood was still recognizable to his eyes, and although she now frowned, her face held the start of a playful smile.

"It's morning." Richard repeated with glee, lowering his enthusiasm a mere pinch. He held tight to the nasally chirp, trying hopelessly not to give into his penchant to yell, even as a giggle twirled behind the singing of his words. "It's morning. The sun is up." Came the additional transmission, as if the news was an emergent bulleting that just had to be said.

"Where? In Britain, Spain or France?" Julia asked gruffly, yet the bite in her sarcastic ode fell remarkably dull. Without waiting for a reply, her head dropped back to the pillow with liberal force, and a tuneful grunt slipped from her throat in bolster of her self-imposed fall.

"Mom!" Richard shrieked haggardly, as if asserting the title alleviated the strain of his multiplying thoughts.

"Richard!" Julia protested with almost matched skill. "It's still dark, there's no sun yet." She whined.

"Can we have hot chocolate in the sunroom and watch it come up?" he asked, shifting his tactics, and in so, dispersed the covet of his first appeal.

"Technically, it's your day. So I suppose that would make it a yes." Her answer came with the affecting of a slow shrug, followed by the careful ascent of her hand. Sluggish fingers traversed the short curls of his hair, coiling tauntingly before falling to his chin. "Did you grow since yesterday?" she asked with a curious scowl, drawing back her hand, she studied him closely.

"I did." He giggled, as if the question was a familiar opening, one he knew well the result.

"I need you to quit that. If I ask you to stop nicely, will you listen?" she asked. The sequel query trailing on the tail of his laughter, sounding drab as the words fell from her tongue. Her eyes brightened as the tips of her fingers waltzed across the lines of his jaw. Richard's giggles grew instantaneously lively, and his body twitched apprehensively under the guidance of her hand, as if his nerves now stood strangely on end.

"No." He hummed, his answer coming in a near wheeze.

"So I guess it's up to me to do something about it then—" she griped, pouncing with a swift grunt, her fingers hooked sharply to the side of his neck. Turning, they twirled mercilessly over the warmth of his skin. Richard's body kicked weakly as a result of her ruthless strive, thrashing under the moil of her hands, it jolt forward in an attempt to stem her relentless attack. The muscles of his stomach shuddered with the clout of his laughter. The melody of which warmed like a cozy fleece.

"Say it! Promise me you'll stop growing this very minute." Julia commanded sternly. "Say it! Say you'll stop." The ultimatum came smothered in her mirth, pressing his small body to the comfort of her pillow. She plowed every inch of his body without sign of relenting. Long fingers worked industriously along the ridges of his sides, climbing to the warm pits of his arms. She heightened the attack, sending his body in a frantic spin. From her back, Rachel's rhythmic giggles mingled well with Richard's phonetic squawks, as if she, too, was under some form of attack.

"Wait! Wait! Stop!" Richard pleaded weakly, beseeching his case through the peal of a cackle. His hands clung tightly to her wrist. "Please! I give! I give!" he cried through a whispered breath, tensing from the remorseless pace of her hands.

"Do you promise?"

"I promise," he shirked with a quick nod, unable to fully command the muscles needed for speech. "No more growing."

"Are you sure?"

"I'm sure." He avowed with a ripening giggle. Constricting his grip on her wrist, he lashed his mother's still moving hands, determined to stall her punishing limbs. Gradually, the pressure eased from its devilish intent, settling back on her heels, her wavy hair fell scraggly from its clip to dangle down her back. Her big eyes shone bright with the dividend of her laughter, and even in the dimness, he could still see the beauty of her face.

"Mwah, mwah," she purred as her lips welded to the small slope of each cheek, and the sound of her kisses rushed through the murky room like the gentle smack of a hand.

Grazing the soft plumpness of their faces, she smiled. "Hey, you," Julia whispered as their laughter fade to a hum. "How are my angels?"

"Good." Their voices came in light unison, pressed still with residual mirth.

As if recognizing the meaning behind the trumpeted waking, Rachel surveyed the shadowy room, narrowing the roundness of her eyes as she worked. "Let me guess," she started in a tempered tone. "Today is Richard's day to crack the whip?" She asked with a stiff smile. Angling her head in question, her enormous brown eyes rolled upwards to an unseen sky. Seeming set to exact harm on whomever it touched, namely the energetic ball now twitching at her side.

"Yeah!" Richard publicized brashly, pride eroding with the word, and much like the parroting of a geyser. It sprung freely from his body with a bold semblance of glee, falling with triumph to the center of the bed. "And I'm not about to waste any of it." He continued in a shrill cry, maneuvering his small body between them, he pounced from the bed. "It's time for hot chocolate!" He called, prancing towards the door like a boastful cock parading the vividness of his feathers, excitement stretched tight across his face. "Come on! Let's go!" He beckoned from the mouth of the room, his body already tense. Wide eyes further widened with anticipation, though his face creased with a deep, definitive smirk as Rachel snorted noisily her response. Rolling her eyes in difference, she stared at the ceiling as if it exhibited some new contraption of art. Richard's jubilant mood persisted without pause, slowly acquiring his mother's eyes, as he knew the matter would be fixed with just that.

"Coming right along, sweetie," Julia answered, decreeing his approaching question with a smile. Dropping a hand to Rachel's arm, she gave the small limb a gentle pat. "Let's go have some hot chocolate." She muttered proficiently, swinging both feet from the bed, she quickly donned the heavy robe draped callously along its edge. "Oh look, sunshine!" She professed sarcastically, emphasizing the words with a superbly feigned smile. Though Richard's frenzied mood, in truth, had no damper fit to do it harm, hardly noticing the attack. He looked ready to jump from his skin.

"Yeah, it's blinding." Rachel's echoing voice followed coolly, rich with matching sarcasm, it skimmed through the unruffled morning air. "What fun." She smiled tersely, radiating this with a halfhearted gust, it exposed the skill of one well past her tender years.

"Why don't you guys go and get your slippers on and meet me in the kitchen." Julia directed calmly, warding off all further comments in its track. "I'll be the one sleeping on my feet." She smiled, raising her brows with a wistful sigh. She dropped a gentle kiss to the top of Richard's head.

Streaks of brightening blue painted a once heavily gray sky. A blast of color adorned the near gloomy horizon, blooming above the distant heads of trees. Orangey-red shocked the far sky, erasing night's dullness from its face. It beckoned like rushing water to a canyon. Julia's breath sailed softly over the dark, sugary liquid in her cup, taking a careful sip, she sighed as warmth raced through her body.

"Beautiful, isn't it?" She avowed then, given as an assertion of fact more so than a query, her eyes seemed unwilling to rescind their appreciative hold. "This is my second most favorite time of the day." Julia smiled, and her testimony came with the serenity of a sigh. A quiet wisp that swept softly over the brooding room, it stirred none but the morning's chill.

"So, big man, what's your plan for today?" Julia asked, locking her chilled fingers around her mug, her eyes moved slowly over his curling head.

"Can we go to the pit? Their racetrack is really cool!" he began as if selling an essential point. "Then can we go see the new Iron Man movie at the IMAX? Then after that, maybe we can go eat at Sogo? It's so much fun there! It's so cool how you get to watch them prepare the food!" Richard eagerly ranted, barreling excitedly through his list of request before he abruptly slammed his mouth shut. Realizing then he had not yet gotten an answer for the first. In his hurry, he lost the remembrance to wait, racing through his demands. He forgot to give her an opening to consider the worthiness of his plans.

"Sure." She shrugged, her answer falling with a light sigh once the opening was had. Certain there was more, Julia waited for the hovering shoe to drop.

"And can we stop at the new toy store? They have the biggest and coolest electronic selections." He assured through a murmur, almost wincing with the question, he calmed the roiling of his nerve. Swallowing, what felt like a mouthful of saliva, he stared nervously at his hands. The room fell silent in reaction to his plea, though his mother gave nothing in the way of a response. Neither did she flinch with the absurdity of his demands, as if inspecting the floor. She stood silent. "While we're there, can I get that new game I told you about?" He asked in finish, rushing through his words. He turned his head with the offering of a smile. A dazzling gleam, of which, mere words would do it ill.

Rachel coughed lightly in rejoinder to his nonsensical solicit, slapping her hand to her mouth. She scoffed loudly at the air. Warning him with the non-too-subtle gesture how stupid a task it was to ask, especially with Christmas being so freshly in the past, now exactly one month to the day. Ignoring caution, he therefore ignored her with proficient skill, since her input was neither important nor necessary at that time, only the woman to his left carried that distinction, and his eyes were already stationed on her.

His mother's gaze lifted from the place on which it hovered in retrospection, lowering slowly. It settled tamely on his, viewing him with a quietness that was more tensing than being scolded by an ogre. Her expression showed the extent of her knowledge, devoid of any note of surprise. She was always good at that. Nothing ever seemed to get by her, that's why they rarely tried. Without acknowledging his question, she lifted the dark, mug to her mouth, blowing softly at the heated vapors as they rose. She quietly slurped the liquid inside, breaking the aching silence that now stood in wait.

"Mom," Richard mumbled hesitantly in start. "Before you say anything, I've given this a lot of thought." He droned, nodding as if confirming his own thoughts with himself. "I'm not asking you to buy it for me. I have twenty dollars left on my gift-card from Christmas and five dollars from my allowance, I'll just use that."

"Didn't you get a few games for Christmas? Your father alone gave you three."

"Yes, but…I really want *this* one."

"Unlike all the others you already have?" Julia smirked, gazing down at his head as it quietly drooped, and she could almost smell the fragranced heat of his brain as it churned in its wish to stay ahead of her. The cup in his hand appeared to have forgotten its mark, and his brows pleated with the strain of his thoughts. "How much is this game?" she asked softly, aligning his mind with a new thought.

"I don't know." Richard slurred with the sprouting of a new frown, realizing then that he had forgotten an important detail in his research. Details in what he once thought to be a good argument well suited to win.

"And what if you don't have enough?" Julia asked softly, giving him the time and opening to recuperate from his loss, for she enjoyed watching his brain work. Putting full thought into the things that they want had never been an element discouraged in her home, and never will. And although the result was not always as they wished, they'd always have her undivided attention as long as they were willing to do the work.

"If it is, then I'll take on a few more chores—your choice." He added quickly. "I'll work without pay to cover the balance." He hummed, nodding sharply as if the gesture would then aid the path of her decision. Richard's eyes flashed bright as the answer slipped from his lips, and pride again assumed its rightful place on his face. While his mind quickly assessed the logistic in the wordings he gave, his body expanded with the heated gust of himself. And in the quiet that followed, one dark brow rose slowly above eyes that studied him with leisured resolve.

"So, you're willing to give up your allowance for an undetermined period of time without even a second thought?" Julia asked suspiciously, needing to be sure he understood the extent of his plan.

"Yes." He blurted without hesitance or pause, and saw his mother's cheek dimpled with her smile. Her interest was piqued and the thought was tremendously reviving to his spirit. "I won't ask for anything until my birthday." Richard dug smartly, going in full for the kill, his face contorted strangely with his mumbled speech. Yet his words came half in question, as he waited anxiously to see which side would take hold.

"You wouldn't be able to afford it!" Julia reminded him then, chuckling almost fully under her breath. "You do realize if you do this, depending on the cost, you may not have access to any money for a good period of time?" His only answer was the vigorous bobbing of his head, and the width of his grin returned again to an immaculate spread.

"Wow!" Rachel gasped, breaking her enduring silence with a single word.

"Impressed?" Julia asked in a dissident tone, throwing the question at her daughter with a smirk, a playful twist now jumped to her brow. Lifting the now cooled liquid to her lips, she stared out the window as if in thought. Proud of the argument he gave, she saw no reason to deny his request.

"Maybe," Rachel mumbled haphazardly, unwilling to give her full concession of his gain.

"Then I'll say it," Julia smiled, gazing down at her son, she ruffled the tight curls of his hair. "I'm very impressed, Richard. You put your thoughts together very well, not bad."

"So I can get the game?" Richard promptly asked. Slamming his mouth shut in an instant as his mother's palm waved like an impending gavel through the air. It then froze staunchly at her chest.

"Richard," Julia sighed in start, his name falling with what seemed a reluctant breath. "The money belongs to you. It's not that I have a problem with you spending your own money. It's that I need you to learn the difference between needs and wants." She intoned sagely, dropping her hands to his shoulders, her fingers curled as she pulled him snugly to her side. "If you spend it because you can, how will you know when to say no to yourself? How will you know when enough is really enough?"

Richard nodded slowly in response to what seemed an esoteric speech, beaming brightly. He gazed into the bright pools of his mother's eyes, hearing only half of what was being said and understanding even less. Captivated with the accomplishment of his feat, impressing his mother was like having his favorite candy on the side. Without lifting his head, he searched out a viewing of his sister's face, eager to capture her expression for posterity. Her mien did not dishearten in the extent of his search, for it was truly what he suspected it would be.

Gaping at his features with what looked like a quizzical gawk, she half smiled in disbelief, and her frown looked almost chaotic in its set, that is, until she recognized the enormity of his gloat. Her eyes slashed across his then with malicious intent, rolling with blood guzzling force atop his skin. She quickly presented him with her back. And he could not remember a sunrise being more brilliant than the one they now had. Or silence being more enriched than this moment that they shared. It was a priceless occurrence to be treasured for sure. One that would last a lifetime with the sweet reverence it held.

Chapter Three

The collective sounds of congestion roared through the thoroughfares like equivocal sequences from an octet. Pared notes echoed off sturdy structures, soaring gracefully above the lesser floors of towering edifices. The breezeways of uptown Charlotte gave no credence to the hour or the day. Midweek was as gruffly coiled in this megalopolis as any other in the week.

Shards of sunlight frolicked across the tall, reflective ingress, mirroring the sky's punctilious glee. Its fervor scorched the edges of winter's voracious bite. Methodically, the doors to The Ritz Carlton sway sturdily shut and the clamor of a city, with the dash emit of a breath, punctually died.

The opened entrance caroled of an oasis. Wedged inside the punishing flay of an asphalt jungle, it gifted sweet serenity to the visitant's mind. Exquisite furnishings adorned the expansive lobby, complimented well by richly colored art. The opulence of such assuaged the senses as profoundly as the etching of a fine picturesque. Lodgers and visitors alike ambled gallantly through the tedium of their day, submersed in the spoils of business or play, yet their discourse hardly ruffled the tranquil poise adorning the room. It simmered, instead, like the distant humming of a strange song.

Upstairs, Phillip lumbered through the doorway of his office. Groaning with the finish of what seemed a robotic sigh. Somnolent eyes strained in their focus, adjusting their determinant nature beneath the sheltered weight of his frown. Gruffly, he scuffed his hand in a rough swipe across the ridges of his brows, taming whatever raked his thoughts with yet another humorless sigh. Stretching his long arms wide, he all but swallowed the room with the powerful aperture he affected with his yawn.

Torpid steps duplicated that of an android. Trekking the wide span of the suite, he staggered impatiently across the threshold of the kitchen. Yawning as long fingers folded tensely around the sleek body of his mug. Pouring himself a third refilling of coffee, in what was still too early in his head, Phillip groaned in expectancy of the taste. Not bothering to add his usual embellishments to the scalding beverage, he fervently swallowed the intoxicant drink black. Absorbing the first mouthful of caffeine, his eyes, blanketed well by wilting lids, rolled upwards in his head, and a long, distended growl rolled forth from the chasm of his chest.

The heat rappelled his insides like the toasted rub of a hand, fanning in every direction at once. His body welcomed the warm bitterness with a slow subsiding breath. Anticipation soared high for the induce adrenaline to rev, as he hoped to rouse the drone still quiescent somewhere in his head.

The day's customary liveliness was slow to torque the mellowing of his mind. And already he was looking forward to its end, needing to recoup a mountain of misplaced sleep.

His lengthy weekend started well earlier than most, hence home sprung foremost on his long list of chores. Thankfully, the short trip to Texas took only a miserly pinch of his time, since his, by then, was already sparse. Knowing this, Phillip filled the modest two days with everything that he could. Aware that his absence, at times, was more than a husband and father ought to have had, and that the plane simulate the succor of home far more than it should. Whether such reasons spout from the anxiety of work or through the rarity of play, the essential craft avails itself more so than the bolstering walls of his house, soaring vast at intervals outside the reach of his control.

New York City rose as his next objective, and first on the agenda was a sequel meeting with Simon Cox—a probable director for their upcoming film. And the man seemed as closely matched to his infuriating quirks as he was to the talents that he had. An evening devoted to charity followed promptly on the meeting's heel. Tending as a strong tribute to his mother, Phillip worked tirelessly in his support for the research, cure and prevention of breast cancer. His mother, now five years departed from said disease, was a constant force as to why. Paperwork necessitating his attention, meant a trip to his office in Los Angeles, where lunch with their potential female lead topped off the crest of his hectic slate. With all this done in a matter of three days, omitting those spent with his family, his body now asserts a litany of complaints, and the lag seriously hindered the jot of joviality still tack to his mood. In that, he suspected it will take a generous heaping of the dark addiction to keep him going on his feet this day.

The suite sat uncommonly quiet, considering the occupants sheltered inside, it simulated the eerie hum of a cavernous womb. No sound filtered the crisp reticence it lent. None but the stammered pecking of their fingers or the sometimes placid shuffling of feet, for none but that dared disturb the lingering peace. As if both men distinguished the fundamental need to languish near the portico of death, they embodied the hush. Reticent, as if their bodies demanded the silence to soothe itself, they each worked on separate task with naught but a few exchange.

Michael set his laptop sluggishly to the waiting cushion of his seat, lowering the lid as if to hide the contents of that page. He dropped back lazily in an arduous stretch. Gathering the dark promise of restiveness in a drink, lean fingers huddled gladly to the heat radiating from his mug. Carefully heaving the steaming chalice to his mouth, he mimicked the intake of a vacuum, slurping the flavorful drink. Michael sighed as warmth bellowed hastily throughout his chest.

Comforted by the antidote in his hand, his head fell slowly backwards. Cradled within the plush cushions of his seat, he liquesced gladly in the muted pleasure that so dominated the room. After the harried weekend he'd had, the morning seemed aberrantly stuttered. Ticking remarkably slow—or so it seemed in his head, though the residue was nothing that a few days by the pool wouldn't cure. Of course, a reprieve of such kind surely needed to be followed by a collection of undisturbed nights in his bed. Hazel eyes flashed lightly with a hint of amusement in their depths, brightening as the quiet supposition rolled pleasantly through his thoughts. Dragging in another mouthful of the searing drink, he smiled at the aberrant thought.

Finance and procuring their means had always been his assigned domain, leaving Phillip to work the pivotal end of creating—which on its own was no small feat. Over the years, he had flourished advantageously better at his job, and his weekend was dedicated to corroborate the revenue of just that. Making certain all parties stayed happy in their appointed post can sometimes be an exorbitant deed. Though locating the right investors was a trick he had since mastered with experience. If not vigilant, the hawkeyed presence affixed to said financier can be an overwhelming force with which to contend. Their fickleness, at times, is of legendary scribing, with God-like afflictions that can render even a mild-mannered man mad, and only the patience of Job can see such moments through. Snorting succinctly at the vision, Michael groaned, and a stingy grin dented the corner of his mouth in concurrence of such truth. Slowly, his eyes tumbled from the ceiling, turning towards the sound of Phillip's stammered steps as he broke the barrier of the room.

"Jeez, you look worse than I feel." Michael teased in a slurring tone, adjusting his body. He took a guarded swig of the dark elixir in his hand.

"Why, are you looking to take a nap, too?"

"I wouldn't turn down the opportunity if it came up."

"Do you think we're getting too old for all this running around?" Phillip asked tamely, as if accentuating the truth, he carefully lowered his body to a chair.

"Speak for yourself, old man. How old is Britney now anyway, twenty, twenty-one?" Michael grumbled, arching his back, he rolled his head with supremacy dotting his eyes. "Soon you'll be able to add grandpa to your list of titles. That should be fun."

"Eleven!" Phillip barked, disgust splicing his word. "And it would do her godfather good to remember that fact."

"Whatever you say, grandpa," Michael smiled, throwing his eyes to the ceiling, his long, muscular arms rose indolently over his head.

"Jealous, are we?" Phillip called from behind his cup.

"Why, are you looking for company in your life of misery? I think we all know who is jealous of whom."

"At least that ego still has you for a mouth piece. Someday soon I guarantee it will drop you for a smarter host." Phillip shot back testily, swallowing another mouthful from his cup.

"Is that what you call the truth these days?" Michael quizzed, shaking his head slowly, he daubed a healthy portion of pity across his face. "It's a damn shame when the truth brings such heavy denials as its reward."

"Someday you'll find yourself wishing that you had—as you say, 'my kind of misery'." Phillip tossed back smartly. Conscious of his friend's softer side, he knew Michael's personality was not only what he allowed intrusive eyes to see. Years of experience have thought him that a deeper river ran beneath the suave exterior that he showed. The truth was just well protected from most.

"If that day ever comes then the method should be easy enough to rectify."

"Is that so?"

"I don't think I need a degree to be successful at it. You put it in, make your deposit then wait for the return." Michael assured with a chuckle, as if his words form an ambiguous picture in his head where only he was privy to the show.

"Are you planning on being selective with which temple you make your deposit in? Or is walking the street until you find one, more your style?"

"I could go through all the work just to rival you and prove I'm the better man. But who has the time? It's easier to just let it be, knowing frankly that I already am."

"You know, I saw a lecture on this very topic just the other day, it was fascinating. What was it they call it…?" Phillip frowned, angling his head pensively toward the ceiling, his eyes glazed as if consulting his thought. "Yes, that's right, pusillanimous!" he howled, lunging his body forward, he landed a satisfied smirk on the figure across the room.

"Whoa! Are you alright?" Michael asked, jolting forward as if startled by a sound. "I know that must have caused you some pain." He averred gruffly, a light grunt following his smirk as he relaxed back on the couch. "That's an awfully big word for someone so… farcical. I'd hate to see you break something."

"Still smart enough to know I'm swinging it better then you, that's for sure." Phillip groaned, touching the rim of his cup to his mouth, a gesture that deepened the rumble of his gargle-like tone.

"Funny," Michael growled, tossing a fixed glare at his friend. "I see jetlag wasn't the only thing you manage to pick up over the weekend. Somewhere along the way you acquired a near humanoid sense of humor. Now all we need to do is hone the darn thing, this way you can use it when the need arise. You know, for those occasions when you're actually expected to make a modicum of sense when you speak."

"How would one discern the difference? All I have is you and your skew on logic as an example. Now that's hardly authentic."

"No fret, I'm happy to help you whet your humor. It's the least I could do to help you right yourself"

"What about my better human example? How do you suggest I combat that?"

"Just look in the mirror and go for the opposite of what you see."

"So that's what you tell yourself every day." Phillip smirked. "Now I know."

"I don't need to do that. I'm the opposite of you, remember? I'm the true vision of what you strive to be."

"Only on those days when the planet gets turned on its head," Phillip rasped, rolling his shoulders to ease the stiffness of his frame, he leaned his back hard against the plush comfort of his chair. Weary limbs took their time in finishing a languid stretch, dawdling as if unsure if the effort was worth the work. His ankles cross in an odd embrace as the bizarre spasm ended. "Usually on those days I just bury myself in the various layers of work and pray the travesty over, which, of course, lessened the chance of that ego popping out in someone's face."

"It's a pity you picked up something akin to humor and lost your sense of honesty, which, by the way, was, without a doubt, the best quality you had. It was the only thing that made you vaguely human." Michael gargled in response, his words coasting with a protracted stretch, finishing the appeasement. He tested his friend. "So, now that your mouth is all revved up, are you feeling better?"

"Actually," Phillip drawled, silently assessing his mood. "I do. Thanks. Stepping on you always helps."

"Careful, wee one, you need to first learn to crawl before you try to walk in this arena or you just may get hurt. Now where's the food? I bet that would go a long way in returning you to your old self. However dull that is."

"How long ago did you order?"

"I didn't order." Michael frowned. "You went to the phone to order…what, more than half-an-hour ago?"

"Oh, right." Phillip grunted, slapping his forehead with the tip of a finger, he shrugged. "I got sidetracked with my need for coffee instead." He explained with a slow roll of his head.

"I can see how that would be a natural with you." Michael apprised with a slow nod, amusement etched boldly on his face. "For such a big head, it's amazing what little goes on between those ears. Sipping coffee and thinking, that's a monumental undertaking for you."

"Now look who's claiming humor for themselves. I don't think it's a good fit on you."

"Listen to you test those puny wings, be careful now. Remember the warning, tot, persistence is not always a good thing, it can leave you discolored and bruised." Michael scoffed, reaching for the phone, he smiled. "By the way, from up here you still look and sound green to me, but I'm prepared to help you out. You can have some of my droppings to aid you in your need. You know, to help you smooth out that void you call a personality. I know you know that even my rejects are better than anything you already have."

"I think I've had enough practice tiptoeing around your droppings, thank you very much. I'll take the zero on that. I'm managing just fine with what I have. My basket still has more than just one egg."

"Why? Is the bouquet not to your liking?" Michael laughed, his eyes flashing as he eased his long body to the opposite end of the couch. "Besides, my one is a world of difference than what it means in yours. Single does not always mean the same to most men." He avowed firmly, finishing with a wry grin. He threw his head back with the ambling of a wide smile, as if the act was to savor the memory of a time past. "What are we ordering?" he asked calmly after a time, returning his attention to the room.

"Get some fruits—lots of fruits. Our writer likes that. I feel for pancakes and eggs, what else is there?"

"Where's the menu? Now that we're talking food, suddenly I'm starving."

"It's your mouth. It's always been the true source of your drainage. Slow down the usage and you'll find yourself better equipped to face the world. But to simplify the gist for you, *try shutting your trap*!"

"Are you sure you know the full meaning of those words?" he asked in a slow meticulous tone. "Or is it really too early in the morning for you to understand the jeopardy of that? I'd hate to have to be the one to give Sarah the bad news about you getting injured somehow." Michael smirked, throwing a stern glare at his friend's advancing frame. Phillip slapped the menu pointedly in his hand, muttering a few choice slurs in his retreat. He made clear the definition of an empty barrel as he slumped in his seat.

The familiar bantering was the kernel from which their friendship sprung. Spurting profusely whenever work was not the leading theme, the rapport was what made their partnership work as well as it had. To him, Phillip was family. The son his parents never had but should have. With William gone, very few people were allowed close, and even fewer pacified the emptiness that remained with his loss. Over the passage of twelve years, Phillip had carved his own notch of importance in his life. Business came four years into the existence of that alliance.

Sarah, Phillip's wife, was an up and coming fashion designer when they met. The unique flare to her fashion was beginning then to start a lionized buzz, and Phillip's name, at that time, was merely a tame form of address. At the budding of their friendship, Michael was at the culmination of his awakening, learning then to start his life anew, when Heather, his then girlfriend of sorts, made the tame introduction.

Phil was so different from the friends he had gotten used to. Different from the boys turned men that he grew up with. His personality was straightforward with an odd logical twist and much like the craving of a chair, what you saw in him was indistinguishable to what you got. In addition, he had a wickedly dry sense of humor, talking with him was incredibly interesting and fun. With Phillip, he did not have to defend his decision to stay clean. Or explain why he no longer ended each evening getting soused or flying high. He was just allowed to be. Taking that time to develop into whomever he was meant to, and knowing it would be without incident whatever the result, for nothing else seemed to be required of him.

Phillip also had an exceptional mind. One he used astoundingly well. Diligently working on the things he wanted to achieve. For him, settling was never an option. The world would knock him back, but he kept striving, reaching farther each time for a little more of the pie, he gathered a little wisp with each stretch. He learned a lot from watching those two, this while fortifying his tractions on life. Yet in the beginning, they seemed almost amazed by the friendship he struck, but it was he who sat in awe of the two of them.

Now the legs that once found no footing could bear their own weight. Capable of trudging through many doors unaided, he commands his own respect. A once no-name screenwriter, he now had a name. With a few master-pieces under his belt, the acknowledgement of his peers stood strongly as proof of such, though he remains a valued anchor to this day.

Resettling himself on the couch, Michael sighed, stretching out his long body; he reached absently for the remote. Hazel eyes, in pursuit, immediately ran to the clock, tacked contemptuously on the wall to his left. It drummed in tune to his brewing angst. With the choices made on their food, the room again fell to a hush, as both men seemed too fatigued to again make work or start the trappings of a conversation. But he needed something to occupy the revving of his mind. Come ten o'clock, the energy of the suite will automatically change to something else, shifting from a slow hum to that of a buzz. Her presence seemed to always affect the room in the oddest sense, and for that he needed the distraction.

As if cued by some strange need, his mind flew effortlessly back to their first meet-ing, remembering her captivating entrance in a voguish boardroom downstairs, he almost purred in accordance with the vision in his head. She strode in then, wearing blue jeans and a black, waist-length jacket over a slinky red top. The tempting blouse gave nothing away but what your imagination was willing to take, and his imagination was surely tested that day. From the delicate part down the center of her long, brown hair, her tress was worn bone straight, with large, soft curls sweeping past the slopes of her breasts. A black coat was thrown casually over the bend of her arm, partly hiding the stylish briefcase holstered in her hand underneath. It took every bit of his strength and that held in reserve to put his eyes back in his head on that day. The temptation to gawk at her for the duration of their meeting was more than a goal. It bore the intrigue of a rare event.

Being out of the country at the time, Phillip had been the one to take their prior meetings. Yet all his longtime friend would commit to relay was that she was very nice, leaving him to wonder whether the avoidance was done on purpose. Her pictures strove well short of doing her justice, and again he could not help but wonder if that, too, was a deliberate infraction on their part.

The quiet rambling spawned endless images in his head, dragging his thoughts to places it should not venture at this time. Thus Michael's mind searched anxiously for relief, twisting his wrist discretely, he again displayed his watch, gifting the time in what now sprouted as his fifth viewing. On their own, his eyes flicked in the direction of the door, and he was again confounded by this odd response. Life, for him, had always been the same in the pleasant palaver of the opposite sex, appreciating the splintering essence of a beautiful woman. He effectively dated more than just a few, and although the truth was he considered her a pleasure to view. The heretical daze made little sense.

Regardless of when or how, whenever she walked in a room, something very disarm-ing and nervy followed her presence through. It gored almost as deeply should he be rocked with contrition while in the midst of being bad, yet it was the same no matter how much the preparation for their exchange. Straightening, Michael shifted his body from its agitated slouch, lengthening his legs on the floor. His eyes again grazed the face of the clock.

"Are you really that hungry?" Phillip smirked, taking another gulp from his cup. His eyes followed his companion's cue. You would have to be truly blind not to have noticed Michael's curiosity with the writer. Not that his subtle questions about her were not all great clues. Although he barely showed evidence of that to her, a fact Julia hardly seemed to notice or care, for whatever the reason. She seemed frankly immune to the effects of his irradiated charm.

"I told you, I'm starving." Michael scowled, almost snarling as he spat each word. Flipping his eyes in the direction of Phillip's chair, he saw naught of his friend, wanting only to squash the topic in its track. His eyes rushed back to the television screen. Hoda Kotb from the Today Show conversed with a panel of women in her usual effervescent way. However, the focus was lost to him, since his mind, already a firestorm of thoughts, barely registered their gurgled murmurs through the quiet.

A light tap echoed through the suite like a throb, and the slow rhythm in his chest ceased its strumming for a short trice, rebooting with a lunge before galloping on high. And he almost laughed at the eccentric nature of that, wondering then if his reaction was due to indecision or was it just nerves? The very nous of his being knew this occurrence as something new. A simple attraction he understood, that was nothing original to him, or to any man, for that matter. But this was something else. This anomalous response to her was a whole new world for him. One he needed to be schooled on.

"Good morning!" Phillip chortled, swinging the heavy door wide.

"Good morning!" Julia beamed back, her oval face creasing into a wide grin, hooked by the contagious exuberance he dealt.

"Come in! Come in!" Phillip beckoned gaily, flapping his arm brusquely towards the open door. He stepped aside to facilitate her entrance. In the distance, a faint ping scuttled to his ears, warning of the elevator stopping on his floor, and he could almost see the doors jerking open in suspense. Phillip waited for Julia to step by him and then paused. Hoping the soft clinks he heard was not just his imagination, but real glasses making inadvertent contact with each other.

He had not long to wait before confirmation came at hand. Displayed aptly in the conjuring of an immaculately adorned uniform, the tall attendant commanded his attention in full, and as he watched his methodic approach. Phillip could not help but muse at the intensity of his stare, deliberating whether it was his eyes or his stomach that kept him rooted in place.

"Just in time!" Phillip called, humming his simulated praise almost two doors before being certain of his terminus, vowing mutiny on the cart if it passed his door.

A small smile registered on the young server's face, showing off a tiny gap in the upper front of his startling white teeth. His effort grew concentrated then. Phillip beamed back almost anxiously, stepping fully in the breadth of the hall, he ushered the young server inside once confirmation was made. His tall body curved high above the clatter of the loaded cart, maneuvering the mobile stand through the door, he smiled his accession. At his crown, short, bristly, red hair swirled almost unruly against his skull, and bluish-green eyes seemed bold against the paleness of his skin.

"That's actually one of the unwritten mottos we have." He announced with a widening smile, and flints from his southern accent stroked his words with pristine warmth. "We aim to always be here exactly when you need us," he persisted, lifting a dome lid. The radiance of his smile blossomed into a garden of its own. "Anticipate, even." He smiled, tilting his head as if to make an important point, he returned the lid as controlled as the sterling top was removed.

Like dust carried on the vortex of a strong gust, the booming smell of bacon swept ponderously through the room. And one could not fault the assumption that that had been the intention behind the display.

"Thank you." Phillip answered somewhat gruffly, almost wincing behind what seemed uncharacteristically tart, hoping he did not truly sound as curt.

"It smells great!" Michael called from the sofa, gulping in a strong whiff of what now taunted his nose. He smiled with inert satisfaction. Quietly, he ambled off to the kitchen to refresh his cup, using the time to sedate both mind and body. He attempted to appease the confusion he felt. At the sound of her voice, his body bounded from the sofa as if compelled to do so by concealed strings. And the potency of his movement seemed truly outside that of his control.

From the distance laid between them, he watched her enter the suite, with what he hoped was casual interest lacing his gaze, and had already noted her manner of dress. The moment the dark coat slid from the slender width of her shoulders, his eyes had paid full homage to the view. Impressively, black stood her choice for today. Though he could hardly ignore, even had he tried, the gray leather jacket she wore. The stylish piece promptly swapped her outfit from hot to a downright sizzling affair, as the topper looked, quite surely, to be sewn to her skin. Carved enticingly about her body, it singed itself to the indent of her waist, held aptly in place by a matching belt. The wavy strands of her hair were swept back from her face to hang vicariously down her back, leaving an unhindered view to her features. Long thread-like earrings dangled past her chin, floating jauntily around the angling of her face. The assemblage was indubitably to his liking.

She stood serenely quiet. Separate of the men. She politely awaited Phillip's completion of his task for further entry in the suite. Collectively, the two had constructed an outstanding rapport, one that worked well even for him. Preferring to leave the hierarchy as it was, it was surprising how comforting he found that fact to be. Fully content to observe their playful dialogue rather than partake when it came to her.

When his mind was fully entangled with work, he was essentially at ease. But the playful interactions were what seemed to give him pause, that being a datum that made little sense to his disposition or logic. In the many pages of his extensive resume with women, he had yet to meet one that had ever toggled madly with his nerves, except in the odd way she affected him, and he had yet to figure out a reason as to why. The door slammed hard behind the server to signal his exit, and Phillip's voice soared to slice happily through the mutterings in his head.

"Julia!" Phillip warbled gladly.

"Phillip!" She chirped back, matching the rhythm of his glee.

"Come in! Come in! Let's eat!"

"Is there something you're trying to tell me, Phillip?"

"What do you mean?"

"I'm just wondering if I should be looking over my shoulder, that's all. Am I expected to be snatched someday soon or do I have some time? You know, it would be somewhat courteous for you to at least forewarn me, I have my kids' wellbeing to consider. At least let me have some time to make arrangements for that. So tell me, is there a witch that's going to be checking the meat on my bones or not?"

Phillip's deep laughter cracked through the subtle tone in her voice, breaking the playful satire that it held. The rhythm bounced joyously from the walls of the dining-room in which they now stood, waking the suite's long slumber. The room shifted as if being sharply stung, and life immediately reared its happy head. Fracturing the sluggish humdrum it once held, all this from a simple jest.

"Are you trying to fatten me up for something or do you just think I look that bad?"

"Well..." Phillip smirked, and his eyes danced with the vehemence of his wit, rushing in that instant to Michael's face. Once again, his friend had gone unnaturally quiet as he was prone to do of late, which within itself was a phenomenon for sure. An eccentricity worth noting, having never witnessed his friend this simmered before. At least not while in the company of a beautiful woman, and the intrigue sparked by his behavior moved him fully to mischief.

"Julia thinks I'm trying to fatten her up to serve her on a platter to someone. Or that I'm trying to tell her she looks bad. What do you think?" Phillip asked calmly, his voice a pinch below a whispered hum, and like a seasoned lecturer, professional sugar buttered every word. Phillip noted with humor the smile his friend gave him, all be it somewhat stiff, before his eyes shot to Julia's face, lingering for a short spell. They dropped like an anchor to his cup. An inner smile seeped forward with the revealing sight, now even more confident with his earlier assessment. He racked his brain on how to better sweeten the pot.

"I say don't trust him." Michael mumbled in what seemed a callous tone, lifting his cup slowly to his mouth. He focused only on his task—another trick used to stay casual in her disquieting presence.

"Even after such long proven simpatico, you still advise me to trust my instinct?" she asked, a pleasant smile washing her face.

"I hardly trust him further than I can see him." He averred, lifting his shoulders casually as if to emphasize the accuracy of his point.

"So there you have it, Phillip." Julia announced with a booming smile, returning her gaze to Phillip's back, she watched him busy himself in the unloading of the cart. Placing a small platter on the table, he chuckled to himself. "You're not to be trusted, Phillip."

"In my defense," Phillip simpered, slashing a stiffened finger through the air, it pointed to nothing but a chalk-white ceiling. "I'd like to state that my action is just a long standing family trait. Blame it on my mother's southern roots." He shrugged, balancing a plate of bacon in his hand, Phillip smiled. "In our household, we all love to eat, and my mother loved to cook. It was the perfect partnership between us."

"Are you saying then I shouldn't fear you making a deal with some evil witch? In regards to me, of course. I mean…whatever floats your boat, Phillip, as long as it has nothing to do with me."

"In all my years, I've only come in contact with one evil witch. Well…warlock would be a more accurate term. But you can call him a witch if you like that more." Phillip assured with a chuckle, grabbing a quick survey of his friend's face.

"Still working out the kinks in that new found humor I see. I'll have to buy you a book on that." Michael nodded faintly.

Snickering in response, Julia returned her attention to Phillip's busy hands. And his expression simplified the relationship they had, looking undaunted like one who had hardly heard the utterance of his friend. He gave neither heed nor response. Discreetly sniffing the flavored air, her stomach growled softly as the smell permeated every corner of the room. Thus it goaded her into accepting the truth, and missing breakfast had, in no way, helped her case.

"Madame, your throne awaits you." Phillip teased, sliding the familiar chair from its place.

"Why, thank you, kind sir." Julia laughed, playfully tipping her head. She watched as he accepted her action by repeating the gesture to her. Lodging himself in his usual seat with Michael now slow on his tail.

Except for the clatter and clinks of utensils against plates, the room fell to a gradual hush. Soft chatter rose cordially from an unseen television housed in an alternate space, aiding the muted chorus of the room. The cadence of their voices in time returned to again dominate the placid calm, setting precedence for what assuredly entailed another arduous workday to come. A promise that none there seemed resentful to embrace.

Chapter Four

The ordinary urgency of the region slowly fell stagnant, and hordes of vehicles, in time, gradually dwindled to none. Trees stood resplendently gallant in place of houses, and the jubilant descant of birds replaced the chaotic roars of exhaust.

Julia steered the black SUV from the small thoroughfare it had journeyed for a goodly length. Turning right onto a narrow, gravely extension, immediately the era terminated from sight, and yore seemed suddenly an untouched reality that lay bare to her gaze. Julia slowed her skulking vehicle to a stop in repute of the eccentric thought, frowning lightly as she consulted the directions at hand. She laid a timid gander out her window into what looked surely like the past. The makeshift pocketed road looked desolate and foreboding in its long lazy stretch, more so than the welcoming alleyway she predicted brashly without pause. Vastly overgrown trees guarded both sides of her passage, most now void of their leaves, remnants of wild flowers and weeds carpeted the ground footing the knotted giants' heads, rich in nature's own natural disarray in their spread.

With confusion mounting, Julia gaped back at the portal's mouth, gauging her wildered surroundings from the folds of an incessant frown. She mentally assessed each turn to her present end. The place hardly seemed formatted for industrial trades, much less residential habitation, yet she had followed the directions as precisely as it was referred. With a moderate draught of air, she gingerly eased her foot from the brake, and watched as a rising dour of dust whistled behind the jarring cracks of her wheels, painting the scenery in grayish-brown.

"Damn!" Julia swore pithily at the rearview mirror, seeing her recently washed vehicle now tarped by a new cresting of dust. *It never fails,* came the seething grumble, eagerly shadowed by a disgusted grunt as she again glanced at the simmering dust, feebly shaking her head at the result.

The first sign of life came in a small, rustic, iron gate, looking the full width of the provincial graveled road, the unassuming postern stood fully widespread. Two equally rustic, metal pillars flanked the heavy posts principal to the gate's ethereal stance, each bearing an amply sized solar panel as a topper for its head. The isolated contrivance was the only indication of possible existence, as the canopied dirt road seemed to stretch for miles, with no furthering clue as to an end. At a duteous mile deep within the woodland's belly, the road eventually split, with both lanes steadily bowing to contrasting ends. Julia's suspicious glint sparred with the scenery before sliding to the decreeing paper holding on her seat.

"Left," Julia confirmed in a low breath, laggardly obeying the directive, she pursued the induced dialogue with a factual sigh. "Man, he's really well hidden sitting in a place like this." And the marvel she bore for the unspoiled environment was fully noted in her voice, rearing evident as she peered impatiently through the thickening cluster of trees. Except for the mistimed quibbling of pebbles and the snapping of twigs, the air was amazingly tranquil. Silent to a fault, it sat unmarred by the impudence of manmade noise, since the only sounds discernible to one's ear were of the things that made, what looked richly like a wildlife preserve, their home.

Stifling a sudden gasp in a needless reaction, Julia slammed her foot irksomely on the brakes, startled by a lone ATV rider that appeared unexpectedly from a curve just ahead. The new motorist, regardless of her response, was well within a safe distance. He, in no way, impeded the procession of her car. In truth, only the shock of seeing observable life on the once deadened road sent her heart on a boisterous sprint. Thudding in her chest, her pulse hammered as she waited to see the rider and his intent. Yet, as like a cynical sigh, the forgotten gate locked soundlessly in the farness, barring the road from further intrusion, and her from quick retreat.

"Good morning!" Michael called with a casual wave, smiling as he shouldered his vehicle within a stone's throw of the place she stalled. His demeanor seemed faintly apologetic for being the cause of her sudden distress.

Julia's smile was instantly dynamic, and a sudden surge of excitement flooded her frame, eagerly stabbing her hand out the window. Her limb flapped with little evidence of a bone, recognizing the man was implausibly more pleasing than it should have been.

"Did you have any trouble finding us?" Michael asked as he drew near, using inert caution in his approach, he repeated his earlier warnings with each step. *Just keep everything short, Michael and you'll be fine.*

"No, your directions were very clear." She chirped politely, her eyes intently following each stride.

"Good. I know we're a little out of the way, but I promise you, there's a livable structure somewhere inside all of this." He reported in a low, unaffected tone, letting his eyes skirt the waned lushness that adeptly swallowed them. Winter's harshness had played havoc on the trees draping, but the enormity of their figures and the diverseness of their mix, kept the integrity of the vast estate well preserved.

"That's good to know," Julia rejoined in an equally low voice, and her eyes strolled the wilderness with an appreciative glow, greatly lessening the intensity that was once displayed in their depths. "It *is* a little bit of a trek." She sighed, apprising him of the simple thought as she returned her attention to his face.

"I know." Michael nodded, again eyeing the greenery with a lenient smile. From the woods belly, it was easy to forget that the city was only minutes from the very spot that they stood, or that modern facilities were not still in the embryonic stage. "That's what I love about it." He expounded lightly, and his sigh gave reverence to the quietly spoken words. His eyes slowly followed the path of her earlier lingering, dropping of a sudden to his ride. He realigned his thoughts. "So…anyway," He grunted, his tone swerving to that of a dry hum. "The gang's all here. So let's get you up to the house." The announcement came in a sobering tone, and the words barely fell before he turned for his mechanical mount. "Just follow me." He explained, and immediately scolded himself for the blunder. *Smooth, Michael. Where else is she going to go?* He grumbled crossly in his head.

"Okay." Julia answered with a polite nod, and watched with interest as he sauntered back to his waiting ride. The menacing carriage resembled the marred ghoul of a rugged steed, though four wheels, instead of legs, graced the stalwart body. Complete with front and rear bumpers, the seats rivaled any luxury car. The bright red vehicle screamed in the silence of a dusty green background, flaunted like some obscured picture once seen in magazines. Michael adjusted his helmet gruffly, moving his attention to the fingers of his gloves. His frame straddled the manmade beast before resting. Giving her the weary sense that somewhere in the gruff swirl of society, a photographer regrets missing the exoticness of that shot. In flawless tempo of the view, he moved with a simple unassuming stroke, and the beast snarled under him like some prehistoric fiend. Soaring like a blast in the encompassing quiet of the woods, the two scurried off ahead of her.

The additional mile did not feel as lengthy in his escort as it had in her timid commence. Although she did, at times, question if there was, in truth, an end before they happened upon a second gate, and its purpose was where all similarities ended between the two. The eight-foot tall minacious guard waited patiently open, and nowhere on the heavy gate, did she perceive a hint of welcome.

Julia's gaze again tunneled the soaring thicket, probing their depths for a glimpse of the phantom house, keen to ease the nip of curiosity from its perch. The massive gate quietly jerked forward as two cleared its reach, slowly barricading the road at their backs in an eerie rendition of a robotic crow. And somewhere in her mind, the peculiar sound of an organ being wildly thumped, jumped mockingly to the forefront of her thoughts. Stirring a new contemplation to life, it challenged her reasons for not giving the subject more reflection than she had, for she truly had not thought twice about accepting the suggested stay. Agreeing fully with the purpose—perchance, due to her blind dedication to work—hitched well on the chance to have two uninterrupted days to finagle the script, this, of course, could not easily be snubbed. It was the only distinction that jumped in her head once the topic was broached. With Phillip and his wife in attendance, there was little left to deliberate upon. Certain Michael Dunhill had no interest in her, since supermodel-slash-actress was not among the many titles in her name.

Their tiny convoy rounded yet another bend in their unrelenting run, and the road began a gradual transformation from its archaic self. Dusty gravel became more smoothly compacted, showing tame evidence of a real road, until an intricately tiled landing welcomed them as easily and as dogmatic as an exclusive neighborhood would. The long cobblestone driveway edged by a waning thicket, soon gave way to a large manicured lawn, walling their entrance with perfection. The vision stole a sharp intake from her breath.

Ahead, a large house waited unobtrusively on their approach, not unlike a stranger who greets you as a friend. The building was not at all how she pictured it in her head. This was not what she expected from a Dunhill. Not *the* Michael Dunhill. A name so synonymous with wealth would be expected to have a grander showing. And although the structure was substantially grander than hers or, for that matter, any she had ever been in. It was not the preposterous gaffe she expected. But then, Julia concluded almost snidely, she was not a Dunhill, and that kind of grandness had no place in her life or her expectations.

The driveway coiled to form an expansive circle against a collection of steps, emphatic in its sprawled eminence. A small island of near lush grass carpeted the center of the curving drive, showcasing a massive sculpture made fully of bronze, now richly seasoned by the elements vended by time. The aged piece was elegantly distinguished of itself. With each layer intricately spiraled within the next, one braid flowed into the other like the continuous swing of a musical note. As if in harmony, they reached dexterously for the heavens as one.

"Welcome to my home." Michael announced in a pleasing tone, though the gesture was more polite than it was friendly. Pulling the silvery-black helmet from his head, he dropped it to the seat. Gloved fingers raked roughly through the short matting of his hair, returning ungloved to neaten the job. His expression verged the line of being aloof.

"Thank you. It's exquisite." Julia remarked kindly as she stepped from the car, gathering her bags, her eyes roamed appreciatively across the stoned facing of the massive manse. Traditionally designed with an odd mix of the castles of old, it stood majestically as a stylish blend of both.

"Thank you." Michael nodded faintly, his retort coming with a smile. Hazel eyes moved with open affection over the wide structure and, as if settling a new thought with himself. Visually, he aligned the theory of some pondering in his head. "As they say, you can only have one real home…." He muttered matter-of-factly, holding the intone more to himself, his smile dimmed as he returned his attention to her. Mentally clamping his mouth shut, Michael stalled the procession of what almost slipped from his tongue. "Anyway…shall we?" he asked instead, motioning to the steps with a tame wave of his hand, he relieved her of the brown overnight bag before he turned.

"I see you found us." Phillip called from the landing ahead, his wife looming eagerly at his side.

"I did. Not too shabby, huh? But you had me doubting my perception there for a minute." Julia warbled with the broadening of a full smile.

"Actually, she found us with no problem." Michael added quickly, singing the praise as if prompted. He clarified the meager accomplishment for more than it was.

"Hi!" her chirp sliced aptly through the small pause, a tuneful Texan drawl veering sharply on its tail. No longer comfortable with waiting, the petite woman readily advanced, thrusting her right hand forward in haste. Her smile was as resplendent as the sun.

"Hi!" Julia sang, returning the wide smile. She took hold of the proffered hand, gladly repaying the firmness in her grip.

"I'm Sarah!" She continued, tightening the clasp of her hand. Her broadening grin looked fondly like the eroding shore of a beach. "Phil's wife," she expounded then.

"Hello!" Julia simpered, nodding politely. She waited the release of her hand.

"I'm sorry. I forgot you guys have never met." Michael hummed dully, his deep voice cutting through the airiness of the women's tone. "Julia Berwick…Sarah Brevard. Sarah, as she so proudly stated, is Phil's wife,"

"Nice to meet you," Julia vowed, again gifting a polite smile, while still awaiting the return of her hand. Sarah nodded affably at the introduction, as if his words carried more credence than that of her own. She flashed almost every tooth in her head with the liveliness of her smile.

"It's so nice to finally meet you." Sarah sang loudly. "I'm a huge fan of your books." She smiled, pulling Julia's hand like a thread through the needle of her arm, she turned towards the door. Lively blonde curls bounced around her petite shoulders with the swiftness of her turn, brushing gently against the beautiful roundness of her cheeks.

"Sarah was the one who recommended your book." Phillip clarified quickly, his voice strong with its usual lively mischief. "Adamantly, I might add. She prides herself on having a good eye for quality and she hasn't been wrong yet. Now you know the secret of my success. It's my better half that makes me look brilliant." He pledged, sending a slight lift in the jousting of his words.

"Now what you need to ask yourself is this, Phillip, what are you willing to give to keep that secret?" Julia asked, throwing the question sweetly over her shoulders, her jest flew as easily as their usual innocent barb. "I'm not easily bribed," she smiled. "But there's always a deal that can defy the odds. It may turn out to be painful for you, but so much sweeter for me with the promise of such an enticing end."

"Perhaps I can get back to you on that. I may need to tally my records, so to speak."

"No rush there." Julia shrugged. "Your secret is safe for now." The lively jest came with a playful flip of her hand, flaunted like a queen dismissing an undeserving subject. She returned her attention to her blonde companion and in this, Julia feted her new cohorts with an exuberant smile bonded to her lips. "So I should be thanking you for all this work?"

"Actually," Sarah chirruped puckishly, leaning her face close, her action mimicked that of old friends sharing secrets of a time long past. "I think that bodes more fitting if it's viewed the other way around. Your books are truly a pleasure to read, inspiring even. The bathtub scene in your first book, 'Friendly Strangers' still culminates its own vision of an undeniably squally session," Sarah purred, her right brow ascending slowly in explanation, as if to deliver, of all things, the manual of a comb to a Rastafarian. "I'd pay to see that on the big screen any day." She laughed, and blue eyes twinkled with the mischief of a teenage girl.

Julia again repaid Sarah's laughter with an easy rejoinder of her own. Already familiar with the passage on which her companion now attested, having had a few letters
from fans explaining just that. Prideful in her meticulous wording of each scene, her
plotting was cast to evoke much havoc on the reader's emotion; so feedbacks were
always a well cherished theme.

Worried of a chance intrusion by the men, Julia glanced over her shoulder to better
judge the volume of the space between them. Michael looked up at the exact minute
she turned, as if sensing she would, his smile seemed almost sunny. Short, wavy hair
still looked matted from his helmet, though the miniscule flaw mattered not in the
encompassing view, as the lapse only served to enhance what was already there. And
in that instant, she understood why he had such mystique with the public at large, that
public, of course, being women. The man was handsome without a visual flaw, and there
was no obscure way of disclosing that. Even the most discerning eyes would likely have
to admit that fact regardless of relevance or profit.

Phillip, the shorter of the two, paused in his discussion to look past her at his wife,
quietly; he leaned with a terse comment on some mysterious point. Spoken in a whispered tone, Michael smiled, nodding his head, he added his own short reply, and again
their conversation resumed its life.

With the muted, brown marble of the foyer forgotten, their footsteps echoed over
the hardwood floor like jumbled taps on a drum. Festal burst of sunlight welcomed
them to a grand living-room space, and a large, elaborately designed fireplace was the
first to grab her attention. However, the furnishings came swiftly on its tail. Neutral
tones dominated the large space, varying from the walls to the furniture. A steady hint
of color was splattered beautifully throughout the calm, breaking the resin of the soft
tints. The decor was classy. Elegantly done, the ambiance's theme seemed cooked with
the natural coarseness of a rustic cabin. It was unmistakably male without the guns,
blood or antlers on parade. A décor that looked to be as untitled as she now wondered
if he, in truth, was. Prideful, with a tone that was tastefully exquisite, but simply done.
This, again, was not as she expected, and again a peculiar swatch of amazement scuffed
at her head. Quite assuredly, Mr. Dunhill was sponging clean all preconceived opinions
she had originally formed of him.

"How about some coffee to ward off the chill?" Sarah asked gaily, her diluted Texan
accent bouncing cheerfully through the quite space.

"I would love some, thank you!" Julia sang, unable to resist the enthusiastic swing
in her voice.

The long, wide hall led them past a prodigious dining-room. Inside, the immense
table looked to be sliced from the extensive bark a tree. The dark inlays within the
sprawling bark were like ancient scrolls of art for the eyes. Fourteen toffee-colored
leather chairs were planted around the smooth, yet naturally sculpted edge, as if they
too, sprouted from the tree itself. Nearing the kitchen, the aromatic pleasure of mixed
spice whirled tauntingly through the air. Of the shifting anthologies of smells, freshly

baked bread claimed the senses as the most distinctive, dominating the spicy aroma of the house.

"I hope you brought your appetite with you," Sarah warned. "Betty has been cooking up a storm. We weren't sure what you like, so, she made everything."

"Why? You really didn't need to do all that." Julia hummed, whipping her apology with sincere shock. "Whatever everyone was having would have been just fine."

"I'm just playing," Sarah laughed, nudging the other woman lightly with her shoulder. "But don't be taken back by the food, that's just Betty. Once she's expecting guests there's just no stopping her. Isn't that right, Betty?" Sarah called teasingly as the two entered the kitchen.

A thin, dark skinned woman looked up promptly from the stove, offering a bright smile. She quickly dropped her attention back to her pots. A splatter of oil nipped at the reedy skin of her arm as the sizzling pot willfully spit its attack. Betty clutched the affronted arm to her chest, mumbling sternly under her breath before adding chopped onions and garlic to a near smoking pot. The smell of freshly baked bread overtook the fusion of the room. Extinguishing all other smells from existence, this as she dipped over the oven and quickly filched a peek at the rising dough. Satisfied, she released the door with a push of her slender hips. Yet her action seemed schooled with enough skill that the echoing thud never came.

Julia smiled in admiration of the older woman's bent, enjoying her brusque movements about the kitchen, for she conveyed the grace and agility of a woman half her age.

"See what I mean?" Sarah chirped. "There's no stopping her momentum." Her affection for the older woman corpulently painted to her voice. "Betty, come and meet Julia." She called to the woman's back. "Julia, this is Betty, the head cook and…Well, she's the head of everything around here. Betty, Julia is the writer we told you about."

"Oh, how nice," Betty smiled, wiping her hands in her apron as she hurried to their side. "Sarah tells me you're very good," she announced. Clasping the other of Julia's hand in that of her own, dark eyes smiled openly in greeting. The harmony of her voice waded like a low, melodic hum, sounding much like a librarian in the giving of her words.

"I'm not sure that's true, but thank you."

Behind them, the grumbling lid of a pot gave argument to that of its own concern, angrily expelling white froth from its mouth to aid in the clash. Betty spun without pause at the sudden commotion, rushing back to the crowded stove, she called. "It's very nice to meet you!"

"And you, too!" Julia chirped back, genuinely pleased with the introduction.

"No matter how much you beg her not to, she out does herself every time." The whispered explanation came with the gentle wobbling of her head. "At times, it's as if she has her own contest to outmatch whatever courtly creation she's already concocted." Sarah smiled, patting Julia's arm as if to settle the point. She glanced absently around the kitchen. "We should get our coffee and go before we get kicked out." She announced with a light frown.

"Good point. Betty hates people messing in her kitchen, and she hates it even more so when they stand around and watch her work." Phillip chortled, as both men, at last, breached the threshold of the kitchen.

"We'll get the coffee." Michael muttered dryly, directing his gaze to the chirpy blonde. "Why don't you show Julia where she can put her things? Maybe she would like to make herself more comfortable now that she's here. Perhaps get her coat off even?" He droned. Full brows rose high with the question, followed slyly with the gentle tilt of his head, amusement laced the composure of his voice. Turning his attention on his guest, he addressed her like a virtuous host. "Your bag is already waiting in your room. Should you need anything, please, don't hesitate to ask."

"Of course you would!" Sarah virtually shrieked, looking ready to camouflage herself in red. She squeezed the svelte muscles of her captive's hand, giving with that a sigh. "Forgive my manners," She laughed almost shyly, no longer looking like an energetic light. "My parents would be so disappointed if they knew I forgot my hospitality. I'm so sorry. Let me start over." She informed in a small voice.

"There's nothing to apologize for. It's fine, really. You've made me feel very welcome, thank you." Returning the earlier pats to her hand, Julia smiled at her petite companion with open generosity coating her gaze, hoping the small gesture would also be of comfort to her.

"Let me take your coat." Sarah twittered as she straightened, at last releasing the arm she had since claimed as her own.

Julia laughed softly, shrugging from her coat. She found two arms stretched forward in wait, each with dissimilar bodies attached.

"I'll take the coat." Michael smiled. "Why don't *you* take her up to her room to get comfortable?" His mandate fell dimly with a soft kick of his head to further clarify intent, yet his voice held the infer of mischief laced within the thin layers of each word. Laying her coat across his arm, Michael turned from the kitchen, leaving the small group behind.

The smell from her coat was distinctive, reminding him of a flower that he had only known in one place. At night, the perfume would permeate the house on his Island stay, giving off the most intoxicating smell. That smell had always eluded him until now, never having smelt it in any other place but in a tropical setting. Not until it whirled up his nostrils from her coat, and the garment seemed an intrusive source of that smell, her smell.

Michael brought the alluring garment close, unsure whether his effort was to confirm or to savor. He took infinite care not to show interest in the deed itself. Filling his lungs with the aromatic fragrance, he was promptly taken back, and the incredible sweetness of those tranquil nights was once again his. Of all the varying smells that pervade the world, he thought it strange that her attar was of the one flowering scent he thought to be a favorite of his.

Chapter Five

As if vetoed from their morning, work seemed a prohibited word, omitted from the gales of their rambunctious chat. The group scathed past said subject without discerning or revising the truth. Hence, by the time they were called to lunch, their only achievement to that effect was on the part of socializing.

With conversations thus distended, Julia was happy to find an opening to reimburse Sarah's kind esteem. For not unlike the sundry of women drawn to her fashion, she was likewise a fan. The aura ascribed to her designs tends to transcend the bearer's mood, and its mesmerism seemed attuned to the ruttiest thoughts. The infrastructure of which, Julia now suspects to be a personality trait. And she wondered on the efficacy of a good bottle of wine on a character such as that. Fascinated by the thought, Julia smiled. At the very least, it would make for titillating research, and she almost giggled at the vision that surfaced in her head, stifling, in a flash, the need to assess further the merits of her plan.

Conversing was to Sarah an unquenchable repute. Falling as natural as her breath, she remained fully fixed to Julia's side. With her passive Texan drawl flowing like warm honey from her tongue, the harmony of her speech intensified once conversation shuffled to the topic of her kids.

Jason, a baseball enthusiast, was named the starting pitcher on his little league team; a sterling accomplishment for which both he and his parents still burbled with pride. At divergent end, sits the younger of the two, and the piano thrived as Britney's forte, preferring to play above all else. Her recitals had her parents equally fulfilled.

"Hence the reason for the piano," Sarah explained then in a cynical tone, happy to brag on the merits of her longtime friend. She enlightened her companion through a dividend smile. "As her godfather, he thought it only natural to oblige her with the piece." She scoffed, trimming the gentle teasing with a slow shake of her head. She aired the full extent of her pity, rolling her eyes drolly over said body. She finished the gesture with a fond smile.

The object of her ridicule gave none but a small dismissive scowl as his reply, seeming somehow content to leave the matter as it was. He uttered naught but a light grunt in his defense. Laughing, Sarah lost no time in furthering the thrust of her attack, seeing proof of Phillip's earlier conjecture come to light. Since Michael gave no answer through the entirety of her jeers, wagging his head at intervals through his conversation with Phillip. A tame glare skimmed his petite antagonist like a throw, and the vision was quite comparable to a squirrel imitating the slouch conduct of a sloth.

It was a quieter kitchen that welcomed their vociferous return. Gone was Betty's frantic waltz of haste. The swift twirls of her skirt were now simmered to a lively hop, for although the rush of preparation stabled, the elderly woman, however, did not.

Her skeletal frame moved with much determination through the luminous space. Arranging the last of her masterpiece, Betty stood back at last with a satisfied smile. Glazed across the edges of her dark orbs was the prominent look of pride, it billowed vast as her gaze surveyed the room. Just as gallantly demonstrated was the elevated comber of her love, emanated warmly throughout the room. It grandly exhibited her sumptuous efforts.

The large, round table was perfectly dressed for the occasion at hand, encumbered with food at every point, all judiciously verified by her silent account. Of a sudden, Betty's shoulders climbed through the simmering air, dropping heavily almost at once; as if to rest a burden she had carried too long.

"Lunch is served," She announced proudly. "Enjoy." And the radiance given in her smile blossomed fully to her eyes, making a quick notation of the occupants' faces. She delivered the mellow invitation to each with a genuine smile.

"Thanks, Betty." Michael called brightly, hurrying forward. He pulled her to his side, and his face promptly shed its usual grimness for a teeming smile. Tightening his arm around her thin shoulders, he dropped a kiss to the top of her speckled hair. "You've outdone yourself—again." He praised through a light mutter, while his eyes walked the wealth of her work.

Betty nodded faintly in response to his courteous words. With gaunt fingers splayed lovingly across the ribbing of his chest, she tapped lightly in forbearance of the pause. Yet her eyes never rose to give heed to his quiet avouch, searching out imperfections in her work. Betty's eyes were fully entangled in their task.

"Thanks, Betty!" came the appreciative cheer, coasting boldly from every lip. It cruised auspiciously above their heads, and equally adoring eyes were attached to every-one. Julia smiled, mouthing her own thanks. She considered the man and his apparent fondness for the cook, and she could not stop the inundation of respect that suddenly gored her regarding that one.

"Everyone, grab your plates and fill them." Michael encouraged with a grandiose laugh, and its richness seemed queued to her modifying thoughts, as if to mock the pre-formed absurdness she once stashed away in her head. "And I do mean fill them," stating the velvety command with the slow lift of his brows, he emphasized the friskiness of his mood. His throaty timbre softened with the purity of his smile, sprouting then with the disparity of night and day in one face. "Now, let's eat!"

With perception newly bloomed, Julia found herself riveted to the man. Deducing the rarity of this strange evince before her eyes, she thought it bizarre that he had never before flaunted that side of himself. Or that she had never seen him come close to looking that relaxed. His persona had always been more reclusive than not, like one who carried a vast weight on his back with no hint of reprieve. Though in its unfurling, his smile strode natural, no longer unbending or reserved. Here the blossom traded his handsome face from princely into a swiftly lethal display. Soft hazel eyes undaunted in their resolve, promptly noted her, and the true effect of his smile touched her then with the vastness of its strength.

"You may have already noticed that these guys like to eat." Sarah began in her melodic drawl, and the music of her voice effortlessly clambered through the other woman's thoughts, puncturing the acoustic clash of their plates with its cheery pitch. "So you'll need to claim your steak before they're all gone." She chimed tunefully, her eyes bouncing playfully over Julia's hesitant stance, and a meek chuckled surfaced with the humor her words profess. "Well…" she started with a crimped shrug, rolling her eyes upwards as if to check the workings of her brain. "If there were steaks to be had," She smirked, elevating her small shoulders, she groaned as if struck by a puzzling thought. "Everything looks so good." Sarah averred in a grumble. "I'm having trouble making a choice, what do you think, Julia, chicken or fish?" She asked, pausing barely a full second before disbursing her request.

The blackened red snapper lay garnished with onions and an ample portion of sautéed herbs. Boasting an aroma that was needlessly persuasive; the choice for Julia was a simple one. "Fish," Julia declared without shifting her gaze from the object of her choice. With seafood being her favorite, the stuffed breast could hardly hope to swerve her attention from its usual bent.

"I'm a Texas girl," Sarah shrugged, having already made her choice. The coy murmur came with an apologetic snort, as did the pertness of her humor, each doused heavily in-between her musical lith. "We live for meat and potato."

"So I see." Julia simpered with a quiet nod, realizing then that the simplicity of the request was only meant as a means to relax, an anecdote, of sort, to put her at ease.

"I'm sure we can manage to leave you something." Phillip charged, his sarcastic manner breaking the continuous clanks of utensils against plates. "If not, Sarah can whip us up something really quick." He advised brightly, his notice cruising like a rough, rumbly chant, thus he fought a dismal battle to remain looking stern.

"I can whip you up something alright." Sarah droned. "Whether you'll want to eat what I've cooked is another question." She informed tamely, a thrifty shrug rearing with defiance, and its vanishing was of little consequence to the effect it intended. Adjusting the plate in her hand, Sarah continued the vim of her haphazard selections before expounding in a syrupy tweet. "I'm hospitable, charming and creative, I don't cook." She smiled, reinforcing the statement with a brusque shake of her head. Her gaze jumped to the other woman's face, and nowhere in the blue fleck of her eyes were there any dusting of compunction to belie her speech. "I've learned to stick with my talents." She shrugged tightly. "They like to give me a hard time, because I've had a few bad blunders over the years."

"A few?" Phillip blurted rashly, and the look his wife sent him confirmed the gravity of his mistake, stalling his blunder without any expanding dictum on that point.

She had a way of speaking her mind without wasting a word, and after more than fifteen years together, Phillip knew those meanings well, even when they're done in a moment of jest.

"Fine, more than a few." Sarah admitted easily with a smile, though her eyes edge a warning to her husband's face.

"Your pots signed a petition to keep you out of the kitchen." Michael inserted quickly, witless of his friend's silencing, he continued the musing unhindered by the same restraints. "They were all tired of seeing so many of their friends die at your hands. My stomach still sends them thank you cards every year." He chuckled, covering his mouth as Phillip sent him an applauding grin.

Swallowing her smile, Julia left her expression blank, unsure of her companion's true feelings, she dropped her focus to the floor. And like a wayward sheep, she was the last in their small procession to shuffle forward for a seat.

"In case you forgot, Michael," Sarah grated sweetly, her gripe flowing with a cool, retarding smile, aimed staunchly at her objective's head. "I do have a very good memory, like an elephant, I never forget. Good enough to remember if or when favors are asked." She smiled, and her serene mutterings sailed with a lengthened stare.

Clearing his throat with a stern cough, Michael's tall body instantly straightened in his chair, and a slow bob grappled with his head. As if the two had had an understanding that was crossed, his sobering words came soft. "I'm sorry." He intoned faintly, yet a brazen smile walked unflinching with his expression of regret.

"I thought you would be." Sarah chimed prettily. The soft comment rolled with an affirming nod, although her accompanying smile held only sugar, and even in its shortened state. It was enough to send his body into diabetic shock—had that been her intent. "Now," she afresh with added warmth pasted to a smile already nearing its max, "as I was saying…" Sarah continued, giving voice to what rang like notes in a song. She returned her attention to the only other woman in the room. "I don't cook, but I'm good with that. Every so often I'm plagued by the urge which never ends well." Reporting this, blue eyes flashed with tinder specks, lingering hard on the men, she awaited the expected jabs to ascend. But all eyes were conveniently, otherwise involved. Well satiated with the power she now had, Sarah gave a rapturous smile. "Do you cook, Julia?" she asked softly, relaxing in her seat.

"I can make a few dishes." Julia mumbled nonchalantly, making less of her answer than the fact.

"Would you like some sweetened tea or—?" Michael asked blandly, hovering the chilled vessel expectantly above her glass.

"Tea is fine. Yes. Thank you." Julia assured lamely, fumbling without knowing why. She ended their interaction before it began, realizing late that he had not yet gotten to the end. Scolding herself sharply for so foolish a reaction, a terse groan trundled through the stun caverns in her head. "Thank you." She repeated in a strained tone, as if to regenerate her reaction to those stilting her manner of old.

"Julia." Phillip called in a raspy tune, his pitch no higher than an acknowledging sigh; yet, for her, it came like the cry of an orchestral harp.

"Yes!" she chirruped sunnily in response, strangely happy for the interruption to her thoughts. Her excitement surged, knowing she could again converse with the one she was most comfortable with.

"What are your plans once you're rid of us? Are you going to take a break? Or will you be jumping right back into work?"

"I think it's advisable I take a break. That's if I want my kids to still speak to me."

"I take it they're having a hard time with the hours you've been keeping of late?"

"That's putting it mildly." She quipped.

"What do you think your next book will be about? Have you tamed the importunate demons as yet?" Sarah sliced through bouncily, curiosity firmly holding her tone.

"Well," Julia started with a coy smile. "I have a few ideas but I haven't decided on anything definitive as yet."

"Anything you can discuss or do you prefer to keep it a secret?" Sarah chortled, her eyes now packed with interest.

"It's not that it's a secret," she defended with a slow shrug, rationalizing the reason for her deeds. Julia searched for the wordings to properly explain her quirks. Though what she found in her survey was the bluntness of their alert faces instead. "It's just a little hard for me to talk about what I have in the works. I guess it makes me a little self-conscious about the whole thing. Or maybe I'm just a little barmy, who knows." She smiled, hoping that her non-answer satisfactorily explained what may be difficult for some to understand.

"Quirks or not, if it keeps you working, I'm all for it." Sarah informed raptly, and rays of her luminous personality rained on the table as fixedly as it would have, had it been snow. "I have my own idiosyncrasies to deal with as well. I think we all do when it comes to being creative."

"That's for sure. There's a little piece of that in all of us, whether we admit it or not." Michael rejoined tamely, his eyes veiled as if the words were fated for the privacy of one. "Doesn't Phillip still stand on his head in the rain?"

"Still preferable to your shorts that's yet to be washed." Phillip snapped back equally sharp.

"There's something so estimable about writers." Sarah tweeted, slashing effectively through the manly banter with her musical lilt. "You give the world so much of what to think. Offer thoughts that change lives and topics to dominate discussions. It's fascinating."

"My wife loves books, can you tell?" Phillip intoned softly, his affection well obvious in his eyes.

"But you get to tell the world what to wear." Julia strummed back keenly, given with equal revere, her voice lifted like a dulcified hum. "You tell us what colors we should or should not wear as adamantly as the when, where and how. The world strives on your say so."

"That's far from the same. Writers take a blank piece of paper and turn it into something that punctures the core of a person's heart. Love or hate, it's of no importance, only the emotions they evoke; and the result always speak for itself. You inspire thoughts and touch lives with just the stroke of your pen. That's a true gift. A gift has no rival. It sits at the pinnacle of achievements watching the others strive to catch up."

"You're very passionate. Maybe you should try your hand at writing. That's what makes most writers good at their job. I'm still learning to hone mine into a worthy skill, so I can't speak for those who have the gift. But I do understand the essentials of what you mean." She smiled, inspired, Julia emitted a lax sigh, comprehending that her own love of books was now rivaled by her tablemate. "I'm easily enslaved by a well written story myself. The more riveted a writer keeps me, the more enrapturing the reading becomes and pausing can sometimes be a difficult task. To those writers, my loyalty never wavers. It's like a love affair that never ends. We're conjoined forever regardless of time." She beamed, shaking her head as a soft gust sailed like a blissful sigh. "There's nothing like a good book that can put your emotions on a rollercoaster ride."

"I see now why your books are so popular." Michael announced in a gravelly hum, his words skating through the room like a purposeful caress, grabbing its intended by surprise. "You speak with such passion for the written word, it's no wonder you're able to convey the same in your books." He remarked coolly, and a small smile flittered behind the declaration he gave. Capturing her eyes in a delicate test, Michael slowly straightened, resting his full attention on her face.

There was no time to contemplate the exigency of his blurt. The eruption came as much as a surprise to him as it did to her, slipping unhindered past his lips, he had little time to stall. Though suddenly he found no need to stop the fermenting curiosity he had pertaining to her.

"That's a very generous compliment," Julia smiled, nodding her head in polite acceptance of his praise. "But I have a long way to go before I get to where I'd like to be. Besides, for all you know this book was the only decent thing I did."

"But you and I both know that's not true now, don't we?" Challenging her remark with a slow, sensual drawl, his timbre rolled caressingly from his tongue, and like a warm breath over kindling timber. He stroked his words to a blaze with the focus of his gaze.

"How is it you can judge what you haven't seen?" she asked with a shrinking knit to her brows. "It's hard to give judgment without a foundation to stand on."

"Who says I haven't?" Michael hummed lazily, his own query leaping forward in place of a reply, spliced neatly with the taunting lift of his own brows. Yet his voice coiled warmly in play. Amiably, his eyes slid down her face in a subtle caress.

"Well…" she groaned, frowning in contemplation of the man. Her eyes were unfalteringly in her need to assess his mood. Unfamiliar with his gestures, it made him especially hard to discern. "I've always thought my books appeal to a different audience." She shrugged, letting the words glide from her tongue with uncanny sweetness.

"And what type of audience would that be?" Michael sauced back in a whispery growl.

"Well…" Julia again started with a stunted sigh, making eye contact with her inquisitor. Her mind dug remarkably deep. It took but seconds for him to rouse her awareness, dashing fields afar the point she intended to allow, though the intensity progressively loomed as if reading a forbidden tale. In the colorful depths, she saw temerity blazing in his gaze, and the persistence in their speckled beds aimed to swallow her whole. The concentration in the beauty of his stare was without rival, and she wondered then who was it that designated blue as the most stunning eye color of all? Since she now looked into the magnificent paragon of hazel that was as spectacular as the sun, and they wrought their eminence almost as strong.

"I'm sure you're well acquainted with my audience." She chanted in a sweet undiluted tone, sending him a half smile. She lowered her gaze to her plate, anything to get away from the intensity in those eyes. Perplexedly, she wondered how she had never before noticed the power or the beauty they possessed. A fresh grumble that churned continuously in her head, this, while she pondered the validity of his words. She decided emphatically that it was more likely that he posed a bluff. "That is, people of a…certain…sex." She intoned in finish.

"Would that be solely in their preference or in their typing?" Michael asked wittily, unwilling to let her off the hook, he sent her a simmering smile. Unprepared for how much he enjoyed the simple banter, he grew reluctant to see what stems as an actual conversation end.

Julia returned his smile coyly, understanding and accepting his game. She persisted with skill. "That would depend on each reader, now wouldn't it? Preference is optional with each book."

"I see." Michael groaned dully, lengthening the deliberate tail on each word, he used the time to discretely admire the variant details of her face. Her eyes were wrenchingly beautiful, like large, dark pools stationed in an exotic display. They gave the most damning sensation with each gaze. Shapely lips formed the marvel that was her mouth, honed with at least a dozen expressive poses; still he knew each one by heart. At rest, they seemed small and rounded, clasped like the budding of a flower when she sits deep in thought. In the movement of a conversation, they become sensual and playful, blessed with a fullness that keeps you wondering on more. "So what exactly does that make me?" he rasped, blowing out the words through a quiet breath.

"I would imagine whatever you want." Julia shrugged, her voice warm and inviting, capable of swaddling any chill. "Such noble decisions are best left to the heir himself." She chirped, her smile widening with satisfaction, enjoying the lavish quirks embedded in their verbal tag.

"Then is it your opinion that a man can read your book and still be…well…masculine? Or do you think that makes him less so?"

Julia's eyes danced with full mischief now stroking their depths, and tiny morsels of witticism erupted in her head from the countless possibilities waiting at hand. A more familiar friend would have already been gutless on the floor, writhing in pain as barbs of stiletto-type riposte sliced meanly through their flesh. "To answer that properly," her sugary voice started in reply, and a stealth smile ran over the entirety of her face. "I'll need to ask you this." She purred, forewarning of her intent, her voice flowed with the gentle massage of her hands. As if hotly intrigued by his question and the ensuing response, she slowly circled each palm with the friction of itself.

"When you look at me, the prospects are enough—I would imagine—for you to decipher that I'm a girl." Julia crooned, filling the small emptiness with an obvious smirk. She made certain he understood the playfulness of her statement. With a bevy of beautiful women at his beck and call, she was determined not to seem destitute for his attention. As she would never be that presumptuous as to think she was his type, though neither beauty nor confidence affected the cause of her decision, knowing in her head neither mattered much. She just never gave the circumstance thought, and she intended to leave the matter as such. In her ramblings, she missed the slow rise of Michael's brow, sojourning the subtle growth of his smile. He pinched the corners of his mouth with his teeth. "If I decided to one day slip into an oversized jersey with just an old boxer underneath, kick my heels up with the boys, and put away a few bottles of beer while puffing on a good cigar, all this while watching a collection of sports; would that somehow change your view on my sex?"

The room took a cleansing breath as she finished her eccentric précis, holding its occupants somewhat angst, it grew strangely quiet. Absent was the pale scrapping of utensils against plate. From her right, she noted that Phillip and Sarah now patiently waited a reply, seeming as if the answer was of the utmost importance to them.

From the subtle downturn of his head, Michael cleverly viewed the slaked smile that now flirted with her face, and he need not interpret further to understand why. His mind, however, was still on the introduction of her mode of dress. The anxious zephyr settled in a flash in his head, unfolding the merits of its details to his mind's eye like a show. Experiencing the fruition of such treat could hardly be snubbed, and even he knew that that, in actuality, was a disparaging truth, since at the very least, he wanted to fully admire the result. Cigar, boxers, beer and sports could do naught to flaw her beauty—not that it would, and he sincerely doubted anything could. Tried as he may, the thought only got more pleasing, and the longer he pondered the scenario, the more riotous it played in his head.

"I can't see your choice of garment or stimuli contributing to me changing my opinion on your sex." He retorted with a casual shrug, fixing her with a steeping smile. Taking assiduous care with his follow-up steps, Michael planted his elbows on the table, acquiring her eyes, his smile escalated to daring. "No." He hummed as if to clarify a miscommunication. "My perception wouldn't change one bit."

"Then you have your answer." Julia affirmed with a defiant nod, crimping her shoulders in a girlish shrug as if to offer an apology or a truce.

"Okay." Michael smiled, returning her subdued nod. He politely accepted her counter as the culmination of a match, aligning himself with the agility of her tongue, for already he looked forward to their next debate. Slowly, Michael scanned the neglected faces of his friends, identifying the awareness well palpable in their eyes. His expression gave way to the already apparent, letting the byline flow obstinate, he answered with a stealth smile. *Yes, she has him well captivated. And yes, he greatly aspires to procure more of her.*

Chapter Six

Morning's gray frolicked with the hems of heavy draperies. Testing the defiance of a piddling dark, frail light merrily flaunted its dingy glow. Toasted air fanned softly beneath the flouncing tails of the casement's dress, charging convincingly through the rooms, warmth smothered the wont of a frigid haze.

Day had not yet aged from night's imposing shadow, for the sun had not yet made its remarkable show. Instead, the bestriding period hovered in a limbo-like wait, locked in a state of dimness and chill. A soft eeriness whispered the promise of the day to come.

Well acquainted with the spoils of a restive night, the evening did not thwart Julia's expectations to that end, for it seemed only minutes passed between each bracket of actual rest. And although respite in a strange bed was almost nonexistent, she was grateful for her fatigue at the evening's end. Thus it brought sleep within seconds of being supine in bed. The habitual waking gave the habit the encumbrance it had, attributing itself to all aspect of her fragmented rest. Night dragged like an eternity in what seemed a polar existence, praying without cure for the opposite to make amend.

Peered like a soft rustling wind through the stillness of a valley, the long sigh came as a whistle, stirring the thinning blackness of the room. Pensively, Julia's glare walked the window's cloaking, analyzing the meager striping for change. As time seemed to have clasped the morning in its claws without the slimmest show of relent. The mopish light displayed little willingness to mature into day, and a maudlin grunt sailed as her answer for its incessant delay.

Sending the covers flying from her bed, Julia brought forth a festering growl from the inset of her chest, and although the sound came sedated within the ghostly walls of her quiet room. It was not intended as such. Gruffly embracing the decision with a brusque shrug, she sent the draperies dashing widespread. Decreeing the ruptured nuance of morning as good a time as any to steer her momentum to work, and what better modus to ensure wakefulness than to meet the starting day now. Jerking the curtains farther apart, Julia gaped out at the pending day, and myriads of syllogism rattled hard in her head on the impeding flaw.

Had she stayed in the expediency of a hotel, she would have already made it to the gym by then, or, at the very least, procured herself the wizardry of coffee to fill the tired edges in. But such freeing luxury did not thrive the same in someone's home, thus waiting for signs of life was her only route.

Dawn's face drifted temptingly close, inciting the drear of the horizon with a brilliant hue of yellow and a soft drizzling of red. Light fog swathed the estate in a milky tegument, looking like fallen clouds waiting to ascend, they hung low aloft the grounds like the corpus of an eerie show. From below the cover of shrubs, a family of rabbits scrambled across the lawn, stopping briefly to nibble scattered tidbits found to their liking. One paused to stare expectantly at the house, surveilling the structure as if sensing it was being watched. The furry creature hovered a prolonged minute, sniffing lightly at the air. It scampered off in the opposite path of whence it came, and in an instant, its small presence was sorely missed.

In the distance, birds docked in assembly on the numerous tiers to their home, looking like clustered leaves in the absence of said sightings. They warmed the morning's misty coolness with their songs.

Resigned with the prospect of her new day, Julia ventured from the window with the launching of a plan, masterfully arranging all options in her head. She set her toils to hand. Meticulous attention was paid to her method of dress. Taking her time, Julia perfected every factor of her choice, even more so than she had in a long time. A side effect, it would seem, for waking up in the same house as a top fashion designer and she suspected said circumstance would cause any woman to feel the same. The extra minutes spent on the spoils of preparation were most likely a common occurrence, since it would surely be so with anyone who had the slightest interest in fashion. The verbiage of such played repetitiously in her head regardless of truth.

Comfort, she understood, needed to take precedence above all else. But style had to be articulated well. Conveying knowledge with a certain amount of allure was her goal, and nothing says casual or comfort like a voguish pair of jeans. For her hair, a long ponytail gave her the best of both results, falling down her back in a sea of treacherous tendrils. Sumptuous devotion was imparted on her face, calibrating her beauty to a magnitude set to stun. Large hoop earrings completed the laidback ensemble she intended, warranting a whetted pout of approval as she surveyed the result of her work.

By the time she descended the stairs, shards of sunlight set the distant sky ablaze. Bleeding its glimmering sparks upon the house, the expansive windows made the viewing a spectacular sight. Resting her laptop and notes to a chair, Julia gaped out at the yellowy bloom, donning her slippers; she admired the full spectrum of dawn's glory. Preened to marvel, it bore extraordinary splendor to the full vaunt of its parade. And all that was missing from the flawless unveiling was the crackling spits of a fire, and a steaming cup of coffee in her hand.

Today her ideas were plentiful. Her night of unrest made certain of that, giving her the time to re-plot certain scenes in her head. Thus an early start should get them all jotted before they tumbled from thought. Introspectively, the morning grew more beautiful than the gray beginning posted from her bed, waking the busy habitants of the woods. Small animals now seem to openly scurry about. Crouched timidly against the shelter of shrubs, a few lingered in pause, as if they too, waited for signs of life to sprout forth from the house.

The golden rays barely thawed the treetops when renewed signs of life tweaked happily at her ears. Betty's petite frame burst into the room as if slowing from a sprint, and she looked no different than her speed of the afternoon prior. Whipping past the furnishings in what could be labeled a blink, she closely breezed through the entire room before catching sight of the already roused guest. Apparently, her rush came with more than just the prospect of burning her food, it seemed, for all comparison, the only gear the older woman had.

"Oh my!" Betty cried airily, stalling in the middle of her hurried stride, a thin hand slammed promptly to her chest. "I didn't see you there," She whispered with a smile. "I'm not used to any one being up before me." She laughed, relaxing her flustered stance.

"I'm sorry, Betty. I didn't mean to startle you."

"Early-riser or is it more that you couldn't sleep?" Betty asked with a sudden frown.

"Both." She professed lightly, offering the other a reassured smile, since the quiet answer seemed almost to be directed at herself. Julia's head followed the retort with a slow bounce, as if confirming to herself that the answer was emphatically true.

"Would you like a cup of coffee?" She asked in what seemed more a motherly tone.

"I would *love* some. Thank you." And her emphasis was well evident on more than just her words.

"I'll be right back," Betty announced gaily, as if the prospect of such chore was most pleasing to her sense. In a noiseless whirl, she slipped from vision and was gone, leaving the room as it once was—remarkably still. *Evidently, Betty loves her job*, Julia conjectured then. Evidence so, with the way each gets done, and doing it well was obviously who she was.

Although it rose at first, faint like the artifice of a dream, it was not long before the sweet, aromatic stench of coffee wafted through the house. "Mmmmm," Julia moaned in acquiescence of the rousing aroma, her throaty yen wading soft through the cool sedated air. Gliding undaunted from a secluded corner of the room, her impatient palate instantly watered with need. Filling her lungs with the fragrant air, Julia allowed her mind to take full pleasure in the decadence of what that meant. Heavy lashes fell like curtains over the transom of brown eyes, immersing her mind in the prospective pleasure that now stood so close at hand. And the loveliness of her smile bespoke the newly awaken gist of her mood.

"Am I interrupting?" Michael hummed, his deep timbre swirling through her body like the soft scratch of a hand, breaking the lingering silence of the room.

"Uh…!" Julia gasped sharply, bolting from her seat. Her mind stumbled to a halt, throwing her to her feet before she realized the needlessness of her action. "I…" she started in a voice strangled with uncertainty and fright, searching her head for the correct opening on where to begin. She stood at a lost. "I-I'm—"

"I'm sorry." Michael murmured then, easing her tension with a softening smile. "I didn't mean to startle you." He averred in his bassy tone. "I didn't realize you were so deep in thought." He expounded, giving a widening grin with his remorse, he hesitated further action in the room. "I can give you—"

"No, no! You don't need to leave!" She implored with a nervous laugh, frowning on the absurdity of such deed—this was in fact his house, was it not? "It's just that…well. I didn't hear you come in." She enlightened in a low breath, dropping the tenseness from her body with the quiet release of said breath. "I was just…" she halted, plunging her eyes to the floor as if suddenly unsure. "I was just savoring the smell of the coffee."

"Then it seems we're of like minds." Michael droned. "Because that's why I'm here." He smiled. "Please, go back to whatever you were doing. Make yourself at home." He coaxed, waving a hand in invitation to the couch, he approached the slumbering hearth. Diligently, he proceeded with its care, setting the room, before long, to a blaze.

Resettled as best she could, Julia found her gaze drawn to the man's back, documenting things she had never bothered to detect before now. Noting at first glance that his hair was still damp, she quickly speculated, from the hour, he no doubt needed a dam to keep his body upright, unaccustomed that he was to early mornings like this. He wore his usual casual attire, blue jeans and a black sweater that gave new meaning to the word. The soft fabric rode each bulge his body offered with enduring grace, leaving little to wonder on his physique, and even less on the foist of the man's dexterity.

Finishing, Michael turned towards the room with a smile, giving very little away with his action. His smile was slow and quiet in its unfurling, though it spoke highly of the man, for it deftly completed the flawlessness of his visage.

"That should do it." He announced in a mumbled tone, intending the publication for himself more so than it was for her. The slaps of his palms echoed though the stillness like the distant claps of thunder. It stirred the quiet no less than the brewing of a storm. Half seeing the morning, his eyes wandered out the window in pretense of taking in the view. Instead, he discreetly regarded the woman to his right.

His hesitation when he entered was not in disturbing what looked to be a moment of succor from what it was, for she had looked sweetly surreal to those of riveted eyes, and a lengthier perusal would have greatly been relished had he had the freedom or the chance, though not at the risk of being caught. "Beautiful." He sighed at last, and was taken by surprise when she assented to such in a soft tweet. *Damn!*

"Yes it is." She smiled, taking a long, soft breath. She sent an appreciative gape at the sun's brilliance. "I never know which one I like more." She maintained in whispery breath. "The beginning or the end, they each give you the same. Yet they feel remarkably new each time."

"It sounds as if you've spend a lot of time admiring them."

"As much as I'm allowed," She chuckled, sending her mind in quick dispatch, she recollected in full color all the times she neglected to throw even a small glimpse in the direction of the sun.

"I guess some days it can start to feel like a nasty cycle, if you let it." He remarked coolly, knowing with certainty where her mind now delved, as his was already enjoying its tenure. Dark residue from the fireplace remained smeared on his hands; showing as plainly as the smudges was felt. Though the effects would neither deter nor prevent him from his new bent. This being their first conversation unchaperoned, he intended to savor the delicacy of the moment to its fullest extent.

Betty, he was sure, would be in shortly enough with their coveted drinks, and he needed a way to curtail her meddling before it began. As his old nanny, she can some-times press forth with a bit of intensity, Michael groaned, though a smile brightened with the thought in the quietness of his head. Since the scant age of four, she'd had the job of seeing to his well-being, and although he no longer needed her mothering, she did not seem inclined to stop. At times, she was more determined than the mother he already had, fussing twice as much. She worries a hundred times more than anyone should, never knowing when to hold her tongue or when to leave him be.

"Yet somehow we can't seem to wait to get on to harvest the ride." Julia mumbled absently in continuance of before, glancing towards the kitchen with a pitying grunt. Her need for caffeine expanded even with the distraction of their near friendly chat, thus anchoring her mind to only that. The taunting smell roused and beckoned her with spite, and without realizing the effectiveness of her deeds. She granted the man the opening he needed to stall.

"Let me go see about rounding up some of that coffee, that smell is almost pun-ishing." Michael groaned, sending her a half smile, he turned from the room without waiting a reply.

Chapter Seven

"What do you think you're doing, old woman?" Michael questioned with a smoldering grunt, hedging towards the older woman's back, he affirmed his prediction on Betty's meddlesome aim.

Already, a sleek, porcelain coffeepot waited at the center of a wooden tray, flanked by the customary sugar and cream in an ordinary exhibit. Alongside that sat an abounding container of fresh fruits, two undersized vessels for the partaking of said treat stalked the brimful bowl. Glistening utensils, and a platter garnished with various Biscotti, further topped the assortments off. Diligently, Betty doted over the large tray, her thin hands working ceaselessly at their task. Seeming innocent in her action, she looked almost oblivious to his scowling presence.

"Getting coffee for you and the writer," Betty proclaimed insouciantly, and although her voice came to him soft, the words spilled fearlessly from her lips. Conveying no apology for the penchants of her hands, or for their current undertakings, nor did the certitude of her stance articulate any such narratives. Without pausing, Betty folded a large napkin in half and then again on itself, tucking each of the four ends back. The crisp creases sat in a diagonal pleat across the serviette's edge. Thus completed, Betty inserted the elegantly rucked napkin through the handle of a cup. Adjusting the spiny edges like a sprouting through the curving stem of a chalice, she gave speech then to the context of her thoughts. "She's beautiful." Betty decreed without lifting her head, grabbing a second napkin, she repeated identical drills. Bestowing no heed to the man now frowning at her back, for she knew well his next words without having sought the mien on his face. "I like her." She nodded as if concurring with her own dictate.

"Will you ever stop meddling, old woman?" Michael asked in a querulous huff, swerving smartly to the sink. He commenced to lathering his hands, knowing his ostensibly peeved words dangled hollowly as they fell, since they sounded no better to the congregating thoughts yet rambling in his head. In a quick, circumspect glance, Michael checked the door's opening, taking care in his effort not be overheard by his guest. He returned his attention to the habitually buzzing mother hen. "I'll take that." Michael declared somewhat sternly, lunging towards the waiting tray. He heard the echoing slap before the commendation for the gesture was felt.

"I'm not finished!" Betty scolded in her usual tone.

"Hey!" Michael protested with shock tainting his tone, though it was well marred by the smile splayed on his face. "You're mean!" he announced huffily, clutching the offended arm to his chest, he gaped at his old nanny as if horrified by her show of abuse.

Vanquish as if consumed by a void, the waggish words fell valueless to an unseen crater and silence again bloated to a heavy spread. As irrefutable proof, Betty gave neither them nor the man an inch of her regard. In so doing, she leveled the altered coffeepot without further wordings of her own. Turning each cup to a precise angle, Betty flaunted a smile as her signal of completion.

"There." She announced with a shallow sigh, appraising the finality of her work. Brown eyes tamely lifted in assessment of her improbable shadow, noting the impatient glare now potently directed at her head. Her thin shoulders imperturbably shifted. In contrast, Betty's lips virtually twitched, seeing nothing past the boy that was once her charge, her smile almost blossomed in full, for, as always, she was deeply susceptible to his charm. "Go!" She commanded in a rush, sweeping the air anxiously with her hands. "Go sit with your guest. I'll bring in the coffee." Betty droned, and although her face showed the set crinkles of a frown, the melody of a song wafted in start from her throat.

"What are you up to?" Michael asked bullishly, folding his arms across the muscular width of his chest, he earnestly awaited her innocuous response; though knowing the notion was an unlikely one. *Does she know something or is this the effect Julia has on everyone?* He grumbled warily, weighing the peppering questions as they crawled through his head.

"I think I'm the one who should be asking *you* that." Betty smiled, and her eyes again took quick survey of the tray.

Michael's numb gape flew back as quickly as her derisory response, setting his mind to a gallop. *Is it really that obvious?* His ego numbly queried, and the perplexing question came as a sharp bark in his head. *Could she already know of his attraction?* After yesterday, he was sure Phil and Sarah knew something of how he felt, but Betty had hardly been clustered within their group. Left to the fervency of their musing, work eventually stole the show, dragging them well into the overture of morning. Not much time was had to enlighten her perceptive ears. "What are you talking about?" Michael probed; retaining an innocent variety to his tone, the furrows on his forehead plunged instantly deep.

"Why? Don't you think I have eyes?" Betty quizzed testily, and immediately reverted her attention to the tray. "Are you coming?" she asked then, balancing the wooden salver between hands, Betty's tone was almost mocking, yet she promptly placed the conversation on repose. Turning quickly from the man's befuddled gaze, she lent him no opening on which to respond. Soundlessly whirling from her place, she breezed from the room, feeling the heat of his gaze as it tattered the clothing on her back, though the bluster dampened naught of her mood.

Jubilant utensils rang like tuned carillons set to enslave, pinging the quietude as they amended their stance. They scratched what badly needed to be fixed. Julia turned inquisitively towards the lively jangle as the music drew near, and a wide, spirited smile, serenaded the elder's entrance in the room. "Betty!" Julia sang. Her voice resonating soft, yet it gave an energetic punch to the other woman's name. With the ottoman readied as a stand, Julia gave full appraisal to the contents of the tray, captivated by the beauty of the undue offer, she smiled. In silence, she waited for the elder to relinquish the burden in hand, this before lending voice to the manifold of words now teeming in her head. "Wow! Betty, that's…Thank you, but just coffee would have been fine." She avowed with a flourishing smile, its radiance emanating like the brio from gold in a darken cave. Betty's face wore much pride for the modish display, and not wanting to offend her generosity, Julia left additional words unsaid.

"It's really no trouble at all." Betty insisted in her usual tone. "A few pieces of fruits could hardly be considered work." She smiled, clasping her hands atop the small mass of her breasts; she paused as if grappled with a fascinating thought. At this, Betty regarded the other woman fixedly.

Betty noted keenly that the young face now brightened expansively as she again regarded the tray's fair. Marked with attributes that gleamed unpretentious from whence they rest, her gesture was almost serene, and she could not help but feel somewhat enamored with the young guest. *No wonder he didn't seem himself around her*, Betty simpered. *She's definitely different from his usual type.* Her inner jury smartly divulged, showing the twinging of a smile. She assessed the younger woman with certain pride, and found that that, in addition to the obvious dividends was truly an advantageous reward. The sudden emergence of possibilities was almost exciting to deliberate upon, enough so, that it was almost work to keep a threatening grin from seeping to her face.

"Michael should be back shortly," she informed in a near sigh. "He's grabbing a collection of needs for me from storage." Betty smiled, clutching the reins on her meddlesome efforts inside. Outside she softly plied, finding no sound reason to further linger or explore her intrusive wonder. "Please, enjoy." She encouraged sweetly, her small voice set effectively to soothe. Posting retreat in the statement itself, she ignored her wont to stay and further catalog her view. Gifting the guest a last smile, Betty flounced sunnily from the room.

"Thank you." Julia replied equally sweet, the mellifluous notes escorting the older woman the entire way through.

In the kitchen, quiet treads marked his aimless browsing as he waited anxiously on Betty's return. Michael's mind roamed unending, although the young writer held her place staunchly in his head, thriving distinct regardless of the many places his mind delved. Rushing in behind Betty would not have looked the casual observer he wanted to project. Since for now, his only definite was that he liked the way she looked, and that that small datum contributed much to the uneasiness he felt.

On her reentrance, Betty skirted the impatient body impeding her path, moving directly to the pantry. She hustled across the threshold without uttering a word, taking the full essence of his query with her as she disappeared inside. Perched as if she carried the rich detail on some essential news, Michael's head toggled with every movement she made, and eager eyes walked, in their quest, impatiently at her back. Betty offered a scant smile as she again turned to face the room, retrieving a canister marked "sugar" from the counter. She gave no further morsel to the man, but resumed the vim of her chores.

"Well?" Michael asked petulantly, his voice coming like a croaky snarl, though it stayed low as it sliced roughly through the quiet room.

"You said not to meddle." Betty stated blandly, rolling her small shoulders with skilled disinterest lounging on display. She gave him no hint on what she already suspected.

"What?" Michael barked disconcertingly, "After all that, that's all you give me?" he griped tightly, pushing a slow gust past set lips, he turned grumpily from his once tethered spot. "I should retire you!" He announced in parting, his words coming in a gravelly grunt, falling without bulk to the older woman's back.

"You'd be lost without me." Betty professed proudly, waving him off no different than she would the pestering of a fly, laughter rattled merrily from her throat. "By the way, you had to get me a few things from storage." She called in parting, polishing an already spotless counter. A slow smirk crept mincingly to her face as his grunt of acknowledgement sailed back tartly to her ears. And its harshness, for more reasons than one, was strangely pleasingly to her. "This may actually turn out to be interesting." Betty exhaled lightly, deepening the intensity of her scrub.

Delightfully caroused with the medicinal perks of caffeine, Julia gave into the dithering temptation that now plagued her thought. *It's just curiosity*. She pledged, frowning at what little ease that explanation carried to her slightly chaotic sense. Wanting to scrutinize a little more than just the man's back, *what's the harm in that?* She grumbled, taking great offense to the derisive grunt her ego so gladly bestowed.

Discretely, she allowed her gaze to stalk him as he reentered the room, and was amazed by the potency and likewise the verve that kept her riveted to his pulchritudinous form. His strides vaunted unhurried. Not in the least disruptive to the stalwart construction of his frame, each movement seemed profoundly precise. Irreproachable, like the mastery shown in a matchless work of art. Such attributes were undoubtedly made to have a wrenching effect, and on him, there was a noticeable sundry from which to pick from, as he was endearingly masculine in every way. From the square set of his jaw, to the deep, dark growl of his voice. The buffet was inordinately set, and the feast, aided by the well assured struts of his walk, was well enunciated with a primal flare. Designed deliberately to keep you baited, the proof needed no subsequent appraisal to make it true.

"Sorry about that." Michael informed sagely as he reached her side, and the erupting words spilled smoothly with an assured ring. Pleasing him inertly with the impervious weight offered in the prearranged lie, even if the effects were not necessarily felt nor did the ruse soothe his rising unease. Her face immediately became a vision, brightening as full, strikingly sensual lips spread wide in a smile, showing off the flawlessness of her teeth.

Since meeting her, an innumerable amount of stolen minutes had been spent gazing at the eminence of that feature, enough so to know well its radiance as surely as the back of his hand. Without a doubt, it was his favorite feature to behold as it pertains to her. Perhaps this was due to the essentialness of her mouth in the meandering of his thoughts, for the beauty of said attribute seemed to have him fully mesmerized, and it had naught to do with the loveliness of its shape. "I had to take care of a few things." He lied, enlightening her in a matter-of-fact tone. He hoped his words did not sound fully what they were. Although lying was in no way a difficult task for him, these somehow felt strange in its offering to her.

As if the circumstance was a natural occurrence, Michael claimed his seat at her side, although the action, for him, sprouted as an inaugural attempt. Usually, he accommodated the furthest joint in this, their eclectic triangle, leaving the space open to Phillip and the comfort they had. It was an understanding that assuaged well his esteem, for it permitted him the freedom of eyeing her from afar, thus allowing the convenience of absorbing her details at will.

"Don't be," Julia assured him with a spirited smile, "As you can see, Betty took pity and came in your stead. She took great care in every detail and I have to say, I'm impressed." Waving her hand towards the tray, she quietly demonstrated her point, not having touched anything beyond filling her cup, it waited fully stocked.

"I can see that." He retorted with an absent nod. Abstractedly, Michael viewed the tray as if for the first time. In quiet cognizance, his mouth twisted with the start of a smile, contemplating the meticulous efforts Betty foisted into a simple serving. He could not help but appreciate the fervency of her work, for in one gesture, she offered him a wide opening in which to skate through. "You remember Betty from yesterday, don't you?" he asked with a frisky air, yet his mumbled words came sounding like a raspy song. Silently, he thanked his old nanny for her meddlesome traits, and a smile—the magnitude of which he would never admit—rose upwards through the barrel of his chest, warming him fully from the inside out. Pouring his own cup, Michael added the usual squirt of flavored cream, swirling in an additional two spoons of sugar for taste. The spoon clanked, clinked and scraped against the warm surface of his mug, assaulting the silence gruffly as he stirred. It snarled in a language of its own, for neither of the two seemed willing, at that moment, to broach the argot of speech. Dazedly, Michael set his attention to the flickering flames.

"Does she always go all out?" Julia hummed, interrupting the stalled muteness with a late rejoinder to break the weightiness of the spell.

"I've never seen anything but, and I've known her a very long time." Michael smirked, offering the remark from behind his mug, his eyes fed on her face.

Clattering bowls rouse the silence that immediately descended on the room. Heaping an ample helping of fruits into the curved plate, Julia erringly tendered the container to her host. A gesture, once dissected, seemed reminiscent of longtime companions than that of an abided guest. The action flew forth as natural as a blink. Like the many unrehearsed procedures in one's day, it unfurled without thought, startling the man almost as much as it did her.

Michael stared dazedly at the vessel in her hand for what seemed a long, clumsy second. "Thank you." He smiled at last, regaining the use of his tongue. He accepted the offering from her hand.

"Oh, I'm...I'm sorry!" she groaned, her eyes widening fleetly with recognition. "I...I'm, I didn't mean..." she further expounded, cringing as she realized late the mild forwardness singed firmly to the deed itself. She stumbled further in a startled daze. "I'm...I'm not sure why I did that." She clarified in what seemed more a question than not. "I didn't even ask you if you wanted some, did I? Here, I'll take—" reaching forward with urgency, she attempted to retrieve her blunder from his hand.

"No, there's no need!" Michael growled, his hands boastful in the acuity of their speed. Hence, they stalled her frail attempt without pause. Clutching the bowl to his body, he anchored it firmly with the other of his hand. "It's fine! Really! There's no need to do that." He reassured then with a building smile. "Really, I was just about to get some for myself, thank you."

"Are you sure?" she asked warily, browsing his person like a mother would an ambivalent child. Angling her head slightly, Julia searched his eyes for the pageant of truth. "You don't need to eat it just to spare my feelings." She explained. "I'm a big girl. I can accept my mistakes." She assured then through the pasty relic of a smile.

"I'm sure. I promise." Michael attested with a nod, and the start of a smile swiftly crimped the corners of his mouth. Slowly, his gaze lengthened with the careful assertion of his words, dousing the scenario with an allusion of truth. In retort, her questioning gape neither faltered nor rested, watching him as if she already knew he fed her a lie. She offered no solace to the pause, and he could not help but be captivated by that.

Leaning forward, Michael quietly returned his bowl to the waiting tray. Feeling the subtle shift of her body as he turned, she skeptically followed the endeavors of his hands. Retracing her deeds, he spooned the bite-size fruits into a waiting vessel, settling the spoon along the rounded edge. He set the container to her hand with a well satiated smirk. "As I've said," Michael reiterated in a soft, lyrical tone. "I'm sure." Touching his bowl to hers, the low clunk of porcelain assaulted the silence that again dove between them. "Mornings mark the foundation for your day." He apprised in a deep, deliberate drawl, spooning an orange wedge into his mouth, he smiled.

Needing to be sure she was not fully the dolt that she felt, Julia waited until he fully swallowed the first mouthful, before turning her attention to the bowl now stationed in her hand. That, Julia carped in a peevish tone, was by far the most prodigious proof that parenting reverts your brain to the grounding of dust. Not for a moment did she sense the budding of that snafu. Thank God she didn't try to spoon feed him as well! Her ego protested curtly, rolling her eyes in agreement, a soft groan rumbled in her throat. *Why did she do that? What sane person does something as inane as that to someone like him? Could she have made herself look anymore idiotic? Let's hope he doesn't think she was angling for his attention with that daft stunt.*

Outside, a thriving morning propagated its beauty across the vast estate, and the merry flittering of birds grew increasingly rampant. Yet inside, the house wallowed in a hush. Silence between the two grew extensively long, with each fully immersed within the familiar trappings in their heads, though the atmosphere between them soared deliciously warm. Void of resentment or remorse. Its texture was neither stiff nor disconcerting. Unmistaken was the sweet, fragrance of equanimity that sat between them. Contentment further bloomed, as the once brusque air grew warm from the dancing amber of a fire's flame.

Seeing little beyond the grass vanishing luster, Michael's gaze again jutted out the window in a yowl of discontent, unable to understand the basis for his hesitance with her. Never having been ambiguous in his methods with the opposite sex before now, such matters had always come with much ease. Contradictory of all else, now he found himself wavering even in thought, seeming practically at a loss in a trot he was well acquainted with. It was sincerely troubling to wade through its blanketing effect, for he, an extrovert by genetic, could hardly muster the right methodology on where to begin a proper conversation with her. *What is it about her that has him so disrupted?* He griped, taking a sip from his cup, he again eyed her from under the slope of his brows. With diligence, he waited for her to swallow before he quietly asked. "Did you sleep well?" the question came soft, rumbling behind the fixedness of his mug as he monitored her. *Unoriginal, Michael,* he chided, knowing the question was a simplistic start, but a start it was nonetheless.

"Yes." She nodded, feeling the lie fall without guilt from her tongue, she smiled. "Very well, thank you." Swallowing hard in finish, as if the content of her mouth came as a sudden surprise, she leaned forward to relinquish her bowl to the tray. Settling the full weight of her mug in the palm of her hand, she allowed the radiant warmth to rope through her body at a searing pace, starting with the well chilled digits on her hands.

"You're up early. Are you always an early riser?" he probed, his question sailing with a touch more thought, bringing a satisfied smile to his lips.

"Not always, though mostly I'm up well before dawn. But…" stuttering to a stop in her thoughts, a jumbled mixture of half-truth raced to her mind at top speed, and for a moment, she lacked the clarity she once had. "Well…" she puffed blithely, giving her mind time to unscramble the alp that now weighted her tongue.

"You don't sleep well when you're in a strange bed, do you?" Michael inquired then, sensing the answer before it came.

"Something like that." She nodded, looking almost relieved. Happy with not having to state the obvious or further the ruts of a lie, Julia offered then a smile, though she felt somewhat transfixed by his swift evaluation. Not that the facts were not already stacked at his feet, but he could have stumbled, just as easily, past the conclusion without awareness seeping through and, of course, she carped, she would prefer not to offend the man. Since it was palpable that if she could not sleep in the luxurious bed he provided, then there was no hope of her sleeping anywhere but in the bounds of her own bed.

"When you spend a lot of time away from home, you end up learning little tricks to help you get around that."

"Please, do share." Julia chirped melodiously, regarding the man with her eager attention.

"Well," Michael hummed, shrugging leisurely. He sipped slowly from his mug, and his eyes moved in rapt deliberation over her face. "For one, you need to learn to sleep through anything, earthquakes included." He elucidated with an abbreviated shrug.

Julia's eyes widen, and finely arched brows rose concurrently with the word. "Really!" extending the utterance well past the short syllables of two. She took a dawdling sip from her mug.

"Oh, absolutely," Michael averred with a light shrug. With his mug affixed to his face, the start of a smile remained hidden from view. "Your overworked brain won't stand a chance once you take back control. Before you know it, you'll be out like a light, and the where won't matter much after that." He nodded, his head falling in the motion of an intoxicated sloth, barking in firm agreement with himself. Michael smiled languidly in the questing of her eyes.

"And that works well for you?" she asked unhurriedly through the complexity of a frown, marred in part by the budding of a snicker.

Plucking the last cube of cantaloupe from his bowl, Michael popped the small morsel in his mouth, taking a lengthy tutorial of her face before giving a reply. Mischief thrived boundless in his hazel depths, seeming afire with specks of gold dust. He at last recaptured the eloquence of her eyes with the start of a definitive nod. In rejoinder, Michael's head slowly dropped backwards, adamant in its progression. It climbed as if to give an extravagant bob, though he simply stalled the chore, well short of its waggish goal, in its track. "No, not really," He chuckled with a soft shake of his head. "I just couldn't resist."

"Funny." Came the coolly stated reply, languidly rolling her head. A slow smile hustled to the strict demeanor of her face. "Who knew," Julia shrugged, taking a protracted sip from her mug.

"Knew what?"

As if the flavor grew more extraordinary then before, Julia dallied over each mouthful of her drink, taking her time, she slowly savored the taste. "Who knew you had a sense of humor hidden inside there. I'm a little astounded with the knowledge." She crowed dryly, holding tight to her smirk. Mutinous with the ration of her response, Julia's gaze slowly walked the breadth of his chest, parking judiciously on the handsome features of his face. She tamely shrugged.

Patiently awaiting her tardy attention, Michael used the time to scout the finer details of her face. Her mouth twitched as she tightened the reins on a fetching smile, though laughter danced boldly in the dark depths of her eyes. "No worries there," he rasped, absorbing the sweetness of her essence into him. "It's an already known secret." He smiled. "At least to those who've come to know me well." He drawled, quietly stroking the outer edges of her fingers, he removed the cup from her hand.

"But—" she started, freezing in accordance of his hand, now stalled between them like the stamp of a five fingered shield. Measuredly, he proceeded then with his plan. Without asking permission, she watched as he refilled her cup, his eyes asking the questions regarding what additives to add, to which she obliged with a simple nod.

"It seems only fair." He advised with the budding of a cheeky smile, guardedly, he returned the rejuvenated mug to her hand.

"Thank you." She muttered in return, giving a small nod, she instantly drove her eyes to the floor.

"You're very welcome." He assured over his own newly fixed mug, stirring languorously as he waited for her eyes to float back to his. "It helps if you have something familiar to curl up with." He proclaimed sagely, dragging her attention back to him.

"I'm sorry?"

"When you're away from home," Michael smirked. "It helps if you bring something that's reminiscent of your base. Pillows and sheets work best." He explained, sipping the heated liquid, his intensive perusal worked even slower on her face, no longer wishing to hide his interest from view.

"Oh." The single word sprouted industriously from her lips, yet it dashed in every direction at once. The intensity of his gaze grew vast, holding her tenaciously under its bent. It refused, in its earnestness, to let her be, and as if to fix fire to flame. The sun set his hazel eyes further ablaze, or was it just her imagination on that? Somehow they looked wonderfully more brilliant than they did the day before. "Is that one of your tricks for staying sane?" she breathed, veering the wont of her gaze.

"I don't know about being sane," Michael laughed, openly amused by her selection of words. Sane was not always a word used descriptively in regards to him, this, in-part, due to the persistent residue of his past, and which made it so much nicer to hear the description from her. "But I've learned a few tricks here and there to help me get through a long night. Although some things amount to an enviable ambition in other places." He smiled, informing this in a casual timbre, his eyes gave new life to what was not said.

"I see."

"Do you?"

"Do I, what?"

"Do you see?" he asked in a low growl, his eyes fastened to hers, fervidly searching their depths. "What do you see, Julia?" he rasped, voicing each word with what seemed prolonged leisure, he calculated her response. "What exactly do you think I'm summing?"

"What exactly are you asking?" she frowned. "Are you asking me to assess, judge or calculate you or the potency given in your words?" Julia tested, shifting disconcertedly in her seat, yet feeling strangely intrigued by the task.

"Which do you find more comfortable?" Michael asked in a mellowed tone, turning sharply in his seat. He faced her fully with the warmth of a slow smile.

"Well," Julia shrugged, muttering the word in a breathless sigh. Brown eyes grew cautious in their assessment of the man, weirdly ensnared by his question. Her curiosity tripled in weight.

"Hello! Hello! Hello!" like the chorus of a catchy song, the blissful greeting tolled harmoniously through a vaguely inebriated room. Startling two, their bodies spun precipitously towards the interrupting expel, almost spilling the hankered drinks in their hands. Phillip and Sarah's smiles were much like a second rising to an already risen sun. The glow on their faces was unmistakably profuse, and the temperature of the room climbed an added degree, wrapped snuggly with the enlivened air that their presence transmitted.

Michael's face was slow to show pleasure in his friends' untimely intrusion, coming closer, than even he expected, in the clarifying of what still needed clarification in his head. It seemed almost a farce to not have had the chance before now. With another swig of his drink, Michael washed the acrid taste of disappointment from his mouth, already missing the morning's unembellished appeal. He reclined with a mawkish grunt, undetected over the newly pulsating babble in the room.

Since meeting her, she had occupied more than a sylphlike portion of his thoughts, although to date, playing the observant tree had been more his forte by choice. Studying and learning as if for a test, he had been somehow gratified with having just that. Their work together was, in part, his biggest deterrent, learning over the years to leave working relationships untouched. Things just ran smoother with such edicts in place, and he could not help but wonder on how much one morning may have changed all that.

Openly excited to see the new arrivals, Julia smiled her pleasantries with resonant zest, giving no further thought to the unique conversation with her host. Julia gave full attention to Phillip and his wife. The man was well use to asserting his charm, and making his guest comfortable would be a priority by far. After all, he had a reputation to uphold. A reputation that had well preceded her visit, and one she had been quite cautious to stay clear of until now. Not that she expected to perceive a lash from Mr. Dunhill's dexterous tongue. Thankfully, curiosity, though pungent, bore not the same color as interest, for she held not the slightest speck of such ambition in her head. The strategy of her goal was already established—work, part company amicably as associates—the end.

Chapter Eight

As if it aggregated its strength from some unseen rift, February crept in as fiendish as the year's genesis vexingly fled. Determined to supplant its predecessor's frigid escort, the rascally weather tarried not from its mulish ambition. Rather, it generously amplified the wont of its intolerant bulk, seemingly unwilling as it was unlikely to abstain.

Winter, it would seem, now dwelt in the Carolinas. Maintaining stringent command of itself, it massaged the icy days in its ever rappelling hands. Nights sprouted with a lengthier ambit. Plunging colder with each descent, it deferred not to the normal disjoined that was immemorially set. And each day meandered awake with a drearier disposition than the one before that. The arctic chill appeared adamant in its intent, exempting a sparse reveal from the sun. Sol's rays were drastically denied the usual access. Hence, darkness only spurred to a dulling gray, as the atmosphere seemed clutched in a perpetual eclipse.

Today throve no different than the four days now erstwhile past. In brewing its glacial guise, the dour day held little in the way of excitement. Anointing the sapping gray into a melancholy existence, twenty-six degrees was speculated to be the high. Yet without a dapple of sunlight to spruce the day's mood, the temperature fell well below the inferred height.

Julia adjusted the snug fit of her robe against her body, wrapping her arms tightly about herself. She buffed the nippy papules from the gradient of said limbs, and a long yawn reinforced the lethargy of a humdrum day. With a sigh, Julia scrutinized the muddy ambiance of the sky. Toting of black, fixed on sabotaging the scant light, already dyed the dusky welkin, and the mood that descended with the sight was no less than it would be had the warmth been physically snuffed. Impelling the soft judder of a chill, it waded through her body like the undulant of a wave. Deepening in resolve as the fated day bowed its ceded head, and in such leaving little wonder as to her thought.

"Are we almost finished, guys?" Julia queried with a coupling sigh, turning from the window. She eyed the children's faces for an equated response.

"Can I have what's left of the Reese's cup?" Rachel blurted in a gusting breath, bequeathing her mother a mesmeric smile. She declared the request an imperative one.

"You know the rules, Rachel." Julia hummed, her despotic tone sailing unbending, yet as a whisper, she negated its irascible bite.

"Yeah!" Richard barked readily, leveling a suspicious glare across the table, his eyes seemed prepared to rend flesh. "What about me?" he probed in a nasally grumble. "Don't I get to share the Reese's?"

"I just figured you wanted the Snickers." She expressed with the casual ascend of her shoulders; as if the assumption had been a natural conceit. Rachel's reply came as a sapling pun.

"The rules are the same, as always, guys. Nothing new has been added and nothing has been taken away." Julia advised coolly, and her announcement came forth no less reverent than a stately address. Competently warding off the inchoatives of an argument, she skated the inevitable bombardments to come.

With Valentine's Day approximate accession, the kids were already athrill, for it seemed any occasion that awarded them candy was deemed worthy of their abounding regard. For them, trading hearts and other specially made gifts was always an enlivened occurrence, and thus far, their afternoon was spent dedicated to just that. Now each was left to personalize the almost eighty sachets of assorted treats, a hodgepodge benefiting two classrooms and a gathering of friends.

It was the simplicity of their joy for moments as this that brought the most pleasure to her day. Shedding light, as always, on the astringency of her world outside of them, a tincture so revered in an otherwise sullied subsistence. Perceptive to her faults, she was ever reminded of her penchant to submerse herself effusively in work. Although her weekend, most assuredly, made a mockery of such sense, if any, it refuted such theory in spades. Still, as if in opposition of the truth, the occasion effectually verified a rapid descent in her patience, bringing to light flaws she never once suspected she had.

Envisioned in its conception as an indulgence for them, the afternoon did not rear exactly as a gratifying thrill for her. Escorting Richard and Rachel along with four accompanying friends—on a self-inflicted junket of sort—left her mostly with a thriving sense of regret than anything else.

A newly released movie was the first tackling of their day, and the event left her more depleted than it probably should have. Although, in her defense, the congestion alone was exacting on the soberness of one's nerves, even in the absence of all else. Closely following that excursion, lunch ensued at an overcrowded restaurant, where patience seemed oddly a scarcity in both patrons and staff. A sightseeing jaunt through the mall reared no easier than the beginning affront, nipping not-too-subtly at her endurance. Though it was their endless high pitch chatter, paired sharply with their squeaks, squawks and giggles that finally severed her calm. The self-proposed outing had successfully left her perversely edgy, and by days end, she genuinely longed for the comfort of her bed and the solace of an isolated space.

"Everything will be divided evenly as it always has. No one is entitled to more than the other; you know that, although bartering still remains a workable option as always." She informed in perpetuation of before, hammering the shrewdness of her dictate in place, she smiled. "However," Julia warned firmly, and a hand fully wadded with scraps of paper and the shredded bits of empty plastic bags, stalled suddenly in its rise. "Each party *must* first be open to the possibility before any such action can begin." The garbage can jerked open as her hand dropped like a gavel to hover atop its lid, sounding eerily like the squawking of a crow. It waited patient as she emptied the fillings of her hands.

"Both parties *must* agree," she reiterated with a gentle, singsongy moan, turning slowly. Julia's eyes dallied decisively on their faces, delaying interminably on the eldest of the two, she resumed her speech. "Before *any* trading can be finalized as a trade," and an austere pitch again trod with her continued preaching, though the gentleness in her eyes truly differed the bruising effect. The innocence of two seraphs stared back as if without sin, seeming oblivious to the meaning of her unnecessary dictate. Only one question was expressed in the anxiousness of their wait. "Have I made myself clear, answered all lingering inquest to your satisfaction?" Julia asked whispery sweet, each word coming like a well-rehearsed ditty through the silence. Both heads moved then almost as one, vigorously bobbing, they noiselessly gave a resounding—yes.

The motto of their home needed no clarification in its bylines. Yet such lectures did little to stem the prospective glitches that sometimes lurked, this, irrespective of what steps gets taken prior to the turbulent result. Julia knew to expect the grumblings as she would the darkness that assured them night. With a recurrent dominant approach, Rachel's coaxing was not always in the form of a request. At times, they resembled an outright bulldozing. Whatever the reason to spawn their discontent, Julia knew at least one, if not two, would appointed themselves master soon enough.

"Good!" she chirped, her head dropping slowly with the playful melody of the word, waiting without movement. Her eyes remained steady on both faces. "Okay." She announced in acceptance of the silence, nodding as if to answer an unheard request. Julia set herself to the task of divvying their treats, M&M, Snickers and the coveted Reese's cup all scattered at once.

"Hello! Where's everyone?" Delia called, her voice drifting to them faint, reaching their ears like the muffled static on a badly tuned radio. It dissipated the very instant it hailed.

"We're in the sunroom, grandma!" Rachel bellowed in response, her eyes fixed on the door.

"There they are!" Delia sang, gliding through the entrance with an ostentatious flare. She looked almost ready to curtail the full use of her legs, conveyed thus by the graceful execution of her flounce. Winged at her side, two small bags dangled carelessly from the tips of both hands, as if to balance the elaborate display. Mostly brown hair, with dusting of sand and the soft highlights of a dusky auburn, swayed happily around the pale, plump lines of her face. Kicking madly from her shoulders, it seemed caught in the throes of a game. Green eyes, resembling the edging of an ocean's end, sparkled with the raptness of her smile. Wading full, her beauty was incontestable, its reverence as enduring as the sun. A loveliness that endured undaunted through the wilt of a half century, posted still in the exquisite tiers of her sixties. A poignancy that now breathed its seasoned breath upon the passing of each day, though she'll remain forever graceful, classic and true in the gulches of her daughter's eyes.

"Hi, mom!" Julia beamed warmly, finishing the mandated doling, she straightened from her task.

"Hello!" Delia returned in an extended chirp, bending, she dropped a kiss to the waiting heads of each child. "Happy Valentine's to you, and also to you," she warbled, placing the small bags in their hands. She stood back with a pleasant smile, openly delighted with her gift.

"What am I, invisible?" Julia griped, spreading her arms wide in emphasis of her query, an exaggerated frown belied the blatancy of her jest. "You do know you wouldn't have grandkids without me, right?" Julia asked in a grumbly tone, dropping her hands as a handle to hips. Her frown deepened as her mother awarded the quip with an undaunted shrug. "I'm supposed to be your daughter. You know, the one you supposedly love so much."

"Oh, don't be a baby." Delia admonished gently, waving off the soft ranting with a quick flip of her hand. Her viscous New York dialect carried a touch of potency to the argument's depths, thickening the meekness of her words. "You had your day. We spoiled you like the baby you were." She reminded with a teeming smile.

"So what am I now, over the hill? I'm too haggard to even get a hello?"

"Cupcakes!" Richard announced at a near shout, removing one of the treats from its housing in the bag, his bliss was fully publicized in his eyes.

The illustriously decorated dessert needed no introduction. Ascribed distinctive, the Edible Art signature was plainly spelt, and from the tailored gawk Julia leveled at her mother, her eyes said as much. For a collection of years, more than seven to be exact, the aforementioned bakery had been her favorite for dessert, heedless of occasion. Their quality, she freely attested without contrition, surpassed the distinction of most. "Mom, you wouldn't?"

"Oh, jeez," Delia grunted in return, waving her hand to ensure silence. She asserted her will in a near dry tone. "If you're going to whine, you might as well make yourself useful and bring in the bags I left by the door."

The invitation seemed barely tendered before it saw Julia whirling from her place. Eager to abide the directives, she almost sprinted to the designated spot. "Thanks, mom!" came her exalted cry, falling backwards over trim shoulders, it needed no addendum to state its case, for it was plainly understood in the magnificence of her bellow. The supposed bags were nonexistent, but that did little to dampen the avidity of her mood, as in its stead. The infamous white box waited like the welcome visage of a friend.

"Happy Valentine's Day," Delia murmured, her face carved with a sardonic smile. "You thought I forgot you, didn't you?" She teased, nudging her daughter's shoulder with a gentle tap of her own.

"Maybe," Julia shrugged, giving forth an impish smile. "No." She countered in follow, waving her head as if to aid her reply, though the answer came with surety then. Confident in her mother's devotion, her second reply foretold just that. "Care to share a slice with me?"

"Sorry, darling, I can't eat another bite." Delia stated with a low grunt, touching a hand to her stomach, she smiled. "Tomorrow, I promise." She sighed. "Come to think of it, I'm too tired to do much of anything. I think all I can manage right now is a good soak before bed."

"Did you ladies have fun?" Julia probed tauntingly, almost singing the words; she turned in time to see Rachel's pinched fingers, now cradled by her tongue, disappeared from view. Assured in her knowledge, she needed no guess on what was held between the padding of those veiled digits, since the mousey chasms were well visible on the small dessert. Richard's cupcake already showed a long trench marring its middle, with two candy bars still clutched deep in the palm of his hand. His attention veered little from the two. Evidently, his difficulty lied with choosing between the sugary treats, and both seemed the wiser decision than actually acceding to the pleasure of one.

"Okay, guys, new rules." Julia interrupted quickly. "I'm sure you'd like to have a cupcake, so pack up all your candy and put them to the side." Smirking at the sudden sight, she was amazed by the swiftness to which the task was then done. Her proposal was met with immediate fulfillment, and with so doing, she averted the dispensing of reprimands from her path. "So, did you?" she asked without turning from the two, resuming her prior conversation with little hitch.

"We did." Delia averred dully, giving then a pleasant smile. She looked suddenly as spent as she felt. Listlessly, she adjusted the leather straps of her purse, feeling suddenly weary, as if someone had syphoned every granule of energy she had, and she could hardly wait to put her now weakened bones to bed. "Key West was beautiful." She shrugged gingerly. "A little cooler than we expected. Except now I need a refuge to recoup from my retreat." She groaned, clarifying this with a soft laugh, she edged towards the opening of the door. "How was your little excursion this weekend?" she asked, turning curiously to the room.

"Wonderful!" Julia smirked, pushing a renewed sense of exuberance in her tone. She threw her eyes to the ceiling at an excruciating pace. "Why, are you sorry you missed out?" she asked sweetly, remembering her mother's chidings for assuming such a job. Her retort came as a taunt. With six pre-hormonal chatterboxes to contend with, it was plain to see why one might find it necessary to avoid any such recurrence.

"A car full of persistent chatter is not my idea of fun. I'm too old for that." Delia asserted with a groan, rolling green eyes to the ceiling, she sighed as if the thought itself wore badly on her nerves. "Besides, there's a reason I only had one child. Two is too noisy."

"You only had one child, mom, because your body wouldn't let you have more." Julia countered in a quick breath, hitched on the tail of a soft chuckle. Her eyes danced with amusement. Cognizant of her parent's struggle to have more children, their concession came on the follow of six miscarriages. Conceding their efforts then, they devoted themselves to the daughter they already had. "Besides, in one, you had perfection," Julia continued, moving her hand as a wand, she emphasized the exquisiteness of her form. "Everything that followed just felt inferior to the prize. They were all awed by the magnificence of what preceded them." Replicating the tale once told to her as a girl, she smiled, this after venting her fervent need for the addition of siblings. The flare, however, was all her own.

"There might be a hint of truth in that argument somewhere. Or maybe it's just been an imperceptible rumor of some sort." Delia intoned tamely, laughter floating from her light, though still dampened with fatigue. It played like music to the listeners' ears. Subtly, she shifted her stance, edging her way closer to the door. She paused.

"Go get some rest, mom. I'll see you in the morning."

"No need to tell me that twice. As it stands, that's my sole intent. Goodnight, guys." She called, whirling on her heels without finalizing the tell. Needing no further encouragement, Delia slipped quickly from the room, her words trailing in her sluggish retreat.

"Love you!" Julia called through the remnant of a smile.

"Love you more!" Dalia sang.

"Thanks for the cake, mom!"

"Thanks, grandma, we love you!"

"Anytime, angels, I'll see you in the morning for my kisses, okay?"

"Okay!"

Retrieving her disciplinarian hat, Julia's palms kissed in the guise of an echoic slap. Effectively, she garnered their immediate attention. "Okay, guys. Put the rest of your cupcakes away and go and get started on your chores. Let's leave the candy here, please, and remember if you will, Valentine's Day is not until tomorrow. So let's save the rest of the snacking for at least the actual day. This way you can essentially enjoy the goodies when you should." She smiled, noting the sudden sloping of their backs, as if the reminder of chores efficiently devoured their zest. Lagging feet scraped the sunroom floor with what hummed well as doom, sounding weighted with lead. They took their time completing each task.

Outside, darkness coagulated upon itself like an experiment gone awry. Setting all evidence of day to its back, fragments of light drifted through the soupy swathing. Broadcasting little, the air stood stark and unmoving, and you could almost hear winter's harrowing breath as it corroded the eerie black.

Chapter Nine

Blustering billows poached an ebon sky, churning wildly, its stodginess slovenly abated with the promise of tomorrow. Darkness blanched to heathery gray after long, ebbing in strength, night begrudgingly assented its will to the crispness of morning.

But for its torpid unfurling, the new day tenured scant assurance aloft its dingy launching, as icy rain combed a frosty dawn. Roily clouds, clasped staunchly to gables and ridges, veiled well the journeying slickness descent. Though not so for the sickles now smeared upon the foliage's edge, glistening on leaves as sparsely as it did the ground. Vestiges of smoke from deadened hearths, loitered the grouchy atmosphere like redolent smog, thus it bonded well with the musky stench of dampened earth. The prickling haze dauntlessly dressed the wintry blend with its own aromatic distinction.

Julia gave the spritzing spectacle only her faintest regard, knowing fully that morning's departure brought with it the façade's end. However, ample sleeting is expected with night's cheerless commence. Irrespective of the irritant weather, the dusky morning dashed onwards as if on massive wings, hence it granted no ease to the litany of her toils. Quietly, Julia lent the clock an impatient gaging, brushing by the mantel, she postured expectantly by a window in wait. Her gaze pasted sharply to each vehicle's approach.

Already, a substantial portion of the morning was spent working on the ironing of her script, and although the laborious task of haggling with her children trailed the immensity of her effort. It bred strenuous when rated in comparison, for getting them off to school remains a commission to be dreaded at times. Tittering over coffee with her mother gave the morning an ample dose of joviality. Thus the effort marked the foundation of her day. A miniscule collection of undertakings came in follow of that; none coasting forward as trivial or excessive in their rank, not the least of which will be her upcoming meeting with the partners, applicably set to follow the morning's planned event.

"Where are you?" she griped in a hushed, anxious breath, wearing a frayed path between her front windows and hearth, Julia searched the neighboring streets for signs of her awaited delivery. Smiling gladly when, as if on cue, or in ode to her irked ramblings, the white van appeared as if powered by air. "You're late." Julia scolded in a mumbled breath, hastily retreating from view. She ducked into the cavern of her bedroom closet, earnestly listening for the signal of a bell while she busied herself. "Could you get that, mom? I'm not dressed." She chanted, sweetening the verve of her voice when at last the chimes swanked merrily through the house.

"Okay." Delia responded, her voice flowing back melodic and sweet.

Julia's chuckle floated like a soft draught before slender fingers stifled an indescribable snort, and none but her fashionable attire witnessed the uninhibited burst. The day's effort was ordained for a mother well deserving. Knowing her father—the genius that he was—reigned as conqueror above all when it came to such things. His talent for making the simplest exertion flower into something breathtaking was unsurpassed, and Valentine's Day remains his absolute best. The token was given in reverence of his impermeable effort as much as it was in recognition of her mother.

"Julia!"

"Yes!" she sang, her answer sailing back casual as she browsed the contents of her closet.

"Julia, you need to come see this." Delia called back anxiously, smiling widely as the recipient of her summons popped into view. With intrigue showing bold in her eyes, her voice rocketed through the room like the frolicking notes of a jingle. "Come take a look at this!" she encouraged with a mischievous snigger.

A frisky simper shepherded Julia's progress in the room, widening with the accosting view. Her treads mimicked the dance of a rooster initiating his prowl. "Nice!" she crooned with candor tainting the arc of her smile, setting her gaze to the corpulent posy of pink roses now clutched to her mother's breasts. Her brows jutted to their max. A second bouquet, nearly half as voluminous as the first, though bolder in red, waited at Delia's feet.

As if forgotten, the portal waited wide at her back, giving evidence of the tapering stream. The door seemed a sudden extension of her mother's hip, held to its place by some unseen hand. Curiosity roped aptly on the reins of her excitement, highlighted now on the features of her face, though only the "who" reared most prominent in her head. And whether the elation she felt was from the joy of seeing her mother's gladness, or from the comical effect of her act. The day's gloom seemed to suddenly shed its disdain. "Someone has a secret admirer!"

"Yes. Someone does!" Delia admitted with a smile, her voice blithesome and rich in its return. "So who is it?"

"What! How do you expect me to know that? You're a big girl. I don't oversee your trips." Julia teased, setting her hands akimbo. Her eyes again stroked the delicate petals with interest. "Who knows what goes on with you on all your excursions? It just might be that you're the talk of the town."

"Well…you can delve into that little anecdote at your leisure, should you wish." Delia warbled, her tone measured like the officiator of a game. "Or to your heart's content if that's to your choosing. But as it stands, dear, these are not meant for me. They're meant solely for you." Delia twittered with a long, satisfied sigh, giving the exquisite arrangement a lengthy appraisal at the argument's end. Her mien was that of a well satiated hyena, revived sumptuously to life by the richness of its meal. Her deportment was candidly mocking. Blooms crisp and unblemished stood erect in their place, looking much like the starting of blush. They waited in a sheet of white elegance. "They're for you, dear." She regenerated in a rhythmic hum, as if to hammer home the exigent of her point. Her eyes danced with unbridled enthusiasm, seeing the dumbfounded look on her daughter's face. Her teeth shone as if they now sat on display at a show.

"For me?" Julia queried tartly, skepticism sharpening her tone. Her face immediately exhibited a condescending scowl, as if the mere suggestion now rendered her mother fully mad. And just the possibility of that phenomenon made her fit to be carted off to an asylum for a long stay. "Did you do this?" she asked, looking somewhat flustered, her frown instantly softened to stunned, well assured the answer would be yes.

"I did not." The quick retort came with an equally widening smirk, as did the sharp rise of her thin brows.

Not bothering with supplementary questions or quips, Julia snatched the arrangement from her mother's hand. Taking flight out the door, she sought to put straight what she knew was, most certainly, an error on their part. "Excuse me!" Julia called in a shrilly tone, adjusting the flowers in her hand, her feet alighted their wings as she virtually flew down an assemblage of steps. "Excuse me!" she hailed once more, heightening her pitch to the driver's back as he slammed the rear door of his van. Stopping short in his retreat, he gave the door a final tug before turning his puzzled attention on her.

"Excuse me," Julia panted as she reined her feet to a stop, specks of her nettling emotion already evident on her face. "I think there's been a mistake. You have the wrong address. These are not mine." She averred with conviction, thrusting the large arrangement towards his hands, a stiff smile wrapped the end of her speech. "Someone would be really disappointed if you left these here," she remarked blandly, looking the flowers over once more, she could not help but admire their beauty. The giver, she saluted in her head, had impeccable taste. "Really disappointed," she groaned.

"Really?" the baffled driver questioned anxiously, and strobes of brindled emotions jumped boldly to his eyes. Ignoring her offering, the perplexed man moved immediately to the passenger side of his van. Swinging the door open with controlled haste, he plucked the waiting manifest from the passenger's seat. In the silence that followed, his dark face grew expressionless, grazing the paper in his hand. His eyes scanned what seemed the full length a dozen times, if not more, before showing the first sign of life. Turning his gaze at last to the flowers still waiting in her hand, he wobbled his head in what seemed vaguely an answer to her account.

"No." His announcement came at long last with finality, and a small show of satisfaction lit his dark eyes at the succinct chant's end. With one last scoping of the sheet in his hand, he expanded on his earlier assert. "This is the address I have for that delivery." He voiced, matching her labeling to his, he asked with a quizzical quirk to his brows. "Julia Berwick?" The question was set forth in a gentle tone, though it stood definitive in its quest.

"Yes." She grunted with an immediate twinge to her brows, and the answer came back sounding almost unsure. A bewildered knot tightened the rut in each individual pleat, eyeing him now with certain distrust. She awaited his blow.

"Then there's no mistake, ma'am." He informed with a small shake of his head. "The flowers were sent to this address, and yours is the name attached. They belong to you, ma'am." He announced with a proxy smile. Resentfully, he dragged his eyes away from the papers in his hand, making contact with hers; they fairly smirked as he furthered the bruising. "Happy Valentine's Day," He hummed, and his voice came nigh to sounding like a jest, adjusting the damp hat on his head. He proclaimed the discussion at an end, and with so doing, turned dismissively towards the van.

"But—but they can't be." Julia cried, her voice sounding suddenly small.

"I'm sorry, ma'am, but my paper says that they are." He rasped. His face folded promptly to that of a dubious gawk, and although he gave no other insight as to his thoughts. It was plain to see his expression held some inkling of shock.

"But…" she hailed lightly, not having much else to offer that would be otherwise convincing. Her words stalled in their place of rest. If this was not an indulgence from her mother, she knew of no one that would go to the extreme or the expense. Without encouragement, no one she knew would take the time.

Delia's stout frame prowled the door's opening like a dog exploring the scent of a decadent treat. Seeming as twitchy or as giddy as a teenage girl, the ocean tinting of her eyes swooned their ebullient swells. They virtually glistened as she watched the disquieted approach from the younger of them. The large bouquet—now nestled on Julia's hip—was almost mocking to her strides, and the long expression, so aptly disclosed on her face, only worked to sweeten the mirth.

"So, darling," she sang with grandiose glee. "Who are they from?"

"I don't know!" Julia huffed, and her answer almost climbed to the altitude of taking flesh. Whipping past her mother—whose lovely form still blocked half the door's opening in exposition of her glee—she stomped the moisture from her feet. And one could well suspect from taking in the view, that that was not the only reason behind the thudding of the floor. Small flexing of slush waited on the fabric of her robe, and from the flogging she gave herself in a sham of dislodging the tiny beading. Her displeasure needed no glossary for a guide. It was well apparent to the blind.

"Perhaps you should try reading the card, dear." Delia expounded with a sarcastic smile, her delight in the moment was well exaggerated in the saccharine tone. Absently catching the door's edging, she let the wooden barring fly. The thud of its snagging was categorical, rattling the windows, it echoed loudly throughout the entire house.

"Try keeping the door on the hinges, mom." Julia voiced then through an appalled smirk.

"I'll pay for any damages." Delia scoffed back swiftly. "Open the card." She pressed in an importunate tone, traipsing behind her daughter who eagerly dashed from the room. Her own bouquet now flushed against her waist.

"I can't do that!" Julia gasped, an astonished glare pulling at her brows. "It's not mine!" she explained as if to an annoying child, setting the collection of pink bulbs on the kitchen counter, her tone came forward almost as a sneer. "They'll be back for it, just watch."

Admiring the monstrous arrangement, Delia sighed wearily to herself. To be sure, there was at minimum four dozen blooms prominently displayed in the tall, basin-like vase, noting again that Julia's name was boldly written on the card. She enlightened her of such. "But it has your name on it." Delia remarked blandly, plucking the card from its resting place, she waved it through the air like a tormenting flag. "Julia Berwick." She enunciated softly, as if reading the title of a book. "That's your name alright. I know, since I gave it to you myself." She quipped dryly, though the cynicism was not lost on its intended. Inquisitively, Delia flipped the card in her hand, surveying the back, she asked. "Aren't you even the least bit curious on who would be sending you such a lovely gift?"

Without lifting her head, Julia sent the arrogant response flying over her shoulders, leaving no doubt as to what the word meant. "No!" feeling certain in her conviction, she knew the only logic was that an error was made. One she expected resolved within the hour, and with that, the inquisition will have been for naught. "Who's yours from?" she asked in a spirited draught, more interested in seeing her mother's response. She aimed her sights on that.

"I'll check mine if you check yours." Delia bargained with a sweetened flare. Temptingly, she flapped the envelope in her hand. The possibility of an admirer had her fully intrigued, showing in her eyes as scenarios flickered through her head. For one, this could mean her daughter will again start the forward impetus of her life. Still stalled from the dissatisfaction of her divorce, she sputtered to a dead stop with the demise of her dad. If this small jolt meant she no longer hid from the world, or as her mother, not having to watch the dwindling, then she was definitely onboard for that.

"What has you so excited?"

"Excuse me for wanting to see my daughter add some form of spice to her life."

"My life is spiced enough. Why don't you throw that advice back at yourself?"

"I'm an old woman, Julia." Delia answered dimly with a slow roll to her head. "I've already had my spice, plenty of it to be exact." Waving the envelope brusquely, she again beseeched. "Come on," Delia smiled sneakily. "Take a chance."

"Mom, there's nothing and no one to take a chance with. I'm telling you, it's not mine."

"Fine!" she thundered then, her defiant grunt sweeping the room like a squall. Flipping the envelope in her hand, there was no mistaking her intent.

"Mom, don't!"

Settling the envelope in her palm, Delia ripped the flap open with one fluid swipe of her hand, snatching the card free. She smiled with approbation in her eyes.

I can find no better way to say you have brightened my day, or to tell you on this occasion when hearts are meant to be expressed, that you, Julia, are my most revered valentine.

Happy Valentine's Day from a very infatuated admirer,

Finishing in a whisper, Delia sighed, smiling with fulfilled satisfaction at the shocked mien that her daughter now had. "Still think it's not yours?" she mocked, her eyes twinkling with delight, daring a rebuttal of the facts.

"I don't know anyone who would be sending me that." Julia shrugged perplexedly, though thoughtfully racking her brain. "I barely have the time to scratch my head, much less get into sparring for a date."

Although all observations were given with love, the green eyes practically screamed their disbelief of such facts, though they held their silence as to how she truly felt. Obdurate in all deed, it had never been an easy task getting a fix inside Julia's head. Once her mind was made, then the fight was mostly lost. Her decision to evade life had been the hardest diktat, as a mother, to remain neutral on, hiding behind her work and her children. She insisted on watching what she should, instead, be a part of.

"So hiding works better for you?"

"I don't hide!" Julia objected loudly. "I'm just happily busy." She shrugged, well contented with her choice. "Maybe I'm looking for someone to look at me the way your guy looked at you."

"How would you be able to tell, dear?"

"I guess when I see it I'll know."

"My dear, that head of yours is buried so far into the crevices of your work and that of the kids' lives, you can barely recognize your own befuddled reflection gaping back at you in distrust, even with the brilliance of the midday sun spotlighting the cause."

"My, listen to you, we're feeling very fervent today. Could it be you have your own tale to tell, mother?"

"I doubt that very much since I've already told my story, and it's a rather long and auspicious tale." Delia crooned, shaking her head at the sudden switch. Well aware the pivot was her signal to put her prodding to bed. Pressing blushed colored lips tightly together, she quietly opened her card.

For that which never dies, like us, love stays eternal, boundless and true.

Happy Valentine's Day, for the man whose heart was his guide, from your little girl whose heart he still has.

Delia's voice again trailed to a whisper as she finished the simple note, her eyes tacked keenly to the small card cradled in her hand.

"Happy Valentine's Day, mom," Julia whispered, pressing a kiss to her mother's cheek. "We wanted you to know how much we love you and how special you are to us."

"Thank you, sweetie, you're very special to me, too—you all are." Delia smiled, dabbing the corners of her eyes with a finger, she gathered her daughter's eyes.

"We know, mom. We just wanted to make sure you remember that for yourself."

"Now look at me," she griped in a shaky breath, wiping her hand gruffly across her eyes. She sniffed loudly in her wont of control. "Sniveling like a baby, gosh, I must look like such a fool."

"Your secret is already out, mom. We all know you're a big softy."

"I don't think I'm the one who cries at commercials."

"What can I say, I learned from the best." Julia laughed, hugging her mother to her side. She gently squeezed her shoulders before again kissing her cheek. "Now," she sighed with finality to her tone, her thin shoulders plunging as if yanked. "I need to battle this heat wave we're having so I can go and prove my worth." Mindlessly tightening the belt on her robe, she peered out the window with a solemn sigh.

"Just be careful you don't get burned." Delia added quickly, still fighting to reset her composure, the swift quip came as natural as her breath.

"What do you think, summer dress? Or should I play it safe and go with my smallest bikini?"

"With this heat, you'll be better off with as little as possible. I'd go with nothing."

"Wild woman," Julia smirked, scurrying gaily from the room, she suddenly stopped. "I should be home before the kids get off the bus, but just in case I'm not, I left Gloria a note."

"No need to worry Gloria about that. I'll be here all day. I'm re-cooping, remember?"

"I remember. I just thought maybe you'd want to rest quietly."

"I'm old, I'm not dying, Julia." Delia objected loudly, making certain her voice carried down the hall to her daughter's back. "You make it sound like having a conversation with my grandkids is too much work."

"I just don't want you to think I take you living here for granted." She countered in a low chirp, returning her attention to her mother. "You already raised your kid. I don't want you to think you need to raise mine."

"I'm their grandmother for Christ's sake. I like doing it."

"I know, mom, but—"

"And I'm not made of butter! I did fine raising you, didn't I, the pain in the butt that you were?"

"I'm sure I was nothing but the perfect angel, so you must be mistaken on that."

"Ask Rachel that in about four years." Delia smirked. "You two perfect angels are nothing alike, so it should be a breeze for you."

"Trying to jinx me, mom?"

"What's to jinx, you're perfect, remember?"

"I most certainly am." She tweeted. "And now, this perfect one must be off." Sashaying down the hall, Julia waved a flamboyant farewell, her robe swaying like a gentle caress against her legs. The morning's accomplishments had severely lightened her mood, verified by the merry tune now drifting from her throat. She whisked hastily through the door of her closet, setting her task on getting dressed.

———

Already convened in expectancy of the day's work, the stylish dining-table looked no less prominent in its swish surrounding. Obscuring but a fraction of its rectangular max, scatterings of notes, pencils, pens and mugs, cluttered the lustrously polished slab like numbered parts in an assembly. In-between the gathering, two laptops occupied their usual space, hissing whispery soft, as if together they traded some coded speech. The smell of percolated coffee filled the expansive suite, swathing the rooms like a welcome hug. Various snacks of pared fruits waited on a large platter.

Absently toying with his mug, Phillip stared fixedly at his screen, absorbed in the appended idiom to her work. He mated her new ideas with those of his, testing the efficacy of their wealth. He, in truth, grew more impressed the further he delved.

"I like Julia's idea to add Jason in the scene at the restaurant," Phillip announced excitedly. "With him there, it gives a better reasoning as to why Beverly decided to leave. It also gives a better understanding to the conversation she later has with her sister."

"Have you seen how she proposed to handle the meltdown when the sisters return home?" Michael hummed, sounding likewise swayed. He glanced up from his laptop with the starting of a smile, and talons of admiration and pride seemed strangely ready to rend his friend's flesh. Having already gone over the projected changes, he fully concurred with the expansion made on the previous synopsis they had. The transformation gave certain kinship to the character's evolvement, and the new broaching does add a more robust body to the version projected for the screen. With such attributes embroiled in the plotting, it should help the story flow with a stronger current in the audience's eyes

"Yes I did." Phillip replied in a husky growl, his octave dropping to the edges of his toes.

"Brilliant, isn't it!" Michael teemed, again feeling an odd pricking from his pride. "Sarah was right. She is good!" He informed without lifting his head, leaving his voice void of everything but his assessment of her work.

"I don't think she intends to ever let us forget that." Phillip advised with a chuckle, already knowing his argument carried some truth. "We'll be beholden to her for a *long-time* for this."

"I sense a very large reward coming in lieu of the mere librettos delivered in a simple thank you. Something sparkling, I bet."

"That I can assure you, with all certainty, is an unquestionable fact. The only mystery here rested in the finale, more intriguingly, the cost."

Laughing at the certitude of that, Michael straightened in his seat, and his eyes, toting a mind of their own, rolled circumspectly over his watch. Discerning the time, his mind, for a trice, went uncharacteristically blank. Lost in the chasm of uncertainty, the correct action befitting his circumstance flew pertinently from his head. *Would she guess?* He wondered. *And if so, what then?* He griped, sounding almost befuddled, he heard little above the noise of the petitions in his head. Aware of nothing but the impending knock, his implementing of a plan took precedence above all else.

Long arms rose awkwardly to the ceiling in a stretch, flecking the muscles in his back. His measured ascension took him from the table in a properly guise sequence of blinks. Lumbering to the kitchen with his mug in hand, he gazed restively at the pot, looking edgy even in his stance. With less casual aesthetic than he intended, Michael ambled from room, smiling to himself as he ducked into the waiting solace of his bedroom. And had he not witness his own pitiful behavior himself, he would not have thought the day a possibility.

Never before now had he ever considered coping with the emotions strewn by the opposite sex—work. *Why would he?* Not when looking was always considered a welcomed pastime, and as one well fluent in the schematics of his masculinity, such baubles were a required treat, although things of such kind were, most assuredly, not so when it pertains to her. More opposite in their personality than not, she prove contradictory to every standard he once thought he knew. Ascertaining as much from his quiet surveilling, he hoped this new approach would stem the foolery going on in his head. Perhaps meeting her on his own term would give his reaction the normalcy it needed.

"Hello!" Phillip's voice rang rich with excitement from the entrance of the suite.

"Hello!"

"And how are you doing on this very fine day we're having?"

"I'm doing well, thank you. So well in fact, that I was actually debating whether I should bring out my bikini for the day. The weather seems ripe to go for a tan, don't you think?"

"Would you believe I struggled with that very concept this morning? I had the damnedest time picking out what to wear, finally I settled on these. What do you think?" he chirped, spreading his arms wide to concede her inspection. Phillip showed off the simplicity of a finely fitting gray shirt, rimmed subtly at the neck with a white T-shirt, blue jeans completed his modish ensemble.

"Good choice! It works well with the color of your eyes. I like it!" she averred spryly. "I came to the same decision in the end, but I do hope to find some time when it's at least a sweltering five outside to put my new bikini to use. Doesn't that sound like a thrill?"

"Absolutely, but I was more thinking of something in the negatives. That should make the party more fun.

"And I'll be right behind you cheering you on."

"Thanks. I think…."

"I'm guessing on days like this a Texan-slash-Californian boy like yourself stays huddled to the fire?" she purred, rolling her eyes with the jest, she smiled.

"Or turn the heat up to its maximum height. But that would only be if there was some ridiculous portent going on with the weather. But…" Phillip shrugged. "Thankfully it's not. The weather has been wonderful."

"It sure has." She affirmed with a chuckle, her laughter lifting to fill the room. "I'm feeling rather sympathetic today, so I guess I could extend some of that momentum to a weather fearing man like yourself." She hummed. "How's everything else going with you?"

"I can't complain, so I won't. How are the kids?"

"Doing their job, testing me every chance they get." She chirruped, and watched as his head bobbed in agreement of what that meant. "And yours?"

"Growing like weeds." He groaned, scratching the short hairs of his beard, amber eyes glazed as if in thought. Rare speckling of white peeked playfully throughout the dark bushing on his face with a distinguished edge. Clustering along his ears, the short hairs on his head showed off the same impending highlights. "Every time I see them, they seem to be bigger than when I left." He informed in what sounded much like a muse.

"I think they do that on purpose to drive us mad. Don't you?" Julia laughed, turning at the sound of footsteps to see Michael's prowling strides as he entered the room, and again she was beset with a new sense of wonder as to his looks. Or was it the entire package? Is it that he oozed sex appeal that had her curiosity a smidgen disturbed?

"Hello, Julia." Michael drawled, letting her name slide purposefully from his tongue, he noted her keenly. Discovering in an instant how useless his approach had been, for his breath now seemed bent on being jagged in his throat. The effect being no different than it's always been, and a new question dawned with the realization of that. Could it be something more than just her beauty that had him off balance?

"Hello, Michael." Julia responded in a low hum, gifting then a friendly smile. Surprise had her pulse tottering unstable in a flash, for his presence now seemed impossible to omit. Hard, tall, powerful and agile, his frame draped the room like some prerequisite of fine art, crafted only by the most prestigious artisan hand. In perfection, dark hair looked inordinately relaxed in the arching of his brows. Accompanying his salutation, the slow ascent made its way to her as a caress. Eyes set on a hypnotic bent, flashed their magnificence from across the room, seeming strangely iridescent as lights strobe their colorful depths as if by design. Affixing them to hers, meaty lips yield their magic in an alluring smile.

"How are you?" he rasped. As if his words were intended for only her ears, they came at an almost whisper, sounding even more rumbly in the gauged dispelling.

"Good. I'm very good. And you?" Julia inquired with a matter-of-fact shrug, pulling the straps of her briefcase from her shoulder. She settled it nervously in the same hand with her purse. It was no secret that Michael Dunhill was a handsome man, gorgeous to be exact, that truth, she or anyone fitted with eyes, was surely sanguine of. And although it was hard to think that his good looks somehow augmented itself, she could not remember him always looking *this* good before now.

"Doing well, and have even less to complain about with each passing minute." He attested in his raspy tone, following her movements with interest. He again noted that the sapid pull, he felt now two weeks past, still had not amended itself. Conversing with her was surely better spent than the usual inconspicuous glance.

"Then that makes you a very fortunate man." She smiled. Emptying the contents of her hands, a light frown funneled her brow, giving insight as to the direction of her thought. Had she been better able to discern the man and his mood, she would have responded with the warped onslaught of her humor. But he gave his answer so blandly that she doubted humor or bragging was, in any fraction, his intent.

"I won't disagree with that." Michael acceded with a slow nod, noting she did the same, as if in full agreement of what was said.

"Oh!" Julia gasped in remembrance of a thought, plucking the small bag from her purse. She waved it through the air with a timid smile, skillfully putting an end to the odd strain in their conversation. "I brought you something." She announced zealously, and as if needing support, her eyes immediately sought the friendly grapnel of Phillip's face. "It's not much, but since we're actually sharing this day together for a spell—the day being Valentine's Day, of course—I thought I'd share my Valentine's gift with you." She explained, shrugging lamely, she placed the small bag at the table's edge. Unsure of their customs or their likes, her smile came slightly strained, for it was especially so when it pertained to food. "It's only a slice of cake from my favorite bakery."

"Thank you. That's very nice." Phillip warbled back with genuine approval stoking his face. Leaning near, he peeked inside the bag, and the sweet aroma of vanilla effectively filled his nostrils. "It smells great. I can't wait to try it."

"It does, doesn't it? But the taste is even better than that."

"Thank you." Michael added in a small voice, noting shrewdly that her eyes never veered to his.

"It's really nothing." She shrugged, feeling suddenly despondent at the meager gift. "It's only a small piece, but I didn't even think of what day it was until last night. Late, I know, but my intentions are genuine."

"Now who's doing the feeding?" Phillip quizzed.

"I figured it was high time I return the favor. Make you nervous for a change."

"I'll have to remember that when we're eating." He laughed.

"It's Valentine's, shouldn't you be home celebrating?" Julia asked with a humorous twitch of her brows.

"We already celebrated our Valentine this past weekend, so I'm spared from the hazard for today." Phillip smirked, sending her a playful wink as he retook his seat.

"Smart man. Good for you! How's Sarah doing with work?"

"Huh, going mad." Phillip groaned. His tone, seeming almost curt, fell dryly from his lips. Wagging his head, Phillip offered an explanation as to why. "She's leaving for Paris in a few weeks for her show, so now she's slowly losing her mind in the process of getting prepared."

"Paris? How exciting,"

"Yes, very. Tell her that when you see her, will you? Since right now, she's pulling her hair out along with everyone else's." He laughed. "It's like that for every show. She goes mad the closer she gets to one. By now you'd think she'd be an old pro at the process."

"Wish her good luck for me." Julia laughed, and vision of Sarah bald, from anxiety of all things, zipped brusquely through her head. And although the image was somewhat amusing, she doubted anyone, including herself, craved the realization of that.

"I'll tell her when I see her tonight." Phillip purred, and his calculating smile required no additional wording as to their intent. "We're meeting for dinner and a few days by ourselves before she gets swallowed up with work, which in turn, will leave me in the role of Mr. Mom."

"Very nice," Julia hummed, her sly smile giving as much in its response as his had in the trenching of its foundation. "On second thought, leave my name out of the mix, will you?"

"How about you?" Phillip asked of a sudden, quickly switching the question to her. "How has the day been treating you, thus far?"

"It's been interesting."

"Interesting? That's not usually a word women use when describing their Valentine." He droned, and a devilish smirk skillfully amplified his taunt. Noted as well was the sudden burst of interest shown by the abnormally quiet Michael Dunhill, as if jarred awake. His attention seemed riveted on her reply. "Interesting, how?"

"I don't even know how to explain it. It's just been a little strange so far." She shrugged, pulling a folder from her case.

"Then later, you must have plans for later?"

"Yes, of course!" she announced with resounding zest. "Work,"

"Oh, come on." Phillip laughed, yet a part of him felt relieved for his friend. Voiced or not, there was definite interest, and it seemed remarkably strong. "You don't expect me to believe a beautiful woman like you has no Valentine?"

"It's hard to make plans when you have me working like a slave." Julia laughed, shrugging at the skeptical gawk thrown in her direction. "A very well paid slave, but…a slave nonetheless."

"Don't forget, we do throw in the occasional meal."

"That's true. So I guess I should stop my complaining then?" She laughed, swiveling in her chair as a loud thud echoed through the suite. Alleviating the need for further clarification, all heads turned sharply in response, and on each face curiosity was clear.

"I'll get it." Michael asserted with a smile, springing to his feet, his strides were determined in their bent, though on him, they resembled the lethal stalking of a feral beast. Returning almost the instant he left, his companion carried at least two dozen long stemmed roses, their blooms as rich as a good Bordeaux.

"Julia Berwick?" the attendant asked, his voice seeming soft, and unsure.

And for the second time in one morning, Julia hesitantly answered to her name. "Yes...."

"Happy Valentine's Day!" The young man smiled, handing over the large bouquet to her hands.

"What? How——" she started in a building pitch, looking and sounding confused.

"Happy Valentine's Day," Phillip reiterated without pause. "Consider it a small token for the day as well as everything else. We know you're not used to the rigor that comes with our line of work, so we just wanted you to know we appreciate your hard work and your dedication. I know it's really been different for you having to put up with us. It's been an experience, hasn't it?" He smirked, saluting her with a wink. He heaved his cup to the air in follow.

"Happy Valentine's Day," Michael added in a coarse whisper, his tall frame almost draping her side.

"Thank you! That's so nice of you. Thank you!" Julia's gushed, surprise well prominent on her face, though she was more amazed with the thoughtfulness of the act than the act itself, as their gesture of kindness was never an imagined one. Glancing profoundly at the flowers in her hand, she returned her brightened attention to the men. "I didn't get you anything." She groaned, suddenly feeling contrite about offering such a meager treat.

"There's no need, Julia." Phillip pledged in a resounding hum, his voice sailing aptly over the attendant's shoulders as he took his leave. "It's a gift of acknowledgement. Relax a few minutes and take it as it is. No compensation needed. Besides, you brought us cake, remember?"

"This is really very sweet. Really guys, thank you so much." She intoned once more, appraising the bouquet in her hand; she could not help but gauge her second delivery to that of her first. Prideful of both arrangements, the extravagance was in no way the same. Their exquisiteness was almost matching, though in some ways, the subtleness of the pink lent the blooms a higher elegance than the boldness of the red.

"They're beautiful." She confirmed in a mumble to herself, stifling a pervading thought that slowly trundled all else in her head. Realizing, with a deep intake of her breath, the path on which her thoughts were so easily led. "It all seems so strange," she droned. "Usually I like surprises, but I hope that's it for today."

"Why? How many surprises have you had?" Michael asked, showing renewed interest in the woman and her words.

"Well, not many, just…one—other. But this was more a snafu on their part than anything else. One I'm sure they've figured out by now. I can't imagine delivering flowers to the wrong person being good for business." She shrugged. "I tried telling him that but…" dropping her eyes to the flowers in her hand, she again offered a small shrug.

"Why are you so certain they're not for you?" Michael interjected softly.

"I just know. They can't be." She averred with a hint of conviction tilling the bed of her tone. Lifting her shoulders without hesitation, her head slowly wagged. "They couldn't be."

"Why such certainty? Don't you think your special someone adheres to customs like the rest of us?" Michael simpered, his query swirling like a low grumble in his throat.

"That would be a valuable point worthy of debate, if in fact there was something to debate upon."

"Then you should keep them, regardless."

"I couldn't. Not when some other woman is anxiously waiting for her beau's gift to show."

"Did you find them at least beautiful?"

"Yes, very! But what does that have to do with it?"

"Plenty, I think that alone makes them yours to keep."

"Why, because I think they're beautiful?"

"No. Because one surely seems befitting to that of the other, and that alone makes it a sure fit." Michael replied slickly, quietly reaching for his cup, he hoisted it to his mouth as a deterrent from the rest. With other words sitting bold on his tongue, his effort was now set on strangling their march before they slipped past his lips. Who knew a childish game would be this perfect to his cause? Michael simpered, for what better way did he have to introduce himself to her?

Julia's frown looked almost stunned. *Was that a compliment he just paid me?* She wondered in quick passing, answering the question just as quickly as it was asked. *No, of course not!* That's more a polite allusion than anything else. "That's very nice of you to say." She hummed. "But it's not up to me, really. The customer and the florist are the ones who get to make that call."

From his customary seat at the table's long edge, Phillip's eyes raced enigmatically between the two. Except for his breathing, he had not moved since retaking his seat, afraid to break the balmy interlude that had since risen between them. Dropping his head, Phillip forced his eyes to stay on the small screen stationed before him, even as his mind jerked at the sound of Michael's voice sailing in response. With curiosity winning for a spell, he resettled himself before long to work, and had he not been afraid of breaking the heated spell. He would have gladly vacated the room and left it to them.

"Was there a card attached?" Michael pried, further feeding his hunger for details of the event.

"Yes."

"Did you read it? It might have helped."

"No! Well…" her eyes rolled with an almost peevish dexterity to its sway, finishing on the tail of a sigh. She gave the disgruntled reply. "My mother did."

"Didn't that help to clarify the confusion?"

"If it had, then the matter would be over, now wouldn't it?"

"Could it be that that's what's bothering you? Is it the secrecy of the matter that makes it somewhat offsetting?" Michael droned. His eyes widening with interest, for any information gathered would be archived for later use.

"Actually, it's neither." She shrugged, her rejoinder given with a casualness that bespoke the truth of her morning. "It neither captivates nor troubles."

"Which only means then that I'm right?" curling slowly with sweetened satisfaction, Michael's smile grew unrelenting. "If the card held your name, then it goes without saying that the flowers belong to you. Your admirer evidently made certain of that—smart man."

"That's yet to be determined." Julia grunted, desperate in her need to challenge his smoldering gaze, for his eyes wandered now strangely familiar in their stroking of her face. "We'll just have to wait and see on that."

"Care to make a bet?" he asked in a deeply sly tone.

"And why would I do that?" Julia demanded sweetly, smiling curiously across the table at his challenging stare.

"For the mere joy of being right, what else?" Michael growled, deliberately taunting the handle of his mug. His fingers all but assaulted the ceramic vessel.

"If being right is that important, what do you suggest I do when I'm wrong?"

"Do I hear you conceding?"

"What do I have to concede? The choice was never mine to begin with."

"I believe the bet was whether I thought your admirer left you a beautiful trinket or not."

"You keep saying that. What admirer would that be?"

"Wouldn't it be your task to discover that?"

"Why? Things have a way of coming out on their own. It's only a matter of time before dawn breaks with the knowledge of what was. The sun has to come up some time or we're all doomed."

"I suppose that's true. But then…" he shrugged, his head angling slightly. "It would depend on the depth of your curiosity, I guess."

"Why should I be curious?" she smirked. Crossing her arms athwart her breasts, she leaned back slowly in her chair.

"You're not sure?" he rasped, sounding almost incredulous, his question rattled in his throat like the arrogant purr of a newly stoked engine. Enjoying her quick barraging response, he dared not relinquish the thorny tips of his needling now. "I mean, a man like that—"

"You seem certain it's a man?" she cooed, clarifying thus at his questioning smirk, and felt oddly pleased with the jolt her remark supplied. "These are different times Mr. Dunhill. Women are grasping just as much incentives as men."

Michael's head dipped in polite acknowledgement of the advice she gave, taking his fill, his eyes lightly fondled her face. "This…admirer," he started, bringing the mug slowly to his mouth, hazel eyes grabbed brown from atop the rim and held. Sheltered by the ceramic mug, Michael's smile grew to a delicious leer before he slowly sipped from the well cool chalice in his hand. "Your admirer," he resumed as he lowered his mug. "Just gave you a small piece of himself, I admire that." He nodded in ending, caressing the curved handle with casual boldness, the long digit on his hand returned to the top as proficiently devoted as it was before it left.

Strangely attentive to his action, Julia's eyes followed the ambling of his fingers. Work now properly forgotten, which, unwitting to her, was his intent. "But from the security of a safe fence." She grumbled, unable to stop herself from responding to the man, she again rose to his challenging inquest.

"You'd prefer it more if he—they…" he corrected with a broadening smirk. "…were more open with you?" Michael drawled, reclining in his chair, he pulled the mug slowly across the table towards its edge.

"Something has to be said for the long standing tradition of a handshake," she countered with a slow grin. "Friend or foe, you see them coming."

"Maybe she…" he rasped, showing open amusement at the thought, as the concept made the corner of his mouth curled into a devilish smile. And with that, he needed an added second to applaud himself for deliberately conceding to her request. *Take the small pleasures wherever you can get them*, Michael chided. "They…" he settled with a nod. "Maybe they thought the flowers would soften the shock of their entrance."

Perfect brows rose sharply in question at the strange suggest. Hearing a collection of doors slammed open on a comment such as that, it was almost too innumerable to count. "Is that so?" she purred instead.

"What better way to say, 'I like you'?" Michael asked in his bassy timbre, the heat in his tone intended as a definite caress, and curious eyes held firm to her near fastidious gaze. "And on what better day than on the one whose very history dictates that you should?"

"Regardless of history…" she paused, a witty reply stalled suddenly on her tongue, as a new thought eclipsed the itinerary of her rants. Strange, but something about his answer felt oddly similar to those on the attached note, but… she halted, shrugging the thought from her head, her laughter was almost an external display. Quickly composing herself, she straightened in her chair, as his gaze, in query, sharpened on her face. She knew better than to harbor the ridiculousness of such thought. Where did such a demented concept surface from? *Michael Dunhill, ah! How dumb would she have to be to even embrace the possibility of that?* She scolded. "Regardless," she continued, shrugging derisively. "It's all no more than a childish game."

"Maybe so," Michael retorted in a flash, further egging her on. "But one with very grown up intention, I bet."

"You know what they say about intentions, don't you?" Julia crooned, leaning forward as she delivered her counter with sugary precision. "It's an awfully long road to travel just to prove you can go to hell."

"I'm sure you've taken a trip or two regardless of destination." He smiled, mischief dancing in his eyes. "Enough to know that preparation for any trek can be more substantial than the journey itself. Especially once words like '*long*' comes attached to the mix. It's how you use that time that defines how you'll enjoy the work. So…be prepared, that would be my advice to you."

"Would your advice be for the journey or for the destination itself?"

"Feel free to pick. Whichever you choose, I'm sure will be just fine."

"I choose my destination with great care, and have for a very long time, and so far I've been quite satisfied with the results. I don't think I'm looking to divest just yet."

"You didn't mention the adventure of getting to the end." He hummed, his head swiveling slowly as if to admonish her choice. "Is that not an interest you share?"

"There's adventure and there's adventure, knowing which is which or when to say when, is a lesson some people never learn."

"And you have?" he asked with a grin.

"I have no complaints." She shrugged, letting her answer fly with detached ease. Her smile was to be revered as it purely dazzled.

"I'm not sure which one suits the other more, Julia." He drawled. "This day or the event surrounding," Michael quipped, and his smile grew leisured as he waited for the thrash of a retort that never came. Abruptly smothered with the blast from a sneeze, the explosion broke the bubble that kept them fully exempt from all else. Phillip's body slumped forward with the force of the expulsion, his face almost level with his lap. Two loud sniffs scratched the silence that followed before he slowly straightened in his seat.

"I'm sorry." He mumbled with sincere sensitivity. "Allergies," Phillip groaned blandly, nodding several times as if affirming this, not only to them, but to himself as well. His eyes again fell with the angling of his head.

Long after Phillip's attention retracted from them, wide eyes filled with dismay gaped at the top of his bowed head. The loud burst from his sternutation brought with it a sour insight that tasted every bit as foul as she felt. In truth, such behavior was not only incongruous; it was incredible offsetting to her. Behavior that was juried by him, and has therefore established a basic for which she could be judged.

Unobtrusively, Julia's eyes sank to the table and stayed, turning just as subdued in the anchoring of her seat. She kept her face hidden from any and all viewing. Though her eyes, as if of their own will, crept across the table to search out her accomplice's face. His befuddled frown eased with the ascension of her eyes, locking, their gaze stayed unimpeded and direct. And in the silence that followed, not even a sigh disturbed the air in the room. Almost sequentially, their chests rose and fell with the workings of their breaths. Michael smiled, and she in return attempted a liken response. Though a stiff show was all she effectively managed, before awkwardly breaking the hold he so competently held.

Scolding herself harshly, Julia's frown gave voice to the ravings in her head. Her confusion on the heavily laced banter, ironically fermented the complexity of her shock, and although she feverishly endeavored to return her focus to work, her turmoil was pervasive.

It was unlike her to be so easily led. Swallowing his baiting, she looked like an overzealous tot the further they trudged, and that had never been a trait closely related to her before now. Usually, her stellar control kept all thoughts and ramblings appropriately intact, ensuring that such nonsense stayed well barricaded in her head, as they should be.

Slinking another glance across the table, her eyes sought out the man. Stirring inquisitively, they explored him at every angle that was there to be had, and even under the pilfered viewing, his handsome face was charismatic in its reveal. Looking relaxed and unbothered, he showed none of the torments she now struggled to hide. In its stead, his face held the new frolicking of a smile, flaring intently, as if something sweet tickled the crux of some memory he had. It sharpened an already grand exhibit.

Of a sudden, Michael hoisted his once dipped head, as if his name had been voiced in an urgent cry, he answered her questing eyes. His own hurling the scrimp hindrance of a computer screen to again take hold of hers, and the reaction her body had to his visceral gaze was not an affinity she planned on cherishing.

Chapter Ten

Paired to a conveyance of freight, angry gusts slammed their belligerent forms against the obstinate structures hindering their path. Indiscriminate in their clamorous assault, the harrowing swells bolstered in strength, instead of dispelled, ingratiating their force upon shelters as if seeking parley from themselves. Yet despite the inferred perils of obliteration, the tornadic guise could do naught to stem a wintry deluging from its own devise.

Snow tumbled puckishly to meet an irrigated ground, skittering about the sky. The rancorous flow rode the erupting blasts as it would a tremulous sigh.

Evening's slumber saw to the sludgy day's end. Although the ireful storm showed no signs of receding then, hence night—in its nonpareil splendor—proficiently saw to the prosperity of a blizzard, sounding much like the disgruntle blather of an eerie song in its cry. The sorrowing babel pinged the crisped night like monotonous notes in an abject serenade.

Already, signs of a worthy dune were well flaunted on the ground. Yet, as of the dispersion of night's inking, the snow's amassing had not yet neared the speculated crest. Though by the time morning birth the new month, its zenith was expected to be a substantial show, as February reluctantly bowed its rowdy head. Although numerically offset by the rest, the squat month was in no means a miniscule tool, grueling in the way of its frigid dispense. It gave an arduous exhibition of itself in proof.

Michael's sigh wafted through his office like the tapered tail to a shout. Solidifying the culmination of a long day's end, he parked the stylish pen to his desk. Falling back-wards in a lengthy stretch, long arms spread wide before climbing above his head.

A listless grunt clambered his chest with the tepid exertion, scrubbing roughly at the air, the heavy chair swayed with the deep arching of his back. In finish, wide shoul-ders rolled as if to assimilate an unorthodox version of a flunked pirouette. Integrating the same therapy for his head, he assuaged the pestering kinks since roosted in his sed-entary joints.

Casting his gaze out the window, Michael admired the frisky flight of the quickening pelts, cascading at times in torrents. The rollicking flakes gave the staid impression of a chase, falling in a pother, before long, to the blanket now waiting on the ground.

The house, of its own, was uncannily quiet. Swallowed in a crotchety dimness, it sat inert in the inlay of its master's stilling. Yawning, Michael's eyes walked measuredly over the rounded walls of the room, scantily lit by the lone lamp near centered on his desk. The surrounding shadows loomed, in their harsh recruit, with a sinister bent.

Beyond the thick shading, blackness drenched the entrance of the large sitting-room. Conspicuously situated behind that, his bedroom sat equally bleak. Built to his specification, the entire house preserved the sanctuary that was that wing. With his office as guardian to the immoderately cozy suite, the rotunda styled room was the true masterpiece of his thought. With its bowed walls and constellation of windows. It was a prideful sensation to be encircled in its warmth.

Richly grained panels enhanced the affluence of the spherical space. Dressed meticulously, an abundance of fixtures resided within the sill-like nooks incorporated throughout, wrapping the room in masculine pride. The area rivaled the exclusivity of a cloistered club.

The location was as precisely planned as the factors regarding the composition of the suite itself. Primly situated in its own ecosphere, it offered seclusion in the midst of a buzz. Having his bedroom nestled far aback the rest, tendered not only a quiet getaway to ensure respite, but impregnable solitude came as an added delight, especially at those times when he surely required it most. Nothing in his design came by way of coincidences or guess, as each detail was diligently strategized for an intended result. Like the certainty that his bedroom sat amidst rooms guaranteed to be used only by him. An insight thus rewarded by years of accumulated distaste for the opposite result, his grumblings had since served him well in that end.

Strolling to the window, Michael watched as a swift draught thrust the pelting snow aside as if in disgust. Stammering their descent, they again twirled sheepishly to the ground. In all certainty, the day had rocketed around him with the fleetness of a blur, leaving behind scorched ridges and charred kindles in a trench that corroborates its haste. Evening came with little in the way of relent. Yet daylight had not taken with it, the lengthy docket from his desk. Oddly, the collection sat boastful, still needing his dire inspection to further wilt the bulk of its growth.

With Sam's tardy return from New York, a mountainous drudgery now sat atop the vintage unit in wait. And as unfortunate a result as that was, the dilemma had no fix, for it would seem the more elongated her absence, the more burdensome his days on her return. Today reared no different than the many prior to its existence, and at the middle of that stood, not the least of what's credited as the reason for her trip. Guzzling much of the hours in his day, time looped almost endless without the promise of reprieve.

With the extensive repair on his apartment nearing its end, he needed authentication on the tiles being installed as a backing for his stove. A faux pas set firmly on reprise, this being their third try in almost as many months, and on that, he was most definite in his intent on it being their last. The damage caused by a busted pipe, had rendered his apartment useless for an extended stretch. A momentous gesture tendered by his last guest, having forgotten, it would seem, to flip an imperative lever, one surely liable to dissuade such calamity as that. Though he doubted such trifling bother would ever be repeated by his friend, since the size of his bill alone would unquestionably see to that flub.

As an assistant, Sam was almost without equal at her job, sitting comfortably at the pinnacle of all others who preceded her stay. She had yet to disappoint on any end. Sporting an exceptionally good head on her shoulders, her efficiency and shrewdness kept him well abreast of everything as it should be.

Still, there are those days that stretch well the peripheries of his patience, and seeing her grates deeply on his nerves. Days when work appears to never have an end, since the issue of his schedule alone can sometimes fray the matter in one's head. A lofty collection of mail further needled his plight, stacked with scores of crucial supplemental all demanding his direr response. Who he was did not change the passage of his day. Expectations, of course, came fully fastened to his name, vaulting all boundaries in their vise. The obligation of that poured in like gales in the throe of a storm.

Nonetheless, the distraction of late seemed more a welcomed gift than a bother. Diverting his mind from its reckless route, work stalled the betraying path it seemed determined to take. Constantly fixed to his psyche, their stirring interchange had her residing, with near permanency, in his thoughts. And he often times found himself exploring the propensity of more than just the workings of her brain. Ruling the ardor of such interlude sweet, her tongue seemed equally spiced for other, thus it lured with more so than just the articulation of speech. The alluring muscle grew more appetizing the further his mind trudged. Quarrying in an endless gorge, it tilled terrains lush with such torrid thoughts, rousing everything amid the short hairs on his head to the nervy tips of his toes. And he yearned deeply to partake of more than the meekness of speech. The astuteness shown in her wit and the rapidity of her mind had him well enticed. A marvel in its tenure that seemed almost unmatched, for to date, he could not remember being so thoroughly enthused about a simple conversation with a girl, and was unsure of which aptitude he now valued more. The beauty that was clearly evident for his viewing or that which was her mind. Since both, he avowed with certainty, was beautifully made for sparring, and he wondered on the gauntlet to be dropped next.

In the two weeks since, emails soared as the only form of communication between the three. Except for their collaboration, all communication remained virtually on hold, taking with it all angles with which to pick a fight. The effect, had he progressed at such, he knew would never be the same as hearing the music of her speech. A dozen probabilities on how, had surfaced in his head since then, all aimed to create an easy prologue for an extended debate. But strangely enough, he had yet to settle on one he thought to be a fitting start without looking artificial. The topic was of little importance when launching his strike, regardless of victor, it was the dueling natter that he sought.

In a matter of weeks, their working relationship will have terminated itself. Muzzling all beholding clout he had since sustained as his guide, and with so doing, endeth the reins he had kept anchored on his tongue. Never having displayed that much discipline before now, he wondered whether that was in recompense of his age. Or was it all in observance of her? Maybe time, in some way, had fermented his mind, and the once treasured decadence linked with donning a chase, had somehow lost a smidgen of its bite. Irrespective of such, he was utterly curious to see where an uninterrupted discussion between them would end. Or for that matter, what his reaction would be.

"Good. You're finished. Come on." Betty hailed, interrupting the warm tender of his mulling with her sudden approach. Cloaked almost fully in the shadows, her stance gave no room for a rebuttal as she beckoned him through. "Come eat something." She commanded, hastening the speed of her flailing arm.

Unwilling to disturb his work, Betty's head hesitantly edged the doorway before making her presence known, and it had taken more than a few trips to see the job done. With the house now back to the skeletal inhabitants of two, there was hardly much to occupy her thirst for work. Beside the pragmatic meals that needed to be tended, not much else was left to be done, as she was not allowed to do much other than that.

The cleaning—be it intense or be it light—was all done by someone else. And much of the laundry—scant as it was—was done biweekly by a private firm. Her only job regarding that was in making sure it got done, though the fun of scurrying her way around each technicality was an ongoing treat that continues to hone the agility of her mind. It was, in truth, the serum of her youth.

"What are you still doing about, old woman? Aren't you usually hiding by now?" Michael returned in a soft grumble. "It's...what...? Seven, seven-thirty, eight?" he frowned, searching the room as if for a clock. "That's bedtime for nanas, isn't it?"

"Well this nana has been waiting for you. Someone has to be the grown-up around here. So I'm here to make sure you eat your dinner like all growing boys should." Betty whipped by sternly, ambling forward in the room.

"You do remember I'm not ten anymore, right?" he inquired gruffly, throwing a harsh frown—feigned that it was—at her slender frame. "You don't need to stay up with me anymore." He smirked.

"I remember." Betty assured with a shrug. "But you and I both know you're terrible when it comes to your meals. If I'm not here to push you around, you'd starve."

"You never give me the chance to find out."

"And I never will. It's my job to make sure you eat, and eat right." Betty sauced in her motherly tone, moving behind him then, thin fingers splayed promptly across the center of his back.

"You just hate anything I eat that you didn't prepare yourself."

"I know what I put into mine. Do you know anything about what goes in theirs?" Betty countered, giving, then, a gentle nudge.

"So I'm never to eat anything not prepared by your hands? Is that what you're telling me, old woman?" he teased, turning to tug lightly on the green scarf, tied like a modish beret, around her head. He filched sharply in retreat, pulling back his hand in haste as she swatted at the offending limb.

"I'll get back to you on that." Betty smiled, quickly setting aside the relaxed expression to brandish an austere frown. She herded him towards the door. "Come on. Come on!" she urged from behind, her small hands pressed hard to his back. "Let's go!" she called, giving him a firm shove. "Out you go. You should have a hole in your stomach the size of your mouth by now."

"I'm going. I'm going. Jeez."

"You've been at it long enough." She announced sharply.

"Yes, ma'am, I have. Isn't that what growing boys are supposed to do—work?" Michael smirked, following the dictates of her hands, he moved through the arching of the door. Stiff limbs both cringed and caroled in exhort of his hustle, yet her pace barely slackened as he expounded on a thought. "Man, this day really flew."

"Maybe for you, but not for those of us who had to sit around and wait."

"You didn't need to wait on me. You could have left me something in the refrigerator."

"So you can end up getting a sandwich instead? I don't think so." She simpered, her expression well dubious of his words. Alert like a mother who knew her child's every quirks and tricks. She paid him little heed beyond that. "Sit," she commanded softly, yet firm enough that he complied without further words.

Michael watched as her tiny frame parroted the pollination march at once, dancing from one surface to another. The view was no different between insect and plant, and she looked as contented as she would with the bursting of dawn. Chuckling at the exuberance she showed in her work. Time bore no difference in her life, even now at this late stage in her years; there was no dimming the range of her efforts. *She'll never slow down,* he mused. They'll have to drag her rigor-mortis riddled body from whatever task her hands were busy at, at that time. Since he was sure she would likely die still in motion. Observing her movements, he could not remember her being faster in her youth. Yes, they were both younger then. But he could not say with certainty that she was any faster at that time.

With as many years of her life—more than half to be exact—dedicated to taking care of him, he wondered if she knew how to stop or what to do with herself, if or when she could not. Yet as bonded as she was to the family, the Dunhills were just as devoted to her. Keeping her in the family when her service as a nanny was no longer needed was not a hard conclusion to draw. Realizing quickly the love she had for food and her talent for cooking, only added to the many gifts she already held. Furthering her knowledge of that gift was the least they could do for her stiller commitment to their wellbeing.

"We need to get you a hobby, old woman." He murmured dryly, scuffing at his chin, he gazed raptly at the glass she set before him of her specially made fruit drink.

"Well," Betty paused, staring out at the night as if it held some clue to the answer she sought. She filled the small silence with a low hum. "If you got me some babies to take care of," she smiled. "That would be a hobby I'd like."

"Should I just start collecting them off the street or do you need me to be more specific?" he groaned, putting no stock to the familiar ribbing, as it was one he had grown quite accustomed to hear.

"Can't you just find some pretty girl and get her pregnant? God knows you go through enough of them."

"That's your new guideline for raising babies these days? Any pretty host will do?"

"I'll do the raising." She vowed, waving him off with a defiant flare. "This house is too big to not have some noise in it—children noises—just one to start." She pleaded. "You won't have to worry about a thing, just leave it all to me."

"You get to have noise when Britney and Jason come to visit." He laughed, stretching his arms wide in the process as if suddenly bored.

"Don't you want to see someone else with your features? A little someone with your name attached? Knowing that after you're gone there will still be a part of you left behind?"

"Nope," he sang, sounding indifferent, he affected a dim shrug. Lifting the glass to his lips, he paused in the launching of a frown. "But if I do, I promise you'll be the first to know." Swallowing half the content in what seemed a single gulp, he returned the glass to the table with the frail edges of a smirk. "Well…maybe the second, or is it the third?" knitting his brows into a tight frown, he angled his head to her. "Somehow the mother, and your back-up—otherwise known as *my* mother—would probably want to know as well. But that's just my opinion. Don't mind me."

"Wisenheimer,"

"Now wouldn't that be like looking in a mirror for you?"

"Bigmouth," Betty griped blandly, the mumbled slur soaring from the back of her throat. She ignored his presence in the continuance of her chores, setting a prepared plate with a generous portion of pepper steak within reach of his hand. Added slurs climbed above the area of his head. Heated vapors ascended the spicy spread, taking with it an aroma that made his mouth water. His laughter was barely contained.

"Why, Betty, I'm aghast. What a disgusting potty mouth you have." He scolded. Looking shocked for a mere blink, the low rumbling of his laughter rang above the muted echoes of the house. It soared like the playful call of some creature inhabiting the denseness of night. Shaking the stillness from its place, it ebbed the desolate cry of a slumbering house.

"Did I raise you like this?" Betty groaned.

"Yes you did, and you love me for it."

"Don't you go kidding yourself now," she warned, slapping his wide shoulder affably as she passed, Betty's laugh came as an airy tune. "Love is a very strong word, and I never said anything about that."

"I stand corrected then."

"Just eat your food," Betty huffed in playful disgust. "Give your mouth a different kind of workout for once."

"Are you calling me a chatterbox?" Michael frowned, feigning insult.

"You never did know when to shut it," Betty retorted glumly, giving a slow wag as she sent her gaze to the ceiling. She then dropped a pitying glance to his face. "Such a sad affliction to have, don't you think? It may just end up being the cause of your death."

"Not with you roosting about, old woman. Those hawk eyes of yours can spot danger miles before it rolls to shore. You don't miss a thing."

"How would you like to sit here by yourself?" she cautioned with a stealthy tilt of her brow. "If you don't stop talking and start eating, I'm leaving you here to eat alone." Betty professed darkly, setting her hands akimbo to heighten the threat.

"Eating," he proclaimed weakly, heeding the warning in her jest. With fork in hand, Michael stabbed crossly at his food, inserting the content huffily in his mouth. He winked at the older of them as he chewed.

———•———

Dwarfed by the plush cushions on the couch, his feet showed no reverence for their location or for the consequences assigned to their engaging. Rather, they trampled the cushions thwarting their path. His knees fell anxiously to the seat that his bottom ought to have had, and scrawny legs all but vanished in the grotto-like trenches they impatiently dug. In addition, his lean stern looked intent on mimicking the actions of a tail—had it had the freedom or length. Pressing his drubbing chest to the pillowy back, Richard gaped out elatedly at the tumbling snow. His eyes flitted hastily over the soft flake's descent, as if each shape was now docked as a memory in his head. Stretched easily across the tan exterior of his face, a smile emphasized the gladness he now had, gamely cresting each ear. It dominated his features in every sense.

"This is so cool!" Richard trumpeted to no one in particular. "It's getting heavier!" he shrieked, grinning happily with his confession, his head bobbed in agreement, as if the action turned his statement most avidly into fact. Marginally frosted by the staggering event, the window's chill hardly deterred his determined intent, in proof; his forehead roughly kissed the misty glass. Forming a circle with his hands, he shielded the light's reflection from his eyes. There he eagerly surveyed the growing bank.

Looming like ominous keepers of the night. Trees stood stark in the darkness, fully garbed in dusting of white. The tall heads of pine bowed with the undulating force of the wind, swaying their thread-like limbs. Their statue boasted the sprawl of a weepy willow than the sinewy giants that they ought to have been. The streets were explicably tranquil, except for the intermittent vehicle crawling by sporadically, the night stayed desolate in view.

Bounding from the couch with the swiftness of a cat, Richard's feet thudded the floor like the weighty limb of a man. The reverberant thump deftly buffeted the kitchen as he maneuvered his way through, turning on the stairs, it echoed through the house like a drum. And had a torch been held to his heels, Richard's progress could not have been any hastier then. Skidding through the door of his room—much the same as he would with a scorching—he halted only when the wall impeded the momentum of his passage. Anxiously working the thin wand of his blinds, he manipulated the slats until they sat fully opened to his view. And the trip, Richard conceded with a slow gush of his breath, was well worth substantiating what it was that he thought. *It's snowing!* Richard beamed once again, and this time the notification was given only to himself. As if he had had some doubt in his earlier sightings, he gawked at the torrential plummeting with something akin to awe.

With snow generously dusted across variant peaks, the view was simply astounding from his prestigious point, as white now dominate the blackness of night. Assembled on roofs, snow rested, rather than stayed on their lofty stoops, as each blasting gust expeditiously scattered the collection from its place. Heavy sprinkling of white sailed rambunctiously through the air, staggering in their descent; they again glided in a stupor to the ground. Richard's smile broadened with the spectacle of their game. His thin body seemed to twitch with the excitement of an infrequent occurrence.

"Yes!" Richard's exhaled in a rush, and the sound of his congratulatory screech whisked through the quite room to its immediate demise. *It's definitely coming down harder*! He reasoned with conviction in his head. Loving the rarity of the snow and, too, the sight of its heavy pelting. He cared not if it grew tumultuous in its descent or if the showering progressed to a gathering of days. His true gladness came with knowing that as long as the spectacle persisted in its plunge, school would always be an improbable datum.

Even with his mother's reminders, his excitement hardly dimmed; for such edicts were of little significance to his way of thinking. Having to make-up his missed days mattered little in the wider spectrum of things, and had it been up to him, there would be no such worries from the start. Such concept as that was incredibly stupid from its initiated state, one undeserving of attention—most especially his. No school still means, no school, did it not? And make-up days were too far away for him to let that trouble his mind from what now captured his heart.

"Richard!" Julia called softly from the stairs. "Richard!" lifting higher, her voice again throttled the air. "Richard, come on down!"

"Coming, mom!" whirling suddenly from the window as his mother's voice penetrated the wrangling of his thoughts. He pondered the prospect of leaving his disassembled window as it was, before thinking better of that fact.

"Come on down," Julia hailed. "It's time to pick which movie we're going to watch!"

"Okay!" Richard smiled. Twisting the long wand until the meager light was extinguished from the room. His feet again were to the floor what a hammering fist was to an empty vat. With each step, Richard thrashed the landing of the stairs until his mother's hand waved like a soundless gavel for the thudding to desist. Decreeing its law, the trouncing abruptly stopped.

"Let's try walking now, okay." Julia muttered almost sternly, giving him a pass on his excitement, she let the matter drop. "Did you already get your pillow and blanket?"

"Oh, right!" He panted, turning with blazing feet. They crowned the fourth step before the first word of reproach was even uttered from her lips.

"Walk!"

"Okay!" his small voice shrieked back. Slowing his pace, the drumming ebbed as his feet skipped to a halt, settling almost immediately to a trot. Barely stunting the motion, he returned to the kitchen with the sound of war-drums echoing through the house. Two specks of red rode his rounded cheeks, and his entire body seemed to anxiously gasp for a sampling of air. Roughly wedged under an arm, Richard carried his pillow. Folded and stuffed to that spot, the padding looked choked and nearing its demise—had it had the need for a breath. In the other, he loosely clutched his blanket to his chest. Sporting a long train, the thick fabric lagged behind his pint-size body like an exorbitant tail.

"Okay." Julia grunted then, rolling her eyes at her audience of one, she bother not with the trouble of her usual scolding. Instead, she barreled on. "We already have our snacks and drinks." She proclaimed more to herself than to him, moving further inside the room, she continued with the familiar inventorying. "Everyone has their blankets?" at their nods she quickly moved on. "Good. Then all we need now is the movie."

"Enchanted!" Rachel hurriedly announced, pouncing on the opening, she looked almost expectant of an affirming response.

"No, Transformers!" Richard bellowed back with just as much zeal.

"I said let's pick the movie, not slug it out."

"He always wants the same two movies or their sequels!" Rachel exclaimed with a frown, rolling her eyes over her brother's face with a grunt. "It's always Transformers or Iron Man. Can't you pick anything else?" she grumbled, throwing her hands up. Her expression was one of disgust.

Julia sighed, already sensing where a long portion of their evening would most likely be spent, she offered a quick solution. "Okay! Why don't we do this?" She verbalized with unapproachable calm, throwing her hand up to stall the starting of a bicker, Julia declared her decision. "Both of you pick two movies and drop them in a bag for grandma to pick from—unanimously, of course. No Transformers or Iron Man tonight, Richard." Julia stated in a bland note, turning sharply to her son.

"But, mom—"

"You can watch them in your room tomorrow or at any other time you feel like for that matter. Let's just try something new for tonight."

"Fine," he whined, his eyes dipping to the floor.

"Yes!" Rachel exclaimed with a twirl, and the soft whisper she intended, came sounding excruciatingly loud. Enough so, that it quickly gained the attention she did not want it to have. Turning a sharp gaze upon her face, her mother's eyes marked her with enough disapproval in a single glance, that there was no further utterance on that.

"No Enchanted either." Julia calmly hummed.

"Why?" her small voice shrieked back in query, though it came sounding much like a yell.

"It seems only fair." Julia shrugged, giving answer in a tame breath. "Since we've also seen that almost as much, it stays out of the pot as well. Why not try a new movie tonight? Maybe we could go to Netflix and pick something we don't already have." She offered in a softer tone, though her finagling got no further than the start, doused in its commence with the sound of an ecstatic cry.

"I'm ready!" Richard shouted with urgency in his tone, as if the word "choice" had titled the scenario a race. Waving his visual decisions proudly, he seemed determined to obtain acknowledgement on that. Branding himself the winner, he awaits the gifting of his prize.

"Avatar and Push, very good choices," Julia smiled, granting him the acknowledgement he sought with the sweetened approval in her voice. With the process moving quicker than she expected, the actual movie watching may just annul the customary delays. Sighing, Julia turned her gaze on the other of them that was more discerning in her choices than her young age should have allowed.

The drawers to the television armoire waited undone, crouching on both knees, Rachel methodically appraised each box. Selecting four from the lot, she set them to the floor by her feet, each lined neatly against the other. Finishing in the drawer, she turned her attention to the waiting boxes. Scanning first one and then the other with trained focus, a long moment passed before she sighed with satisfaction at attaining her goal. Smiling, she returned the rejected movies to the drawer, turning to her audience with the full indication of her pride.

"I'm done!" she announced proudly.

"Going for the classics, I see. We haven't watch Lion King in a while." Julia smiled. "Everyone made such good choices tonight." She acknowledged with a soft chuckle, grateful the process was over; she quickly dropped their selection in a bag. Not wanting to chance anything that could cause a delay, she moved the proceedings along with selfish intent. "Now, mom, if you please?" In a merry bounce as if to start the spoils of a game, she gave the small bag a shake, taunting the pause before relinquishing the chore to the other woman's hand. And as if to announce their distaste of such handling, the cases barked loudly in their grumblings of such negligent care.

"And the winner is!" Delia called playfully. Reaching in slowly, she plucked a winner from the bag.

"Happy Feet!" Julia announced excitedly, and watched as her son's shoulders slumped with the loss. Rachel's own grew inches in the mere seconds that it took, twirling about the room in glee. She neither pondered nor did she recognize the dejected look on her brother's face.

With the air mattress wedged against the sofa in a long standing trend, she pranced to the waiting bed. Throwing herself to the surface, Rachel rolled with little effort to her spot. Heavy with disappointment, Richard dropped his leaded body to his place, anchoring himself dead to the spot. The force pushed Rachel from her pillow through the air, bouncing. It dropped her coarsely to a place on the bed, and a soft giggle immediately rose from that corner of the room. Quickly standing, Rachel returned the favor in spades. Sending Richard's smaller body climbing higher behind her force, muffled shrieks and giggles suddenly filled the once brooding room. Together they took turns pouncing while the other sailed and bounced across the airy bed, winners and losers now well forgotten in their play.

Chapter Eleven

Dollops of yellow stealthily incised an ominous crown, dulling the dusky showing. The stale hue of morning gradually lessened its intransigent grasp. Amongst the mosaic of changes, the gelid day stingily assented to its inevitable thawing. All signs of a perpetually dense overcast were emphatically disbanded. Dispelled with the aid of a gentle breeze, the sweltering light again plundered the earth with the balminess of its rays.

Julia appraised the stylish leather tote at rest on the passenger seat with affection. Inside the tawny-brown case was another deed with which she could delineate her career. Through diligence, she nurtured each pursuit to ensure the certitude of a vocation as well as its breadth, cognizant of an intrinsic need to procure that success. Though irrespective of such, the rewards established in this extraordinary venture, deposited her well beyond anything she had a right to reverie with the launching of a new profession. Thus marking a new stage in the varying junctions of her life, to date, they have both intersected well.

Formatting her writing to fit the abbreviated facets of a movie script was a rudimentary undertaking for her. One she found terrifying from the onset, most indubitably since her agent insisted the obligation done as such. But working with Phillip had made her involvement less threatening than the envisioning she once held in her head. Having had more fun than she anticipated she would, the copasetic ambiance now allowed her the fortune to recollect the experience with true fondness for years to come.

However strange that it was, gladness was but one of the many sentiments that had surfaced when the news of their interest was first proposed. Kathleen, her agent, was almost beside herself with the gleeful summary of a conversation she just had. *They want to make a movie out of one of your books!* She had opened with the call, and the initial besetting of shock had kept her completely speechless for the duration of her address. Sounding more excited than Richard at Christmas, Kathleen had barreled through the unabridged proposal with verve, almost running out of breath with the speed of her sketch.

The negotiation after that felt as if it dragged for months, finally coming to an end, ten days before Christmas. Two days later she was appointed an introductory greeting with Phillip Brevard over lunch. And much like a soft wetting to ease the prickling of shock in a necessary perforation. It gave them both an unobtrusive way to assess the other person's intent. That reserve only lasted them mid-way through their lunch. Past that, conversation flowed between them like old acquaintances rebuilding parts of a neglected fence.

With Michael laboring in Africa on a charity event, it was not until the middle of January that the three sat down to their first true conference. The mission for the celebrity's convergence was projected to draw attention to the needs of orphans in that part of the world. Requiring a hefty sum for the continuance of such work, their efforts raised funds that were of dire importance.

Growing uncharacteristically nervous with the pending event, the morning of their introduction matured to find her feeling unwieldy and strained. Hence, Julia walked into the large conference-room not fully herself, and was completely swept, for a moment, from the perch she harbored as her home.

Michael Dunhill, she realized then, was not fully what she expected. His tall, casually attired body was a remarkable instrument to assess. Handsome without a soupçon of flaw, he emerged like an exquisite gem. Cradled lovingly in jeans and a long-sleeve cotton shirt, his muscular body demanded a second appraisal. And although she was prepared for the well-advertised persona that they sold, his unspoiled appearance still stunned. Looking more rugged and naturally attuned than she expected he would, he had caught her completely off guard with the distinctiveness of his features. He was not supposed to do that.

The man was handsome. But… she had quickly stalled then, scolding herself harshly for the immense slip. Her resolve saw to the quick reset of her thinking. Good specimen or not, she would much prefer to admire him from a distance. Preferably, one well protracted of her.

Six months now loomed within reach of their grasp, this, since Kathleen's hysterical call. Piloting their adventure to an end, the finale shared some bitter with a quantum of sweet. Now that the caudal swiftly tapered in their link, her meeting with the partners seemed suddenly constrained to her sense, and she wondered if this was, in part, due to a smidgen of the bitter she now felt.

Julia perused the burly giants that stood munificent about the secluded manse, blissfully captivated. She absorbed the quiet splendidness of her surroundings through the smudged window of her car. Quite laboriously, the day had matured into a beautiful splendor of itself. Cosseted in the stirring arms of March, it blossomed more avidly with each warming hour. Roused from its slumbering bent, the sun's rays blanketed the sky with a small gifting of heat, and for the first time in an allotment of months. Winter was not the sole topic on everyone's tongue.

The drive today was nowhere as taxing as her primary venture had been. Navigating the graveled road with confidence, she slowed as she neared the original rendezvous point. Half expecting Michael to again guide the remainder of her passage, though he granted the occasion no such indulgence. He was not in attendance as she had somehow expected he would, and although she anticipated much the same result as before. She did not hear the tormenting carps of an organ blaring in her head when the heavy gates juddered close at her back.

Despite the vastness of its girth, it had much the same propensity of a home, look-ing genuinely unperturbed from its enormous perch. The large structure propounded tranquility in its welcoming pitch.

Michael watched as her vehicle shouldered the curve of the long drive to a stop, eyeing this from the shelter of his garage, he smiled rigidly to himself. Long fingers worked determinedly through a collection of drawers, hardly seeing the nifty appa-ratuses clearly clogging his progress. He blindly brushed the hard metal of each tool, shuffling their placement. Michael set each piece noisily back in a sham. With numb defiance to his hunt, he slammed open another drawer, again unable to settle on that which he did not seek. His whole reason for being there was a well strategized farce. Only needing to look her over for a spell, the garage put both discretion and aloofness comfortably in his hand—if only for a minute.

Discreetly, Michael eyed the long, slender legs as they slowly alighted to the ground. Leisurely unfolding her body from the car, she looked as delectable as any banquet he'd ever had. Glancing over at him then, she smiled, and his response again was not what it should have been. Waving back, Michael returned the greeting as spontaneously controlled as he could. Turning back to the drawers, he selected the largest plier that he had, inspecting its worth. He dropped it for one smaller with a longer nose, and there again he repeated the auditing process.

His body was disturbingly tense. Too tense for him to shake with a simple shrug, and although he had no need for the tools he sought. The scavenging kept him from pounc-ing the minute she drew within reach. This whole thing was like an unnatural geyser that showed no means of rest, not having experienced anything of the sort before. He felt almost ready to crawl from his own skin.

"Welcome back!" Michael called softly as she neared, looking much like a cat out for an afternoon sunning. His leisured steps brought him through the open mouth of the garage.

"Thank you. Thanks for having me."

Now there's a thought. Michael smirked in silence, and it quickly became work to drag his thoughts away from a sudden vision of her undressed. "Anytime," He growled softly, answering her statement as well as his errant thoughts.

Julia's steps stalled almost three feet from his person, smiling politely at her host, her eyes swept the lawn in one encompassing wave. "I can't believe how nice the day turned out." She murmured in a single breath, taking her first stab at small-talk with a Dunhill. The surrounding grounds were evocative of an island, guarded by a large mass of the willow-like giants. It stood serenely obscured by itself. "I was beginning to wonder if winter was here to stay."

"I guess then, the cold is not your cup of tea?"

"I'm a summer baby, through and through." She avowed proudly, gifting then a smile that was more than the usual polite sheen. "I'll take the heat over the cold any day."

"I can see you being a summer girl." He rumbled with a slow nod.

"Why is that? And if you say it's because of my sunny disposition, you and I will be at war."

"No." Michael countered coolly, his eyes moving steady to her face. Broad shoulders rose slowly and then rested before giving further reply. "You just do." He expounded in a husky tone. His hazel eyes locking with hers, and the silence that followed grew intimate in its unfurling.

"Is…Is Phillip in?" Julia stuttered softly, dragging her attention away from his grasp. She again gazed out at the lawn.

"He's in the house." Michael answered in a rumbly hum, drawing a potent conclusion there and then. He announced his decision in his head, as if needing to confirm it with himself. *I'm going after her.* He established with a silent shrug. *Work and everything else be damned!*

"Oh." Mouthing this, instead of giving actual speech, the single word fell like the mimicking of a rock. Skimming the shallow surface of a pond, it immediately fell stagnant behind the initial splash. Tentatively, Julia swiveled from the intensity in his gaze, turning towards the front entrance of the house. She but took the first step before he stalled her progress with his speech.

"Why don't we go through here?" Michael interjected with a quiet sigh, motioning towards the mouth of the garage. He stepped wordlessly from her path. Feeling suddenly unfettered by his pledge, he ignored the stuttering silence that had since pressed itself close. Her perfume drifted calculatingly along the narrow chambers of his nostrils as she passed. It floated about him as a mocking reminder of his favorite flowering scent, and on her. The fragrance was not only sweet, it was alluring. Wafting from her person, it moved like a hypnotic breeze over the guarded walls of his senses. Intriguing and beguiling every region of his mind and body, it goaded his immeasurable yearns into wanting more. But already, her eager feet neared the threshold in their rush for escape.

The heavy door swung open with a sure jot of haste, and the aroma from Betty's work greeted their procession through the entrance like sunshine after a good rain. Phillip froze mid-step on the landing of the stairs, flashing recognition like a bright beacon from across the room. He hastened his descent of the stairs.

"There she is!" he gushed, his arms slowly spreading wide.

"Hi!" Julia's voice sailed back high, grinning happily with the address. One could easily suspect that relief was also enclosed with the exalted pitch in her tone.

"Hi." Phillip answered back, placing a small peck on her cheek. His smile stayed characteristically wide, and as if to bolster her strength. He gave her thin shoulders an affectionate squeeze. "I've been reading the last email you sent me," he declared in a lighthearted tone. "I love it!"

"Wait until you see what I've brought you. You'll really be in love then."

"Somehow I sincerely doubt that."

"So why am I here then, if not for the accolades, what then?" Julia baited, posting a pseudo frown with her tease. "If you're not going to let me have any fun, I might as well just take my toys and go home."

"No need to do all that. I've already conceded the obvious; the game would be so much less fun without you in it."

"Smart man, now I remember why we get along so well. Such skill is a priceless fine. How does one give that up I wonder?" She praised, patting his arm with a playful dip of her head. Julia awarded him a smile. "In honor of that, here, I brought you a treat."

"Fully finished?"

"Hmm…" not wanting to be presumptuous, Julia hesitated in giving her response. "Barring a few tweaks here and there." The stealth answer came with the sluggish ascent of her shoulders, knowing their view on the final results determined her next step.

"Wonderful!" Phillip gushed, clutching the case to his chest. His eyes almost sparkled.

"Now there's a look that suits you. You should accessorize more often, Phillip. It brings out that other side you keep hidden so well." Michael warbled.

"Thanks. Now I know what to get you for Christmas. One in every color should be just about right, don't you think?"

"As long as you know such generosity will not stay discounted for long." Michael grunted, his voice hardening, as did the glare he delivered to his friend's head.

"Oh, there's no need for thanks, Michael." Phillip assured in an ignorant guise, repaying the stern gesture with a generous smile of his own, such that it returned the whimsy of his youth. "What are friends for, if not to enrich one's life?"

"Are you two at it again?" Betty probed, interrupting the richness of their masculine hum. Her voice broke through the rumble like a gentle draught.

"At what?" Phillip asked in the sweet facade of a whisper, looking fresh with the innocent air of a child, both men promptly lost the competence of speech.

Waggling her head, Betty turned questing eyes on what still looked to her like children squabbling in a room. Lingering long on Julia's face, Betty noticed the charred residue of her response in the form of a quiet shrug. Depositing itself as quickly as it began, her experience gaze discerned the weak gesture in a flash. Stabbing her hands to her waist, Betty slowly nodded, and her small frown showed the measure of disappoint-ment she had. Quietly, her eyes jumped from one to the other on the men. Reproving their behavior as if they were but trifling boys caught in the middle of a naughty ordeal. Betty's frown stayed.

"Be nice, you two." She gently scolded. "No need for you to let your guest know you act like children." In finishing, her eyes waited on Michael's face, as if the brunt of her admonishment rested on his head. They lingered in their gaze.

"Actually, I think it may be a bit too late for that." Julia interjected then, wrapping the statement with a teasing smile.

"Maybe for him," Phillip grunted, stabbing his thumb towards his friend, he assumed his most dignified air. "I'm always of the highest caliber of good behavior, you know that."

"Is there some new concept to the meaning of a snitch that we somehow missed?" Michael grumbled, leaning closer to his friend as he spoke. "Can you believe it?" he asked through a gathering scowl, his eyes registered disbelief on their slow descent, with both now aimed, like a narrow muzzle, at the accused head.

"Not that I'm aware of." Phillip muttered blandly, dropping a small scowl on the accused himself. Half smiling eyes conveyed their own shock.

Feigning disbelief herself, Julia's voice flowed to them like a song. "I'm not sure what you thought you saw, guys, but I did not snitch."

"Really?" Phillip sang back in question, folding his arms snug across the wide span of his chest. Both men showed their skepticism regarding her remark.

"I was non-committal." Julia whined, touching a finger to her chest. "There's a difference, I assure you."

"Shouldn't she be punished?" Phillip grunted, knitting his brows with the question as if suddenly confused.

"What do you have in mind?"

"I'm not sure," he shrugged. "Something really good though. Do you have any ideas?"

"I'll need some time to think on that, I need to find something…appropriate." Michael groaned, setting his gaze to hers.

"Good." He hummed, watching her keenly, Phillip juggled his thick brows, and a gratified smile played in the deep cognac-like depths of his eyes. "I'll leave the matter in your capable hands then."

In response to the ramble, Betty sighed and again wagged her head at the arid endurance of their jest. Hints of her prior scolding still lingered in the dark shimmer of her eyes. It veered shrewdly from one to the next of the men. "Lunch will be ready soon." She muttered then, turning her full attention on younger of them, she continued in a thick honeyed tone. "How about a little appetizer while you wait?" slanting her head with the question, her eyes jumped to Michael's face. "Maybe if you're feeling generous you could share it with the boys. I'll leave that entirely up to the goodness of your heart." Betty simpered, and her thin face creased to show off the rare swooping of her smile. Escorting the younger woman from the room, that smile remained expansive on Betty's dark face.

"Thank you, Betty. I'll give that some thought." Julia donated her own beatific smile to the cause, throwing a second glance over her shoulder in the direction of the men. She confirmed their stupefied gape, and she could not help but muse on the consummate flair of the small woman at her side.

With astute perception as her guide, Betty gave the distinct impression that she was hip to every trick in the book, and perhaps even some that were not yet scripted into words. At most, Betty's small stature stood at five feet. Abnormally reedy, her slight frame neared being gaunt, she barely tipped the scale at a hundred pounds—if not quite less. With hardly any wrinkles to her supple dark skin, her age was only a series of guesses. Neither was there enough silver in the short ponytail she wore pinned to her head to hazard a proper estimate on this. Sporting a pleasant countenance, her personality bore of intrigue, yet she seemed hardly willing to stand still to hearten a chat.

"Make yourself comfortable." Betty directed sweetly. "I'll be back in a minute." She smiled and virtually floated from the room.

The large family-room felt remarkably familiar, primped in its guise like a cozy friend. Sunlight blasted through every window like diluted beams of the Aurora Borealis itself, thus it emerged as paradise displayed for her. To one corner, the golden light rested in casual comfort across the knotted oak of the floor, warming it like a rug. It reared with a notable essence, seeming as if she had spent numerous afternoons in that very spot.

"Betty likes you." Michael rasped as he settled in his seat, his voice warm and silky as if intended as a hand. Sitting marginally close, the two retained almost the exact positions they had on that faithful morning some weeks before.

"I think Betty likes everyone. I don't think she can help it."

"True. But there are subtle differences to each. You just have to look for it."

"Why?" Julia probed, wondering on the possibility of that. Since conversations with the older woman had been but a few, as was the proximity in their length.

"If I told you that, she'd kill me." He smiled, tipping his head in the direction of the kitchen. "You'll just have to take my word for it."

"Since I don't have the base suited to form a proper judgment, I guess I'll have to concede to your assessment on that."

"Good." Nodding stiffly, Michael garnished the stingy reply with a polite smile. Entombing a tinge of regret, his discontent fizzed, as the chance of a squabble had surely been missed.

Phillip showed no interest in the conversation transpiring between the two. Languidly procuring his seat to the couple's left; he offered none of the usual witty conjecture to expound on his friend's annotation. His eagerness now rested on the canvas of work. Phillip opened the tawny case as he would the wrapping of some peerless prize, sinking his hand inside. He immediately fished out the object of his interest. Slowly extracting his hand, the hulking manuscript followed his withdrawal to light like a newly tamed beast.

Rocked with an odd sense of anticipation, Phillip set the assemblage of pages to his lap, leafing slowly through the volume. He started his rummage, of all place, near the back.

His progress captured Julia's anxious attention en-route to its end, grabbing her interest. Her eyes dashed curiously to his face in wait. Phillip's eyes scurried across the pages like a chameleon's close kin, his amber orbs seeming to drink in all details to be had at once. Nodding immediately, he smiled lightly to himself, bobbing twice more as he scanned the full length of another page. Three pages brought two additional nods, each with an interesting smirk shadowing its body. His demeanor vaunted of one intending laughter for some unknown jest, but thought better of the chore ere attaining mid-tread. He resumed an austere composure instead.

"Phil," Michael hailed mildly, and the sound of his gravelly voice interrupted not just the absorption of his friend.

Phillip's head jerked back sharply in response, and a faraway look mingled with his show of surprise, shielding any show of a verdict he may have had.

"Are you going to read all day?" Michael asked dully, not yet ready to buckle down to work, his voice dipped with the arch of a natty brow.

"I'm sorry." Phillip sighed, setting the manuscript and case aside, he smiled. "It called to me." Phillip explained with a slight shrug.

"Here we go!" Betty heralded in her reentry to the room. Balanced in her grasp, the elegance of a large wooden tray leveled a platter almost equally as wide. Perfectly sliced smoked salmon and seared tuna centered the platter on the tray, circled by an assortment of wafers, crackers and crisply toasted bread. Rivaling the service of any fine restaurant, the display was as appetizing as the spread itself.

Julia smiled her appreciation of the splayed treats, realizing she had come to expect no less than the extant results, since distinction seemed the only govern Betty knew. "Betty, I may have to sneak you home with me when I leave. Can you tolerate bickering?" Julia asked, finally lifting her head. She smiled up at the older woman who now surveyed her presentation with pride.

"You have children?" Betty asked with a modicum of shock pinching her tone, instantly transfixed as to a reply. Her brows shot to the ceiling and stayed. Usually, the women Michael tends to commingle with, seemed as obdurate as he about children, at least that's how the scenario appeared sanctioned in his life.

"Yes. Two." Julia informed her proudly.

"How nice!" Betty sang, taking a quick stock of Michael's face with the comment. She adjusted her stance to that of an inquisitor. Deftly ignoring her gape, he showed no interest in the direction of her quest. But absent was the usual scolding he normally hurls at her face. "How old" Betty asked in her soft, motherly tone.

"Ten and twelve," Julia chirped, giving the retort like a rhyme as she selected a slice of smoked salmon for her wafer. She offered the older woman a pleasing smile.

"I'll have to send home something special for them when you leave." Betty announced in her small voice, and a newly elated smile cracked the elder woman's face.

"Oh, you don't need to do that, Betty, really!"

"It's no trouble," she assured, waving Julia's objection off with skill. "It's my pleasure. I love kids." She explained with a broad smile, sending a sideways glance to her boss, she offered the younger of them her most inspired regard. Over the years, more than thirty-five to be exact, the two of them, as does the entire family, had been through a lot, marking everything from sickness to death, and an ocean of disquiets in-between.

With none being more pronounced than those bracketing his addiction, but through all that, one thing retained its luster afar the rest. He was a good man. Unconditionally loved by his family, he eventually grew to be exceptional as she knew he would. His well-being had always been her first concern regardless of time or age, and if that meant getting nosey at times. Then that's just how it had to be.

"I may just take you up on that offer after all." Betty twittered back. "I doubt that I'll be missed around here."

Again ignoring her jibe, Michael stood without adage or frown, looking as cool in his bent as if no words were being uttered pertaining to him or his life. Quietly moving to the tray, he skillfully snubbed Betty's editing glance, already confident as to where her mind now gallops. Though the difference here was in the result, for the woman now sharpened in her sights, also had his interest fully locked.

"Enjoy," Betty mumbled at last, turning as if to go, she paused to give an added broadcast to the small group. "Lunch will be about thirty minutes." She called back softly then, flitting from the room in silence. It was as if her feet never touched the floor.

"Thank you, Betty." Michael smirked at her back, seeing her answer in the hardened glare she shot him as she disappeared from view. His laughter waded soft in his chest. "Told you," He whispered leaning close, as if his words were given in the strictest of confidence. His smile further warmed.

"Maybe you'll really get her to stow away with you if you play your cards right. Sarah and I have tried…but…well." Phillip shrugged, gifting his friend with a stern roll of his eyes. He dropped his gaze to the waiting tray. "She has some weird attachment to *him*."

Julia's laugh came as a soft cackle, already aware of the truth in that remark, only needing to observe the interaction between the two to get full evidence of that. "I'm sure she'd be back in less than a day. The thrill of two active kids can wear thin very quickly, especially when you're not used to having that chaos. It can be something of an acquired treat." She chirped, and for half the revolution of the clock's hand, conversation veered this way and that like the curling of a warm breeze.

Lunch was served at exactly the time Betty proclaimed that it would, and as usual, the spread was an extraordinary one, appeasing the palate as well as it did the eye. Dialogue flowed with its usual syrupy bent, whilst in this; the men's friendly banter knew no end, though Julia fitted her own jibes to their squabble whenever the occasion demanded that she should. Eventually, the topic turned fully to work, bringing the room to an abrupt halt, silence was stroked only by the occasional crisp twist of paper or the pecking of keys. All eyes widen with inexorable interest then, and the frisky chirrups that once were, was no more. This, Julia thought somberly to herself, this she was sure she would sorely miss.

Felicitations supplanted all aspect in their effectuate work, imparted freely. Julia glowed under the spill of their continuous praise. So inducing the verve in which she acceded to their enlivened request. Defenseless against the vim of such sheening display, the invitation came varnished with charm. Wrapped in the warmth of a deep, lyrical tone, an opulent smile flowed forward like a subliminal spell, capping the potency it held. There was no vindication garnered to nullify that. Tentatively set for the summer, the pool festivity commemorated the success of their partnership and, too, the ease with which it prevailed. And in so doing, they solidified the demise of their union, avidly done with an exquisite flare.

Subsequently, the concept of a stroll was brought forward, and once again her usual hesitance fell completely lax, immediately concurring. Julia bounded with the thought. After enduring their lengthy forum, it granted her the chance to stretch her limbs, and although she thought of little beyond the sun's toasting. It was unlike her to be so easily led. Vacating the house through the side entrance, the three sauntered across the large verandah, and was immediately welcome by the beauty of a newly uncovered pool.

Ablaze with sunlight, a gentle breeze skimmed its lagoon shaped body, sending soft ripples trembling in an endless wave atop the surface. Julia admired the tranquil scenery with sincere raptness spilling forth, basking in the feel of the prodigal sunlight. Her mood almost seemed to be eclipsed by someone else. Except for the generous plains surrounding the large house, most of the property remained untouched by man. Manicured lawn swept far inland of trees, and, although dormant, the scenery was no less splendid to view, and it was easy to grasp the admiration he had for his home.

Like clouds being darken with the brewing of a storm, Michael's face grew suddenly tense. Throwing a threatening scowl in Phillip's direction, he scored the man's face with a harsh, penetrating stare, and definitive demands sprouted bold in his eyes. Julia missed the frown that anxiously shadowed the first, so, too, Phillip's puzzling gape. The small kick of Michael's head in the direction of the house was as discreetly done as the inaugural ploy itself.

Phillip's swift wit was quick to recognize his friend's request, nodding gently in riposte. The inaudible dictate ended before it began. Blind to the dialogue at hand, she could not have seen the skilled conversation passed between friends. In whole, it occurred in mere seconds.

"Oh, damn! Wait, guys!" Phillip called, sounding faintly exasperated with himself. He dropped an anchor to each leg, immediately stalling his momentum to said spot. Frantically, he patted each pocket as if searching for a speck. "I think…" he choked, taking a shallow breath, he elongated the pause. Yet his hands never wavered in their hunt, slapping the back pocket of his jeans, he clarified the delay. "I think I forgot my cellphone and I'm waiting on a couple of important calls." Phillip announced dryly, clouting his pockets yet again. He dug suddenly inside, as if his phone had grown paper thin in the process of his search. "Let me run back and get it. I'll be right back!" Phillip vowed. Not bothering to wait on a reply before turning towards the house, his urgency seemed high.

"Do you want us to wait?" Michael called after him, his own face showing concern.

"Ah…no, you go ahead." Phillip shouted back. "I'll catch up. You're not going far, right?" stopping abruptly in his tracks, he waited for an answer, as if that was somehow an important premise for him to know.

"No. We'll just stay around here." Michael affirmed dazedly, giving an inclusive sweep with his hand, he indicated a small portion of the striking backyard. Quietly seething in mirth, he watched as his friend milked the farce better than he ever expected he would. "Shall we?" he asked at last, turning to his companion as if uncertain, he made the decision hers.

"I guess we could go slowly, this way he'll have time to catch up." She replied, seeming somewhat uncertain, yet at any other time or place, she would have deemed the decision a simple one.

As if contemplating his choice, Michael glanced back at the house with hesitation now showing in his stance, though inside he watched raptly as Phillip disappeared from view. With his conflict now looking pronounced, he allowed another minute to tick past before turning of a sudden to resume their stroll. Starting wide, he left a generous gulch between them. Moving steadily closer the longer they strode, they soon trod the canopied path in unison. Shoulders only inches apart, they almost seemed one.

"It's beautiful here." Julia sighed at last, breaking the lengthy silence.

"Yes it is. Thank you." Michael hummed, his voice hardly stirring the quiet that blanketed the woods.

"It's like being on your own little island." She laughed, and the soft airy sound felt as natural as the area that nestled their walk.

"That's what I like most about it." Michael replied smoothly. "I like that you recognize that." He hummed. His eyes touched her softly, and a cunning smile settled in the corners of his mouth with what reared as a roguish thought.

"How long have you lived here?" Julia asked, ignoring the possibility of a compliment in that speech.

"I've owned the land for about eight years, but I've lived here now for six." He drawled, watching her intently as they moved. At a point, the path abruptly narrowed, and with slackened steps, they promptly adjusted their strides. Pausing at the entrance of a cluster of trees, Michael granted her the opening to step past. Wide barks and low limbs shielded all view of the house by then, thus granting him the solace that he craved. He took his fill of the view as they maneuvered the roughened terrain, having gone further than he had proposed at the start.

Her foot scraped the edge of a protruding knot that sprouted from the root of a large tree, catching the heel of her boot. She looked, for a moment, as if preparing to fly. In a flash, Michael's hand flew around her waist, pulling her close to balance against his frame. He settled her alongside the hardened cliffs of his body. The encroachment lasted but seconds, if not a faction of that, but the repercussion felt as if it lasted a year. That is, as least, until she looked up. Eyes, wide with a glazing of shock, drew him like the whispery chants of some forbidden place, murmuring words he found himself straining to hear. Without moving, her lips seemed to sigh the syllables in his name, falling slightly apart, they waited as if for an answer to something asked.

"Oh!" she sighed, her hand tightly slung around his neck.

Barbs of electricity coursed through his body, stammering in his chest. Michael's pulse raucously sped. Ironed to every arc of his frame, she rested excruciatingly close. Such that it was, that he could feel the softness of her breasts persuasive against his chest. Smell her with every intake of his breath, and feel the faint residue of each exhale on the lower portion of his neck. For the moment, it was as if everything ceased to further act, including the very air that rustled the trees, as their surrounding grew astonishingly quiet. Not wanting to release her just yet, Michael waited, and for a minute she stayed, their eyes locking as if compelled by the lure of a magnetic flux.

As if startled from a deep slumber, Julia's pulse lunged, throbbing madly from deep within the cavern of her chest. Her senses swiftly galloped past the point of being nonsensical. Emboldened tingling raced determinedly through her body. Growing pronounced, it churned inconceivably sweet, and for a moment she was strangely confused on what to do with herself. "Uh…" she voiced then, her hand moving like a warm slither to his chest, pushing softly. She retained what little balance she had. "I…I think we need to wait for Phillip to catch up." She intoned in a breathless sigh, straightening from the safety of his chest. She waited as his hand stayed stationed at her back. Slowly uncoiling his fingers from her waist, he allowed her to move quickly from his grasp.

"There's a bench just ahead." Michael mumbled hoarsely, pointing in the direction of the seat, he cleared the asphyxiating press from his throat. Her head bobbed slowly in response, quickly turning from his gaze, she moved earnestly towards the proffered seat. Following her lead, Michael watched her fixedly, noting her expression and the lovely sway of her hips. He scolded himself for a squandered opportunity now lost. At any other time in his life, he would have gone in for the kiss. *Why didn't he?* He asked numbly, his mind grumbling tersely as the two silently took their seats.

"Julia," he whispered after long, mouthing her name like the waking of a tempest from a dream. Michael set his full attention to the task at hand. She turned slowly to him then, keeping her gaze no higher than his chest, she waited quietly in expectation of speech. Again swallowing the sudden tightness in his throat, he waited for the feeling to pass, for the urge to kiss her grew agonizingly strong. Her mouth, he avowed for the hundredth time, was an incredible force to behold. Its fullness played havoc on his mind, and he would really love to have tasted her then. "I'd love to have a cup of coffee with you this weekend." Michael asked calmly, thinking it best to start small.

"You already have some changes you'd like to make?" she questioned, her mind automatically thinking of work.

"No." Michael answered slowly, as if giving her mind the time it needed to adjust. "This has nothing to do with work." He murmured in a rumbly tone, his gaze lingering attentively on her face, most predominantly, her mouth.

"Then…why?" she asked with a tight pull of her brows, looking almost at a loss.

Watching her openly, Michael waited before giving response, taking his fill for all the times he restrained himself. He gave fully his appreciation of the view, and although her eyes plummet from his to gaze questioningly at the woods, it was well worth the partaking. "I'm asking you out—on a date." He drawled, his voice grating the restricted fringe of his throat, tight from holding the reins on his restraint.

As if contemplating the validity of his words, she remained silent, her gaze parked on the bark of a large oak tree. "Why?" she asked in a small, befuddled voice, frowning confusedly at what she deemed an impossible occurrence.

Certain he was not the first to notice her loveliness, Michael laughed, amazed at the stunned boom stoking her question when he could hardly narrow his adjectives to one. And nothing she could say would otherwise convince him that she had never been told that before. The woman was downright stunning. "Were you looking in the mirror this morning when you got dressed?" he asked in jest, softening his smile, he almost relaxed. "If you must know, I like very much what I see looking back."

"Oh." Julia crowed as she straightened in her seat. "Oh…!" she groaned, her eyes widening with the word, brightening as if she suddenly solved the mystery of a rare puzzle. Sending him a timid glance, recognition jumped boldly to her eyes. Nervously interlocking each finger, she stammered her response. "Huh…thank you." She stuttered, taking in the view of her hands. "But, I…huh, I don't…really…date." She announced in a low mumble, lifting her head, she tentatively gathered his eyes.

"You don't?" Michael asked in a grunt. "Never?" He persisted in an incredulous tone, summing all that he could not in the quick pull of his brows. Her head rolled softly in response; side to side it went and then dropped, giving then a definitive "no". "You haven't had a date since your divorce?" and his tone again gave way to something parallel to shock.

"I know it's a bit strange, but…" she shrugged. "I just find it easier having my life uncomplicated. The men don't get to feel as if I'm looking to them as a potential catch for my kids. My kids, in turn, don't have to deal with a throng of strange men traipsing in and out of their lives, and I don't have to deal with the madness of both."

"You've given this a lot of thought." He groaned, his mumbled statement seeming calm, though he was far from feeling that. In truth, he sank deeper in a state of disbelief.

"I've had some time to deal with it." She shrugged.

"How long have you been divorced?" he asked softly, already knowing the answer to that.

"It's…been a little while." She nodded.

"Too much for you to say?"

"A little bit of that and a little bit of…" thin shoulders gently teased the angling of her chin, dropping roughly back in place, she finished with a simmering sigh. "This."

"I see." He droned, the soft tone stated more as a whisper to himself, unable to think of much else. It was all the words Michael found that resembled an answer in his head, for his mind was a lightning bolt of thoughts.

Around them, a gentle breeze brushed the threading on lean limbs, rattling the twiggy arms on others as a slow wave danced through the coppice-like setting where they dwelled. A whisper rose around them like the augur of an audience's murmur following the jolt of an unpredicted show. Cognizant of the game being played, the trees almost smiled with the placid tickling, seeming eager in their sway to join the frolic. Yet it was a dissimilar truth that now plagued the consciousness of the man. A well devised plan in all rights, nigh impeccable in the executing of itself, though irrespective of the adeptness shown. A startling setback now thwarted his objective, and the end was neither expected nor foreseen. To recoup his loss, he now needed to overhaul his entire thinking. Reassessment of his method and preparation was incontestable, these fated to be principal in his call to arms, for he needed, with all surety, to formulate a new plan. This was not over. Not by any means. Certainly not when she draws him so decisively, the game, with all sureness, had only just begun.

Chapter Twelve

Rousted from the nadir of slumber, Rachel yawned as the tuneful chirrups of birds drifted through her room. Soaring without end, the cheery ballads romped where the rafters skewed. Thus it pervaded the entire chamber entrenching her bed.

A strident sneeze brought her consciousness to further wake, rebounding harshly through her body. Its potency roughly rattled through the cavities in her skull. Sending another behind that, her body sharply convulsed with the shudder that was then dispatched. With a brusque stomp of her hand, the alarm clock stalled its harmonious play, and the room again fell to an unperturbed hush.

"It's my birthday!" Rachel proclaimed in a hoarse cry to an equally perked room, vaulting from her bed with a single lunge. A flutter of purple formed a helpless puddle at her feet. Sacrificed in her drive, she hastily started the preparation for her day. It took mere minutes to see her stylishly dressed. Jouncing through the doorway of the kitchen, her walk looked much like a choreographed dance.

Already strikingly dressed in black, Julia's slacks clasped the aptness of her curves like spandex in a glove. Likewise for her blazer and white cotton shirt, though each completed the ensemble in a more relaxed display. Adjusting her fingers around the slender coffee mug, she looked up and smiled, beaming her pleasure as the smaller vision of herself gamboled in the room.

"Good morning, birthday girl!" Julia chirped, grinning jauntily over the rim of her mug.

"Good morning, mom!" Rachel beamed, skipping to her mother's side.

"Are you ready to get started?"

"Where are we going?" Rachel asked anxiously.

"I guess we better get started so you can find out." Julia chortled, setting her mug to the belly of a stainless steel sink. She turned with a question on her sharply inclined brow. "Shall we?" She asked, hugging the small shoulders, she gave a gentle squeeze.

Rachel nodded eagerly in acquiescence of the query, gazing up at her mother, her soft, brown eyes, by now, ablaze with glee. And no words were needed to further expand on how she felt, as she gave it all in the transparency of her expression. Her buoyant smile then waded wide, as the two, in unity, turned from the kitchen and so departed the house.

The Original Pancake House launched the exploits in a laggardly planned day. A favorite of the family, their Swedish pancakes were among Rachel's favorite foods to have, and the trip only cemented her delight in the day. Conversation as usual grazed on the lushness of everything. Layering boys, school, and a list of accessories newly purchased for her character on the popular internet game, MapleStory gave its tale in a huff of excited shrills.

Time sped without reason or thought, and in what felt like a blink, it dragged with it a goodly portion of a dyad of hours. And although it was not wastefully spent, the remaining ventures needed to be divulged—if they were to be enjoyed.

Reaching inside her purse, Julia pulled out a small gift bag from the interior fold. Placing the bag on the table's middle with a measured show, she smiled musefully as if contemplating the gift inside for herself. Her gaze fully singed to the soft, teal colored bag.

Rachel scrutinized the tiny omphalos between them with a curious frown, smiling cautiously, she looked almost afraid to venture inside. "What is it?" she asked softly, quickly cataloging a list in her head. She summarized all the things she had boldly designated as wants for her upcoming day, and not one came close to fitting inside the near palm-size bag that now hovered in wait.

"It's your birthday present." Julia remarked calmly, holding back the urge to laugh at the puzzled look painted on Rachel's face.

As if the miniature bag was a strange appetizer she was leery to try, Rachel gingerly peeked inside. Seemingly, the gift was the farthest thing from the imagined endowment she expected to have. The imperturbable sound of tissue paper assaulted the terse silence as she pulled the first from a collection free, and the table, in response, held its breath in wait on the probable result.

"Ah…" she groaned, pulling the last few of what seemed a never ending supply. "Oh. Oh, my God! Oh—my—God—!" Rachel ranted, flipping through the content of the bag, she squealed sharply in glee. The plastic cards clicked softly together as she flipped through the growing collection in her hand, suddenly seeming beside herself.

"Happy birthday! I thought maybe you might like the idea of a shopping spree." Julia smiled. Savoring the radiance daubed on Rachel's face, as the reward now surpassed the coordinating efforts in her plan. Instead of the hassle of hunting for the so ordered specification of her presents, she had everyone purchase cards from a list of her favorite stores. Now *she* controls the harmony of her own shopping destiny and that of her wants. "Ten cards, each from a different store. I think that should do you nicely for a spree. So what do you think? Would you like to spend the afternoon shopping? Or, we could do something else if you prefer." She shrugged.

"Shopping! Let's go shopping!" Rachel squeaked loudly. Attracting a few quizzical gapes from the other patrons, she giggled without a speck of remorse.

"Good!" Julia crooned almost as elated as she, paying no heed to the lingering stares still trained in their direction. "Since I believe as a rule every girl needs a good purse, there's an accompanying present in the car. Especially when shopping is the objective, a girl needs someplace chic to transport her wealth. Now, let's go start your spree!"

"Okay!" Rachel sang as she sprang to her feet, beaming with unceasing gladness. Already, this birthday topped any party she'd ever had.

Augmented by the emotional drip of her new found patronage rights, the first store held her fully enslaved. Rachel entered the large edifice with eyes twice their normal size, showing more teeth than what seemed a normal display. Her feet staggered to a stop in the middle of the glitzy entrance, gaping with wide open enthusiasm, her brown eyes gleamed as if seeing the store and its filling for the very first time. Straggling feet scraped and scuffed loudly at her back, stuttering as a handful of customers touched their feet to the polished entrance, parting peculiarly around the living statue she created. Rachel held without care or contemplation of their eyes. Lost in a world of her own, she basked in the feel of her new power and the pleasure she felt in what she now had.

Although Julia remained closely stationed at her side, she gave her the room needed to devour the prospects that now laid in wait. Patiently, she allowed her the time to enjoy the thrill of the moment and what that brought. "Are you ready to get started?" she asked as Rachel touched big, bright eyes to hers. Seeing her head bobbed in answer, Julia offered a reassuring hand, and long, slender fingers closed gently over the smaller edition of themselves. Both bodies turned placidly towards the core of the structure in which they stood. Laden with trinkets, the smaller of them gave the offerings her most thorough esteem, assured of her authority in the result of each choice that she made.

———

Three dozen yellow roses posed tastefully in greeting on her wearing return to the house. Julia recognized the familiar arrangement the moment she walked through the door. Sending the flowers a disconcerted glare, she immediately felt depleted by the sight. Not knowing of a way to stall the persistent bluff, grated even heavier on her nerves.

The small white envelope sat as a desolate being in an ocean of walnut. Stranded in the center of the kitchen table, it waited as if to be rescued by her hand. Lured perplexingly by a vast sea of yellow, Julia cautiously approached the canary vaunt, looking further perturbed the closer she got. Her eyes narrowed as if like a vise, though she could not deny the vision the offering gave. Truly beautiful to regard, irrespective of sender, perfection molded the motif of each bloom.

Below the hang of a receding frown, Julia gazed at the impressive display, ogling the uninvited token for far longer than she envisioned she would. She examined the cheery disposition of each bulb. Weeks of thorough inspection had brought her no closer to unfolding a clue. Neither did her search find a definitive solution to the predicament she now had. Vague curiosity wafted idly forward now and then, although that was solely directed towards what new stanza would be added to the mix, for she could not help but ponder upon that. Julia's eyes browsed the forsaken envelope as if it whispered her name, seeing said appellation printed neatly across the front. She sighed, ignoring the taunts that implored her to further delve.

In resolve, her shoulders lifted with the weighty intake of her breath, dropping heavily in place, she grumbled to herself instead. *This is getting really strange*, she admitted with a frown. Valentine's Day she could easily forgive, for that could be blamed on the pressure of the day. But he'd since sent her two more. *What in heaven's name does he expect in return for his gifts, and how the hell does he know where she lives?*

A deep breath followed the troubling questions now a constant in her head, sending it flying in a rapid exhale. The sound was no less the howl of an angry gust. Being ignorant of his identity was a definite bother to her fraying nerves, especially since he evidently knew hers well. Solely encased in the dark, she had no way of explaining her rules as it stands then. Or commanded the matter over with when she deemed it done—as she does now.

Rattling the same reasoning repeatedly for weeks, Julia scoffed grumbly to herself, and again she studied the small printing of her name, and although she was unsure of her intent. Her fingers walked across the small envelope with a nonchalant twist of her hand. Slick paper skidded eagerly across the smoothness of wood, resting almost fully in her hand. The inquisitiveness of her nature was enough to compel her then.

A quiet breath I have held, though I have seen you, I seek you more.

"Who *is* this?" Julia sighed, noting his continued signature on the cards. *Very infatuated admirer,* she frowned, hearing the questions percolate inside the hollow of her head. Yet the writer in her did like the varying aspects of his words, as there were qualities there to be admired. And had she had the motivation to date, she might have been curious as to who he was, just to see if he could live up to the alluring qualities of his words.

Rachel's voice bounced from the ceiling as she cackled in the middle of her relates, having had the phone pasted to her ear since the moment they reentered the house. Julia knew the end was nowhere near to being broach, and Kayla, she suspects, now knew the tenuous details regarding the events of her day.

Puttering about the kitchen with no particular intent, she turned eventually from the room. Her mind rummaging each crevice it held for clues, curious on the identity of her supposed fan, or of the purpose behind his plan. And although she dug remarkably deep, no face wafted through her consciousness, this regardless of how hard she tried.

A large bouquet of white roses, nearing its limit, cheerfully greeted her loom. Julia's eyes roamed over their petals with affection almost as bold as her guilt. Placing the flowers in her office had given them more importance than they really had, but white orchids were her favorite, and…Well…. They were beautiful enough to be considered close. She saw no need to waste them because of an aversion to being blindly pursued.

At the far edge of her desk, two cards sat staid, both identical to the one she now carried in her hand. Plucking them from the polished surface, Julia's eyes moved slowly over each word. *Maybe there were hints she missed in his words before*, she reasoned in her search.

Press with care for she slumbers here. Take caution to gently wake her, for in her wake she will kindle the hearts that greatly mourned the length of her rest.

To this he signed,

Just because it's Wednesday,

Utterly confused by the gesture, Julia shook her head in frustration, unable, in her search, to find anything she could use to identify the man. Even her dealings with the florist had been unsuccessful after more than a quarter-dozen tries. Patrice, or something within the context of that, refused, quite blatantly, to be of any assistance to her plight. Announcing in no uncertain term, how unethical such engaging would be—had she divulged information expected to remain confidential. Of course, the size of the bouquet and their frequency had nothing to do with the loyalty she had. Only offering an apology, the woman was of no use to any revenue not her own, seeming almost jubilant when she offered the only tidbit of information she gave. Her joy, it would seem, was to inform her that the deliveries were all paid for well in advance, restricting her involvement, there was nothing that could be done—had she wanted to try.

Evening signaled its departure as it would the flame on a wick that's frayed. Slowly, the radiance faded from sight. As usual, the sky flaunted its most brilliant array for the show, like the ever changing wallpaper on a screen. The sun finished its easterly voyage; skating past the tops of trees in a rapid descent, it bid the long day's end. Gazing out the window, Julia gave a distended sigh, but the beauty holding her eyes was not what clung to her mind. Wishing, instead, she had more details to better formulate a plan, thus forming a counter-strike to an evident attack. Yet it seemed her only recourse was to sit around helpless and wait, and she did not like the vulnerability of that. A sitting duck had never been her cup of tea, not on any level.

Chapter Thirteen

The day began as it would any other during the week, sifting slowly like the plunge of a feather. It soon spun dawdling minutes into frantic. Fastened within the midst of a chaotic press, tarrying feet drudged lamely through quiet corridors, and rappelling shoulders endured to sweep the low edges of walls, heavy with the platitude of glum.

Julia hustled to the front entrance with embers streaking her subsequent path, summoning her children with a firm exclaim. She heartily urged that they mimic the haste she now exhibited in her steps, hoping that the urgency her voice so clearly divulged in its climb, would be enough to incite a prompt reaction. The crusade, though fervid, neither jostled nor nudged. Hardly scoring the surface of their skulls, her words never penetrated the armor that assured comprehension of her simple mandates. Instead, they showed near no response.

In minutes, the school bus was expected to show at the predestined stop, and her children's expressions was of one who still had hours left to go.

"Let's go, guys, we need to move!" Julia chanted eagerly, striving unsuccessfully to rally their brains to the exigency of their action. "Let's go!" she trumpeted yet again, using her arms like a bird, they flailed like one who had not yet learned the full use of its wings. She slapped the side of her thighs with the force of a full applause. The sound cracked hastily through the drowsy silence, stunning the ears, it sounded astoundingly more menacing than the act itself.

It was lucky for them, that their house sat comfortably across the street from the stop, or that the sound of the heavy engines could be heard effortlessly from a far. Such startling facts seemed the equivalent of frost slicing through the ardor of summer's scorch. The appeasement was but a minimal fix. Working amiably on those dreaded wintery days, it swapped itself as an abject disadvantage on others, rearing more frankly as a fret. It rendered her task an utterly problematic one, since riling them from their stupor and out the door on mornings as this, can sometimes be a maddening struggle. Fortunately, their buses shared not only the same stop, but a marginal difference in their arrival schedules. With each collecting their zombie-like load within minutes of each other. Thus allotting her the fortitude to quickly treaty the morning battles. It was like getting two kills with a single shot.

Determined to galvanize a reaction from her kids, Julia listened for the ornery timbre of an engine's roar or the loud screeching of brakes as it slowed in provision to stop. However, the neighborhood relayed no such regaling to her ears, but remained, instead, reclined in a whispery hush. Affably spliced with assurance of spring, the cool-ness of morning softly brushed over her skin, bequeathing a crisped fragrance. It tattled effusively of winter's death.

Across the street at the purported stop, the waiting kids clustered in a wan mob equaling two, each seeming oblivious of the other. Indubitably ranked, the newly dis-passionate middle-schoolers waded like embittered runts in their stalking of one end, while the ever spirited elementary gnomes, twittered afar the other. With the older of the two disregarding the younger crowd, this as they would a pacifier offered in place of a meal. Yet all who assembled wore an odd strain of the same dowdy expression. It was a countenance she'd grown to know well. One that besets her children on the onset of each day, it vaunts as the irritant look of indifference.

"Rachel! Richard! Let's move it!" Julia barked from the door, darting her well trained eyes hastily up the street in yet another search. Rachel's feet scraped hesitantly over the polished planks of the hardwood floor, almost scrubbing each slat to a dulling as she shuffled glumly towards the door. Behind her, Richard stumbled to a jerking stop. His eyes widening as he skirted the rounded edge of the small table in his path, dropping his backpack then. He rotated back from whence he came.

"I forgot my book!" He announced almost jestingly, taking no time to say what type or the importance it had. "I'll be right back!" he yelled, drubbing the floor gallingly under his feet.

In the distance, the hard, irate sound of an engine pierced the once lax morning air, and the purity of silence was immediately lost. Julia flew past Rachel who still dallied in the foyer's mouth, her devotion inappreciably earnest, working now, somewhat fever-ishly, on the fitting of her arm through the sleeve of her denim jacket.

"Bus!" Julia yelled towards the ceiling, her tone rivaling the beatific assonance of a crow. Spinning, she pulled the twisted jacket free from Rachel's small hands. Expertly fitting the diminutive garment in place, she folded each cuff, this while towing its occu-pant through the door. "Bus!" she announced once more, her voice again projected high. Relying on the precision of her ears instead of eyes, she affirmed her son's descent, for his feet now thrashed the last rung on the stairs. "Faster, Richard, faster! Let's go!" she cheered then, and watched as two buses instead of one, slowed in preparation to stop. Behind her, Richard skidded to a wild stop at his bag. Heaving the loaded satchel high over his shoulder, he breezed past her out the door.

"Bye, mom, love you!" Richard gurgled, sieving each word through the last bite of his toast.

"Bye, mom!" Rachel supplemented through a yell, already racing down the long driveway. "Love you!" augmenting the afterthought over her shoulder as she waved.

"Love you both! Have a good day!" Julia rejoined with a tuneful blurb, waving with the rhythm of such, she watched them dart athwart the front of the first bus, disap-pearing in a hummock of yellow. She again waved as the carriers rolled from their stop, turning onto the next street, though both took dissimilar routes. The smell of the heavy engines swam acridly through the frail morning air, vexing the gentle draught, the putrid bath stayed long past the culprit's escape.

Drained from the morning's pursuits, her body imparted a visible sigh, and a quiet house stared back at her sluggish approach. Seeming as fragmented as she, the house yielded a fatigued breath, and she could almost hear the expulsion of its relief as undoubtedly as she could the clatter in its settling creeks. Julia collected the used wares from the table on her return to the kitchen, rinsing the crumbly particles from their faces. She stocked an almost brimming dishwasher drawer.

Already, coffee contaminated every crevice of her thought, having had no time to savor a taste of the aromatic drink; she was now impatient to annex a jolt from the fluidic surge.

Now that the constraints of the manuscript had ended, a few hours of relaxation were a desperate need, and the daring step would evidence her first, in regards to that, in a goodly collection of months. In the past twelve months, her splintering pace had hardly slowed—let alone stopped. Moving seamlessly from finishing her book to working with the partners. Relaxation did not swim aloft the cream that yet toppled her bowl. Preserving all unmanaged time exclusively for the kids, sleep was the only luxury she had since managed outside of that.

With their final meeting scheduled for the end of the week, her goal was to take, at least an hour just to be, this in-part to stifle the droning of her mother with the baring of proof, just to say that she had. Though at the very least, she could walk in feeling rejuvenated from such strive, and with her mother volunteering at the hospital and a house to herself. She had no demands on which to set the blame should she not make the effort to try.

The sturdy aroma of coffee generously blanketed the room, casting its distinctive vapors through the air like a plume. It slinked up her nostrils in a heady rush. As if to deliberately toy with her senses, the enthralling smell flew in every direction at once, wrapping her snugly in its warmth. Julia dried her hands and folded the towel neatly in the provision of her wants, dropping it over the left edge of the sink. She turned anxiously towards a grumbly coffeepot. Of a sudden, warbling chimes blared sharply through a once quiet house, stalling her revered fantasy of attaining first taste. She jerked to a stuttered stop. Turning towards the intruding sound, Julia frowned, hesitating in her action as if to contemplate the choices she had. Begrudgingly, Julia moved towards the ingress, varying her tread with openly mawkish steps. She stalled all subsequent effort as she detected who the visitor was.

"Good morning!" Michael called brightly from the landing of her stoop, and each word seemed to rumble as it rolled from his tongue.

Julia stood silent. Her eyes wide with surprise, and it took her a lengthy minute to unstuck her mind from the obvious or find her tongue. "What? W—what are you doing... here?"

"Since you won't let me take you out for coffee..." Michael enlightened with the aid of a shrug. Raising the two bags he carted in his hands, he waved them temptingly across his chest as if to bait her with the offer of a treat. "I brought the coffee to you." He smiled, brushing quickly past her paralyzed stance.

"Michael..." she voiced, seeming almost breathless. Turning as he stepped past, her eyes shot to his back in her sought to clarify a point. "Michael, y—you can't. We—you—"

"Why and why not?" he rasped, flashing a small piece of what was inevitable his most perfect concoction of a smile.

"I already told you why." She grumbled hesitantly, turning from the door. She faced him squarely with determination well set, though in rejoinder of the chore, she became fully enmeshed in the man's allure. His body loomed in the entry like a monument of sort, ode to the perfection of a masculine figure. He made a fetching sight in more ways than just one, and strange though it seemed, it felt, at that moment, as if his presence swallowed what she once thought to be a large foyer, leaving her little room to regulator the expenditure of her breath.

"We're only having coffee, Julia." Michael drawled, flashing yet another charismatic smile. His gaze penetrated the dark depths of her eyes, and like some oracle of old. They further syphoned her will. The gentle swing of his hand grazed a shoulder now taut with the building of her angst, reaching past her. He pushed the heavy door shut. "And to prove the validity of my intent, I won't even venture outside of this spot." He vowed in a thundery swirl, flaunting a gauged dispel of his elite charismatic brood, he waited boldly on her response. At her continued silence, Michael rested both bags on the floor, pulling from one a woven shawl for the base on which they stood. Deftly, Michael threw open the soft, green spread, heavily fringed on two ends. It rode the air like a wave, sending a small gust behind the brandishing. He dropped the cushiony fabric at her feet like a rug. "Madame," he rumbled as he bowed chicly, gesturing a hand to the floor. "The best table awaits you."

The nervous smile she intended came favoring a sneer. Unable to add further adage to her earlier oath, she reluctantly relinquished her place at the door, seeming then to have lost the use of her quick tongue. Dark eyes grazed his person with a troubled frown, finally taking a seat. Her sigh drifted like the spent residue of discontent. Michael nodded in acceptance of such, yet a triumphant smirk singed his face as he took his own seat at her side, though he sat far enough to accede her some comfort in that. Although in him, the action bought some sureness of control. Crossing her legs at the ankle, she braced her back comfortably against the wall, liberal in assuring the space she placed between the two of them. She gingerly accepted the tall cup he fixed to her hand with a nod.

"Thank you." Julia mumbled meekly without looking up, content to quietly attend the cup that he gave.

"You're welcome." He answered in a rich, gravelly tone, barbs of humor spiking the bassy timbre he gave, and although well hidden amidst the pitch. It soared brashly for the listen—had she been settled as her usual self. Handing her packets of sugar and cream, he smiled as he remembered how she took her coffee from watching her at the house. *Mostly dark, but sweet,* he hummed, as that was staunchly reminiscent of the woman herself. Together the two stirred in silence and the sound of plastic—fashioned into modish straws—scratched coarsely at the bottom of two paper cups. Thus it filtered boldly through the nervy calm.

"Why are you bothering with me when there're so many women that would gladly go out with you?" she asked in a strangely distant voice, finally breaking the silence that had pressed oddly close.

Michael turned his gaze over her slowly. Caressing her face, he let his eyes drop to her mouth and there they stayed. "Because I like you, that's why." He stated bluntly at last.

"Women, I'm sure, who fantasize about you, and would probably do anything for a chance to show you how they feel. Doesn't that sound more like a better plan?" She persisted quietly, elucidating her point as if he had given no answer to her probe.

"Do you fantasize about me?" he asked slowly.

"I left fantasies behind with pom-poms and pleated skirts." She informed him tepidly, aided thus by a shrug. "I don't have the time for much, let alone fantasies."

The smile on Michael's face boiled with the flavor of a grungy leer. Ardently, he mulled the appealing visions that catapulted through his head, taking his time before voicing a response. "I'd love to hear more about the pom-poms, actually."

"Of all the things I said, that's all you heard?"

"I heard you." He shrugged, and a careful smile touched his lips as he spoke. "And I'm willing to bet that you do."

"Bet that I do what?"

"Have the time for a good fantasy. You just have to be willing to take it."

"Spoken like a man with little cares."

"Why is that?" Michael asked gently, his dark brows pulled curiously tight.

"Why is what?"

"Why is it you think I have no cares?"

"Well," Julia paused, casting her eyes to the floor. She stared as if the answers were penned within its gains. "You're extremely wealthy, handsome," she certified, raking the titles as if they were considered faults. She quietly flicked a finger towards the ceiling with each descriptive that dashed past her lips. "You can go anywhere in the world you want. Do anything you want and you have your health?" she chirped triumphantly, seeming suddenly proud, she shrugged. "Those are usually the big ones most people worry about."

"Do you have cares?"

"Of course, almost everyone does!" She answered with a stupefied gape. Her countenance twisted in emphasis of such.

Michael's eyes strolled over the exquisite paintings that dominated the wall to their left. So, too, for the others dispersed about the elegant living-room space, dropping, they lightly touched the tailored furnishing as well. "You seem to be doing well, why do you still have cares?"

Julia frowned impatiently as she waited for the logical answer to come, one befitting the point she endeavored to make, though none came the harder she bade. Her mind seemed to have halt its momentum in blackness, this from the validity of the answer he gave, granting her nothing pertinent to add to the judgment she so eagerly dispatched. An audible sigh breeched the silence she birthed, skidding all assembled argument to an untimely halt. "I'm just trying to stop you from wasting your time." She announced in a grunt like a parthian shot.

"I'm here. Shouldn't that count as a care?"

"What do you care about?" she asked, and the words slashed from her mouth with defiance neatly wrapping their tart edges.

Right now I care to kiss you. Drink the taste of coffee off your lips and just delve. That should do to start—if you must know. Michael groaned, cringing inwardly as the thought altered his pulse, and it was not disgust that churned within his core. Instead, he muttered steadily. "My care is to get to know you better." Sweetening each word with the warmth of his husky voice, he smiled. At less than an arm's length away, he could just lean in and push that issue right now, take control of the situation in a flash. *Why is it that he hadn't the inkling to try?* Michael probed, again debating the bothersome point with himself. He stared at the wooden barring that was now walled only inches from his toes, and a silent chuckle bubbled in his chest as a result. Realizing then he was truly literal in his petition for an entry, and may need to tunnel his way through the blockage to make himself an intrinsic affiliate.

"There's really not much left for you to know."

"I beg to differ. I intend to learn all there is to know about you."

"Now there's a waste of your time."

Wide shoulders lifted slowly in response, stroking the air softly as they moved, his smile was inciting. "It's my time to waste." He declared coolly, reaching across with his cup, he touched the papery goblet to its loosely balanced kin in her hand. "To interesting endeavors," he murmured drolly, shifting his position on the floor, he resettled his back to the wall. The bite of the hardwood, and the rigid wall at his back was certain to mark the most cumbersome way he had ever started the workings of a date. Especially so, for the tenseness that's sometimes clasped to the ascribing of a first date, but cumbrous or not, the crude transpiring would have to do for now.

"I suppose since you brought me coffee, I'm expected to play the proper host an invite you in?" She groaned, her words sailing almost like a tease. Noticing his tentative search for a comfortable position, guilt walked as an ogre through her mind, this, in addition to her own stabbing discomfort, gored, as if by gradual degree. A twinge that soon lanced the flesh of her buttock and the high portion of a thigh with determine resolve.

"Oh, of course not," Michael hummed, feigning dejection as he rolled his head in reply. "I told you I wouldn't leave this spot, so I won't."

Rolling her eyes at the saintly verbiage given in the sell, she shifted in ready to push to her feet, groaning tersely at such with a pitying shake of her head. She commanded in a low moan. "Come on."

Pushing nimbly to his feet in a gallant show, Michael offered her his hand. "Here, let me help." He purred, reaching forward to aid her without waiting a response. Long fingers tightened along the upper curve of her arm, pulling her gently to her feet. He unhanded her the minute she drew vertical as if he somehow needed to.

Unprepared, Julia swayed, caught sudden by the numbness in her thigh. She stumbled backwards, tightening her hold on his hand for balance. She steadied herself against the wall.

The quick impinge of his action was meant to be only of aid. His sole objective for treading near held the purity of such intent locked in its encoding. It wielded the only reason why he then gathered her close, or why his body now pressed hers as intimately. So, too, his body's motive for staying corporal in the way that it surged, and why his eyes foraged hers as raptly as his pulse now sped.

Flattened against the wall, Julia's back rested smooth upon the surface hindering retreat, for his body, to her front, prevented anything but. Waiting for some sign of clarity to spurt bright, she gazed into his eyes, though she could not say for sure why. The smell of his aftershave swept recalcitrantly through her mind, holding it strongly as his, and without intending to abide. She swallowed, feeding his warm, masculine scent to her own body, and likewise of the first. A scrumptious tingle sizzled hotly with the taste. Starting at the very tip of her tongue, it moved swiftly through her body in waves, as those magnificent eyes drove uncannily deep. Holding her captive, they willed naught but obedience in the tincture of their delve, and without understanding why, she readily complied with the efficacy of such. Her pulse thence cantered in start of new life, lunging in her breast. It slipped quickly to madness.

The subtle press was all it took to give warning of a forthcoming threat. Julia felt him lean, saw the intent in his eyes, and although she knew what was about to come. The knowledge came of little importance or help. Fear drove home her panic instead. Turning her head just in time, his lips rested soft against her mouth, catching the outer edge. They loitered in the place they rested.

Michael's breath came like a heavy squall, drawing deep. It whirred loudly on the descent, coiling roughly through the small space in which they stood. His labored intakes were well discernible in the new silence they brewed, waiting eagerly for his head to clear. He simply stayed. She—her scent, and the lunacy of his body's response, all permeated his mind at once, and the heavy pull of his breath only contributed to the odd drive. "I'm sorry." He whispered against the corner of her mouth. "I don't know why I did that. I mean...well. I know why..." closing his eyes, he sighed, and the gush of his breath slid warmly down her cheek like the feathery touch of one's hand. "I'm sorry." He repeated in a firmer breath, though he duly lingered at his designated roost, showing no sign of stirring from said spot.

Her hair was pulled back with a simple twist, knotted on the top of her head like a short tail, and from his best guess, she did not look to be wearing makeup, nor was her outfit an enchanted affair. Sporting nothing more than a long, oversized shirt with dark leggings to match, she rattled every facet of his nerves, and he wanted badly, in that instant, to devour her whole. He had the strongest urge to turn his head and work industriously on her mouth—but he held. Choosing, instead, to just stay, he enjoyed the feeling of having her near. She had not moved an inch since turning her head. Instead, she stood like a warm fragrance against his skin, and the sweetness such ambiance tolled could neither be ignored nor ordained.

"May I ask you something?" she murmured weakly, at last finding her tongue.

"Of course," he mouthed in reply, his head falling in a gentle nod, abetting the discreet stroking of her lips with each bounce.

"Am I able to move now?"

"You need my permission?" Michael inquired then, slowly shifting his stance. He stroked her with the warm, flavor of his breath.

"You're blocking my way. It *is* the polite thing to do." She gurgled, making no attempt to remove herself from the intimacy of their stance.

"Polite...maybe, necessary..." he drawled, his shoulders climbing with the implied assault, caressing her on the ascension of a purposeful drive. "You do know it's okay, right?" he asked in a low growl, though a half smirk played with the corner of his mouth, and therefore, played with hers.

"Okay for what?"

"To like me," Michael smiled. "It's okay to like me. I like you." He breathed, touching his forehead to her hair. "And I think you like me."

Turning her head a mere minimum, Julia strengthened her resolve. Quietly, she let her eyes take in his features at will, and from the angle that she stood, he looked even better to her. Although the vision, in its magnificence, was more sense than sight at that time. "I don't," she uttered in a flat tone, and the denial sounded false even to her own ears. "Not in the way that you think. Even if..." she droned, her eyes moving then with an edge of boldness over his face.

"If what?" Michael simpered back, his brows waiting high on his forehead with the inquest.

"Even if you have...looks" she shrugged, taking a deep breath with the tame twitch. Her breasts swayed in their slight clamber up his chest. Julia smiled contrarily, liking the feelings that it gave, her eyes again moved with quiet danger over his face. "Because I won't spend the money on the art piece, does not mean I can't recognize the beauty that it has."

"Usually, if you enjoy the view the art brings you. That's a good enough reason to buy." Michael smirked, taking a long breath, for he knew the subtle movement gave him another brush with her curves, and the returns were definitely worth the provoke.

"Not if the price is too high."

"Doesn't that usually bring the best profit in an investment as that? Sometimes it exceeds what you once thought was too high to start."

"That's a gamble I can't afford, much less the price."

"Isn't everything a gamble? Life itself, isn't that a gamble?" the softly spoken words vibrated against her mouth with purposeful resolve, shifting slightly in his stance. He let his body further sway against hers.

"To some degree," She nodded tritely, pretending to ignore the feel of his exerts. *Why didn't she just move? Why hadn't she the urge?*

"Sometimes the best things come at the greatest risk." He murmured in acquiescence, as if privy to her thoughts.

"Is that how you live your life?" she chirped. Tipping her head back, her lips stroked his with the ascension of her eyes.

"It depends on the risk. Some things are worth more than others." He affirmed, lifting his shoulders, he gently caressed her cheek with the edge of his broad frame.

"That concept seemed to have gotten you in a lot of trouble. So I think it's defunct as a constructive resource in which to search."

"Now are we talking live or lived?"

"Is there really that much of a difference?"

"You, of all people, have to know that there is."

"How so?" she purred, her voice wafting like the melody of an incredulous chant, sharpening with the intent of her gaze.

"You tell me." He shrugged. "You've seen me these few months, tell me. Am I a man or am I that boy?"

"You expect me to judge the whole book just by reading a few excerpts?"

"But haven't you already done that?"

"How is that?"

"By refusing to see me, you did exactly that." He smirked.

"That's not a judgment, that's a decision, and there's a huge difference in that." Julia frowned, barely bothered by his lighthearted words, though she could not say the same for his unintentional intentional caresses, as it had her braising from the heat of each touch.

"But a judgmental one nonetheless,"

"Not judgmental, sensible." She smiled, and in reply, her shoulders gently rocked. Purposeful in her bent, she thrust her breasts to his chest. Julia's body thence swayed, feigning the need for a deep breath, she slowly turned her head to implement her crave, deliberately allowing the warm feel of his lips to fully stroke hers. And in so doing, she savored the coffee that still flavored him as a result.

His growl was near audible in reaction, wading soft in his chest. It simmered like the expectant judder of a bear, for he wanted badly to lean in and change her mind with the aptitude of his tongue. Having never had a conversation this closely pressed before, at least not one with his clothes on, the newness was, of itself, a soft quaver of shock. Yet it rose nicely as a scintillating treat to gulp from at the very least. The thrill was amazingly sweet, staggering his tangled mind how much he liked the systematic taunts, and how much he craved the decadence promised with the rest. "Is that what this is, you being sensible?" he growled.

"You could say that." She whispered lamely, each word drifting from her soft; they die in their soft spilling against his mouth. For reasons unbeknownst to her, she was completely off her normal axis, as she could not get her body to stop the strange antics it now eagerly dispelled. Even her thoughts did not seem to veer straight this day. *Am I shaking?* Julia grumbled tartly. In reflection, her eyes skidded sharply down his face to his mouth, hovering on the curve of his bottom lip, they stayed.

Michael saw the migration of her eyes, felt the heat of her gaze as it landed on his mouth, and all thoughts paused as his eyes dropped to also feed on its liken. Quietly, his hand traveled to her cheek, cupping the smooth curve, he stroked the side of her face. Wielding his thumb like the satiny brush of his breath, his finger walked the plump edges of her lips, feeling them part like the slow opening of a door, they invited him in. The invitation warranted no hesitance, but full compliance. Turning his head at once, he aligned their lips, eager to savor her taste. Excitement surged with just the decadency of a touch, and the warmth of her breath stroked strange fires that muddled his mind, for she was—

The loud crash sounded like the toppling of a thousand plates, followed by a strong thud—of what one could only deduced as the shelf. Shocking the silence, it jolted her back to her senses. Julia flinched. Turning her head, on a sharp swivel, towards the sound, she froze in expectation, as the boisterous blast came from a room at their backs, someplace nearing the back of the house. Michael's groan festered as a result, a well audible rumble that boiled deep inside his chest, ballooning around the sequestered spot. He turned, his much delayed attention, towards the sound, though his focus hovered someplace else. A door slammed with the force of an angry blast, causing both bodies to recoil abruptly in response to the thunderous thwack. Straightening, Michael turned guardedly towards the sound, shielding her body with his. He searched the small area for *any* usable weapon that could be of aid.

"Hello! It's only me!" a woman's voice hailed loudly. "Miss Julie, are you in? I brought you that thing we…well, never mind, it's just fit for the trash now." She explained in a grumble, though the rest of her ramble sprout incomprehensibly to them, as she slipped decisively into her native tongue.

Releasing a heavy breath, Julia's sigh showed her relief. Though still heedless as to who that was, Michael's frown asked a necessary question, turning to her sharply with already woven brows, he bidden her response. "Housekeeper," She spat in a rush, sighing, she closed her eyes and waited for calm to return.

"Oh." Michael groaned then, dropping his back against the wall in relief. His eyes closed as he drew in a ragged breath, settling the tumultuous swirls in the pit of his chest with another behind that. The sweetness of their frolic had perished with the sharp intake of a breath, leaving him submerged in a strange void. One he had no way of reasoning its eccentricity. "I should go." He muttered lightly, his voice sounding oddly pained, darker than he intended the simplicity of his words to be.

"Oh." She sighed, straightening slowly from her lean. She swallowed the gulping of a full breath. "Yes…okay." Snorting the shaky exclaim, she moved tepidly from her place at the wall.

Stepping immediately to the door, Michael gave her no time to complete her bent. "So I'll see you on Friday then." He mumbled tamely, his hand already on the handle of the door.

"Wait!" she called in a hurry. "Your blanket…" quickly grabbing a fringed edge, she waited to pull it clear, only needing him to vacate the position he now held.

"Keep it." He shrugged. "Something for you to remember me by," liking the idea the longer it revolved in his head, Michael smiled. Maybe she'll remember how nice the conversation felt. A time when two people stood so close that the other's breath could be tasted as their own. As he most certainly will not.

"But…" finding no words to give him in parting, Julia paused, unable to fashion a worthy homily to further add to the eccentric farce. Was she really disappointed to see him go? Did she want him to stay? She asked, sounding dubious to her own ears, she quickly resolved the point in her head, *of course not!* She stated with surety bruising her tone—this from the wiser of her analytic self—used in all consultation that's of importance in her head. "Bye." She murmured then, though only she knew truly what was said. Yet he nodded in reply as if the word had been broadcasted from the joists of every room, turning immediately. He disappeared out the door.

Julia stared at the barring with a queer tinge of what reared faintly like dismay now seeping from her pores, her confused body almost feeling drained. Amplifying the current arching through her body, the foible accorded her no way of discerning what was real and what was not, hence, her emotions whirled like a jumbled mess. Lamely, she collected the discarded items off the floor, listening to Gloria's footsteps as they trampled the stairs on her hurried descent, each step seeming louder than her usual thwacking. Julia rushed back to the kitchen to quickly discard their cups. Willing herself to again return to her calm existence of old, as the delay only made her more edgy than she needed to be.

Chapter Fourteen

Not unlike the choreographed glissades of a mirrored cant, the swank elevator doors glided shut. As if in a trance, Julia followed each salient step from ignition to its languorous end. Pasting the scant flesh of her back flush against the wall's warm wood graining, narrow shoulders then rose, flattening on the ascent. It crudely plummeted to its once reposed stance.

Irrespective of her distress, the nervy climb thence replicated itself, and each gust openly gnawed at the passiveness of the space. To the casual eye, her impeccable posture emulated a regal comport well equated with her. Yet, that was not how she felt.

The stagnant ride greatly infused her with weird but thrilling pangs, and much like the residue of a dream, the experience felt oddly inveigling. Nonetheless, she was utterly perplexed by their strength. As each troublesome surge waded through her like the reverberating quivers of an aftershock, thus making it impossible for her to retain control of her rational self.

Okay, is this fear or am I just feeling guilty? She asked with a billowing grunt, well prepared to rationalize the silent reproach ere it augmented itself. Though a new thought sprouted its quills in the midst of her rant, singeing her wrath like the striking of a match, it smothered the fire of her assault. And its brashness was no less an affront, than had an adversary shrieked the absurd comment to her face. *Could it be excitement?* Her troubled mind blurted through a soft sting of shock, slamming her brain to a halt. It ambushed all inferred excuses she had organized in defense of herself.

Seemingly appalled by the audacity of the inquest, Julia almost growled her response. *No! Of course not!* She asserted with pride, shaking her head profoundly, she physically answered her own befuddled thoughts. *It's just anxiety!* She groaned, tightening the accordion-like folds on an already woven brow. *Hard, uncomfortable anxiety, but that's all it is.* Thus scolding herself with a decisive sneer, Julia pulled tense shoulders back. Straightening with a new show of resolve, she again altered the rigidness of her posture.

The steel chariot vaulted each level on what seemed truly like gargantuan wings. Landing on the sixtieth floor in what felt like a flash, it effectually deposited her at her stop. Garishly broadcasted as such by the hammering of a bell, the blast sounded no different than the echoic bang of a firing squad. Purposely setting her pulse to its thrashing pace with the jeering announced.

Jitters once thought to be stabled, abruptly sprang bold, startling her with the fervency they disported. They thoroughly encumbered her thoughts. A wicked tingle compellingly surged warm crevices still aquiver from their prior exchange, and at such, it stirred what needed no bolster or aid.

What is this? What the hell is going on? She screamed, and although no sound came with the exasperated inquest, her expression spoke of her confusion in spades. Having walked these halls for weeks, her destination had always been the same, and she'd maneuvered such chores with the simplest skill compulsory to the task. *Why is this bizarre phenomenon happening now? Why would it wait until the extinction of their dealings to affix this new perception of guilt? This is it.* Time now lunged to an end for their fecund tie, so there can be no continuance of this embryotic idiocy. This was not the time to adopt some teenage affliction. Just finish the job as it began and walk away clean, she encouraged, swerving her thoughts from the impetus of wonder to a decisive result.

In the distance, the elevator bell again pinged through the quiet hall, jarring the smoldering silence like an eroding ricochet. The grating sound splintered through her head like a shot, quickly stalling the internal storm she now struggled to slake.

Julia's hand divulged full proof of the spawning chaos now foraging for control. Gently rumbling through her body, it showed the instant she hoisted her affected limb to the door. In dismay, Julia yanked the offending arm back, stabbing it roughly to her side. She crossly disputed the basis of her reaction. *It can't be that I'm nervous about seeing him, how could I? Nothing happened for Christ's sake!* She avowed brusquely, though the defiance was ineffective in enlivening her mood, for the betraying nuisance sped wilder yet.

Since the strange interlude between them, it had grown alarmingly hard to ignore her mind's compulsion with the man and the fine features that he had. Rerunning the essence of the incitement they had, her subconscious knew no rest. For even in sleep, her mind roamed easily where consciousness should never freely rout. Hence the impediment she now had in harnessing the madness, and her effort to ignore what should be of little or no importance, grew continuously taxing on her nerves. As it is, it seemed a constant fight, and she greatly looked forward to bidding their affiliation a decisive farewell and seeing the weirdness garner its demise.

Gradually, Julia steadied herself, willing her body's composure. She assumed an apathetic persona before entering the suite.

As usual, Phillip was a limitless fount of joviality. Greeting her with exuberance, he gently touched his kempt beard to her cheek, and although it was unlike her to take support from others, Julia leaned effusively against his frame like she would an old friend, therefore affirming, if not only to her skewed view, she was nowhere near her customary self.

"Hello, Julia." The shrewdly coifed murmur came lodged in the center of a deep, husky burr, floating to her like an indelible sigh. It emanated a warmth that was sweetly rousing.

Startled eyes rushed towards the source that bodied the raspy voice. Upon contact, already skittish pulse eagerly dashed, as his patient manner had effectively simulated an eagle surveilling the action of a prey, and as always, the vision that he gave was well worth the price of a gander. "Hello." The murmured salutation came with a soft bounce of her head, as does her search for the fading features of indifference.

"How are you today?" Michael asked, and his throaty question sauntered as a soft rumbly wave.

"I'm doing fine." Julia answered nattily, swallowing a surge as his eyes scooped her body like spoons in a bowl of ice cream. She dazedly continued the casual inquest after a nervous cough. "And you?"

"Working hard," Michael shrugged. "Still trying to tackle the complexity of my cares," he droned, stilling the smile that pinched the corner of his mouth.

"Sounds hard," she slurred, swallowing a sharp twinge, yet not knowing why.

"As is everything that's deemed a worthy reward. I wouldn't expect otherwise in this case." He countered in a methodic tone.

"Oh." A light nod sufficed well as her response, and although her frown alluded him to her insight into his connotation. She dared not elaborate on that. Not if she expected this craziness to have the end she so deemed. At her side, Phillip dimly shifted, turning abruptly as if summoned by a soundless cry, he checked the numeric scribing on his watch. Amber eyes anxiously followed that exert with a quick fire down the hall.

"Excuse me for a minute." He droned, dropping his gaze on both faces. "I need to finish up an important email before we get started. I promise I'll make it quick." He vowed. Sleekly reminiscence of tussore, the lie flew to them smooth, so, too, the unflappable gesture shown as he darted from her side. Disappearing in the modish bedroom, he offered no other account, nor did he wait on their reply.

Phillip smiled approvingly at his evasive tack, hoping his talents would then pay dividend for his friend. He congratulated himself on coining an opening for such result to be had. In observance of Michael's attraction, he had no need to dawdle in the room, as the tension between them grew persistently thick, and something about their conversation skirted on intimate lines. Still, his agreed deception did come with a sprig of averseness, genuinely torn with his fondness for her, the act marred his stealth chaperoning with guilt. Now with Michael's expected dally, his morning now verged on long, a beginning that may require more resuscitation than he can drink.

The room ceased all functions the moment Phillip scurried from view. Racked with apprehension, it remained suspended like a monger in the throes of a sell, lodged between the frazzled intakes of their breath. A worrisome frown gauged Julia's expression, although it was the nervous excitement that truly hampered her will. Bleakly, she coerced her feet into taking a step, avoiding the potent urge to turn and run, she slowly advanced further in the suite.

The apartment-size suite sprouted as the quintessence of luxury. Offering every distinction of home to its exceedingly pampered guest, very little was left to be had that was not already in account. With an adequate size dining-room and kitchen sprawled chicly to one end, both of which were only mentally visible to her view, this due to the rooted stance she procured near the entrance of a spacious living-room. A grand piano waited in the corner of the elegant room, seeming as reserved as she, it eyed her with certain trepidation attached to its tone. To her left, two bedrooms, Phillip and a study sat in wait, while the exit remained distantly protective at her back. Yet all this, successfully simulates the quietude of a monastery, as two people stood earnest on the precipice of something new.

The silence between them grew abundantly rich, as did the pleasant intoxicant that it lent. Wrapping itself around them with a flavor that grew increasingly fervent, the sensation was strangely electrifying to the soul, and with it, she could find no effort nor urge or reason to move from the heat of his gaze. She, instead, remained quelled. Warmed by the intensity of what he gave over in his scrutiny of her. Skillfully, he stroked tinder along her spine, stoking its sparks until the spasms felt were not only isolated in her chest. *This makes no sense*, she reasoned, having such reaction to a mere look. How can that be? Nonetheless, the substance that it gave was undeniably sweet.

Michael drank in the arc of her features with reverence. Absorbing every morsel that he could, as the urge to taste her soared fiercer than it ever had before, finding her exceedingly appetizing, though it was not only his eyes that she fed so enticingly well.

"May I ask you a favor?" she whispered at last, and the quiet question startled the taut stricture of the room, dispelling the shock like a shrug. The room took a calming breath.

"Yes, of course." Michael hummed, forcing his eyes from the object of his want. He recaptured the pooling of her dark eyes. The dark orbs waited his ascension as intently as he awaited her request. Though she gave none in reply, instead, she took an advancing step. Pausing nervously, she visually swallowed before adding a subsequent step to her plod, and as if the gesture granted her the strength she needed. Her progress soon took her within reach of his hand.

"Could you put your hands in your pocket, please?" she asked.

"What?"

"Put your hands in your pockets, please." She repeated blandly, her voice now strained in her throat, forcing her directive to spill in a soft, croaky tone. Slowly digging his hands into the copious depths, Michael guardedly complied, his confusion now evident in the curious gaze that he dropped to her face. Ignoring the silent inquest, Julia waded close. Averse in her plotting, she flouted clarification of what bore no sound reason in her head. "Do you promise not to move?" she asked in a low voice, and watched as a slow nod came as the means of his assurance, thus prompting her to take the final step.

Tentatively, she stopped just short of touching her breasts to his chest. Willing the action as an assertion of self, something she needed to do to retake control, for in her mind that's all that was needed to rescind his hold. All the strange emotions her body now expelled were all due to his relentless attack. They could hardly be considered real or carried any substance to their bite, and therefore needed to be dealt with, with the swiftest of haste. Evidently, she was not as immune to his charm as she once thought.

But that, too, would also have an end, as she intended to stunt the problem in its tracks. Be the instigator and watched the madness die.

Michael stood with his hands confiscated in the ample depth of his pockets. Having responded to her request like a dutiful slave, his interest was aptly piqued. Steadily, her scent moved around him like a curtain, walling him off pleasantly from everything but her. The heat of her body boldly stroked him wherever it rest, as did the soft zephyr of her breath, and it felt no different had she fanned her fingers over the skin of his chest. A touch of mint minced the spicy air between them, and until then, he could not remember ever wanting a mint more.

Indomitably, Michael's fist tightened into a hard ball, fixedly making his pockets their temporary tomb, now grateful for the insight she had in securing his promise. For had she not procured such pledge, he would be nulling a fraction of space with them locked at her back.

Julia's heart thumped in her chest like a wild equine treading up a rancorous hill, and it showed no sign of steadying its pace. This was not the consequence she predicted when she initiated the attack. Was her body really responding to him or was this something else? There were urges being stroked conscious that could not be. Feelings that were making itself known that should not. Steeping, they seethed to a familiar hanker that fund no outlet but one. How could this have happened? When? She was so careful in retaining her focus. Staying divorced of the man regardless of who or what he was. Griping the censure in the stadium of her head, she welcomed the thick, shelter of darkness as she closed her eyes, taking a deep breath as she drank in his scent.

His smell was like a virus not yet known to her body, affecting it in ways that was utterly foreign to her. It commanded her will. Hailing her body soundly from the chasm that it dwelled, and in answer, she fought the urge to drop her head to the cradle of his waiting chest. Or beg to endure the comfort of his arms and just rest. Did she want this? Did she want him to kiss her? She groaned, her copious thoughts soaring to no end, twisting, they turned inside her head like an excavation gone awry. It was hard to discern reality or what just madness was. Everything flew by so quickly, she was well beyond the rocky edge of confusion.

God, he wanted to delve! For the provocation was no less maddening than being a hungry peasant in a patisserie. Having no means in which to partake of the food, you're left to savor the distinctive flavor of both sight and smell. Stilling the rantings in his head, a low grunt sailed from Michael's throat in reply, and in the silence that followed. The urge to eat grew increasingly strong. Not one part of their bodies decisively touched, she was fastidious in her certainty of that. But the stance was no less erotic had foreplay been a mutual undertaking between them. And he could not help that his mind swallowed the bait on that thought, dragging his torment further than a sensible man would allow.

Much like the start of a dance, her body swayed towards him in a dozy show, though she quickly stilled the predisposing of her action. Lifting her face from its hover near the bed of his chest, her eyes walked slowly up the broad width, yet the brown gaze came no farther than his mouth. A long, torturous minute passed before she gave a tame nod, dropping her gaze, she slowly retreated from the inferno she so adeptly created.

"Thank you." She mouthed then.

And with that, the moment was gone. Lasting only minutes in full, he could still feel her presence where she once stood, though the place had gone precipitously cold with her hasty retreat. Their stance had been like a sapid seduction, and he had never been so beautifully seduced with so little contact before. He indubitably wanted more. Decisively, Michael hands slid from the crypt that once held them in wait, easing coercively behind her back, they pulled her close in a leisured tow, signaling his go. It was now his turn to start a new game, his time for seducing, and his approach on how to get the job done.

"Do I get a turn?" Michael whispered hoarsely, his face already pressed close, each word brought a caressing to her cheek. The firm muscles of his chest swept the swells of her breasts as he eased her closer yet, stopping just short of steaming her to his flesh. He conceded the magic that the contact brought with a rakish smile. She made no effort to resist the directive of his hands, neither did she look surprised by the new turn of event. Her eyes looked, instead, like a magical pool, and in every way he longed to dive in and go for an extensive swim.

Julia's gaze shimmered nervously from his mouth to his hazel eyes, noting that a touch of green played magnificently in their depths. The mossy color danced mildly in the darkening edges of his eyes and was, in truth, quite stunning to look at. *I can do this.* She scoffed, and a slight tremor rolled mockingly through her body as if in disagreement of that. "I—"

"You have the most beautiful mouth…." Michael blurted, not meaning to give his reflection voice.

Julia swallowed the judder of her nerves then, taking with it a multitude of emotions that sat high in the back of her throat. She shrugged. "All the better for the biting of knaves I think. Pretty things are not always to be trifled with." She hummed, growing suddenly feisty.

"A little bite here…or…there never hurts anyone." He growled, his smile a wondrous bloom. As if working with a mind of their own, his fingers stroked the sun's touch along the side of her neck.

"But a bite…there, could be…devastating." She smiled, her voice dipping with the salty implication.

"I would imagine it being the same…if such spoils were reversed, maybe even worse. Such…delicate trappings and all," he leered.

Julia paused in contemplation, understanding his meaning, she conceded him the point. "I suppose you could be right, since…delicate things should never be bitten. A gentler approach would give a much greater reward."

"I'm inclined to agree, I—"

Phillip's sneeze erupted through the suite like bugles portending the call to arms. And the harsh tang of disappointment descended promptly on both, as neither of the two wanted to see the provocative spell end. But with the affright sound, they both knew playtime was at its end.

"You owe me something." He whispered against her mouth.

"And what exactly would that be?" she purred.

"You owe me a kiss." Michael hummed with a slow stroke of her mouth, tasting what little he could in haste. He breathed his answer into the very depths of her soul, efficaciously warming each lip. "It's the least you can do to repay my being so…still."

"Maybe you should stop trying." She smiled, lifting her face on the pretense of viewing his. She tasted the warm freshness of his breath. "This could be considered harassment."

"Then you haven't seen anything yet. I'm just getting started." Michael averred, stepping quickly back as Phillip's sneeze again soared through the suite. The modest disruption only helped him to realize the need for a new approach. Should he ever want that kiss to come to fruition—and he most definitely wanted to achieve that end—he'll need to be officiator and king of his own stratagem.

Phillip's cough loudly fringed the entrance of the hall, and as if maliciously melee by dust mites, he cleared his throat what seemed a dozen times, miring his steps before entering the room. Crinkled in stern concentration, his forehead seemed almost glued to the illumined face of his phone. Swiping a finger to and fro, his gaze worked diligently on each page. The purposeful delay, he hoped, gave the two what they needed in warning, not wishing to intrude on the privacy of their time. But he acknowledged that anything longer would have strained the circumstance as it was, and in so doing, bled the truth into obviousness. The occupants turned from separate sides of the room, and both innocent stares were now trained on his face.

"I'm sorry that took so long." Phillip murmured in mid-stride, giving the lie reverence, his eyes skittered over each face. Michael gave him what looked like a curt smile, turning from his view. He seated himself on the couch.

"Everything okay?" Julia asked then, managing to show a modicum of normalcy in her tone.

"Yes." Phillip nodded gently with the word, clearing his throat, he smiled. "Everything is very good."

"Good." Declaring this with a wan smile, she lamely bobbed her head as if to mimic a new trick. Timidly, Julia turned her attention to work. Fishing through the laden, leather purse, she set the small laptop at its usual spot. With sloth-like care, she retrieved each page of her notes as individuals, this while the others assimilated their customary seats. A strange current stalked the tasteful texture of the room, except for the soft shuffling of papers and the clinks of fingers on keys, the space had gone eerily dead. This it had never been before, not even in their somewhat strained beginning. Thankfully, she came well prepared with work, taking the time to draft converse ideas. She gave each problem a list of conceptual response, all to be debated and resolve.

Intending to steal an unfiltered look at the molester of her instinct, Julia's gaze jumped discreetly to the visage of the man. Soft hazel eyes waited on her sluggish approach, as if sensing she would. Trimmed superbly with an alluring smile, they disrupted her intent on remaining aloof. Julia's pulse quickened with the decadence awarded in the view, and the start of a smile played with the corner of her mouth, but she quickly stalled all evidence of that. Sobering with a quick sigh, she cleared the lump now distended in her throat with a forced cough. Awkwardly shifting in her seat, she dropped her eyes to the work still waiting in her hand.

Michael's deep voice cracked the silence like a whip, jolting the stillness with the gravelly depth of his cough. A calculating smirk slid tepidly across his face in recognition of her rebuke, though no remorse shadowed the waggish show. He was enjoying the goading, Julia vowed, she was greatly confident of that. The corner of his mouth further dented as if privy to her thought, and again a thunderous cough barked through the air. It teased the silence into aiding his impish provoke.

"A-hem," he snickered, his hand quickly eclipsing his face. "Excuse me." Michael gargled, casually singing the words over the rim of his mug. He eyed her above the vapor's ascension, affecting a quiet nod as she bestowed him yet another frown.

"So," Phillip muttered, much unaware, without looking up, his attention now fastened on his notes. "I was thinking," he elaborated, slowly dragging his eyes from the paper to her face. "In the bar scene, before Nicole walks over to the jukebox, I thought it might be a good idea if we lengthen that scene. It's a great scene—" Phillip added quickly, noticing her frown. "It's the tipping point to everything—I know. But if we have her talk about leaving Beverly at the hospital, I think the audience would understand sooner why she had to do the things she was later forced to do."

"But that scene is too crucial a platform for that. It's a necessary catalyst for two people, who separately, life rode maliciously raw. It needs to stay simple. To lengthen that scene, you'd either have to fill it with awkwardness or with a glut of words. You can't muddle a scenario like that with a surplus of words. Too much explanation and they'll talk their way out of the need for that intimacy into the dinginess of a simple one nightstand, which would only lessen all the benefits that came from that one encounter." She stressed, twisting her body determinedly in her chair. She continued her argument with passion. "I don't disagree with you on giving a broader explanation about Beverly and what happened at the hospital, but I don't think that's the place to put it."

"Where would you suggest we put it, then?"

"I'm not sure." She shrugged, searching a single page of her notes for an indication on that. "Maybe in the scene where she's leaving," Julia hummed, glancing over the page contemplatively. "Or perhaps the scene where she cleansed herself of everything pertaining to her past; actually, that's even better." She chirped, brightening with the flip of her creative switch. "Think about it. She voids herself of everything in her effort to start her life anew, which includes ridding herself of the books they collected when the two were but precocious girls. What better time to look back on why you're now treading this desolate road. Suffocate and die, or live as a quarantined tree. That's the dilemma she faced with her decision, and that's your place to add that. That's where you expound on her life."

"That's good. I didn't even think of prying that crisis open." Phillip gushed, his head bouncing in agreement.

"We could always put the notice of Beverly's death in one of the books she unloads." Michael added.

"True." Phillip acceded, a finger sighting the recipient of his short retort, though his eyes remained locked on his notes. "Even though the story unfolds a little differently in your book, you really never disclosed what she did with the notice beyond tossing it aside. That could mean anything." Phillip shrugged, and intrigue skimmed the surface of his amber eyes. "She could have appended it to the books out of some weakened sense of reverence." He smiled. "Maybe we could explore using that as an opening to unlock a little more detail on her life. You know…" Phillip exclaimed. Slicing the air with said finger from his left hand, his eyes again dropped to his notes. A terse silence then tumbled through the room, waiting. It stilled the very blitheness in their debate, though it was only so for a spell. A propitious solution soon eroded the spindly delay. Hours flew on the sails of similar debates, with work at the helm, their conversations were again energetic. Playful bicker parked easily between creative dialogues, lengthening their zealous drudging. It paused only when the discussion turned to their choices for lunch.

The sharp knock came in value like the whistle in a miner's shaft. Signaling lunch, it quickly dispersed the three from their task. On the guise of making a call, Phillip darted hastily to the back, again leaving the two duelists to themselves. Julia stood slowly, arching her back. She listened to the familiar clinks of the approaching cart. On his reentrance, Michael's leisured strides promptly halted, and his eyes spoke boldly of mischief in their fiendish depths; widening, they swept her in one elongated glance. The cart held itself like a sentry at his back, hovering near the entrance, only it stood privy to what he now held at his back. Slowly, he brought his vision to light.

"What are you doing?" she asked, her question directed to the small bouquet in his hand.

"Has it really been that long?" he smirked and his expression wavered jauntily between an incredulous taunt and surprise. "The rules haven't really changed all that much, Julia. Allow me to refresh your memory." He smiled, stirring its aim with the professional tender of pure sugar bonding its edge. He augmented the show with a tame drop of his head, flicking his eyes towards the crimson colored flowers in his hand. "I'm wooing you, and these…are what you give to the person you court."

"You're what?" she asked, her words sounding much in the favor of a squawk.

"Courting you. You know: pursue, hunt, tempt, chase, flatter, admire, ravish—respectably, of course." He explicated mildly, affecting a light shrug. His eyes twinkled on the last like the visual augury in the caveat of something grave. "All of the above for certain, with a few cessations perfect for…talking." He smiled, lengthening the able limn of his lure, his eyes, as ever, thrived vivid with the pigment of mischief. "Consider this notification of the proceedings to come. I'm coming after you, and as per my earlier presage, I'm just getting started."

"And I told you, I don't date."

"That you did." He affirmed without elaborating further. "But you do know it's okay to take it. It won't bite you," he smiled. "I'm the only one who does the biting." Michael hummed, his brows twitched roguishly as a result and incredible eyes drove home the meaning behind his puckish words. "It's okay. Take it." He coaxed. "Just like it's okay to kiss me back. The world will not fall from its axis on that, I promise you."

Julia smiled but made no move to take the flowers from his hand, not knowing whether she should. He stood patient in the face of her pondering, looking casual in his stance. His dashing smile neither faltered nor fade. And a soft sigh came as the first hint in her collapsing restraints. Drearily, her hand extended to take the delicate bulbs from his hand.

"Thank you." She mumbled guardedly under her breath, leaving her immersion on the flowers, she asked. "When did you find time to do this?"

"I have my ways." He shrugged, moving a step closer, he stalled. Remembering Phillip's presence in the suite, he thought it best to avoid the temptation. "Have dinner with me this weekend?" he drawled.

Julia's pulse instantly leapt with the sultry inquest, liking the raspy way the question rumbled from his throat. It fostered a smile, for something deep inside her wanted greatly to say yes. Should she even be contemplating this? *You don't have flings. Isn't that what this is?* Her inner voice warned. Two people having fun, that's all this is. "I'm—I'm afraid I can't."

"Why?"

"Why can't I?"

"Why are you afraid?"

"I'm not afraid!" She frowned defiantly.

"You said, 'I'm afraid I can't', why are you afraid and of what?"

"I was just being polite."

"About what and why do you find it necessary to be so polite?"

"What do you want me to say? Would you prefer go to hell?" she laughed, though uncomfortable with the insight he had in her head.

"If you feel it, but you don't. Do you always fight yourself that much?"

"Not usually." She hummed, and her shoulders played softly with the air in reply. "It's also not usual that the bright lights of the big city come to town."

"Do I dazzle you that much?" he asked with a soft dip of his head.

"Only as much as I allow, I just need to get new shades, that's all."

"Then you'll need to buy a few. You're going to need them, because I'm just getting started." Michael affirmed in a raspy tone, drafting each word like a solemn oath. They held no hint of his usual wit. Confident her feelings were not all that she proclaimed them to be, it was with surety that he elaborated his point. "I'm coming after you, Julia, so armor yourself suitably for the hunt."

"What do you know about courting, anyway? Don't you just usually go down the line and make your selection for the week?" she teased.

"I'm sure you haven't noticed," Michael shrugged tersely, ignoring the implication in her jibe. "But, I am a grown man, a very healthy one, too. I…have…had some practice at dating." He smiled, raising his right hand, his eyes immediately jumped to the fingers on said hand. In a flash, two quick snaps promptly clucked through the air. "It's not just a matter of me snapping my fingers." He droned, shrugging weakly behind the act, his head wobbled in disappointment at the failed stunt. "Nope, that old trick's been on the fritz lately, but I'm willing to give it a try." The fast press of friction skin came forward like a parroting clap, and with each, his eyes fleetly jumped to the couch. "Come on. Get on the couch." He rasped as the irregular rhythm continued. "Come over here and kiss me." He rumbled, looking numbly at his hand as if suspicious of the finish, he then glanced at her. "I told you it's been on the fritz." Michael laughed, shaking his head, his eyes plucked at her skin. "If I had that power, I wouldn't still be wondering what it's like to kiss you. I would have tasted you weeks ago."

"Weeks?" she asked curiously, unable to fathom the concept as he hardly spoke to her then.

"Weeks," he affirmed.

"But-but you hardly spoke, and when you did you hardly spoke to me."

"I was being polite." Michael smirked.

"Funny. So let me guess, you're supposed to be a funny nice guy, right?"

"I am a nice guy. But nice guys also want the girl."

"But you always get the girl?"

"I want you. Do I get you?"

"To play with. You'll be over it soon enough."

"Okay. If that's how you want to play it." Michael nodded, expounding no further on the point, he set the candid warning to a plate. "We'll just leave that for a later discussion. But remember this, Julia, you've been duly warned."

Chapter Fifteen

Awe bathed both faces while dust winged the tinted windows of their car. Slaying the spiked peal of their voices, wide gapes—by then greatly distended—bolstered further arresting as the stout vehicle meandered the petrified road. They blistered bold once the majestic manse laid denuded to their view. With the odd semblance of some rare avian species, the elegant structure sat sprawled to the ardor of the midday sun.

Julia's glance strode over the rich architecture with zeal, feeling strangely content with its welcome, she ushered her kids towards the artfully wrought entrance.

"Hello, hello, hello!" Phillip sang in greeting, his eyes touching each face, and his customary zest, as always, was greatly welcomed.

"Hello, Phillip!" Julia chimed back warmly, and immediately felt the tamp press of her kids, as each promptly grafted themself to her side. Timidly, Rachel conceded a small smile, quickly dropping her head. She smothered the budding before granting it the median it needed to shine. Frills of a nervous gawk tightened across Richard's thin face, and the vivacity he bore only moments before, seemed the wilting roe of an enigma. Julia's arms closed supportively around the meager expanse of their backs, urging their progress. She gently piloted their ingress in the house.

The resonance of music suddenly torrent the long hall, booming from the walls. The hum came with a sequential trouncing of the hardwood floor, and the pounding was as familiar to home as her own bed. In celebration of Sarah's success with her new line, the afternoon's festivity was described as a simple expansion of lunch. Packaged sweetly with the sumptuousness of his charm, the invitation had descended directly from Phillip himself, how could she say no to that? Though with Betty as matriarch of the event, she was sure the occasion would be far removed from being just that, since simple did not seem a word listed in Betty's book.

"Now let me see if I have this right." Phillip frowned. "Richard and Rachel, right?" at their nods, Phillip smiled, and amber eyes searched the contour of their faces as if for assurance of such. "Now maybe one of you can tell me which one is which?" he grumbled, looking thoroughly confused. The melody of their giggles wafted in merry mingle to the drubbing beat of the song, breaking the tension they once held. Their mood seemed suddenly relaxed. "I just wanted to be sure." He shrugged. "With names like Stone, Apple and Moon, you just never know these days."

"Julia!" Sarah hailed in her usual lively tone, flouncing in the room as sunny as the break of day. Her smile was, within itself, a confectioner's paste. "You made it! Thanks for coming."

"Sarah!" Julia sang back, finding it hard to resist her contagious mirth. "Thank you for inviting us. Congratulations on your new line!"

"Thank you! Oh my goodness, look at you!" Sarah preened, dropping her eyes to the kids' faces, her blue gaze cuddled Rachel's frame. "You're beautiful!" She proclaimed with an awed sigh. "You look so much like your mother. And you, wow! Look at those lashes, so handsome!" She smiled, cupping the cusp of Richard's chin, she gave an affectionate squeeze. "What do you say we go rescue Michael and the Wii from my little angels?" She chanted, dropping an arm upon his shoulder. She turned him towards the thumping of the bass. "You know, come to think of it. I don't think my kids have even noticed they're not at home. I think it's time we shake that up a bit. What do you say? Let someone else have the use of this place for a change." She sang, cementing his small body to her side as she skirted ahead, not needing a definitive response to her convivial ramble. Her twitter sailed like the choreographed cadence in a hollow aviary.

The beat to Thriller blared like an anthem through the stereophonic room, pulsing as Britney danced her way through the highlighted moves on the game named after the artist himself. Fanatic slaps soared wildly from a foosball table across the room, puncturing the illustrious rhythm of the song. It bred almost blustery, as Jason and Michael strived to defend their prospective goals.

"Hey, guys! Our guests are here!" Sarah announced in the rhythm of a song, and the sound of the slapping instantaneously stopped—though only in part.

"Yes! I score!" Jason screamed, pumping his arms, he then threw them above his head. "I won! I won! I won!" he chanted, showcasing a slow celebratory dance as his reward, he prolonged his taunt. "I rule! I rule! I—" the lyrical jeer ceased as surely as a hand depressing the volume control. Jason's body froze in the midst of a twist, his excitement crumbling to a halt. It died without taking an added breath. Amber eyes eagerly scaled the gap to then feed on Rachel's face, staying as if compelled. He missed the full gist of his mother's address.

Like mother, like daughter, Michael mused in the silence that followed. Cognizant his primary response had been no different than that. He empathized with the young boy's plight, for only age had helped him to better hide that fact. Although her complexion was of a creamier tan, Rachael's features bore remarkable resemblance to those of her mother's. It was almost scary to think what the possibility of ten years could bring. Jason's focus remained glued to the pint-size beauty, not having taken a breath since the jarring pause. He stood as if in wait. Finally, Rachel gave him the acknowledgement of a shy smile, glancing up at her mother in question. It, too, slowly died.

"Jason! Jason!" Sarah piped, and waited for a reaction from her son, finding humor in the sudden smitten look on his face. Jason's head wobbled lamely, and a frown darted between his eyes before he peeled his attention from the girl to then focus on her. "Maybe you'd like to meet our new guest?" she hummed, her witty remark bringing an instant reaction. Painted bright across the slopes of his cheeks, it eagerly washed down the full length of his neck. His face displayed at least three separate shades of red before his head dropped. "Remember the author I told you about?" Sarah asked softly, quickly changing her tact.

"The one whose books you're always reading when you say you need to relax?" Jason voiced, his red face quickly angling up.

"Ah…well, yes." Sarah fumbled, embarrassed by the frank manner in which his answer came. She sighed, as the meek retort had successfully tendered more honesty than she had intended to give at that time. Truth be known, she was a diehard fan. Not only did she own her stellar collection, but the assortment had matured into the strategic arc of her creative rituals. The lady truly had a way with words, making descriptive language an art. Her books worked like magic when she needed them most. "Well, this is her." Sarah mumbled, pushing the start of a casual smile to her face, she further expounded on the introduction. "This is Julia Berwick, her son, Richard, and of course…her daughter, Rachel."

Bright, hypnotic amber eyes again jumped to Rachel's face, lingering heedless of the others in the room, his voice came surprisingly small. "Hello."

"Hello, Jason." Julia muttered then, understanding that he may have little care that she spoke. She sweetened the tuning of her voice. "It's nice to finally meet you. I've heard so much about you from your parents." She crooned, offering a warm smile. She watched as he attempted to mimic the incomplex chore, failing, he attacked the floor with his eyes instead, and a slow nod followed as his means of acknowledgement of what was said.

Of a sudden, the drubbing of the music stopped, and Britney's body, with the aid of a loud pant, crashed feebly to the floor like a discarded sack. "Yes! I got four stars!" she shrieked in a small voice.

"Britney, come say hello to one of my favorite authors!" Sarah called with a swell of excitement again fringing her voice, her blue eyes jumping to the small body sprawled on the floor. "This is Julia, her daughter, Rachel and son, Richard."

"Hi!" Britney smiled, already showing great comfort with their guests.

"Hi!" Rachel smiled back, and although the meek word made its way to Richard's lips, no tangible sound made it past. Quietly, he nodded his head instead.

"Hello, Britney, I've also heard a lot about you. Are you still practicing the piano?" Britney's answer came in the form of a brusque nod, and eyes, an odd variant of what seemed blueish green, twinkled with the enormity of the pride she felt.

"Do you think you can show them the ropes around here?" Sarah asked in her musical drawl, brushing back a loose strand of straw colored hair almost identical to her own.

"Sure, mom!" Britney chirped, seeming to display much of her mother's infectious disposition. She smiled at the waiting guests.

"And this is Michael," Julia quietly added, lowering her head to the kids. Her eyes travelled to the place where his tall body loomed in wait, well riveted by the view. Swallowing the start of a surge, she continued with a soft smile. "Michael is one of the two people I've been working with these past few months."

"Hello, guys," Michael rasped, sauntering forward with a smile—the gauge of which promptly shot to high—chiseled beautifully on his face. The grandeur of his charm oozed with every step, arcing from his body like the glow of a static charge, and one could only wonder if such opulence came with its own switch. "I'm really sorry that we've kept your mommy away with so much work. But she's really good, isn't she? I'm sure you're very proud."

"Do you really make movies?" Richard blurted elatedly, firing the imperative question with gusto. His eyes bulged past what one could deem a natural event.

"I do." Michael nodded, widening his smile in accordance of Richard's excitement. "We both do." He hummed, and a finger indicated Phillip's quiet entrance in the room. "Phillip and I are partners, which only means he takes the credit while I do the work."

"Anything we've seen?" Rachel promptly asked, finding enough of her voice to fire the reinforcing shot to her brother's critical probe.

"Ah...no, I don't think so. Not yet. But now that you mention it, we'll definitely look into that."

"We sure will." Phillip added, looking truly resolved with the point.

"Sarah is Phillip's wife, and of course, you've already met their kids, Jason and Britney." Julia smiled, directing the placid intro to Rachel, though both kids stayed anchored to her side. "I'll give you two chances to guess what Sarah's job is. It's something you love and it has nothing to do with ice cream."

"Ah, I...I don't—"

"Designer!" Britney whispered, leaning close. Yet her small voice easily enlightened the entire room.

"Designer!" Rachel yelled. Giving her answer as if the thought was all her own. She beamed brightly at its end.

"That's right," Julia confirmed with a strained smile, although laughter gently spilled about the room. "Sarah just got back from Paris where she showcased her new designs. Quite successfully I'm told. Congratulations again!"

"Thank you. Thank you." Sarah bowed, gracious in her acceptance of the praise. "Oh! Speaking of my show, I have something for you."

"You do?" Julia frowned, and her countenance showed her perplexity of such thought.

"It's not much, just something you inspired, that's all. I'll get it to you after lunch." She avouched with a swift nod. "Come on. Let's go unwind while the kids are occupied."

Although curious about her gift as well as the reason, Julia aptly held her patience and her tongue. "Okay." She calmly responded instead, observing that the kids were now involved in the tentative steps of conversation. She offered the gentle reminder with a smile. "Be good, guys." She called not expecting a reaction, and was not surprised when none came in return.

March coasted well past the midmost of it prime, and each day steadily grew warmer than the one before, giving full evidence of the impending with the merry twitter of birds. Today evolved no different than yesterday's incredible unveiling, ripening to an astounding seventy degrees. The sky was without a single flaw. In observance, lunch was to be served outside on the large verandah, the day's warmth being conducive to that. Set for dinning, refreshments and snacks already waited on a long console dressed as exquisite as a summer garden in the blossoming of spring. A cozy living-room space postured at the opposite end of the spread, looking as elegant as any showroom for the advertised pieces it sold.

"Hello, Julia." Michael muttered in a leisured tone, moving close. His breath brushed the soft skin of her lobe.

"Hello." She breathed in return, swallowing a shiver that lunged through her body from the mere warmth of his breath. The single word was released as one would the tension on a rein. It crawled seductively off her tongue with purposeful intent.

Michael smiled, appreciating the affinity of their game, as it was so much better than any he'd ever had, and a thousand times more exciting than any he could have imagined himself liking. Having been known for being more direct than not, what some considered a clumsy beginning, came to him with a modicum of ease. So to this vagary, he was uncertain of the rules. But for her, he was willing to stay the course and do the study, eager to learn all things her.

"You're looking..." wagging his head with what seemed a muted growl, his eyes crept intriguingly over her frame, taking his fill before giving voice to his thought. "Mm...Deliriously appetizing this day," He sighed, gargling the words in his throat, he murmured them with the intent of them falling to none but one ear.

Appeased by the sparks from the timber that he lit, Julia smiled, liking the rumbly swirl of his voice. She slowly looked over her attire as if assessing its worth. "I'm just trying to stay in step with the queen of fashion." She shrugged, lifting brown eyes to the speckled gems of hazel, she willingly plunged their depths. *What is it about his eyes that tethered her so well?* She sighed, meekly surrendering to whatever yearnings they had. She felt their heat as surely as she would his hand. Slowly, they walked over her body at will, stirring the thrill ever onward as they landed on her mouth. Conscious that the effect had grown vastly exciting, though that truth, she was certain, would never be told.

"Trend or not," Michael hummed, again bowing his words to her ear. He took remarkable care with the enunciation of his speech. "That...dress..." he drawled, his eyes dipping on the raspy expel, they again caressed her body at a tired snail's pace. "It makes a rather generous donation to a...very good cause."

"And what cause is that?" she sang.

"The secret to any success in this Dog-Eat-Dog world is, knowing what to hold. What to sell and when to go public is another practice one has to master to be trium-phant in work." He smiled, murmuring the cryptic response. His fingers skimmed hers as he took the glass from her hand. "Allow me." Michael rumbled in continuance, pour-ing a glass of the freshly made fruit drink, his thumb caressed her palm as he returned the chilled tumbler to her hand. Smiling, his eyes gave minute hints of the filth that romped freely through his head, it tattled on the longings that churned in the pit of his stomach, though he quickly swallowed the exhibiting of that.

Phillip and Sarah seemed in the middle of an intimate chat. One he was sure they instigated to aid in the furthering of his cause, and he intended to use his time well. Now that he had made his attraction known, a generous portion of his thoughts had since been taunted by the sultriness of their interludes past. And his imaginings, triggered by the unavoidable traps that it bade, had somehow soared to new height. Every occasion begets him an inaugural promise of something else, yet, like viewing water through a sealed bottle with an unbreakable lid, they've all kept him nicely at bay. His body still wilting from thirst.

"Betty, hi!" Julia called in a soft shrill, noticing the older woman's approach. She quickly bolted from his side, looking as guilty as kids caught in the flurry of spiking their drinks.

"Julia!" Betty greeted spryly, hardly slowing her speed. Her eyes stayed on the brusque toiling of her hands, adjusting the platters already in wait. She added a server to the newly allotted space. "How are you doing?" she asked without looking up.

"I'm well. I'm very well." Julia smiled, still amazed by the energetic drive she showed. "And you?"

"I'm just fine!" The small shoulders shrugged. "You brought the kids?" she asked, suddenly slowing in her task.

"I sure did."

"Good, good! Then I'll get to meet them." She smiled, showing off the full loveliness of her face.

"I'll introduce you myself." Julia laughed.

"Then I'll hold you to that." She smirked, throwing back a chuckle as she swept from the room. Behind the two, Michael groaned softly in abject discontent, having had another stolen moment invaded upon. He was flatly tired of that. All hindrance, he vowed decisively, would be addressed posthaste.

By the time the group sat down to lunch, Julia was near famished, and as usual, the spread exceeded expectation, this, even while knowing Betty's tendency to excel.

"No, no. Children inside," Betty announced softly, stopping the kids' rush staunchly at the door. Her thin shoulders curled softly as she leaned close. "Let the grownups have their food. We don't want that." She whispered, giving then a soft shake of her head. She offered the answer to her speech. "We have better food in there." She winked, pointing a finger discretely towards the door. "Hamburgers, kebabs, root-beer float…" she hummed, leaning in close. She quickly pressed a finger to her lips. "Shhh…" Betty again warned, straightening, she cleared her throat as if to heighten her concern. "If they knew, they'd want to be invited. So let's just back up quietly and act like it's no big deal, okay." She bade sweetly, glancing back at the grown-ups who were well engrossed in a lively chat. "Just follow my lead, okay." Murmuring this, all four heads eagerly bobbed.

Betty turned her small body with the precision of a luxury car. Replacing the soft expression she once had with a stern glare, she started the austere announce. "Ah, I'm having the children eat inside the house with me. It's easier this way, at least conversation wise." She shrugged. Behind her back, Betty patted whomever stood closest to her hand, giving their body a slight bump. She asked. "Right kids?"

"Right!" The choir sang in agreement, all voices chanting at once. Small feet shuffled backwards in retreat, goaded into doing such by the coercing dictates of Betty's hand.

"Okay, Betty." Sarah chirruped, slashing any possibility of a rebuttal from the new-comer to this game. She smiled.

"Okay then. Bye." Betty grunted, turning immediately, she smiled victoriously at the kids, following the rarity with an even rarer wink. Her arms spread like wings in preparation of flight, encircling her brood. She encouraged a faster departure from the scene, one they promptly complied to with zeal. Triumphant giggles followed their guarded escape, erupting as they entered the kitchen, yet as a group their volume remained startlingly low. Betty's giggle was almost as blissful as the kids themselves, giving each hand a smack. Her enthusiasm soared as limitless as they.

Dressed for the occasion, the table held brightly colored utensils and plates. In accordance with such festivity, oddly shaped hamburgers waited in the center of a teal tray. Alongside that, almond-crusted chicken strips, fish steaks on kebabs with an assortment of vegetables waited on corresponding trays. A sprightly colored fruit salad sat in avid display near the right hand of everyone's plate. Four root-beer floats waited in blue goblets on a small red tray, looking almost pompous like the superintendents of a fair, implants of long straws centered the thick drinks.

"Cool!" imparting his admiration of the view, Richard's exclaim clambered the room like a blast, tumbling through the air like the tail-end of a howl. It broke the lively current of the space. Richard's small hands barred the gaping evidence with a hard slap to his mouth, instantly bombarded with their collective "shush." He dimly expressed his regret. "Sorry." He whispered, slowly dropping the cover from his mouth, his eyes rushed to the door.

"Let's eat before your parents come in to see what we're up to." Betty nudged with a quick peek at the door. Lifting the first chair, she offered Richard the seat. Consecutive chairs then followed the maiden deed, bereft of even the smallest bark, as each child brokered their action with care. "Now, let's get started. Root-beer float, everyone?" she asked, and all heads bobbed eagerly in concurrence of such, smiling their thanks as the tall drink was placed within reach of their hands. Jason was the first to take a long drag on his straw, lifting his head. He found Betty's eyes already trained to his face. "Remember," she prompted then. "Slow does it, and…?" raising her brow in question, she patiently waited the finishing in his own timbre.

"Always with food," Jason mumbled dully, putting the drink aside, he adjusted himself in his seat.

"That's right," Betty smiled, her soft voice falling to a near wheeze in its whispered state. "The rules for enjoying your floats are very simple, guys." She announced, strolling to the counter, she deposited the empty tray. "Slow always makes it better every time. You can't enjoy your food when your brain is chilled, now can you? So, enjoy your food...with your drink. As delicious as it is now, it won't be tonight when you get a stomach ache from not eating." She warned, smiling down at her audience who seemed riveted to her words. "Too much of anything is never any good. Besides, how will you explain what made you sick? To do that, you'll have to let the secret out, and if we want to keep this little party of ours going, we'll have to carry ourselves as responsible beings. So, can we follow the rules so we can keep our party going?"

"We can follow the rules." They muttered singly, remembering to warily proctor the height of their shrilly tone, though their excitement was not lost with the murmured speech.

Pleased with their enthused response, Betty nodded her appreciation with a full smile, her dark eyes brushing each face. "Now," she whispered like a cherub above their heads. "Let's all dig in!" Betty charged, ringing the starting gong with the exhilaration in her speech, she took her own seat in readiness for the show and watched as bantam hands hurriedly fixed their plates. The sound of giggles broke the festal air often, and conversation vaulted in-between at a virtual whisper, that, when paralleled with the acute normalcy of their tone. The preparation, Betty warbled with her mollified self, was well worth the sights. Now all that remained was to await their reaction to the taste.

"Maybe I should go and make sure my kids are staying on their best behavior. I'd hate for poor Betty to be playing fetch instead of me." Julia muttered absently, throwing a worried frown at the door.

"You can't. Or you'll spoil the whole thing." Michael smirked.

"What thing?" she asked, looking and sounding confused.

"The game Betty makes out of things; everything, actually."

"Game, what game?"

"Well," Sarah chimed in pleasantly. "Betty has this thing she does with the kids, sh——"

"She probably has them eating their vegetables and begging for more is what it is." Phillip smirked, cutting through the crux of his wife's speech.

"Betty has this way of working with kids. She can get them to do anything." Michael groaned, expounding on his opening warn. "It's a gift," he continued softly, remember-ing the many tricks she used on him, and knew the very same was probably being used as they speak. "Thankfully, she uses it for good."

"Their hamburgers are most likely spiked with vegetables and they won't even know it." Sarah laughed, covering her mouth with the willowy tip of a hand; she hid the evidence of her chew. "For as long as we've been coming here, you'd think my kids would have caught on by now, but..." she shrugged, "they haven't yet, or so it seems."

"It takes a little while for your acumen to catch on; that's the problem." Michael carped. "And, even then, she has an answer for everything." He assured in a low, raspy tone, rolling his eyes to the sky. He denoted in a single gesture how badly he was doped himself. "She always made it so much fun. I think that's the trick. After a while you don't really care that it's not real, you just focus on the parts where you're having fun."

"You're kidding?" Julia droned, splicing the start of a smirk with the richness of her frown.

"Nope," Phillip retorted gaily, his own smirk brightening in amity of the first. "Ask your kids when you leave about their food or the revelry they had inside. They'll blunder their way through an answer, but they won't tell you the full truth. That's the hold she has. She goes out of her way to make them feel special, and they go out of theirs to protect the sanctity of that. They won't give it up."

"That's brilliant!" Julia snickered, casting her eyes at the door as if to garner a peek at the cabal holding inside. Yet the egress, haloed by a sliver of sunlight, remained the same, and only the chorus-like chirps of crickets seemed missing from the silence that gushed from the house. "That woman intrigues me more and more each time I see her. Getting kids to savor their vegetables and repeatedly return for more is no small feat. Where did she come up with that?"

"We have no idea. But it works and we never talk about it. Unless, of course, she's asking about their likes and dislikes, which even then you'll find that Betty has…this… way." Sarah sighed, her face creasing into what seemed an uncertain frown. She curled her shoulders with the show before expounding on her point. "Betty has a somewhat eclectic way of dealing with people. It's not usually what you're used to, depending on the mood. The illusory strictness can sometimes be a tough shell to get past. She has the best heart, though. But if you don't know her, she can literally scare you to death, and will if you mess with her big baby over there." Sarah chirped, kicking her chin towards Michael's tall frame. She laughed. "She's worse than any mother hen when it comes to him, and is not afraid to let you know it. Even his own mother has to wait her turn when it comes to letting those protective fangs fly."

"But we love her despite her underlining weakness." Phillip crowed, snorting frailly behind his words, he inciting the table to merge with the chorale of a tuneful snicker.

To the edge of the verandah, a wiry squirrel bounded from the gnarly branch of a tree, as if in a race. It sprinted across the lawn with another just as earnest on its tail. Zigging this way and that, they darted up the next tree at a reckless pace, disappearing behind the wide trunk. Their existence was immediately doused as if the two had not been.

Conversation augmented affably throughout the entirety of their meal, and at every opening, Michael's eyes subtly scuffed the alps of Julia's physique. Leaving no part of her body untouched, he made certain she retained awareness of his earlier oath. And again, she felt betrayed by the reaction her body insisted on giving over to his gaze, as she was constantly sentient, not only of his person, but of a goodly portion of his thoughts. Small stirrings in the house indicated the children's festivity at an end, and the faint drubbing of feet flawed the full vanishing they most likely intended. Darting back to the game-room in their pursuit of fun, the grownups eventually drifted to the family-room in continuance of their own tame revelry.

"Okay." Sarah chirped, returning to the room after an extended break. She meekly flourished a beautifully hand-painted gift bag from her back. "This is for you." She whispered, leveling the bag as if its content was inexplicably fragile. She carefully placed it in Julia's hand. "I hope you like it. It was inspired by you."

"Thank you. But you didn't need to do that, Sarah."

"Open it up!" she cried excitedly, rubbing her palms together in an eager show as she waited a reaction, thus ignoring the softly intoned comment.

Julia studiously obeyed the impatient request. Carefully undoing the flap barring the top, she slowly widened the bag's mouth, smiling with fondness as something shimmery gaped back as she stared. Cautiously, she pulled the soft fabric from its artistic cradle, believing the object to be a scarf, though it was far from being that. "Oh my goodness!" she rasped. "You're giving me a dress?"

"The design was inspired by you. So who better to have one of my designs than my inspiration?"

"It's beautiful!" Julia sang, gazing in awe at the silky red dress. Covered with what looks to be subtle flecking of black scales, it was an extremely sexy piece, and off the top of her head, she could not think of one place she would want to wear a piece like that. "You said I inspired the design?" she asked, soundly almost incredulous.

"When I was working on my designs for the show, you popped in my head and this popped out as a suited garnish. Come on! You have to try it on!"

"Well, I—" Julia started, stuttering to a stop as Sarah yanked her to her feet. Reluctantly following the tow, she allowed herself to be closeted in a vacant bedroom at the top of the stairs. Aversely, Julia slipped the slinky garment on, and had Sarah taken her measurements to assimilate the right fit, the dress could not have been more perfectly done. The silky piece fitted her body like the supple textile of a glove. Hence the reluctant admit, for she had to concede that the piece looked especially sultry wrapping her form. Yet nothing about the sexy outfit was befitting of her style. Neither did the meager garb scream PTA.

Such thoughts were but a few that awkwardly weighted her mind as she retraced her steps. In reticence, Julia cleared the tightening in her throat, and all heads spun in response to the small cough she bade in aid of her nerves. Sarah's face immediately went flushed with the magnitude of her pride, palming both cheeks, her eyes brightened with her smile. Phillip slowly mouthed what looked like a "wow" as his eyes sketched her person. Keeping her focus locked on the two, she left Michael's expression, unwittingly, for the savor, unearthing the odd urge to relish his response.

"You look…amazing!" Sarah sang through loosely clasped hands. "I knew it would look amazing on you! This is my sassy take on the little black dress."

Though awkwardly done, Julia turned slowly in exhibition, granting Sarah the enjoyment she sensed came with viewing the fulfillment of one's work. Her description of the piece, though far from a lie, only offered the truth in part. The dress was indisputably small. Yet "Peppery and Vivacious" suited the miniscule piece well. Strapless, the silken body glove tapered to a stop near the middling of her thighs. It sheltered only the necessary parts needed for one to be considered clothed. Although, had the length carried a few added inches, it would not be quite as inane to her taste. Since it was, in truth, a beautiful dress. Something she would actually wear if she did not feel so explicitly bare.

Carefully walking her eyes across the rug, she set her gaze to the place where Michael reclined in the cozy molding of his chair. He had not moved nor did he speak since she entered the room. And his gaze, with all certainty, did not disappoint. Hazel eyes worked like hands over the sudden swellings now swathing her flesh, drawing her closer with every brush. They were, in truth, like tasting the apogee of a dream, granting the bold visage of what one would wish to see in the eyes of a lover. *A girl could drown in a look like that.* Julia purred ravenously, for his leer was as bright as any star in the blackest of night.

"Very nice," Michael rasped, breaking the slight pause. He quietly leaned forward in his seat, dropping an elbow to his thigh. He complimented his imagination with the measly authenticating of her body, and the smile that grew on his face, was reminiscent of a hunter spotting the pleasing eminence of a revered prey.

A warm tingle slithered up her thighs with the licentious ogle. Ricocheting through her body like a hum, it settled enticingly in the warmest fissure her body had. In follow, the heat of her skin shot swiftly to braise, and she was sure sweat now pimpled the arc of her buttocks. A puerile reaction from just the sweetness of his gaze, as if her body somehow hungered for the wont of the scrutiny he gave. Julia expelled a soft sigh in her rummage for control, dragging her attention from the man. She gave herself over to the others in the room, both now eyeing her with an odd showing of pride. "Thank you, Sarah." Julia mumbled, sounding almost calm, she flaunted the making of a smile. The intensity of his gaze, though shunned, could not be easily forgotten, thus her sense of complete exposure grew to a lofty height. For with all certainty, such that the blind could attest, she truly doubted he saw any part of the racy dress.

"Yes." Michael nodded, though his eyes never left the woman or the dress. "Thank you, Sarah."

"You're welcome." Sarah chirped, crimping her small shoulders in response. She turned to her husband and smiled. The two exchanged an extended glance, stealth in their absence of dialogue, yet the gesture seemed knowing, nonetheless. Phillip's smile came flanked with a small nod, returning his attention to their guest. He again surveyed the dress.

"I'm not sure how I inspired this, but.... Thank you."

"It's a sassy little piece, isn't it?" Sarah chirped, walking a slow circle around the live mannequin in their midst. She admired the fitting of her handy work, having guessed right on the finer details of Julia's figure, Sarah gushed with pride. Years of experience had done her well on that front.

Julia nodded exaggeratedly. "Yes. Very little," she gasped. "It's hard to imagine that this is what you see when you look at me. I'm not this sassy." She laughed.

"Then you and I need to set aside time to have us some girl talk." Sarah chirruped, tilting her head slightly as she gazed thoughtfully at the near flawless creature now showcasing her creation. Looking not unlike the many used to do just that, Sarah murmured her thoughts. "The dress is a gift. The kind mothers don't normally buy for themselves. Don't worry. I don't expect to see you wearing it at our next get-together." She assured with an understanding smile, pausing in her rambling, she frowned. "Consider it a totem. A source, if you will, one where all things come from. It's your rejuvenation point; a point you should always keep close for when you need it."

Julia gave the petite woman a slow nod, half understanding yet half caring past the expectation patented to the skimpy dress, as all focus dipped once the issue was confirmed in her head. Symbolic she can definitely do, and do well. There were shelves covert enough in the back of her closet that can keep symbolic well tucked. Anything to not feel as naked as she now did, especially in front of a man that already made her feel just that. With the fixed way he leered at her of late, it's hard to remember what his gaze looked like in the months before now. Did he always look at her like that? No wonder he hardly spoke. He was probably ogling her body this whole time—the pervert. He probably has the sickest mind, too. No wonder he'd been able to have such enticing conversations. She grunted, saying nothing as to the raunchiness of her own. Or of the fiery flavor she had deftly added to the fusion to further pepper the pot.

Julia's grumbles grew endless as she discarded the miniscule garb, retrieving what she appropriately deemed "clothing well suitable to wear". She again felt a semblance of her normal self. His warm, mellifluous gaze had had an adverse reaction on her body, and that, she knew, needed to stop. Yet even so, her pulse leapt as she recalled how her body responded to just the will of his eyes, wondering then on the potency of her response had the culprit been his hands? Shaking her head brusquely to dislodge such thought, Julia stopped the descending train her mind seemed so determined to be carted on. Hence she forced her attention back to where it needed to be, and it was not on Michael Dunhill or what he can do with his hands.

The day bolted with great speed on the ensuing of their rambunctious chat, and in no time, evening pervaded the air with its dusky tint, bringing the group's festivity to an end. The drive home was as usual garrulous, with the kids eagerly recapping the highlights of their day. Julia watched the expressiveness of faces in the rearview mirror and smiled, deciding to test Phillip's contention. She dove directly to the point. "How was your food, guys?" she began in a soft voice.

"Great!" they both chirped.

"Did you enjoy what you had?"

"We did! It was really good." Richard tweeted, and both heads bobbed eagerly in concurrence.

"I'm sorry I didn't come in and help you, what did you finally pick to eat?"

"Hambur—" Richard twittered in start, wincing suddenly from the pain of Rachel's elbow hitting his arm. "Ouch!" Richard squealed, turning sharply in his seat. He gave his sister an angry glare, one well suited to cause harm itself. "Wha—" he halted. His words again froze in his throat, held there by the firm shake of Rachel's head, reminding him of their promise. "Oh, ah…" Richard grunted, rubbing his arm as he searched for a suitable reply. "Chicken I think." He mumbled finally.

"You don't remember what you ate?" Julia probed, sniffing softly under her breath.

"It was chicken." Rachel added in aid, quickly taking control.

"Did you guys at least enjoy it?"

"Yes!" they squealed, both eagerly nodding in response. "It was a lot of fun!"

Chapter Sixteen

Cogent hands boldly walked the apogee of her breasts, blazing like stoked embers across her body. They shrewdly roamed the venues that tendered the most gratifying delights. Lips persistent in their wont, seared in their coaxing, wrangling the flavors of an aptly engorged fission of itself. He urged further submittal to his lascivious plight, renewing the potency of his ravenous feed with skill.

Drinking deeply from the moist furnace of his mouth, Julia immediately complied with his ferocious drive. Avidly accepting the pleasures that came with the intensity of such toils as that, she imbibed a fire that bred exceedingly sweet. His hardened form thence grew extraordinarily fierce. Igniting memories once extinguished, they burned vindictively through the parched regions of her body.

No longer assuaged with skulking amidst the dingy shadows of her mind, desire sauntered brashly to the helm of both mind and body. In reply, a hungry sigh wafted warmly from her throat, gifting her appreciation from the crux of her soul. She accentuated thus with verve as his hand journeyed the smooth length of her thighs. Deftly, he inhabited the heated cavern, softly playing the bedewed edge. His tongue orbited her with superb dexterity, and had she not intended further use of him then, she was solely tempted to roll and ravage his length in full, for his caresses sent waves of delectation crashing through her entire being.

A rousing groan came as his answer against her mouth, pulling her closer yet. His breath came like a warm fan aloft her cheek, brushing his lips upon a soft lobe. He plunged greedily into the fiery morass of her body.

"Mmmm," she moaned in acquiescence of the euphoric glide, her sugary tone sailing through the darkness like a predacious howl. It curled like fingers against one's skin. Now slotted firmly atop hers, she savored the electrifying pressure of his body, for it nestled the ridges and valleys of her form well. "Ohhh," she acceded once more, elated with the sensations billowing from his strides, her own answering cant madly stirred the intoxicant drive.

Trembling hands quietly caressed his chest, stroking the wall of his inspired physique. He suddenly mellowed the zest of his enraptured pace, veering their dance to an objectionable stop. Under the waltz of her hands, his once hardened body now relaxed, morphing into a sad sham of itself. Julia growled roughly in response, though it was not pleasure that triggered the guttural cry. Ire by the abrupt change, disappointment washed her from inside out, eroding the purity of her pleasure. Rapture retreated with the moroseness of a tide retrieving its treasure for the sea. With a litany of words already prepared on her tongue, Julia's eyes flew wide, well prepared to confront the cause of such malicious display. She, instead, was near blinded by the spray of an officious light.

Morning thoroughly minced a once gray room, erupting gaily. It sang the exalted cheer of a new day. As if to thrust home the day's mandate and the tormenting of why, birds chirrups drifted pleasingly overhead, posting the obvious, in a slow crawl, to the forefront of her head. The distant snarl of a dog's bark further impelled the lingering fog to fly.

Alone, she rested fully tucked within the vacuous confines of her bed. Still tasting the putrid flavor of something lost. The nauseating stench of famine still sat apparent in her hand. It curled suffocatingly around the pillow she now clutched to her breasts. Dubious of the truth, Julia's body shot forward in haste, frowning, she searched her bed for proof of other than what remained to her gaze, certain the foolery would prove to be a lie. The memory of his touch now drove the intensity of her quest, cruelly strumming her mind while her body yet hummed. Thus, it rejected what it already knew to be true. *Oh, God!* She moaned, finding no such proof. *It can't be a dream! Damn! Not another one!*

A long grunt kissed the sweetness that well lined the cheery morning air. Diced by the sound of frustration, it marred what was truly an impeccable display. Vexed, Julia settled back to her lonely place in bed, well mindful of that fact, this being the third time this week that she has had the same results, and with each, the intensity grew stronger yet, seeming so real that her body still pulsed with need. Without ponder, she could still feel his hands on everyplace that he touched. Even her lips still stung from the marauding pressure his kisses yielded, and his aftershave still played on the vibrissae of her nostrils.

"Come on. *This has to stop!*" She barked. Irritated with the weakness her body continued to show. Julia advised herself of a necessary truth. "It's not real, Julia. He's not real. It's just the glitz of the fantasy that he represents. That's what you're feeling. That's all this is. It will pass. It has to." She instructed gruffly, now fully appeased with the wisdom of her counsel, again confident a handle would soon be had. She was not one to have flings and was not about to start now. So the decision was well clear, there would be no furthering of that.

A spray of sunlight streamed jauntily through an uneven slot in her blinds, giving great promise to the day ahead, though, for her, the premise just felt odd. With the kid's absence, her loneliness was magnified in spades. It further mocked with the tingling her body still gave, and even the house now seemed unsettled in the suspense that she felt. Voided of energy, it seemed the very bricks felt no less the despondency of her mood.

Already, the weekend was upon them with its swift fiery breath, slicing the hours of her day in its ever demanding palm. Saturday marked the finish of a short respite the kids now had. Thus far, she had chauffeured both kids to their destination of choice, conceding to a sleepover with their prospective best friends. The occasion had gone forth without hassle or glumness creasing it edge, and although it was not easily done— due fully to the schedules of the parents involved—accommodating the exactness of the invites was, for her, like procuring aspirin to ward off the certitude of pain. By simply allowing both to enjoy the fruits of their wants collectively, complaints were not among the leading quarrels for that day, and she avoids the stress of having to deal with all that, by simply holding to a plan.

Still clasping the pillow to her chest, Julia reached for the slim remote, needing something besides her own thought to ease the sturdy pull of Michael's hands lancing her body. She aimed the invisible beam at the black screen primly clipped to her wall. Arching her body in a long stretch, Julia closed her eyes and searched for an untormented place in her head, yet finding none to where she could hide. None that did not already have the man waiting with ulterior intent, or was not already drenched in the memory of his touch, though knowing fully the stir was not real.

Incensed by the dawdling twinge she now harbored, Julia sprang from the betraying comfort of her bed, muttering her disgust as she tossed the once coddled pillow to the floor. "It's not him that you want, Julia." She grunted. "It's just the evidence of your absence talking, that's it. That's all this is. It has to be. Isn't it?" she sighed, uncertainty wrapping each word. "Besides, it wouldn't feel that good anyway. There's no way it could." She again warned. "Definitely not!" she spat, forcefully affirming her thought, she decided to rid all evidence of the man from her mind at once. And what better than a cold shower to properly do the trick of that?

The slant of a familiar face jumped to the television screen as she veered from her bed, catching her eyes as she turned, it froze the propulsion of her feet in mid-tread. Julia gawked bewilderedly at the angling of his face, and every dark memory from her dream flooded her body at once.

Michael's smile was quietly animated, looking comfortable on the set of the Today Show. His conversation with Matt Lauer seemed truly in-depth. Julia stood transfixed by the beautiful sight now plastered on her wall, forsaking all dictates made only moments before. She keenly watched the language his body spelt, and he seemed to have studied well for that test. His specimen was truly worthy of the adoration it gets, for he was, without malice, *astoundingly* good to look at. Quietly, she conceded that in her head. Shifting in his seat, Michael's eyes seemed then to slowly gather hers, as if aware of her thoughts. His hazel gaze was almost mocking as he smiled in response to Matt's ensuing probe.

His answer came obscured in a mute wave, as was Matt's subsequent retort, both shrouded in anonymity by the near imperceptible volume hissing from the television amps. With little grace aiding her exert, Julia threw herself towards the bed, clumsily slamming her shin against the footboard of a wrought-iron bed. She screamed coarsely in her throat. "Ouch! Damn!" the bland expletive came in the guise of a loud grunt, "Ouch!" she sang tartly once more, cradling her injured leg. Julia grabbed the coveted remote, working her thumb firmly atop the volume button. She flashed bits of a dourly snort between each soft pant.

"We make the process quite easy for everyone to get involved. All they have to do—be it to donate time or money—is go to our website. Once there, they'll be walked through each step from start to finish. It's that easy. There is no limit to what we ask. So whatever the amount they can afford or whatever the time, it's all greatly appreciated just the same. As you know, Matt, a gift can never be too small, or too large for that matter." He chuckled, pulling his leg across its partnering knee. "We consider every dollar donated a gift, with all the proceeds going directly to the Red Cross to continue the fight."

"It kind of puts the whole anxiety we carry on life in prospective, doesn't it? It really is amazing how easy it can be to forget how truly fortunate we are. It's so minimal a task to not give thought or to take such things as a trip to the pharmacy for granted when you see them every day and at every turn. That's such a great cause to champion. We wish you enormous success with the auction and with the consequent gala as well." He droned, shifting the paper in his hand as his eyes jumped to a new monitor. "All the information needed to be a part of this crucial effort is now listed at the bottom of your screen, and can also be found, for further details on getting involved, as a link on our website." Supplying this smartly, Matt leaned back in his seat with the start of a smile. "Now that we've covered the important aspect of your visit—not that this makes you unimportant, mind you—but other topics swim forward on cue with their own need to be resolved. I'm sure you already know the direction my next questions will take." He shrugged, his smile verging the lines of an apology. "It's not a good segue, I know, but you know I have to ask. It's a tough job, unfortunately, but someone has to do it, right?" He smirked, folding the papers in his hand. He pinched a long distracted seam down the center of the page. "As always with you, ears have been tuned to the rumor-mill for any tidbits they can, but so far, they've turned up nothing. Your name has not been linked to a supermodel-slash-actress in months, or with anyone for that matter. So…" he droned, as if to make an inaudible petition for his case; his open palm waved forward before he again ironed the emphasized fold along the paper's edge. "It falls to me to ask," Matt probed, lifting his shoulders almost apologetically. He tapped the creased paper to his knee. "How is your love life?"

Reminiscent of a panther's snarl, Michael's laugh came soft, seeming disentangled from the man as it gurgled in his throat. He glanced thoughtfully at the floor. "Well," he began, giving a soft shrug as if the question yielded him no bother. "I'm no different than the next guy, Matt." He rasped, offering a placating smirk to couple his reply. "We're all just looking for that one, aren't we? Someone different than the rest that you can connect with, hoping that if you're lucky enough to find that, you'll be smart enough to know how to hold on." He shrugged, looking up in finish, he again smiled, well happy with the obfuscated answer. "So I guess it means my love life is the same as every guy. It's a work in process."

"Somehow I doubt it's exactly the same for all men." Matt averred with a frown. "Does this mean you're in the market or at the market?" he asked, rolling quickly forward as if reading a prompt.

"Oh, man, my brain just rolled over in its bed with that one." He groaned. "Well...I... um, I think I'll need to get back to you on that, Matt." Michael frowned. "I think a question like that requires a little self-council before I can give a proper response. Jeez, it's way too early for that, Matt." He griped, seeming to suppress a shudder before ambling on. "I'm barely awake, much less cognizant of the thought process needed to resolve that type of contemplation."

"Wouldn't that be something already fixed as a part of your thought process?"

"Maybe so for smart people like you, Matt, but for nitwits like me, it takes nothing less than a summit to get one foot to move in-front of the other."

"Oh, I didn't know that." Matt smirked, shifting artfully in his seat. "But it does explain a lot." He nodded. "Once you've resolve the matter, I expect you'll come back and let us know?" he smirked, again skirting the tangy tinge of a jibe.

"You're a sly one, aren't you?" Michael drawled. "As always, you're first on my list, Matt, you know that."

"Yes, I'm sure. I see the proof of that every day." Matt retorted sagely, chuckling, he tapped the creased paper to his knee. "Sorry about the questions, but I had to ask. Are you going to be doing a new movie soon?" he inquired then, expertly changing the topic onto a less invasive path.

"Man, you're all over the place this morning aren't you?" Michael smirked, looking somewhat perturbed. "Do they know you do that around here? You know, that's not a real good trait to have."

"It's not, huh?"

"No! That's actually considered an impolite trait to broadcast so freely. I'm not sure if anyone has ever told you this, but I've known you a long time, Matt. So, I'm only doing you a favor when I say it. Not an ounce of malicious intent is involved in the wordage whatsoever. In fact, it hurts me just saying it."

"I just bet it does." Matt smirked, looking almost sincere in his response. "In any case, that's very thoughtful of you, Michael. But I think they already know a little bit about my chatty side around here. So tell me, anything new?"

"Tenacious aren't you?" he asked with what surely held the tangy flavor of a taunt. "I'm always busy, Matt, you know that." Michael shrugged, shifting his body forward in the stylish chair. "I have a few irons in the works, but nothing definite enough to talk about at the moment."

"Well, we'll be glad to have you back when you do. Come back and see us, soon." He smiled, confirming this with a nod.

"I will. Thank you."

Julia groaned pitiably at the television screen as the interview ended, almost glaring as the weekend host gave the introduction for an upcoming segment, noting again that the interview was previously recorded from the day before. A Huggies commercial advising the merits of their brand, blared gruffly across the screen, swallowing the stillness that descended on the space. Confused by the emotions that yet romped through her body, she sighed, as it was inconclusive whether the viewing had been a threat or treat. Straightening, Julia glanced at the indent left behind on her shin, and although the weight of the pain had since ebbed, the soreness still stung. Drawing her peripheral attention, the time sat boldly on her clock, snapping her focus from the bruise on her shin. It spurred a prompt reaction.

With her standing date with Carol and Vanessa now barreling through her head, Julia dashed off for her once intended chilled shower. Inseparable since high school, the three women remained devoted to each other to this day, surviving well the rigor of college, careers, husbands, kids and everything thrown in-between. There was little that was done by one that did not involve the other. Unconditional in their support, the three remained a reservoir of strength in the face of other's need, staying well apprised of the each other's lives regardless of schedule and by any means. Theirs was a bond that would forever endure untouched. With the coordinating of calendars, occurrences and the continence of an iron will, the three got together at least once each month, instituted as a tenet since college, and just let loose.

———•———

Not yet inundated with the usual lunch rush, the Thai House sat amazingly quiet, with sparse patrons littering the restaurant's unruffled ambiance. Only the whispered whistle of each diner's speech, feathered through the splendorous silence.

Julia entered to find Vanessa and Carol already seated at a booth, each woman looking, as ever, the perpetual professional, spliced with a flare that was all their own. Already, servings of Jasmine tea, crisp noodles and spring-rolls sat on the table in wait.

"Sorry I'm late, guys." Julia began, smiling brightly after their usual lengthy greeting. "Mmm, that smells so good. Did you already order?"

"We did, but we also ordered for you. We got you the spicy shrimp and scallops." Carol informed softly, her long, dark hair cascading in playful tendrils across her breasts with the swift angling of her head. Pale skin looked almost void in the restaurant's dim lighting, and muted circles floored her once sparkling gray eyes. She looked deathly tired from every angle sweeping to view. Although, being the mother of a nine month old can somehow have that effect.

"You look tired, Carol. Is Nathan still keeping you up? I thought you said he was better and was sleeping through the night." Julia commented dimly, adjusting her position on the padded bench.

"He is, normally. But teething is kicking my ass."

"Maybe you should have a drink and serve him one, too." Vanessa groaned faintly, though the words were still flanked with her habitual spunk.

"Tried it, it only makes me feel worse. The next morning finds me even more exhausted."

"It seems like a million years ago when my kids were teething. I know it's tough but it gets better soon." Julia sighed.

"You're not kidding about the tough." Carol groaned, rolling her eyes in the process, she hastily jumped ship. "By the way, how did the touch up on the script go?"

"Yeah, how'd they take the finishing touches to that Oscar winning manuscript of yours?" Vanessa chimed.

"Well," Julia hummed, her face immediately brimming with pride. "They seem to like it. At least…that's what they said."

"Of course they do. There's nobody better than you." Carol frowned, posturing as if her statement required no further discussion on such topic.

"Thank you, Carol. I'll make sure I pass that along if there's ever any problem." She smirked, gathering a cup of her own. She poured herself a sampling of tea.

"Well?" Vanessa grunted, the question sailing with a sharp lift of her brow.

"Well what?"

"Have you had a chance to fully assess Mr. Dunhill's lovely attributes as yet?" she groaned, leaning forward. She grabbed her friend's hand and squeezed, and cold fingers stayed against the branding warmth of the other woman's hand.

"What is he like? Now that you've had the chance to be around him more, is he still nice?" Carol asked, chiming in like an echoic song.

"I'm not sure. He…" Julia frowned, straining her shoulders upwards as if unsure of the answer she held. "Seems the same… He's nice, I guess." She smiled, answering both women skillfully at once, this without showing the complicated smut burnishing the underside of her hand.

"Is he really as tall in person as he seems on the screen?" Vanessa eagerly asked.

"And does he look as good?" Carol reverberated yet again.

"Do you know he dated that supermodel, what's her name?" Vanessa asked in a mumble, not waiting for an answer to her opening quest.

"Naomi Benue." Carol quickly announced, nulling the pause in a flash, her gray eyes grew suddenly bright with the tickle of gossip now looming near.

"My, god, have you seen her? She's gorgeous! Now there's someone who can effortlessly stomp out your self-confidence, and all just by simply being near. Can you imagine being put to stand next to her? No matter how good you look, she could make you feel downright inferior." Vanessa snorted, taking a slow sip of her tea.

"So what is he like to work with now? I want details. Give us some juicy details for Christ's sake!" Carol urged. "We were good. We left the interrogating until you finished your work. Is he still quiet? You haven't said much about your work lately, and when you do, Phillip's name carries a goodly share. Too bad he's married." She smirked. "You didn't even tell us what his house looked like. Was it like a John Travolta type mansion or not?"

"Or is it worse? Does he also have his own runway, his own plane or both?" Vanessa smirked, leaning almost halfway across the table for a response.

"And is he really as loaded as they say?"

"Carol!" Julia screeched, singing the rebuke in a less than lady like tone. Surprised by her underlining need to be evasive, feeling somewhat protective of him, yet not understanding why. Perhaps it was due to the intensity they bestowed so freely in their welcome. Though whatever the reason, it just felt wrong to air what she learned in the privacy of one's home, even with the trusted comradeship appended to those of best friends. "I'm only working with him, Carol. I'm not his financier. That's your job, remember?" She assured sweetly. "And…Eschewing quite nicely, I'll ask, still loving it at the bank?"

"I do!" Carol shined, showing additional bites of life in her darkly ringed eyes. "You know how crazed I felt about going back to work after Nathan's birth, but, I'm more comfortable with it now than I thought I would be. I think. At least I am a little." Carol laughed, sounding almost bashful. She flipped her dark hair with a gentle swipe of her hand, dropping the silken mass like a curtain down her back. "It's a little hard, at times, you know?" she shrugged, her face wrinkling as if to compress itself. "Nathan is almost a year old and I'm still having trouble with separation anxiety." She groaned. Smiling serenely as all three paused for the waitress to unload their meal, with each instantly plucking samples from the other's plate. Conversation again became the focal of their want.

"It's hard, I know, but it will get easier. Maria is a great nanny. We did a great job picking her, didn't we? You just need to get comfortable with finding the medium between extreme and apathetic, that's all."

"I know. But some days…still, I just…" Carol groaned, squeezing her shoulders tightly about her ears. She sighed "I just wig out, you know." She laughed, slowly shaking her head as she gathered her Coke. "It's kind of pathetic and sad when you think about it."

"Nothing pathetic about it, it's a part of the requirement for being a mother. Didn't you read your dossier from end to end? Just wait, soon he'll be running into your room with a list of demands for both your time and money, and you'll be looking to work like it's a vacation. Alec will be wondering what got into his wife."

"You promise?"

"I promise. Mommy coming home in the evening is still mommy, isn't she? Isn't daddy coming home too late for bedtime still daddy?"

"That's right, look at the hours Alec keeps sometimes." Vanessa added with a stern knit to her brows. "Yet Nathan still thinks the sun rises with his daddy."

"That's definitely true. Who knew an engineer could be so wrapped up in his work. Lately he's been thinking of splitting that time with home, at least this way he'll be available for a few more hours during the week."

"That's both good and bad," Vanessa shrugged. "But it's mostly good in the impor-tant sense. Babies don't know why daddy or mommy is home, just that they are. It may be more frustrating for all involved with him being at home than being away."

"Listen to you," Julia teased, drawing herself upright in her seat. "Giving advice, huh, an expert, are we?"

"Hello, I did manage to not just go to medical school, but finish. I am a practic-ing physician, you know. Why is it you guys always look so surprised whenever I say something that sounds smart to you? I am able to think for myself, you know." Vanessa carped, glaring as she received a chorus of snickers as her resounding response.

"Anyway," Julia exhaled loudly, leveling her gaze on her friend's glowering stare. "Anything you want to report on the baby front?"

"Yes!" Vanessa chirped, her expression flipping as easily as a switch, moving flaw-lessly from scowling, to now show the full breadth of her glee. "A-hem, after careful deliberation, we've decided it's high time we start building our family."

"And by *we*, you mean *you,* of course?"

"Of course, it's not his career or body that will be going through all the changes." Vanessa grunted, seeming unconcerned with the subtext. "Anyway, we'll be starting right away. Well…as soon as I'm finished with this pack of my birth control that is."

"It's all so exciting, how can you wait?"

"Because, having one menses per month is more than enough for me, thank you very much." Vanessa replied stiffly, her answer closely favoring a snarl. Brown skin wrinkled softly with the exaggerated expression, tightening the pleats atop her forehead, dark eyes slashed sarcastically across Carol's smiling round face.

"Oh, yeah, I forgot that that happens if you stop before you get to the end." Carol frowned, ignoring her friend's outlandish display.

"It *is* very exciting. So, what about you Carol, are you going to play catch up with me?"

"Soon, let me at least get my old figure back before you have me knocked up again."

"Why? You're only going to lose it again anyway." Vanessa informed her blandly.

"Now look who's throwing in their two cents worth, should we tell her all the things that are going to happen to her body; Miss designer outfit. I can't wait to see that waistline you work so hard to keep; you know that figure you're so proud of. I can't wait to see it all stretched to smithereens. I'm going to happily document that protruding belly button of yours, from innie to outie. Let's see what those designer outfits will do for you then." Carol simpered, mockingly throwing out each word, yet her underlining mirth was such that it voided all prospect of a bite.

"For your information, I'll still be wearing my designer outfits then. I earned these babies. I didn't spend all that time in medical school to not enjoy the fruits of my labor, miss financial officer, with CFO wagging in the winds. Where are your outfits from, the Basement Barn? Don't make me out to be the bad guy because I kept my knees together longer than the two of you."

"What? Who would that be, and what knobby knees are you implying to?" Carol squawked, and her look of shock was more priceless than any word she expelled.

"Don't forget who was there right after you lost your virginity, first year of college, to that slug Veroski? Steven Veroski." Julia laughed. "That's when you learned the hard way that being logical when you choose your sexual partner is a bad idea. A fact I know we both tried to talk you out of. But noooo, you wouldn't listen to that. You knew best and it showed. You thought waiting around until you developed a strong attraction was a waste of your time. I wonder what's the result on that?"

"Ugh, that was a callow encounter." Croaking her avowal on the shadow of a tart note, the awkward sound swam forward with what looked vaguely like a painful cringe. "You had to remind me, didn't you? To think, I had completely wiped that whole debacle from my mind." Vanessa grumbled, wobbling her head with a look of disgust. "That's it, I need some new friends. We've been friends too long." She groaned.

"That's perfect. Carol and I were just saying the same thing. We think you're holding us back from our full potential."

"That's right. My son is going to have to find a new godmother-slash-aunt, but that should be easy enough. I think there's a website that offers that or there should be."

"Vanessa as a mother, did you see that coming?"

"You guys knew I wanted kids. I just wasn't sure when and well…it's when."

"How excited is Roger that you finally agreed? He's been after you for about a year now."

"Roger is excited, he's also…very excited."

"Yes. They do like the practice and the tries, don't they?" Julia smirked.

"Yes they do. That kind of work they tolerate well, it's the other side of the work that has them piddling out." Carol purred.

"Have you guys come to a decision as yet? Will you cut your hours at the hospital or just hire a live-in nanny?"

"Actually, we've decided to do both, so you guys have another arduous trail ahead with the fine tuning of that. The nanny comes in quite handy when either or both of us have to pull a late shift or run behind on whatever procedure is being done. The emergency room just doesn't seem to believe in breaks or adhering to the stringency of schedule. But having one for those times when I need my husband to take me out and remind me I'm still beautiful is a good thing."

"Like you'd ever forget that. Every time you get to a door, we essentially have to shave some girth off your ego before you can pass through. There's no insouciance in that." Julia countered with a smirk.

"So anyway," Vanessa scoffed, thrusting another hateful glare at her friend's head. She persisted in her speech. "As I was saying, the late shift can take its toll, but if I'm having trouble doing that then maybe I'll go private." She shrugged. "I'd rather not, but…"

"It will all work out. You'll find the right decision before it all comes to a head. You may not want to do that now. But it may end up being the right thing for you in the long run."

"That's true." Carol added softly.

"I know. I know. It's just getting the decisions finalized that seem a little iffy right now. But anyway, we'll figure it out." Vanessa shrugged, giving her usual runt clue of the subject's change. Her eyes slashed across Julia's face with the obvious brewing of quest. "Now, as of six days ago, are *you* still celibate?" she asked with normal ease, and Carol's eyes, in concomitance, jumped immediately to said coordinates on the other's face, as if Vanessa's words had rested within her very own mouth.

"Are you guys really going to do this every time? It's been *five* years, guys."

"Yes." Vanessa stated with finality. "So don't skirt around the question. Has that body of yours gotten touched lately?"

"No. It has not. Thank you so much for asking. Happy?"

"You've got to stop this. I mean...I understand your reasoning, I really do. Your career takes up a lot of your time and you want to give all that's left, especially since the divorce, to the kids to maintain stability in their lives. But can't you find a jock and take out your pent up frustration on him, for medicinal purpose, if nothing else? No relationship needed for that. Just good old-fashion fun. You remember what that's like, don't you, grandma?"

"So now I'm old because I'm not letting some jock feel me up? Didn't we leave that behind in high school?"

"No. You're old because you're letting that gorgeous face and body of yours go to waste. You do know that all this," she grunted, gesturing with a finger in Julia's direction, her hand formed an exaggerated "O". "It all goes away. It doesn't last forever—"

"But even old she'd still look good, better than a lot."

"Thank you, Carol." Julia huffed. "Backhanded that it was, it was still very nice of you to say."

"Yes. We all know this. We all know you'd look good regardless. But will you still be able to have fun? You're missing out on fun, that's the thing."

"You do know we're only talking another two, three years at the most? That's the entire sabbatical I'm taking, and in any case, I haven't met anyone worthy of the effort. I just haven't had the urge to put myself out there. I haven't felt the need or had the time." She groaned, knowing deeply that this was somehow a lie.

"That's good. I'm glad to hear that you're at least sticking to that damn timetable you started with. But we're still talking two or three years without fun. You need to get yourself some treats for the road. Some form of snack to tie you over until then. I'll even go shopping for you. Come on, Julia, you have to get back on the horse. It's been a long time."

"I know it has, but it just doesn't feel that long to me. Anyway, what fun do you think I'm missing? I have a very full life." She asked, ignoring the deeper pull on the other side of that statement.

"You mean besides a warm body in your bed?"

"I hav—"

"Not under five feet tall." Vanessa warned, cutting past what she knew was about to come. "One that has a working appendage that can make your body moan. Or hands to squeeze those pretty little things you wear on your chest."

"Besides that."

"You mean that alone is not enough for you?"

"Nope, by itself it's still not enough." Julia shrugged, sensing the bite of her lie as the drab words touched her ears.

"Okay, there's talking, cuddling, fondling, kissing—"

"Then that should leave me only two things since you guys already covered two."

"We'd better be thinking of the same two," Vanessa warned, rolling her dark eyes sternly. "I love you, but not enough to fondle or kiss you."

"Why, are you afraid if you do you'll become my bitch?"

"That's right, and one bitch in this trio is enough."

"Which one of us is the bitch?" Carol asked almost wide-eyed.

"Why, me of course." She chimed, patting herself on the shoulder, she smiled. "None of you are tough enough to carry the name. You guys are too sweet. That's why you have me to do the barking and biting when you two won't."

"Should we be addressing you by your new name?" Julia hummed. "Will Vanessa Bitch be sufficient or Miss Bitch Vanessa will do?"

"Whatever you guys want to call me is fine with me. Just remember we had this conversation when I'm fat and hormonal, and I better see buckets of understanding at my stubby feet."

"I'll bring the ice cream and the heated tub for your feet." Carol chimed.

"So I can get fatter, of course?"

"Don't worry. We'll just swaddle you in designer cloth and roll you through the door." Julia teased.

"Like I said, you guys are terrible friends. I should just go out and get some new ones right now." Vanessa groaned, shaking her head, she took a long drink of iced tea. "Hmm, that reminds me," she started, "have you decided yet if you're going to let Rachel get the shot?"

"What shot?" Carol chirped, her voice again climbing high.

"The HPV vaccine. It's recommended for girls starting at about Rachel's age." Vanessa explained, her medical background quickly spilling through.

"No, I haven't. I want to do some more research first."

"I brought you some things I found. Remind me to give them to you before you go."

I'm glad I had a boy, there's so much to learn with girls." Carol whined, her tired eyes looking almost despondent.

"But you always wanted a girl."

"I know, and still do. But it's so different when you have a boy. It seems like attention and understanding is all you have to give. Girls get so much more complicated."

"But as a girl yourself, I would think it would be easier, since you already went through a lot of the things they'll be going through." Vanessa frowned.

"What do you want, Nessa?" Carol asked softly.

"You are the only person that still calls me that, and the only person that can get away with it, too." Vanessa groaned, shaking her head, she continued with a quiet snort. "I don't know what I want first, but I do know I definitely want a girl somewhere in there."

"How many kids are we talking about here?" Julia teased.

"At least two,"

"I want two more."

"Man, listen to you guys. I remember when I wanted a big family. You guys all looked at me as if I was weird! Now listen to the tales you spill."

"Do you think you'll ever get married again and maybe try for more?"

"I can't let myself think about that, Carol. That's a road I won't let myself go near much less travel. I'm much better off leaving thoughts like that alone."

Conversation between them continued on the same endless rung, jumping disjointedly from one topic to the next. Time moved like the wind under the flap of a bird's wing. A trip to the salon came as their next treat to each other, followed by an afternoon of shopping. And again, before they knew it, time doused the day's gaiety from its bent, refusing to adjourn the fervor in its apparent haste. It bought their gathering to an end.

Chapter Seventeen

What kind of problem could they possibly have with the script? Julia questioned tartly, running a sundry of scenarios in her head. She sharpened a registry of summations for any argument they purportedly had. Yet, those were the exact wordings Phillip used in the inexplicit fifteen word email he sent her proclaiming such folly. Twenty-five, if you count the ten digit phone-number he also included. She knew this, due in full to the incessant reprising that went on in her head.

Nonetheless, all attempts at an explanation since have stalled with the lyrical voice of Phillip's assistant. Who, in earnest, had fended her probes like the goalie Dominick Hasek himself. In concession, she eagerly dispatched Phillip's heartfelt apologies for not having given a response. Judith then informed her, in that same sun-drenched tone, that a meeting was scheduled at the house for noon the next day, and that all explanation warranted would be forthcoming then.

In remembrance of the havoc such ambiguity had laid bare to her brain, a concise breath slowly whistled through the silence of her car. Ruffling the nervy pulse of the space, her eyes again grazed the leather case with pent frustration. A coalescence of many that mingled well with the frenzied emotions now swimming through her body. None of which, Julia stubbornly declared in a rush, had to do with the prospect of seeing their host.

He had nothing to do with the dulcet smile that was somehow plastered on her face. Neither did he cause the euphoric combers in her state of mind. The day's exquisite vaunt was responsible for that. She promptly reasoned, for it was frankly too gorgeous a day to let anything interfere with the beauty of its reign. Nothing beyond nerves was the motive for her heart's wild antics as she verged on the avenue to his house, likewise for the tremors now juddering through her limbs, all of which required more than a few added gulps to settle the disruption in her body.

In emphasis, an unsteady hand laid gently across the doorbell in constrained haste, depressing the small button. She felt the rousing lurch worsen in her chest.

"Get a grip, Julia!" she scolded through tightly clenched teeth. "He's not the first good-looking man you've ever been around." She scoffed, taking yet another breath as if in settlement of the fact.

Michael came to her vision almost before she fully retracted her hand. Framed in the prominence of a heavy glass door, his sinewy form moved towards her at a leisured pace. Smiling, he pulled open the barring with undisturbed affluence mincing his deeds. The act, in taut fruition, looked almost torpid in its deliberate dispense, and the suppleness of the deed loomed strongly of an allurement, though the process was quite beautiful to watch.

Julia smothered the rumble that percolated noisily in the dark recess of her chest. Smiling boldly to herself instead, as she was inept in her efforts to pull her eyes away from the fineness of his stance. His impeccable physique draped the doorway like the supreme weapon of temptation itself, built by the devil's own hands. Talons of torrid zest radiated from his body like hands through the many layers of her flesh. Churning mightily throughout her ebullient form, it warned as aptly as it bade.

Classically polished in a tailored jacket, its salient tint etched fitly somewhere between midnight and blue, sported atop a pinstripe shirt that softly mirrored the sky. The ensemble further screamed the lyrics of an already known song. Stealing her breath with the entrancing vision, she had to concede that blue jeans had never looked that mesmerizing before. And although her exult swooned from the pother caused by the clothing itself, it drew nigh expiry from the felicitous fit the man presented to her view, for together, they looked good enough to feed on.

"Wow!" Julia sighed longingly, drinking in every inch of his tall physique. "You look like you belong over my bed."

"Really?" He growled, and hazel eyes danced into hers with more than a dollop of intrigue.

"I mean...um," shaking her head confusedly, her expression sharpened in a blinding flash. Realizing her error, she adjusted the meaning of what was said. "On a poster, I meant on a poster."

"I see."

"You look...nice. Good." She sighed, stumbling over each word as if afraid to give them life, yet being somehow compelled to do just that.

"Thank you." He murmured in the parity of an embryotic roar, his smirk rearing with certain sinister bent, as bassy timbre drifted purposefully slow. Taking his time, his eyes stroked her in a staunch, manipulative caress. And the branding, one could ardently attest, struck the incendiary flint of a pristine game. Today's hairstyle had large, bouncy curls hugging the right of her face, shadowing the hem of that eye. It fell in a silky wave down her shoulders and back and the look, he averred in a mute rumble, suited her well. Purposeful and unerring, Michael's gaze then dropped slowly to her mouth, noting the coppery-brown tint staining her lips. He deemed himself hunter with a penchant to enact as a prey, further pull by the sassy display, as their fullness wickedly beckoned him yet. *Perfectly ripe for snacking,* he groaned in the dwindling solace of his head. Her mouth had been an endless source of yearning since their first encounter, goading him even while he slept. Their eminence forever remains a constant in his head.

"You're staring again." She whispered with an easy smile, truly savoring the rousing he gave in his openly desirous gaze.

"Am I?" he asked softly, not bothering to shift the wont of his gaze. He granted the full spectrum of his attraction in the exhibit he gave. "I thought I was merely reassessing a foregone conclusion." He smiled.

"And what conclusion is that?"

"Just a mere attestation as to the trove of your physique," he shrugged. "Openly agreeing, that is." Looking more the predator sparring with a formidable prey, his smile was a lecherous sight.

"So we're leaving no stones unturned today?" Julia smirked, incisive in her resolve. Her eyes calmly edged his body.

"Some…not all," he drawled, witnessing the diverted route of her gaze. His eyes brightened in reply, knowing full well what it was that she sought. "They're still those that will be left untouched."

"Should I be getting a second armor for this?" she chided.

"Why?" like a rough, rumbly gust, the growl came with the slow descent of his eyes, strolling warmly down her body. He drank her in before returning his gaze to her face. "When you wear this one so well?" he smiled, appreciating the subtle sway of her simple black skirt. Lurked like a taunt mere inches above her ankle, the uncomplicated garment showed no exceptional design beyond being just that. No unique sparkle embellished the soft fabric or distract from the purity it gave, nothing except the way that it fitted itself to her form. It glided over her hips like new skin to rest seductively against her thighs. Thighs well displayed to his gaze through a long opening in the front of said skirt.

"Have you had your fill yet?" Julia asked jauntily.

"Would you care for the truth, or should I just lie?"

"On second thought, I think I'd best leave that one alone, so neither." Shrugging lamely with the reply, her eyes again searched the foyer for scant signs of a familiar face. Confused by the uncharacteristic delay, her gaze grew almost anxious in her need to squash the ferocious inferno that was her body. Although the blockage preventing her entrance would have greatly amplified that fact, for he had stationed himself in the threshold like some great sentry of right, something neither he nor Phillip had ever done before.

"Was that fear I heard twilling in that answer, or was there a hint of disinterest drizzled within the tone?" he droned, his brow arching almost whimsically with the probe. "You know, I really like the lyrics you choose when we do these dances."

"Does it matter?" Julia asked in a drabbed tone, her hair oscillating softly atop her shoulders and back with the placid wave. "Did you hear fear?" she asked contemplatively. "I wouldn't know if you do. You seem to only hear what you want."

"Is that how it seems?" Michael queried tamely, his mien adopting the guise of a conspiring rodent on the trail of something sweet. "Why don't we let that jumpstart a new debate inside?" He countered, the gravelly retort staying firm in the back of his throat. With scant appraisal, it would seem she had an answer for everything, this, irrespective of the what, where, how or why. A factor that truly suited her well, he mused, and one he well liked. "I believe the battle cry just pealed in an assonance that was frankly unmatched, it should be nigh time to rally the troops, don't you think?" He teased. "Shall we? I wouldn't want you standing here all day, regardless of a fondness for the added fixture you make." He hummed. Dropping a hand to her in offering, the eloquence of his smile further brewed its decadence in his wait.

Confounded, Julia hesitated in accepting the proffering he gave. Smiling reticently, she considered his waiting hand as if searching his palm for a written rejection from which she could abscond. Finding no such solution waiting in the tan bed, she slowly rested her fingers to his.

For a quick trice, Michael's hand remained unclosed, savoring the small triumph that such a moment had. Long fingers gently enfolded her in warmth, thus sending an instantaneous tingle through her body. It was deliciously appetizing in its kindling verve, surprising even her with the avarice of its surge, as it bit like a fire being lit. Michael's movement then mired in the spot that he stood, gazing at her hand now loosely bedded in his. His eyes trotted measuredly up her arm, gathering the dark tint of her own. They whispered secrets long held in a place of reverence.

Ignited further by the heat relinquished in his gaze, she perceived that the heightened sensation reverberated through him as sumptuously as it did in her, for instead of turning, he stayed. Looking prepared to syphon a kiss in lieu of his next breath, his eyes fondled the soft edges of her mouth, and for a moment, she thought surely that he would. Though had he bothered to try, she doubted she could have resisted the effort or the drive, but he stayed such inkling with a quiet breath. In its stead, he offered her what looked like a wan smile, turning from the balmy lynch of her gaze, he quietly led her through the entrance, and it was an indisputable fact that something newly sweetened deposited on the two.

Together they strolled from the entrance in harmonized silence. Her body shadowing the masculine aura of his in their ambling dance, and it felt strangely comforting to have her hand so strongly sheltered in his, as it added sagely to a pleasantness she could not explain. The silence between them was almost surreal, blissful in its quality. It wrapped her body in warmth. Intensifying the drive, the persistent whiff of his aftershave blew back to her nostrils, cajoling her already turbid senses. It scrambled thoughts once distinguished as facts, and at the moment, she could walk like this for an undetermined expanse of time, though eternity ended at the entrance of his suite.

"I have a confession." Michael mumbled as he turned.

He wouldn't! Her mind screamed, and all earlier ramblings of comfort were quickly forsaken in her madcap haste, as she stood then truly arrested by the direction of her thoughts. *Would he?* Her internal arbiter snarled. Would he try this as a game? She had flirted with him—yes—shamelessly so at times. But there had always been an implicit line marking their drive, one well toed though not crossed. Would he really try to push her past what she was willing to give? He had tried to kiss her—a factual score amidst all else—but had never forced the issue on any other such attempts. Would this then be the inception of a new approach?

"There's no—" Michael started in a pleasing tone, pausing the instant he noticed her growing distress. A large bouquet, now stalled numbly between them, held to its place like a delicate shield, though braced in the other of his hand. Languidly, his eyes traced the path of her focus, seeing the source of her concern, he sighed. "When I take you in there," he purred, nodding toward the intrinsic opening. His eyes stated, in full prudence, their truth. "It will not be as a surprise."

For a moment, a sigh of relief flared bright in her eyes, spiraling through her body before her mind rapidly sobered to his words and the tacit promise they supplied. *When?* The word rooted through her svelte frame on the full surge of a tempest, screeching onto the bed of her tongue with pinpoint urgency. Her need to give him a thorough enlightenment blazed with an intensity beyond this realm. Riled by the forwardness his words thence implied, as he, most definitively, had presumed his conquest of her. It was no longer a wish or a request as to his cause, but a full drawn conclusion verged only on time. But she was no starry eyed female starved for affection, therefore ready to succumb. She was strong enough to say the word "No" without guilt. Asserting this with full ire streaking her tone, her arbitrator gave a satisfactory nod, mollified with the explicit grandeur of her rile. She awaited his retort with full readiness to set him lolling on his heel, unaware she had not bothered to let a single word fly, but stood, instead, gaping as if under a spell. Without spilling a drop from her lips, her scolding librettos never funneled his ears and so needed no reply.

Michael rested the bouquet against his chest and coercively smiled, slamming the door shut on whatever amendments once begged to be said. "As I was saying," he continued with a soft breath. "I have a confession to make."

"Do I need to sit down for this?" Julia whipped back palely, stroking the delicate edge of a petal as she resuscitated her ambling mind, not bothering to notice their obvious similarities with the previous deliveries she'd had.

"That would be at your discretion, though any option is fine with me." He smiled

"Then set yourself free." She chirped, at his smirk, she quickly clarified in a light sardonic tone. "Your mind,"

"Okay. Well, we're not having a meeting," he rasped, angling his head apprehensively as he ripped open the sutures on his deceit. And although worry troubled the fine edges of his gaze, charisma still dripped like warm honey from his face. "So to speak..."

"Oh." She blathered in the guise of a grunt. "I wondered." Julia apprised coolly, dazed by how little the truth mattered to her at that time. The longer the banter had prevailed; suspicion had flailed its arms like a pungent fruit, ripe for the taking. It blared like a klaxon in her head, as she had never known Phillip to delay a meeting before now.

"For you," He smiled, handing her the reason for their pause.

"Thank you." Already bothered by the heat he tendered in his gaze, her body further warmed by the entrancing circumstance he now presented for the partaking of. More so than she cared to admit or even pondered upon, this, even in the privacy of her own head. "But I—"

"Just stay and have lunch with me." He breathed, his eyes warmly caressing her face. "A mere hour of your time, that's all I ask." Rumbled like a soft, cohesive snarl, his long body crowded the sprite radiance of day now seeping from a window at his back, taking a step towards her. Michael shortened the small void that yet hovered between them, looming above her like an effigy bathed in the impeccable tinge of sunlight. He smiled his acquiescence of an answer he hoped would surely come.

"I..." Julia stammered in a light breath, gazing at the flowers in her hands instead of the attributes ascribed to the man. Tame, as like an absurd contrast to the chaos in her body, though bold with a vivified blush of orangey-red, smidgen of yellow brushed the fragile blooms. Assuaging her mind, they bred as a bribe to her wavering focus, soothing what etiquette narrates that she should while in the midst of trading speech. So much of her wanted to say yes, but should she? She asked almost guileless, as if expecting an answer to be quickly dispatched from someplace outside her head. The silence grew near that of being taut. Her sigh was almost an audible gust as his fingers continued their rousing display, stroking the palm of her hand in a delicate brush. Her pulse, in its traitorous fashion, did a showy somersault. "I-I guess I could give you an hour." She hummed, and her eyes dropped, as if tethered, to her hand still curled freely in his. He showed no inclination in releasing said limb, and she made no attempt at being freed. Both seeming, for the moment, content to leave things as they were.

Without lifting her gaze, Julia felt the heated brush of his eyes as they roamed at will, and knew he studied her closely as a result. Grasping the sweetness like the building of a bridge, recognition flared as kindling sparks, and there was something greatly stirring in knowing that fact. Yet she knew not the why or how. *Where is her untiring strength now?* She asked curtly, wondering on the ease with which she gave in to his enticing request, not having offered, in her placid strive, even a clumsy return as proof of a battle. Where's the good in that? She carped. With what bubbled through her like a groan, her metal flogging stopped as abruptly as it began, seeing the graceful flip of her hand. She felt the furnace of his breath as he brought the limb to his lips.

"Good." Michael whispered against the soft skin of her wrist, allowing his words the freedom to vibrate warmly into her. He hovered in his place of rest as he again gave speech. "Let's eat then." He smiled, and it was one of sugary charm that he then displayed, rolling unnervingly across his face. The slyness buried in the hazel depths could not be denied.

Deftly, his lips brushed across the silken spread of her skin, and every part of her betraying body reacted with craving and in accordance, she almost openly sighed. Quickly straightening, Julia gathered herself as he raised his head, giving him naught but the taut indication that she was well ready to move their lunch engagement along. Michael smiled, and it felt somewhat sardonic as he watched her. As if aware, her response was not fully what it appeared to be, though he made no comment on any such facts.

In adjourned candor, the two turned from their tarry, both bodies held in reticence as their feet tapped the wood floor in arcane contemplation. Absorbedly, Julia followed his leisured escort, pointed in the direction of the kitchen, her hand still held as a prisoner to his heated embrace. And although the day's strangeness grew increasingly vast, the fact that contentment soared as she sidled at his side, made her more eager for the hour to end, impatient, in her need, to go back to her normal self. Michael led her to the entrance of the kitchen and stopped, stroking her palm with a thumb, time seemed surely to have mired itself. A soft glow illuminated the doorway with an aura of its own, its radiance looking like no sun she had ever seen. Quietly, he offered her the opening, removing the blockage of his body without the tangle of words; a resplendent smile then marked his face.

The kitchen was no longer the place stamped in her recollection. Looking like the thick of night, the once cheerful room was submerged completely in black, with yards of said drapes obscuring the vivacity of daylight from every window. A dozen candles lined the surface of the island in wait. Twice as many of the dancing lights floated on each surface around the room. Casting their distinctive hue upon any shadow the room might have had. Gone was the large, round table upon which they once partook of their meals, replaced with a small, intimate piece for two. It sat exquisite in the space, looking, to all eyes, like it belonged. Crisp, white linen covered said table to hang loosely on the floor, where two similarly dressed chairs rested primly in wait of their tenants, well tucked beneath the pleated body of the skirt. A small crystal bowl, centered on the table, made the flickering fire enclosed a dazzling sight. Softening the room further with their blooms, four accompanying bouquets graced a place on each counter except one, with a fifth vase waiting diligently on the island as if for something grand.

"Another confession," Michael rasped, bringing her attention back to him, he smiled. "This will be dinner instead of lunch." At her blank stare, he expounded in a light tone. "Again, since you won't let me take you to out, I brought dinner to you, so to speak." Michael hummed, shrugging coolly as he picked up a small remote from the island where it patiently sat. Pointing the tiny resistor to the air, the soft melody of a soulful jazz singer kissed the silence in an impressive display.

With a calculated infer to each movement made, Michael took the flowers from her hand, filling the once empty vase. He reclaimed her fingers as his, effusively setting the ambiance between them. "By my watch," he drawled. "It's about seven, and our reservation gives us the best table in the house."

Julia's tongue was slow in returning an answer, the room—the gesture and the beauty now displayed all had to have taken much in both conception and process. She had to admit, even amidst the sparring in her head, she was greatly impressed. "I wish I had prior notice that we would be dining here." She grumbled almost voicelessly. "I would've treasured the opportunity to dress better for an occasion as this. I hope my attire is still suitable for this place."

"On the contrary, you're by far the best thing here." Michael droned, setting free her hand, the gentle scraping of wood eased through the quiet like a burp, gurgling as he seated her and then himself.

"You went through a lot of trouble just to have lunch—dinner" she eagerly corrected, flashing the start of a tame smile.

"You don't think you're worth it?"

"My worth is not the question here." She assured, interlocking her fingers, she laid them to the table in an effort to contain her focus. "Just the results given with the work,"

"I disagree," He drawled, his voice drifting uncannily slow. "You don't shop the same for everyone on your list, do you? The importance of the recipient is usually the decider in both the price and effort. So I ask you again, don't you think you're worth it?"

"For your information, my value has no number. I'm priceless, but that was not my question to you."

"Precisely!" Michael exclaimed, the sound seeming almost sinister in its bent. It floated from the back of his throat like the salvo of a perilous warnig. "You know, I think we agree more than you care to admit." He announced in his gravelly tone, leaning forward in his seat. His eyes hinted of some knowledge that he held. "Now, what can I get you to drink?" he hummed, letting the question neighbor his speech, as if to dismiss further comment on a subject that might have been. He put the discussion to bed.

"You're serving?" she asked with a hint of surprise, quickly scolding her apparent daftness for neglecting the obvious clues. If the responsibility of such onus had fallen at Betty's feet, she would've surely made an appearance by now.

"I am." Michael muttered softly, dipping his head in a formal display, he offered then a sly smile. "I'm completely at your service."

"You're alone today?" heavily weighted in her tone, the question flew, and in adjunct of the other, her frown showed not only disbelief but discontent.

"I think I can manage being alone with you for an hour." Michael growled, waving a hand towards her in assurance, his smile slowly warmed, and there was dark mischief lining his pupils as he spoke. As if suddenly aware of a threat, her eyes scurried about the room, rushing to the far walls like a bird in flight. Brown eyes cagily lingered as if for a means of escape, dragging further the furrows of her brows. "Don't worry. I promise I'll be the perfect gentleman." He averred as he rose. "Your food is the only thing on the menu this day."

This was an astonishing occurrence for sure, Julia speculated warily, though in-spite of her unease, she watched almost fixedly as Michael sauntered across the room. Unsure, in both mind and body of how or what to think of this new turn of event. Indisputable were the facts sutured to the occasion at hand, mingled with the madness of how he affected her body. Could she barter her level of unrest for the wont of something else? She was alone in the home of a known playboy on the guise of lunch. Should she really trust him to keep his word?

"Could I interest you in our finest bottle of wine?" he sang, his voice ringing playful. Displaying the sleek bottle, labeled almost by the color it held, like a connoisseur's dream. "This," he continued, "is one of our finest."

"It sounds perfect, thank you." Julia laughed, feeling slightly more at ease. Her eyes discreetly veered to watch the man while he worked. With definite panache guiding each bent, he poured orange-juice to the near brim in champagne glasses, slipping the bottle in a waiting bucket before retracing his steps.

The golden gleam of the candles only enhanced the bronzy gambit of his looks, for had he looked any better. He would be mounted in a gallery as art. "This is very nice. Very…special. Thank you." Feeling the need to compliment his painstaking effort, politeness won the struggle over fear. No one, in the not too measly length of her life, had ever gone to this extreme before now, most certainly, not in a long time. Michael paused in his action as she finished her speech, gazing at her intently as if her words had defamed him somehow. "You seem surprised." She muttered then, straining in an effort to sound unconcerned.

"I am a little taken back." Michael admitted, serving then a small bowl of salad, he retook his seat. Riveted by her apparent discomfort, she slowly sipped from her glass before looking his way.

"I am, too." She confessed in a hushed tone, dropping her eyes slowly to her bowl. They moved leisurely to her hand. A finger slid gingerly down the lean stem before she again gave voice to her feelings. "But…" she shrugged, turning her head to scan the room as if unsure of what needed to be said. "You took the time to do all this, and it's…" thin shoulders again climbed the stocky air, turning back to the table. She allowed her eyes to settle once again on her glass. "Very special,"

"Was that really that difficult or are you just that out of practice?" he teased.

"I may be out of practice, but that had nothing to do with it. I think you know that."

"Tell me, what was it, then?"

"You analyze everything I say," she shrugged; genuinely tense with giving such truth. "Sometimes drawing unexpected conclusions, you question my questions, and I feel as if I'm always on guard with you. It feels as if I need to look for an answer less leading than the prior exchange."

"And yet you hardly skip a beat. I always got the impression you liked a challenge."

"I do. But I don't think at every turn. With most men I can say 'no, thank you' and say it well enough to get my point across. With you…it's…different. I don't think you hear me."

"So I'm your challenge?" Michael queried, bringing a forkful of lettuce to his mouth. He watched her shoulders roll in a noncommittal response. "Why do you think you can say no to other men, but with me it's different? Why haven't you said no to me?"

"But I have!" Julia barked softly, her eyes complacent in the exhibit they held, widening across the table in emphasis of her words.

"Have you?"

"Yes. I have." Her tone sharpened, yet not enough to spell annoyance to even an onlooker's gaze.

"You've said you don't date. You've said you can't. You never said you wouldn't date me. I made it very clear I was coming after you."

"Polite just doesn't work with you, does it?" she grumbled. "You need me to say the words?"

Though it dashed to the bed of his tongue, Michael's retort quietly stalled in his throat, as the comment that surfaced was less necessary to the point than logic would suggest. Instead, his shoulders slowly lifted, returning her earlier reaction as his. He bundled the vague gesture with a vaguer smile.

"Okay, then." Julia grunted, staring at her glass as if wishing the substance was stronger. She slowly gathered her nerves, and in an almost whisper, she sighed a solitary word to emphasize the sincerity of her wish. Giving answer to what she could barely defend in her own head, "No." she squeaked. Her tone drifting to an abrupt halt with the anemic expulsion. Falling neither firm nor convincing in its plunge, she knew this with scant assurance before she granted it life. Undoubtedly, from the look on Michael's face, he heard the pathetic pule just as plainly, if not more. A look of affirmation slowly streaked his smile as an added reward, nodding his awareness of this. He collected their half-finished salads as if unseeing. His strides seemed to mock her in the silence that crept in, and she could almost swear that that phenomenal stature of his, looked taller in the grace he displayed.

The oven door closed with a petulant huff, this behind the silence her defiance infused. Michael placed the contents on the counter with a modicum of skill, removing the protective covers. He slowly served the ingredients to their plates. Widening her observation, Julia's eyes then pawed at his back, thankful for the solace of discretion now wholly at hand, she exploited the vision at length. His jacket, in its swathing, was worth its weight in gold, beautifully fitted to his body, as if the design had been done solely to enhance his physique. It offered a promise that was more taunting than not.

Broad shoulders tapered slightly at the waist, shifted with the efforts of the man's hands. Presenting a cinched fit, though it moved easily with his stretches while he worked. It insinuated boldly of a feast just beneath, counseling this in the comfortable, yet daring, way the garment rested against the arc of his muscular buttocks. He was an incredibly sexy man. So the stories have been told, and in that suit, she would have to make that foregone conclusion irrefutable. A perfect ten. Any woman who gets into a… relationship with him, would find it hard to keep her hands off such superb packaging. She purred, and the pictures such wordings thence availed to her eyes, moved fluidly through the darken corridors of her mind like an erotic scene. Skillfully undressing him in her head, while she pondered further on the nicety of that. The delicious reverie ended as abruptly as a raucous blast. This, when her eyes travelled up his body to his face. For although his body showed no eyes surveying from a place on his back, the face attached most certainly did just that; and it now wore the most devilish smile. Apparent, by the look on his face, her predicament was more than amusing; it was recompense for an evident debt. And she wondered if his reaction was due to her looking, or the fact that he caught her *feeding* on his physique. Since his smile was more than approving, it was applauding.

Unsticking the lock on her eyes, Julia dropped them to her glass, offering a breathless apology as she cleared the smog from her throat. "I'm sorry." She whispered almost without sound, wishing for the deadly strike of an aneurism to drop her in that spot. Or for the gift of a sudden floor splitting earthquake to slam through the room—one most specifically under her chair—one that would take her with it. "I got—"

"Don't be." He murmured in a roughened tone, swaggering back to the table, a roguish grin slowly slithered across his handsome face. "I like your eyes on me." He announced warmly. *It's a captivating start.* Michael added in his head, biting back the words with strenuous effort.

Julia's eyes fully averted his as he hovered at her side, as if riveted by what was to be next. She planted her eyes sorely on the plate he placed to her face. Sedately, his hand brushed hers as he retreated from her side, and without looking, she knew it was no mistake.

"Blackened trout with crab." Michael explained as he retook his seat. He had given great care to those prominent in his selection. Selections he made from the details he collected these weeks. Seafood was her favorite, and he hoped that the choices made were to her taste.

"Mmmm, it smells fantastic." She cooed, still averting her gaze. In truth, the smell was indeed amazing, savoring the appetizing aroma with each breath, she smiled. "Seafood is my favorite."

"I know."

"How did you know that?" she asked, looking up for the first time with confusion stalking her brows. "Never mind," Her hand fluttered through the air to a sudden stop, not needing the sweetness of his words. For his explanation would only be another way for him to impress, and she saw no need to further bother with that, as she was already well mesmerized as it was. Anything else would only be adding wood to a blaze, and what she needed most was water.

Michael shrugged off her refusal with a lengthy regard, brimming behind a wryly smirk. His manner looked then like the sinister stalking of a fox, seeming once again to have garnered some secret insight into her.

"This is very good." Julia mumbled, genuinely loving the food. "Tell me, Mr. Dunhill, will you be doing this often?"

"Which, lure you or feed you?"

Julia's fork paused midpoint to her plate, her eyes lifting slowly as if to assess a new find. She smiled impishly into what was the fantastically bright prism of his eyes. "Are you flirting with me, Mr. Dunhill?" she asked through a sweetened purr, his name rolling enthusiastically in her mouth. Brushing over her tongue as if tasting each word, she let the stirring syllables fly, each coiling slowly before touching the rim of his ears.

"I thought the days of clubbing women over their heads were long gone, but I'll be happy to oblige you if you think it would help. Just pick out whatever you find suitable for clubbing, and I'll get right to it." He pledged, his gaze lingering fondly on her face. "I didn't think I could be any clearer," he shrugged. "Short of using my hands that is."

"Why, Mr. Dunhill," she sang, her honeyed tone further warming as his name again coiled through the balmy air, already knowing the answer to the counterfeit question she posed. Since, with full certainty, she would have to be utterly dense not to have amassed that fact. But he had a way about him that made her tongue eager in a way it normally would not. "I—"

"By the way," he rasped through a soft chuckle. "Just so you know. Your use of my name has more of a contradictory effect than anything else." He apprised in a rumbly soft roar. His eyes ogling as he leaned close. "Somehow I don't think it's coming out quite the way you may have intended. I feel almost certain of that, and I just feel I should clarify that there are special numbers one call to hear text convert that well. But, please..." he chanted, and the flash of his smile was near dazzling, hitting its mark across the table. He continued in a drawl. "Don't stop. Please feel free to...call my name out whenever you feel the need. It's quite inspiring."

"Is it just that you like playing, or do you just like playing specifically with me?" she taunted, deliberately keeping his gaze.

"Do you really want an answer to that question?" Michael probed, retrieving his glass. He eyed her over its translucent rim. *And do you really need one?* Groaning this in the silence of his head, he left the words to rattle and stay dead.

"I don't think you'd like it if I played with you." She grumbled, gathering a few leaves of spinach on her fork. She shrugged in approbation of the thought.

"Care to put that theory to a test?" Michael asked in a low breath. "What sort of... play would you like to begin with?" he simpered, showing full fondness for the probability of such rout.

At the seditious test, the thought of him as a rooster grew strong in her head, brightening the smile on her lips as she further expounded on the notion. He knew his trade well, that much was certain, and it would be her guess that he implemented said skills just as deftly as the galvanizing start. It really was not a question of *if* when sighted in his path, but *when*. His fork sat loosely on the edge of his plate as the silence stretched, waiting patiently in this their adversarial game, and the smile he gave her was regaling in its behest. Thus, it fostered well the thought of stealing a kiss and the sweet potency of his taste. *It would probably shock him into shutting up*. She smirked. It may even be worth it just to see the look on his face. "What do you have in mind?" she challenged in a newly sweetened tone.

"This day belongs to you. I'm completely at whatever deems amicable to your choosing, yours fully for the bidding." He declaimed, rumbling this through what waded like a sugary growl. His demeanor distinctly serene, as if the words had been a practiced monologue in his daily routine, thus he skillfully returned the sword to her hand.

"At my bidding?" Julia queried amusedly. "Whatever I choose? Those are powerful words to hand over to a novice in the game."

"I'm aware of the power that comes with it." He hummed, his elbows bridging the table as he leaned forward in his chair. "But I trust you to be wise. It still stands, Julia, whatever is your bidding?"

Without thinking, Julia leaned in an equal portion of the way, gifting him a wicked smile as she tabled both hands, and the urge to kiss him surged inexplicably strong the greater the lean. "What could I possibly need you to do for me I can't already do for myself?"

"You tell me." Michael countered in a slow, deliberate tone, his eyes brushing the seductive hue of her lips. Lingering long with intent radiating from the mystic gems, his smile, of a sudden, dimmed to an inimical smirk. Its variance now balanced as if a warning shot had rocketed through the space. He then eased back in his seat as if so bade.

A strange twinge of displeasure, mingled greatly with loss, walked through her brashly as she watched him retreat, already missing the verve that he dished. Though she held close the verity of such facts, adamant in her refusal to let the obvious show. She eyed her almost empty glass with a frail sigh. "Perhaps I'll have another glass of that delicious wine."

"One glass of wine coming right up," Michael chimed, nodding politely as he sprang to his feet. Benevolently, he took his time in the chastened filling of her glass, reminding himself repeatedly of a promise previously made. Needing to earn her trust, this being his focal goal, preferring to have her unafraid of being mauled every time he came near.

"Thank you."

"My pleasure," He rasped, a seductive lilt stroking his tone.

"Cheers." Julia whispered, lifting her glass with a collapsing smile.

"Cheers." He grumbled in acquiescence of the word and its meaning. Their glasses touched in a swift, gentle gesture, and the soft chime from the crystal goblets whistled, between them, like the dinging of a recess bell. It aptly swallowed the verve stilting their voices.

The music of a saxophonist gusted through the quiet room. The melancholy melody sawing astoundingly deep, twirling maliciously, it gnawed until it held you compressed within its enervated grasp. As if synchronized in a ritual play, each rested their glass at the same time, their eyes touching in the gesture of an unseen hand, denoting, in the deed, the perfect opening to start a new topic. Though neither felt inclined to speak nor did they avert the intensity of their gaze, stretching the taut silence to a new rendering of infinity.

"I like this music." Julia muttered tensely, clumsily pointing a finger through the air, she gave him a quick glance before her gaze flew wide to encompass the room.

"Would you like to dance?" Michael asked wryly, half expecting her to say no, though she contradicted his guess, as she instead grew quiet.

"Okay." She sighed, mostly mouthing the word, Julia straightened in her chair. Of a sudden, she was a buddle of nerves, as she had not meant the mention to be an invitation of such. But when he gave the offer, something inside her had jumped happily at the chance. Prompting her to take hold of his hand with a lazily smile as he helped her to her feet.

Michael walked her to an opening in the breakfast-room with a deceptive ease he did not feel. Closing his arms around her, he quietly held his breath, hoping to stop the fluttering in his chest.

A familiar tingle rose through her body as she leaned timidly against his frame. Relaxing in his arms as the soothing rhythm wrapped itself around the room, effectively swaddling them. Her heart pounded wildly in its place of rest, jutting to its mad as the unfamiliar grew irresistibly renowned. Unprepared for the sensation it gave, or how much she liked how it felt, Julia's body seemed no longer her own but a bale of need, and the longer they stayed together. She prayed he could not feel the franticness of her pulse, though she, most certainly, could feel the welcomed hardness of him. Tall, lean and firm against her, he felt the way she thought that he would, with unfathomed masculinity that was incontestably lethal. An armament that was surely dangerous to be near. His arms tightened around her with the subtlety of a new tenure, pulling her closer the longer they swayed, and without fear or falter. She adjusted their stance, exhaling gently as she rested her head on his chest.

The dance seemed to verge on the pretext of forever, if forever could be bottled in minutes or a day. And the excitement that danced along with them was exquisite in its least, as was his scent. Wafting up her nostrils as his body warmed against hers, he was, to her, like smelling her favorite dessert. Lifting her nose to his neck, she saw that he watched her closely, his hazel eyes seeming to grow dark. A simmering hint of desire sat bold in their transmuted depths, and the sight was glorious to look at, as was its solicit. Burning through her with an abetting gust, the rousing started from the very tips of her toes. Julia waited in agonized suspense for his cravings to burst upon her, stoking her own ardor mad, as the intensity lengthened instead. Michael's head slowly descended, miring of a sudden as the music stopped. A deadened silence fell inquisitively on the room. The two then stood inert in the fevered space, unwilling to relent the moment or see to its enhancing, expressive eyes warred with each other instead. A new song started, and the room was as melodious as it once was, changing again the ambiance of the space.

"Dessert?" Michael breathed, his breath falling against her cheek.

"What?" Julia cried in hoarse reply, her throat tightening on the unexpected return. Spelt thus, by the deep furrows now dragging on her brow. The sour taste of disappointment thrived like the mantelpiece of an impressive display, intrepid in its flaunt, nigh boastful with the new turn of event. It seeped through her body in waves like the eerie consonance of a chant.

"I think it's time we have dessert." Michael proclaimed in a raspy growl. "Come." He sighed, and unlike the bolstering display he was known to sport, his smile came stiff. Almost delicately, Michael led her to a chair at the edge of the room. With gaze averted from the vision she made, he set her to a seat, gathering her slender limbs from the floor. He let his hands glide slowly down the length of her calves. Spilling her shoes with the gentle persuasion of his hands, his palms moved over the souls of her feet as if to administer a warming. Not wanting to look into her eyes, Michael's gaze stayed on the drudging of his hands. Yet, he could not miss the tumbling tail of her skirt, as the long slit offered him a tempting view of her thighs. Thwarted in his endeavors to abstain from that which was surely his wont, Michael growled, and the sound bled as a long, deep, murderous grunt, locked too far in his oscillating head to be heard. Quietly straightening, he pushed the oversized ottoman to form a platform in aid of her legs, lifting the cascading skirt from its path. He gave her toes a gentle squeeze, offering then the placid expound. "I'll get dessert," he mumbled as he again retreated.

A timorous hand rose, uncertain of why, though it paused before making contact with the other. Silently, it dropped to the chair in her own show of retreat. Surprised by the measure shown in his control, she held tight to her own restraint, for she had not thought that of him just minutes before, and definitely not after the quality of their word romp of late.

"And for dessert," Michael heralded as he reentered the room, handing over the small, white bowl. He quietly smiled, moving without pause to her chair's twin. His gaze rimmed the lines of being aloof. "Mango sorbet," he clarified in a light rumble. The two overstuffed chairs were arranged cozily for the purpose of a verbal exchange, one directly in front of the other, though conversation did not come as willing as it once did.

"You put a lot of thought into your selections," Julia muttered at last, still keeping her eyes veiled from his. "Thank you for that—for this."

"You're very welcome." He nodded, also cautioning his gaze from its usual bent.

A quiet nod affirmed her acceptance of his response, unsure of what else to add, she fell awkwardly silent. He, in all his distinctions thus far, was unlike the many visions she had eagerly presumed, unlike so much of the stories she'd heard. It was a perplexing feat to discern what to accurately think or how to behave. Especially with the penchant of her body of late, even now as she watched him, she found she was well drawn to more than just the view. Yet, he appeared fully engrossed in his bowl. A small frown worked his brows as if troubled by some austere thought, and the spoon that now touched his lips, carried less than a third of its capacity. *Maybe sorbet is not his thing*, she scoffed.

"May I ask you a question?"

"Sure." Michael drawled, his head slowly lifting in wait.

"I'm curious about something," she smiled, nervously blurting the inquest. "Why haven't you tried to kiss me today?" Her tone came uncertain and soft, unlike her usual self-assured ditties of late. It sounded as if the words came from someone else. Julia's eyes stayed anchored to her bowl as a defensive guise, but she did not need to see him to feel the intensity of his gaze.

"Did you expect me to?" Michael asked in a hushed tone, reining control on both voice and body.

"No." She lied pithily. "I just wondered."

"I was trying to be respectful—especially here." Michael rejoined steadily. The words trailing his emit of a jagged breath. Was she relived or disappointed? His turmoil mind asked.

"Is that the secret then?"

"The secret to what?"

"To you. Is this your trick to get me to spend more time with you?"

"That's no secret, Julia." He smiled. "I've made myself known and have showed you my hands."

"Yes, I suppose you have." She sighed succinctly, feeling like a nervous cat in her effort, as she was doing a poor job broaching the subject of her wants. It would certainly be easier if he just took the hint and came over and kissed her. But what hint does one give? *Where's the bad-boy now when I need him?* She griped. "What if?" she started in a weak breath, slowly easing to her feet. She turned promptly from his view, clutching the bowl as her support in this unaccustomed drive. Embracing the gesture, as it granted her the fortunes needed to collect her nerves and gather some strength.

"I'll take that." Michael called, bounding to his feet. He reached for the emptied vessel now clutched tightly in her hand.

"No, no." She assured then, waving off his determined attempt. She veered around the barrier he posted in her hurry towards the sink. "I'll do it." Julia vowed, though he followed her headway without pause, his steps staying only a half-a-pace behind hers. Placing her bowl in the sink, she turned to him with a victorious smile. "See! Safe and sound."

"Wondering what?" Michael questioned without further tarry, as if there had been no break since the start of her query. Oddly, she shifted uneasily under the keenness of his gaze as he waited, and although the polite thing to do would be to grant her the decorum need for some space, he did not. Well certain, at that moment, he could not.

"What if I took the intrigue away?" Julia whispered at last, feeling the heat of his body, as he stood extraordinarily close. If she but leaned in, it would be all over—so to speak.

"Which intrigue would that be?" Michael breathed, his pulse dancing to the tune of her inebriating scent.

It took less than a step to close the meager space between them, letting his scent persuade her further still. She filled her lungs as she stabled her nerves. The music of her pulse thence carried no name, as it went enigmatically mad the minute she stepped near, warming her body the longer she stayed in the electrifying pose. Without shoes, she stood almost a full foot shorter than his towering frame. Still, her gaze jumped immediately to the beauty of his.

"What if I kissed you?" she blurted hurriedly, thinking then that the words did not sound as ghastly as it did in her head.

Chapter Eighteen

A pubescent boy might have trembled with the thrill of such question as that. His mind might have crackled from anxiety melded with the offering she gave. Drunk with anticipation, he might have thenceforth guzzled the air to thwart the flux of emotions now wafting through his body.

Conversely, the man divulged no such discharge to the cause. Yet, although he exhibited naught to substantiate any such employ, the bourgeoning in his body was no less sweet, and its newness was no less an athirst worthy of savor.

"As I've said, I'm utterly at your bidding." Michael rasped coolly, cherishing not only the thrill of her request, but the form sojourned so favorably to his.

Her small cough came strained, chipping at the thickness that now pressed affably through the room. She softly cleared the distended frog from her throat. Edging her body more intimately to the weaponry of his, warmth clasped firmly to the solidity of warmth. And memories failed, in their rummage, to fetch forth another period in time when he was this enlivened with the proceedings that verged a mere kiss. The excitement was unlike anything he'd ever felt and the hammering in his chest made true its point with every thud.

Julia settled her body snugly against his, seeing the flicker of the candle's fire in his eyes. It set to blaze orbs that already sparkled on their own, though her own danced with the dividend of intrigue. Embarking on the short climb to the balls of her feet, she felt the heat of his breath as he lowered his head to hers. Resting his face gentle above her, he left her the first move in the sizzle of an electrified abeyance. The air around them grew fastidiously calm, ripened with anticipation like the onset of a storm. But that this air was astoundingly sweet, permeated with the opulent smell of mango sorbet and the intoxicated scent of each other.

Composedly, Michael stayed suspended as her lips brushed across his. Standing perfectly still, he allowed the melody of a first kiss to play. Her lips were soft in both flavor and touch. Plied with its own distinct sweetness, it emblazoned the senses with the inking of a date. Much like one's first taste of cotton candy at a fair, the decadence was now etched within the fabric of time, and she rattled every nerve in his body with the piquancy it gave. His arms ambled her body like a serpent on the hunt, slowly encircling her waist. He held her firmly to his frame, and although everything in his body screamed for him to forage, he held.

The thudding in her chest knew no bound with the empirical tasting, pushing her further onward. It chanted one solitary cheer, one she already intended to pursue irrespective of the recipient at hand, for more was, without a doubt, her one objective. That familiar tingle rattled her entire being as their tongues met. Each touch thence lingered as if sampling something uniquely exotic or sweet. The explosion came when she allowed him to fully taste her, welding their bodies together with the force of a puissant embrace.

To her back, the counter's edge seemed adamant in its charge, wedged deep in the soft tissue of a hip from the force of their drive, though no more so than the man's effort to her front, for she could now feel every ripple and bulge that his body held. Jarred, the room stood further on edge, thickened with the bolstering gales from their concocted storm. It, too, held its breath, watching. It cheered them ever onward in their hunt. The deeper he dove the more eagerly she gave, taking him with her through a thoroughfare of intensifying pleasure—that which heeded no bound. Pleasures she had long starved for and had missed. *God, has she ever been kissed like this?* Julia panted. Though her doyen in matters of such seemed otherwise involved, too much so, in titillating substance, to elucidate such point. *Not likely*, she asserted without pause, and a moan of acquiescence extended its long tail from her throat. *She would have remembered something this erotic and wild.* Affirming such dictates, she trembled under the verve his mouth then dispensed, thus goading her to blur the lines of discretion that was so far observed. Slipping her hand inside his shirt, eager fingers strolled across the matting of his chest, clambering up his neck. They ambled softly through his hair.

Michael's breath came warm against the aperture of her mouth in follow, setting his lips to work along the soft lines of her neck. He played above the opening of her shirt. Dark hair feathered the angling of her chin as his kisses skied the slopes of her breasts. Tasting the sweetness of her chocolatey skin with certified greed, a low howl of manumission came from his throat.

Nipping his ear as he ascended the slender angling of her neck, she caught the soft lobe between her teeth. Her tongue then played on the supple edges with skill, seeming distinct in her knowledge of him. The intensity that came with the kisses that followed was like nothing of those in just the moments before. Nor could either discern an equal to attribute the exquisiteness of their pain, as the two only knew desire in their hunt. In a blink, she was off the floor and in his arms. Hers fastened fixedly around his neck as he carried her from the kitchen to the opulence of the family-room couch.

Gingerly, Michael rested her back against the thick cushion of the couch, tempted greatly to seat her across his lap, but knew any such action would slaughter the restraints he had yet tried to show. His movements bore caution in the very core of his approach, fearing she would fly, as greed now smoldered like a visible plume above his head, and he was grateful when she made no attempt to flee from the leery tilt of her perch. Her mouth was exasperating, enticing and worrisome all at once, reminding him in an instant of a rose, delicate and sweet but damaging to the touch.

For a moment, Julia's face broadcasted a hint of surprise, yet her shock was not attached to the action itself, but for what she now felt. All logics from her prior governs seemed to have forsaken her then, for she held him to her as if he but granted her life. Effusively imbibing the electricity his mouth so sweetly roused, for forever had since come and passed since she'd been kissed. So long since she'd been kissed like this. She just could not stop.

To substantiate the verity of her need, her body shivered sweetly the deeper his kisses plunged, slinging desire well beyond the point of persuasive. There was no hiding the effects of her wants. Atremble with the potency of her covet, her hands shook as she reached for the buttons on his shirt. Heaving breasts strained in their effort with the drag of each breath, weighted now with her yearning sighs. Michael paused in his effort, helping the moil of her hands, though his endeavor unfolded like the wild gust of a hurricane instead. With what bode like a single gesture, he sturdily ripped the enclosure free of his shirt. Tossing the garment to the floor, his jacket fully incorporated in the discard. The scattering pings of buttons across wooden planks went unnoticed or unheeded by both. Pulling her roughly to his chest, he again devoured her mouth. Enticing her to accompany him on the inebriated climb, one she eagerly adhered to without pause. The cushions spread with the shifting of position, falling to the floor as her back bedded the couch, though she took him with her like a willful pawn on the descent.

Michael followed eagerly without pause, lying fully atop her body. He taunted the tense peaks of her breasts, sending her body in a wild spin, well past the point of recognition of self.

Again the need to hold barreled through his head. *Tighten the handle on your control*, so the words echoed through his head, but that was becoming downright arduous. It was near impossible to preserve such point if they continued like this. Unsure why the nous of that goal felt so significant at a moment as this—just that it was. Still, his hand slid up the long slit of her skirt, caressing the smooth length of her thighs, for the urge to feel her softness dragged him near the point of being mad. Long fingers slowed as they moved over the delicate fabric of her underwear, stroking softly. He waited as if to garner permission for a tour. A single digit slowly slipped beneath the sheer protection, testing her warmth before immersing in the dank furnace itself.

Generously coiled, it boomed like cannons rending the succor in a midnight raid. So, too, the unfurling that next came. The imprudent melody of a chime came loud through the room, dispersing in every direction at once. It devoured the sweetness of the silence that once was, instantly robbing the room of the ardor it once held.

As if from a trance, Julia jumped, her body jerking under his as if receiving the flash of a charge. Breaking the ardent spell as the tune ciphered slowly through the fog in her head. "Wait." She panted, giving aid to her cause with a shaky breath; her body juddered with greed even as her words flew. "Wait." She whispered taking yet another breath.

"Why?" Michael asked hoarsely, his breath like a scorched blast against her neck.

"What…? *Oh, God*, what–what am I doing?" she asked in a panicky whisper as her eyes rounded the room, seeing it now, it would seem, for the first time. "We can't do this. I-I can't do this." She murmured frailly, shaking her head as if to clear the soupy mixture of some delirious fog. Still feeling the tilt of his finger as it deftly worked the inset of her body, he built further on the inferno already braising her frame. "Oh, God… please, mmm, please…stop that!" She sighed, holding her breath. Julia squeezed her eyes tightly shut, hoping to cool the sensation he gave.

"Why?" he again groaned, his breath falling heavy as he, too, vied for control. "It's okay to let yourself go a little." Michael rasped, his lips stroking the corner of her mouth, wishing he could go back to tasting the many flavors she gave.

"I'm sorry." She grunted, shifting her body under his, now desperate to get away from all reminders of where she almost went. "I'm really very sorry." Julia again sighed, pulling the front of her shirt in a tight clasp. She barred her exposed bosom from his view. Only four of the six buttons teetered undone, but enough so to cement fully the extent to which she had almost delved. *How could she have come this far?* She groaned. Not unlike the pages in a book, confusion was written in his eyes, as boldly so as the desire yet oozing from his body, that which was now pressed staunchly to hers. "You have to let me up." She informed tightly.

Michael's head fell gently to the curve of her neck, taking a slow breath. It sailed like the sprouting of a howl. "Stay. Please." He hummed in what favored a breathless sigh.

"I can't." She breathed back dejectedly, shaking her head to reiterate her resolve. Michael's nod came slow like a gentle wisp, as if he had expected none but the answer she gave. He again took a long breath, lifting himself from her without further utterance or plea. "I'm sorry." She sighed, voicing the words like the imparting of some secret tryst. She flew from him before he fully seated himself, rushing back to the kitchen where she collected her things, though without shoes. Her feet were almost silent on the wood floor. Only the fortitude of her pace gave her action its voice. Scurrying towards the entrance, she was almost through when he whispered her name. "I'm sorry." She cried in lieu of an answer, barely slowing in her pace. She gave no heeding beyond that, nor did she wait for his approach. "I'm so sorry." Julia called, flinging the excuse over her shoulders, she winged out the door.

The car's enclosure scorched like the well of an oven, for the midday sun had done well in seeing it fully so, though she hardly noticed such measly effects for what it gave. Instead, her body sat in a quiver, amazed, even then, that she still trembled from his kiss. Authenticating the cuff of its strength in its persuasive force, as her hands still plainly bore the evidence of such, shaking irrepressibly as she tried, to no avail, to start her car. The heavy clinking of keys froze as she tossed them to the seat. For the thudding of her heart was almost violent in her chest; it echoed rowdily in her ears. She could still feel his hands grazing her body. Everywhere he touched seemed to morosely denounce her and her decision, oddly choleric in its vaunt, regardless of a virtuous tenet.

The way he kissed her was truly hypnotic, and in concurrence, her hand displayed a tremor as she brushed it across her lips. As if needing to soothe the throbbing from its place, she repeated the test, though her action served as a prompting instead. She was hungry. Ravenous to the very depths of her bones, so much so, that she almost ate him for lunch. The sensation now was no less demanding than it was then, climbing from the nadirs of her soul. It just would not ebb. And for some peculiar logic, she could not seem to make herself leave, regardless of her tries. As if armed with a master key to her body, he had flung wide doors she had carefully locked with just the partaking of lunch. The rest he offered as an extra on the euphoric combers of dessert. Skillfully releasing every lust, cravings and hunger she had so neatly tucked aside. All now roamed freely, and they rocketed forward like the gnawing that came with hibernation's death.

Tender cravings sweet with anticipation now felt vengeful, wanting nothing but him. They spiraled further onward with their goad. "Go. Just start the car and go. It will get better once you leave." Her whispered promise came with a nod, yet her effort grew progressively harder, as stubborn fingers closed tentatively around the keys. "Damn! Damn! Damn! What's wrong with me?" She cried, resting her head on the steering wheel of her car. "It's just a kiss! Well…" she groaned, knowing it was so much more than the simplicity of that, and so much better than what the labeling suggested. Long, deep, sensual kisses that was breathtakingly good. Better than good. Better than any. And the more the flavor surfaced through her thoughts, the more gluttonously her body spoke of its wants. Was she caught up with the man or just the fantasy he sells? Could she lose herself for a spell locked in his arms? Women do it all the time, could she?

Michael's grunt jangled the newly strained silence like the warning bay of a wolf, sweeping gauchely across the rafters. It gaped back from whence it came as he again settled on the couch. Once again, the day had not gone as smoothly as he had planned, though in this, it careened the banks of a precipice with certain destruction at hand. He had worked so hard to harness himself and his greed. So hard to not end up the way that they had, trying his best to earn her trust. But all that effort now summed for naught. After today, he'll be lucky if he could convince her to have tea in a public shop. Even their playful banter now sits dangerously at risk, and after this revelation, she'll need to be extremely vigilant in her guard, since it was certain he most avidly wanted more of everything she possessed. He could not remember ever being kissed like that, being kissed so…well. It was electrifying at the very least. How could he not want more? He'd never been this much of a gentleman to any woman before in his life, granting over the lead to her hands. But gentleman or not, she'll know his thoughts the minute she enters the room, for there would be no hiding that fact.

Coerced by the potency of her desire, Julia staggered up the steps to his door, trembling with indecision as she leaned hard upon the bell. Still shirtless, Michael appeared almost in a flash. His strides vaunted sleekly of a new hunt, mirroring a lion in its stalking of a mate. Swinging the door open, he left it wide as he leaned against the jam, looking remorseful and relieved all at once, while he summoned the necessary wording to declare his case.

"Okay." She sighed the instant the ingress widened at his back, the sound vaulting low from the back of her throat.

"Okay?" he repeated with a nod, hesitant to show his delight.

"I'll sleep with you." She whispered hurriedly.

"You'll what?" Michael exclaimed, and the sound came very near to being labeled a squawk.

"I'll sleep with you." She again apprised in a hesitant tone, though still feeling the need to clarify her point. Name the terms of her submission before they furthered the deal. If her body won't allow her to forget his kisses, then she needed to make the terms and conditions of what came next.

"Why?" he asked tamely. "That wasn't my intent, I-I wante—"

"Isn't that where you expected things to end?"

"But I—"

"I'm just cutting out the time and drudgery of an entree so we can get to dessert."

"You're offering me dessert without sampling the first course?"

"Is that against your guy code?"

"No!" Michael barked, shaking his head to assure the absurdity of such point. His answer came quicker than it should, quicker than he intended. "I wanted...I-I just thought..."

"You don't want to...?" Julia asked softly, suddenly afraid, as she had not thought much on what decision he would give, or that he might refuse.

"Of course I want to!" he grunted, again answering faster than he should. "I mean... yes...but...well." Sighing, Michael simmered the rousing of both body and mind. "I just don't want you to feel...pushed."

"I didn't. I don't." She assured with a heavy sigh, dropping the prim angle of her head. "Actually, I don't know what I'm feeling. You have me somewhat...topsy." She sighed, her eyes moving back to his face. She then paused as if expecting her next words to be displayed in his eyes. "I have to say, I'm a little surprised." She groaned. Her voice trailing as she turned nervously to gaze at her car.

"So am I." Michael frowned, wondering why he hadn't pounced the minute he opened the door.

"Have I sullied your opinion of me?" she asked, her eyes falling to his feet.

"No! Not in the least." He vowed in a sharp convincing tone. Stepping close, Michael calmly gathered her hands, touching his lips to each palm, he smiled. "I'm very attracted to you, you have to know that."

"Before you say anything else," she rasped, her shoulders lifting almost laboriously with the heavy haul of her breath. "I need to know something. I need to be certain it's really me that you see. So I need *you* to see me." She hummed. "I need you to see who I am." Groaning this, she stepped past him into the house, her fingers working on the buttons of her shirt, quickly undoing each. Her fear soared in its goading for the job at hand; knowing if she slowed any she would lose what little courage she had summoned for the job. "I need you to see what it is you're asking for, Michael." She declared faintly, dropping her shirt to the floor. Julia hurriedly stepped from her skirt. "I'm not a twenty year old supermodel, Michael, nor am I a Barbie Princess. I'm a mother, a thirty-five year old mother of two." She muttered dryly, dropping her bra to the stack. "Do you see *me*, Michael? Or is there a vision you perceived in your head? If so, you need to take your fill now and state your truth."

Michael's eyes scurried across her body like a chipmunk gathering food, not knowing where to lay his gaze. He fed on everything his eyes touched. She looked as he had long since imagined she would, delectable down to the very last drop. Long beautiful legs were exquisite down to her toes painted bright red. Her breasts, though luscious, were not fully round. They stood less at attention than he surmised they once did—motherhood, he suspected. They did not give him their full attention in this their mock-impasse, but they most certainly had his. Wavy hair jeeringly draped a fair portion of one breast, and he fought the impulse to step close and push the obstructing strands from his view. Nervous hands rested atop her most savory part and, as if acquiring the nerve, she dropped them slowly to her side, and warm, almond colored skin shifted uneasily under his gaze.

For a trice, he thought of closing the short distant to offer his response. But he suspected that was not the answer she sought. In truth, she was stunning. Even more so than he'd established in his head, and he could not imagine her thinking anyone seeing less than just that. How do you convince beauty of her beauty? Or was beauty trying to convince him she was something other than that?

"Julia, I'm not asking you to be anything more than what you are, that would be an impossible feat. You're incredibly stunning."

Julia watched his eyes as he spoke, heard his words in the spry spilling and thought they rallied the components of truth, and a sigh waded her body like one who had been holding their breath. One less familiar with her strength, might presumed her action ascertained a certain lack of confidence in herself, though the opposite would be in fact true. But real and reality were both like stores titled within the pages of magazines where he's from, and her type of real could sometimes be rare. She just needed them both to be aware of where they stand.

The feel of his eyes did not bring with it the discomfort she expected. In fact, there was something quite carnal about the way his eyes walked over her skin, especially so with the residue of lust still weighty in their depths. "Do you...?" she started, knowing she could not stay to expound upon any thought he might have. With Rachel and Richard getting home in less than two hours, there was hardly enough time to truly savor what she wanted from him, or in any way savor him.

"I accept." Michael growled, finalizing any further thought she might have. Long legs ate up the gap between them in two strides, pulling her into his arms. His mouth was almost bruising as he drank her in. Compressing softness to the stalwart backing of his, skin smeared roughly to skin, and without his shirt to hinder the stir. Her breasts felt like warm silk against the hardness of his, making the rummage even better than it was before. Her breath came heavy against his hair as his kisses trailed to her breasts, savoring their taste with the warmth of his tongue. A circular climb that saw persuasively to the dulcet drive.

"Michael…" Julia called, her voice shearing through the soft waves of his hair. "Oh… mm, wait. Michael…stop." She cried in a hoarse breath, and in an instant, his body went frigidly taut. "I'm sorry. I'm so sorry." His eyes were almost stern as his body slowly straightened from its bent. "I'm…I'm sorry." She groaned, shaking her head in an apologetic show. "I'm sorry. I really am. But, I have to go. My-my kids…" she announced softly, dragging her hands heavily across her face, she again sighed. "Please don't be mad. My kids will be home soon. I have to be there. But…I'm free tomorrow.…" She proclaimed with a soft lilt, lifting her eyes, she awaited his response. His eyes worked slowly over her face as she waited, and although he gave no words in answer, the question was plainly asked as much as it was felt. "I promise. I'm not trying to frustrate you. Really I'm not. I'm…" she paused, letting her breath fly like the whooshing of air through a long tunnel. She buried his hands between the swells of her breasts. "My body does strange things around you and even stranger things when you kiss me. I'd like at least a full night to work on that. I'll even give you the entire weekend if you'd like."

"All weekend and no interruptions?" Michael asked curiously, immediately intrigued.

"If you want it."

"You wouldn't be playing with me, would you, Julia? I don't trust my instincts with you. They seem to get all muddled when it comes to you."

"I don't play, and certainly not this type of game. That would be cruel. Do you really think me that cruel?"

"Yes." Michael gushed, softening his expression. He gifted her, the full swag of a smile. His first since their playful exchange at lunch. "To do this to any man is cruel." He grumbled, shaking his head. His hand moved slowly over her breast. "But to do it twice in one day," he growled, his breath bathing her ear. "That does surpass the cruelty line."

"I'm really sorry. But I promise I'll make it up to you."

"Oh, you will." Michael assured in a rumble, his tone sounding like a deep, gravelly song. Bending, his kisses skated the swell of her breasts, taking his time on each. Warm kisses eased in a leisured stroll down her stomach, stalling at the edge of the black swatch she wore. His teeth then played along the inner curves of her thighs, taking turns with his tongue, he drudged the crevice of her body until her fingers locked in his hair. Slender legs trembled softly against his mouth as she called him by name, and although he knew the reason was not what he intended, he liked the sounds that floated from her throat. "So you can remember me." He whispered as he straightened.

"You didn't need to do that for me to remember. But I get the hint. Now who's cruel?"

"I can't believe I'm saying this to you, but…" Michael groaned, and his eyes rolled as if in search of the heavens itself. "Please cover up before you get eaten."

"I'm sorry." She muttered tamely, reaching for her clothes. She quickly stepped into her skirt, shoving her arms awkwardly in the sleeves of her shirt. She left her bra behind like the forgotten runt in a litter. Attempting modesty, her fingers worked clumsily at her buttons, hurrying in her wont to cover her nakedness from the riling of his gaze. "I'll go." Mumbling this hesitantly, she turned from the heat of his gaze, for he watched her so greedily that it made her entire body quake.

"Here," Michael grunted at last, pushing her hands aside. He began the tedious task of buttoning her shirt. With only a miniscule collection, the task should have, in fact, been a snap, but time bore no essence in his drive. Thus he lingered in his task, letting his fingers brush the soft swells as he worked. "What time should I expect you?" he asked in a raspy voice.

"What time do you want me?" his glare came without veil, as was the sarcasm given in his laugh. Realizing her error, Julia hastily adjusted. "You know what I mean." She scolded. "Give me a time and I'll make it."

"I'll be here all day, what about first thing?"

"What is that for you, dusk?"

"Funny."

"I wouldn't think you got up before noon." She smiled.

"You would be surprised what can get me up." He growled, touching his mouth to the place where her collar brushed the edge of her throat. He made certain his point was well understood.

"How's ten?" she whispered then.

"Ten sounds very good to me." He murmured, his husky burr lifting through the kisses he now pressed to the delicate skin on said spot.

"Good, then its set. Well…bye…." She muttered then, enticing his fervor to stop, and wishing badly for the thrashing of her pulse to ebb as well. "Michael…I—"

"Go." He insisted without pausing in his toils, feeling her pulse react to his bent. He wickedly wanted to drive it to a gallop as his seemed wont to stay. Her sighs, however, encouraged him to lift his head. Quietly taking her hand, Michael walked her to her car, opening her door, he watched keenly as she seated herself behind the wheel. Gathering her keys from the dash, she looked up at him and sighed, her hair now a faded radiance of its earlier self. The elegant vaunt of her clothes was now gone, disheveled, her beauty was even more pronounced in his eyes. Dimmed by the obvious unease she now felt, she appeared softer than she ever had before, defenseless, sweet and a pistol all rolled in one. A vision so unlike her usual poised self, that, to him, was sexier than had she wore an exquisite gown.

"Well." Julia muttered feebly, gazing in his eyes.

"Well." Michael answered dully. Already aware of the risk when he leaned in and started the kiss. Each taste bred sweeter than the last or so goes the story stated by his body, and he was solely tempted to take her in the very place that she rest. But an hour in the car could never beat a weekend in his bed. The math proficiently attested to such, making the stall a necessary martyr. A dark, rutty moan thundered through his body, climbing from his throat before he spoke. "Go." He breathed against her mouth. "You need to go now."

Julia's nod came like a weightless bob, knowing he was right, but could not shake the oddity of her mood. Leaving him just did not feel the proper thing to do. "Yes. I should go." She affirmed shakily, twisting the key in the ignition behind her words. The arrogant cough of an engine then solidified her intent; purring, it timidly pawed the silence that fell. With a last wobbly smile, Julia again gazed into his eyes, perplexed why leaving felt so strange.

"Until?" Michael droned, smiling tightly, he tunneled the dark depths of her eyes.

"Until," She nodded, feeling a sudden ease from the word, Julia offered him a faint smile.

Michael's return came with a stiff nod, his expression seeming as bewildered as she felt, their objectives now being of a solitary thought.

Chapter Nineteen

The afternoon lagged relentlessly long, and evening surfed the atmosphere without pace, parking its talons deep. Torpid hours demeaned the torments she now faced, or so conferred logic recites through the tauntings in her head.

Julia had not stopped moving since charging through the entry of her house, hastily changing her clothes. She realigned the vaunt of her disheveled veneer. The interior, she neatly bottled to a shelf. Rachel and Richard then brusquely followed in exactly twenty minutes on the nose, thus granting her no time to reminisce the occurrences in her day. Having only that with which to shed her frazzle, she brought forth her most perfect parenting guise. Milking the disguise with skill, it guided the procession of a highly devoted chore.

Old work, tests and a mountain of flyers were the usual corpus ushering the school week's demise, with all needing to be weeded through or discussed. Julia readily stacked the array to a basket on the kitchen desk, delaying the tedious task for a later tackle. Line of sight, she knew, greatly guaranteed the probability of their resolve.

The kids' annual trip with their dad quickly torqued the afternoon's pulse. With packing swiftly sliding to the forefront as the mandate they most needed to confront. Remarkably, procrastination of the crucial chore had effectively carted the group to such end. As was the norm in their house, conversation on their day easily dominated an immensity of time. Spilling tirelessly from each child, it effortlessly stalked the ambit of their engaging. Rachel scored a ninety-six on her once dreaded math test. This she proclaimed, in a thorny shrill, to be a hefty two points higher than that of Kimberly Stratum, her supposed nemesis of a hundred years, or so the feud postured itself to those listening in.

"You should've seen the look on her face, mom, when the teacher said that I had the highest score. It was beyond cool!" Rachel exclaimed, her big eyes rolling with excitement. "Because her dad is a professor at some college, she thinks she knows everything. She's always bragging about how smart she is. Even when my answers are right, she always tries to make it seem as if hers would've been better. Then she tries to say it's because she's so good at explaining things. I wish she would just go away!" Rachel grunted, shoveling a handful of tops in her bag on the grounded denounce. "God!" she growled, rolling her eyes back as if to inspect an inscription on her brain. Still, her hands, in their eccentric selection, never once slowed from their task, as yet another set of pajamas made it in her case, her third thus far. "I can't seem to get rid of her! She's been in my classes since the fifth grade! When is she going to impress NASA or something, so they can come snatch her up and take her someplace far away from me? When, mom? When?" Rachel huffed loudly. Straightening from her task, a hand flew to her hip in wait, as big eyes switched their focus to then settle on her mother.

"Before I answer that," Julia stated calmly, "What did you score on your math test again?"

"A ninety-six," She announced almost as calm, a small lilt to her voice.

"So that makes your score the…" Julia frowned, as if somehow confused. "The second highest?"

"No, mom, *I* have the highest!"

"Oh." Julia hummed. Showing then the start of a smile, svelte arms folded like a leisured hassock behind her head. Leaning back in her chair, she looked, of a sudden, like a well contented cat. "I thought you started out by saying that. *You got the highest score!* Take the time, sweetheart, to be proud of yourself for that. Forget Kimberly. Be happy for you. She maybe a smart little girl, but you seem to forget, *she* is in all of *your* classes, and as you've stated yourself—since the fifth grade." Julia counseled kindly, seeing the confused expression on her daughter's face. She gave a long sigh before simplifying her point.

"Sweetie, there's always going to be someone smarter than you, prettier, better dressed or more insightful, and that's just to name a few. The trick to coping is to remember yourself through all the strife life offers you as the result of just being alive. Is a ninety-six the best you can do? And if it is, can you be proud of your ninety-six even if someone else scores a hundred? In school, life, work, relationships, whatever the title, it's never about just being the best. It's about being *your* best; and if your best makes you *the* best, then that's what having your cake and eating it too should mean. Got it?" she hummed, smiling as Rachel nodded lamely in response, and her eyes glazed as if consciousness now beckoned from a distance.

"She's always had one or maybe two points above me." She frowned, dropping her eyes slowly to the bed. She paused as if to ponder the essence of her noting. "That's not a lot, is it?"

"Not even on an alternate universe." Julia grinned musingly.

"I still have an 'A' in math, just like she does." She continued then, her eyes lifting in question to her mother's face.

"I believe I saw something to that effect when I signed your report card."

"I got a ninety-six on my pre-algebra test. The highest in the class; that's pretty good!"

"I thought you might eventually see it my way," she cheered sagely. "It was a little touchy there for a minute, but you pulled through with flying colors. Good job!"

"Thanks, mom!"

"Anytime, love." She crooned, loping to her feet. Quick steps aided her progress across the room. Hugging Rachel's shoulders, she planted a kiss on the top of her head. "By the way, if you're planning on having actual outfits to wear, you might want to unload your suitcase and try again." She muttered matter-of-factly, playfully waggling her head, she laughed. "I don't think you'll be too much in love with the things you've already packed."

Rachel's eyes bounded to the overstuffed case waiting on her bed, confusion showing on her face as she turned to her mother with a frown.

"Maybe you could start with some of the things I left out on your chair. Who knows, they might help." Julia shrugged, stepping through the door's opening. She called the reminder before advancing down the hall. "Don't take too long packing, your dad will be here soon, and don't forget to pack extras!"

Already stuffed past the realms of its capacity, the striped duffle carrier looked ready to explode. Preached crudely over his back, Richard's haste was immense, colliding with his mother. His body jerked to a sudden stop. "Sorry, mom!" He squeaked, his face instantly budding alive.

"You're all done, already?"

"I got everything!" He exclaimed eagerly, answering the next question without addressing the first.

"Everything?"

"Yes, mom," Richard groaned, looking almost frustrated with her inquest.

"How many pants did you pack?"

"Five." He blurted quickly. "And some shorts for the warm days, shirts and a sweatshirt in case there's a chill." Wagging his head to the hum of his own voice, he visually showed his count. Richard then itemized the contents of his bag as if memorized for a skit. "I have socks, underwear and pajamas." He finished, showing his pride in the veraciousness of his smile.

"Very good, and I'm guessing you don't want me to double check your bag?"

"I'm old enough to pack my bag, mom. You don't need to."

"Fine," Julia shrugged, giving in to his request. Unconcerned with the consequence of mistakes, she relinquished the point. There were enough duplicates waiting at his dad's house, to smoothly cover whatever pieces forgotten in the establishing of his independence. "Did you pack your travel bag?"

"Yes, mom," he groaned, looking again offended.

"Then what's that I'm looking at on your bed?" Julia asked drolly, and watched as his small body twisted towards the door, seeming ready to snap. His eyes bulged from its place.

"Oh." Richard groaned, spitting the word abruptly from the back of his throat. "I thought I put that in."

"I'll take this," Julia informed quickly, rolling her eyes with the budding of a smirk. Patient hands heaved the duffle from its place on his back, though a groan sailed dimly as she leveled the weight in her hand. "What do you have in here, Richard, rocks?" she grunted. "My goodness! Go grab the bag off your bed and meet me down stairs. I'll try to make room for it, but…." She sighed, gaping at the bag with disbelief now trolling her face. Julia calmly shook her head, doubting she'll accomplish such feat without losing a great few of his treasured belongings.

Another thirty minutes passed before their packing was considered fully done. By then, the kids' excitement was well brimming, woven nicely alongside the exhilaration was the prospect of no school. Thus, the thrill of their trip toppled the torrential flow. For the past five years, Fontana Dam had been a staple in their lives, a ritual for which they continue to implore. Each year for Easter break, David rented a cottage in the same quaint Carolina town. There, they spent four days fishing, horseback riding or just enjoying the company of each other, and, it's figured something they still looked forward to with bliss.

"Daddy!" the kids proclaimed with glee, their voices blaring through the house in echoic aid of the musical chimes that announced just that. And the only thing missing from the commotion that followed was the constant yelping of a dog. The usual pleasantries passed affably between parents, dawdling in a near cheery twitter, while the kids lugged their belongings to the car. Though the stubbornness they exposed in their haste was quite nearly an affront, and had she not been secured in herself and their love, she would have been insulted with their staunch determination to be on their way.

In a compromise of solace, Delia laid an arm around her waist. Both looking almost inert in their stance, they watched as the lone vehicle, in its hurry, swallowed the length of the street, waving a final goodbye as they dwindled from sight.

"I could use a cup of tea, care to join me?" Delia bidden tamely.

"Sure, mom," assenting this on the shadow of a sigh, Julia raked a hand absently through the heavy spilling of her hair, openly despondent as they reentered the house. Tea was her mother's remedy for any and every affront, similarly so for the merest ails. You name it, and her mother will cure it with a cup of herbal tea, or at the very least, start the onset of a miracle ministered in a cup. Still, she grew to cherish those times for the monuments that they are, finding them more special the older she got. She'd since learned the secret of life's most titanic troubling over the imbibing of tea. Yet, in all truth, the ailment that now plagued her this day, would take a river damming at her door to calm the tumultuous riles she obviously had.

"Are you feeling okay, dear? You don't look yourself today. Maybe you're coming down with something?"

"No." Julia shrugged lightly, putting on her most relaxed façade. She smiled, "just tired. I think doing this script took more out of me than I expected," she droned. Knowing that that was, by far, the most truth, in her circumstance, she was willing to give.

"You could always come with us. You know we'd love to have you." Delia encouraged sweetly, placing a brimming cup on the counter. She quietly studied her daughter's face, a hint of concern showing in her eyes.

"Actually, I'm thinking of going another route." Julia hummed, wondering what her mother's response would be, should she offer her a hint of her weekend plans. *I'm going to satisfy my cravings, mom.* Julia smirked nimbly, imagining well the look of shock that was certain to mask the beauty of her face. "I'm thinking of going to a resort." She announced instead. "Maybe treat myself to the spa." She smiled, proud of the half-truth given in the statement itself. Michael's home, as it stood, had much the evocative presence of a resort in its exquisite features, and she did so intend to treat herself to the amenities he offered, or, at least, have him treat her. Whatever it takes to get her body back on the road to being itself, she'd gladly pay, at least for the duration of a weekend. Besides, spending a weekend with her mother's friends was not to be rumored, by any, as her idea of fun, no matter how much she loved her mother. Iris and Gail were two very sweet women, both of whom had lost their husbands, as well. But their children's and grandchildren's' lives only stay fresh for so long, yet the stories were constantly replayed regardless of the tales themselves.

"Good! It's about time! God knows you're too young and too pretty to live your life like a widow." Delia assured in a soft grumble, hitching her body to a seat at her daughter's side.

"Don't start, mom. You'll get your blood pressure all fired up." She smirked, hoisting the cup to her mouth. Her eyes dipped carefully over the rim to acquire the green tinting of her mother's.

"Start what? I gave you a compliment. All I said was, it was about time you did something nice for yourself. I don't see how that's starting something." She protested with a light shrug. "I mean, the fact that I get out of the house and see more people in a month than my daughter does in a year. A daughter almost half my age, mind you, what's there to say about that?" Delia shrugged.

"So I guess that means I should be getting out more often then? Is that it? Will that make you happy?" Julia asked with a sweetened smile.

"Immensely. Now do you see how little it takes to make your mother happy? You'd think you'd be falling all over yourself to do it more."

"This is really good tea, mom. I really like the mint. It's one of my favorites."

"Fine, I can take a hint. I only have one last question." At Julia's sluggish acquisition of her eyes, Delia discerned it best to make the matter quick. "Have you heard anything at all about your secret admirer?"

"Nothing," she grunted, her eyes sobering in a flash.

"He's still sending you flowers, I see. I'd love to meet him."

"Me too, so I can set him straight. And, if all else fails, he can have a cool piece of my mind."

"That's probably why he hasn't shown himself, dear. Maybe he knows you more than you think. Smart man." She smiled, barring its full radiance behind her cup. "I like him."

"You would, wouldn't you? You'd like anyone who has a penis to hijack my life." Julia gently mocked.

"There's nothing wrong with having a penis in your life, dear. In fact, they come in quite handy." Delia smiled, giving a light shrug. She clarified. "And no, not anyone would do. But you don't know until you try, now do you? A man, who takes the time to send you flowers and poetry without any attachment, deserves to be listened to. He deserves a chance."

"But there is an attachment, mom. He wants something; namely me."

"So?" She asked blandly. "It's good to be wanted, and I never said you had to marry the man. I said he deserves to be given a chance. That's all. Dating comes in many forms, dear. How many spouses or near spouses can say they've gotten poetry from their partner? The effort one puts into their cause speaks much of who they are. That's something worth remembering, above all else." Adopting a casual poise to the matter, she sampled another sip of her tea, knowing it best to curtail the length of her point. "I'm going to finish packing. You think about what I said. A woman needs more in her life than kids and work, Julia." She sang sweetly. "She needs someone to whisper her hopes and dreams to. It's a necessary antidote needed in life." Delia assured coolly, wheedling her way to the door. She gave her daughter a regaling smile as a precursor to her departure before vanishing through.

Slightly irked, Julia sighed thickly; her mother's needling now strumming in her head. And her eyes, in reticence, scrubbed neatly at the contour of Delia's disappearing back. It was not as if she hid fully from life, she groaned in answer to herself. Her accomplishments, thus far, spoke other than that. Nor had she been unhappy with the way she'd managed her time. Until Michael, she'd never felt the urge or need to question any element of her choices. In all her travels, had she met someone that made her feel as he does, she would have happily given him the chance needed. It was just too bad the baggage that trailed who the man was, his life being too fast, too fake and much too invasive for her to ever be swayed. Too much of the caged compartments of who a person is, emerge like a spatter in the public's eye, and smeared too perfectly so for him to ever be a comfortable fit. If a mistake was made, the sorrow of that was not only his to resolve, but for everyone else to judge. Only family should be able to do that. Yet, in a matter of hours, she would need to put all that aside for the sake of this hunger she now had.

Just thinking about him made her body respond. Coasting forward like a ripple, the memory of his kisses still stood prominent in her head. She could still feel, quite profoundly, every nibble that he gave. Julia's groan grew curt in the heckling silence, already needing something to shave the smoldering edges of her yearn. This, starting with the soothing scent of lavender in a bath. The relaxing fragrance, she hoped, would grant her the succor she so badly needed for sleep.

Kismet, it would seem, rebuffed all strives or pleas. It contrived its own plot. For, the two hours that followed, saw near no effect in her strategy. With a bath, a glass of wine, and a movie behind her, she was no better composed than she was at the afternoon's start. Inside, she was fully angst. It took another two glasses of wine and a documentary to finally grant her the respite for which she begged. Yet that, too, was a temporary mend, as she woke two hours later from a dream that near singed the edges of her sheets. They still glowed in crimson sparks as she lay panting. There was no cooling her mind or her body then.

The house quietly drew a somber breath in the midst of her body's turbulent surge. Exhaling softly, it waits patiently for the liveliness of the kids' return. Julia felt the arduous nips of melancholy drifting mercilessly through each room, chilling the space with its icy breath. For it was not only the buoyant silence that slings itself upon the house, but the quiet breakfast that would surely come. Scrambling for one, did not come with the same gaiety, when four was the usual amount.

Julia's groan trundled loudly in the darkness of her room, unable to find comfort or sleep. Her mind simply refused to take solace or rest. Morning yet stood at some distance, so told by her clock, and a glance in the direction of her window promptly attested to the verity of that. As if wishing the blackness gray, Julia glowered anxiously at the blank slats of her blinds. And another groan sailed weakly through the muted space. Frustrated with the ongoing verve yet stapled to her body, Julia sprang from her bed. In a slow lope, she jogged quietly through the house, hoping the exertion would somehow do the trick to distract her mind.

"One thirty-six? Jeez, what the hell?!" She gasped, coming to an abrupt stop, her brown eyes cut crossly athwart the offending display. "Could this be anymore pathetic?" she grunted, rolling her eyes towards the window with her query. The inaudible strut of a cat caught her eyes as she peered through the ebon mask of morning's inaugural stance. Wiped from vision like some conjured apparition, in an instant he was gone, ingested in the shadows, as if but a meal. "This is ridiculous!" She grumbled to no one but the denseness of night. "You're not eighteen, for God's sake, and it's not your first time!" she scolded. "Just settle down. Please, just settle down and be cool!"

Upon return, her bedroom stood as desolate as it was in her leaving, seeming to sense her unrest. She paced the interior like an animal about its cage, now badly in need of being freed. Julia closed her eyes and allowed her mind the freedom to wander as it willed. Yet, all that surfaced was the magnificent features of his face.

Michael's face still yet pressed to her breasts, waded to view the instant she closed her eyes. His tongue sweetly bathing her body, or a hand working the inside of her thighs, setting her body aflame. They screamed brashly, what she already knew. Another quick look at the clock confirmed the obvious truth, only thirty minutes had thus far been eaten off the time. "Well," Julia shrugged. "If ten was perfect then three should be outstanding." She asserted, and her stomach immediately plunged with the news of her declaration, feeling, suddenly, laden with rocks. *Shouldn't he be at least a little pleased?* She asked in her head. In a macho, egotistical kind of way, shouldn't he be a little glad to see her? To get the girl to succumb is masterful, but to get the girl to come to you in the middle of the night, that's ingenious.

A bevy of reasons were quickly slung by the wayside in her call to arms. Reasoning she needed to help her out the door. "What if he's with someone else?" she sighed. After the way he felt against her, she could not fault him for accepting the readiness of alternative route. She did refuse his every request, and regardless of urges, she had no claims to stake. "If he's with someone else, wouldn't it be best to know now?" Julia again asked, finding no place to set her comfort, as no answer sailed back to her in response.

A quiet fume seethed through her as she entered the stylish bathroom, staring at the dusky reflection of herself, while her mind yet galloped. Why would he go after her if he had someone else in mind? She griped, unable to let go of such thought, feeling as afraid as she was anxious. *Isn't that what he's known for?* She reminded herself dully, unsure of what should be her next move. With sleep forgotten, her body only wanted one thing, and that one thing was her biggest concern. "Let's get this over and done with." Julia tartly advised her replicate self. Solidifying the decree with a firm nod, she then ducked in her closet. Stuffing a few necessities in her overnight bag, she hastily got dressed. Drafting a quick note to her mother, since getting interrupted was the last thing she wanted for the weekend she had planned.

Chapter Twenty

Propelled by the cadence of time, her forty minute jaunt came to a terse end, erstwhile than that which was planned, discernible thence by the stupefied glare she now fired at the rustic metal gate.

Thoughts on security surrounding the great manse, had not surfaced once during the animated rows she perpetually had with herself. Although, now with her sensibilities fully reinstated, it also dawned that she had no means in which to contact the man, none that were of consequence at this hour of the day. His email-address, now, did her no good. Not if she expected to have a solution before the designated hour, or the next day. But his number, be it private or the professional twitter that went with one's office, had not been disclosed to her, and at the moment, communicating with his house was what she needed to accomplish most.

Phillip had always been the poignant anchor in their corporate alliance. The principal in whatever she needed to discuss, and in all that time, she had thoroughly enjoyed the comfort of having their association as such. Thinking him reserved, Julia thought it sensible to stay clear of their host and the palpable irkings he roused in her. She saw no need to have his number then, when an email-address provided all the contact obligatory to their work. That is, until this minute.

So, what now, Julia? Her frenzied mind asked, and the condescending tone rending her question, did not go fully undetected by its host. Julia pressed her lips together firmly in thought, consulting the many realms of logic, she rifled through her predicament and the possible solutions available for use. There was no room to drive around the antediluvian-looking gate, and no intercom on which to announce her presence. A horn would likely wake the neighbors faster than it would him, although she somehow doubted that fact. She had yet to see any signs to substantiate life in the vicinity outside of his. Still, she had never thought it necessary to ask, and therefore need not attempt that route, should the reverse be true.

"Well?" Julia asked in the silence of her car, waiting as if expecting an answer, she sighed when none came in return. Would she have the courage to come back if she left? She asked, and a dozen questions tumbled through her head regarding that fact, all of which now only aided her fears. "Well I'm not going back!" She announced defiantly to the car, her tone summoning no reproach from the silence as if expecting there would be. "And sitting here until morning is definitely not the option I want." Reticently, Julia shouldered her purse, stuffing the overnight bag in the back. She covered it with an odd collection of towels and toys. Smartly taking her cellphone in hand, she palmed a small canister of pepper spray in the other. *Just in case,* Julia muttered through the whirlwind in her head, remembering the functioning flashlight on her phone. She proficiently settled her mind to the petrifying thought. With another quick check of her surroundings, Julia cautiously stepped from her car, manually locking her doors. She then tepidly charged the obstruction in her path.

The morning's crispness quickly swaddled her with its chill, kissing the soft skin of her face. It immediately rewarded her choice of attire. Wearing the matching jacket to her stingy top seemed the one decision to pay dividend this day. As the air—for one ludicrous enough to roam the premature dawn—could be perceived as cold, it nipped frostily at the skin. The color of her clothes was also a happy plus, black rendering her virtually invisible under the dense cover, since unwanted attention was not her intent.

Charily, Julia stalked the archaic, metal gate, looking like a matador sizing his bull. She established her point of attack. Crouching beneath the straggling limbs of trees, Julia gingerly dodged the rustic post, crawling through the barb-like cluster. Shrubberies and weeds tore angrily at her clothes. The deterrence was compelling to say the least, and had it not been for her fortitude in advocating her progression, her strive would have ended in exactly the place it began.

"I can't believe I'm doing this," she whispered cheekily in the dark, shaking her head sadly at the thought. And as if to add injure to the exclusivity of pain, it occurred to her, in what seemed like the flipping of a switch, that her shoes were highly inappropriate for the excursion she was currently on. Thankfully, her mules offered aspects similar to that of its kin, protecting her feet in part like a sneaker would.

The night stood as a blithe symphony of sounds, and the woods around her part-nered its splendor with the accompanying of an auditory bliss, though for her, the music sat as a mere backdrop to her grumblings. With every step, Julia grew more staggered by the impetuousness of her choice. Understanding the truth in the danger she now faced, yet furthering her drive regardless of the ruction going on in her head.

Senselessly traipsing through the pitched belly of a forest at an asinine hour—one purportedly reserved for thieves—to then offer her body on a platter to a man. "*What are you thinking?*" She asked, a hint of derision spiking her tone. "This is not you." She counseled with a sigh, grinding to a full stop. "How do you live down an exploit like this?" Julia catechized in a lame drawl, followed quickly by the explosive blast of her breath. She gazed out at nothing but black. Swallowed in the thick of it, it surrounded her at every end.

The new moon's feeble glow barely penetrated the compressed blackness itself. Ingested fully, she stood obstinate, though fear and indecision clutched her boldly, as well. Squared by the empty offerings of the woods, behind her, the security of her car beckoned, while the comfort of a man waited to her front, though knowing her disgruntled feet had already carried her far. Should she close the book and consider this matter done? She groaned, again peering through the dark in wonder. Fear of the unknown shrewdly rattled her nerves, pushing her onward. It gave little beyond the usual trimmings in answer of her voluminous inquest. Not wanting to retrace the darkness, Julia passively ambled the graveled road, though it did not ease the unending ramblings in her head.

One by one, Julia evaluated, argued and rebutted every decision she made. Until the massive gate lay bare to her gaze. The thick iron cordon reared unyielding, barring further progress, it stood stark between her and where she wanted to be.

Every summation, once made, now barreled through like an anchor in her head, willing her, like a blazed weapon, to the very place that she stood. *Once you touched that bell, there will be no going back, are you prepared for that?* Julia's mind hastily asked, and the words, slogging like iced fingers, clambered up her spine. A shudder swiftly stirred through her body. The frightening warn amplifying the intensity it lent, and whether it materialized from the question itself, the barraging thumps in her chest, or the night's chill. The reason was patently unclear at that time. Does she really want to know if he's with someone else? She groaned feebly, tasting the bitter zest of something not quite understood. The unknown and the hour were like barbs in her brain, growing intensely in height, it made choosing harder than she expected it would.

"How angry will he be with a stunt like this?" She asked with a heavy sigh. Three fifteen is a horrid hour to call on a friend. With an acquaintance, it was an indefensible act. Of a sudden, her lonely bed did not seem nearly as hostile as it once was. In fact, tossing alone now seemed an enticing treat, far preferable to the wretched unknown that now awaited her.

Swerving in a flash, Julia trotted in the direction of her car, her feet thrashing the hardened dirt as it would an enemy from hell itself. One who had since whispered her name, her movement bred faster than the onset of her journey to that very spot. Quite suddenly, the flogging eased its demented pace, and the progress of her retreat precipitously stopped. "No. Finish this, Julia!" She scolded through a stern yell. "Just get it done. Whatever the result, you end it tonight!" Sedating her qualms with an assemblage of reins on her galloping pulse, she greedily drank in the brittle morning air. Returning to the towering postern, in what favored a snail's crawl, she inched closer on her second try.

The stern structure gaped menacingly at her timid approach. Seeming to show a broadened sneer in its breadth, it wondered on the audacity she showed, and why she dare to venture near. Ignoring her dread, Julia mimicked the deceptive charge of a bull, jamming her fingers against the protruding knob. She lingered longer than sanity expressed that one should. The old, brassy name plate grabbed the light from her cellphone as she shifted it in hand, "Hills and Dunn's Holdings" it read, and the age of the plaque felt somehow judgmental to the choices she made.

All at once the night's noise abruptly stopped, as if the bell rang, like a shot, in the surrounding wilderness. The woods continuous chatter seemed to quaver no more. In the silence, Julia wondered on his security and the state of his sleep. Was he a deep sleeper? Her nerves asked then, and her heart pounded anxiously against the barrier of her chest with her wonder on that. Shaking her already trembling body, every negative thought then boiled through her overwrought brain. If he answers, what kind of reasoning could she give him that would make much sense of the occurrence or make it okay? "God, what am I supposed to say." She asked in a whisper. "I'm sorry. I was just—no," she groaned, tossing the opener out, Julia searched for the perfect explanation, one that could lay smooth in the telling. "I'm sorry. I couldn't sleep." Julia sighed distantly, thinking back on the afternoon's euphoric display. "The truth is," she murmured, taking a long breath, her words fell like a plea in the voice of another. "I couldn't get you out of my head, and I really need you to make me feel like that again." She tested, her voice seeming breathless, submersed raptly in the memories of his kisses.

The heavy gate groaned loudly in response. Jerking with a start, it slowly relaxed its stance. Like a soldier standing down from his post, it relinquished its guard. Julia stared at the ghostly opening in awe. Shocked, she looked unsure of her next act. A gaggle of seconds passed before awareness dawned. Jolting her into action, she hastily bypassed the iron guard. The gate's growl pierced the atmosphere's chill, echoing from the blackened woods. Its cry sailed like the judder from a clowder of feral cats, straining against the quietude of the place, as it again retrieved its menacing stance. Suddenly, a wash of headlights flooded the soupy black, lighting the gravelly path. The deep throttle of a truck's engine stroked the surrounding softness, quieting as the blinding beams converged on her body.

"Are you alright? What are you doing, where's your car?" Michael rumbled, his tone verging the knoll of a reprimand—or so it seemed in her head. It soared light over the throaty twang of the truck's engine.

"I had to leave it at the gate."

"Why? Why didn't you call me? I would've met you."

"I'm sorry. I don't...well. I don't exactly have your number. I'm sorry." Julia crowed wearily, adjusting her stance as if to brace herself for an impending assault. It's now or never, she groaned. "I know we agreed on ten bu—"

"Get in the truck before I paddle you right here!" Michael growled, taking hold of her hand. He towed her to the truck himself. Opening the door, Michael parked her in the passenger seat without spending another word, and was around the truck in what felt like a blink. With his smile locked tight, he settled in his seat, though he shortened the volume it displayed. Brandished without the usual flash of porcelain to brighten the spread, a strange expression convoyed the modest exhibit, looking, in part, unlike his witty self. He pushed the truck sharply in reverse, depriving the silence of further adage as he drove. In what felt like a trice, the grumbling of the engine stopped, parked expertly in front of the expansive house in the likeness of a docile bull. A new tick saw Michael posted at the passenger door.

With a deep, cleansing breath, Julia collected herself, knowing this would be the last phase to her adventure, one last hurdle to climb before the end. Michael's hand rose for the handle of her door and her heart promptly sped. He had not given a smile or uttered a word since she entered the truck, and she could not help but wonder on the reason for that. Was he mad? With anxiety well spiked, her body mimicked the engine's putter like leaves caught in the eye of a persistent gust.

"Would you like to come in?" Michael asked in a low whisper, seeing her hesitation, he left her the space to gather herself. With a slow nod as her response, she tentatively took the hand he offered. Icy fingers crawled atop his, almost freezing to the touch. They trembled as he swallowed them in warmth, tucking them against his body as he led her to the house.

The heavy door closed behind them without pause, folding like the entombing flap on an envelope, the house suddenly went still behind the culminating deed. At long last it was the finale. All that was left now was for her to collect the prize. Julia turned towards him with an explanation on her lips, fighting her nerves in what she knew needed to be done.

"I'm sorry. I…I, I couldn't sleep." She began in a stumble.

"Me neither." Michael shrugged. "Would you like something to drink?" he asked like a prodigious host, his tone almost friendly, though it seemed somehow tight.

"I know this is a very bad time to call," she again started, growing more nervous with each breath. She ignored his request. He did not look very interested as to why she was there hours ahead of the schedule they planned. Was he mad? *Oh, God, of course he's mad! What was she thinking?* "I'm sorry. I shouldn't have—I–I should just…well…" she stumbled, sighing weakly. She attempted her cause once more. "I was thinking maybe…I, I'm sorry. I should just go. I'm sorry to have bothered you. I shouldn't have come. I don't know what I was thinking." Muttering this, her shoulders turned as if preparing to walk the extension of a ship's plank.

"Please don't." He rasped, his deep voice cutting through her thoughts like a siren's dissonant warn, advising of the dangers to come. It halted the evolution of her steps, terminating all protest at once. "I'm trying, Julia." Michael rumbled as he stepped close. "I'm really trying hard to give you the space you seem to need. I don't want you go." He hummed, grateful for the normalcy of his tone, since he was certain, could she read his thoughts, such knowledge would not, nor could it have alleviated any splinter of the disquiet she now felt. "I'm really very glad you're here. But you seem to need some time."

"I thought maybe you were angry."

"About what?" Michael grunted, his face showing off a skeptical glare. "Having a beautiful woman wake me with specific intention?"

"Well, it wouldn't be that if you were not alone," She countered nervously.

"You wondered if I moved down the list?"

"Well…."

"Since I couldn't have you I must have, right?" Michael groaned, shaking his head, he smiled. "You know, contrary to what you may have read about me, I'm not the rolling moss they say that I am. I've done some growing."

"I'm sorry. I'm…I'm just…" grinding to a halt, a heavy sigh plummeted from lips already parted with angst. Quietly, she offered him a tame nod, exhibiting a tinge of understanding she did not feel. Her eyes fell to his chest in reticence, wanting badly to explain what it was that she felt, though not knowing the answer herself; words failed to unravel from the jumble in her head. As if to taunt the roiling in her body, his robe draped further open to her view, showing off the arc of his muscular chest. It dragged her interest like water to a thirsty rug. Obeying the call of her body, Julia slowly rested her forehead to his chest, closing her eyes as if to rest. Michael's arms swathed her in an instant without limit or pause, pressing her snugly against his frame. His body warmed against her like a heated cape, dispersing its warmth to the very crux of her being. His scent scaled up her nostrils like an hallucinogenic on the hunt, and he smelled even better than what she remembered of his usual scent.

The minty flavor of mouthwash drifted close, draping them lightly as he pressed his face to her hair. His lips then walked gently down the side of her brow, touching warmly to her skin, it lingered in its place. Julia lifted her face to his and he tenderly brushed a kiss to her lips. Soft like a feather, Michael plied her and she stayed, hungry in her want for more. A tremor waded hard through her body, touching him almost as boldly as it did her, and his kisses instantaneously stopped.

"You're still trembling, are you still scared?" he asked in a whisper, his breath wrapping warmly around her lips. Her head slowly bobbed in answer, and she promptly buried her face in the slopes of his chest. "Of me?" Michael asked in follow.

"I don't know. I think…I think it's of me." Julia sighed, wagging her head as she spoke.

"What would you like to do?" Michael asked softly, needing her to be at ease, as regrets will only leave a putrid taste in her mouth come tomorrow, thus being of little benefit to him then.

Julia stood silent, pondering the prospects slated to his question, though still yet feeling the heat of his touch. Should she take the out he now offered? *I could be back in my own bed before dawn.* She debated in her head, though already knowing the correct answer to choose. "Maybe I could borrow your shower?" she asked finally in a small voice. "I think a hot shower might help me to relax." She reasoned, and the effort was as much, for him, as it was for herself. "May I?"

"Whatever you need," Michael smiled, quickly dispelling a seditious vision of her naked from his mind. He regulated the erupting thought, dragging his hands firmly down her arms in a long caress, before taking hold. He eased her from his chest. In silence, he led her to his suite, past the very point that was once the source of her worry. "Make yourself at home." He mumbled as they entered the modish bathroom. "Do you need something to wear? There's a robe in the closet." Michael announced without waiting a response, pointing clumsily towards the closet door. "Take as long as you need." He assured hoarsely, his eyes lingering on her face. Abruptly, he turned from the room without further adage, sharply pulling the door shut at his back.

Hastening feet carried him from the room faster than he remembered traveling, with visions of her wet now playing in his head. Michael groaned sharply from the promise offered with the perceptive show, dropping his body to the chair behind his desk. He wondered on whether she was truly aware of her looks, or of the effect she had on him. She smiles in that decadent way and completely misses the sparks she lights. There was nothing about her that did not have him panting for the wont of more, and the reality of that had him turned inside out of himself.

Michael scrubbed his hands roughly across his face, smearing both palms, in a sluggish descent, over his eyes and forehead as if to wipe clean the puzzle from his mind, and a long sigh sprayed from the vessel of his hands in reaction to such musing. He had spent most of the night thinking about the beauty of what transpired between them and the feelings they roused, and the other part with her well immersed in his dreams. The tormenting was his only reason for being awake at this hour. and why it was so nice to hear her private conversation outside the gate. It's hard to believe she walked all that way to adhere to a pledge, and most especially so at this hour, putting herself in danger. Tomorrow he'd have to rectify that.

Quietly moving through the halls, Michael hovered and waited from a safe distance. Cautious in his deception as he strolled pass the room she inhabited, for his inquisitive parts were unremitting in their push. Yet, only the sound of rushing water came back across the barrier to his ears. Aimless in his wandering, he secured the residence as it once was, while his thoughts, in its raucous musing, grew riotous. Angst gnawed incessantly at both brain and body, and the urge for a drink now nipped at his gut, anything to quell the edges of anticipation that sprouted stronger yet.

With her shaking finally ebbed, Julia stepped from the shower and grabbed an oversized towel from the rack. Now all that remains was the wide variant of her nerves. Wrapping the towel to her body, Julia stared at the reflection of herself, seeing the heavy tendrils of her hair fall about her like slackened cloth. Her expression seemed unrecognizable to her, as if she gazed at someone who shared her salient features, but was yet unknown. All the usual attributes remained intact, yet something about her felt different. "What are you doing here?" she whispered to the rattled replica of herself, smoothing a hand across her face as she spoke. Though only an anomaly of herself gaped back in awe, and it gave no answer to the issues she shared. Contemplating the isolating barrier from the mirror, Julia sighed, knowing he waited for her on the other side. "Is it really time for this?" she asked woefully, squaring her shoulders as if to buffer the sting of an attack. "It's been long past months and years in time, Julia. Go get something for yourself." The answer sailing to her in a sharp, amplified pitch, sounding unlike her own, and she knew the message was no lie. "It's time to get something for you." She answered stoically at last, nodding as if to confirm the answer with her reflected self.

For the fourth time in as many minutes, Michael's rounds took him through his office to his suite, strolling with an illusory mien. His eyes slowly browsed the room as if admiring the marvel of the space. On his fifth tour idolizing the wondrous sight, the bathroom door creaked. Wearing naught but a towel, she paused hesitantly in the arching of the door, her hand rested gently across the plush mat as if to prevent its descent. Dark hair, now wavier than it was straight, draped heavily around the narrow shape of her shoulders, seductively cupping her face. Soft light drenched her body in full warmth, radiating alluringly across the caramel of her skin, it published like the dim silhouette of a spotlight showcasing its find, and he took his time drinking her in. She stood stock still while he savored the deliciousness of the view, as if rooted to the floor. No smile came in greeting, and no words were exchanged between them. She just stood tranquil watching him watch her.

"Are you…? I'm sorry I——" Michael croaked tightly in start. Clearing his throat, it took him but four steps to capture his prize, his mouth plunging as he engulfed her in a forceful embrace.

Everything she felt, wanted and needed since the onset of their rousing, flooded her body at once, and she happily answered every demand that he made. Julia's body swayed against him in a hungry caress, singeing every hair on her body with its heat. The towel slipped sharply from her breasts with the force their bodies lent, dipping further still with the intensity of their clasp. The firmness of his chest caressed the soft mounds as proficient as the stroke of a hand, grazing the tips of their soft bed. His hand moved over her body in an enchantingly firm stroke, aiding the drifting towel to the floor. The sensual slide tenaciously pressed her naked body further into his, enticing her to mold profoundly to the hardness of him, and through the fabric of his robe. She became well acquainted with the stalwart form of his body. His kisses then dove deep, controlling every thought. He made them forage as one. Julia sighed hungrily as a result of his stringent demands; no longer feeling the cruel stab of her fear, for only the sensation of his mouth clambered through her senses, driving her onward up an arduous climb. His kisses sweetly drenched her in delight. Trembling hands moved to the inside of his robe, undoing the loose tie, she felt his pulse quickened under the surf of her hands.

Michael drank her in as if dawn bore them no promise. Taking all the sweetness her mouth offered and more, this, in recompense of the nigglings he has had to endure, and she was oh…so…very sweet. Obliging her roaming hands, his gentle shrug gave aid to the prohibitive robe's descent, brushing his calf as it fell silently to the floor. His mouth then slowly trailed down the slender lines of her neck to her breast. Taking possession, she closed her eyes and held him close, while he, in his primal forage, savored their peaks with controlled greed, moving from one to take the other in his mouth like a feast.

Heated kisses again recaptured her mouth, taking great care in the climb. His hands manipulated the balmy regions of her body with skill. Julia's hands walked boldly over his chest, falling tantalizingly down the hard cliffs of his stomach. They sank assertively inside the waistband of his shorts. Pushing the garment slowly over his hips, she followed the measured descent, escorting the scrimp slacks over the hard curves of his buttock to his thigh. The laggard fall left no barrier stable between them, pasting the sensitive layers of bronze skin to its deep caramel liken, hunger steamed staunchly to the toxicity of famish. And in approval, he stroked her with a firmness that granted a delicious promise of things to come, watering her with a fervor she had long missed. Michael swept her from the floor in a pall of muted swiftness, carrying her to his bed, while his mouth yet fed.

Her skin, with the subtle scent of a bloom, scraped him like the dainty petals themselves, searing like heated silk as she moved against him, and it was almost painful not to plunge and devour her then. Instead, he ravenously requested her mouth, knowing, with all certainty; he needed to take his time.

Smooth and robust against her thighs, he acquainted her with every inch of his body as he grounded the fullness of his bulk against the sweetness of her frame. Growling his desire like a dark warn, his mouth thence worked every inch of her slender frame. Almost bruising in the most magnificent way, he forced torrents of desire to burn through every port that she held. Michael's hand dropped slowly down her stomach and across her thighs. Touching her with a gifted gentleness that swept her up in its intensifying howl, a long, slow moan of acquiescence slipped past her lips. Warm kisses ambled the swells of her body with the sureness of a scorch-less fire, moving leisurely across her navel, he kissed her crevices fervently and to every avail, pausing only in earnest to edge the bed. Gathering a condom, he sat back and promptly dressed himself. Gifting her, by scripted decree, her first view of his stellar physique, and he was truly...beautiful to behold, even to glutted eyes. Though to famished senses, he sat simply at the cusp of pulchritudinous. Looking like a well forged weapon, consummate in its design, its warranted to bring one, with each quarry, to their knees. Michael recaptured her mouth with a ravenous verve that matched her own, feeding hungrily from lips that were well parched. A mingling of tremors stole her body and her breath, as firm strokes nestled him home.

Julia sighed darkly with the sureness of his stride, throwing her head back with the deliciousness of a fire that fully consumed. Her breath wafted like the sequence of a familiar song. One that had been too long since expelled and well repressed in its verse, though memory hailed as tides of pleasure waded through her body. She had almost forgotten what it felt like to be penetrated. The sweet, blissful fire that such filling ignited, or how such dulcet surge heated the very balls of your toes. Her hips rolled greedily to his in a test of will, as if retrieving the memory of something that had suffered the spoils of neglect, though, in its minute facets, was well missed. She hugged him deep inside, purring affably on his slow retreat.

His groan answered the melodic hum lifting from her throat, and the dexterity of his hands was unsteady as he caressed her breasts. Her embrace grew bolder with the fervor they built, gluttonous in the sustenance of her drive. She squeezed him tighter each time that she moved. Michael's body replied more ravenous with each climb, each movement more lyrical than the first. Indulging the mellifluous dips, he basted her body in a sweetness that was wild. From both inside and out, she trembled with the potency of her unconstrained appetite, not knowing whether the feed or the feeding drew her hunger more. As if on the last gradient of a hill, Michael's breath grew jagged, slowing his pace, the exquisite deploy of his waltz uncannily stopped.

"Wait…" Michael whispered breathlessly, a long groan vibrating in his throat. With his eyes shut tight, his lower lip was snugly caught between his teeth. "Don't…move." He whispered then, aware of the precipice at which he now rested. His body trembled as he lowered his face to hers. "Shhh…Just–just give me a minute." He sighed against her mouth, searching his mind for something less stirring with which to place his focus. He blew out the content of his lungs. He had had fantasies about her, and his creative contemplations had gotten him close, but they were mild in comparison to the sweet inferno of the actual ride. "You—" he rasped in a heavy breath, rolling his eyes heaven-ward. "—mmmm." He growled and tested his movement once more.

Julia waited the propensity of his wont. She waited until his strides were once again rhythmic, rolling her hands over his body in acceptance of his pace. Her hips swayed deliciously to the riff of his mating dance, squeezing him tighter with each rise. His breath again grew heavy with the maddening pace, and of a sudden, he pressed himself taut against her. All movements, as one, instantly stopped, and the room, in answer, fell unexpectedly still. The weight of his breath slapped the air with a harsh, almost angry boldness, suppressing the quietude of room. It soared no different than a shrill. A low hiss sailed from him then, conveying more to the listener than just the discomfiture he felt. He rolled his slackened body from hers, settling indignantly on his back.

"I'm sorry." Michael whispered throatily, grounding out yet another long breath. He threw an arm across the hard doming of his brow. "I don't know what…this–this has never happened to me before—ever. I don't…" he sighed, coming to an abrupt stop. The room again went instantly still.

With her body still ablaze from the ferocious petition he pitched, a long breath was needed to squelch the magnitude of her regret. Julia's head turned slowly in the thick mat of her pillow, her eyes quickly assessing the exquisite physique of the man, now laying almost crumpled at the far edge of a king-size bed, a sullen stench now wafting from his body. She could well see the strain of his bruised pride advertised full in the way his body stayed, and could also imagine how he might think she feels about his matinal finish. But she had come too far to stop before the desired end. She would not be that easily deterred.

"I'll take that," she murmured as she rolled to his side. "As a compliment, of sort." Julia smiled, pulling his arm from its cover of his face. She gave him a quick kiss. "My turn!" she grinned invitingly, her eyes still dark with myriad of possibilities as she rolled over him and sprang from the bed. Her smile grew wicked as she turned to look him over. Mischief and hunger boiled as the dominant showing in the expression that lingered on her face. The length of her strides was profoundly measured, deliberate in its unfurling. Shown thus from the lazy sway of her hips to her purposeful wait by the door, granting him a long view of her curvaceous form. She confiscated herself behind the door like some act in a cabaret, awarding him the time and space she sensed he needed.

Once alone, Michael released the heavy groan that had long since waited in his chest. The quiet room only making the thick, guttural howl seem almost nascent in its dispensing. *What the hell just happened?* His mind grumbled perplexedly, normally the duration of his stamina was like a perpetual drive. Charging like a thoroughbred let loose until spent, his actions had always been purposeful and clear, and of any, he really wanted to spend his time enjoying her, relishing every aspect she had to give, and taking his time to offer his own.

Michael heaved his frazzled limbs from the bed much in the way that she had, though his action lacked the seductive grace publicized in her own. Divesting himself of the condom behind a hard jerk in its knot, he snatched his robe from the floor where it still waited. A simmering groan further threatened an already restive room, bubbling like sequential waves as he shoved his arms grouchily through the sleeves. Moving with agitated steps towards the couch, he dropped to a seat as his breath pushed hard against the extended rounding of his cheeks. Michael's eyes walked without interest across the crisp, white carvings on the ceiling, his mind grumbling madly as he retraced every chink of his steps. The ride was simply astounding, catching him off-guard as to its saporous zest, something he, most definitely, needed to address before the next try. Since disappointment, shock and the absurdity of his pride had had him frizzling before seeing the venture to its rightly end.

An assemblage of minutes passed, at what seemed a snail's pace, before the bathroom door opened once more. Julia stepped out wearing the proffered robe from the closet, smiling almost playfully as she took a seat on his lap.

"I'm really very sorry about that." Michael offered in a low, grumbly spill, his eyes scooting by her face to linger quietly on the wall at her back. The beauty of his body spoke in details far more than he was willing to say, looking almost rigid. He slumped awkwardly under her. "I don't know what happened, I—"

"How do you like to be kissed?" Julia asked softly, cutting through the spattering of his words. She was not the least interested in his homily on regrets, nor did she want his apology, since as far as she was concerned, the matter was already done. What she needed most from him was to be given more, and she needed that expeditiously. It was now time for them to start the preface of a new game.

"What?"

"How do you like to be kissed?" she purred.

"Haven't we kissed before?"

"We have. But a kiss, as with everything, comes in various methods." Julia smiled, letting her fingers play through his hair. She stroked the edge of his mouth. "I could kiss you soft," she hummed, and her mouth brushed his in a touch that was no stronger than her breath. "And slow," she purred, again stroking his body with her lips. She moved slowly to his cheek. Pushing his head back onto the pillows, she covered his body with a compilation of the downy kisses, each as soft as the air she breathes. "Or," she smiled, her gaze delving into eyes that now twinkled of their own volition, arousal marring the speckle gems. "You may prefer something a little more…giving." The words rolled from her throat with a decadence that twirled through the heart of one's soul, and the robe fell from her body with the skill of a magician's hand. Caressing his body with her own, her kisses grew firm, drawing from him the very essence of her need. She hungrily nibbled and caressed along the hard edges of his body. "Or—"

"I believe I've shown I have a profound inclination to whatever route you take." Michael whispered as her ear came near.

"There is something of a consensus in that, isn't there?" she breathed, giving answer against his mouth. Her kisses scorched like a spindle of fire itself, inciting the decadence of their passion as she went. With knees wedged firm against his hips in the resilience of her drive, she lowered herself to him. Julia rolled the fiery marsh of her body over the fiercely taut dowel of his, hearing his reply fall in a jagged breath. Michael groaned coarsely as he moved further into her, burying his face in the cliffs of her breasts, he kissed them sweetly in answer to her forge.

"Who are you?" he sighed as he lifted his face to her.

"I'm the same girl as before." Julia breathed back, taking in fully the sustenance she needed. His hands moved like flames upon her skin before settling on her hips. Allowing her the right to take all she needed, he left her to set the pace to their ritual show. Quietly abetting the ride, he moved in matching lifts to her, soaring as one in a blissful dance. They passionately devoured the other in a maddening journey through the stratosphere and back. It was a fire that burned and consumed all at once, splitting into a thousand shards before returning as one. Leaving them spent, they collapsed in stillness against each other.

Michael smiled at her lazily, his breath coming rough as he kissed the corner of her mouth, dropping his head back onto the sofa. A long, heavy sigh moved quickly through the air, rustling loose strains of her hair before crossing the top of her cheek. There was hardly a place on his body that did not still tingle from her touch, and the sumptuousness she gave seemed familiar somehow, as if from a memory fended in fog.

Julia raised her head from his shoulders and smiled serenely. In return, Michael gave the same, tracing a finger over her mouth. She purred before kissing the lean tip. "Your turn," she hummed.

"What? But I've—"

"The first one doesn't count," she teased. "I was just warming you up for our game."

"Okay." Michael droned, unsure of what else there was to say.

"Give or get?" she casually asked.

"What?"

"Do you want to give something or get something?" she explained.

"Do you mean I can choose to get what you just did to me again?"

"No. It doesn't work that way. It's about following the leader. When I lead, you have to follow and vice versa. The leader picks how and what to play, unless it's too twisted then the follower can resist. A simple 'no' should suffice there." She shrugged, kissing him softly, she smiled. "So, I hope you're ready to play because you just became it."

Michael looked her over with awe brightening his eyes, not knowing what to think, his expression showed his thoughts. "Who are you, really, and were you always like this?"

Julia laughed wittily in answer, smoothing the frown from his brow. She kissed his cheek while offering no speech. He had vehemently succeeded in informing her just how famished she really was, and in remedy, she intended to make him the buffet. "I'm just playing catch up. Disappointed?"

"That would make me a fool now, wouldn't it? And I'm no fool, at least not today. Surprise is more what I'm thinking."

"I like surprises."

"Me too, more so now than I ever thought,"

Julia's smile was almost impish, feeling no shame in her actions past. None on the radar she so diligently used as her guide. Only knowing she needed more and she needed it like she needed food. It had been a long, five year dearth to get to this end, and there will be no sleep for this stag for the residue of this night.

Chapter Twenty One

Shrouded in a cloud of black, the room sat lifeless. Void was the frisson yielded in its verve, as it, too, slumbered in wait. Julia's eyes opened slowly to wakefulness, and even through the dimness, the mewling of daylight came to her clear, though evinced behind a thick rampart of drapes. Radiant and warm, the day's brilliance merrily hailed from its blockade, clambering the dark with diminished pomp, as only a hint of sunlight touched the dormant space. Hence, it lazily speckled a mere corner of the floor.

Michael lay enervatingly on his back. His arm flexed with marooned solace across the wide sweep of his chest, the other at rest, like a trilby, above his head. The muscular slope rose with the evenness of his breath, dropping as subtly as the climb. His breath delicately walked the darkness. A thin blanket sheltered only the narrow width of his hips, leaving the protruding riffs of his body fully splayed for her perusal, and of that, she took her utmost fill. He was, without doubt, a truly beautiful specimen in every sense. Tall, lean and immensely toned, his body rivaled the predilection of a seasoned athlete. Muscular, yet agile, he lurked primed and ready for use, and even repose. She was again reminded of a stalking lion.

The dark furring on his chest was hardly visible in the dull luster of the room, amassing again below his navel. Julia's eyes lingered with interest on said display, her appreciation parading well in the darkness of their russet depths. Chiseled within that plane, his runnels flaunted a scintillating treat, more delightful to endure than it was to simply regard. The man, Julia respired with zeal, spawned an amatory reliance for sure.

Wedged almost fully to his side, the inverse end of the blanket laid across her breasts, edging the high curve of her thighs. Julia smiled in avid content, as reminiscing on the why and, too, the where, flashed as a vibrant movie in her head. Stretching languidly, her eyes again caressed his long physique, ardently applauding the display as well as the eminence of its grind. There was not much left that they had not already done. Filling the sprouting hours of the morning with their amorous vaunt, a commission approached doggedly like the exploits of a need. One that had ignited the cinders of her abstention like a sheaf of paper caught sternly in the pyre of a brush. Without glimpsing the time, she was certain not much rest was had. Arching her body like a cat, her sigh then mimicked the assonance of said animal's show of content, while her eyes, in marvel, slowly rounded the room.

Dressed in naught but the essentials, the renderings were minimal for a room of such size. Flanking the large bed, two richly toned Bombay-style nightstands, offered their opulent balance to the sleekness of the bed. Each differently carved, yet fixedly belonging as a set. Paired leather benches sat uniformed at the foot of his bed, pillared like sentinels atop a massive Persian rug, they tastefully concluded the stylish accoutering daubing the room. The space brandished, in its sparseness, a well refined grace, complimented nicely at such by a scant collection of art.

With sloth-like resilience, Julia exited the ransacked bed, silently maneuvering her way to the shower. She rejuvenated the exuberance that romped throughout her body. Everything about her felt better than it had in months, which, when dissected and researched, comprised gushily with the absence of sleep, since between them, only a minimal sum was gotten in the hours past. Seemingly freed from a compendium of herculean fret, the very air held a sweet redolence to each draught she inhaled.

"You moved." Michael rumbled as she reentered to the room, his voice sounding deeper than she remembered from just the hours before. Stretching his long body, his smile was openly welcoming. The blanket tentatively shifted with the infer of such exert at hand, almost falling clear from its place, it cleave tauntingly to his pelvic instead.

"I'm sorry." Julia smiled, adjusting the towel around her breasts, she modestly shifted her stance. Grateful she had at least remembered to brush her teeth—irrespective of the fact that her fingers were the implement used to achieve such task—the task nonetheless was done. Except for the previously offered robe, she had no means of clothing herself, not even a toothbrush to remove the musty stench of sleep. Since her bag was still tucked away safely in her car or so she hoped. "I thought a shower might be a refreshing treat." Julia quipped, eyeing the crumpled robe on the sitting-room floor. "Even an artist needs a new canvas here and there." She smiled, her eyes playful as she watched him roll from the bed, the act unfurling with a simple fluid-like stab. Michael held the blanket loosely to his front, heedless of the opposing end. It dragged like a beauteous tail at his back. With his eyes now trained to her face, his advance was not dissimilar to the picture she held in her head of a prowling lion. A beautiful glow of mixed colors shifted avidly across her skin, as if searching for a new port of attack, his smile then widened as if acquiring such goal.

"I guess I'd better get the brush elutriated then." Michael murmured in a raspy tone, giving her a last hungering look. He stepped past her to the room recently vacated by her. "By the way, whose turn are we up to now?"

"I'm not sure," Julia shrugged, her hand still propped gently across her breasts. "After such a tamp spell, it's a little tricky to keep the numbers straight."

"Hmm, why don't we just start at the top and say it's yours." Michael smirked, eyeing her through the half closed door. "I don't mind following orders."

"I'm beginning to see that." Julia smiled.

"Good. Now make yourself at home. I'll be right out." Michael invited, kicking his head towards the bed, a mischievous smile broadened before he closed the door.

The sound of rushing water danced through the silence the instant the ingress sealed, marking the air with a faint hiss, notable so only by a near imperceptible pinch. Julia quickly stripped the towel from her body, wrapping herself in his robe; she glanced numbly at the empty room. Unsure of the proper etiquette for occasions as this, she stood ridged to said spot. Should she take his suggestion and get back in bed, or would that be giving the wrong impression? And if she ventured past his bedroom door, would that be considered an invasion of his space? Deliberating such, her mind churned as a continuous storm, rolling with swells of contradicting thoughts.

His home was exquisite. There was no doubt in that fact. Everything tastefully highlighted his personality through and through. A personality she felt somehow more enlightened on, with none more obvious than the sculpture of a yawning mouse sitting drolly by the hearth. It truly articulated the humor she had since been confronted with. On the other side of the room, a small clock quietly whispered the time through the gray cover swathing the room. Perched prominently on a round, pedestal table, its rhythmic warbles seeped well through the silence. "*Noon!*" It gabbled with a flourish show of its hands. Stating the obvious in its bellows, a sudden pang granted it aid, as she had yet to have a proper meal since their lunch the day before, though at the time, it was not food that held her interest in its vice. Yet, she could not say the same for the gnawing now, for her stomach now groused otherwise to belie her decision past.

As if waiting in awe on his return, the air grew cautiously still, and the gentle hiss of water, as it hastened from the pipes, suddenly stopped. The bathroom door creaked before long, and Michael strode out wrapped in a vision of white, the stark color resting low on the breadth of his hips. A soft mist trailed his sumptuous physique like a cloud, haloing the crest of that room. It dimmed as he advanced further into the vastness of the other space.

Stopping only inches from her breasts, Michael gifted her, a slow, seductive smile. The effects of which were instantaneously fluxing, and a low purr welled in the back of her throat on just the radiance itself. Short, dark strands seemed almost black, worn slicked against his skull. It accentuated the stateliness of his looks, and again a purr pulsed from deep inside the gulch of her body. A gathering bead of moisture dripped from his still wet locks, swiftly riding the arc of his chest, in what reared wholly, like a taunt. And she could neither fathom nor reason her sudden bout of envy towards a simple droplet of hydrant. Wanting badly to lick the intrusion off his chest herself, she stifled the inkling with an indiscernible groan, letting her eyes smother the floor instead in her struggle.

"Hungry?" Michael quizzed through a coarse drawl, as if reading her thoughts, his breath stroked the wavy strands of her hair.

"The thought of eating did cross my mind." She remarked tamely.

"And what is it you see when eating comes to mind?" he asked in a warm breath, his gravelly tone softening with the dual review, stroking her fingers in a most sensual display. He smiled. "There's food, and then there's…"

"Preferably something I can masticate." Julia assured with a tame grin, liking the sensations wading through her from his hand.

"I guess you would need to keep up your strength." Michael droned, implying the absurdity of that with a wayward sigh. "To the kitchen then?" he asked, turning in the direction of his closet, he stopped. "Would you like to get your car first? We could do that quickly and get it out of the way."

"But I don't have any clothes."

"You look over dressed to me." Michael teased, crossing his arms atop the spread of his chest, his eyes lapped at her form. "You could drive my car. No one will see you either way, or you could wear something of mine. It's up to you."

"I guess what I'm wearing is fine, since no one will really see me." She shrugged.

"Good choice." Michael nodded as he exited the room. Returning in minutes to her view dressed in a soft white T-shirt and loose, athletic shorts, the look was no less appetizing than the one he wore through the many hours prior.

April now brandished its most exquisite display, as spring flaunts a splendor that paralleled none, stirring the air with new life. It called forth rapture from all things that partake in the sweetness of its air. Julia wrapped the oversized robe around, what seemed the entirety of her body, tightening the belt. She again cuffed the long sleeves, and was grateful in her adjustments that the robe was not considered full length.

Navigating the route to the showroom-style garage, an arm rode the soft curving of her hip, enforcing his presence like the steady flame of a torch. He kept her cinched to his side. Three cars gaped back imposingly as she followed him through the entrance. Each seeming to summarily ridicule her lax manner of dress, already knowing she did not belong in their midst. Of the three, only two were remotely recognizable to her limited view, that being the sleek styling of the Mercedes AMG, and the muscular domi-nance of a Buick Gran Sport. On the third, she had no clue on its make or what posh distinctiveness it possessed, situated at the far end of the room. There was no way for her to espy its name, and she felt no need to probe on something as that, though it's beauty proclaimed boldly its expense. The fourth space, she presumed, rightly housed his truck. And she could not help but wonder why they had not taken the vehicle already parked outside. As if to answer her wonder, Michael stopped at the prominent tail of his AMG, his expression brimming with mischief.

Julia's smile was almost knowing in the bold way it dispelled, shaking her head at the spectacle advertised before her, she asked. "You want to take this to the gate?"

"Can you think of a chariot that better suits you?" he intoned huskily, his smile say-ing more than the music of his tone.

"I don't think I'm dressed for this car." Julia smirked, eyeing the lustrous vehicle with a sardonic note.

"I think, actually, the opposite is truer." He rumbled, and his smile again gave voice to that of something else, easily imparting the strutting of a leer. "Get in. Let's see if we can fix that." Michael invited in a low growl, his smile widening as he skirted the car. Julia stared at the chic vehicle for a long, pensive moment before following his lead, settling herself almost timidly in her seat. She shot him a knowing smirk. "Aren't you going to straddle my stick?" he asked, his deep tone seeming to thunder through the reticence of the space.

"You don't have one."

"I can get one," he rasped, his tone dipping low, and there was no hollowness to the promise that came with his smile. "Custom made especially for you."

"Should I be holding you to that promise?"

"I was hoping you'd ask me that." He growled as he fired the engine, filling the large garage with the throaty grumble. Michael flashed the sprightliest of his smile, winking in assurance before backing the showpiece from its perch.

In the light of day, the large gate did not seem nearly as foreboding as it once did. Perhaps being seated beside the overlord himself helped that matter some, since the metal giant's devotion was well clear to her eyes, creeping open with a smooth swing. It worked in silence rather than give the usual begrudging jerk. Julia's car looked almost dejected in its abandoned state, standing desolate within the mouth of the engulfing woods. It patiently waited their methodic approach, though it stood otherwise untouched.

"Give me your keys." Michael asked as the small gate began its unbarring.

"Who's going to drive your car?"

"You are."

"You want me to drive your car—*this car?*" Julia asked in disbelief.

"I think I can trust you to handle my baby on a driveway without any other car in sight." Michael grinned, waving sarcastically at the window, he emphasized his point. "If you damage her, then I'll just have to get the repairs out of that big check we gave you."

"I don't think that check is enough for this car."

"Maybe not, but it would do nicely for repairs." He chuckled.

"Let the record show," Julia warned, dropping her keys in his hand, she flashed him a tepid smile. "I do this under the advisement of the owner himself—one Mr. Michael Dunhill, and should any damage befall his property, he will remember that this service was done solely under duress."

"The record is duly noted." He grunted with an impatient bounce of his head. "Now get in the driver's seat." His advisement coming prompt on the tail of his gruff reply, pressing his hand swiftly across her breasts, he stopped the inception of her exiting plans. "No need for that," he smirked. "Just climb over."

"Don't you need to get out for that?"

"Then I'd miss all the fun now, wouldn't I?" easing back in his seat, he smiled. "Come on over. It's not that far. Just a little stretch and you're there." Michael invited, putting the full breadth of his charm on display. Her smile, however, was more mocking than not, solicitous in its paraded. She rolled her eyes as well as her head in aid of that fact, and the luster of her suspicion gleamed remarkably bold. An audible sigh quietly scraped the silence as she touch a heel to the flat of her seat, stretching a slender leg towards his thigh. Michael shifted, widening his posture, he watched appreciatively as the bottom half of her robe fell wide. Taking the hand he offered for balance, she eased her way to his lap.

"Okay. I'm here." She announced to his beguiling face, and in assurance of such, the top of her robe fell open to his gaze. Realizing the instant it happened that it was already too late to see the rousing exhibition undone, for his hands were already moving, like a warm, slithery extension, up her thighs. As one, they rounded her buttocks in a slow stroll, gliding temptingly up the spread of her back. He guided her closer to his face, kissing the soft peak of a breast, a soft hum, given in the wild guise of a purr, crawled from his throat. "So this is why you wanted me to drive?"

"It may have crossed my mind." He droned, his voice soft against the skin.

"You want to fondle me here?"

"My car, my property, where else should I fondle you?"

"Well…" Julia started, though she could find no suitable answer to deter his ploy. After all, was she not the one to originate these rules? Her eyes searched the surrounding woods fretfully, hoping no other eyes stared back while she gaped. Since she was greatly tempted to let him do whatever he willed.

"Don't worry," Michael whispered against her throat, again as if privy to her thoughts, he softly added. "It's only for retrospection." He sighed, pulling her fully onto his lap. He guided her head to his, covering her mouth, he endowed her with a series of long, slow kisses. "Mmm…See, I told you I could get one custom made just for you." Michael murmured spryly, pushing the robe further aside. His eyes drank in the full breadth of her beauty. "You're…so…*damn* beautiful." He growled, the words climbing warmly from his chest.

"Please." Julia snorted with open cynicism. "Beautiful is hardly the word I'd use to describe me right now, I believe I left that somewhere in my closet last night."

"Are you saying my eyes lie?"

"You'd be surprised how much one's eyes can deceive them."

"If they are," he hummed, eyeing her slowly, his hands fell in a slow caress over her breasts. "Then I like what they're telling me. I like it very much."

"Then it may just end up being your downfall to be so easily duped." She groaned, trying hard to ignore the workings of his hands and the able partnering of his mouth. "Do you really want to do this here, Michael? Wouldn't it be much better inside?"

"Don't worry. I'm only tasting, that's all. But you're right. This will be a lot more fun inside, void of trifling deterrent, that is." Lifting his head, Michael pulled her robe closed, giving a last kiss to a pliant peak, he smiled. "For later," he declared then, scooting his body from under her, he exited the car. The wing-like door closed with him sending her a leer, gazing up her thighs as she adjusted herself in the driver's seat.

Julia glanced nervously at the dashboard of his car, thinking it reminded her of the cockpit of a plane, she slowly straightened in her seat. The dark leather seats were pushed almost fully back, too far for her comfort, yet not enough for her to fiddle with his car. Turning, Julia surveyed her assignment through the back windshield, knowing she'll need to drive his car in reverse. The sound of her car's engine towed her focus from its gauging, and she turned in time to see Michael throwing her a playful thumb, looking well full of himself.

With timorous resolve, Julia's foot slowly eased onto the gas, and the car virtually glided in the direction of whence it came, crunching the gravel loudly beneath its wheels. The two cruised guardedly along the narrow path, getting to the fork sooner than she expected, she quickly used the mock cul-de-sac to her advantage. Righting the direction of the car, Julia felt an instant lift from the disquiet that accompanied her task. That ease then saw her safely to the house.

"What would you like to eat?" Michael asked, setting her bag by the entrance of his suite. He steered her in the direction of the kitchen.

"What do you have?"

"You've met Betty, right?" Michael smirked, lighting the still blackened room, he swung the refrigerator door wide. "So.... Let's see. She usually leaves me everything under the sun when she leaves for a few days. So there is..." he paused, picking up a container, he popped the lid free. "Waffles—wheat waffles, fruits—lots of fruits, ham, eggs, a stir fry if you want to go for something heavier, and of course, there's the leftovers from lunch." Michael droned, airing this with a slow smile, his deep voice dipped with an oath of something else. He then looked her over as if affirming his intent.

"I'll have that." Julia chirped, explaining further at his cynical frown. "You can never go wrong with seafood. Besides, it's lunch time."

"True enough. Then leftovers it is." Michael rasped. Liking her choice, since it offered him the prospect of righting the few wrongs he had done. Warming their food, he set it to the same table they drew repast from only the day before. Lighting what was left of the candles, Michael turned out the light.

"What are you up to now?"

"Call this my do over, at least on some things."

"Why? It got you the result you wanted."

"Maybe, but there were a few key places I would love to have handled differently."

"Such as?"

"Don't worry, its coming. Just enjoy your food for now."

"Do I have to worry about it hitting me on the head like a brick?" Julia frowned, savoring the flavor of her food, as it was even better, to her astute palate, the second time around. Perhaps getting one craving out of the way had helped the other, she snickered, though the guffaw stayed deep in the privacy of her thoughts.

"And risk hurting that beautiful head of yours? Not a chance."

"Then where do I fit in this…little plan of yours?" she shrugged, again adjusting the sagging fit of his robe.

"Are you looking for a hint or just eager for the results?"

"Are you asking, or does the result already have you giving a standing ovation."

"That mouth of yours is very…skilled, isn't it? I like that." He growled. "I like it a lot. Do you think you've had enough yet?"

"And of which enough do you speak, exactly?"

"You have a list of enoughs you're not quite tired of?"

"You tell me yours and…" she smiled, her slender shoulders moving upwards through the air, though the result was not as she intended. As if coerced or paid, the robe fell, without care, away from her breasts, laying her bare, in its negligence, to his gaze. "—maybe I'll tell you mine." She finished, swallowing another sampling of her meal.

"Shouldn't that be, 'you show me yours and I'll show you mine'?" he asked, his eyes following the work of her hands as she repaired what little modesty she had left.

"What exactly do you think I should be showing you?"

Michael's smile brightened, holding her gaze. His answer came like a vaulted gnarr. "Why, everything of course."

"That you haven't already seen."

"It's like studying for an exam. You need to know the questions from all angles before you can give a proper reply."

"Are you studying the questions or the answers?"

"I'm trying my hands at both, you know," Michael shrugged. "To cover all my bases," aiming the small remote at the air, the mellow sound of jazz again fitted the darkness. "Care to dance?"

"I'm guessing I do?" Julia teased, though seeing he was already to his feet. Taking her hand, he again led her to the middle of the room, his action no different than that of the fortuitous day at their backs. Michael smiled as he pulled her close, resting her solidly against the wall of his chest; the two slowly began to move.

The angst of anticipation from the day prior did not hover as it did before, but what now bade them was no less thrilling than the first, as her body now tingled from the incessant pressure his body lent. And the fact that she wore naught under the oversized robe, only seemed to enhance his cause. Michael's hand slowly glided up her back, moving through the unruly mass of her hair, he cradled her head as his mouth descended on hers in a wildly amorous kiss. Growing deeply passionate, it took every bit of her breath. Astounded by her continued response, Julia clung, almost gasping as he pulled the very air from her lungs. Feeling her body move with the force with which her heart drummed, Julia sighed as she savored the strength he tendered in his embrace. Slowly, his mouth reduced the depths of its voracious feed, sweeping a hand down her breast. He undid the tie of her robe, pushing the ornery wrap open. His mouth then worked as ardently on her body as it had on her mouth.

Taking his time, his kisses mined her body, grappling past her navel in a continuous fall. He dined wherever he docked. Tormented by the sensation of his mouth, Julia's head fell weightlessly back, her body now atremble with the decadence of his work, and a long sigh escaped the back of her throat. Not entirely on its own, the robe slid from her body to the floor, yet modesty was not the subject that now rocketed through her mind.

"Michael." She called in a low breath, barely teasing the air with the timbre she chose. "Point taken, now can we go?" she grumbled breathlessly, taking hold of his hand. She led him from the kitchen to his room.

Retarding her progress, Julia hesitated at the foot of his bed, folding his arm around her breast, she stood as if in yearn of being consumed. Michael pressed her firmly against the muscles of his chest, kissing the lines of her throat. His fingers frolicked upon the taut peaks of her breasts. Dropping her head to his shoulder with a sigh, he played just as fervently on her mouth, venerating the sensation her mouth brought him with every touch.

Julia's body again shivered under his relentless attack, realizing quickly that her appetite had not yet been quenched, as she greatly longed to savor every aspect of his body. Decisively, her fingers slipped inside the falling waist of his shorts, pushing the garment from his hips. It rappelled to the floor in haste, and the relic left behind was almost scorching to the touch. Julia purred as awareness riddled her body in the thralls of anticipated delight, almost tasting that which could be touched. Hands firm and imperious, wandered across her navel as he bent a knee to the bed, easily taking her to his desired end. The weight of his body roofed hers with skill, and the sweet warmth of his approach swallowed her fully in it blaze, though it was his movements that ripened supreme. Their breaths then rustled through the quiet with distinction, and as like a painter, his strokes spoke of his talent. His techniques then showed in the answers she gave.

"Mmm," Michael growled, sweetening the fervor of his trot. "You…feel…soooo… good!" he breathed, his voice coming like a braided sigh against the skin of her back, and had it not been his own words, he would have missed its spilling, as she had. His muscles flexed with prodigious vigor against her, taking her with him through a torrent of sensations, an ecstasy of their boisterous passion at its greatest bequest. Michael clasped her body roughly to his as the music ended, and a deep growl escaped the barrel of his chest in answer of such, his head dropping instantly to her back with the culminating soar. The ragged spike of his breath blustered over her in haste, cuffing her skin like the gales in an incensed storm as insanity ebbed.

In the silence that followed, the two laid fastened together as one. Michael shifted after long, without releasing his hold. He rested his weight to the bed. Her hair laid spread across the curve of a shoulder, burying his face. He absorbed the scent that had his body in a state of continual upheave. Kissing said shoulder, her neck and her back, Michael traced his fingers down the smooth skin of her side, and the contact was immediately alluring to his sense of touch. Her head turned slowly, and a smile, sweet as the first day of spring, softly jetted from her eyes, and everything about him was immediately hauled further into its giving.

A sigh wafted from her throat as his hands continued its exploration with feathery strokes. With his body still pressed to hers, the heat of his skin was like a shawl to her back, lending her the oddest sense of content. Tomorrow will come, Julia noted with a quiet sigh. Tomorrow she will leave him behind, and all the coercive feelings he cultivates inside her would remain a mere memory of a time past. But for now, she would make everything of the time they had. She had no plausible explanation for her body's response, except that a five year drought had left her body overly parched.

"Thirsty?" Michael asked in a whisper, his breath caressing the soft veneer of her back.

"Uh-huh," she hummed, feeling a weird sense of familiarity with the question.

Taking her with him in a roll, Michael snatched a bottle of water from the nightstand where two sat in wait for an occasion as this. Twisting the cap free, he tendered the bottle to her hand. His eyes then fed intently on her features as she drank, feeling the spill of the cool liquid as it trickled onto his chest from her chin. He watched the light dance in her eyes as she laughed, offering an impish apology, she returned the bottle to her mouth. Michael smiled, waving the giddiness of the matter off, he wiped the liquid from its place, and for reasons unbeknown to him, his thoughts fell suddenly frazzled as she again rested her head to his chest. Michael waited for the brooding sensations to rest. He waited for her to subdue the inexorable need she roused in his body, but the armistice in that had yet to surface or make itself known. Instead, he lay virtually as ravenous as he had been since the very moment they met. Wanting, always wanting that much more of her.

Returning the bottle to its place, long fingers softly stroked her face, turning her head in his aim. Michael towed her close, taking her mouth as she drew within reach. Her answers came then as sweetly as it had in the hours before, and her taste soared just as piquant as it was with very first sampling. Twisting his body, he aligned her under him, pressing her back to the pillowy matting of the bed. Their tongues played chase as their kisses grew delightfully long, enchanting them the deeper they drove. The more he asked, the sweeter her answers came, inducing the fervor of his greed, for it was the more he found that he wanted of her.

A sigh bathed the slope of his cheek as they caught their breaths, her brown eyes seeming to have grown black with the emotions of her body. Michael pressed himself provocatively to her in a firm caress, moving tantalizingly sweet around her soft, womanly cavern. Her lips parted with the deepening of his stroke, releasing a long, slow, sweetly intoxicated breath, he reclaimed them with desirous bent. His body was insistent in its quest for her, moving to her in slow powerful strokes, he pressed the riven of her body with no desired end. Shifting her hips against him, she welcomed his descending focus. Thus stalling his breath in the back of his throat, as his body grappled with the potency of the pleasure that came with the heated imbibes.

Julia's eyes floated open and their gaze punctually locked, holding as if in the relaying of a tale, a long breath past the luscious crest of her lips, trailed by the soft flick of her tongue. Her hands stirred over his chest in a soft caress. His movements bred hypnotic with its strong, fiery strokes, deepening the intensity that harnessed their drive. Her hips rolled like the commencing motion of an exotic dance, exciting him further. It drove him slowly wild. Her cries floated to him as if like the rousing of a hand, and his deep throaty answers fell spirited to her in reply. The ferine sensation intensifying the longer they went, growing feisty until myriad of needling sparks burst upon both, granting them magnificent release.

A shudder passed through Michael's body as the feeling ebbed, and a provocative thought surfaced with the clarity that came. *Okay, it has to be less thrilling the next time*, he reasoned. He should be happily gratified, not greedily seeking more. They'd spent the wee hours of the morning getting very well acquainted with each other. He should be, at least for the moment, sated. Instead, he was being catapulted higher each time. Each pinnacle growing stronger than the first. Each leaving him wanting, wondering what the next would bring.

Julia almost purred as he leisurely kissed her, following him as he lifted his head. She fed with gluttonous vim, wondering what wine seeped from his mouth that had her so inebriated for the want of more. "If you keep this up, I won't know what to do with myself when I leave here." She crooned, her breath brushing soft against his mouth.

"You always know where to find me." Michael whispered back, shifting his weight again to the bed.

"Yes. But...do you really want to become someone's slave?" she teased, letting her fingers follow suit along the hard lines of his rib as if in the onset of a game.

"Now that would depend on the...who as well as the what, wouldn't it?" He shrugged, and a quiet smile settled on his face as he pondered the thought. "I believe I could force myself to live with this. It's tough but...what can I say, I'm selfless."

"Hmm," she groaned, her eyes twinkling with their own mischief into his. "Handsome, rich and magnanimous, however do you make it through the day and still be single? Those, I believe, are the true callings of a gallant man."

"And yet it only took the elaborate scheming of a lie to get you to have lunch with me." Michael drawled, his lean fingers soft along the curvature of her hip.

"I have to admit, that was pretty slick. Rather sneaky of you, really." She assured with a nod, retorting this, Julia's brows slowly wove into a frown, even as her lips parted with the start of a smile. "And there I was getting frustrated with Philip."

"I bribed him into forwarding all his calls to his assistant." Michael informed lightly, lending then a tepid shrug. "At least for the first half of the day, it remained the entire length out of fear you'd find out."

"Does he know about this?" she bayed. Distress heightened her pitch, thus widening her eyes.

"No! How could he? Unless you had it planned all along. It wasn't on the menu for lunch."

"Not even at the bottom with all the fine print?'

"Well…" Michael groaned meekly, resting his face between her breasts, he kissed the soft mounds upon contact. "A man always has hope, Julia." He smiled. "I tried to be a gentleman. I really did. Well. Until—"

"Will this be highlighted in any discussion between you two?" she plied, pushing past his play. Her voice soared almost sweet, yet his answer was of great interest to her. She would much prefer to keep all details of their tryst just that, solely between them. No one needed to know her name was now added to his long list of conquests. Cheap and easy had never been her suit, and an easy lay does not go well with one's career.

"Contrary to what you may think, Julia, there are things I like to leave as my own private business, even with friends. Do you tell your friends everything?"

Ignoring his question, Julia continued her query, wanting to know with certainty that this was truly only between them. "Does he know that we had lunch?"

"He's been in the room with us, Julia; he knows I like you." Michael droned, sighing dubiously at the thought. Was it ignominy or remorse that seized her body so tightly? "He only knows I wanted to ask you out." He explained. "If you want the answer to be 'no' I can convey your polite refusal if the topic comes up."

"I'd like that, thank you." She sighed, revived by his offer. Not having to wonder what or how much his friend knows is preferable to the alternative.

"Mum's the word then." Michael shrugged, feeling at odds with the sudden weightiness the moment lent. He rolled from her side, collecting another bottle, he offered it to her. Accepting the proffered, she drank almost half the liquid before handing the bottle back. Throwing his head back, Michael emptied the content in one continuous swallow. Resting the empty bottle to the floor, she retained her position on his chest the instant he reclined to his place, this, irrespective of the discomfiture that now swirled like an agony in his head.

Day deliriously hurled itself into the sheathing of night, spliced with activities as regaling as such. Night gently blossomed into a new day, though very little hours, it would seem, were wasted on sleep. Conversation came with unfathomable ease between them, and the two filled parts of their time exercising that right, although the physical simile of the word was far more enticing to both.

Julia felt almost giddy as she crept from the warm sachet of his bed, ducking from the room, she admired the blooming of a new day. Faint streaks of orange, amber and red, paraded the spread of a baby's breath blue, brightening the luster in the furthest corner of the sky. The day's promise was not without hope. With today being her last in this, their amorous diversion, reality now returns like the yielding of tides. In mere hours, the demure mother would again revert to her stature of past, leaving the absurdity of her lustful demands behind.

Michael flexed his body in a long, powerful stretch, his muscles bulging with the stark force of each squeeze. Honing his gaze, his eyes slowly walked the room. Heavily darkened with the residue of night, the room sat reticent. Six-thirty not being the usual projection in his weekend start, unless work required otherwise. His weekends tend to take a longer means to relax. A groan wafted forward with the finish of said stretch, sounding oddly like the soft ranting of a bear. The melody promptly coddled the room. His body should be tired; he was well mindful of that. Nonetheless, he had never felt better than he did then. It was as if he had slumbered for days, for his body now conveyed a feeling of complete content. Like a subset of himself, he knew before he opened his eyes that she was no longer at his side, and he wondered was it just that he missed the warmth she emits, or was it in the scent she supplied?

The sound of rushing water suddenly died, and everything stilled as if waiting in solace on her to return. Michael clicked the drapes opened, showing off the most brilliant glow of a bright orangey sky. Palatial in its rendering, he felt the room's intake as it sighed in welcome from the beauty of the show.

"Good morning." Michael greeted as she reentered the room, his voice sailing to her in a throaty whisper.

"Good morning." Julia whispered back, not understanding the reason for the quiet, since the two were the only occupants in the house. Rolling from the bed, Michael sauntered towards her with a panther-like precision, leaving everything behind but his smile. His gaze bore the keenness of a hawk. Julia watched his progress with interest, trying hard to keep her eyes on the towering level of his face.

"My turn," he hummed, moving slowly around her. He pressed his chest to her back. "I'll be back to collect on that." Michael droned, slipping through the door with his pledge still swirling in her ears.

In retort, an entrancing smile flowed across her face, the implications in his oath already tugging on the strings of her imagination, taking it on a stroll that was as pleasant as a lazy afternoon cessation. Dropping to the bench at the foot of his bed, she hugged the soft robe to her breasts. Leisurely, Julia reviewed the place she'd spent nigh every hour of their weekend, and the room bellowed their actions in every corner that she gazed.

Remnants of their late night snacking waited at a corner of the bed, seeming more than it was. A half-eaten apple rested eerily on its side in the discard, looking almost untouched in the sly way that it rested. Two sickly remains of grapes were all that lingered from the twisted twiglet that once carried much more. An opened box of Wheat Thins and the crumbs from a slice of Godiva cheese cake, all littered a waiting tray on the floor. On the bedside console, an empty wine bottle sat as if in defiance of the rest. The glasses still prim at its side. Yet, those were but a few on what was a continuous list.

Predominantly casted on the floor, the blanket laid crumpled to one end of the bed, the remaining edge waited diagonally on the opposite junction of said unit. Julia smiled, well pleased with the happenings of their days, so, too, for their nights, as they certainly will go down in her memory as a grand experience.

The door opened with a slow crawl after long, and Michael stepped out wearing the usual swathing. Hanging low on the muscular plane of his hips, it immediately drew her eyes to the soft furring cresting its edge. Michael smiled as he drew near, bending to her. He tilted her head back with the gentle abetting of his hand, gifting the sweetest apportion of a morning kiss. The soft plying was incredibly sensual in its dispel.

"Good morning…again," Michael whispered as he lifted his head.

"Good morning to you…again," she sighed.

"Are you tired?" he asked in a murmur, his fingers strolling through her hair.

"No."

"Care to join me for a swim?"

"The water is too cold for—oh." She groaned, her voice slamming to a sudden halt, sending a wirily smile with her gaze. "I forgot you have another one inside." Julia frowned, throwing him a smirk for no reason beyond the fact that she could. "I didn't pack my swimsuit."

"I'm sure whatever you have is fine. Your bra and underwear works quite adequately to cover the same things." He hummed, assuring this as he pulled her to her feet. Turning her towards the bathroom door, he encouraged the fulfilling of his plea. "Go. Put something pretty on."

In a matter of minutes, Michael had them crossing the threshold to the pool. Smaller in size than its exterior kin, its deficiencies were amended in the grandness that showed. Beautifully lined in royal blue, navy blue squared in contrast along its sides. Like wainscoting, the pattern ascended the walls no different than the scribing of art. A wall of windows offered a generous dispersion of daylight to the room, while sconces sat high on pillared ends in adduce of added light. Three navy blue chaises sat primly at each short end of an oblong shaped pool, four on opposing ends. They sat as the overseers to a magnificent display.

"Coming?" Michael solicited, his eyes bright with the challenge of his ask. Noting that she had again wrapped herself in her robe, and his intent was to see the garment fully off.

"You go ahead. I'll be in in a minute." She replied pertly, taking a seat along a curved side of the pool. She dangled her feet in the inert ripples of thawed crystalline water. Michael dove in immediately, the splash echoing loudly from the walls of the room. It rang twice that of what it should for a simple splash. Her eyes stayed trained on the agility of the man as he swam from her, working the entire length of the pool and back before easing his pace. Standing, he dragged both hands across his face, laggardly removing the excess liquid from his hair, he smiled. Black trunks slid low on his hips like the raunch factor of a promise, clinging deliciously to every detail of his body. The muscles in his arms flexed as if to sweeten the taunting view.

Julia's groan vibrated high in her skull in distrust of her senses, for had she thought him beautiful before, then he was, most definitely, breathtaking once wet. Her repast had been a long time coming, but now it seemed she could not get her craving for the sight of him, out of her head. Those beautiful eyes were now locked to her face; watching, they studied her with a knowledge that gave her more than a smidgen of unease as to their skill. And in answer of such audit, her gaze quickly fell to the tiles adorning the floor.

"I would have thought after the past few days you would have gotten used to seeing me by now." Michael murmured with a warm smile. "I could have sworn I wore less then." Droplets dabbled along the lap of her robe as he tugged at her belt. "Come on in," he coaxed softly, his fingers gently working the robe from her arms. "The water is waiting."

"Can't I just watch?"

"The sidelines are off limits today, maybe next time." He drawled. Her robe fell in a crumpled pile on the stoned floor at her back, revealing a coppery-brown bra, that cleaved nicely to her breasts, and a swatch-like showing in her underwear to match. The stringed garment was trimmed with the same colored lace along its edges, and Michael's eyes were more than appreciative of the view. Hazel eyes swept over her in a long lingering gaze, slowly tracing her body from neck to navel and back, before a smile teased the corner of his mouth.

"Haven't we already been through this?" Julia asked in a small voice. His leer being so bright, it would hardly be lost on any who had eyes.

"Yes. Yes we have." Michael smirked, dropping his eyes again to her body. "Although the word 'through' has such finality braided within its meaning." He smiled. "And every great entertaining act is usually layered to heighten the enjoyment before the actual... finale is got."

"What act would you say we're on now?" Julia challenged with her usual sweet smile.

"Did you lose count?" he asked, his eyes jumping to hers. And an already bright smile further brightened with the impish probe. Lunging backwards, he allowed the water to swallow him whole, immediately resurfacing to her view. He rose to his feet like a chiseled myth created only for the insidious heist of a woman's dream.

"I didn't know I was supposed to keep count." Julia purred, taking the time to slow her galloping pulse, as it refused to halt its madness or regulate the flux of a near ludicrous pace. How can anyone look that good, she griped; and shouldn't her pulse be settling by now? "Are you?" she asked in a whisper instead.

Michael's smile waded forward in place of an answer, searching the immediacy of her face. He perceived the sly sweep as her eyes move over him with dulcified appreciation marking their depths. Absorbing the nostrum gifted with the act, he found that he fully liked what it was that he saw in the dark givings of said feature. Yet, it was not his ego that it fed. He gave no mention of motive as he spread her legs, setting them wide, he stepped gamely between her thighs. Strong hands worked in facade of a winch as he locked her legs at his back, securing her body to his before he turned. He strode leisurely towards the deeper end. "You've seen me stare openly at you," he hummed above her ears. "What makes you think I wouldn't gladly welcome yours?" he asked, squatting low as the water climbed towards his chest.

"I would think you picked your teeth with such treats as that."

"But not all treats taste the same, now do they? Do you eat every candy ever made?" he probed, and his face quirked quizzically with the eccentric test. "And do they all appeal to you with the same reverence, or taste the same for that matter?" a small chuckle was her only response as he adjusted her legs, aiming for a surer fit as he settled himself as her seat. "I would have thought," he breathed against her ear. "Seeing me would have been more natural to you by now. You saw more of me then?"

"I didn't think you wanted me looking then, I was a little…busy."

"Oh, I'm well aware of that fact." He hummed, his smile widening as he took her with him in a slow, backward lunge. His strokes, though leisured, slowly towed her around the pool, stealthily falling further beneath the surface with each pass. Her arms tightened around his neck as they left the surface behind, and a strange smile stole the frown she once held, as if suddenly acquiring new insight into his head. She lengthened her frame atop his. Her hair floated about her like some mystic angel of the ocean, and for a moment, it was as if he watched a moving piece of art.

On his second pass, the two rose to the surface gasping for air, the tranquility of the moment broken with the sting of their echoic cough. Michael's hand stayed on the small of her back, pressing her wet body to his. He noted that the lace of her bra was now singed to the swelling of her breasts. "My turn," He breathed roughly against her, waiting a long minute before stepping back to garner his view.

Julia arrested her thoughts and stilled all actions with the dispensing of his words. Knowing she had to stay her grounds and allow him to attain his pleasure, or anything else he deemed of his choosing. Hadn't she given him the rules herself? Strangely, she found his attention more delightful than not. His eyes granted her the empathy of a choice dessert, what woman wouldn't want that? A slow smile turned the corner of her mouth as she glided both hands down the length of wet hair, lifting the heavy mass from her shoulders. She allowed it to hang freely down her back. A sluggish turn thence followed the birth of an elusive taunt, waiting with her back to him then; Julia gave him the time to capture all aspect of the view.

"You recognize me, I see." Michael muttered hoarsely as she turned, his eyes matted to the clinging underwear, now smeared to her skin like paint, and he doubted if she wore nothing it would have captivated him as intently.

"We've been introduced," she smiled. "Acquainted even,"

"Then why hide from me?" he asked as he stood.

"It's like you say, some things you just keep private."

"Unless a need comes up, right?" he asked, letting his hand roll slowly over the edge of her breast. "But I'll gladly give it to you. So I'll tell you this." Michael shrugged. "My appreciation speaks better for itself when it's sometimes left unsaid. But no words is not always silence, now is it?" he rasped, maneuvering his body in a slow caress. Intending to be soft, Michael's head slowly dropped to hers. Though when she touched him, his hunger stole the moment from his hands, and it was he who trembled against her with anticipation.

Minutes dithered in their ardent commencing, but dashed after long in a fiery blaze, halting at others as if to partake of the view. It was a long time before the rapturous sensation ebbed. Two bodies now spent. Exhausted, they sprawled across the pillowy cushion of the chaise. Julia nestled her face against the matt of his chest, drawing a leg high between his thighs as his was with hers.

"Stay with me for another day or two." Michael asked softly, his hands playing along the slope of her back.

"I can't." Julia whispered on an exhale, her breath warm against his skin, luxuriating in the softness of his caresses.

"Yes, you can." Michael retorted in a deep drawl. "Your kids are away and they won't be back until Thursday, stay and spend a few more days with me. Stay at least until Tuesday."

"Mmm, I can't." She hummed, unwitting to the fact that it would be the master key to her undoing.

"Come on. Stay." He whispered, brushing his hand along her breast. He softly kissed the brown peaks, his tongue gliding over each rise as he sweetened them to a stance. "Stay." He pleaded, his breath coming like the surge of a desert stroke.

"Mmmm," she purred, her lids fluttering closed with the release of said breath. "Maybe I can do another day."

"Two." Michael bargained in a rumbly purr, nibbling the soft edge of her mouth in his unwillingness to give. He was not yet ready to see their weekend come to an end, and he willfully employed his tactics to stay that result.

"You don't play very fair." Julia crooned, her fingers soft through his hair.

"I have to. You don't make this easy for me."

"I'll stay." She whispered with a slow nod, feeling at peace with her decision.

"Good." He hummed back, satisfied with his achievement. He balanced himself on an elbow, showing off a rascally smile. "Now, say 'my turn'."

"Why?"

"Just say it. 'My turn,'"

"My turn," Julia mumbled tentatively.

"Yes it is." He nodded, easing himself from the chaise. Long, leisured strides carried him to a stack of towels at the far end of the room. Collecting two of the plush body sheets, the same measured strides saw him returning to her side. "How was that?" he inquired softly, resting the towels across her breasts.

"How was what?" Julia frowned, uncertain of the meaning behind his inquest. Still, she had watched his action with veiled appreciation.

"Did you need a little more time, or did you get more than a glimpse?"

"It was a little more than a glimpse." She twittered coyly, not yet at ease with admitting her lust.

"Oh, don't worry," Michael simpered. "You'll have more than enough chance to take note of the view."

———

The musk of spring wafted through the air stirring dormant to life. Trees cheered, and songs flitted merrily high. Evenings grew long in their visits, lengthening as the once dour cover repealed its hold on a previously latent ground. In balance to the suffusing boon, the wings of time swept the atmosphere with a meteoric gust, bringing all pleasant things to a rapid end.

Julia set her bags to the bordering edge of the sitting-room floor, this being the primary step to saying goodbye. Straightening, she absently leaned against the door's frame. Lifting her shoulders lamely, she answered his questioning gaze. Like the epilogue to a stories end, there was nothing left to be said, only that of the postponement's demise.

Michael sat rigid at the foot of his bed, watching in silence, his usual witty soliloquies now dwindled to an awkward halt. Or was it just her feeling somewhat disconnected? There was nothing left to be said that was not already said. They both knew the weekend had to have a preemptive finale, and both knew the rules going in. If things, time and circumstances were vaguely different, she would be willing to reason the whys, but such intrusions were better left unsaid.

"I need you to do me a favor." She asked.

"Sure. What is it?"

"Can you get rid of that—before Betty gets back?" Julia droned, her finger flying reticently through the air to then point out her request.

Michael's eyes followed the direction of her aim to the corner of the room housing the trash, nodding his understanding. He stood with a tight smile. "I'll take care of it now." He sighed, not knowing much else to do.

"It's a bit…much." Julia whispered, leveling her gaze with his hand as he tied the small bag, and she instantly lost sight of an irregular collection of plastic wrappers. Michael nodded in what seemed an answer, resting the bag on the floor at his feet. "I just don't want…" she shrugged, her voice trailing softly, and the explanation seemed locked in the words not said, for there was nothing left that she needed to add. Yet he seemed to understand her meaning well, nodding as his eyes touched her gently. The room wrung itself suddenly quiet. Swallowing, Julia quieted the angst in herself, sensing his intent to move towards her, but he held. Dropping his back securely against the far wall instead, he shifted composedly, as if realizing he needed the distance to further pacify the moment, yet his eyes sank uncannily deep.

"Why are we doing this?" Michael grumbled at last, his voice soft in an already quiet room. "I understand your argument, I really do. You like your privacy, and I understand that. I can't guarantee that for you and your children. I get it. You want to keep their lives as stable as possible, but there has to be a way around this."

"There isn't." Julia stated flatly, leaning her back against the door. "Whatever I go through, will always trickle down to my kids somehow. It's my job as their mother to filter and weed that out, and if it means some sacrifice then…that's just what I'll do. One divorce is enough. A series of broken relationships is not."

Michael nodded faintly, vaguely agreeing with her explanation, his eyes quickly dropped from her face. He had no argument fit for a rebuttal to such staunch conviction, nothing that was not already offered in the propositions he gave. Her feelings were understandable, factual in some sense. She had to protect her children from any and all foreseeable harm. He fully understood that. But understanding does not always mean acceptance, and he was not yet ready to sit back and accept. She captivated him truly, more so than anyone or anything he had ever known, and their weekend together did not wane the veracity of that. Not in the least. The lure of such dulcitude had him firmly entrenched in its grasp, with needs roiling within him he'd yet to understand. No, he would not be skulking away.

Chapter Twenty two

As with the afflictions following the wrath of a tempest, an empty house awaited her return. Somnolent in its demeanor, the rooms respired much like the empty vestibules in a monastery faced with its own demise. A vapid air hovered grimly within the starched vaulting of the space, and quiet nooks tendered their maudlin through a whispery sigh. It sifted through the house with a deafening drift amidst the silence.

A strange hollowness strolled the halls of the house, clipped staunchly to her side. It mocked the monologues yet campaigning in her head. *Am I really brooding?* Julia questioned gruffly, though she quickly heckled the absurdity of such thought. *It was a tryst. That's all, a means to an end, nothing more.* She griped densely, recapping the reminder for the yearnings that now cultivated her body. The weekend was, without qualms, exquisite. Their togetherness was inclusive of everything, unending in its trudge. It surpassed her remembrance of such. Hence, she should be full for a worthy spell, therefore back to her old self in a matter days. So her mind gently attested with each day's beginning. The adjustments, she professed logically, were just slow in coming. She needed only to recollect the patterns of her existence before him. *That's all*.

With their working relationship now at an end, there should be no known reason for their paths to ever cross, and like everything, these memories in time would die. This she assured tartly to herself, as if to soothe her own worry on such truth. The strict reasoning scrolled continuously through her mind, flashing like slogans in advertised slats. They brightened the moment the memory of his impressive physique permeated her thoughts, so, too, the decadence of his kisses. Yet, it was not their physical aptitude that troubled her mind the most. Nor was it what she reached for at varying intervals of the day. Instead, her subconscious insistently lunged for the playful conversations that streamed so easily between them. In truth, their connection was genuinely gratifying. A camaraderie of sorts, like old friends with centuries woven between them. It was like a familiar place in which to rest your head, such verity, she stingily admitted with a shrug. Though such sentiments bred as the trappings of a different time, one she had no intension of traversing the borders again.

Normalcy returned in what seemed an awkward flash, redepositing her, less than ecstatic, kids back in school. Julia's days, through fierce determination, became an organized ramp. Starting immediately on the papers neglect left to grow to a massif on her desk. She wheedled her way through to again espy the mute luster on the surface of a well-aged oak desk. A backlog of errands now badly in need of her focus, aided in the dissidence of her cause. Each providing her an outlet well sought.

Although laden to its max, the usual expectations brokered no vary, and the hours in her day flew, at time, as if aided by a gust. Homework, story-time and their playful gatherings, consumed only a minor portion of her evenings beyond that of her cause. Yet, she tackled them all with inexorable zeal, as it was her nights that gave her the most reasons for pause. Waking, at times, it seemed, in an eerie trance, still feeling the warmth of his body in her bed or, too, the effects of his hands as he manipulated the fissure of her body. In counter to the psychological clash, her bed, in odd remedy, had become more of a torturous venue than a place of relaxation of late. Emerging from the fallacies often, thoroughly roused, her confusion was without bounds, unsure of whence the sensation came; only that it held her fixed within its lancing grasp.

"This, too, will die." Julia vowed, repeating the simple mantra in the darkness of her room, for the struggles were continual in their pungent boast. Though irrespective of the notes fastened to those in the relapsing hymn, such stable assertions had yet to take root in her mind, nor had it stayed her body's wont to reminisce. The wild, impulsive introduction to their weekend, appeared, quite frequently, to be a broadening probability. A certainty, in truth, if she did not get her wavering mind under some semblance of control.

A new delivery came within days of her return. Arcane in its flourish as always, it arrived in the middle of the afternoon, this, on a day that beckoned with magnificent promise. Pleasingly so—until the spoiler trampled her mood. The driver, with a familiar twinge, eyed her wearily as she opened the door, pausing to recheck the manifest he carried in his hand. Though in candor, his hesitation went triply long, longer than rational need said that it should.

Julia watched his dawdling action with a peevish knit set to her brow, finding his behavior somewhat slighting, since his manner suggested that she was less than polite in the encounters they had. Yet she was confident that her only guilt was that she insinuated he made a mistake. There should be at least a good mile between that and berating, which, undoubtedly, is what his actions now strongly implied. Her impatience, however, was not solely vested in him and his ridiculous feint, but that she abhorred the symbolism behind his presence. Knowing it meant another arrangement from her supposed admirer with a pseudonym instead of a name.

To her surprise, the flowers were nothing like the expected show of the past, these being as different as winter was to the livelily of spring. *Lilies of some kind*, Julia quickly guessed. Almost blood red, they hailed exquisite. With buds of green spritzing through a plume of red, the contrasting shades looked more like a primed canvas against the dotted red petals.

The cagey man smiled as he relinquished the bouquet to her hands. Or perchance so, as she was irresolute on the chore, since she was truly uncertain if the strange tick he demonstrated could be labeled a smile. Julia nodded kindly, intending to repay the effort by offering him one of her own—if not just as a gesture of goodwill. But his retreat was instantaneous, in so, that she barely had the time to acknowledge much beyond the murmured obligation required in the exchange.

The flowers gifted a sweet fragrance. Remarkably pleasing to the senses it touched, it feathered an aroma well gratifying to the mood. Her smile brightened as the attar wrapped itself around her like a cloak, enveloping the room. A sudden pang of excitement furrowed through her body without reason or cause. Ignoring the quivering sensation, she daintily set the flowers to the tall counter of the bar. Confident of the sender, his name popped in her head like the answer to a quiz. Her hands nigh shook with the thrill that such moment brought, a reaction suited to another but her, yet much like an ecstatic teenager. She tore open the envelope with raw homage dictating her deed, snatching forth the small card in a ceaseless ripple, eager to read his thoughts.

An aromatic beauty for one truly sweet, J.D.

Ps. my swims have not been quite the same since....

Julia's body prickled deliciously as the memory of their time together tumbled through her head. The strange, hypnotic pull was inanely mesmerizing—even if sorted by the feign ember of indifference—as its swells built like tides in rejoinder of a full moon. And she could not stop the intensity of such remembrance from engulfing her frame. And for once, since her lengthy repast ended, she did not want the brewing to stop.

Once more, a long week grinded to an excruciatingly slow end, triggering a sigh of acquiescence and relief, such lassitude begetting the oath of a lazy day in bed, since an unscheduled weekend was surely the medicine to soothe whatever ailments she had. Conceivable, it would seem—until her phone rang. Bobby's mother chirped happily in greetings from the other end, confirming a play-date that both were ignorant of. With the two forgetting again to invite the grownups to their talk, the boys, it would seem, had been busy making plans of their own. Thus, they thwarted the relaxation she had planned. Although not fully reluctant, Julia acceded to the visit. Mindful that the boys had been best friends since their first day of kindergarten, Bobby was to her, like her own son.

"Can I have Kayla, too?" Rachel asked anxiously, her long hair swaying behind her as she burst into the room.

Julia's answer came in a languid stretch, arching her back with the budding of a yawn. She slowly straightened her slackened body on the bed, and the quiet room almost reiterated the long breath of her sign. Leisurely, her eyes climbed to the expectant gleam on Rachel's waiting face, admiring the features at first glance.

Rachel stared wide-eyed at her every movement with untiring focus, the brown iris following her actions with great zeal, as if her gestures reared like the preview of a greatly anticipated film. The oval face sat strangely, like a replica of her own. Rachel's skin, being lighter, gave her large, dark eyes a more exotic vaunt, though her lips were less pouty and her hair was considerably less rowdy than that of her mother's.

"Since Richard has his best friend over, can I have mine?" Rachel continued impatiently, her hand waving back towards the door in emphasis of her words.

"Rachel, what exactly does a lazy day mean to you?" Julia asked calmly, wanting desperately to hold on to the quiet day. They could watch a thousand movies; if they so wish, have a daylong picnic in the sunroom should that be a simmering covet. It all made no difference to her how the hours unfolded. Her only sureness was that she did not want to leave the house for any reason outside of a pending demise or, in any way, cater to another person's child this day.

"But Richard gets to have his best friend!" she countered, imploring her mother in what sounded like the start of a shriek, yet not answering the question placed before her. "Why can't I have Kayla?"

"Because I deserve to have a weekend without having to cater to another person's child, I should be able to have that!"

"But mom, you won't even know she's here! We'll just stay in my room. I promise. Please, mom!"

"Fine, fine!" Julia grunted brusquely, waving off her daughter's beginning whine. She was not in the mood to hear the pitch climb, or to know how far she'd be willing to take the rising timbre now affixed to her tone. Having had already anticipated the beseeching, she was surprised the petition took as long as it did. "You can have Kayla, but on our next lazy day, I'm inviting my friends." She warned, though her words fell unheeded to Rachel's back, already screaming in glee as she raced from her room.

"Did you hear?" she mumbled discreetly to her phone as she entered the hall.

"I will not be picking up, or dropping off today, thank you." Julia called, hurling her voice at the door, though doubting Rachel heard much past her consent. Her coveted laidback day was quickly drawing to an eminent end, since despite their promise, it was certain her name would soon be on everyone's lips. Aware her second guest was most likely already on her way, Julia begrudgingly dragged herself from the comfort of her bed.

Not unlike the challenges appended to a race through a frigid swamp, her muscles seemed weighted with lead, and in that, her small reserve of energy had been expended on the task of accomplishing breakfast, and she badly needed to recoup that loss. So excited was she by the prospect of lazing, that she forgot to wager the simplest rule of parenting "101". She forgot to expect the unexpected. Julia took her time piddling, almost mindless, about her room, using the anabasis of, what seemed, a snail's crawl. She entered the bathroom to examine the condition of her hair. Deciding then to twist the long mass into a bun, she secured it with a large, toothy clip. Long, wavy wisps fell down the sides of her face from its loosening clasp in stubborn reply, sagging wildly down her back. She could not help but smile at the picture such vision conveyed, agreeing fully with the unruly look, for it seemed to mimic something of her mood.

Doused in sunlight, the cheery spill of the kitchen became her destination of choice. With her previous cup of coffee now only a memory, her need for a new cup was grave. Delia brandished a small smirk in greeting as she entered the room, offering what seemed a halfhearted condolence in the keenness of her gaze. Julia's eyes rolled to the ceiling in cynical answer to her offer, and a large puff of air flew, as an added supposition, from her lips. Her eyes grated across the chilled coffeepot with annoyance, seeing that the small machine was no longer warm. She conscripted a series of begrudging steps. A soft grunt of pleasure chafed the stingy silence as the newly warmed cup settled in her palm, taking a tentative sip. She stabled her slender body to the surface of the couch, crossing her legs at the ankle. Her song of felicity became truly distinct.

"Mmmm," she chanted heavily, dropping her slackened head to the soft pillows at her back.

"Maybe you should try the spa again, sweetie. You're not looking as sprightly as you did when you first got back. You really should treat yourself better." Delia scolded with a tight, obvious frown. "You can more than afford it, and you certainly deserve it. Why don't you treat yourself to something good?"

The sluggish inspect, once offered, amassed to her senses laced with definite distrust. Uncertain of how to take the subtext of her mother's words, as it felt almost invasive—knowing to some extent. "I'll be fine, mom." She shrugged shakily; putting on what she hoped was her best smile. "I just need to take a few days and relax. I'll be even better after that."

Delia reviewed her daughter with faltering resolve. Perceptive of her stubbornness, it made the diligence of the picture not sit well in the observer's eyes, something was definitely off. Julia was as stalwart in her decisions as her father had been in his prime— if not more. There was no changing their minds once a conclusion was drawn, at least not directly. Comforting them, at times, meant giving them the space they needed to just be. It's the very reason she knew when to say what, how to say it and how far to go. Their entire relationship was built on the stricture of knowing that fact. A compulsory govern to abide, it helped to know when to let a cranky teenager have her space and when she should not.

Although those teenage years were well behind them, Julia still had her own obscure way of thinking things through, which has made the frequency of her getaways even more imperative than they seemed. Those absences, tendered like a donation of sort, had been her own way of leaving her daughter open for the prospect of something else, the prospect of facing something new. It was not that a woman needed a man to be happy outside of all else, it was more attributed to the less than rounded way her daughter now lived her life. All work, all the time does not make a happy life, no matter what doctrine you preach.

"Not you, too, mom," Julia sighed dishearteningly, noticing her mother's pensive stare. This was not the time or the day to have this talk, as she was not in the mood to hear any such scolding on her life. "Not today, mom," she warned in a low grunt, taking another mouthful of her coffee, she sighed. Desperate in her need for this day to find its end, for maybe tonight she'd recoup a goodly lot of her less-than adequate rest. Of late, more often so than not, she routinely got fewer hours of sleep in each erratic session, and the dwindling was not wearing well on her mind or her body.

Another week stuttered by as typical as the others in all things branded routine. Yet the monotonous grind sparked no new insight for controlling her thoughts, or a manner in which to quell her subconscious and savor the full sum of her sleep. Julia grew more languorous with each week at her back, and the tallied deprivation now had her mood bordering sadly on morose. Giving serious thought to her mother's suggestion of a spa, she contemplated the advantages to her choice, knowing something had to be done to lift the drear of her mood, since her gloomy disposition did not seem willing to lift on its own.

Julia feigned her cheery self as the children hustled to leave for a weekend with their dad. Hugging them close, she sent them on their way with the usual barrage of kisses.

Only one plan dominated her subsistence for the week's end—rest. The lone topic surfaced in bold letters on a broad screen in her head, with neon lights flashing at its back. There would be no out—even had she had one planned—as she had not the energy to resist its persistence. Now with the house to herself, she intended to do nothing but see to the resolution of that, and first up, was a leisured soak in a fragrant bath. Sequencing promise beyond that was to stay in bed, leaving her mind blank was her most avid ambition.

"Gail and her son will be here any minute," Delia announced as she entered the kitchen, fussing anxiously with her bracelet, she peered pensively at her suitcases already crowding the hall. "Let me say goodbye now before I lose my head." She smiled, again glancing at her bags. She made a mental count of her belongings, nodding dimly to herself as she finished.

"Bye, mom," Julia smiled, loosely throwing her arms around her mother's shoulders. She tightened the closure with a firm squeeze.

"Bye, sweetie," she crooned, kissing her daughter's cheek. "Please take care of yourself, and be safe. Okay."

"I will, mom. Now you do the same." Julia chanted, again tightening her hold as she returned a kiss to her mother's cheek. "Calm down, mom! I'm sure you have everything." She teased, noticing her mother's flustered appearance, as her eyes again shifted to her bags.

"Oh, darn! I forgot to put that little gold-leaf earring in my purse. I think I left them on the dresser with that heart necklace I was iffy about taking, shoot! Let me go grab them before I forget." Delia muttered with a soft groan, turning much like an agile cat, she scurried off to her room.

"They're here!" Julia cried, lifting her voice as the sound of a car's horn summoned her attention. Opening the door in acknowledgement of such, she waved, dragging the smaller of the two bags to the waiting minivan. Gail's son politely relieved the bag from her hands, fetching the second for himself, he loaded the growing collection. Julia smirked as she assessed the assortment now splayed in the back, seeming well above the necessary reach of their need. How much need could possibly arise on a five day cruise? So her intellect prodded with a waggish spike.

"Bye, darling," Delia chirped as she rushed forward from the house, almost bouncing down the steps in her haste. She gave her daughter another warm, lingering hug, pressing a soft kiss to her cheek, she capped her earlier guide. "Now you remember what I said." She whispered, giving a last squeeze before getting in the car. A spirited wave saw them turning from the driveway onto the road, leaving her daughter to gape at the back of their vanishing vehicle. Silence fell like an atmospheric pause.

An empty house sighed upon her reentry of the dourly space, its breath mimicking the weighty spill of her own, listlessly flowing through her body to the swing of her hands. Julia leaned her back against the hard surface of the barring, bolting both locks. She stared into silence that gawked back. Her thin shoulders lifted in recognition and then dropped. Dolefully, she turned towards her room, feeling the weight of every step in her weary tread. The past few weeks had been like an oppressive vise upon her body, bleeding her dry, but one for which she now intended to make amends. Stopping in the kitchen for refreshments aimed at aiding just that, the sight quickly stole her attention from its intended route.

"Damn!" she exclaimed in a grunt, spotting her mother's small purse waiting pitifully on the counter, she veered from her task. A quick check inside confirmed the enormity of her fears. Housed in the small bag was all the essential features needed for her mother's trip—not the least of which, though highly revered—was her wallet. The assemblage of such was now clasped loosely in her hand, giving little aid to the one who needed it most. On propensity, she dialed her mother's number, looking almost shocked when the music of Beethoven's Fur Elise broadcast pleasingly from the purse in her hand. Julia snorted at the small bag, rolling her eyes in charging, yet grateful that no one witnessed the idiocy spliced to the act itself. Gail's number raced speedily across the small screen of her phone, as if sensing the urgency at hand. Hence it took only two rings for Gail's heavy Bostonian accent to sing the usual greetings in response.

"Hello, Gail! This is Julia!" She began, relating the information on her crucial fine. She thence followed with an in-depth version once the phone was passed to her mother's hand.

Delia apologized immensely for the stupidity of the act, refusing Julia's offer to meet them mid-point of where they were.

"There's no need for that, dear," Delia explained sweetly. "Julian says he'll just swing back after we get Iris. Have you started your relaxing as yet?" she asked tunefully, her tone switching easily from instructive to probe, highlighting the depths of her motherly concern.

"I was about to." Julia chirped, a hint of mirth scratching the lilt in her voice. "But alas, my leisured bath still waits."

"Then you go ahead, love." Delia nudged, unwilling to hinder any portion of her pre-planned relaxation, since such things were not usually considered or taken as a treat in Julia's over-burdened life. "We don't know how soon it will be before we get there, it all depends on Iris and the traffic. I'll just use the emergency key to let myself in."

"Really, mom, it's not a problem." She offered calmly. "I could cut a lot of driving out of Julian's time."

"Maybe, but the traffic is already thickening its bulk, and there's really no need for both of us to get stuck. I think it's best if we left the purse where it is and let us work our way back to you. Just put it by the door and go start your relaxing. I want you to take the time to pamper yourself. No skimping, do you hear me?" she warned, her voice coming as a mother to a child.

"Yes, mother." Julia groaned, feigning a perturbed grunt with her laugh.

"Good. You work too much, and you don't take care of yourself enough."

"Don't worry, mom. I'm definitely going to treat myself this time."

"Glad to hear it. Hopefully you'll get a taste for the habit. Now go get started, I'll see you in a few days."

"But, mom, I—"

"Now do you understand why we start out so early?" Delia laughed, cutting nicely through her daughter's protest. "It's so we can make up for being old, dear. It gives us time to fix little mishaps like this."

"Are you sure, mom?" Julia questioned yet again, feeling guilty about the matter without knowing why. She propounded yet again to meet them halfway, though she understood fully the logic behind her mother's refusal to budge. With the purse safely stationed at home, the chance of a mishap was far less than the possibilities that waited ahead.

As per her mother's request, the small purse was left to sit in the foyer by the door, and Julia almost skipped to start the process of her bath. The ingredients were painstakingly mixed, and with the props fanatically set. Her eyes made a quick note of the things that surrounded her bath, affirming in a steady sweep she had everything she needed.

A thick mat lined the broad face of her tub, with another spread wide on the floor. Cold drinks waited in a cozy container within reach of her hand. Along the side of the portly tub, a caddy waited with two novels meant to dissuade her galloping thoughts. Flush along the opposite edge, further necessities sat in wait, her toiletries, extra towels and a comfy pillow to assuage the back of her head. Sitting on an abutting ledge, her phone waited outside of her reach. An indispensable link, though something she hoped not to use for the entirety of the weekend—except in the case of her kids. The small stereo was set to give a grand performance of the classics while she uncoiled the lock from her mind. Beethoven, Schubert and her favorite Bach, were all queued to serenade the unraveling.

Julia sighed as she settled back in the steaming liquid. The water near scalding as she liked it, and her eyes, in rejoinder, instantly fluttered closed. "This is just what I needed." She muttered dimly, adjusting the pillow at her head, she acquired the perfect position to elicit rest. Julia's eyes remained shielded as her body relinquished all goals except one. Annulling all others but to liquesce in the sudsy sauna and rest, and she quickly resolved herself to that endearing fact.

Settling deep in the depth of the large tub, her chin jutted high as she hummed to the music of Bach's Fugue in D minor. Julia's fingers jerked sharply through the air as any skilled conductor would, rising and falling in complete rapture with the tune, dimming in verve as one song waltz with little pause to another. Signs of the pervading tension weakened its hold, wafting like vapors from the heated muscles encasing her limbs. Her body sighed contently the longer she stayed, and minutes surpassed their transient self to settle on the realm of aeons. Suddenly parched from the perpetual heat, her thirst then compelled the exploits of her hands. Julia's eyes opened to acquire the ordinance of her thoughts, and the sight that accosted her thoroughly heisted her focus from that which it intended.

With an abrupt start, Julia's body jolted forward in surprise, a tinge of fear roped tightly to her deed, though the emotion stalled as quickly as it bade. Unsure whether to trust the sight for what it was, Julia stared wide-eyed, time seeming to stop as she waited for clarity to come. Though both now teetered between the rifts of her hammering pulse. Her eyes had deceived her on all other occasions as this, why should this occurrence be any different than the many before now? She had thought about this moment for far too many nights, refuted too many illusions to trust the moment as real. Waking to think he rested at her side, only to be proven wrong. She expected this instance to be no different than those before now.

The door creaked fully open after what seemed a century or two, the eerie sound falling to her ears like the slide of an electric guitar. Corroding the steam filled air with its sharp nasal pitch, it ballooned on the semblance of rising dough, and had she not been so deathly frozen, she would have remembered to at least be scared. A half stride took him across the shrinking threshold, looking taller than she remembered. He looked even more delectable then to her hungering view. Each inch of his striking physique like the gusset of a wicked taunt, as both face and body reared better than the pictures she kept well hidden in her head. So were those amazing eyes that looked ready to set fire to her skin. Indiscriminate in their crusade, they grazed her longingly, feeding wherever they touched. They roused more than just her wonder in the exigency given in their work.

Julia's heart leapt through the opening of her throat, juddering in haste, it receded in a blurred trice. Answerable for such action, the organ wielded a cluster of summersaults within the restricted cavity of her chest. Thus, it danced chaotically as she waited, for what, she was yet unsure. Her body grew warmer than the heated liquid states that it should, and supple nipples grew taut just below the surface of the suds. In aid, a delicious tingle worked hard between the tense crevice of her thighs. The metamorphoses ensuing without as much as a touch, and it amazed her at the level to which her excitement rocketed. It soared wild just from the intensity of his gaze, and in concurrence to the puzzle. Her principal elation was to feed upon his actual presence.

"Michael! What——?" Julia murmured in start. Swallowing roughly, she quieted the useless question from its intended path, as it served no purpose in her body's resurgence. Knowing whatever his reason, at that moment, she truly did not care.

"Hi! I..." Michael rasped, his words coming with a faint breath. Intending to say something casual, all his well-rehearsed lines wickedly barricaded themselves in his head. He could think of naught to say beyond what was already said. Only his eyes worked to articulate a portion of his thoughts, taking their fill of all the things that had held him captive until now. Long strides took him to her in what seemed a blink, and before she could respond with anything other than such, his mouth plummeted to hers in a ferociously avid kiss. Michael groaned coarsely as her tongue glided over his, her arms locking instantaneously around his neck. Taut muscles flexed roughly as Michael's arms slid under the smooth skin of her thighs, plucking her body from the tub. He sent scented suds splattering across the floor. Though none seemed to have noticed the mishap for what it was.

Melting her body firmly to his, Julia sighed with the triumph of having him near, and their passion, in its erupting swells, grew to the resemblance of barbaric. Hungrily dragging the shirt from his body, her fingers worked with a greedier bent on the fastener of his jeans, pushing the garment well below his knees. Her caresses grew bolder still. Demanding in their drive, her intent was unmistakable. With need regulating the dictates of her hands, she stroked the smooth, heated form of his manly body. A cavernous moan rose from Michael's chest in rejoinder of her strive, smothering the soft nips of their lips. His hands bit roughly into the flesh under her arms, lifting her from the floor. Her legs undauntedly became his belt. Dampened hair spilled wildly down her back as the two savagely became one, and a long sigh rose like a gentle caress through the humid air. Luxuriating in the exquisiteness of the moment, their bodies forged together as if at war, each pushing the other harder still.

The coolness of the mirror gently touched her back as he rested her on the counter. Yet, her focus lied not on the venue itself, but on the exploit attached. Having squashed the median with which to consult the workings of her brain, she could but feed, as the enactment fully imprisoned her devotion. Her cries assaulted the air as he quarried deep, burrowing harder with a cadence pace, though it was no menacing pain that compelled the lyrics of her song. Like cohorts in a sumptuous brawl, their bodies at last went taut, surged together in passion, they summit the rigorous climb. Michael ravenously commanded the warm cleft of her mouth, tasting the last of their passion before it ebbed. He fed without rations. Clasped wearily together, their breath came as a wheeze in the silence that followed, each waiting inertly for calm to descend.

An eternity passed before Michael, at last, lifted his head from its dais atop hers. Each face wearing an almost stupefied countenance, oddly set, like a mirror of them- selves, though both with dissimilar reasons attached. Michael's face creased into a slow smile, as if in finish of an imperative edict. His eyes immediately dropped to the angling of her face. Guardedly, Julia returned the favor as best she could. Touching the back of her head to the mirror with a dispelled breath, clarity reverted at once.

"What...? How—how did you—" she stuttered, her earlier question stumbling clear at long last, as if it had sat patiently in deferment waiting to fall free.

"Your mother let me in," he answered calmly, his hands resting softly on her thighs. "She did say you may be a while when you didn't respond to her announcement. I fol- lowed the music and...Well...."

"Why?" Julia smiled, aware of his implications. "Why are you here?"

"I wanted to...talk to you." Michael smiled, glancing down at her legs still locked at his back.

"Now you want to talk?" Julia teased, unhooking her legs from his back. "Don't you think you should've mentioned that earlier?"

"I guess I lost the use of my tongue back then."

"It looked to be working perfect at last check."

"Hmm, it's amazing what a good technician can do." Came the tickling retort, escorted by a short, deep chuckle from the back of his throat. Returning her legs to his waist, Michael carted her from the counter to the bed. Stealthily shuffling his way to the edge, he kicked the trappings free from his feet, cradling her prettily on his lap.

A chill ran over the once roasted surface of her skin, fanning her body with the suddenness of the change. Michael's arms slid over the smooth skin of her back, pressing her close as if sensing an immediate need. Julia rested her head gently against his chest, listening to the rhythmic drumming of his heart, as both bodies now worked to relax.

"Will this be a new routine of yours?" she asked in a quiet voice, though knowing she was the aggressor in the funneling of their act.

"Yes. I still want to see you. That has not changed with time." Michael droned, knowing, without a doubt, that that was in fact the truth. It was the sole purpose of his visit, and after today, he was sure it would keep him coming back. "I've been thinking about you—a lot."

Slowly nodding in response, Julia's gaze shifted, though she seemed unwilling to give whether that was in concurrence or comprehension of what was said. "It seems my body keeps betraying me with you. You keep getting me to...well..." her sigh came sounding ambiguously wrench. "Maybe we should...I mean, maybe...we can come... to...an agreement." She stumbled, asking this in a strained voice. She brandished a timid smile, slowly gathering his eyes as she waited. Again apprehensive of his answer, as she now felt suddenly exposed.

"Is that a 'yes' I'm hearing?" he asked in a cautious tone, suspecting that with her, it could just as well not be that.

"Not for dating, just…this," She grunted, jutting her chin towards his chest, she enunciated her meaning with the rigid bow of her head.

A deep frown furrowed the smooth skin of Michael's forehead, tensing lightly before he spoke. "You're still saying no to going out with me?" he asked lamely, almost afraid of the impending decree.

"Consider us buddies," Julia smiled, suddenly playful, she shrugged, well pleased to finally get the matter off her chest. "Very, very, very, friendly buddies."

"We can do this again—whenever, but…I can't take you out to a nice restaurant?"

"All the benefits, none of the heartaches," She smiled.

"Why?"

"You know why." She sighed, giving him a halfhearted shrug. "Maybe we just need something that the other person has to offer right now. I'm not sure. I only know you're on my mind—a lot. So why not satisfy each other's cravings by walking in with both eyes wide open. If there's no expectation then there can be no heartbreak."

Lowering himself to the bed, Michael held her close while his mind reeled with a sundry of thoughts. As nice as she felt, she seemed almost as troubling to his nerve, with decisions that left him scratching his head in confusion. Her offer was vaguely familiar in its relaying, having had the same proposition spilled from his very own lips. Why then does he hesitate in his decision with her?

"I'm going against everything I stand for, Michael." Julia grumbled through the pause. "Well, what I thought I stood for."

"You're offering me your body," he questioned softly, needing for some reason to be sure. "And nothing else?"

"To do with as you wish, and I was more thinking of…us, as long as the other is available that is."

"I get carte blanche over your entire body?" Michael asked with a sense of uncertainty, though smiling with intrigue at the thought. Her eyes gently fell from his face with the query and, as if her mind still wrestled with her choice, taunting lips pressed together in thought. Michael's eyes settled on the hypnotizing feature, and like a highly enthralled youth. His gaze stayed. *What was it about her mouth that keeps drawing him back?* "You can't possibly think I would turn you down?" he asked, easing the awkwardness of the moment with the broadening of his smile. "I think "yes" goes without saying." He rasped, noting the small frown she wore as he rose to syphon a kiss.

"Not so fast, Michael," she grunted, her hand screeching to a stop against his mouth. "There are rules you have to agree to abide by first."

"Of course there would be." Michael smirked, the corner of his mouth almost twisting with the humor that spilled with such thought. "Such as?" He asked softly, returning his head to the mattress in wait.

"I don't like lies," she began in a new voice, sounding more like someone other than herself. "And I hate cheats even more, so you need to consider everything before you agree." Julia warned sternly, her voice growing almost sharp. "With that said, these are my rules. This has to be exclusive." She declared then, pausing as she quietly studied his expression, though there was no tell to his face that she could aptly read, nothing definitive with which to pick from. "I don't play second chair to anyone, and I don't share my men. So tell me now and we can end this without anyone getting hurt. Do you have this arrangement with anyone else?"

"No, I don't."

"Are you sure? Are you seeing anyone? I know it's a little late to ask that but… it's better now than never." Julia informed stoically. With her eyes keenly fixed to his, she watched as he toyed with her hair, looking well relaxed through the moil of her inquisition.

"No. There's no one." Michael answered simply, keeping his answers short and to the point.

"Is that the truth, Michael? Or is it Hollywood's truth?" she asked firmly, her voice sailing back with a heavier edge. Her frown then deepened as she eyed him with a meager show of distrust.

"I promise you, that's the truth. Hollywood or otherwise. There's no one currently in my life."

"Is there anyone you think you may be attracted to?"

"No. There's only you."

Julia waited in uncertain silence, her eyes trained like a hawk to his face. If she was going to do this, then it had to be made clear. There can be no surprises. Not when it pertains to something like this, and she had to be certain he understood that fact. "Do you understand what I'm asking, Michael?"

"I understand what you're asking." He murmured softly, refraining, with little effort, from spoiling the obvious facts. In her own round-about way, she managed to ask for all the benefits that came with a committed relationship, one that usually starts with the simplicity of a first date. For in that, she now sternly requested all the things that he'd been asking of her.

"Then the deal is this, we can…play…however often, there are no limits, only restrictions. This is my home. My family…my kids are my first priority. When I have them, we are away from home a lot. So those occasions are simply excused as off limits. I just won't be able to be there, nor can I do anything about that. But when I'm free, I'm all yours—if you're available. Lastly, if you feel you're becoming attracted to someone else, tell me before you enter into a new arrangement with her. Next, this is between us and us alone, I will not be the topic of discussion for anyone. I like my business to remain just that, my business." She grunted, tilting her head back, she cautiously gathered in his eyes. "Did I leave anything out?" she murmured in a softening tone.

"No. It sounds as if you've covered everything." Michael shrugged.

"Are my terms acceptable to you?" she quarried, further softening her tone.

A heavy silence consumed the room as she waited his response, waited while he allowed her words the reverence they deserved. Evidently, she had given the matter great thought, which told him, quite convincingly, he was not alone in his discontent. "They are. Do you need me to swear?"

"No. Nothing that drastic," she shrugged, and a small smile flirted with the corner of her mouth.

"I swear to you," he groaned, his deep voice ruffling the new silence of the room, resting his hand gently to the top of her left breast. Hazel eyes burned into hers. "From this day on, to abide by all the rules so stated by you." Finishing with a grin, Michael rolled, pinning her nicely under him. His mouth settled upon hers, soft, sensual in its gifting, he vehemently sealed their agreement with the sizzle of a kiss.

"Are you sure?" Julia whispered, her breath curling soft against his mouth.

"Are you?"

"No. But it seems I'm over ruled. You've turned my body against me."

"Have I? And you…" he questioned, touching the tip of his nose to hers. "You had nothing to do with any of it?"

"Not so much," she sighed, knowing he could feel the thudding in her chest. "Not willingly."

"You're an intriguing woman, Julia Berwick," he mumbled with a slow shake of his head. "You peak me at every turn."

"So I'm a puzzle to you?"

"Not exactly put, but…" Michael's head swayed in contemplation, and an odd downturned twist to the corner of his face, came in the aiding of his reply. "Not fully wrong either."

"And what happens once you've figured me out?" Julia asked in a whisper, lifting her chin as his kisses breached the slender lines her throat.

"I'm not sure," he murmured against the indent of her neck. "I guess I'll know when we get there."

"You do know the empty box loses its intrigue just as much as that new toy will?"

"Which one do you suppose you are?" Michael asked, frowning lightly.

"I'm sure that's a decision suited for the giftee himself. I can only be what you see." She smiled, demurely batting her eyes as she spoke.

"The fickle child or the new present, which one of us do you think will have clarity first?"

"You tell me."

"That's going to take some time to figure out." He mumbled, propping the weight of his body to an elbow, he smiled.

"So you're not sure either?"

"But isn't that queued to the purpose of a date? Two people getting to know each other, taking that time to figure out what comes next. I'm the same as any man who's hoping to find that distinctive fit. No different."

Definitively, he was right. The sole purpose to drinks, dinner or a movie was to make that electrifying connection with someone else, hoping there's enough sparks to build upon. But dating does not seem to be his world's forte. Relationships barely last a month, and marriages, in that, were more like the punch-line of a joke than not. Why would she open herself up to that? Why would anyone? He unleashed a part of her that seethed like a roaring furnace, pushing her ever onward. He floats constantly through her mind, fervently reminding her of all she had missed. Five years is a long time to not have the touch of a man, a very long time. She just wanted to enjoy it now while it lasted. "It is." She stated simply, a mellifluous smile swallowing her entire face. "But I've given you the greatest part of that. It stands inimitable without any of the other trappings to muddle its path."

"And I get to do whatever it is I want?" he asked raggedly, a smirk floating forward while his fingers caressed the silkiness of her hips.

"The same rules apply from the weekend, just with a little more leisure attached, I suppose." She affirmed with a coy smile.

"How long exactly will your mother be gone?" Michael growled, his voice twirling friskily in her ears.

"The house is ours and ours alone for the entire weekend. Are you up for playing?"

"First things first," he counter with a light frown, glancing curiously around the room, he asked. "Where's your cellphone?"

"It's in the bathroom, why?" she asked in a soft twitter, her brows hiking in aid of the question. Michael simpered in response, giving no words in answer. He bounded from the bed, quickly ducking from the room. Long fingers worked absorbedly on his return, looking up at last with a smile, he waggled his brows as in the wont of a game. "So we don't have a repeat of the last weekend we had." He explained through a rough drawl, his voice dipping as he repositioned himself in bed. With his tall frame again topping hers, he connected all important parts to their likely structured kin. "Now, what was it you were saying about playing?" Michael asked with a lazy grin. "By the way, I'm JD."

"Yes, that's right! I'm loosely familiar with JD's exquisite taste. The flowers, by the way, were especially beautiful. Thank you."

"You're welcome. Now, what was that saying? Oh, yeah, 'my turn',"

Chapter Twenty Three

Wildly indicative of a hive, the hums were unremitting. Whirring perpetually through the spinney blades of pines, the wind's cries aptly drowned the afternoon's clamor. Batting the heads of burgeoning vegetation, the breadth of its antics lectured of an imminent storm, summoning night rashly with its assault. Darkness brought naught to reprieve the cogency of a querulous wind, giving aid to its scalpeling arm. It loitered while the lively gust skillfully sheared the new warmth.

A new week arrived with the emergence of morning, rocked heavily on the sails of the harrowing wind. It, too, gawked at the enigmatic occurrence. Ribbons of gray trolled a chalky ceiling, vaguely conceding light to the dusky swallow, still the wind refused to lessen its gust. Much like the gestic of a dance, the trees chronically swayed, lending their nonpareil voice to the droning. Lanky limbs flailed exhaustingly amidst the gusty force, and time evolved through the bother of a merciless tick, aging the surly morning. It weakened the breadth of a tarrying gloom, as hints of gold breached a dissident sky, and, although faint, the tiddling of birds came as a chorus through the rollicking gales.

Seeing only beauty in the day's wavering grayness, Julia's gaze strode the aeonian malcontent, an ardent smile notably carved on her face. Recognizing the verve of her old self, her body arched in a long, lingering stretch, and a dreamy sigh leisurely emitted the silky yielding. With her sleep now granting the serenity of old, she was again her phlegmatic self. Undisturbed by the irksome struggles of the past, her body greedily recouped the losses it had. Thus, it buried itself deep in the arms of Morpheus for a goodly spell. Gone were the heavy components that had descended on her mood. No longer hounded by denials, she was again free, granting herself permission to enjoy the peppery morsels of her imaginings.

A balmy air cradled the soft rhetoric of her voice, lifting the notes to the ceiling. Her hums straddled the halls, ascending the curvy passage of the stairs like the distant chirp of a bird. Ensuring her children's progress, Julia's treads were almost nonexistent on the descent, floating to the kitchen on the absence of clouds. Humor structured the essence of her intone and her strive. Remaining unperturbed in her efforts, such lightness marked the recurrent prodding of their drive, for as is customary in their morning routine. The school-bus did not rear as an important entity for which they strived. Instead, it leapt forward as a nuisance to be tolerated in their tapered view.

In an act symptomatic in the likeness of a reincarnation, Julia moved through her days seemingly inspired by an unseen force, tackling each task with rejuvenated vim.

She whittled through the day's contribution with the daubing of a smile. Consequently, her jovial comportment captured Delia's ecstatic regard, delighted with the startling transformation. She openly seethed with excitement at the show. "*It's been a long time coming,*" Delia expounded with a smile.

"I think you're right, mom." Julia retorted with a wry grin of her own. Rinsing the dishes from their pioneer meal, she stacked the dishwasher drawer. "I don't treat myself enough and I think it's time I change that." Elaborating this with a nod, she soaped the walls of the large sink, her head bouncing brusquely as if to affirm the decision to herself. "From now on, every opening I get. I'm going to do something for me."

"That's great!" Delia applauded in what richly favored a squeal, throwing her hands behind the exuberant exclaim. Her face bloomed with the brilliancy of her smile, as did the lively green of her eyes. "I'm so glad to hear you say that, sweetie! That's such a great first step! Do you have any idea where you want to go?"

"No. Not yet." She droned, dropping the lie like a gentle hum. She quickly bent her attention back to the task at hand. Usually, secrets were a rarity between them. Anything of importance was typically discussed, to varying depths, with amicable results. But this was not one for conversation nor warranted her aid, not with the prurient things she had planned in her head. Since she strongly doubted any part of their deeds fell under the category of friendship. Knowing, with all certainty, it did not, although it would surely be otherwise titled in the eyes of her mother. "I'm just going to play it by ear and see where the wind blows me each time." She chirped.

"That is such a wonderful idea! Just keep your mind free. Keep yourself open. I like that!" Delia again chirped, truly elated with the decision, her mind eagerly assessed the significance behind such change. Maybe the crucial step would now steer her towards incorporating other things—equally significant in their purpose—in the dim arches of her life. Perhaps even open her more to the possibility of dating. Who knows the potentials this has? She beamed. "It's so good to see remnants of your old self coming back! I've missed the energy it yielded."

"I've been here, mom. I didn't go anywhere."

"No, darling, you haven't. You haven't been here for a long time. I think the divorce, the shock of daddy's illness, his death—me. I think it all affected you more than you think. More than *I* think you're even willing to admit. You haven't been yourself since..." Delia sighed, lifting her shoulders in careful abet of her words, her green eyes gathered those of her progeny's brown. "Darling, you take remarkable care of everyone," she resumed with a soft shake of her head. "And a toll like that would have taken a lot out of anyone. It's taken a lot of life's fire out of you."

"I'm fine, mom, really. I am." She croaked, her voice ringing loudly its somber note. Dipping with the falling of her head, dark eyes lazily shimmied to the sink. "They were hard times, I know." She shrugged. "Especially daddy's death, but..." obliging the weak descent of her shoulders, her voice trailed to a doddering stop. In challenge of the pause, the murmured music of water callously bombarded the smooth surface of the sink, complementing the riotous howls of the wind. Its tireless whines cloaked the room now swallowed in silence, censoring the tenseness of their breath.

Painted on her mother's face was a stirring concoction of pain, as was the evidence of her love. With both now heavily compressed into a gauche smile, the two together then jutted from her eyes. Such topic was not usually a conversation piece fitted to their home, stringently cleaving to her aspiration of such. She therefore avoided the vale of unpleasantness that accompanied the undesired result. Unless instigated by her mother, all discussions referring her father was tactfully left from their exchange. Afraid, as ever, to revisit the terrifying abode from whence they escaped. "I handled it. I didn't see the need to…well. I miss him. I miss him every day, but…" She sighed, swallowing the tightening in her throat. Her eyes quickly tackled the floor. "I know he wouldn't want me to mope forever."

"No, he wouldn't. He wouldn't want that at all." Delia replied tamely, seating herself at the table, her gaze grew unwavering in their search. The gentle words given were thence promptly devoured, wolfed by the incessant hiss at the sink. Its stubborn chorus filled every corner of the room, as aptly so as the trill tailored to a scream. "He also wouldn't want to see what you've done to your life either, since that would pain him. Daddy loved life, sweetheart." She whispered hoarsely. "Yet you seem to be hiding from yours."

"I'm not hiding, mom, I'm just…" the sound of her breath sliced the abruptness of the silence, and a weighty shrug swallowed the non-existence of words. "I don't…I, I just don't…feel it." She stuttered, letting her eyes move jaggedly over the counter to the dishwasher door. The sound of rushing water slowly penetrated her cochlea to imprint softly on her brain, and an almost doleful hand gently depressed the waiting lever. The room fell precipitously tranquil, as if a cacophonous stereo had been behind the ruckus in the room.

"You can't know what you're never a part of, darling. Try stepping onto the ride. I promise you, you'll find something there for you. It's a struggle every day I open my eyes to go on without him, but I keep reminding myself how much he loved to experience life. When I go on my trips, I know he's with me for the haul. I go because of him, despite myself, because of what was. Assured that the things I experience while I'm there would truly make him proud, and that's worth the effort of taking an added breath." She expounded dimly, brushing a finger across her eyes, she roughly wiped the progression of her tears. "Daddy wouldn't want us to not go on living, sweetie. He wouldn't."

"I know, mom. It's just…hard. I can't seem to…" she shrugged. "I don't know.… I don't know what's wrong."

"You buried everything then because you had to. Maybe it would help if you unearthed the culprit for a while. Perhaps smooth the pocks that have since quarried deep."

"I've never really thought about it…well…" she shrugged, her eyes again falling to the counter.

"We've never talked about…this. You know, daddy…."

"I didn't want to…well. I was afraid it would hurt you."

"I know, baby. I know." She sighed, her whispered answer straying no further than the reach of her hand, almost stagnant in its unfurling. It hovered in the stodgy silence they created. "But I'm better now, sweetheart. Much better, thanks to you. I promise you, I won't break if you lean on me some. It's my job. Actually, it's the best job in the world, and it's my favorite thing to do above all else." She smiled, again wiping her eyes.

Julia's head slowly bounced in response, and fretful eyes, in their wonder, skulked across the counter from the floor. Gathering the red tinge of her mother's gaze, they lingered in place, as if to test the currency of the truth she now offered to be solely that. "Okay, mom," she mouthed, her words falling tardy behind a soft expel, breaking the staunchness of the room. She again affirmed her decision with a nod. "Do you remember the time we rented the cottage in the mountain and daddy forgot to pack the bag with the maple syrup in the car?" she asked, her voice extruding weak, falling as if from a distance like an afterthought to something else. A hand awkwardly daubed the outer edges of her eyes. The brown orbs hazed as if she eloped to a place in the past, gazing through some far off window with the query. "And we had to drive, something like, four miles to get to that tiny general store. Remember? Daddy ended up paying almost five dollars for a microscopic bottle of syrup, all because he promised us pancakes for breakfast and he wanted to right his mistake." She sighed, and an odd smile touched the corner of her face.

"We kept that bottle for a whole year just so we could rub the reality of that price in his face." Delia hummed, nodding her head as she offered a smile. "I remember. I remember everything, and that's why I keep going on. And I need you to start doing the same, sweetie."

"Okay." Julia whispered with a gentle nod, uncertain of the validity tamped in the answer she gave. Was it really truth or did she speak a lie? She groaned, the words twirling madly in her head, only knowing she meant the word as it was spoken then, yet understood the strangeness of the promise itself. Her mother did not appear to be fractured by the pessimistic dialogue. Neither did she look as despondent as she expected she would. Her mien seemed almost relaxed. Sorrowed, yet somehow contented, as if relieved of a burden she had carried for far too long, and was now quite happy to set the cumbersome weight free.

"How about the time we went to Canada and he bought tickets for us to go to that historic theater? Remember that one? We got all the way there only to find out that the tickets were for the following week?" Delia chuckled, adjusting her body on the chair.

"Yes! And we ended up spending hours at the hockey museum instead!" Julia finished with a revivifying smirk.

"Well, until we quite literally couldn't stand another minute of all that sport drivel. Lord! Whew, that's boring, Canadians and their hockey!" She chirped, her eyes jumping to the ceiling. "Thank God for the workability of hindsight, that's when we finally got so mad that we left him there to go out and eat. That restaurant was amazing!" Delia added coolly, rolling her eyes triumphantly at the finish, she laughed.

"Do you ever wonder if he did that on purpose, you know, just so he would have company to go to the museum?" Julia asked with a festering frown. "As I remember, neither one of us wanted to set foot in that place, remember. No matter what bribes he offered, we flatly refused."

"You think?" Delia answered with a question of her own, puzzled by the premise, her scowl profoundly deepened. George Waltham was often a mischievous devil, more so at times than not, something fiendish stayed hidden beneath his sleeve. And knowing the sporadic extravagance of his games, she wouldn't put it past him to use such rascally behavior to get his way.

"Daddy was always playing little tricks on us, and in counter, we were always eager to try and outmaneuver his pranks. I wouldn't be surprised if he did that on purpose." Julia shrugged, smiling pleasantly at the thought.

"That little devil! You know, he probably did, just to get us back for something we probably won."

"We didn't have such a bad time." Julia smiled, "At least we didn't once we got to the restaurant."

"Do you remember that bill?" Delia smirked victoriously. "I think we won the game that day."

"I remember the bill. But I also remember how surprised we were when he wasn't as incensed as we expected." Julia snickered, looking somewhat confused with the tale. She stared puzzlingly at her mother, mirroring the confounded expression her parent now flaunted. Silence then fizzled into rapturous laughter, kindling the once dejected room with new life, as both women achieved an epiphany as if by the turn of a page. George Waltham became the topic of discussion in the hours that followed. With both giving recollections of one supposed mishap after another, analyzing each. They marveled at the intricate brilliance of the man. A slow dawning then brightened, as the extent of his trickery was elaborately dissected and revived.

———

Diversely, the Berwick's residence received three unforeseen deliveries strewn throughout the new week. Launching the surreptitious arrivals, a stunning arrangement of pink orchids enhanced an already spectacular day.

To the beauty of taking turns, JD.

"That it is." Julia smiled, concurring with the inference of his words, she sighed. The expulsion drifted from her lips in the wont of a passive breeze, coasting playful in its rise, like the tuning of a key. Her mind assembled the cause of her inducement as well as their depths, and the list grew profoundly enticing in the pictures they disclosed, thrilling her with the potential of events already set. It heightened the frayed edges of a patience she now rightly needed.

Prompted by the new covenant, an appointment with her doctor was an imperative step. With the pill being staunchly efficient in endeavors of such, it was a far safer bet than the alternative practice. Thus it persuaded her decision without pause. In the five years since her divorce, she has had no occasion to deliberate matters of such, not until the beatific features of Michael Dunhill. No one else had ever come close to upheaving the serenity moored to her quite world, and she was yet unsure how or why he had. Something about him draws her regardless of plot, and resisting seemed a futile toil to no benign end. No matter the fortitude applied in the tries. One she appears destined to lose, at least for a spell.

Wednesday brought with it the intrigue of a new delivery, one well opposite of the rest. The small package incorporated a uniquely carved Styrofoam box, housed inside the refrigerated case. Another container prettily displayed four ample slices that summed a scrumptiously decorated cheese cake.

Since you've refused to have dinner with me, I'm opting for dessert. Join me at seven. I made reservations, JD.

Ps. check your listing. I'm certain you know the place.

It took an impressive show of tenacity to keep her eyes from persistently mauling the clock. Julia grumbled in silence as her eyes again clobbered the dark, orbicular face, this being her fifth tour in the short stint of half-an-hour. The evening's length was almost sardonic, creeping by on well-aged feet. The hours seemed surely to pause at intervals for rest. Unable to squelch the anxiety of waiting, she meagerly plied herself to her task, picking through her dinner, though she made sure she left ample room for dessert.

On the pretense of making an important call, Julia disappeared to her room at six-fifty on the dot. Locking the door at her back, she eagerly marched to her closet, this while butterflies fluttered through the crater in her stomach with the advancement of each step. Julia gazed appreciatively at the gesture, sliding the chilled container from its hiding place, she smiled. A small stack of icepacks surrounded the elegant presentation, keeping the content well chilled in its frosty bed.

In readiness, Julia garnered a seat on the closet floor, tucking one leg beneath the other, as if to start the serene process of introspection. She pulled an extra pillow from a shelf just within reach of her straining hand, dropping said prop to her back in provision of her paltry wait. With phone in hand, she stared excitedly at the small clock, feeling girlish in her bent. Her enthusiasm reverberated through to the clammy tips of each hand. Barely allowing the minutes to celebrate the naissance of the seventh hour, Julia pressed the highlighted green button, getting an instant response. His deep voice coasted like supple leather from the other end.

"Hi!" Michael exclaimed, the deep timbre coming slow, stroking more than her ear with its vibrancy.

"Do you really have to have a reservation, or is anyone allowed at this restaurant?" she quipped, tracing the outer rim of the Styrofoam box, her body contently sighed.

"Strictly by reservation only," Michael murmured huskily, stretching his back against the pillows on the couch. Having taken much the same precaution as his companion, he reposed in the privacy of his suite. "If you're calling, then it must mean you found your invitation. So that makes you safe." He smiled, and the essence of said feature fell to her, much the same as it would, had she witnessed the unfolding. "How are you?" he drawled.

"I'm good. How are you?" she purred, lying back onto the pillow, she propped her feet to a shelf housing her shoes.

"I'm good—busy. How are the kids?"

"Keeping me busy—and Betty?"

"Keeping me in line," he smiled. "I like this voice you're using, it's nice. Where are you calling me from?" he mumbled low, the rich tone toting the scraps of a smile.

"My closet, where are you?"

"My bedroom, what are you wearing?" Michael drawled, his voice lowering to a deep hush against the phone, as he again adjusted his long body on the couch. Lying flat on his back, he tucked an arm as a pillow to his head, dropping his legs atop the furniture's arm.

"Hey! What kind of restaurant are you running here? You can't harass your customers like that!" she objected with a feigned groan, yet fully prepared to describe her manner of dress.

"Fine, we'll stick to food then." Michael griped, straightening on the couch, his eyes rushed to the waiting dessert, presently exposed on a small table abutting his seat. "Open up your container." He directed as he gathered his fork, and the body affix to the other end quickly obeyed his instruction without pause. "These are from one of my favorite restaurants, 'Annu'. Let's start with the white chocolate, take a bite and tell me what you think."

Savoring the velvety texture, the flavor scraped the receptors on her tongue. Easily melting in her mouth, it washed her with a pleasant sensation. "Mmmm! Oh, that's good!"

"You like that, I see?" he asked in a gravelly drawl, allowing the inveigling sound to spread through his body, Michael smiled. "Do that again." He murmured to the phone.

"Do what?"

"That sound, make that sound again." Michael bade, twirling a finger around the handle of his fork. A slow, lazy grin migrated across the chiseling of his face, widening as her voice drifted back in compliance with the elfin request. "I like that. It's…nice, very nice." He rasped, giving full credence to the evoking. The small sound provoked memories that were better left untouched, memories that granted no out, especially for one now slumbering alone. "Okay, let's move on." He grunted, quickly shifting his thought.

Knowing exactly where his mind went, Julia's smile widened. Her insight touring the shadowy regions of his thoughts, seeming to have a weird perception of its workings, her smile further expanded. His introduction on the remaining pieces ensued, and although she deeply loved her tasting of each, the white chocolate remained her favorite of the four. The experience was incalculably new. Sharing something so simple, yet the interlude itself was profoundly elite.

"Do you see how easy it can be to share a meal with me?" Michael teased, electing a bottle of beer from a small bucket on the floor. He crudely wrung the cap free, guzzling the first mouthful in wait of a response.

"I promise to keep the statistics in mind." She smirked, donating the sly answer. Julia set the barely eaten pieces aside. Returning her head to the pillow, she propped her legs atop a waiting shelf. "Wha—"

"Mom!" Richard called, his voice exploding as a bellow from her door. Hardly waiting for a refurbished response, his fingers worked the handle of her door.

Startled, Julia bolted from her position on the floor, snapping the container shut. She returned it to the Styrofoam box. "I have to go. I'm being summoned." She whispered, pushing the parcel under the hanging hems of her dresses. Her voice dipped excruciatingly low.

"You go ahead then. Thanks for dessert."

"Thank you for having me, and thank JD for the flowers, will you? Again, they were exquisite."

"An endowment accordant to the heir, it's a perfect match, you two."

"Mom! Mom!" Richard cried repeatedly, his voice again resonating through the tranquil aura of the house. The click of the handle promptly followed his nasally beckon, wafting like an exclamation sign behind the single syllable. It emphasized the urgency of his resolve.

"I really need to go. I'll talk to you soon." She hissed, her voice now coming in a hush, dipping with every word.

"Until then?" Michael asked, as if confirming a promise already made, the rich baritone of his voice gave the words a wealthy life.

"Until," she replied, immediately knowing the meaning behind his question, she paused. Savoring the simplicity of the word along with all the possibilities it had, and the combining effect felt the equivalent of a dozen calming breaths all taken at once. It soothed and excited in a single utterance.

"Goodnight, Julia."

"Goodnight, Michael." She breathed to the phone, gazing at the screen as if to verify the conversation's end. She strolled from her closet feeling again renewed. Julia ignored the range of the chorus now coming from her door, simply swinging the egress wide. She calmly remedied the grating beckon. "Yes, Richard." She muttered with a sigh, her voice coming cool. It sailed to him like a light breeze on a blistery day.

"Mom, I need a new glue stick for school. Can I have one?" He announced calmly, stepping sharply backwards with his proclamation, as if expecting an instant profit on his words.

"And for this you bellowed?" Julia asked in what seemed an incredulous squawk, sighing, her eyes rolled to the ceiling and back, as did the ascending resonance of her breath. "This is your reason for howling at my door?"

"But I'm all out! And my teacher said I need to bring in a new one, or I'll be in trouble." Richard stated flatly, rattling off the information in one continual gust, a flustered look then teetered on his face.

"And you choose now to tell me this? Why? It's almost your bedtime, Richard."

"I was busy with all my work, I forgot." He protested, his retort flying back promptly, and ceaseless fingers aggressively fidgeted with the stitching on his shirt.

"And what work would that be, Richard?" Julia asked sternly, moving her hands precariously to her hips in wait.

"Ah, homework…and…" Richard stammered, fidgeting with each finger, he then moved to the bed of each nail. "My chores!" he announced gladly, his eyes widening as if the words carried an armor of their own.

"All of which were done before your bath and, the hour you requested for your stint on the video game."

"But…but I didn't, I—" he croaked, his voice stuttering to a stop, shifting his weight from one leg to the other, his breath whistled from his nose. "—I need it!" Richard squeaked, hastily capping the negotiation with an eloquent précis of his own.

"Then you should have asked earlier now, shouldn't you?"

"Mom, please! I'm going to be in trouble. I need it!"

Julia's sigh sailed blandly through the threshold yet whelming their form, seeing his small body twitch nervously under the sharpness of her gaze. She relent the intense edge stalking her probe. "Let's go before you bruise that beautiful brain of yours." Muttering this in a drab tone, she dropped a hand to his shoulders, turning him jestingly towards the closet that housed the aforementioned supplies. "You remember this closet, don't you, Richard?" she asked, her tone sailing overly sweet.

"Yes. It has the school supplies." Richard replied proudly, his eyes once again wide.

"And did you bother to look inside for the item you needed? Let's say, something like…um. Let's see, ah…glue stick? Did you check the place that would carry that?" she asked again in a sweetened chant.

"Oh." He grunted, spitting the word with little more than a short curve of his brows before resuming his strides.

Of course not! Julia smirked in the silence of her head, pulling the small door open. She waited for his eyes to scan each shelf. A stack of five twin-packs sat in a clear bin on a shelf perfect for his height, the orangey publish almost mocking in the place that they rested. "Well look at that, Richard, glue sticks!" She exclaimed, smiling teasingly, she asked. "How many do you need, Richard?"

"Two." He mumbled dully.

"Oh. I'm not sure I have enough. I'll have to see, Richard. Um, let's see, one. Oh, look! It already has two in one package, imagine that!" She smiled, plucking the tiny parcel from the bin. Her eyes trundled his face. "The things you could discover if you just let that big brain of yours do the work. You would be dangerous, Richard."

"Thanks, mom!" Richard cried, hardly hearing a word of what was said, he smiled fondly as he relieved the packet from her hand. With his only concern now resolved, his elation now rested on the fact that he was no longer one on the verge of being punished for an idiotic deed.

"Did you brush your teeth?"

"I was about to——" He started in a piddling voice, stopping as his mother's hand ripped through the air like a flag suddenly starch.

"Then get to it." Julia grunted, knowing that she stalled the sequence on a heavy batch of excuse. "I'll be up to say good night shortly, and I will be checking those teeth, so scrub them well." Richard whirled from his place as if by unseen hand, already racing down the hall, his small feet pummeled the floor in exaggerated haste. "Walk!" she called, her voice coming as a song, scraping the ceiling with its might, it left no room for speculation on its intent. The drumming instantly eased to a hardy tread, continuing down the hall, though halfway up the stairs. It again returned to a brusque stomp. Julia groaned tersely at the ceiling, shaking her head, she sighed. A smile then edged the rigid expression on her face, leaving the matter untouched, as she knew no better antidote for her ire than the deversion of laughter.

The third delivery came as the loath glazing to an utterly hectic week, though as usual, it wielded a beautiful exhibition of the best. Julia groused at their continued showing, yet she thoroughly admired the exquisite vaunt they displayed. Hence an added delight soared with the bestowal itself, grateful in her guilt that they were, at least delivered by someone else.

Sweet fire of my heart, come softly me. Sweet fire of my heart, give yourself to me. Set your flames to my ardor. Engulf me in your warmth. Take me from my misery and set me in your heart.

Yours, infatuated admirer,

Julia grumbled on the oddity of the moment as she deposited the card to a small draw in her desk. Grazing the delicate bloom of a rose, she sighed, as her gaze was not fully dominated with aversion towards the magnificent presence itself. "Who sent you?" she asked, directing her question to the rich burgundy bulbs, yet none gave an answer in revenue of her appeal. "How could anyone waste so much time, money and effort without showing himself by now? What exactly does he intend to gain? Can you tell me that?"

———————

Friday brought with it a fresh palate for the start of the coveted week's end, sending waves of excitement through her body. It held her fully enthralled within its grasp. The pesky irking mattered not where or what task was being done, only the extent of the intensity it lent. Since in supremacy of will, the delicious sensation claimed her attention at odd intervals throughout the entirety of her day, sweetly reminding her of what was to come.

Julia gazed enthusiastically at the illustrious house, knowing once inside, she would lose all aspect of her lucid self. The man inside would adroitly make certain of that, and in commemoration of such truth, her heart pounded as if it belonged to something wild. Jarring her fiercely, her hand nigh trembled as she reached for the protruding bell. Wrenching the offending limb back, Julia waited instead to find calm. For her body now seemed burdened with naught but anticipation, desire and lust. Spliced in a fiery brewing, it would not ease the elixir it fed. She has had dreams in expectancy of this pending, and she hoped their treaty did not change the potency of their alliance, as she would hate to temper even the smallest pinch of what they shared. Not when it gifted such exhilarating outcome, and certainly not before she has had her fill.

"Don't look so desperate, Julia," she scolded in a whisper. "Try to maintain a little dignity, will you? Calm yourself before you enter the house. And for God's sake, stop making this so important!" she rebuked in a grumble. Forcefully swallowing a large gulp, she instantly partook of seconds, this just to acquire a pittance of calm. Her body felt strangely like a puppeteer's toy, almost ethereal in her personality. Nothing about it or the moment seemed anything like herself.

The whirring of her breath sailed as if from a long tunnel, dragging her shoulders with the heavy plunge, it weighted the lids of her eyes. Raising a shaky hand to the ornate doorbell, Julia repeated her earlier warns, though the effort seemed an unnecessary bother to her ear. As her pulse further heightened its gallop the minute Michael's tall form came to her view. Deposited to the door in minimal treads, the elegant barring swung immediately wide, and his smile was like a beacon that immediately captured her eyes. Yet she could not help but wonder whether such radiance was sent to pull her to the darkness or through. *It's unfair for anyone to look that good*, she griped, understanding first hand why he had been voted the sexiest man alive two years in a row.

No words sailed in greeting from the bodies that so affably draped the entrance, only the sizzle of their smile screamed of their proclivity for each other. Seconds passed, and still the two stood taut, planted on the edge of their elected precinct. They smiled warmly in the pertinence of a conversation not heard, though understood, consuming each other; their eyes fondled the other with its heated touch. Michael's hand glided slowly through the sweetened air now nestled around both, his upturned palm waiting like paradise's offer of rest after a lengthy quest. Julia's thin fingers eagerly repose atop the heated skin, gently closing the warm cloak of his hand. He promptly ingested her in warmth. The contact was deliciously erotic. Decadent, like the taste of a sinful dessert, and both eyes, in unison, registered the excitement it brought. Michael's gaze instantly lowered to her mouth, lingering, they roamed eagerly over her body, and his entire being grumbled with the delicacy offered with such sight.

The evening sky had slowly grown dim, with darkness now smothering the last splotch of an orangey glow. Its brilliance rested beautifully at her back, and she looked especially beautiful standing under the withering sun. Thus the urge to pounce and syphon her dry grew compelling—but he held. Instead, strong hands gently pulled her through the threshold that once separated the two, closing the door behind them. Michael set his back to the wide barring, hazel eyes, in longing, further obtained their fill. Admiring the lean fit of her blush colored dress, his smile slowly widened. Ditto for the silvery sandals, well haunting in its evocative prominence, upon her feet, completing the assemblage with her toes painted to match the beguiling frock. The garment's hem sat high, stopping well short of her knees. The design's only job was simply done and done well, as it wrapped itself nicely to every curve that she held.

"You look...amazing." He whispered as his eyes further ravished her body.

"Thank you." Julia smiled, taking her own time to enrapture the view. Looking comfortably elegant in his usual attire, the sleeves of his shirt were folded back to display a portion of his bronzy arm. "So do you." She murmured, softly biting her lower lip, her eyes roamed the features of his face. Julia watched as he pushed himself from the door in silence, stepping towards her. He paused before again taking her hand, leading her to the kitchen without further wording on his thoughts.

A lone candle sat in the center of the usual breakfast table, as was the setting for two. Bequeathing a certain comforting grace, the quiet room seemed content with all things again righted.

"No props this time?" Julia teased, looking playfully around the room.

"No. I decided to impress you on a grander scale. I ordered the backdrop to surround the house instead." Michael smiled, waving at the window. He indicated the last remnant of the setting sun. "It cost me a fortune. But it's beautiful don't you think?" he smiled, and for a moment he looked almost nervous.

"That's impressive."

"I know."

"It's beautiful. But I'm sure you're good for the expense." She shrugged, her eyes again playful.

"Yeah, I'm good for it." Michael muttered faintly, wanting badly to kiss her then, though he again held. "We should eat." He murmured dryly in the silence that followed.

"Okay." She answered with a nod, and a hint of disappointment laced the soft spilling of her voice, though she hid the effects of that well.

"So what have you been up to?" he asked in a low voice, leading her to the table, he quietly seated her. His gaze lingering as he worked.

"Not much, just busy with the usual," She murmured absently, and her gaze hungrily shimmed the ridges of his body, resting on his hands. It thence walked over the muscular form of a thigh. "I took the kids to see the new opening at the Mint Museum. We liked it. It was good." She rambled, unable to stop the roiling of her nerves.

"I read about that. The reviews were good." Michael countered with a nod, pausing. His eyes dropped to his hands now bedded on the table between them. "I'm sorry." He murmured without looking up, his voice stroking the tense silence of the room. "I'm trying. I'm really trying hard not to turn you off right now. I'm trying not to make you feel like a piece of meat. But…" he sighed, looking her over with venomous hunger in his eyes. "I really need to kiss you right now." He groaned

"Oh, thank God!" she exclaimed loudly, relieved by his confession, Julia brandished a nervy smile. "Oh, that's good to know, since I've been turned on all day just thinking about you." She breathed, her voice coming like a purr, and her dark eyes devoured him as aptly as the fervor he deported in his. The barking of wood sailed in answer to their admission, as his chair was sent flying with force, followed closely by the echoing snarl of her own. His mouth crushed her with a force that drove her instantly back, stabling her in the closure of his arms. His kisses grew deliriously sweet, savage and intoxicating all at once. His mouth gave as freely as it demanded, and he demanded everything of her, delving long the deeper he went.

Michael grunted softly against her mouth before he swung her from the floor, turning from the kitchen—

"Wait, the candle!" she called, stalling his rush from the room, for the flame still flickered from a lone candle.

"Grab it." He grunted, whirling with her in his arms, he returned from whence they came.

"Grab it?" she frowned, repeating the oddness of his ask.

"I get to watch you by candle light, what can be better than that?" He smiled, again swerving from the table. He carried her to his room. "Lock it." He commanded in a coarse whisper as his heel caught the low edge of the door, parking it roughly in place with the finality of a rowdy thud. "So you know. You will not be leaving this room anytime soon." He growled, setting her slowly to the floor.

"I had a feeling you'd say that." Julia smiled. Her fingers moving to the hidden portal of her dress, stylishly tucked within her side, the zipper softly glided. The trim dress loosened with the slow slither of her hand. Falling open, it granted him a captivating view. "So then, where would you like me first?" she asked in a whisper, stepping from the garment, she watched his eyes darken with delight.

"It's always ladies choice around here." Michael drawled, savoring the view, as she wore nothing more than the radiant glow of the candle and the warmth of her beautiful smile. Her eyes were reflective of the fire as she watched him, moving to his side, her body swayed like a musical note. Forsaking her shoes, she kicked the heeled tauntings toward his bed, and each skidded, as if directed, to hide along the skirted edge. Her fingers moved lightly to his chest then, gliding like a smooth song across the skin of his neck. They ambled through his hair, pulling his head down to hers. She lit fires like never before, for her kisses consumed and filled him in a single tasting.

"In that case, we'd better get to bed." Julia breathed, her hands already working the button on his pants. "Perhaps I can assist you with these." She asked with a smirk, not needing an answer in return, her fingers labored without pause. Unbuttoning the weighty textile of his jeans, she left it to hang loose on his hips. Her fingers thence promptly glided under his shirt. Caressing the hard ridges of his belly, they walked languorously over his chest, detaching the fasteners as she went. She thrust the garment from his body. "Mmm, you smell so good." She sighed, brushing her lips across the top of chest.

"So do you." Michael sighed back, rolling his fingers through the curly strands of her hair.

Each kiss touched him like the teasing stroke of a feather, with her tongue following in a heated glide. She aroused him with her play on his nipples. Standing complacent under the moil of her hands, his breath came as a hiss, the soft expel then perched stagnant in the room. Aided by her hands, his pants fell from its rest on his hips, compelling him to step clear of the trappings it laid. Pressed fixedly against her, the heat of his body was like a dulcified mix, as the fire was promptly sweetened at every turn. Touching her breasts to his back, the soft curves of her body caressed the hardness of his, while her kisses, in a convoy of pure spite, came soft along his spine. Her hand moved attentively over the hard manliness of his form, enticing and exciting him with the dividend tangled in each stroke, and the gentle clasp of her maneuver grew bold and dynamic in an exquisite caress.

Readdressing her toils, Michael's hands were far from placid. Crudely yanking her to his frame, he crushed her against the heated rapier, now thoroughly perceptive to its task. His mouth sought hers with hunger, urging her to obey his drive. He drew all measure of dewiness from her lips. Freeing a heavy groan from his throat, his hands again moved to the back of her thighs, lifting her from the floor. He pressed her to the pillows on his bed.

The stalwart gifting of his body edged the supple lines of hers as his kisses gently roamed her breasts. Travelling the length of her body, his tongue played the edges of her warmth. Tempting and teasing until her body writhed deliciously in beseech of procession. Michael rose to her then, pressing firmly in ignition of their bid, the dank furnace swallowed him whole. Wrenching through his body like flames in a newly banked hearth, the rivet was exceedingly sweet. Slender legs curled possessively, instigating their drive, they redeployed like twines about his waist, both bodies swaying conjointly in a mesmeric dance. With ravenous fervor piloting the crusade, it heightened the endurance of their drudge, spilling them collectively, at last, upon a rapturous plateau as imbursement for their trudge.

Assuaged by the exquisiteness of their physical endeavor, the room again grew still, though the rustle of their breaths badgered the new silence with an odd coarseness abraded to its tumble. Wrapped in the sachet of her arms, Michael's body remained taut. Submersed in the runnel of her pillow, his sweat dappled the wildness of her hair, hers now quietly singed to the side of his neck, and with each lusty expel, her breath further roasted his bronzy display. Turning their heads on the softness of a single pillow, bemusement flared bright in the foreground of their eyes, speechless for what seemed an endless sigh, wonder slowly blossomed into laughter. *Damn, that was good!* He groaned roughly to no one but himself.

Late into the night, the two sat nestled together on the floor, both working avidly to refuel the throngs of energy spent. Michael watched her intently as they conferred about work, life and all else that swam to the forefront of their thoughts. The candle's light thence bathed her magnificently, tanned skin in a sputter of gold, and cat-shaped eyes aptly sparkled with each flicker of its flame. Its dimness shadowed, almost fully, the plumpness of her lips, looking, to his eyes, as if she was made from the flowery heat itself. He decided, before long, quite effusively, that she most certainly had to have been, since she was definitely a fire to him. Her radiance was pure, like the dancing flicker of the flame itself. She left him no doubt in that. Something about her captured him intently, and he was innately curious to know why.

Chapter Twenty Four

Winching the curtain of night, darkness conceded its rest, and morning launched amidst a whispery breath. Like the turning of a page climaxing the chapter's end, a gentle breeze fingered the foliage's edge, plodding the troughs of their flowering surface in its search. The air's freshness grew somehow sweet.

Although pleasant, segments of the morning's visage seemed almost solemn in its view. Bridled with the expectancy of dawn's splendor, the dull atmosphere simpered with the insertion of color, tinged with globules of which flaunted a resplendent display. Peppered across a grayish-blue sky, yellowy-orange abraded a near saturnine horizon, sending shards of pigments in an eddying burst. The air caroled its gladness with its dance, as the fiery ball prepared to summit the willowy giants in a show.

Julia gaped out at the erupting beauty with a pensive sigh, awed by the flamboyant parade. She avidly devoured the transferal. Already, the robust aroma of coffee wafted pleasantly through the house, appeasing her senses, it assuaged the doltish status of her mind. Cradled cautiously between the ruche of her hands, Julia adjusted her fingers around the febrile mug. Whiffing the fleeing vapors as they rose, she tentatively touched the cup to her lips, sighing as the dark elixir enthused her body to life.

Built with a notable banner of its own, the day was far from an ordinary diurnal showing. It stood inherently unique of the rest. Bested by none preceding, the morning evolved with a fervency that fully ensnared, hence, the harmonious flavor in the music it dispersed. Garrulous in its songs, May seventh's emergence commemorated the enraptured babel of Richard's birth. Complete with the pomp of a stately event, the day's grandeur surpassed all with just its mere existence.

With all else stricken from his mind, his birthday remained the sole topic blitzing from his tongue. As always, his excitement had been thrilling to watch, exuding from every pore. It puddled with every step that he took.

Thankfully, plans for his upcoming celebration had already been set into construction long before now, with all twelve guests already confirming their attendance. His wait was at last at an end.

Envisioning the habitual pre-dawn trouncing, Julia thwarted the jolt of his attack with an early advantage of her own. Though the strategy unfolded, thus far, it would seem, without merit, since as of yet, the house showed no signs of a stir.

At forty minutes past the hour, a faint pitter-patter gave the seventh hour new life. Richard staggered across the threshold of her room trussed in a fog, tottering to a stop. His body swayed as if soused from other than the torpor of sleep. Above him, the grubby stench of sleep still soared uncannily strong. Crudely splayed upon his face, his eyes registered naught but the inferred clearance needed for his feet. Seeming almost reclined, his stance tilted weakly in its place of rest, and as if tethered to his chest, his head bowed without the authority of a bone.

A slow yawn widened the tense corners of Richard's mouth, stiffening his frame. He gazed blindly about the room. His eyes lazily inched the occupant of the bed, landing scruffily on the angling of her face, they lingered on the syntax of said feature. Sitting with a pillow tucked haphazardly at her back, his mother's eyes registered the quiet yielding of a smile. Surveilling him curiously from across the room, her countenance seemed somewhat expectant. In slow procession, she brought the vapored mug to her lips, her eyes still lashed to his face. Sipping the steaming liquid, she quietly returned the mug to the console next to her bed, folding her hands atop the flattened spread as if waiting to hearken something vital.

Confounded by the lingering haze, Richard's face further pleated with a frown. Shielding the bothersome light from his eyes, he rubbed what felt like granules from their beds. Slowly, the viscous fog rescinded its hold on his brain, and a sluggish grin smoothed the trenches of his brow, widening as awareness gradually dappled his wake.

"Happy birthday to me!" he sang, jumping onto the bed, Richard rushed to the vacant estate at his mother's side, almost spilling her coffee in his haste.

"What a coincidence. I have a birthday thing I have to do today, too!" Julia exclaimed with the launch of a playful frown, chuckling lightly as he tucked his head beneath the fold of her arm. "If you're good, maybe I'll let you come." She teased, running her fingers through the short curls of his hair. "Happy birthday, angel," She whispered, placing a kiss on the top of his head, she tugged the soft lobe of an ear.

"Thanks, mom," he hummed, snuggling closer still. He curled his small form to her side.

"You're late. Did you have trouble falling asleep?"

"A little," he muttered dryly, the answer coming fresh on the tail of a yawn. Richard then donated the weak remnant of a smile with his response. "I was so excited. I kept thinking about all the races I wanted to have."

"We don't need to be there until eleven. Would you like to go back and lay down?"

"No. I don't think I could sleep." He grumbled, shaking his head to amplify his response.

"You don't have to sleep. Just rest a little."

"I don't know." Richard groaned, dropping his head across his mother's lap, he again yawned.

"Are you hungry?"

"No."

"Do you think maybe you can think of something you'd like to do, if not rest?" she asked skeptically, again throwing him a playful frown. Julia watched as his body shifted languidly in reply, setting his head to a more comfortable position on her lap. He yawned as he nestled himself in place. "If you don't get some rest, you won't be able to enjoy your party or your friends."

"But I'm not tired!" Richard grumbled, his words lifting strained through an ensuing yawn.

"Really, and what's this, Richard, your new show of bountiful energy?" Julia quipped, smiling as her son again adjusted his body to her side. His lids gently coupled on the tail-end of a resultant yawn, and the faint smearing of a smile quietly dented the corner of his mouth in response. "Okay, that's it!" she announced at an almost whisper, patting his back, Julia eased her body from the bed. "Come on. We're going back to bed. Let's go!" Murmuring the intent, she lifted his arm in assurance of such, readying his body for transport.

"But mom!" he whined, rolling from her grasp, Richard's body curled promptly to the second pillow on the bed. "I'm not tired!"

"I can see that, love, but we'll try anyway. Come on! I'll lay with you for a while." She smiled, coaxing with arms outstretched. Julia's voice was gently swaying, though in show of his protest, Richard tendered a generous frown to cause. His mouth gaped in readiness to reject the implication of what her offer now suggested, yet none came in prospective for the bargain she posed. Slowly, he clamped his mouth shut, choosing to take the hand she offered, he instead shuffled from his roost. Julia's arm folded immediately around the weary drooping of his shoulders, while his, in turn, alighted to the indent of her waist.

Comfortably back in his bed, Julia wrapped him snugly in the solace of her arms, resting serenely at his back. She listened to the changing resonance of his breath. Asleep in the true perception of minutes, Richard's small body laid curled in exhaustion, looking almost angelic cuddled in the plush matting of his bed. Gingerly, Julia tiptoed from the room, smiling in amazement at the evidence at hand, her mirth, she knew, was not without worth. For it would seem, her son's effervescent personality had somehow met its match, vanquished, at least for a spell. It transpired on the one day that his vivaciousness was needed to aid him the most.

The day groused its rowdy duration like the persistent squawk of a crow, bowing its enervated head at long last. Evening roosted auspiciously in a vibrant Carolina sky, boasting a soft crimson. Its prim disposition capped the threading on a dynamic day. Upon return, the Berwick family marked the rostered occasion as grand, one that by any standard would be considered a success. With Richard reverting to enough of his old self, he enjoyed the days bequeathing with little delay. Again spirited, he bounded through the activities of choice.

In his usual haste, Richard's feet drummed the living-room floor without pause, hurrying through the entrance. He raced up the stairs to his room, missing his mother's soft glare now aimed at his back. Julia sighed, not bothering to give comment on the thudding or his rush, she smiled in tolerance of the day's significance, shaking her head at the waning sound instead. Too drained to be bothered with much beyond seeking

solitude for herself, her only thought consisted solely of rest. The day had grown excruciatingly long in its endeavors, wedged wildly between the elevated chatter of kids,
and the never-ending throttle likely in a parade of engines. The compressed setting of a
speed-park depleted much from the liveliness she once felt.

A long shower brought her within semblance of her old self. But it was the rejuvenation that came with the indulgence of sleep that truly beckoned her will. This she
aspired to attain at an early end.

Without coaxing, the house rested as if in a lull, holding its breath in wait, the
halls somehow mirrored the occupant's mood. Rachel's voice came as a rhythmic
murmur from the walls of her room, no doubt inventorying her complaints on the
phone, as the day, she contends, was overly taxing to her nerves. Sprawled on the
soft, conforming cushion of his chair, Richard zealously tested the spoils of his new
game, and from the slope his body offered, he was very near the point of being spent
himself. It was not tenuous to surmise that his evening would have an early end as it
did for her mother. Delia in her maternal effort, dwindled, in time, with the yowl of
the raucous flock, and by the second half of their stay, she looked completely outside
of her realm.

Accepting the much needed solace for what it was, Julia happily scuttled to the
sanctity of her room, flinging her wearing body to the bed in exhaustion. The succor was
immediately embraced as one would, a miraculous gift, thus it bolstered the intensity of
her sigh. The submersion bloated like a gratifying current in the ocean itself, wrapping
her in the soft fragrance of spring and the fresh spill of clean sheets. Her mood was
instantaneously boosted from its glum. A notable riff promptly broke the tame impetus
of the room, startling the once entrancing space. Julia groaned sharply at the rend peace
that was now rendered null, lunging at the nightstand in haste. She plucked the offending object from its place with malicious intent.

Two letters, though somewhat nondescript in their unveiling, garnered a titanic
reaction, as her body was immediately enlivened by the sight. All trace of fatigue vanished with the fluttering in her chest. Smiling, her entire body welled with a remarkable
resemblance to that of joy.

"Hi!" she answered in a rush, her smiling voice sliding through the phone in an
exalted caress.

"Hi!" Michael's deep voice strummed back, rolling like fingers over the raised follicles of her skin in a slow stroke. "Can you talk?"

"Yes. Well, for at least a little while—what's wrong?" she queried with the composing of an instant frown, striding across the room. She gently pushed her door shut, and
the lock jumped in place as quickly as she did on her return to bed.

"Nothing, I just wanted to talk with you for a bit."

"Aren't you supposed to be in New York?"

"I am in New York." Michael droned, his eyes distant as he soaked in the panoptic
scene. With a wall of windows wrapping the entire first floor, it gifted the breadth

of a spectacular view. The earth's fire flaunted its brilliance across a galvanized sky, splattered and stained like the husk of a painter's palette. The evening's distinction held him fully transfixed. Prompting the pretext of his call, as she had sprang to mind with a clarity that would not sunder its hold. Having had the urge on countless occasions as this, her vision now stayed prim, like a monolith in his head, refusing to set his addled mind free from its trap. Yet, respecting the boundaries set, had made the matter harder than he expected it would.

"Oh! How's work going?" she asked, pulling a pillow to her chest. Her fingers gently worked across the surface of a silky cotton edge; tepid in her movements, as if afraid the fabric would bruise under any show of strength.

"It's going well." He shrugged, strolling back to the sofa. Michael gruffly lowered himself to the seat. "We may be close to finalizing a deal with the director."

"That's great! I know how hard you've been working on that. I'll keep my fingers crossed for you."

"Thanks. I appreciate that."

"How does the apartment look now that everything is all finished?"

"The same," Michael retorted with a slow shrug, his eyes bouncing in assessment about the room. "A few changes here and there, but...it's still the same." Expounding on the thought, he quietly reclined to a more comfortable station on the couch, and the deep baritone of his voice came then as a raspy whisper in her ear. "So, what have you been up to?"

"Not too much," she shrugged, rolling onto her side with the answer. She again tucked the pillow to her chest. "Today is Richard's birthday, remember, so we spent the day celebrating at the speed-park."

"Speed, sugar and a collection of friends to share it with, that's the perfect combination for a boy. He must have had a ball!" Michael laughed, propping a pillow under his head.

"I think he did. He's tuckered, but he had fun."

"You sound tired yourself."

"I'm definitely ready for bed." She groaned.

"Can I join you?" he rumbled darkly, his voice falling like a deep, dissolving hug.

"Hmm, tempting," she smiled, resting her chin against the pillow on her chest. "But a little hard to achieve with you all the way in New York."

"I could hop a flight out in a few hours, and be at your door well before midnight."

"Hmm, really?" purring to the phone, she gave the offer more thought than she should. "As tempting as that offer is, I'm going to have to decline. We don't seem to be very good at being demure, remember?" she smiled, her voice suddenly dipping as a tingle zipped through her body.

"I remember. Things of such fomenting nature are not easily disregarded." Michael assured hoarsely, shifting his body on the couch, he clarified his meaning—some. "You're very hard to forget." He sighed, closing his eyes as if on cue or in ready for the conjured show. In the stillness of his head, he saw her wading in the shadows of his pool, standing wet and practically naked. Only a hint of cover veiled the full vision from his view, and that was just one of the many pictures now stored in his head. "What are you wearing?" Michael growled, his voice now husky, laced with more than just the humor that he showed.

"Is your mind always going to go there?" Julia teased, playing with the fringed edges of her pillow, she smiled.

"I never left. Now, tell me what you're wearing so I can see you?" he murmured, his voice deepening to a leer, thus sweetly stirring in its fall.

"Black leather thong and a whip." She whispered with a spirited sigh, hastily assessing the gray bottom and black tee that she wore.

"Mmm, nice," he purred. "Is this one of the things I have to look forward to?"

"Do you want to know or be surprised?" she asked sweetly, further extending the tease. She smiled, adoring the warm, intimacy of where the conversation now led them.

"Maybe it would be better left unsaid, this way I coul—"

"Mom?" Rachel chirped faintly from somewhere close, her voice hardly stirring the mood, though it stalled all ancillary answers in their tracks.

"You'll have to hold that thought for now. It seems my time is up." Julia apprised tepidly, rolling to the edge of the bed with the tattle. She sighed, already missing the balminess of their chat.

"I'll see you soon?" Michael asked in a whisper, his deep voice rumbling like the start of a storm.

"Very soon," she purred, her body answering the invitation set forth in his ask.

"Until then," Michael droned, savoring the warmth now tilling the softened quality of her voice.

"Until," she sighed back, her breath falling almost mute to the phone. His smile was plainly felt, answering her with a rich, rumbly grunt, though no words followed the lusty breath. "Bye."

"Bye." Michael drawled, comforted. He listened as her voice rang back in answer to whomever beckoned, before the line went dead.

Susceptible to the perils of leisure, the weekend fled. Bolted to the bracket of a sigh, it initiated the advent of a pristine week with the culmination of said breath. Moving thence without the force of gravity's tug, each day crawled exasperatingly slow. As orchestrated by her phantom donor, Tuesday dispatched another of his weekly contributions to her door, and as always, their radiance highlighted the room. Between the flails of a bird's wings, a smile skimmed the tense surface of her face, refuting, for a moment, her averseness for the bribe. Reluctantly, she acceded to a small strip of pleasure now funded by his words. And had she not had her own weird battle to contend with, she might have taken the time to relish the significance more. Julia read his words with ambiguity attached to her mood, thought the connotation woven in its lyrics fell to her faintly sweet, taunting her imaginative sense well.

The sweetest beauty walked my way. Doth she see my heart's display? Can she hear my whispered songs? Whilst I linger in the dainty folds of suspense, should my truth yet be distinguished, would she render thusly the sweetness I yearn? Forsooth, my heart muse her goings each day. In patience it awaits a flicker from her smile. Patiently, my heart awaits her.

Signed,

Infatuated as ever,

Fully baffled as to the fervency given in his words, new questions toppled like torrents through the storm raging in her head, wondering on the character of such a man. Should she admire his creativity and the generosity of his words, or should she fear his apparent obscurity? Perplexed by the cadence of her thoughts, her turmoil further heightened its cause, though knowing the mystery rest solely on one. Not yet able to discern his identity, she wondered further on who he was.

———

For him, the week sped like the parched trajectory of a torpedo's tail, propelling the hours of each day. It again rested at its end. Like clouds trolling a windswept sky, so, too, the minutes waded betwixt the hours in his day, trudging without encouragement or aid. It twirled without end.

His projected brief stay in New York had stretched longer than his vastly distended schedule once planned, though the venture itself had not been without cause. To facilitate the purpose, Michael plotted through every charted step with verve, finagling each exert. He cleared much from an inexorable calendar. Buttressing his time well with a handful of meetings with his lawyers, he finalized, what had begun to seem, a repetitious kink in a contract that looked, at times, to be dead. His usual appearances for charity passed without delay, so too, his statutory dinner with old friends, followed promptly by lunch with the swank disposition of another prospective lead. All this to further flatten the wrinkles ordinary in the grueling concoction, so imperative, in the assembly of a film. Time flourished like a whirlwind without beginning or end, dragging in the places it should not, it juried the proceedings of his day. Yet it was the hours spent with those holding the purse that truly took its toll on his will. Consuming the majority of his time, ideas and changes are never rationed once in their presence, but donated freely as with the offer of a mint. Thus they left him, at day's end, fully sapped.

However operose the hours bled, in truth, the strain mattered not, since by contributing his time for the period at hand, he eradicated any possibility of a weekend face to face. An honor he had no intention of imparting on anyone but her.

The house seemed utterly enlivened with the possibilities to come, already anxious, as if it, too, awaited her return. Having already seen Betty off for a weekend at the spa, Michael gave his mother her usual lengthy call, updating her on all the happenings in his life—except one. Strict instruction was given to Sam in regards to his weekend and the expectancy of his plan, as work was, in no way, a part of his objectives, at least none that could be dictated or set to print. Working diligently that very morning, they both conquered a mountain of obligation on his desk. Mowing it to a respectable hill, though knowing by Monday, it should again rival Everest. But that would neither prevent nor interfere with the carnage he had meticulously planned for her.

The truck's engine roared crossly athwart the wooded estate, backing the vehicle from the shelter of the garage. Its throaty snarls grated the serenity of a simulated island. Strange though it was, the tactic was little more than a precautionary step. Implemented to stem the prospect of budding curiosity, should one be stricken with overzealous madness or be infected with an inquisitive flare, his action now warded off any probability of such. Making room for her incoming car was but a measly step to assure no such repercussion with her stay, for the two could sometimes be a detrimental pair. A new car of itself stands only as curiosity. Not so for a new car staying the entire weekend. Such gesture starts the seedling of a question or two. But said car continuous influx, breathed needless life into the dangerously sharpened tusks of the paparazzi themselves. And he'd be damned if he wouldn't do everything to protect this—whatever the combustion between them denotes.

The sun's diluted light quietly dipped into the shadowy sea of the horizon, enabling streaks of gray to smudge a dimming orangey-red. Michael gazed at the approaching blackness without seeing the arresting beauty it so boldly displayed. With his thoughts now locked on the strangeness that environed his life, and the eccentric world in which he worked. His mind offered no rest. Wondering of the many men throughout the world, who else would deem it a necessary task to hide all evidence of a prospective date? *Hardly any*, Michael reasoned in response, not unless infidelity was the culprit behind their act.

His world consisted effusively of lies, imagined or otherwise. Lies were, for them, another language used to supplement their native tongue. Sometimes it's used to protect one's self, and at others, it's in spite of that self. With so much of the imposed magnate's life already exposed, blunt characters find themselves, at times, saying the opposite of what they should, trying desperately to retain a miniscule ort of who they truly are. Everybody lies, but where he's from, it's a lifestyle. It's no wonder she's hesitant to venture in his world, when even he does not always trust the words given by his peers.

Timed spotlights blazed across the sculpture centering the cobblestone drive, flooding portions of the contiguous property, it illuminated the house like a sculpting itself. The atmosphere darkened as blackness swallowed the last of the sun's rosy hue. Michael smiled shrewdly, assured of her timely arrival. He turned long strides towards the house, stopping short to answer the melodic serenade from his phone.

"I'm here!" Julia sang, her excitement creeping easily through the phone.

"Then come start your party!" Michael rumbled back, his voice cascading like warm rain. A finger rolled over the buttons of a small remote, setting his command instantly to task. He turned back to the opened door of the garage, swallowing the short space with the length of his strides. With eyes pressed to the long thoroughfare, Michael's pulse quickened, and the restive wait incited a mad pounding in his chest. Julia's car rounded the bend in, what surely equaled, hours in his wait, and his enthusiasm, at such, sprouted very near that of an impatient youth. Yet through it all, the thought of kissing her welled with a vociferous bite.

Directing her to the vacated venue in the garage, he parked himself at the indent of her door, zealously awaiting the stutter of the engine's death. Their eyes met, and hers danced with undisguised bliss. Sweeping warmly over him in a timid glide, the glance seemed oddly reminiscent of a teenage girl. One, who, after some anguish, had at last, noticed that the boy she's long watched, also watches her, too, and something about it was quite beautiful to observe.

Embarrassed by the candidness depicted in her eyes, Julia's gaze hastily fell to the floor, shocked by the level of lust that now careered through the inset of her body. As of the two weeks preceding, she had looked forward to seeing him since getting home from their last sparring, yearning the ravenous ways of his play. Every morsel of every act had been exhaustively ruminated, analyzed or relived in her head. The prospect of a repeat had her body shuddering with excitement.

The click of the door's latch fell like a hammer in the gapped silence of the oversized space. Swinging the door wide, Michael offered her his hand. Julia smiled, taking the proffered limb. She set her feet to the checkered pattern of the floor. Cautiously biting the flesh of her bottom lip, she rolled the soft, pillowy bed between the sharp edges of her teeth, holding herself contained, as his closeness madly provoked her body's will.

"Hi!" He smiled, his deep voice dispelling the word as air. It warmly caressed the softness of her cheek.

"Hi!" Julia whispered back, offering him a flash of her incredible smile. A tight silence followed, and neither moved from their procured perch or saw to its end. With each gaze holding the other captive, their bodies stood inert as trees, brushed sweetly with the warmth of the other's breath.

Michael broke the nervy impasse with a soft growl, pouncing like a hunter on the attack. His assault was like the first sampling to a meal and, he was, but a man, discarded in the fray and left to starve, so proven by the ferocity of his drive. Working his tongue industriously over hers, he demanded that she respond in the same sweet way she had before. Cupping her face as if to drink, his breath came as a gale across her cheek. Her fingers curled instantly through the hair at the base of his neck, locking to said locks. The intensity of their rummage was well matched between the two. His body then pressed hers with the adamant nature of his intent, teasing the aggravated tips of her breasts. He syphoned every drib of nectar she possessed, and every taste was a reminder of their encounters past, as well as the dreams they carried for the day's elapsing in-between.

"God, it's good to see you!" He murmured roughly between his gluttonous delve.

"Oh, I know!" She sighed, half humming her answer through the press of his lips. His passion was unmistakable, boiling through his body. It grumbled in the recess of his throat. His was a body so firmly pressed, she could feel the subtle raise of his chest, so, too, the rapid beating of his heart and every other throbbing muscle his body lent. The heat of his mouth lingered long after his kisses passed, searing her skin. They move down her neck to play betwixt the soft rise of her breasts. Julia donated a slow sigh in reaction of such, dropping her head back, she held him staunchly in place, wanting to feel his mouth frolic freely upon her body. She thrust her breasts further in his path. Unexpectedly, his intensity eased before the feasting stopped. Michael's eyes lifted to hers in question, looking dazed as to a reason for the pause. His eyes skimmed her face before jumping to survey the room.

"We should go in." He murmured hoarsely, looking reluctant to move. His face loomed above hers like an instrument of incitement, and his eyes, in open beseech, again fell to her mouth.

Julia gave her agreement with a slow nod, fighting the urge to draw him back to the relinquished task at hand. She swallowed the prodding of her bubbling lust.

"Come." Michael rumbled at last, walking his fingers down her side, he gently took hold of her hand. Slowly easing the press of his body, he turned towards the entrance of a house cloaked in silence. He'd had two weeks in which to lust her. Two weeks to relive all the things they attained before then. Two weeks in which to conjure up the multitude of things he wanted to do to that gorgeous body. Not one of which was quick enough to involve the inflexible space of his garage. Still, she would be a sight to behold spread across the hood of those in his collection.

Hers was the last slot accessible in the showy room, the furthest bay from the entrance of the house, and in angst, the two walked in silence through the low light cast by a single chandelier.

Michael said nothing as they left the garage behind, moving in silence through the long halls of the house. His thumb stroked the soft skin of her palm, looking like a fenced beast fully tormented. He seemed to plot his next port of assault. And with only the strength of his gaze, she could almost feel him removing her clothes, a sensation that brought a warm glow to her skin.

Reaching the threshold of his suite, Michael's steps quietly stalled. Blocking the arching of the door, he draped the shadowy opening with the beauty of his physique. And whether her ingress was through him or around, there was no margin left to allot her further entry without the pairing of their bodies.

Feeling his libidinous gaze loosened the spicket of her body, Julia stepped close. Swallowing the intoxicant air wafting warmly from his frame, the erotic flavor scored remarkably deep, strumming the chords of her body with skill. Without the spoilage of words, her hands moved over the snaps of her shirt. Undoing all, it fell to their feet in silence. Michael's eyes lowered to the trim waist of her skirt, followed methodically by his hands. His fingers were set eagerly to task. Undoing the short zipper, he slowly pushed the garment free from her body, while his eyes, in their gifting, avidly aided the sluggish descent, caressing her as he guided the garment from her hips. Hungering eyes brushed greedily over almond colored skin, almost tasting the sweetness while his fingers worked the fly of his jeans. Kicking it clear of his legs, his hand found the handle of the door without pause, and the sound thudded through the silence with extraordinary force.

His mouth crushed hers savagely in follow, driving her back to the hard barring. There was no gentleness in the greed his kisses bespoke. None in the greedy way his hands maneuvered her body, delving deep, his tongue thrusting deeper. Nor was there any indication of gentleness in the way his body compelled hers, or so, for the raggedness of his breath, fleeing in a blustering gust from his nostrils. His sighs came from the deepest region of his throat, vibrating through his body like the pulsing of an engine. The excitement he woke was incontrollable.

The muscles in his chest flexed against the aroused peaks of her breasts, crushing her body to his as he pulled her from the door. The savagery of his kiss eased as he pulled the brown circle into the warmth of his mouth, working his tongue slow and willful around the savory tips. He gave no signs of relinquishing his drive.

Julia's sighs drifted through the short follicles of his hair, holding still as his hands slid over the curves of her buttocks. Rounding her hips, her breath slowed as he played along the junction of her thighs, taunting her with his kisses. Her back arched in offering, feeling her womanly processions effectively ravished as quickly as she avails them to him.

Mercilessly foraging, Michael fed as if she bled sweet on his tongue, taking all she offered—except one. Though for this, his appetence commanded that he take his time. Holding himself firmly in check, Michael waited until her eyes held the same fire as his, until her cries pushed him near the point of madness. Further braising her body, he waited until his own throbbed with the most delicious pain. Only then did he partake of the dulcified forge she so avidly bestowed. Climbing together tangled and aflame, their bodies wielded collectively as one. Breathless and spent, they slipped to the coolness of the hardwood floor, with bodies thusly entwined. They quietly waited sanity's return.

"Do you think we'll ever have dinner first?" Michael asked when at last words flowed to him with clarity, placing a kiss on the corner of her mouth. His voice came as a raspy breath.

Julia smiled in utter content. His kisses felt almost as good as the very first that touched her. "Maybe when it's not so new," She crooned, running her fingers through his hair.

"I made dinner." He whispered against her mouth.

"You cooked?" she asked in disbelief.

"Not well," Michael shrugged, his voice seeming to rattle in his throat. "But I wanted to make you something. I really only followed some directions, that's all." He explained, cocking his head as if to study her face. He traced a line along the column of her neck.

"I can't wait to try it." She giggled, knowing that that was in fact the truth. "Anyone who'd take the time to cook for me deserves to be indulged."

"You could have told me that sooner." Michael smirked, shifting his weight against her. "It would have saved me a lot of headaches, knowing all I had to do was cook you something."

"Do you really need to be treated any better?"

"I won't complain. How could I?" he smiled, looking inquisitively about the room. Pacified in his notice that they had not made it very far, and the bite of the hard floor now accentuated the distance left to his bed. Michael rolled languidly, pushing himself to his feet. He lifted her from her place on the floor, his arm immediately encircling her waist. "That's better." He sighed as they tumbled to rest against the feathery pillows on his bed.

"What did you make for dinner?" she asked, smiling into eyes that instantly gathered hers, and she could not help but wonder on what he saw in his study of her.

"Broiled salmon." He mumbled with a grin, pulling her closer to his side. He stroked the long, silky contour of her thigh. The feel of her skin had him fully entrapped, seeming always to want more. The way she felt against him had his body loitering outside of itself, almost buoyant, like the eerie effect of a drug.

"Wow! I'm impressed," Julia chirped, throwing her head back, she studied his face.

"It's nothing to write home about, really." Michael warned, shrugging stiffly, his eyes again caressed her face. "I just thought we could have something to eat…before"

"But the effort is." She assured with a gentle smile. "Are you hungry?" a single lamp offered their only lighting in the room, easing the darkness within. Outside, the sky rested in full blackness, reaching far into the room; it shadowed the recesses and corners well.

"Not enough to move right now." He drawled, and a finger sketched the tip of her nose in aid of his reply, outlining, in follow, the fullness of her lips. "I like our quick runs for replenishment at nights; they're fun." He smiled.

"We do give ourselves a workout, don't we? Maybe we should shorten our expectations of what we want when we see each other. Perhaps come up with a plan?"

"Like what?"

"Well, maybe we should start with a snack or something small like a drink?"

"I think we tried that." Michael retorted softly. "Does it bother you that we always end up like this?" he asked in a gentling tone, though his interest went deeper than even he understood.

"If you look at it in the grand scale of things, it is why I'm here. Why…we're here."

"I know, but maybe you would like to catch your breath before you get so ravenously devoured."

"But isn't that what keeps us coming back? I can't explain it, but…" Julia fell silent as she studied the expanse of his chest. Conscious of his action, since she could feel his eyes watching as always, but nothing came to better rationalize what they had. There was no explanation to better clarify what hovered between them, none but the obvious—lust. Every time he looked at her or kissed her, she sank deeper down a lusty dark hole.

"Maybe we should try not kissing hello." Michael hummed, his voice chiming softly through her thoughts, quietly shrugging as her eyes rose in question to his face. "We could try."

"It does seem to be the main culprit in our plight." Julia smiled, though she wondered whether she would consider depriving herself of such a seditious treat, still knowing, without any doubt attached, she was not yet ready to relinquish that indulgence. "I don't think I…" she started, a small frown building. "I don't think I want to do that just yet." She sighed, catching his eyes in the process. "It's…"

Michael watched her quietly as she dithered in her reply. Cognizant his suggestion was only that—a suggestion. Not kissing her was the last thing, if any; he would be willing to sacrifice when it came to her. "I like kissing you." He drawled, his breath combing her hair. "I'm not willing to give that up."

"I noticed," she nodded. "You're…very good at it." Julia pledged in a low breath. "I like it."

"Says the keeper of the flames," He sighed, turning fully unto his side, he smiled. "Maybe a new guideline should be put in place. Getting the greeting out of the way should be the only plan we make from now on. No dinner, no drinks, just us saying hello, and we say hello quite splendidly, I might add."

"So I have your permission to fully ravish you the moment you set foot on my property?"

"I don't think you need my permission for that," Julia countered with a slow smile, rolling her shoulder, her eyes softly fingered his face. "I seem to remember getting just that. Why else would a woman drive out to see you wearing just about nothing?"

"Oh, trust me. I could be much worse. I told you. You're very hard to forget."

"I seem to recall a few disturbances to my rest as well."

Michael smiled slyly in response, pausing in his study of her face. His hazel eyes danced in the low lighting of the room, as the warmth of her smile roused a quiver in his chest. Dazzling his mind, his eyes fanned the features that she gave. With her hair now straight and unmarred by curls, the long tress spilt like the streaming cleft of a waterfall down the center of her scalp. Runnels of brown draped the doughy edges of her pillow. Already etched in the recess of his mind, her beauty further sealed itself to his brain, as the vision he behold sprung riveting in every way. Never had he been so utterly drawn to anyone. Nor had he ever enjoyed anyone more, not in all his years of consorting. The level of his attraction was, for him, a new world, one that should probably have him floundering or distressed, though for reasons unbeknown to him, he was not. The forte was much too scrumptious to be that.

"Have I ever properly expressed how absolutely beautiful I think you are?" he breathed, his whispered words flowed like a warm misting from the ocean itself. It then flourished sunny in the quiet darkness of the room.

Julia smiled, greatly pleasured by his words. The sight of his fire-lit eyes was, for her, a treat all on its own. "You've mentioned it once or twice." She shrugged, being drawn to his eyes. His touch came like the tender brush of a breath, walking the slope of her cheek. A thumb traced the warm curvature of her mouth, and without thinking, she kissed the caressing limb, touching her tongue to the firm padding in a slow climb. In response, Michael granted her the warped glimmer of a smile, swapping his thumb from its place, his mouth then delved.

"It seems I'm having some trouble keeping my hands off you." He whispered as he lifted his head, although his lower half remained firm against her thighs, pressing her further still.

"I wasn't aware you tried." Julia teased, feeling his fingers inveigling along the outer swell of her breast.

"Oh, I've tried. So be warned, Julia, be very warned. For there are much imaginings that now draws the praxis of these hands, and control seems a futile strive to harness the depths." He smiled, dipping his head. His breath came soft against her skin as his kisses wandered her throat.

"Man, I'm glad I went back on the pill, or we could be having an interesting conversation one of these days." Julia groaned, lifting her chin, she offered him the entirety of that which he bade.

"The no-pause definitely has its merits as well." He murmured hoarsely, working his way to her mouth, his mind reeled with the sensations she gave. Her attar soared strong in his head, as it always does, driving his senses. He rapaciously rummaged for more, and he wondered then, which of her many enchantments drove him the most insane. Was it in her taste or in the fervency her body dispensed? The maddening suffusion of her scent seemed pillared in a class of its own, an essence that truly governed the actions of his body. A tame smile emphatically answered his musing on that, already knowing the riposte to such query. He set the peculiar mulling from his mind, preferring to satisfy the hunger he held instead.

Chapter Twenty Five

The day reared blisteringly hot, unforgiving in its render. It scorched the dermis of those who tested its clout. With limbs seeming in wait, the trees stood starchily fixed, for not even the draught from a whisper fraught the air on this wretched day.

The sweltering month had proficiently subtracted all the nuances of spring, pushing the impatient season directly to summer. Already, the atmosphere sizzled from its guide, boasting a staunch ninety-two degrees. The midday sun seemed eager to demonstrate its infinite power.

Raking a hand through the wet strands of his hair, Michael swabbed the gathering moisture. Dismissing a grand expel from his chest. He glanced through the trees in suspect at the blinding vision, as if questioning its intent. His shirtless back glistened in the blaze of noon's masterful surge, drenching the waistband of his shorts. His body exuded sweat from every pore.

Tapering on the apex of its long tail, the arduous pace of his run lessened. Setting the house again in his sight, Michael's eyes rushed the bench he titled instrumental to his present affiliation with the fire in his life. Blotting the lines then, he had somewhat ineptly made his attraction known in that very spot. The day, and those that closely followed, did not evolve as he had hoped, but with such consequence springing from his persistence, he had nothing with which to lodge a complaint. He had wanted to kiss her then, but did not. Or was it that he could not? Whatever the reason or cause, it was probably a lucky thing that he had not. Not with his usual wont to devour her the way that he now does. Unable to stem the urges she riled, it would not have progressed well for him, had he attacked her then.

Almost woefully, Michael cleared the cluster of trees, squinting at the new brightness as he grumbled his disfavor of the heat. The sun's rays callously pelted his body; starkly toasting the bronzy exterior to an instant griddle, sweat, in remedy to such sear, tripled its production, as in the wont of crumbling dam. Michael smiled as he further mused on the partnership they now have, marveling on the anomaly of this new occurrence in his life. How is it that his control gets squandered so easily with her? Thus far, he's been unable to categorize his fixation with the sultry beauty. There was no tidy partition with which she fits. Though, for that matter, neither did the feelings he harbored for her. All his previous instincts seemed more an obsolete entity than not, unable to govern his steps or offer him aid. With her, it all seemed a new script, though contrary to those in his past, the rewards were most extraordinary.

Betty's countenance barely showed awareness beyond the actions of her hands. Turning tamely from her chore, her eyes gave no reaction as Michael staggered through the entrance of the kitchen. As if for herself, Betty gathered the chilled bottles left, waiting on the counter, for the better part of five minutes, stopping by the refrigerator. She grabbed the damp towel left inside.

"Thanks." Michael panted, straightening his crouched carriage, he accepted her treats. "Whew! It's hot!" he exclaimed in exaggerated relief, wiping the cold wetness across his face, he dragged it slowly down his neck. Sitting the coolness on his back, he then draped the warming cloth across the span of his chest, forcing the descent of his body's temperature. Guzzling half the bottle's content, Michael roughly buffed the short strands of his hair, staying the determined streams escaping his pate. Without comment, Betty's back again fell to the room, and as with her wont, her hands grew busy with their toils, sparing no minutes outside of such. She tarried not in her labor. "What are you up to now, old woman?" Michael asked gruffly, his voice stifled by the towel's press.

Again, Betty's hands gave little heed to his ask, neither did her expression waver from the quiet mien it displayed. Barely lifting her head, she eyed him from the deepest corner of her dark eyes. "Why? Would your palate prefer some pretzels and a beer?" she asked, her soft voice cruising with an underlying bite, as skilled fingers worked the skin of the small mango in her hands.

"Don't knock it till you try it, old woman." He countered, a mocking tremor seated within the core of his voice. Drinking almost half the bottle of Gatorade in one swallow, Michael smiled, setting both bottles to the edge of the counter before furthering his taunt. "There's nothing wrong with pretzels or a good beer, I relish both every chance I get." He teased, knowing how much she liked to govern the things he put in his body.

"Not on my watch, you don't." Betty rebuked gently. "Not without a good foundation to start."

"I know!" Michael grunted, furthering his torment, he smiled. "That's why I have it every time you're not around." Betty's head turned then, giving him a thorough scolding with her eyes. They moved over him like the harshly maneuvered tip of a whip. Michael's smile widened, well gratified with the results of his fib. His satisfaction bloomed further as he finished the last of his stretches. Grabbing a bottle of water, he gulped the first few mouthfuls before she uttered her next word.

"That must be what your weekends have been all about." Betty murmured matter-of-factly, passing him close, she turned towards the refrigerator door, the container of diced fruits now balanced in her hands. A quiet smirk crossed her face as she noticed the urgency of his swallow, feeling well satisfied with the result of her own taunt.

"Only to start," Michael groused guardedly, trying his best to recover quickly from the shock. With Betty, he knew the danger of where he tread. "I'm having all the things you won't let me have, like everything and anything on a sandwich."

"Are you enjoying it?" Betty muttered in her usual soft voice, reaching in the cabinet for a skillet. Her eyes remained on the undertaking of her hands.

"Absolutely," he shrugged, eyeing her warily with each disciplined step that she took.

"Is it everything like you thought it would be?"

"Better." He grumbled, finishing his water. He again shrugged, quieting the effects of her ask. "More than I ever expected."

"I'm glad you're having such a good time." Betty smiled, setting a bottle of olive oil by the stove. She set the surface to heat. "How is Julia?" she asked without looking up, and felt the room tumble to an instantaneous hush.

"Julia! Why?" almost shrieking his response, Michael frowned, rocking his brain for a reaction more natural than that. He'd never been able to hide behind a lie when it came to her. With such swift insight, she could read him like a book. "Why do you ask?" he ventured softly, his voice reigned tightly in his throat.

"Oh, no reason," Betty shrugged, still yet holding her gaze from his face. "I like her, I was just wondering."

Michael rolled his eyes slowly to the ceiling, and the start of a sigh wafted from the basement of his body. Smartly, he guzzled the telltale sound, smothering the show of his discontent before it rushed past his lips. Choosing, instead, to stuff the bottle in his mouth, he feigned being casual. How does she do that? His mind grumbled. How is she able to know so much, and still appear to be so disinterested? "She was fine the last time I saw her." He muttered near the window, walking casually to the glass, he gazed out at the sky.

"I'm glad to hear it." Betty muttered softly as she swung open the panty door. "Someone like that, you just always want them to do well. You know, see that they're always held in the highest regard." Popping her head around the open edge of the door, she garnered his attention with the weight of her gaze. "Do you know what I mean?" she asked calmly.

"Uh…I guess." Mumbling the lie, Michael shrugged. Already knowing exactly what her caveat meant, this being her sly way of telling him not to mess up. But to answer would be to acknowledge what she seemed to already know.

"Would you like to eat something now, or grab your shower first?" she asked in a sweet, casual tone, giving him the out she knew he wanted.

"I'll shower first." Michael affirmed hurriedly, happy to let the matter drop, and even happier to put some distance between him and the room.

Betty watched him dash from the kitchen as if the smell was repulsive to his sense, smiling at the spectacle with more mirth than she should. The sound of a snicker escaped the tight press of her lips. She would have had to be blind not to have noticed the way he looked at the writer when she visited the house. A man does not contemplate a woman like that and just let the matter drop. Now of late, every other weekend he sends her off to someplace nice. Not that the prospects was never made available before, but lately, he'd been downright adamant in his request. Also, there were subtle changes evident in him, less restless than he once was. He almost seemed content in his own skin. The premise had been amusing to watch, strengthening the layers of, what she predicted as, an utterly interesting phenomenon.

———◆———

Julia gazed at the new arrival with a bemused glare streaking the staid demeanor of her face. It now neighbored four months of the same since the first delivery, and still she has had no contact other than the vivacious baubles to reflect upon, nor does she have any indication of the sender's intent, not the least of which, was his name.

Today's bouquet shared much the same distinction as its predecessors—excluding one. In these, the colors waxed an unusual shade. As if pulled from the ocean's floor itself, the coral-colored petals seemed individually brushed with a vibrant orangey-peach. Their beauty was, without doubt, an indisputable fact, and she grudgingly admitted the same of his taste.

My breathless wonder: sweet, perfect and divine; spill your spirally tress upon my breast and rest. Stay with me, so I can gaze upon that which heightens but never dies. Stay and let me bathe in the sweetness of your breath. Stay, so I can touch paradise, for it is within you that such opulence rest.

Utterly infatuated with you,

Julia drew in a long breath as his words emptied from her lips, filled with her own mince of wonder, she sighed. *There's no way these words are meant for me!* No one has shown that kind of interest in her, not in months. It has to be that they have the wrong address. Hopefully, he'll recognize his error soon and the gestures will stop.

The billowing of music pulled her sharply from the crux of the uneasy thought. Without reluctance, Julia sprinted from the room, catching the phone on the third ring. A smile replaced the once tight frown rutted on her face, sweetening the chorus of her jolly salutation.

"Hi!"

"Hi!" Michael sang back.

"How's Cannes?" Julia chirped. Her voice softening as she strolled to the couch. Lying back, she curled her toes to the soft bed of a cushion.

"Beautiful. How are you?"

"I'm good. How are you?"

"A little jetlagged, I think." Michael sighed, stretching back in his seat. He squinted as he stared past the French doors of his suite, perusing the actions of the vessels littering the water just outside the dwelling.

"I'm sorry. You should try getting some rest. It does help."

"I will." Michael smiled, easily accepting her instruct for its nurturing brush. "Have you had lunch?"

"No. Not yet."

"Care to join me?"

"I'm sure you've already had lunch. It's almost dinnertime for you." Julia smirked, and keen eyes immediately rushed the clock in assurance of such. "It is dinnertime!" She affirmed then.

"Does it matter what they call it?" Michael asked, a gentle rumble stroking the edge of his voice. Taking a drink of water, he again gazed out the door. A tray stocked with the anticipated repast already waited his regard, having previously ordered once the spry thought stabled in his head. "As long as we're sharing it, there's no difference."

"Okay. Then let's do lunch." Julia laughed, strutting eagerly to the kitchen. She scavenged the bowels of the refrigerator for something quick. "What are you having?"

"Roast Hen,"

"Hmm, I see your hen, and raise you…um, a turkey sandwich. What do you say?"

"I'm all in." Michael growled, touching the glass to his mouth, he smiled. "But you just upped the stakes. Maybe I should put my own addendum to the policies before we go any further."

"And what would that be?" Julia asked, dispensing the ingredients for her sandwich across the counter. She waited for what was, sure to be, a prurient response. "I've already procured such a high debt with you. I'd hate to add anything more to the pot."

"Looking the way you do, there should be a rule. The drooling shmuck gets to have you whenever he wants."

"So I should just start preparing to be attacked everywhere I go, then?"

"No. I already licked you. That makes you mine. Besides, the rule only pertains to me."

"What does that make you?" Julia smiled, sweetened by the man and his words. "I believe I've left some saliva on several parts of your body."

"Yes, yes you have." Michael growled, dipping a finger in the raspberry sauce waiting on the side. He brought it to his mouth. "I've had a few dreams on just that effect alone."

"Okay. I'm ready."

"For me?"

"To eat," Julia laughed, swallowing a meager sip of iced-tea. "That would be a little hard don't you think?"

"It's as I've told you, I can fly back faster than you think."

"What about Jean-Paul?"

"Yes. That would foster a slight problem."

"Have you talked to him as yet?"

"Not too much. He's been pretty busy with the press and his other obligations. But I'll be seeing him at the congratulatory dinner schedule for tonight. I'm told they envision it to be a grand showing, since this one is put together by his family and friends. We're expected to have a ball. We should be meeting in a few hours to start the revelry."

"Then why are you eating now, won't this spoil your appetite?"

Michael shrugged warily in a bland response. Jean-Paul Bertolucci had been his favorite actor since he pinnacled the age of ten. He had every movie the man had ever made stocked in his library. Jean was the one most responsible for him becoming an actor, and who later encouraged him to direct. The two had since grown closer with the elder waning in years, and when it was announced that Jean would be honored at the Cannes festival, he did not hesitate to fly out to show his respect. But if she asked him, he honestly could not say, with full candor, what his answer would be.

"I much prefer eating with you." He smiled.

"Even with my clothes on?"

"Now whose mind sank into the gutter?"

"I'm sorry. You just bring out the worst in me."

"Don't be. I like the company." He smirked, leaning back in his chair. His expression was coherently pleased. "And you are...very good company."

"You're gloating. Didn't anyone ever tell you it's not polite to gloat?"

"What makes you think I'm gloating? I just gave you a compliment."

"It was all over your voice."

"Fine, maybe I was. So let me pick up the shovel further. What are you wearing?" he asked, his voice dropping to a husky whisper.

"Nothing that would interest you," Julia laughed, throwing her head back in the process. She caught sight of a single strand of hair, tenuous in its show, it dithered precariously on the bent arm of the chandelier.

"Why?"

"Because I'm not naked, you seem to have a reverence for me that way."

"No, not true. But...well, if I do, can you blame me?" he smiled, strolling to the balcony. Michael stared out at the brusque blue of the sky. Doming the water, the two converged in the unseen distance. Vaguely marred with a soft tinge of orange along the far edge, the onset of evening was as breathtaking as the day itself. "The view is magnificent." He whispered, speaking of the person as well as the place.

"Do you see how different our lives are? I'm spending this weekend at Carowinds, and you're spending it at the Cannes Festival in France."

"You could always come with me." Michael shrugged, already knowing her answer before it came, yet not knowing what else to add.

"And do what?" Julia laughed, putting her plate in the dishwasher. She gave the phone a condescending frown.

"I can't wait to see you." Michael whispered, skillfully changing the subject with the truth.

"When will you be back?" she asked tamely, feeling the weight in his voice, as it skillfully gouged a shiver through her body.

"Sunday,"

"Then five days from that." She informed then, hearing her voice change. The phone fell silent, and neither spoke in response to the placation she gave, nor did they offer, as consolation, a new topic to debate upon. The heaviness of his breath descended on the silence that followed, it crawled about them like an ill-fitted cloak, and she felt oddly drawn to the essence of said sigh. The length and the weight that it gave penetrated the deepest place inside her chest, stirring something restive from its place. "I'm glad we could have lunch." She whispered almost hesitantly, yet feeling the need to break the sudden melancholy that descended on her mood.

"Me too," He murmured back, his voice barely distinct on the other end.

"My turkey sandwich beat your roasted hen anyway." Julia smiled, needing more than anything to hear him laugh before the last word got spoken.

"I'll say it's a draw." Michael smirked, leaning his shoulder to the frame of the door. He stared longingly at no particular object in his view. "We'll need to play again to determine a winner."

"You got it. Anytime, anyplace,"

"Details then to follow?" He growled, turning back to the room.

"I'm counting on it."

Heaving another sigh, Michael again settled on the couch. "I better start getting ready."

"Okay."

"I'll see you soon."

"Michael."

"Yes?"

"I'm anxious to see you, too." She whispered after a pause. Michael smiled then in reply. She knew this, for it was warmly felt, knew it as plainly as if he stood by her side and her body again responded to both.

"Until then," Michael queried, feeling somewhat at ease.

"Until," she purred, her voice flowing across the line soft, ensued by a short hesitation, the line at last went dead. With the phone still clasped tightly in her hand, Julia leaned her back against the cushions as a sigh rushed past her lips, feeling now strangely saddened by something unresolved. The peculiar sensation lingered long into the evening, long past the time that it should. It was not until sleep overtook her that she was free of the interesting pique.

Growing restless through the long hours of wakefulness, Julia's mind stayed distractedly on the man, as slumber only offered her its solace in spurts. Something about him and his voice troubled that moment in their talk, and she could not dark the disquiet from her mind. Whatever it was that descended on him, affected her as profoundly as it would—had it been her very own fret. *It's just concerned*, Julia shrugged, *the same as I would have for any of my friends, this is no different*. She vowed, grumbling this as her fingers hastily scraped the buttons on her phone. With the bulk of her morning routine behind her, this was her first chance to see the task done, and her heart, in eager response, knew no action but one, sprinting with excitement as the phone rang.

"Hi!" surprise and pleasure braided the pitch of Michaels's voice in answer.

"Hi! Feeling better?" her question came soft, yet her tone seemed weighted with concern.

"I am now." He hummed, his deep voice coming like the melody in a song. Slowly, his hand fell from the handle of the door, paused there in the middle of his exit. It now raked the skin on his chest. Invited to go sailing with friends, he had only stopped in the room to grab a light jacket for the blustery trip, but that delay now gifted him luck.

"Care to join me for a drink at the bar?" she asked, taking a seat on the couch.

"I'd love to!" Michael retorted swiftly, his voice now a deep raspy sigh. "How will I be able to pick you out in this crowd?" he asked, turning towards the coziness of his room

"I'll be the one wearing the little red dress. You'll find me sitting at the far end of the room."

"Nice. I can't miss you in that. What are you drinking? I could order for you." He asked, his smile transmitting easily through the phone.

"Not so fast. How will I know you?" Julia probed in a soft, silky timbre. "What are you wearing?" she asked, letting her voice fall in a hush to the phone.

"Mmm," Michael sighed, enjoying the effect. His eyes raced over his casual attire. "Tux,"

"Tux?" she questioned, lying back, she propped a pillow under her head.

"I just got back from an awards dinner, and I'm still wearing my tux."

"Okay, tux then. What are you drinking?" she continued in the same sexy tone.

"Whiskey and Coke, what are you having?"

"A Long Island Iced Tea. So, do you come here often?"

"Not too much, only when I'm in town, how about you?"

"I'm here often enough, I like the music. Do you like music?" she asked sweetly.

"Love music." Michael growled. "Care to tell me your name?"

"Jules, what's yours?"

"James, you remind me of someone, Jules."

"You remind me of someone, James. Are you in a relationship at the moment, James?"

"I'm trying, how about you?"

"Kind of…well, it's complicated."

"Any room for me in that complicated life of yours, Jules?" Michael asked softly, stretching his long frame across the bed.

"I'm not sure. Do you want some consideration, James?"

"I'd love a little more than consideration. I have to say, Jules. I'm loving that voice of yours. Do you ever get to Charlotte? I'd love it if you looked me up."

"Do you usually work that fast, James?"

"Only when I see something I want."

Julia's laugh sailed sprightly with his witty reply, tilting her head on the pillow, she asked. "How long would you like to continue this? We'll be out of small talk soon."

"As long as you want to, I love it."

"How are you?" she asked softly, sobering from their play.

"I'm fine. Just tired, I guess."

"Are you sure?"

"I'm sure. I'll be better once I get home…back to my own bed." An extended silence fell then, and just as it had before, it lingered until she broke the persistent hush.

"I just gave you a kiss." She whispered to the phone.

"Where?"

"Where would you like it?"

"You know where I'm likely to say."

"Okay then, let's pursue that thought. Close your eyes." She ordered and heard him sigh, feeling him relax in the process. She knew this, because her own body grew tranquil as well. "Do you see me?"

"Yes." The murmured answer sailed to her soft.

"Good. Now hold on to that and I'll do my own parody of the picture when I see you."

"More torture? You're wicked. Now I'll have you even more on my mind, as if you're not already there enough."

"I'll make it up to you." Julia smiled, suddenly feeling light.

"I know you will. This goes to your accrual."

"My tab seems to be getting pretty fat."

"That's what you get for the havoc you wreak."

"I should let you go…." She sighed, hesitating behind the awkward announce.

Suddenly remembering his friends, Michael begrudgingly agreed. "Thanks for the drinks. You looked especially good in that dress, by the way."

"So did you in your tux." Once again, that hungry silence fell upon them like a comet from the sky, eating up all the things that could have been a prologue to something else. It staunched a vestal endeavor between the two.

"Until?" Michael whispered at last, wondering why the sudden bout of melancholy, as it seemed determined to hamper his mood. He was fine only the day before. It must be jetlag as he suspected.

"Until, she breathed back, still liking the sensation funded to her by a simple word.

"Bye, Jules." He growled through a dispelling breath.

"Bye, James." She purred, pausing only shortly before terminating the call. Julia smiled, arching her body in a tabby-like stretch. She returned the phone to its place on the counter, again feeling her vibrant self.

Chapter Twenty Six

Thoroughly roused from the roadway's ruffled bed, a light breeze cosseted the canopied woodland, stirring a curling cloud of dust. The billowing grayness veiled the scant sunlight beneath the clustering spread, so propelled by the thrust of a subsequent draught. Dirt danced disjointedly amongst the trees crowding heads, shepherding the choked momentum of her car.

Quaffed insides a grotto of verdure, the evening stood remarkably tranquil, drenched with the rich, alluring fjord of bliss. The air reeked strongly of excitement. Swept with nature's own bolstering breath, the dusty shower steadily weakened, vanishing fields afar the furor it so rashly incited.

As with the customs she had since been acclimated to, the last cove of the garage stood gaping in welcome, like warmth at the terminal of an arctic trudge. It awaited her behest. Julia nested the SUV inside the sleek, architectural space, looking more at home in the designated roost than not. Her actions conveyed little difference in its dispersal than the lord of the manor himself.

Gathering her purse and the small overnight bag, Julia veered towards the entrance of the house, alleviating her anxiety's edge with a slow emission. The composed procedure belied the necessity of that. Of a sudden, the subtle hum of a motor chipped the concentrated silence, besieging the large space. It broke the dedicated voyage of her steps mid-point of their drive, stuttering her motion to an immediate stop. Whirling from her projected route, Julia's eyes jumped to the door's descent, seeking out the cause of the ghostly barring, they quickly garnered the reason and stayed. And brown orbs passionately devoured the picture that was so deftly displayed.

Michael's tall frame donned the entrance like a newly erected effigy, beautifully salvaged from the past. He exemplified a decorator's dream of an adorning. Worn astoundingly low, the smoky-silk boxers seeped as his only mode of dress, iced well with a scrumptious smile. The inspiration was, indubitably, an indulgence to later educe in the convivial shadows of one's dreams. Unreservedly decadent, it raptly enchained, and wicked tingles effectively manipulated the cusped regions of her body. Slowly enrapturing her mind as a vassal for itself, submission was instant, for the rendering, as it stood, was without a single fault. David, of Michelangelo's own hands, held no splendor beyond the sculpting of that which lied before her eyes, and had he been privy to the view, the artist himself would have deemed the vision well worthy of such praise. As if privy to the label she gave, Michael's smile slowly widened, bringing a hand forward, he touched a berry-colored rose to the cliffs of his chest.

"Coming, or are we starting in here today?" he asked, his husky voice stroking her skin like fingers, mowing sweetly on the ascension of her thighs. It skillfully pitched fire to the kindling already there. Except for the soft light waiting to be extinguished at her back, the two were almost ensconced in darkness, and its dim glow doused the breadth of his olive complexion in the radiance of bronze.

"New outfit?" She quizzed with a slow, methodical smile, resisting the urge to rush. Her murmured jest scaled the large opening like the fall of a sigh, though her body quaked with everything but. "It must have taken you forever to come across that piece."

"I'm only trying to even the field." He countered through the furnishing of his own charismatic smile. "You seem to be ahead of me at every turn. With a little work, maybe you'll allow me the chance to make up some grounds. What do you think? You like?"

"Oh, it's…" moving her head in a slow wave, a purr sailed forward like the start of a grunt, eyeing him then with ravenous glut. "Mmm, so…nice…."

"Hi." Michael breathed, immediately pulling her close; his voice stroked the soft arc of her cheek. "This is for you," he growled in counsel, touching the rose to her fingers. He relieved the encumbering bags with the other from her hand. The sound of the carriers striking the marble entry was comparable to a small explosion, waking the stillness. It echoed through the halls of the house. Under any other guide, a clatter of its like would have been disturbing for the inhabitants within, though neither seemed to have heard the unnerving sound. "I won't be insulted should you happen to drop it." He rasped against her mouth, his voice rumbling over the plumpness of her lips. A hand moved in mandate to her waist, guiding her through the door's opening before it soundly slammed.

Suddenly impatient, Julia yielded her restraint, conceding to her hunger. She initiated the feed, and the devotion, as always, accentuated everything she yearned and more. Crushing her in the usual demonstration of his passion, his ardor burst upon her raw. Prompting the release of the floret from her hand, she showed no delay in locking them at his back. Neither did she waiver in the tethering of her leg, firmly cradled in the notch of his waist, she made clear her intent. With the quickness of his hands, Michael furthered the torrents, lifting her from the floor. He pressed her to the hard bracing of the wall.

"Mmm," he growled, wielded like the lengthy end of a staff, the vibration crossed the rift of her mouth, and she aptly swallowed the flavor it gave. "Should we try and make it to the bed this time?" the raspy query came with an avid caress of her tongue, thrilling the sensory bed of both, their breaths trounced the air with its depth.

"Okay." She returned in a hum, that being the only conjure so managed by her brain, as his kisses had her honed for only one thing. Michael's hands dropped, like a narrow sill, to her buttocks, turning, he carried her high about his waist. Half staggering in his haste, he compensated the gesture with the hungry pursuit of his bed. Julia hurriedly peeled the simple tank from her body, pausing briefly; she smiled in offering of the meze she so zealously displayed. Accepting the proposition as a treat, Michael smiled back, placing the appropriate appreciation on each breast. The two darkened the threshold of his suite as they would the finish of a race. The door clapped like the warning salvo of a squall, forcefully hammered in place with what seemed a nominal swipe of his hand. And not unlike the structured ire of a tempest, silence quickly reclaimed the elegant manse. Softening like the peaceful streaming of rain, it fell unhindered and free.

Time aged before Michael's head again rose from the indent of her pillow. A smile distorting the angling of his face, lingering pleasantly in the speckled gems of his eyes, they caressed her features in-depth. Julia stared back with the same fusion of amazement showing on her face, though her eyes glistened with fire yet smoldering through their dark depths. Michael's head gently lowered, touching a kiss to the corner of her mouth, his lips walked as soft as the spilling of their weakening breath.

"How are you?" he asked against the warmth of her cheek. His voice trundling in a low, raspy purr, sounding everything like the overture of a lover, it tingled on its descent. That voice grew increasingly sweet the longer its heard, befitting the rune that trickled with the ripening of night. A cadence that aptly enslaved the prodding of one's will, streaming effective when the lyrical flow bred fervor too pleasing to ignore. It was the way it roughened the delicate passages it probed.

Marveling at the degree with which his voice now captivated her ears, Julia smiled. Of late, everything about him was like a bedeviling. "I'm good. I'm very good." She sighed, drawing in a long breath. She savored the moment's offering, most of which spotlighted him.

"You look good." He murmured, tracing the lines of her body with his hand. He again gave his appreciation with the widening zest of his smile. "As always," he grunted, balancing comfortably on his arm, his lower half lingered in its intimate press.

"You're looking like something from the dessert cart yourself."

"Really, can you say where you'd like to partake of first?"

"Didn't I just do that?"

"I don't recollect any definitive eating just then."

"Maybe not, but there was definitely an avid amount of…swallowing going on in that mix." She teased, removing the tight pull of her hair from beneath the determined press of her shoulders. She smirked at the resilience of her oratory gift.

Chuckling, Michael rested his head to the pillow adjoining hers, savoring the spice of her wit. Its finesse has yet to cease regaling his mind, adding fuel to a forest already aflame. It amplified his esteem of their talks. The topic was of little consequence in the undertakings, only the melody betrayed by the process or its end, so, too, for the buoyancy of its hum. "Yes. I guess I'll have to concur, since there was definitely a significant amount of swallowing involved then."

Reveling in her verbal victory, Julia's smile was near blinding. Her eyes showing the full fervency of her pride, though, in truth, the matter started as such. However, the finish was without precedence or sort. Those eyes were again regarding, and they seemed persistent in their wont, tenderly feathering the sensitive layers of her skin. They penetrated the hidden alleyways of her soul, holding her steadfast without will. "Tell me something truly beguiling about yourself." She sighed with little evidence of thought. Though her eyes immediately registered her startle at the intrusive query. The brash words had bolted from her mouth without qualms, giving her brain no time to evaluate the rift from such logic. She had always been contented with the things he deemed suitable to share, having never intruded on his personal life before now. The matter felt profoundly strange to her sense of self. But, too, it felt surprisingly right. Finding it an essential need to garner a more intimate morsel of the man, the offering of such was, for her, an odd pull.

"What would you like to know?" Michael asked with what seemed an inviting smile, seemingly unbothered by her inquest.

"I don't know. Anything. Whatever you judge okay to tell." She shrugged, her eyes dipping with a sudden surge of nerves, unsure of her reason for taking the venture into such realm of his personal life.

"Anything?" Michael asked in a low groan. "That's a lot to filter through."

"I'm sorry. Maybe I should not have asked, and you don't have to tell me, if you prefer that I leave that side of you alone. I really don't have a problem with that." She rambled in a whispery voice, suddenly rocked with guilt. It paralleled well the bour-geoning swells of her unease.

"Do you want the good, the bad, or the downright stupid?"

"Wherever you feel the most comfortable," she shrugged, answering this with a sigh. Her body furthered the taunt as a ripple boosted the apprehension she now had, and without deliberating the facts. She knew the sensation was not just hers to bear. "You don't have to give what you don't want." She quickly added in start.

Michael nodded, rolling onto his back. He stared absently at the ceiling, and a long, spiraling gust bested the silence.

"Are you thinking that I'll judge you?" she asked in a soothing tone.

"That's…well…I don't know. I'm not sure." And although soft, his murmured answer neared the pitch of a grumble.

"Does that bother you?" she probed in a gentle breath, afraid of what she sensed in him, as the connection between them bred outstandingly clear. Detecting scraps of his emotions was almost as distinct as the steeping she weathered from her own, and at the moment, he was plainly unnerved. "I wasn't asking for you to list your faults, Michael, I just—"

"I just can't figure out where to begin." He groaned, hesitant to witness even a nominal stitch of disapproval in her eyes. Michael held fast to his tongue. Should he enlighten her on how asinine his actions had been? How much detail should he give her on what he was like then? How much before disappointment or disgust slinked as a mirror on her face? The edgy questions rocketed through the jabbering in his head at an unrelenting pace, though the answer offered no easing to his thoughts.

"The past is a very interesting thing, Michael. The things you store there have a weird way of owning you until you reclaim the power you expelled on keeping them fed. No one has the right to fault you for your past, Michael, no one; the least of all me.

If you've already left that part of yourself behind, then that's just where the imps will remain locked. That's why we call it the past."

"But I did a lot of stupid things in those days." He apprised tamely, turning his gaze upon her. A faint streak of anguish peppered the marble-like depths. Magnifying his confusion, as he could not fathom why her opinion held him so fully transfixed.

"Then leave them there." She shrugged, not needing to have specifics, nor did she want to see him hurt. "Are you proud of the man you are now?"

"I've had to work very hard. Mend a lot of fences, but…yes. I am."

"There's no better reverence for the keeper of time than growth." She smiled, feeling his discomfiture relax with the easy flow of her voice. "Besides, I wasn't asking for the details of how many women you've been with." Julia teased, nudging his arm, she widened her grin. "I don't need the particulars of what you did with them or how. I already know you've been with a lot of women, how could you not? You possess the two biggest qualities that would enable that outcome."

"And what's that?"

"Money and looks. Money by itself will get you a lot, but when you combine the two…um." She groaned, shaking her head as if scolding his actions past. "Well, let's just say I'm glad you were adamant about condoms."

"I've been around the block, that's true. That doesn't bother you?"

"Why should it? I can't do or say anything about it now, can I?" She shrugged. "Short of climbing aboard my moral throne to put an end to all this," emphasizing her point, she waved an arm across the intimate sprawl of their bodies. "There really isn't much left for me to do, now is there? Just remember what I told you when you agreed to our deal. There's a reason why they call it the good old days, Michael. If you get the urge to relive them, then you'd better grant me the courtesy I asked, or our passion will be of a whole other sort. I won't guarantee how it will leave you, but I know it will leave me somewhat fulfilled."

"Why would I need to?" He smiled, turning onto his side, Michael propped his head on the pillar of a hand. "When you lay such feast at my feet," He murmured with a slow hike of his brows, wondering who could truly best the spicy dishes she served. What skill would another woman have to possess to keep him more satiated than this? She had him confused, smitten and titillated all in a single breath. What more could a man want? "Drugs were my thing," he droned, dragging the words slowly through the pause. "Any, all, and eventually in amounts that was less than sensible for my health." Murmuring the annotation as if to himself, his words gave way to a need, needing to share a part of himself with her. He continued in a passive tone. "I almost killed myself a few times, usually while I was high out of my mind. And it wasn't much better for my mother, since I almost killed her with worry. My parties lasted days, and the women…they were many."

"But I'm sure she's proud of you now, any mother would be." Again feeling his unease, her voice fell like the gentle swing of the wind. "You grew up, changed your life. That's all any mother ccould ask for." She smiled.

Studying the tilt of her face, Michael responded with a slow, enthralling smile of his own, his eyes searching as if for something veiled in the answer she gave. As if settling a thought in his head, he leaned to her with the warm tender of a kiss, stroking the readied fullness of her lips with his own. He lingered in his effort, plying her with much of what he had yet to say. "Have I mentioned how much I like talking to you?"

"My ears are always at your disposal." She whispered back, understanding the difficulty in the synopsis he gave.

"What would you like to know?"

"It doesn't matter really." She sighed, moving her head softly under his. "Whatever you'd like to tell is fine or we can just drop it as it stands."

"Ask me a question." He rasped, still resting against her mouth.

Again feeling his hesitance, she stroked the soft outline of his lips with her own. "What are you the least proud of?" she muttered, turning her mouth fully to his.

"There are a few, actually." He muttered after a pause.

"Like what?" she asked in an airy whisper, brushing her fingers along the edge of an ear.

"Like indiscretions," he shrugged. "Or the lack of them, mostly, a mountain of ungentlemanly behaviors lined much of my past." He rasped, his pitch faltering like dialogue being carried by the wind. Teetering to a stop, his eyes glazed as if watching a movie from his past, they grew distant before veering back. "But..." he shrugged, breaking the self-imposed pause with a low grunt. He offered no further comment but a stiff smile.

"Did you really total your car turning into your garage?" she crooned, continuing her maneuverings of his ear. Her fingers walked the lines of his jaw.

"I thought you didn't follow gossip?"

"I don't. But neither can I escape it." She smiled. "How long have you been clean?"

"Completely? Twelve years, eleven months, three weeks...and, six days," He rumbled swiftly, drawing his brows immediately tight, as if empting a putrid stench from his past. Reciting the answer in a rough, monotone chant, his pride for attaining such ascension was still unmistakable in his tone. It transmitted sagely through the reserve he showed, and in that instant, Michael's mind stormed in a backward spin to his past. A place rarely frequented, he abided little relish for his behaviors of old, as the barbs, yet sharpened on few, persisted in their irking still.

His most lucid venture, thus far, was in suffusing himself with the people he admired most. That verdict, within itself, had helped him at every junction of his struggle. In the many years since, he'd learned that danger bodes in everything that one does, not only in the lure of the drug itself, but in the expectation of time, things, and the harsh penalties sometimes tacked to innocuous events.

In the eyes of most, it all seemed as if two lifetimes had elapsed since then, though it was not so for those with a struggle of their own. He had since separated himself from everyone who embraced his lifestyle of old. Longtime friends were of little difference to his cause, slashing everything and everyone in a clean sweep was like a cleansing within itself. Since his last encounter with that world was the most frightening yet.

Celebrating his twenty-seventh birthday, Jeffery, his best friend at the time, threw him, what was considered, an amazing birthday bash, lasting, those in their clique, a staggering four days. On the sixth, he woke up in the hospital with a horrific aching in his head, added to the nuisance of that was his sudden inability to walk, as both legs were now broken. Four cracked ribs, a fractured arm and a severe allergic reaction to something he took, reared as latecomers to his mounting stack of belated gifts.

Reaped from the many retelling, it seemed he had forgotten his ability to take flight, though he tried doing just that from the third floor balcony of his friend's house. He then watched as his mother collapse outside the dim corridor of his hospital room. Thankfully, her debility was only due to dehydration. But the effect of such had already taken its pound of flesh. That, for some reason, helped, in conjunction with a sprouting stack, to scare him straight, knocking some sense into his thick skull. For as it turned out, she had not eaten almost the entire time he went missing. The experience had had him wondering if that was, in anyway, near the way she felt in regards to the foolery he had always instigated. What must it feel like to watch him repeatedly toy with his life, after having lost so much? Until this day, he'd never had the courage to ask. Though he had wondered how she coped with watching the people she loved dwindle from her life. Having to witness him barrel forward on the fury of that, well eager to follow suit.

Strangely, stupidity actually saved his life. Informed by the doctors later that had he not jumped, he would have most likely died, judging from the severity of his allergic reaction.

Determined to change his life for the better, he threw everything into rehabilitating himself. Travelling for a while, he left the familiarity of his life behind, experiencing that through the eyes of others. Africa became his most ardent lesson, more than the visual paraded of poverty. It opened his eyes to resilience, something he had never taken the time to do before then. Sitting on the floor of a one-room hut with a family of four, all inhabitants of the small space, as each, in selfless generosity, offered to share, without reservation, from the meager tithing they possessed. That was a humbling experience of itself.

He lived two weeks with that family he branded his own, learning from them how to be productive as a human being. From them, he learned how to be a man. After leaving, he volunteered as work, eventually starting his own charity. He grew tall from the dirt roots of said hut. "Abnormal though it seems, it took me leaving one home, traveling halfway around the world, if not more, to then grow up in a one room hut." He hummed in conclusion of his tale, his eyes growing again distant, though he furnished the moment with a pleasant smile.

"Are you back?" Julia asked softly, seeing that his mind had drifted miles from the husk of his body.

"What?"

"You went away for a while."

"I'm sorry."

"Don't be. Wherever you were, you looked peaceful. It must have been a good place."

"It was—is." He shrugged.

"Good. It's good to have that. So that's what you mean when you call yourself a late bloomer? You know, that only means you should love the whole thing more."

"What things?"

"Everything, since it took you longer than most to get there. You can appreciate it more. At the age you accomplished these things, that maturity can only work in your aid. You can see better the things you were missing. You can also see where you've been and how to treasure your prize."

"That's true."

"Did you stay in touch with the family in Africa?"

"We write back and forth constantly, and I see them at least once a year."

"They must be so proud of you."

"I hope so."

"If you're so proud of yourself, and should be, why is it so hard to talk about?"

"It's not, well…not normally." He smiled, and nicely tanned shoulders slowly lifted in accordance of his words, brushing hers on the descent.

"Okay." Julia smiled, nodding in understanding, more so, than she understood why. "Are you okay?"

"Never better," He smiled, pulling her with him as he rolled to the other side of the bed. The wavy strands of her hair cascaded around them like a curtain, filling his nostrils with her scent. "Hmm, are you hungry?"

"No. Are you?"

"Not yet. But I plan on working my way to that point." Michael drawled, brushing his lips along the inside of her arm.

"And just how do you plan to do that?"

"Why don't you come down here and find out." He hummed, his murmured words again stroking the skin of her arm.

"I'm guessing spilling your soul gnaws well at your appetite?"

"Leaving me the most ravenous cravings," he growled.

"And what of the other occasions?"

"Well," he smiled. "That's a whole other story for a different time."

Julia smiled, holding tight to the start of a purr, though the shiver she could not. Wading through her body, it radiated to the top of her head. How is it possible that she keeps getting this incited with so little effort from him? Shouldn't the thrill be tapering by now?

Chapter Twenty Seven

Skiing the shapely length of a thigh, the sensuous feasting so savored the spread of another, salaciously engaging in its creed. The act warrants well the proof with the flooding it so ardently assigned. Much like the keeling of a reservoir's door, anticipation reared robust, fostering that which compelled the yen for a satisfying end.

Treasuring the raunch scorching of his breath, Julia awaited the surge of ignition, so pledged by the ravening reins of his approach. His kisses came like the tasting of a rare treat, hot, moist and soft in the sampling. It grew proficiently sweet. Bringing pleasure with the competence of its touch, thus testified to aptly by the tailored expression now fashioned on her face. A sigh slowly wafted through the silence, though in time, it transmuted to the airing of a cry. Vibrating softly in the edging of her throat, it lengthened once his tongue instigated the cadence of play.

Frissons inundated the svelte splendor of her body, commanding the will of her hands; lively fingers rend the covers from its place. Trembling, Julia caught what came more like a coo, seeming the mutterings of his name, though the yielding hardly ruffled what yet governed her brain. As the flick of his tongue was like a balletic whip. Purposeful and roguish in its wont, the rhythmic flagging thenceforth heightened its pace. Not unlike the tenacious exert brandished in a butterfly's wing, each lash ceded ascension atop a euphoric alp. "Yes! Yes!" her body avidly screamed, blurring the lines of internal dialogue with that of external speech. A caldron of explosions then rocketed through the abyss of her body, locking her shuddering limbs to the orifice's bestowing. She held, as the rapture impeded all process of thoughts.

Moistening the parched fissure gone dry, Julia quieted her body's bliss with the pilfering of small breaths, as consciousness restored the once befogged regions of her brain. Wielding an equally satisfied expression on his face, Michael rose from his low perch. A kiss then skimmed the soft den of her navel, trudging upwards to her breasts, he lingered in said place. And the decadence of his smile was unequaled once he flaunted the implement thus.

"Good morning to me!" She sighed, returning his smile, her eyes yet vibrant with, what haughtily seemed, adoration's kin. "Every woman ought to have that come special order with their morning coffee." She purred, and her eyes quickly skirted the discarded tray in affirmation of her jest. Laden anew with their emptied wares, the evidence was well exhibited on the elegant bench. The morning for them had grown well-seasoned with age, partaking of breakfast in the idle hours before, residue of eggs, waffles and fruits stained the faces of their plates, conversation being their skirmish of choice. That is, until then.

"Should I start sending out flyers?" he asked from the edge of her ears, touching his tongue to the smooth pocket of that spot.

"Not just yet." She smiled, her voice floating the same as his whispery probe. "I haven't used you up as yet."

"Is that so?"

"Well…." She shrugged, offering a frisky visage with the structure of her smirk.

"Then I guess we'll just have to see about that."

"Testy? Or was that your delivery of a challenge?"

"Let's just say I find the statement…interesting."

"How's that?"

"I'm sure you'll figure out the answer with time."

"Do you give hints with your cryptic spitting, or do I have to unscramble the quandary in my head?"

"I doubt it will require you to put in that much work. Everything you need for grasping the facts has already been disclosed."

"Is that so?"

"I think so." He shrugged.

"More mysteries? Man, this morning definitely has you on a roll!"

"No mysteries, I'm just leaving you to access what you already know. That's all."

"Fine, I guess I'll leave the probing at that then."

"Good choice." He teased, tweaking her nose. Michael dropped his head to his own pillow with force, voicing his next question through a languid stretch. "Now, what should we do with ourselves today?"

"Are you sure I'm not interfering too much with your work?" she questioned with the starting of a frown, already conscious of his answer before it came. "I know how crazy your schedules have been, and I don't want you to feel obligated to put things off when there's really no need. I have more than enough to occupy me for the month."

Flaunting the trappings of summer, the warm, evocative days of June now trolled with its usual charm, shouldering well the promise of adventures to come. The last day of school saw Richard and Rachel off for a staggering three weeks with their dad. Thrilled at the pledged furor of having no school, the prospect had had them patently brimming with glee. Julia's excitement was near matching in its comber, though her reasons, quite surely, unparalleled their own, knowing that while they celebrated their respite from rigid compliance, she most definitely intended to play. With her mother off in the Bahamas for almost two weeks, the window stood wide open to do just that. And she meant to reap every ort of the time she had.

In his own unique fashion, Michael deftly broached the subject of her plans. Revealing, quite boldly, he desired an ample segment of said break. She just wasn't sure if two weeks would hurt the harmony they had. God knows their festivities were beyond the mere depicting of words, and to lose any portion of that would eventually sour the outcome, an outcome she was not yet ready to see croak its last breath.

"Will you stop?" he scolded, threading long fingers to the smaller of hers, Michael smiled. At the prospect of ogling her for more than the usual two days, he had leapt at the chance, rearranging most of his schedule for the want of that. Two weeks was a lifetime when compared to the specks of the past, summed to almost three months to be exact, there was frankly no way, short of a catastrophe that halted his breath, he intended to miss out on a treat like that. "If I recall, I had to pretty much seduce you into saying yes. You don't beg to have something because you hate to have it done." Gentling his voice, he kissed the back of her hand, and again he brightened his smile. "But, we do need to discuss Betty."

"I was wondering about that." She sighed, feeling the full weight of the statement itself. Well aware of the bond that existed between them, she had deliberated some on the duration of Betty's absence, and how that affected the administering of his house. Was it unfair of her to insist, so drastically, on the privacy of their deal? "Where is she?"

Still holding her hand, Michael quickly captured her gaze. "She's in California with her family. But I think she already knows."

"What! But…how?" she gasped, her head rotating with an urgent snap.

"I don't know," he frowned, tightening his grip on her hand, his thumb soothed the tense tendons now standing on end. "But Betty is like that. You think she's not paying attention or that she has no inkling of what's going on. Yet, she has a way of giving you feedback that completely bowls you over in your track."

"Oh, no!" Rolling her eyes, Julia hazard the start of a groan, deepening the tone as humiliation distorted the viewings in her head. "What did she say?"

"I think she warned me to treat you with care." Michael shrugged, relaying his thought, her quizzical glance lingered as the two exchanged their own wondering gaze. "I told you she liked you."

"How does something like that even come up with you two?"

"I wish I knew. One minute we were discussing food and the next…well. Just out of the blue she asked, 'how's Julia'?"

"What did you tell her?"

"Nothing! Well…actually I told her the truth. I told her you were fine the last time I saw you."

"That's it?"

"That's it."

"I don't hear a warning in that." Julia frowned, seeming more confused than before.

"Well, when I asked her why, she said she just wanted to make sure you were doing well." Clarifying the point, Michael's eyes rolled upwards in pause, as if searching his memories for the accuracy of his thought. "Or something like that. I know Betty, and I know she was warning me to be careful with you." He smiled, turning, he propped himself on the column of an arm. "You seem to have a weird way of getting people to fall all over themselves to try and please you."

"Now she thinks I'm one of your easy treats."

"No, she doesn't." He countered in a rumbly breath, his fingers toying with the smooth strands of her hair.

"How can you be so sure?"

"Like I said, I know Betty. Betty only talks when she wants to, or when it's necessary to be polite. She didn't talk much to the other women I brought home in the past."

"Okay, first, I'm going to ignore the part where you just fashioned me with the other women in your life. God! That sounded so cheap!" shaking her head, she bequeathed him a partial glare. "Besides, she didn't talk that much to me."

"I'm sorry! I'm sorry! You didn't hear that." Michael chided, waving his hand above her as if to wipe clean the memory of his words, his fingers gently stroked the slope of her brow. "Not only did she talk to you, she went all out. She even sent you home with treats for your kids."

"She did, didn't she?" answering what dangled more like a statement than the jarring of a quest, a wayward sigh preluded the empting of her words. "What do you want to do?"

"Nothing much really, just say it's okay to have her come home. That's all. She'll stay away from this side of the house, I'm sure of it. The only thing that will change is that she'll know. Well, she'll have confirmation. But Betty is trustworthy, I promise you. I trust her with my life—have trusted her with my life. She wouldn't tell anyone, not even if her life depended on it."

"Fine," spitting the versatile word like a protracted whine, a weighted draught spiraled from the sluices of her nose, skewing the wary stillness like a howl. She scuffed the rafters with said breath. Objectively, she had no right to any answer but that. Thus far, he has been downright accommodating. Yet that hardly vetoed her prospect of being labeled a cavorting minx. She was, in actuality, one of a sundry of treats known to the man. And while the soberness of the act bares no shame, it did not change the fact that the consequence of said act can be, at times, shameful. What titles would they add to her name should their liaison be exposed? A probability she prefers to have shelved, not that such exploits could be prolonged for any length. The newness will eventually erode from what they now have, tempering the prerequisite of their union. The inferno, as with everything, will in time staunch, putting to bed the very thing that had once set them ablaze.

"Good. I'm really glad we got that settled." Michael smiled, dropping a kiss to her chest. His breath basted her skin with a force of warmth. "I have to tell you. I've never been able to lie to Betty, not just because she knows every nuance I have, but…well." His shoulders rose slowly through the pause, emphasizing his meaning before he granted it life. "Call it respect. Call it her own weird powers of intuition—which she does have, by the way!" he grunted, quickly adding the thought through a frown, he jutted a finger through the air with what came more as a warning than not. "—I've just never been aptly skilled at that, and had she asked me, not that she would, not with something this personal. I couldn't say with certainty what my answer would have been."

"Are you trying to tell me that underneath that bad-boy facade, you're just a choir-boy? I didn't sign up for that. Don't tell me you used your charm to lure me with false pretense, because I expected the full package. Drugs, sex and rock and roll, that's the excitement I want!"

"I bet! You wouldn't even have given me the time of day then! Not that it was much different with the changes, mind you. But I doubt that even a consortium of charm would have carried you to my bed. Yeah, you would have really loved me back then. You got the full package alright, just…a little tame." Shrugging lamely behind the statement, he smiled. "And a little wiser in part,"

"And a whole lot smoother, that's for sure." She teased, stroking the fullness of his brows, she smiled. "All those changes were certainly not for naught, look at all the things you've accomplished." She added with a slow incline of her brows, dipping her head in a slight bow to her chest.

"Oh, I'm well aware of my accomplishments thus far, and the payout tells me it was well worth the fray. Of late, it seems more obstinate in its reasoning than it has been in the past." Sagging the gravely depth of his tone, Michael's eyes fell intently to hers, holding the heart of her gaze. He gave strength to the simple rendering of his words.

"I–I think I'll take the tray back to the kitchen," she fumbled in start, feeling drawn by what she found utterly spectacular to gaze in. Julia deftly alleviated the chance of furthering their talk. "When I get back, I may have something of a treat for you."

"Really, what kind of treat?"

"I thought you liked surprises?" she asked stiffly, clearing her throat. Julia rolled promptly from his side, and immediately clamped tense fingers to the waiting tray. Something in his wording tickled her fancy more than it should, and things of their nature were better left untouched. Dressed in another of his shirts, the length rivaled a small dress. With sleeves roughly pushed to her elbows, the enclosure remained loosely that. Starting well below the swell of her breasts, the hem winged with the slightest shift, bypassed by the last two buttons, the depiction saved the imagination much. Lately, such attire has been his singular request. Leaving the garment out at the foot of his bed, she found no reason to deny him that. "Don't make yourself too comfortable." She teased, turning promptly, she sashayed from the room.

The morning, though riddled with age, remained uncannily dark, resembling the dregs of an artist's brush. The heavens now tallied two days of purging itself. Thunder and lightning had chorused the swathing of night, though the music of that had since stopped. It left behind a heavy drubbing of rain. The resonance of which still tickled the roof like skilled fingers plucking on a musical string. A peaceful breath whittled the trouncing, donating solace in the crackling's wake. Grown indolent with the hammering rain, the day yet gifted a happy edge, almost enlivened. The sun's absence seemed hardly that.

Empting the trash from their tray, Julia stacked their plates in the dishwasher draw, moving about the kitchen as efficiently as home. She returned the large platter to the cabinet colonized with similar stacks.

"Coming?" she called from the entrance of the suite, smiling as his body shot forward in response to her spoken caress.

"I didn't know we were going on a trip." Michael countered with a playful smirk, bounding from the bed, blue boxers, as dark as midnight, sagged from the hard bones of his hips.

Sleek, powerful and beautifully built, his physique was not one easily ignored, and again she was reminded of a lion, for his swagger told much of the dominance he bred. *My goodness what a treat you make,* Julia sighed, muttering the appetizing thought in her head, she fought an odd urge to lick her drink from the trenches of his stomach. Instead, slender fingers wrapped softly around the larger of his, piloting their slow exit from the room.

"Where are we going?" Michael asked as they entered the garage, certain they would not go much farther from their manner of dress, his smile gave an inkling of knowledge. Her only answer came in the stuttering of her steps, pulling open the wing-like door of his AMG. She voiced a simple query.

"Driver's side or passenger's side?"

"What?" Michael waited with eyes keenly fixed, sending her a daft frown. His question bounced from each wall of the space, swallowing seconds before the fuzziness lifted. "Oh! Passengers!" he assured gladly.

"Then get in!" She answered with her own widening smile, enjoying the swiftness of his compliance, though his tall frame tangled in the mist of scooting, scaled another level in the humor they shared. Julia promptly followed his ingress, moving languidly across the leather seat, she perched beguilingly on his lap. Looking like a rare dove cloaked in the rosy aura of light. "Now, what was it you said about your car...your...what?"

Instantly, a twitch deepened in the corners of Michael's mouth, skipping through the depths of his eyes, anticipation rode her proposition wild. Happy to give over the rights of his body, his mind was already dreaming of aberrant ways to repay her indulgence. "I said something like...my car, my property, where else should I fondle you?" he groaned, and much like a predator's growl, the mutterings rumbled coarsely through the small space. Fastening the gems of his eyes on the laboring of her hands, Michael watched intently as she unclasped the last button from its place. Slowly opening the shirt to his gaze, her shoulders gently rocked, freeing the garment. It fluttered to his feet in its haste.

"And what exactly was it you wanted to fondle?" she asked, stroking his ear with the plump warmth of her lips, her breasts abnormally pillowed his chin.

"Just…well, here…." Michael growled as his hand trailed the side of her breast, falling slowly downward, his fingers trundled her body. "There…and…Well…" turning his head, his lips brushed hers, and as if sampling the flavor of an ice-cream cone, his tongue slowly walked the soft bed of her lips. "And…This" He sighed, covering her mouth in a kiss tasting strongly of concupiscence; the dark fusion soon blazed, sweeping them in a current too exquisite to not delve.

Emotions trudged every inch of his frame, wielding his indurate limb as her hand moved to the inside of his shorts. Masterfully taunting her body, his own grew primitive, growling with carnivorous focus as she shepherded him home. Her hips danced like the excerpts from a spell, taking him on a journey exceeding all else. The hungrier he grew the more ravenously she ate. Forsaking all but the ecstasy she gave, his hands were incessant, rummaging her body at will. They clasped her in the throes of flight, as both bodies, in time, pinnacled the stars. "*Oh, God!*" Burying his face between her breasts, his grunt wafted low from the barrel of his chest, still tasting the sweetness she gave.

He could feel the maddening rhythm of her heart, and the thudding was well matched by the thrashing of his own. So, too, the quivers yet rappelling his trunk, arcing no less vivid in the tremors wading through his hands. His breath sailed ragged in the small space, tolling loud in the hollowness of his head, as each drag extinguished like work. She gave no movement since their quenching, and he greatly hoped that she would not, knowing with all certainty he could not. Had his life depended on that action, then doom would have surely conquered without ruckus or fray. As the sensation was too gratifying to let go of, for the will was neither present nor able, nor was the strength. Was this the work of his attraction, or is it her that makes this so… very good?

With what barely tendered as an effort, her head turned, and the sweetness of her smile waded through the shadowing of her eyes. Eyes that yet mirrored his sated gaze, looking like dark pools he wanted to dive in. Craving, above all, to live inside her for a spell, dwell as he was, and take up residency inside the cloaking she gave.

"Nice treat?" she purred.

"Oh…mmm, the very best," he sighed, holding her gaze, his voice came like a grated bass. *What is it about you that contradict prior rules, that makes this sooo…good? How?* Mulling on both sensation and thought, Michael leaned to her for the annexing of a kiss, stopping any chance of the question slipping from his tongue.

"I thought you might like that." She cooed, adjusting her legs on the seat. Julia smiled, though his answer came as a soft, eddying grunt. Kissing the side of her neck, he kept her pressed to his chest, and a soft moan dripped from her lips in rejoinder.

Necessitating his one clarifying thought, powerful arms yet caged her. Tightening the coop with every breath, she blazed hard the roughened texture of his appetite. Soft, warm and smooth against him, she evolved more like the anamnesis of a dream, awed by the beauty itself. He feasted from outside of himself. Growing tranquil, Michael worked on stilling the thundering in his chest, swilling her flavor with the potency of his work.

Outside, rain thumped the thick width of the doors like the tight skin of a drum, sending conduits of water down the windows in a vexing rush. The melody grew magnetic, soothing the occupants inside. It was the perfect morning to be ensconced with a lover. She being the perfect lover to scabbard his body, and there being no place he would rather be than their venue of choice.

Rain pummeled the earth for another doublet of days, lessening on the morning of the third, though the couple inside hardly seemed cognizant of the torrential sluice clouding their windows. Sealed in the pervaded luxury of their room, the two ventured elsewhere only when their bodies deemed such piddling a must, calling for the pleasing sustenance of food at bizarre hours of the night. At intervals, laughter tumbled through the eclectic silence, not so for the acoustic descant of their murmurs and grunts, as play roused well between the crestings they bade.

Day in time tilted its floundering head in its sought of rest, launching the curtain of night. The atmosphere's glum shaded the evening in a powdery gray. On return to the kitchen, thus dictated by a potent need, the two busied themselves with the preparation of dinner. Her in the role of instructor, and he, an apprentice eager to learn, chatting fervently on an immensity of topics as they work.

"Come sit on me. I mean...with me." He drawled, setting her plate at his side, Michael relayed the dictum with a slow smile. Stretching his hand to her in wait, his eyes gave little evidence of a slip.

Confident the assertion was no mistake, Julia chuckled at the dry mien he so innocently displayed, knowing well the magnitude of his thirst, though her own indulgence was neither trifling nor lacking in its strive. She wondered, truly, on the level to which such cravings root. Of late, even the dungiest petitions bore no consequence of thought, for her appetite, since their scorching induction, had grown rabid. Things she had never tried, or wanted to before, now easily traipsed through her thoughts. Putting them to fruition without a modicum of modesty or fear, he had her epoch afar what she once measured that side of her personality to be. "Not filled up I see."

"Not even close." He vowed in his usual gravelly timbre, watching intently as her hips waved in his face. Swaying like the loosely tacked hinge of a pendulum, she slowly lowered her rump to his lap. "Comfy?"

"Quite."

"Good." He grunted, lifting her hair from the shoulder adjacent his chest. Michael savored the fragrance fixed to her shirt. That scent being truly one of her most beguiling facets, he groaned. "I'm glad I could be a source of comfort. Anything else I can do for you? Because I do so...aim to please,"

"I'll let you know if the need comes up." Julia smirked, blowing a simmering vapor from the sliver of ravioli on her fork. She sunk the smothered pasta in her mouth, chewing it clear before voicing her thought. "I'd like to know something though, why am I always naked when I'm here?"

"Because it looks so damn good on you," he groaned.

"I can say the same for you, but…you're not naked."

"Do you want me naked, Jules?" he whispered leaning close. "You know, I'll gladly comply with whatever you want."

"Are you talking to me, or to some alter ego of yours?"

"I never did get to finish my drink, did I? I wouldn't mind it if Jules and I picked up where we left off. Her voice was simply inspiring."

"Maybe you can look her up one day, though jet setter that she is, it could prove quite futile a task." She shrugged, sending him a soft glare as she sunk another sliver in her mouth. His chest offered full respite for her back, but his eyes were incessant in their work, studying her as they spoke. They amassed her details as if they were but scribings in a book.

"I love the color of your skin!" He informed in a rough breath, voicing the words in lieu of an answer, his deep timbre came with the reverence of a maudlin youth. Gifting their concurrence of such, his eyes instantaneously dropped, slowly. The pair strolled the length of her thighs. "It reminds me of chocolate with a swirling of caramel inside, or is it the other way around? It's exquisite either way!" he rasped, lacing his fingers through hers. His thumb stroked the back of her hand before lifting said limb to the light. "I swear I can taste it every time I kiss you." Tacking his eyes to the fold of her hand, he brought the limb to his lips, and perfect teeth flashed their brilliance in a smile. "That may explain why I can't seem to get enough."

"Sweet talker," She jeered, trying not to be affected by the fixation of his mouth.

"You think that's sweet?" Michael quarried with the start of a frown, his deep voice vibrating across the smooth skin of her arm. "I have much sweeter things I could tell you, and even sweeter yet to show you." He pledged, and the other of his hand moved like the intro of a promise to her thighs, lightly sketching the inside of each, he smiled. "So much sweeter,"

"You're a menace, you know that?" Julia griped, feeling the effects of his kisses and, too, the working of his hands, as both played well their prospective sport. "A bully and a menace, that's what you are. You're always going to search for ways around my resistance, aren't you? You just won't let my body say no, will you?"

"Do you still want to?"

"I've grown accustomed to you." She groaned, answering the troubled subject with a shrug, as the truth was far too complicated an answer to give. It wasn't just that her body reacted to his touch, but that she, uncannily, reacted to him. But why muddle things, of such complexion with the entanglement of words? Candor could only serve as bedlam for the situation they're in. Didn't she already give enough of herself in the furiousness of her response? The rules remained as simple as they once were. Two con-senting adults in a mock relationship, the advantage was but one. Had she not brokered that arrangement herself? She had not overlooked one thing in their odd affiliation. Walking in with her head facing forward and her eyes pinpoint on the target at hand, well conscious the fervor would not last, though perhaps that sentience had yielded her the incentive for saying yes.

"Interesting," Michael smirked, his hazel eyes looking like polished gems, as the light further brightened their depths. "I haven't grown accustomed to you."

"Maybe I'm just too complicated for you."

"No, not complicated. More like…intriguing," he drawled.

"You keep saying that, what is it that makes me so…'intriguing'?"

"It's an amalgamation of things, really." He shrugged, pausing as if to ponder her query, his eyes dipped slowly to their joined hands. "If I were to go to the market—wait, I said if…"Adjusting quickly, he answered the dubious shot of her brow. "If…I were to go shopping," he again started, fixing her with his own look of sanction before continuing his speech. "An onion is always the same every time, peel away the layers and you get the same thing, no matter how many you peel or for how long. But an orange, on the other hand, is rarely ever the same, visually, yes, or at least mostly so. But to the lingua of one with a discerning palate, it's of another matter completely. There's sweet, sour, juicy, sometimes it even lacks flavor on a whole. All of which can fall, in rarity, from the same tree. Usually, they say the hunt is to find them with all the right percentages in place, and that, in of itself, can sometimes be quite hard, even rare."

"Was that an explanation that I'm being likened to a fruit?"

"Something like that." Michael shrugged, resting his face against the back of her arm.

"What makes you think I'm a fruit?"

"Oh, you're definitely a fruit alright." Michael groaned, and a slow chuckle rose from the back of his throat in response, pushing her hair from her shoulder. His lips brushed the nape of her neck. "Yes. One with a sweet, exotic flavor for sure." Pressing his lips together, his tongue slowly glided across the soft beds, as if tasting the residue left by her skin. "Definitely a fruit,"

"An orange?"

"A surprise is always best when left as that. Why would anyone want to know what the gift is while they're in the middle of unwrapping? I like surprises." He shrugged, taking another taste of her skin. "Something's are just better when you take your time. Some are exclusively erected for that. This way you make sure the work is fully satisfying for everyone involved." Lifting his face to her ear, his breath cuddled her skin. "If you start slow, you can always build on that. Work until the rhythm catches you both, this way the end grows equally copious for two. I like taking my time." Michael hummed, his tongue slowly skating her ear. "The more layers there are, the more time it takes to undress."

Under his prodding, her pulse loped, tilling urges in the grazing of her skin. The soft swing of his finger bloomed antagonistic to her nerves. Perched against the tail of her shirt, he stroked her with malicious intent, and of their own volition, her legs slowly relaxed. His hand wittingly shifted then, electing a new spot, it reposed though his finger did not. Continuing the persistent rock, the man eyed her from atop the rim of his glass.

"I've never been likened to a fruit before. Obviously, you're a man of many words. It seems to compliment your hectic adventures, and no doubt you're a master of both." She smiled, looking forward to the instant his hand brinked the warm cove of her thighs.

"The subject has more to do with that than not." He shrugged, and his deep voice strummed, like arpeggios of a chord, on the walls of her senses as a result. Loitering along the junction of her thighs, his fingers goaded of an imminent attack.

"Something tells me you can make art out of even the greenest mold."

"And what do I make out of you, Julia?" he asked with an odd sneer to his smile. Shifting his hand, his fingers coasted her navel, stopping below the swell of her breasts. He stalled all action in wait of her response.

"What exactly are you looking to make out of me?" she asked in a small voice, perceptive of his touch, she shrewdly awaited more.

"Why don't *you* tell me for a change? Tell me what you'd like instead? I promise you, I'll do everything I can to see your wish come true." Again leaning close, his words came purely of air.

"And what type of information would you need to help you with that?" she chirped, turning her head. Julia offered him the favoring of a smirk, though the composite flecks of hazel was all that she saw. The pair gaped back like thinking jewels attached to a face, seeming to syphon her secrets without exerting much work. His hand then slowly rappelled her body, returning to her thigh, his finger resumed its devilish taunt. "I'm at a loss of what else you could possibly need."

"One thing can be as good as everything some times." Michael shrugged, enjoying the feel of her skin, though the topic carted its own clout. "Information is golden, Julia. You would be amazed at what even a simple nod could tell."

"So, you're saying if I but nod my head that would give you all the ammunition you need?"

"Sometimes, but sometimes a little more works best." He smiled, stopping the tidal rock, his hand turned as if to rest. "Information comes in many forms, Julia. You'd be surprised where or how you can gather what you need."

"Which grants more proof of mastery, and if that's so, shouldn't the feel be more satisfactory than the tale?" Disappointed with the stilling of his hand, her legs unwittingly shifted, chilled in said spot by the loss of his warmth, she guardedly sieved through the remains of her food. His hand then clambered her side to rake the skin on his chest, ruffling the back of her shirt in its wake, thus furthering the strategic taunt.

"A certain feel, yes. I'll concede you that, but that's not mastery." He smiled, returning his hand to her thigh. The pendulum resumed its drive, though its method mimed of an imminent demise. "For instance," he growled, breaching the misty threshold, his stodgy tone seeped like honey over the heat of her skin. "When someone touch you and you like how it feels, shouldn't the rules be already clarified on that?" Gentling the rough hum of his voice, the workings of his fingers entailed a new name. "Take me for instance. I really like touching you. I like the way your skin feels against mine. You know this, because I tend to always seek more. So if you like my hand on your thigh and want me to use it, any simple gesture you choose will get you what you want. But you have to tell me, Julia." He droned. His lecturing breath warm upon the cording of her throat, while his finger sought but a solitary goal, and its mission, bodes astonishingly well. The second of his hands moved to inside her shirt, cupping her breast, his thumb played the soft peak. Partnered greedily by his mouth, he heightened the attack. Directed by the sound of her sighs, he slaved until her head fell with a decisive cry.

"You're a devious one, aren't you? I should be running for the hills, shouldn't I?" Julia whispered in reflection against his mouth.

"Why, because I can see more of who you are than the piddling you show?"

"Who am I?"

"I'll tell you that when I have it all figured out." Kissing the tip of her nose, Michael smiled. "There's still much to acquire and assess."

"You know, you may not like what you find. That onion may just be all that there is." She warned, running her fingers through the waves of his hair.

"Oh, I doubt that. I doubt that very much." He drawled, and the thrust of his smile was well assured, touching his lips to hers. He felt the budding of her own baiting smile. Yet he knew, with certainty, she found candor in his words. Outside, dreariness morphed with the blackness of night, whispering the songs of evening in an obvious serenade, they jointly swallowed the grounds like the smothering of a wick. Locked in the arms of the other, the two stayed press, unconcerned with none else but each other.

Ascribed as a day of reckoning, the petrifying day sprung the same as every other. Absent was the gloom that once suppressed, as the sky again gifted a softly diluted Maya blue, and its beauty baffled one's mind with the absence of flaw. Today, information once thought to be shared by two, will be divulged as facts to a third. For today, complaisant or not, Betty returns to her neglected post.

As with her usual comportment, Betty's entrance was almost stealthy in its gentle disperse. Hardly varying the aura as she entered the room, her smile wade the same as it always had. Noticing the couple on the couch, her expression wavered not, brandishing no different had she happened upon a meeting between the two. It was as if she had seen them together their entire life.

"Julia! How are you?" she probed, her soft voice inching forward like the lyric in a song, riding the tail of a stir. A smile brightened the dark inset of her eyes.

"Betty, Hello!" Julia rejoined with an almost timid smile, yet feeling esteem towards the elder of them. "I'm doing well, how are you?"

"If I'm still on my feet after dinner, I hope to have an answer for that." She laughed, and the soft lithe again played like a song, as it floated remarkably sweet. Drifting free, it disarmed the disquiet like gesso to a painting. "Family! They do require a lot, don't they?"

"I take it your trip was more work than you expected?" Julia asked, not intending to pry, her voice softened. Something about the older woman changed her disposition to relax.

"Oh, I expected the work," Betty shrugged, her thin shoulders moving brusquely through the air. "I just always get surprised by how much I end up doing." She frowned, touching a hand to her chest. Her eyes slowly waded out the window to the yard. "I see we had a lot of rain."

"We did! Almost a week's worth." Julia answered with her own gentling smile, tracking the direction of her eyes. The two gazed at the new lushness with pride. "How was it on the coast?"

"Smoggy," Betty groaned gruffly, returning the younger woman's gaze, she smiled. "I love the place, but I certainly don't miss it when I'm not there." Shifting her focus, her eyes rolled affectionately over the other in the room. Seeming heedless of their chat, his face showed little interest in the surrounding view, though she knew better of that act. His hand lounged lazily on the seat between them, as if waiting to take hold, they looked almost anxious in their linger. Thrilled with the sight, Betty smiled in satisfaction of her earlier surmise. The girl was nothing like his usual type. In fact, she was almost the opposite of his norm. Her beauty was the only understandable part in this phenomenon, for the others most certainly was that. Still, much of the personality was off, different, though better in so many ways. His demeanor, of late, sprouted frankly relaxed, seeming almost happy with himself, and she hoped to see more of that. "Did you miss me?" Betty teased, stealing his attention away from the girl whom he discreetly watched.

"Are you talking to me now?" Michael asked, sounding almost gruff, though a smirk seemed stapled to his face. "I didn't think you knew I was even in the room."

"Always needing attention?" she asked, responding much in the manner of a drone. Her voice dipped, hardening as if to sharpen its point of attack. Yet a mere three steps carried her to his side, and as with the wont of a mother, her hand gently rapped the stubbles on his cheek. Michael's hand covered the small fingers the instant they touched, smiling fondly, though neither acknowledged the other with the full gamut of their gaze. "So, did you miss me?" she asked with the taking of a breath.

"Why would I miss you, old woman? All you ever do is tell me what to do! Why would anyone miss that?" he grumbled, giving his full attention to her then. He noted her face, making certain her complaints of being tired was just that.

"I'll have to go away more often to get more welcomes like this. I don't think I'll know what to do with myself today. All this gushing has me speechless." She teased, holding his gaze, the thin arch of her brows rose with the ending of her speech.

"I could combine a promise with that request." Michael smiled, and watched the small head nod, satisfied with the state of his health.

"Have you already eaten?" Betty smiled, returning her gaze to the woman at his side.

"No, but I—"

"I'll have something fixed in a jiffy." She muttered through a sharp turn, slicing through the words being said. The tail of her shirt flapped with the speed of her twirl.

"But you don't need to do that, Betty. Aren't you tired?" Julia hurriedly asked, turning in her seat. She gazed bafflingly at the older woman's back.

"I can rest when I'm done. There's nothing to it, really." Her small voice sailed back as a promise as she ducked from the room.

"Aren't you going to tell her she doesn't need to do that?"

"I learned a long time ago, more than twenty, really, that Betty does as Betty wants. You can't make her do anything. She hates wasting time, and finds sitting around a waste of hers. So…" Michael shrugged, curling his fingers through hers, his eyes lowered to their hands. "I just let her do what she wants. It's faster, easier, and a lot less hassle than the alternative." Pulling her back to his side, he set his shoulders to the soft cushions of the couch. "I told you she liked you."

"She's just being nice." Julia assured then, looking down at her hand in his. She glanced at the entrance as if worried by the show. The thought of unhanding herself trotted through her mind, but the sensation he gave surpassed all feeling of ill. Warm, safe and assuaging, it's rendering nurtured more like the comforts of home.

"Come, let's go for a walk." He rasped, his breath stirring a light fragrance from her hair.

"But…Betty is cooking."

"We'll be back in plenty of time. I know her. She'll be at it for a while."

"Where are we going?"

"Around," he hummed, pulling her to her feet, his hand caught hers as they turned for the door. "We're taking a walk, old woman! We'll be back shortly!" He yelled, straddling the threshold in wait. Betty's voice sailed back immediately, acknowledging his call with an answer seeming almost as tart.

Blue sky wiped clean all memories of the erstwhile days' dreary past. Boasting its dominance, the sun again gushed like a furnace gone awry, eliminating the sodden grounds with its ecstatic show. Untarnished by words, the two strolled hand in hand in silence. Pulling her to his side, Michael's hand slowly encircled her waist. Julia smiled as he planted a kiss on her brow, well pleased with his continuous affection.

In the shadow of the house, Betty illustrated her own stow of emotion at the sight, watching discreetly from the window. She smiled.

"Good boy. You keep holding on to that one." She awarded with a widening smile, praising all manner of his action in her head. She studied his body's speech. "I'd say that's well beyond any school boy crush." She mused, observing the couple until they disappeared beyond the trees. "Good boy."

Michael's hand rode the hard curve of her hips, keeping her tucked to his side. They walked through the coppices in silence, each absorbed in the tranquility it gave. The rising songs of birds accentuated the peaceful aura, muting much from their steps, their music chorus the whispery rush of a distant brook.

"It's so beautiful here." She chirped, her gaze blanketing the lush ambiance of the woods.

"I was just thinking that."

"Do you come here often?"

"I make it a point to come at least twice a week when I'm here. You know, I think you're the first to truly get the enormity of what this place means."

"I sincerely doubt that's true." She smiled, ignoring any meaning beyond that of a jest.

"Always dispelling, aren't you?" He smiled, leaning to her, his mouth drudged soft. Like a warm breeze before the unset of rain, his kisses told much. Relishing the fervency in its touch, the two regaled each other through a distended silence. Locked in an embrace with time, the relevancy of the moment was not lost.

Chapter Twenty Eight

The seventh month was indomitably poised to be her test at asceticism. Curbed by the excess of planned excursions, the busy month would leave her no time for indulgence outside of activities already set. Nor would the chaos grant her the option to abscond for a night or two.

Like rations amid the challenges of war, her gluttony in the weeks prior should effectively serve her in the dearth to come, as life again comprised solely of decorum. With Rachel and Richard due home the next day, Julia's mind was purely governed by the chasteness of motherhood and it's like, with few things, of late, to do with work. In another few months, she'll revert to the rigorous dawdling at her desk. Work being a proficient lure from staying idle, pushing her, as always, in the throngs of something new, it soon punctuated her every thought. But for now, puttering past her office would have to be enough.

The days shadowing their weekends had always left her feeling odd. Plagued with a nagging sense of something unfinished or undone, dark fragments of loneliness dogged her nights well. The verity of such was inexplicable, yet the sensations remained just that. Much like furnishings being moved in her absence, the familiar pieces prevailed bold, only their placement cataloged the dissimilar sense.

Gamely, her usual lingering on the topic of Michael was quickly deferred, perceptive that the luxury of a leisured inspection was not readily at hand. As three days initiated the naissance of their family vacation, and her days, thus far, had been utterly swamped. Ensuring a tranquil trip, Julia plowed through an extensive list of errands, whittling through the necessities needed to enable that fact. Everything that was not already done, tolerantly waited abolition, and the list, it would seem, grew almost eternal. Overseeing the stoppage of her mail, newspaper and the delivery of a community weekly was smartly stabled first, so was the slating of her bills.

Fourteen days on the beautiful Island of Jamaica, should soothe even the faint sediments of her unrest, and the work now safeguarded the foisting of her bliss.

Prompt on the tail of their return, Michael's pool party was set to be their next undertaking, a task she branded as an interesting strive. Judging by their conduct of the last few months, the mingling should be an intriguing occurrence, since they had yet to hone the basis of control. Scheduled for the twenty-third, the celebration applauding their alliance, embarked in a matter of weeks, and all vested parties and their families are expected on hand. The festivity could not have been more perfectly placed, since the long days of summer had adopted one route, and each day grew hotter yet.

Evening at last descended on her drive, and although sluggish, it bolstered defiant in its bent, smothering all trace of liveliness from her limbs. It extinguished the glee of daylight without qualms. Julia crawled into bed ready for the shrouding of sleep, yet she drowsily awaited the gambol of Michael's call, this, since their morning conversation had ended abruptly. Finalizing a few details for their trip, David's untimely call was the disinclined culprit that terminated their chat.

"Hi!" answering his call after only one ring, the whispery greeting came sweet, and her entire body convoyed the ecstatic joist to her smile.

"Hi!" Michael's deep voice juddered to her low, falling with equal zest, it gave her mood wings.

"How are you?" she immediately asked, sensing something troubled him from the morning past.

"I'm good, how are you?" he smiled, his voice coming through like a shrug.

"Good. Busy." Having the distinct notion something was off, her voice whipped back like the ambling of a shrug, as the perception had gnawed her the entire day. "Are you sure you're okay?"

"Come take a drive with me."

"What?"

"Come take a drive with me. I want to see you before I can't."

"You're here?" she asked through an incredulous shriek, springing from her pillow, all trace of weariness instantly fled.

"I'm pulling up to your driveway as we speak." Michael expounded with a smile. "Come on out and see me."

"But I'm in my pajamas!" Julia cried, holding the soaring pitch firm in her throat. A giggle bounded from the nasally gaps of her nostrils, sounding much like the anthem of a love smitten girl. Her haste was no more eloquent than a child, dashing without reserve to the front window of her house. She gaped, wide-eyed, as his truck rolled to a stop in the middle of the long driveway.

"Even better," He growled, his raspy retort trolled deliberate like fingers gliding down the slope of her spine. He tormented her well. "I get to view you at your best. Now come on out, so I can see you."

"I'll be right there!" she gushed, needing no further prodding to marshal her thought, Julia hastened to do just that. Fitted with only her keys and the phone, she gingerly exited the house. Utilizing the modish arching of the front door, as she feared the stoic chants of the garage would give voice to her escape. The headlight's blinding beams streamed her body like spotlights showcasing its mark, though these seemed to charge fully at her face, forcing her to squint as she neared. "Hi!" she chirped through a broadening grin, cautiously pulling the heavy door shut, though the engine's grumbly hum was plainly published through the expiring night. Michael smiled, straightening from his reach for her door. His eyes unleashed the full measure of his assault.

The windows of the cab stood gaping, and a light breeze tussled with the mild cabin air. Yet she was immediately swallowed by the warmth of his scent. Roused by the strong masculine aura, the small space escalated its dominance in a flash, jumping to erotic with a single gulp.

"Hi." Michael answered in what drifted through the space like a growl. His eyes then fondled her face, dropping to her mouth. It lingered before progressing down her frame. Taking his time to garner his fill, he slowly put the truck in reverse, easing his foot from the break. The grumbly vehicle stealthily rolled to the street, getting then a small touch of fuel to fire its life. Her hair was loosely bound to the top her head in a wild bun, with wisp of curls, falling in an impish game, framing her face. Her pajamas, as she called it, was no more than baggy shorts and a fitted tank, nonetheless, her looks yet rivaled all. *Still scrumptious*, Michael muttered inside, and a smile of affirmation slowly wafted his throat.

Julia gazed in silence as he turned onto the first neighboring street, thoroughly amazed that he was actually there at her house. "What are you doing here?" she chirped.

"Taking a drive with you," He smiled, his hazel eyes catching hers, seeming afire in the interchanging dark.

"I see." She returned in a nasally hum, shaking her head at the vagueness branded to his speech. Julia pressed the distended button cradled near the handle of her door, watching wanly while tinted glass amended the sound of a querulous wind. The truck fell silent as Michael followed her lead. Turning down a second street, he adjusted the air before making a left on the third.

"Where are we going?" she asked, undaunted as to where their destination might be.

"Does it matter?"

"No." Giving her answer true, she amplified it thusly with a slow wave of her head.

"The tide's low, and the weather is balmy over here." He hummed, and the murmured invite seemed to float, roughly, from a silo in his chest, catching her hand, Michael gently tugged. "Come on over and enjoy the ambiance." He goaded. Julia smiled quietly in reply, though she followed the prompting of his hand, snuggling, as best she could, with almost a full stretch to her lean. Enveloping her without delay, his arm tightened as her head fell to the wide ledge of his shoulder. Michael pressed his face to the wildness of her hair, filling his lungs with her scent. He touched a kiss to said place on her head, and her scent, as always, was contentious to his sense.

On his next left, Julia guardedly shifted, flattening her face against the warm cording of his neck. She savored the scent emitting his frame, as it drifted about her like billows of steam on a frosty bay. The attar was deeply enticing to her mood. Michael's pulse hastened against the press of her cheek, staying in a dance as she swabbed her body against his. The streets then flew by unnoticed, each looking the same as the others passed, as both now relished the tour in silence. Another right and Julia's mind finally took note, recognizing his intent, as the new street delegated the way to the neighborhood park. Desolate from the hour, the truck rolled to a soft stop, roosting in the darkest corner of the curved road. A meek turn of his hand brought the engine's death, and everything at once went ghastly still.

In a slow heave, Julia's head rose from its nesting on his neck. Her eyes jumped to his face in what seemed a silent query, catching his botched attempt at a lax smile. The effort came remarkably strained, though his eyes gave dark snippets of his thoughts. His breath then broke the silence, seeming for a moment prime to give voice to his thoughts, and although he held, she did not. She knew not why, only that he taunted something in her senses, driving the weight of her attack. Her mouth collided with his like a ravenous boar, and his taste wrought better than it was when she left him last. Heightening her feed, her kisses grew wolfing. Capturing him so hard that she almost drew blood, her need propelled well the plunder of her mouth. Anxious in her want to taste the sumptuousness he so ardently yielded with his work, her rummage adopted a new title in its plunge. Vehement in her yen to feel the brawn of his body or ingest the breadth of his powerful strides, sinuous in its quarry, shimmying deep over and under and grubbing from her back in the professing of its will, needing fully the wizardry of that decadence that comes from him.

Without hesitance, his hand moved under her shirt, cupping her breast. The firm strokes incited her climb, scaling the console in a flash. She further straddled his lap, flavoring the intensity of their hike with insanity braided within its heat. In her zealous verve, her back slammed the steering wheel column, and the blare of a horn blasted the interlude like cannons in a disarming salute. Both bodies sharply tensed, plummeting from their high, two sets of eyes scrutinized the girdling dark. Curious as to what attention they attracted to themselves, their pulses further sped. Yet only the night's stillness gawked back in reply. Julia groaned in charging, turning her head to again gather his eyes. She dropped her forehead to his, a hint of humor clipped to her face.

"We should go back." She groaned, her breath sailing like a tremulous gust, waking the fetid stench of disappointment. It tunneled forward with the obviousness of his frown.

"Not so soon." He grumbled in a hoarse tone.

"If you want to stay here, I'll stay with you. But if you want me to finish what I started, I think its best we go back." Already cognizant of his answer, Julia smiled. Knowing every nerve in her body now stood on end, and was certain it bred no different in his. She could feel, taste, touch and smell his yearning and the piquancy well matched her own.

"Oh, no, let's just stay here." Michael groaned, lifting her promptly from his lap. "We could…just…talk, get to know each other a little more." He persisted with a smile, reaching forward, his hand moved faintly with the keys, shattering the silence of the night.

"Well…" she started, though his quick look of fake sanction stalled all further wording in her jest.

The drive back boasted quicker than their wily exit from the house. Michael parked more than two houses further than the need perceived, settling on the opposite side of the street. Precaution, he insisted, demanded that he should. He then strolled across her lawn looking strangely detached, while she, discarded two houses erstwhile their destination, ambled in from the opposite end, meeting at the entrance like acquaintances once slighted, but with little chance of repair.

Tranquil as if so bade by night's enchanting shadows, the house remained sojourned in slumber, though both ears perked in their scour for signs of life. Michael treaded close as the two warily strode through each room, listening for sounds of wakefulness in any other but them, their breath sailed in relief as they attained their aim of seclusion. The heat of his body dwelled prominent at her back, brushing her arm as she secured the door to her room. He gave her no chance to launch an attack, taking first strike. He claimed the advantage his.

Pressing her back to his chest, his hands dallied not. Gliding under her shirt, he caressed the pliant peaks, while the other rose in a keen instant to her face. Lifting her face to his, he brushed a kiss along the side of her neck. Working slowly upwards in his forage, he claimed the warmth of her mouth as his hand gently dropped. Rappelling the plateau of her stomach, his fingers pursued their laboring inside the confines of her shorts.

Julia moaned hungrily as the two staggered towards the bed, neither discharging the other from their determined pace, not even in the collapse. Fiendish hands moved with impatient zest, ripping the shirt from his body, hers, in return, flew with equal appeal, each falling to the rug in silence. With a sprightly swipe of his hand, he took the shorts from her hips, though his followed promptly with twice the fervor he showed. Yet her deed disclosed none of the styling honed in his skills. Michael rolled the instant the garment cleared his body. Pinning her beneath his frame, he reclaimed her mouth for his customary feed, and his kisses soon blazed a fire through the forest of her room. Her legs clambered his waist the moment he touched, locking as he came to her swift and unyielding, burrowing deeper with each enthralling descent.

Pleasure deluged her body as she met his quarrying drive, pulling him deeper still with her climb. She met every crash with an impetus of her own, giving as sumptuously as she got. She facilitated the ride with her vigorous pace. Sparks flew yet their bodies clung, and thunder grumbled through the darkness as a result of their strive. Yet the two remained unperturbed in their established sought. The inferno exploded at long last, mushrooming from sternum to tail. Michael's mouth plummeted as a deep, raspy growl escaped his chest, locking them in a merciless kiss. He feasted fully of the combustion.

The room went wistfully still, and the loud rush of their breath followed the sprouting silence. Holding true while his face stayed buried in the padding of her bed. She could feel the thundering in his chest yet holding wild; hear his breath trilled, aided by a visual descent. And each thud of his heart was like the marching of hooves on the soft tissue of her breast.

"Was this hello or good bye?" murmuring the query in his ear, she brushed her lips to the cartilage with a teasing smile.

"You tell me, you're the one who started it." He whipped back in retort, the grumbly tone sailing as his gaze turned upon her. His eyes playful as he gifted her the full warmth of his smile.

"Fine, I'll take it back, then."

"And how are you planning to do that, have me take you from the back this time?" he smiled, kissing her long upon the mouth.

"I'll let you know once I've worked out the scenario in my head." she shrugged, her reply coming like a grumble, though her hand gently stroked the side of his face.

"No need to trouble with all that work when you have a willing participant. If it makes you feel better, I'll gladly annex you from the back." He smirked, turning his head. He kissed the palm of her hand. "Just give me a few minutes. I'll turn you over and complete the job."

"Did you come here expecting this?"

"I told you. I just wanted to take a drive."

"Liar, you know what happens every time we get together. You wanted this."

"Aren't I allowed to…miss you?" he asked, knowing he spoke the truth.

"You can miss me." She groaned, seeming casual in her affecting of a shrug, though liking the fact that he now laid in her bed.

"So then I can also dream, can't I?" He smirked, again kissing her on the mouth.

"I knew it!"

"But I didn't! You did!"

"What did you think would happen once we got to the park?"

"Conversation, what else?" he shrugged, adjusting his elbow next to her head as he balanced his weight. "I only wanted to talk to you," he smiled, passing a hand over her thighs as he further explained. "You know…talk. I really like how we do that." Michael averred slyly, rolling onto his back. He stared at the ceiling in thought, his shoulders lifting with the weight of his sigh. "So, this is it for you and me?"

"At least for a little while," Julia purred, rolling instantly onto his chest. She rested her chin on the flat of her hand, feeling compelled to do so; she complied without question or pause. Drawn intimately between his, her thigh draped the spread of his hip, while his arm, in return, nestled the swell of her breast. Soft strokes took her finger over the ruts of his brow, smoothing their lines. She in turn soothed him.

"When do you get back?" he asked, turning his head in wait of a reply.

"The twentieth," She droned, feeling a sudden tinge of loss for something not quite understood. "Back with enough time for your pool party," she smiled.

"At least I'll get to look at you then." He drawled, tightening his grip on her body as he steamed her to chest. "I should get my fill now, shouldn't I? Since I won't be able to have you for an entire month, I need something of substance to stash in my reserve." He rasped, touching his lips repeatedly to hers as if tasting something sweet. "You're a very difficult woman to forget, Julia Berwick, very difficult."

With fun being the chief word on everyone's lips, their days on the small Island were generous in its bequeathing of anything such. Respectively, each day came laden with activities to occupy all facets of their lives, and each day they unraveled more still. Rafting on the Rio Grande bloomed especially pleasing in the lauding of its assets. Drifting on a bamboo craft while nature soared abundant each place that one looked, the experience boosted astoundingly serene. On what looked like a conga line, they climbed the Dunn's River Falls. The hike being an odd combating of itself, for the feeling of an eminent tumble greatly dominated the entire ascent.

Rachel and Richard experienced their first bonfire, sighted as a momentous occurrence in a compendium of many, and complimented by the dazzling eminence of a twirling baton. A Show, so claimed by the peal braided to their timbre, now beheld as the evident pride of their trip, with all planned activities coming in a meager second to the roast.

Julia drank in their adventures with the fullest intent, treasuring each experience with throngs of enthusiasm attached. She made certain her days were packed with a cask of activities to spare, needing such pursuits to fatigue her mind. Since of late, nights bred as her biggest challenge yet. Refusing to rescind its hold, her mind would not let the memory of him go, thus his attributes, undiluted in their trudge, scrolled as a constant through her head. Deep, dark and grumbly in its bequeathing, his tone wheedled persistently through her skull. A tone that, by now, had surely frayed the sensory layers of her skin. One feature, in a vastness of many that had since sprouted as a pillar in her brain, setting roots since the moment she left. Finding the urge to converse with him stronger than she ever anticipated such piffling would be. An impulse that now seeped into all aspect of her wake.

Not once did she contemplate the loss of their usual chat as anything but an indispensable pause. Not being able to call never bounded her thoughts, nor did she think to perceived the deficiency as an arduous effort. It was almost disturbing how difficult it now seemed to stay away from the man, and she was beginning to suspect that it mattered not what factors she perceive as a want. Only her body now seemed to master its will. With her trip now resting on its tenth day, four yet remained in their lengthy stay, and they have not had their usual parley in almost fourteen.

On the eve of the ensuing day, Julia's desperation broke. Sending him a simple text, she smiled at the context, once again feeling resilient in her bent. Scribbling the small diagram on her stomach, she snapped the inciting picture with her phone and immediately dispatched her message with a measly touch. Smiling, she spent the next few minutes scrubbing the brazen note from her skin, while awaiting his reply.

Depleted fully from his abounding quest, Michael reclined on a sofa in the sitting-room of his suite. His hand flung haphazardly atop his head. Between work and the weekend with Philip and his family, his exerts had taken more from him than he thought, draining the strength from his body as, surely as, the impulse sighted in a leech. From sun up to sun down, the kids had had him going nonstop, running him ragged without end. He was confident he never thought of work once while sheltered in their home, though he wished he could say the same of her. After all that clatter, his house now felt unnaturally quiet, something he had always thought to be a favorite of his. Yet of late, that stillness just felt somehow off.

The loud twittering of his phone swept through the room and his thoughts like the blaring of a horn, startling the quiet, and in so doing, startled him. Noticing the sender's identity, Michael smiled.

Wish you were here.

Her text read, with detailing art of an arrow that extended well past her navel.

"Mmm, man. So…do…I!" Michael growled, and his eyes brightened as they scrutinized the picture she sent, mauling the small patch shielding her most erogenous parts. He immediately decided on his reply. Relocating to his bed, he pulled the shirt from his body in haste, tossing it to the floor as he plopped atop the surface. Lying on his back, Michael stuffed a large pillow against his chest, enfolding its softness in a gentle embrace. A flash of light signaled his intent. "Wish you were here." He mumbled as he typed, sending his picture in reply, he smiled.

"Would be if I could." Julia giggled from the bathroom of her suite. "Just keep it warm for me. I'll be there as soon as I can."

"Can you talk?" Michael mouthed as his fingers pieced the opus of his words, hoping her answer would be yes, for he had missed talking to her almost as intensely as he did having her in his bed.

"Not really." Julia sighed, staring long at the phone before strumming her fingers across the keys. Almost instantly, his timbre soared in answer, and his voice sounded to her like the melody to a gritty blues song.

"Hello, you!" He hummed, his deep voice swaying through soft, yet the tone vibrated richly through her body.

"Hello! Julia purred, her body feeling suddenly whole.

"Thanks for the invite. I'll have to take you up on that the next time I see you." He muttered in the usual gravelly grunt, the leer in his voice sailing easily through the phone.

"I doubt you'll be able to do that, not unless you want to shock my kids." She whispered, lowering her tone with each word.

"That's right, I get to look but not touch." He groaned, stuffing a pillow under his head, he sighed. "That should be interesting."

"Well, if you're good, I'll let you pet me in a dark corner somewhere." She whispered through a giggle. Opening the bathroom door, she checked that the coast was still clear. Her trepidation went without saying. Since the last thing she needed would be to find her kids listening outside the door, playing the naughty lady was not aimed for any audience but one. It most certainly was not intended for kids, and most of all—not hers.

"Will you now?"

"It's a good possibility." She smiled, looking cautiously over her shoulders to gauge the frankness of her speech.

"I'll have to be on my best behavior then. Then again, I'm always my best when I'm with you."

"I can't have this conversation now," she smirked. "What if my kids walked in?"

"Fine, but you owe me." He teased, kicking the sandals from his feet. He stretched lazily across the bed.

"What's the price?"

"I'll let you pick. You do well enough on your own."

"And what do I get in this?"

"The store is always open for you, Julia. All you have to do is be ready to shop."

"That's an awfully tempting slogan you have." Smiling sweetly in response, she left his words to frolic through her head, rousing memories and visions in their trampling.

"That was the intention." Michael avowed in a rough murmur.

"I think I may be willing to accept that policy, though I'll raise the purse with something of my own, which we'll have to discuss at a later date." She crooned, glancing anxiously at the door. "I have to go." She whispered in a sugary tone, strolling to the entrance, she again surveyed the room. "Acceptable terms for now?"

"No." Grunting the impetuous response, his voice softened as his breath sailed in follow. "But it will have to do, for now." He groaned. The line grew rapidly quiet with the dwindling of his words, hesitant to bring the call to an end, he lingered in thought.

"I'll see you at the end of the week." Julia explained without knowing why.

"I'll see you then." He replied in an almost solemn tone.

"Michael."

"Yes?"

"Definitely until," she sighed, and the silence seemed almost listless in its lengthening before his answer came.

"Until, then," he nodded.

"Bye."

"Bye." Michael breathed in answer, his thumb quickly tapping end. "I miss you." He whispered to an already sedated phone, dropping the small, rectangular lifeline with force to his bed. A low growl skimmed the silence. It was getting stranger by the day, his connection with her. Almost lugubrious the further apart they were, stammering his thinking as if half his being remained wherever she was. His attraction was enigmatic enough. Never had he been so totally consumed by anyone before, nor had he ever wanted to return every act so intrepidly. Having his mind so affixed was surprisingly foreign, and it had him blindly trudging through the oddity attached.

———

As promised, her call came at eleven a.m. on the dot. His phone counseled him thusly with a lively cheer, announcing her promptness as he neared the threshold of the garage. Michael smiled shrewdly at his luck, knowing everyone was otherwise occupied with their task. It left him free to cherish such sightings at will. In the months prior when he brokered the idea for the quiet event, the concept was meant as a strategic step, one to guarantee the fruits of his ambition. A ruse, if you will, to have her close at his side. It was not intended to goad, nor was the inferred fated to be torture.

Exiting the house through the heavy door, Michael skirted the showy pieces housed in the garage. Needing an undiluted glimpse without having to hide, he wedged a shoulder to the frame of the stall-like door. His eyes effusively pinned the long driveway, though an eternity passed before her car rounded the corner, turning on the straight towards the house—towards him. Having not seen her for weeks, his pulse tilted and turned before opting on mad, roiling in his chest the closer she got. It forsake all erstwhile gear but one.

The vehicle slowed as she neared and their eyes locked, a pleasant smile sculpting the loveliness of her face, and time seemed almost suspended before the car stopped. Serene and graceful like the lineages of a gazelle, she alighted looking like a goddess garbed scantly in white.

From the back, her hair looked almost wild, managing a simple upsweep from her face. A long braid hung tamely down the center of her curls, touching the open back of her dress. The garment seemed tailored to the riling curves of her body, and it did not look like much could be worn beneath the trim fit, though his hands quickly volunteered to pioneer that quest. Richard bounded to the ground in a brusque show of agility. His expression patent of one well ready for the ruckus of the day, or, at least set to put in motion that of his own. Michael straightened from his lean with the starting of a smile, watching raptly as they gathered their things. His pulse strummed as if to the tempo of a tune, demanding freedom from the caging of his chest. It hastened its hammer as the family turned in greeting. And he was definite in his scrutiny that it was not just the bestowing of her smile, lovely that it was, that bade his body so profoundly from its sleep.

"Hello!" Julia called from a distance, appreciating the datum given in his wait. Her smile was revealing of the excitement she felt. He looked as magnificent as ever in the advertising of his navy-blue trunks, his sex-appeal being downright brimming.

Beautifully bare without the concealment of a shirt, his muscles poised like a regiment waiting their orders to attack. It was a beautiful thing to watch and even more so to partake of.

"Hello!" Michael called back sprightly, his eyes lowering to the shapely length of her thighs, jutting from beneath the hem of her dress. The fringed midst held him transfixed. *On any scale, she was off the chart*. He groaned. A connoisseur of beautiful women, yet he had found no comparison worthy of her. They just did not equate. Not on any level, for none had ever affected him quite in the manner she had. "You made it." He murmured hoarsely, though his eyes said something else, flaunting a raunchy piece of his thought as she drew near.

"Yes, we did." Julia smiled in answer, holding his gaze. She said "yes" to the many questions his eyes now held. A small pause, tightened with electricity, spiraled through the space between them. Drifting as assuredly as the smoldering of a fire, it weighed the moment before he abruptly turned his attention to the kids.

"Hello, guys. Welcome back! I hope you're planning on having a good time." Michael warbled, looking from one to the other, and seeing her features boldly anchored in both. He mused on the eminence of such traits. Straightening brusquely, Michael tensed, feeling the strain of his thoughts as it swept him down an anomalous new road, pouncing on their own probability for kids. It pondered on what features, of his, would remain unmistakable should they have children. Realizing what just entered his mind, he almost grunted the answer aloud. Marriage and children had never been a praxis that held any interest for him. Kids especially, they don't go with the oscillation of his lifestyle. It's for that reason why he cherished having Britney in his life. On her, he can dote to his heart's content. Spend himself on her and her brother extensively and still triumph with the wont of his carefree life.

"We will!" They chirped, their voices sailing back as one, waking him from the worrisome vision.

"Good." Michael chimed back, shoving the temporary barb from his mind. He titled the episode ludicrous and ended it at that. "The game room is in need of some serious attention, I suspect I can depend on you guys to give it your best." He asked in a playful tone, his eyes falling to Richard's face. "Can I?" he droned, and watched the boy's head vigorously bob in answer, before actual words sprang from his mouth.

"You can!" Richard smiled, remembering the merriment of his last trip, and hoped the day brings much of the same result.

"Good! Everyone's inside." Michael announced as he returned his attention to her, though her eyes were already fastened to his. "We should go in." He sighed, again conveying something else with the intensity of his gaze.

"Okay." Julia nodded, turning the children towards the entrance of the house. She tossed him a gingered smile over the slant of her shoulder. Following closely, Michael made his presence immediately known. Ambling her body with reverence, his hand slowly strolled the notch of her waist, falling gently down her hip. It rode the curve of her buttock like a second skin. Without veering from her task, Julia placed a hand on the fleshy slope of her back. With fingers splayed in expectancy of his hand, she had not long to wait on his reply, as strong fingers instantly locked to the leaner of hers, holding as if to foster the other life. Together the two walked in restrained distress, clasped in a phantom embrace known only to the other. Frustration was but one entity that brewed between them.

Abutting the entrance of the house, Julia's eyes again darted to his face, and an intense longing darkened their already dark depths. Her thumb thence delved into the fleshy center of his palm, answering a question without having been asked. She gave to him the full extent of her affection in the simplicity of her touch. It was with profound hesitation that the two released their hold on each other, stealing one last glance before they entered the house, and had their deed been witnessed by any, it would have seemed oddly reminiscent of star-crossed lovers, for both were wholly in compliance of the requisite needed for such.

The smell of Betty's cooking was the first to attack their senses. Grabbing their attention, the spiced aroma permeated every corner of the house. Music drifted to them low from the small speakers housed in the ceiling, yet the atmosphere bred vivacious, labeling the day perfect for the gaiety to come. Britney's voice rived the music as she called to her mother, tilling the calm. Sarah's voice then quickly followed, her melodic accent sounding sweet.

"Coming!" she bellowed, running for the stairs, though her eyes quickly jumped to the new arrivals instead. "Julia!" she exclaimed, swerving from her path, her long, blonde hair almost trailing behind her in her haste.

"Sarah! Hello!" Julia mimed, finding her effervescent vim infectious, for every emotion she had was well displayed on her face, and much like a buffet. The offerings were ample. The only disparity being that the assortments were all a variation of sweet. It would be a hard task not to like her, Julia mused. Even if that had been her intent, the petite blonde was just too sweet to ever try. Sarah was immediately upon her, wrapping her in a bear-like embrace, a startling venture for one so small, and as with the custom of aged old friends. She lingered in the dispensing, her perfume drifting warmly around them, and smelling amazingly good.

"How are you?" she asked brightly, and as with her usual wont, her hand dallied meekly on the other woman's arm.

"I'm good! I'm very good." Julia smiled back, feeling truly engulfed by her warmth. "How are you?"

"Busy. Nuts!" Sarah shrugged, her slim shoulders taking her entire upper half on the ascent. "You name it, and I'm there." She laughed.

"Working hard on your next show?"

"Something like that." She smiled, her blue eyes seeming to mirror the radiance of the sky, and the soft blue of her dress appeared to only intensify their depths. "How about you, are you working on anything new, your next book, perhaps?"

"Not quite." Julia chirped, shaking her head in answer, she smiled. "I usually take a little time during the summer to spend with the kids. After that, we'll see."

"Mom!" Britney sang, her voice slicing through their chatter to sit clear in the space, and all eyes jumped to the balcony as one.

"Oh!" Sarah shrieked, realizing her lapse, she immediately spun. "I'm being beckoned!" She explained, releasing Julia's elbow as she rushed for the stairs. "We'll talk later!" She waved as her foot touched the first step. Recognizing she had not yet acknowledged the children, her voice sailed back cordial to the group. "Hi, Rachel! Hi, Richard!" Sarah hailed, chuckling behind the greeting. She bounded each step with determined haste. "I'm coming!" she announced formally to her daughter's waiting ears.

Julia's smile followed her on the entire ascent, finding humor in the picture it gave, her smile further widened. Like a bear guarding the innocence of his cub, Michael hovered patiently at a distance, as if reluctant to release her from his presence. He busied himself with the angling of a piece of art. At her side, the kids grew anxious in their wait, specifically so—her son. Swinging her arm madly as if it was precariously tethered by strings, he leaned his body full into her side. "So, what would you like to do first?" she asked, stiffening her arm in the process, she stalled the propensity of his drive. "Do you want to get in your swimsuits now, or play a little first?"

"Play!" they sang, both voices ringing as one. They concluded all further questions at once, and the excitement was not lost in the shrill.

"Fine, go ahead then. Just remember what we discussed about the behavior you should use, and let's not forget the consequence you'll each have if you don't."

"Okay, mom," Richard nodded, being the first to answer. He dazzled with his smile.

"Can we go say hello to Betty?" Rachel asked timidly, her eyes turning in question to Michael's face.

"It would really make her day if you did that." Michael vowed, knowing his old nanny would find that an amazing treat. "She's in the kitchen. If you follow this hall…" he paused, his hand stretching past them as he pointed the way. "It will take you right to her. Just follow your nose if you get lost, or better yet—yell." In answer, the kids turned anxiously in the direction denoted by his hand, scurrying off to the kitchen with their feet already in a trot. Michael's smile dimmed as he straightened, his eyes probing the surroundings before capturing her gaze. "Come here." He rasped, kicking his head towards a far closet shouldering a corner of the hall.

As dictated by his rumbly lilt, Julia promptly followed, her pulse galloping wildly in answer before she expended the first step. Rounding the corner, she threw a last look of caution at the room, making certain the coast was indeed clear before stepping in.

His mouth stirred with bruising voracity in the harshness of his attack, torching the stowage of her reserve—had she had any to start. And had it not been so good, it might have been viewed a chastising for some wickedness done in her past. Pleasure hiked through her body like a jolt of lightening, excavating every need that she had. His hands slowly glided down the firm slope of her back. Caressing the roundness of her

buttock, he pasted her to his indurate frame. A groan sailed from his throat in reverence, lengthening in the rough guise of a plea; it deepened before his exploits abruptly
stopped. The weight of his breath dragged his shoulders in a rapid descent, elevating
almost as laborious on the ascent. The warm rush buttered both sides of her cheeks, as
his face remained fully pressed to hers.

"No! Don't stop!" she implored in a ragged breath, and every sense in her body
screamed for him to persist as he was. Wanting most to savor his taste, she took the steps
needed to retain what it was she wanted of him. Standing on her toes, she pulled his
head sharply to the angling of hers, instigating then her own form of attack. Their kisses
waltzed from fiery to outright rage, and it took both sometime before the grungy sound
of rhapsody penetrated their ears.

Only when he had her legs coiled like loose twines around his waist did the matter
enlighten her some. When the deep press of his body stroked her firm, or when the urge
to further indulge had her hands well poised to comply with such need. Only then did
the haze lift from her mind, understanding then the reason behind his earlier stemming,
for it needed to stop before madness descended. "I'm sorry." She panted against his
mouth, feeling the heaviness of his breath; her own strongly raked his face.

"It was a bad idea to start with." Michael groaned, his voice falling like a raspy whisper, and although their bodies struggled for control. The two remained tightly pressed.
"You should go. I'll stay here."

"Okay." She nodded shakily, fighting to calm the raging in her body. For the decision
was, in truth, an asinine attempt. Knowing what their chemistry brewed when they got
together in the past, it was with true certitude the foulness such activity would breed,
one they should never have endeavored from the start. Considering the fact that they
hadn't seen each other in almost a month, it was pure luck that they didn't ignite. "I'm
sorry." Julia whispered breathlessly, stepping from his body. She turned, intending to
leave before urge goaded her into doing more than she should. But his hand on her
waist gently prevented her will. Slowly, it moved over her hips, slipping under her dress.
His fingers leisurely ambled their way up her thighs, settling over the thin fabric of her
underwear. A smirk slowly streaked his face, wading mischievously in his eyes.

"Just checking," Michael murmured then, widening his smile.

"To see if I still have one? If that's so, that's not quite how you would check." Julia
teased, her eyes travelling to the hand resting comfortably between her thighs.

"I was curious what you wore under there."

"I only dress like that when I come to see you—in other capacities." She elaborated
as his brows rose in wonder. "Are you going to move your hand?"

"It wants to stay."

"It will, soon. Very soon," She sighed, turning for the door. His hand reluctantly
dropped, freeing her to exit without pause.

Phillip stemmed sole conqueror of the water by the time she made it to the pool,
stopping on her way to say hello to Betty. Who, as usual, harbored the kitchen like the

possessor of a rare prize. Phillip waved happily as she neared, swimming towards the steps, he heightened his greeting with a wide smile.

"Hello, you, I was hoping you would make it." He smiled, leaning forward. He kissed the air on each side of her cheek. "There's a real Hollywood kiss for you. I guess you've changed your status since I saw you last." He teased, pointing to his wet body as if to further explain. "I'm a little too wet for that pretty dress of yours." He added quickly.

"So I didn't go Hollywood, you were just baiting me?"

"I'm afraid so." He shrugged, looking expectantly at the house. "Where's everyone? Sarah and Michael were just here." He mused loudly.

"I saw them inside. Sarah's with Britney and Michael…is, I think he's talking to Betty." She murmured, giving the half-truth with calm.

"Care to join me for a swim?" he asked, turning again for the pool. "I usually get mine in while it's early." He announced spryly. "If you can believe it, melanoma runs in my family. I'm married to a fair skinned blonde, yet, I'm the one who has to run from the sun. Peculiar, don't you think?" Phillip apprised matter-of-factly. "What kind of bizarre madness is that?"

"Who knows, but I'd love to join you. Just let me get into my suit." She hummed, turning back to the house. She garnered a discreet wink in return for her smile, as Michael sauntered passed on the way to the pool. The kids' voices were enlivening. Boosting the energy of their game, it transmitted gaily through the house. Curious, Julia poked her head inside. Enraptured in their task, all four seemed engrossed in the reigning exploits of table hockey, and from the look on each face, it surpassed being just a game.

By the time she returned, everyone except the kids was now lounging by the pool, and all eyes turned to her in welcome as she entered their clique. Michael tactfully watched her from the water, being the last to look up. His gaze followed the working of her hands, sharpening as she undid the white sarong from her waist.

Hazel eyes lingered in full awareness of the view, knowing it wise to detach his gaze, but knowing somehow he could not. Her suit was no different than the many he had seen through the sum of his life. Just a simple set dressing another beautiful body. So, why then, did it affect him so? He could feel his body responding to said vision the closer she got, and could only be grateful the water effactually masked all evidence of that, as image of another time morphed with the sight at hand.

Furthering her taunt, she dove in from the opposite end, swimming a full lap before she again rose to her feet, and with the simplicity of the act, she took what little breath was left in his chest. Past visions, well tucked in his head, suddenly had a contender, for the image was, in truth, something worthy to behold in the wakefulness of one's dream. This day was beginning to look like a colossal mistake. Not only can't he touch, but neither could he admire the feast, and the sight, in all sureness, was definitely that. It was about to be a long day, a very long day.

"So what have you been doing with yourself, Julia?" Phillip asked from the opposite end of the pool.

Right, conversation, that should help, Michael's ego gladly advised, filled with gratitude for the disruption his friend effectively gave. He grumbled as his body sliced through the water with verve, needing to exert some energy with a few laps. It took him four rounds to calm his body, and another four to wipe the impression from his mind. Not bothering to listen or partake in the conversation as he swam, his mind stayed sharply on his task. Unwavering in his hunt for solace as he slipped from the pool, it was for that reason why he ended his grind in the kitchen with Betty.

"Put your tongue back in your head and hand me that spoon, will you?" she muttered calmly as he entered the room.

"You are a menacing old woman that should be locked away from people, you know that?" He barked. How in heaven's name does she know what he's thinking!?

"Only on my own terms, sulky. That's the only way you'll get rid of me."

"Who says I'm sulking?" he grunted.

"Certainly not me," Betty shrugged. Brushing by his shoulder, she seated the colander in the deep inlet of the sink. "I only thought your eyes looked…bigger, that's all." She smiled.

No sly return came in counter; neither did the ramblings necessary to fill the gaping her words fell to in a flash. Instead, Michael strode across the room, looking almost listless as he came to stand by her side, plucking a wedge of carrot from the mixed vegetables inside. He popped the chip in his mouth. "What's happening to me?" he whispered after a stringent pause.

"That's something you're going to have to figure out for yourself." Betty advised sagely, her soft voice sailed back in answer as the water stopped, and the room swiftly fell to a strange hush. Listening to the carrot being crushed between his teeth, Betty stared out the window at the yard. She could tell him what she thought, but knew it would not help his cause to interfere thus, for such things needed to be unraveled sagely by the source. This, he needed to figure out on his own. "You know, there are specials everywhere you turn." She began in a matter-of-fact tone. "They come at you unending. You can find them everywhere you look. The trick, however, is knowing which, or when the specials pertain to you. Having the insight to grab what you want before you lose out on what it is you need. That's a lesson some consumers never learn." Without clarifying the strange thought, Betty smiled, turning back to her job, she shook the water from her hands.

"But…wait? What?" Michael grunted somewhat confused, only half aware of the wisdom she dispelled. Julia's voice broke the quiet that followed, announcing her intent in a rich tone. She called to Richard from the hall, informing him of her destination. She hastened to collect his goggles from the car.

Suddenly, Betty turned to him with a sharp frown. "Darn! Could you get me that clay pot from outside? You know the one. I only use it once in a while. It's on the highest shelf in the far left corner of the storage room. I forgot to remind you I needed it for today."

Michael's own frown exhibited ample doubt in its plunging weight. Betty has never forgotten anything in her life. "Is your age finally catching up with you, old woman?" he teased, smiling as he turned to do her bidding, and although no answer came in response, the faint sound of euphonious humming rose from the kitchen as he left.

"I was hoping you would come." Julia greeted as he entered the garage. She had particularly announced her intention loud enough for all to hear, hoping he would take the hint and come. She delayed in her task just for the purpose of that. "Are you alright?" she asked softly, touching a hand to his face.

"I'm fine." He rasped, pulling her close. His arms locked at her back like bars on a cell, imprisoning her without lag. Their suits mocked his preference for being bare, for he has always liked the feel of her skin next to his, and it bodes no difference now in their stance. "It's just…well; I think I'm having some trouble with you in that suit."

Taking his hand in hers, Julia led him to the shadowy side of his truck, and the wide structure instantly screened them from the prospect of inquisitive gander. Instantly, she pressed her body intimately to the hardness of his, feeling his form bold against her in the surge, she smiled. "I promised you I'd let you pet me." She purred, gliding her hand over his frame. "Would you like to pet kitty now?"

Michael's voice rose from his throat in a heavy grunt. His breath stretched warm against her throat as his hands moved down her body in a steel-like caress. "I want to do more than just pet kitty." He grumbled, kneading her body further into his. "I want to eat, feed, lick and bathe kitty, that's my problem."

"Mmmmm,"

"Don't do that." He whispered against her mouth. "You're already driving me crazy. No added sounds are needed in this asylum."

"Would it be better if I left?"

"No! Stay. Just…cover up a little, please." He smiled, taking a nibble of her bottom lip. "God, I want to kiss you so bad."

"Too much trouble?"

"A whole heaping of it, since I don't seem to want to stop at just that," he groaned, taking a small taste of her lips. "We need to go back before they start wondering."

"Are you feeling better?"

"I am." He nodded, clasping her body to his in a powerful embrace, he sighed. In actuality, he was feeling better, and was unsure if that feature had to do with their talk or just being with her. Or was it both that facilitated the harmony of that?

Chapter Twenty Nine

Julia glowered at the hemic occurrence in dour distress. A dark smolder eclipsed the path of her stupefied gape. Staggered by the sight, a rousing breath was thence wrenched from the recess of her chest, saturated well in her wrath. Promptly lost in the surging tide of a tremble, disbelief and shock swam torturously through her slender frame, bringing with it awareness for what that now meant.

"No! This can't be happening." She growled, gaping again at the sight. "Not now! Hasn't this month been hard enough? Come on! Couldn't you just give me one day?" she whined, her voice snipping the air like the bittered squawk of something newly caged. It jarred the walls with its near deafening pitch. Dismayed by the unwelcomed sight, a growl again winged the scaled space, stalking her exit from the room. Julia crumbled on her bed as if unexpectedly pushed. Sprawling her irksome body with force, the bend of an elbow dropped dully to her face, as if to bar the significance of all things from her mind.

Drained of the sustenance surrendered in the pockets of a once laid plan, frustration shrewdly edged her to the brink of tears, as all trace of her earlier fervor instantaneously vanished. Cognizant of what needed to be done, her sighs faltered not, pelting the starched air like the rending of cloth. They lingered long through the tense silence. Loathsome of this new reality with every fiber of her being, she seethed starkly. For each grunt mocked not the severity of her ire, but screamed it true in the harshness it dispelled. Indolently, Julia reached for her phone. Scrolling through a lengthy call-log, she elected the third number from the top, and a loud sigh accompanied the broadcasting ring.

"Hi!" Michael hailed with an obvious smile, his voice drifting through like warm rain against the skin of her ear.

"Hi." She answered in a heavy grunt, her eyes clambering to her bag already waiting by the door.

"What's wrong?" he asked, his tone instantly falling soft, and all signs of discernible mirth departed the gravelly pitch without pause. A deep sigh came in answer from the other end, followed then by an elongated silence. "Julia, are you okay?"

"I can't come." Julia whispered at last, her voice, strangled with the tautening of her emotions, quivered as it vacated her throat.

"What? Why? What happened?" Michael sharply asked, anxiety staining his bassy tone. It soared apparent even through the small amps of a phone.

"My friend is here." She retorted dimly in a small voice, one hardly sounding like her twitters of old. It withered to a swift halt in the very place it began.

"Your friend? What friend?"

"My…special…friend," she groaned, again sounding like a drone. She waited through the silence for clarity to surge forward and take hold.

"What? Ohhh, that friend!" Michael exclaimed drolly, smiling at the despondency in her tone, realization came with the very next breath. "Oh." He grunted.

"I'm sorry." She sighed, groaning as the painful sting of disappointent mated madly with his.

"Can't you still come?" he probed, unwilling to rescind any of his time with her. "I'd still love to see you. We just can't…"

"But I want to. I want to…I want to very badly." Julia vowed, her voice sailing with life, though it died on the tail of a groan.

In answer, Michael's eyes rolled tersely to the ceiling and stayed. *Of course he wanted to. This drought has been mutually menacing for both parties involved, not just the grousing of one. God, she has to know how much he wants to.* Obvious were the bylines given in his words, slitting the prospect of a shield from his pride. He'd been looking forward to this date since the sultry month began, feverishly counting each day. Their braising conclave that fogged the crevices of his closet had not helped his rational cause, as his body still throbbed for fulfillment, and memories of her still hounded large facets of his dreams. "We could have dinner, stay up and talk all night, and still raid the refrigerator in the wee hours of morning."

"Are you sure?" she asked in a small voice, relief staining the uneasy timbre.

"Of course I'm sure." He hummed, his retort sounding like a smile through the phone. "I want to see you."

"I want to see you, too, but…." She sighed, her gaze again moving to her bag by the door. Strange—Julia thought with a lingering sigh—but it looked almost as solemn as she felt. Only minutes before, its aura seemed practically impatient.

"We can still have until."

"Yes, but one with an asterisk assigned." She groaned, sending him a dim smile with her words, still not yet alleviated by her plight. The effort was a meager attempt to ease the disquiet felt, though the insight was, in no way, a meager truth.

"True. But…" Michael shrugged, and his breath came, in follow, like a heavy squall through the phone. "We'll be together. So that still makes it until."

"Okay." Julia announced in a vivified tone, resolving the thought in her head. "I'll see you in an hour then." She declared as she sprang from the bed, feeling almost inspired by his talk. Her bliss was not of the usual amatory tenseness, but with the visit, she'll at least have him close for a spell.

"Great! I'll be waiting."

Apprehension remained pronounced in her thoughts as she dashed from the room. It gored her that she hadn't taken the time needed to be better prepared for an occasion as this. If only she had given the small dial ample devotion, then the pending would be astoundingly clear. Since she would, in all clarity, have noticed the start of her non-active pills, and would have henceforth taken the steps essential to forestall the predicament she now has. Yet, irrespective of all that, her leeway typically spanned a varied corpus of days, staggering, usually, between three or four before the flow finally starts. And on scant occasions, she'd had as many, probational margins, as five. Why couldn't this be one of those times? *One night!* Was that asking too much? It's been over a month since their last liaison, the eminence of which had been sorely missed. Now that the kids were back with their father for a week, she had the next seven days to do with as she willed, five of which would now, undoubtedly, be with her legs properly latched.

Michael awaited her entrance by the mouth of the garage. His sedated stance a paradox of his gaze, so, too, the mongrelized emotions pacing beneath the walls of his chest, warring through his body like a rebellion collapsing on itself, they mangled his thoughts. Everything about this moment was dissimilar to the man he once predicted himself to be. When did he start behaving like a pubescent boy? He had never been one whose insides got knotted at the thought of seeing a girl—excited, but certainly not anything this extreme. Yet his argument ceased its importance as her car slowed to a stop, for a smile, rich in flavor, brightened well every angle of his face. Watching her made the world stop, *God, am I going nuts?* He asked with a decisive grunt, its dull residue echoing through the privacy of his head, this even as his arms hungrily claimed her as his. Locking her in a solid embrace the instant her body drew near.

Julia leaned against the hard brace of his body and clung, savoring his essence with every breath. Together the two gave life to their longings with the strength of their press. Wrapping the other in the warm tenure of delirium, time paused as they each waited for the sweetness to end.

"Hi." Michael whispered above her ear, breathing in her scent.

"Hi." She hummed, her muffled answer warming the skin of his chest. "Oh, I've missed you." She groaned, tightening the lock of her hands at his back.

"I've missed you, too." Michael drawled, his voice a raspy whisper, taking a long breath. He slowly unlocked the entrancing circle of her arms. "Let's go inside." He sighed, taking the bag from her hand as he turned her towards the house. Wrapping his arm around her shoulders as they walked, he held her firm to his side. She looked up as they crossed the threshold with a sweet, desirous smile, pictured for the world to see like a mirror of his own. And a long moment passed before he was able to alter his gaze from that sight.

The house stood quiet on their entry of its cavernous space. It did not shake with glee as it seemed to routinely do on her visit. Fermenting in the coolness instead, it grew superior with each pass of the clock's hand.

"Are you hungry?" Michael asked as they strolled through the bedroom door, placing her bag on the floor of the room-size closet, his expression oddly taut.

"No." She replied with a terse wave of her head, while her eyes, in audit, slowly noted the room. In the last few months, she had spent infinite minutes in this one space, and none of those had been with her body locked in a state of excited angst. Not until now. "Do you feel for something to eat?"

Yes, you. Michael groaned, leaning a shoulder to the framing of the door, his eyes indexed her features. Her beautiful face was turned in expectation of his next response, with lips parted slightly in the start of a smile, and he'd never wanted her more. Nor has he ever wanted anyone more than the moment portend. "No. I'm not hungry." He grunted, *not for food*, his mind quickly spat, adding the afterthought like snacks flanking the isles of a grocer's till. His shoulders then twitched in answer, and the solemn words fell lifeless at his feet. Taking a rough breath, he whispered her name. "Julia,"

"Yes." She breathed in answer, looking almost greedily at his face.

Michael waited through the pause that descended on the room, as if to garner clarification for something not said, his eyes shifted in their search. Letting the thought twirl in his head before giving voice to the contemplation he now wrestled with. "I have a rather…massive shower, don't you think?" he asked in a grumbly breath.

"Yes…." She frowned, thinking this a weird introduction for a conversation piece.

"Big enough for…well, a very large someone or two…not so…large…some…ones? Wouldn't you agree?"

"I suppose if—yes! Yes! If you don't mind that kind of…sharing," Julia rejoined wisely, suddenly filled with a sea of excitement from his implication.

"I can't say. I've never…tried that kind of sharing."

"Never?"

Muscular shoulders slowly climbed through the silence that fell, escorting the incline of his head—that being the most competent of answers that he had, reluctant to acknowledge that he has never needed to wait. There was always something else in which to divert the weight of his needs, and someone else with which to attain it with. "But I'm…oh…so…very eager to have you as my first."

"Give me five minutes then come and join me!" She called, already heading in the direction his topic suggested. Her shirt sailed back to him in play, trailed by the melodious tail of laughter. Its music mauled a suddenly expectant room.

Five minutes felt like an eternity when waiting. Michael spent the full volume of this eroding a path outside an unobstructed door. No longer concerned with looking anxious, he would have already burst through had she not asked for the time.

Her upturned face creased into a generous smile the moment he entered the room, a steady rain flowing slickly through the strands of her hair. "Keep your eyes up here on me." She advised in a whisper, touching a finger to the corner of her eye. She lifted the water-laden strands from her shoulders with the adjustment of her stance, dropping it like an amputated cloak down her back.

Michael smiled as his arms erected a wall around her. Wondering where else she expected his eyes to go, as they seemed to be utterly taken with the sight of her. With enthusiasm woven in her climb, she met him before he concluded his descent, her mouth feeling like fire through a torrential pulsing of rain, igniting whatever it touched. Her tongue glided across his in an offering that he took; taking from her all the sweetness he had long starved for. Needing desperately to taste her dry, he foraged her depths. A small tremor scuttled her body the deeper he dove, and the wall of his arms grew rapidly smaller with the intensity they bred, sighing soft against his mouth. She disbanded all thoughts from his head.

Languidly, he fed on her breasts, delighting in her taste as raucously as her touch. Doyen fingers showcased their skill as she stroked the lines of his body, dropping to claim him in the most enthralling caress, and like a grating through the misty air, her hand transformed his breathing to a coarse, lyrical song.

Firm hands, impatient in their need, moved to the small of her waist, turning her in his arms, he pressed hard against the curving slope of her body. A moan rumbled through her chest as heat slid definitively against heat, and the ambience made his body tremble in reply. Sinking deeper, he stirred the zest as each taste grew more inadequate than the first, driving him harder with each surge. His jabs then escalated its bent, tilling pleasure with each ardently dank dip. Her cries softly scratched the air surrounding their dance, jangling faint as he lost himself inside her. The quivering seemed unending, and an irrepressible growl wafted from his chest like the answer to a question asked. The moment would indubitably pass, but the sensation it bartered lasted long after the explosion, long after the whirring ends, and well past the emptying. It was those times that drew him to her most. Those were the occurrences that replayed in his head like an indelible song.

Pressed against the warmth of her back, he felt the energetic spray of water cascaded down their bodies like a waterfall goaded by a flood. Felt too, the heavy heaves of her shoulders from the weight of her pants, and each plunge well-matched the thundering in his chest. Her smile was quiet as she glanced back at his face. Michael kissed her shoulders in response, tasting the sweetness of her skin as their eyes locked, and a tranquilness daubed the moment as profoundly as it did her face. And not unlike the perceiving of a rare bird, with wings widespread, in the throes of flight, her beauty was implausible to his eyes.

Julia watched him as if his eyes held the answer to some wonder she sought, unfaltering in their drudge, as was his arms. Never leaving the warmth of her skin, they continued their press. As if compelled by a whisper, their lips brushed like a gentle breath, tasting of a nectar now newly brewed. It was a vernal experience for both, yet it abides as ancient as the erudition of time. Freshly imbued, the piquancy strengthened once cherished. Coxed on a venture not yet taken or understood, they drifted amiably past avenues never before acquainted with. Together, the two drank from an unwavering chalice, each getting equally enamored the deeper they delved.

In the three days that she stayed, Julia had never before been so thoroughly clean in her life. There was enough showers had, jointly, to last them more than a month, and had there been some fallowed way to avert the impending truth, she would have gladly stayed the entire week. But there was no easy way to fix the cumbrous event. Her friend just did not age well, and with no evidence of her holding herself rigid, it was the only choice left to be made.

———

The afternoon wrought brutally hot. Blistering air reared like demons from the asphalt's sweltering plains, while neighboring lawns endured the torture of a harrowing faith. Like the eerie echoes of an erratic piece, one could almost hear the grass whimper erstwhile their death.

Julia adjusted her sunglasses before lounging back on the chaise, squinting through the tinted plastic of her lenses. She gazed up at the pelting rays. The large pergola excelled well at its job, blocking the blare of the afternoon sun, though it did naught to stem the heat from its shade. Smartly provisioned for the scorching haze, a chilled glass of lemonade sat on a small table at her side, as did a bowl of mixed nuts. Water, notepad, pencil and her phone, completed the orderly settings for her afternoon's laze.

Clambering on the brink of an hour, ideas for her next book thrived profusely, fitting her fingers with wings. It efficiently staunched the bent of her meandering mind. Of late, it seemed quite apparent she'd veered from being astutely controlled to a woman with a one track mind, earnestly contemplating the strategy of the next ride, wanting only to watch him quiver at length as a result. *Now what's wrong with that picture?* She groaned, *and for that matter, what's wrong with her?* Those eyes of his could make her do anything. Why is it that every rule sprouts insignificant in his presence? More importantly, where has her tamped verdict on celibacy been vanquished to? Where was the temperance she once savored as a notable treasure of herself? What of that self? Would she even recognize that woman again should they meet? Wasn't this thing between them supposed to be an intermezzo? And judging from the man's past, isn't all this destined to die? Julia groaned, sighing perplexedly at the worthy litigation now swirling in her head. Dropping a hand blindly for her drink, her head rolled on the cushion to locate the intended glass. The tame movement sent the ice on a merry clatter, sounding almost playful in their endeavors. Beads of condensation trickled rashly onto her top.

"Julia?" Delia called enquiringly from the house.

"Out here, mom." Julia chirped in response, her eyes following the orbit of a small plane, as it bellowed no quieter now than it had on its first pass.

Delia's brows twisted together in a sharp frown, as sensitive green eyes reacted to the blinding glare. "What are you doing out here? It's hot!" she probed, fishing feverishly inside her purse for the glasses she recently dumped inside. Her expression seemed almost stern.

"I know." Julia shrugged. "I just wanted a few minutes. I'm going back in shortly." Closing her eyes, she again reposed against the plush cushion of her seat.

"Still loving the sun, I see?" Delia smiled, slipping the sunglasses over the sensitive flecks of her eyes.

"Until it kills me," Julia smirked, sending her mother a non-committal shrug.

"You're back early. Weren't you supposed to be taking a week for yourself?" She asked dully, still yet wearing her frown, she swung her legs onto the adjacent chair.

"I had a visitor. It didn't feel like much fun after that." she droned, and a tinge of shame slowly surfaced with her lie, though the fact that it was, in-part, true, helped to squelch the pesky invasion.

"But there are ways to get around that. Didn't you try?" Delia chirped, her question coming almost serene, though her eyes were fastened on the tilt of her daughter's face, set to scrutinize all aspect of the reaction she gave. She was not too blind to notice the slight, though undoubtedly palpable, changes of late, and was certainly not too old to suspect that such behavior entailed the sinuous affliction of a man. Seeming almost harmonious in her amblings at times, these past few months had been the happiest she'd seen her in years.

"You know how it gets," Julia gingerly shrugged, keeping her expression bland. "I just wanted to be in my own bed after that."

"Did you at least have a good time?" the older woman asked, dropping her head to the cushion of her seat.

"Sure." Humming this, she nervously adjusted the position of her legs, not wanting to use many words to aid in the description of her time. It was a fantastic occurrence, in truth, and although her words may not say that, her expression might. "I feel rejuvenated." She announced dully.

"I'm glad to hear that, sweetie. You look like you are. You should definitely keep doing this. It's been good for you."

"Thanks. How was it at the hospital?" she asked, skillfully turning the conversation away from her lies.

"The same," Delia shrugged. "Deborah whines, as usual, about the severity of her pain, and how many pills she needs to take to ease the effects of her hurt. Yet, she does nothing remotely new to help herself on that front. Elizabeth, on the other hand, works way too hard to hold on to her youth. She's beginning to look like a distorted figment of herself." She groaned, and a brusque smirk coupled the dryness in her tone. "Soon, not even her dog will recognize her with all the changes she's made." Delia droned, waving a hand before her face as if to swat a fly. She broadened the vaunt of her smile. "It's a little scary when you think about it. But it won't change, not until they all wake up. Anyway…I've been meaning to talk to you about something." Swerving immediately from her rambling, the dimming words came heavy on the tail of a sigh.

"What is it?"

"Well...I've been thinking..." Delia opened, sobering her tone, her head pointedly dropped. "I've been with you a long time, Julia. I was thinking, maybe—maybe it's time I got a small place of my own. You know, leave you to your privacy again." She muttered in a weary tone, weighting each word carefully before uttering one.

"What? Why?" she squealed, her upper body jarring forward with the note, rocketing her to a pin-straight pose. "Mom, why would you want to do that?"

Delia rounded her shoulders tamely in response, again weighting her words before giving them voice. Her eyes dropped to the desolate press of her hands. The assumption that her daughter felt she needed to hide her undertakings, made the matter more urgent than not. A grown woman should be able to bring a man home if that's at all her intent, this, without having to worry about what her mother thinks. It's the sole purpose of growing up. "Well...I'm so much better now than I was." She began, her voice sounding suddenly small. "The kids are getting older, and I hope to see you eventually married, what's the purpose of having your mother around?"

"Nobody is going anywhere. This is your home, mom, that's never going to change. Even *if* I was to get married—someday down the road—that would not change. Besides, why would I marry someone who didn't like my mother?"

"It wouldn't necessarily have to be because he doesn't like me. It's just the privacy required with getting to know someone that would make the circumstance an uncomfortable fit."

"Do you really want to leave, mom? Honestly? Do you?"

"No. But..." she sighed, wobbling her head against the murmured words. Her grandchildren were the single most important things in her life, keeping her stable throughout each day, even on the days when she didn't want to try. But should the need arise, she would gladly loosen her hold. "Well...not really."

"Then you have my answer."

"Don't you want the privacy to share your life with someone? Especially as you get older, isn't that something you should put in your plans?" she asked, the soft test coming in her usual buttery tone.

"I'll let you know if I ever find someone I like." Julia shrugged, pushing back the vision of Michael's face as it rushed to view.

"Are you sure, love?" she hummed, her voice lifting again small, wanting desperately to give her daughter an out. For as much as she would miss the limitless interaction, she had missed seeing her daughter happy. The samplings she'd had these past months had been something of a treat, one she wouldn't dare spoil with the bother of an inquest.

"Mom, if I wasn't sure, I wouldn't have begged you to move in."

"That was a while ago, dear; people change. Besides, you did that because you were worried about me. You always worry about me. Yet, you insist I'm not to worry about you. Who's going to worry about you, Julia?"

"Thankfully, I don't have anything out of the ordinary worth worrying about. So you don't need to fret on that fact." She smirked, choosing to ignore the meaning behind her mother's words. "Are we settled on you moving out?"

"You're not tired of having your mother live with you?"

"Why would I? I barely see you as it is. You're always flying off somewhere or another. It's like having a college roommate all over again. When I start throwing your things on your side of the house, that'll be your first hint to get out, or is that too subtle for you?"

"A little bit." Delia laughed, recognizing her husband's humor in the jest. It's amazing how much of his personality she had; no wonder the two were so close, and why his loss has been so hard on her. "Get the hell out, written in pig's blood on the lawn, could be a subtle start." Delia chimed, pulling her mind away from the sadness that came with the thought. "A few broken windows, my tires slashed; maybe some sugar in the gas tank could all be offered as hints. Then, you can throw my things out. It's all in the process you choose." She quipped, rolling her head on the cushion, her shoulders crimped with a light shrug.

"I'll have to remember that, especially the pig's blood that may be the subtlest of all." She laughed, bringing the glass to her lips, she took a long drink. The music of the ice was, by now, subdued, courtesy of the heat. It whispered more so than it sang. "With ideas like that, I may have to consult you on my next book."

"I notice you've been scribbling, are you thinking of actually starting the next one already?"

"Just a few ideas swirling in my head, that's all."

"And which exotic place will you have the characters romping this time?"

"Actually, I've been thinking of keeping them closer to home."

"Really, like where?"

"That's a part of the pieces I have to finalize. I'm just a little hesitant to burrow too deep. I don't want to neglect the kids or feel burnt-out in the process."

"Then stick to the way you've done it all these years. It's worked successfully until now, why change it when you have no need?"

"It's just a little hard to put my brain on pause sometimes. The grumblings never stop."

"Speaking of brain, I notice you have another delivery." Delia smirked, eyeing her daughter then. "Has he at least given you a hint as to who he is?"

"No. And it's getting ridiculous. All that money wasted, and still not a word. It's bordering on creepy."

"Why? Did romance suddenly go out of style? Don't you get it? He's courting you." At her daughter's stunned face, Delia threw her head back with a tuneful cackle, reveling in the annoyance yet funneling her eyes. Whoever this man is, he already warranted the richness of her respect. Evidently, he had figured out an important key, recognizing an effectual port of attack, since he could not use normalcy to challenge the folly of her thinking. No. Her thick-headed daughter needed something wilier than that. "You young people these days. You say you want romance, long for it even, but when it happens you hardly notice that it's there." She scolded, ignoring Julia's frown, Delia adjusted her body on the chair as if preparing to enlighten a child. "A long, long time ago," she started through a pesky jeer. "This is a small piece of what a woman would get when she's being romanced. The man would start out by sending little notes, flowers, maybe a sonnet or two as his way of getting her attention."

"Well, it's not working. And I don't think he'll like the attention he has."

"Isn't it?"

"No! I don't even know who he is. Besides, I couldn't be interested in him any-way I'm with—I'm…I'm not interested in anyone right now." She lied, stumbling over the correction. Julia straightened her frown, turning slowly in her seat. She sealed her mouth with a drink from her glass.

So, there's definitely a man? Good. Delia smiled, immediately wishing for the revenue of a face to face. Succeeding where so many had failed, if nothing else, had garnered him that. "Life has a very strange way of dealing with us, my darling. Never lock a door with-out first knowing what you're locking away; it maybe something you eventually need."

"You're loving this, aren't you? You don't even know him, yet you like this guy." Already knowing the answer, Julia frowned her displeasure at the thought. Her mother had expressed her wishes enough times for them to be well-known; a dictate that, by now, was transcribed into every language under the sun. Ushering her to the dating scene, she would probably encourage her to give the delivery man a try.

"I do. Because he's a thinker, I like thinkers. He's found a way, not just to intro-duce himself, but to keep himself in the mix. He's offered you insights, while keeping your mind fully engaged on him. All without suffering the usual rejections you dish. See…thinker." Delia smiled, tapping a finger to her temple, she continued her address. "Evidently, he knows who you are, and knows being straightforward won't work." Chanting her view, a subtle laugh rumbled through her chest in finish. "I like a man who's in firm control of his mind. You'd do good to hear out the rest of what he has to say. I'm curious how he'll articulate the rest."

"You know, mother," Julia started, tightening the knit on her brow. "For all you know, I'm just the wrong girl with the wrong name. Any day now, the sender or the florist will figure out their mistake, and all that intrigue will have been for naught. What then?"

"That would make it handy for you now, wouldn't it?" Delia asked, watching as a frown deepened on the young face.

"It would save me a lot of trouble."

"Well," Delia grunted, and her long sigh sliced through the thick air like a blade. "I guess we'll just have to wait and see."

"I guess we will." Julia muttered with a dismissive sigh, lying back in her seat. She threw the curly ends of her ponytail atop the cushion. A sudden breeze rose in the far corner of the lawn, taking a sprinkling of leaves in its rush. The gust bowled over the parched lawn like a wave towing its treasures to sea. Determinedly, it brushed the heads of every blade before vanishing as quickly as it came. In the distance, the afternoon sun started its dip, peering through the stern heads of trees. It showed no easing in its brag.

Night brought little to boast in the way of relief. Heedless of the waning hours sweeping its back, the musty thickness remained oppressive in its surge, leaving most to seek respite behind the cooling doors of their homes.

At its fullest, the moon sat high, painting whatever it touched in its own reflection. Darkness blushed like a radiated gem. Julia laughed as she gazed out at a silvery lawn from the window of her room. The hour, by then, had grown well late, though she hardly took notice of the time, surpassing her two hundredth minute on the phone. The luster of her smile gave no presage of an end, with such chatter now being as routine to their affiliation as the air they now breathed. Turning back to the room, her knees sank into the conforming mat of her bed, wading to her pillow. She asked.

"What do you think I'm wearing?"

"I don't know. That's why I'm asking."

"You always ask that, why?"

"So I can get a picture of you in my head. That's why." He drawled. "Is it anything like what you wore the night I stopped by?"

"Actually, I'm not wearing anything." Julia purred, straightening herself on the bed.

"Prove it. Come let me in wearing nothing."

"You're not—" her head vaulted the pillow as if yanked by invisible hands, setting her body like a reluctant pole in the center of the bed. "Did you?" she asked as she scrambled from her place, running to the front door on the balls of her feet. A hand waved slowly across the shadowy opening of the door. "Oh, my, God!" she gushed, excitement cracking the shrilly timbre.

"Let me in, and I promise to take my time at whatever the job." Michael rasped, his tone climbing from the balls of his feet. The locks clicked immediately in reply, first one, then the other, before the door swung wide. Her smile brightened in greeting, looking like a nymph, she leaned her hip against the thick slab. "Liar," Michael rumbled then, stepping close, his deep voice tumbled forward like a soft grating on her skin. "I had my heart set on seeing you naked at the door, now you just shattered that dream. Shame on you for playing with my head."

"What are you doing here?" Julia sighed, angling her face to his. She rested her head invitingly against the door.

"I could tell you this way," he hummed, his bassy timbre grazing her cheek. "Or, I could tell you this way." He drawled, and his mouth glided over hers in a soft, sensual sampling, easing across her lips like a delicate breath. It bred unlike the ferocious tasting he was notorious for. "Just tell me which way you want it." Michael growled, his long fingers sliding to the back of her head, holding her face to his while he meandered the furnace of her mouth.

Julia's body gave answer in no uncertain term. Sweetened by the concupiscent sug-gest, though it granted such speech the moment she swung open the door. The vision, it seemed, was all that it took, and the hurried waltz in her chest sprouted almost tame—if compared to the heat now surging along her thighs. "Why don't you come in and explain yourself further." She purred, not bothering with quips on how, she quietly locked the door as a definitive rejoinder to whatever offer he had.

Michael followed without further banter or play, saying nothing when her bedroom door locked at his back. He granted no speech when she stepped alluringly from her shorts. No utterance wafted his lips while he peeled his clothes free, tossing them gruffly to the floor. No words came while her hands strolled the arced muscles of his chest. None when her kisses rappelled the ripples of his stomach. His breath came ragged and hoarse, but words—coherent or not—seemed somehow extinct. Not until her body arched in pleasure. Until a thousand sparks went off at once. Only then did he follow, his body surging on the rigorous climb, then and only then did an utterance past his lips.

"*Oh, God!*" he cried in a guttural pant as he pulled her close, his mouth immediately seeking, taking whatever she had left. He took until they grew weak.

Michael's eyes opened slowly, glimpsing that the shutters of her dark eyes rose almost in sync with his own. Her gaze was sweetly intimate in its dispel, moving over his face. She touched her lips to his with a smile.

"Is that what you came for, did I get it right?"

"Perfect. You're very good at reading minds." Michael rasped, his breath like a balmy stroke against her mouth, brushing her hair back from her face. He smiled.

"Why did you come here?" she crooned.

"I already told you, I like talking to you." He shrugged. "After a while, I just wanted to see you."

"Thanks a lot, now I'll have to shower again." She groaned, playfully gargling each word in her throat.

"Can I wash you?" Michael asked, his deep voice gliding through her hair, trickling in a warm slide down the length of her spine.

"Is that going to be your new side gig now?" she sang, shifting her body against his.

"Just putting my application in," he smiled, stretching his long body on the bed. His left arm bent as a pillow for his head.

Julia gazed admiringly at the man from her roost on his chest, and she could not help but acknowledge how beautiful he looked lying in her bed; and had it been at all possible, he was more beautiful tonight than all the others combined. Those eyes of his looked twice as playful as ever, and five times as brilliant in the soft lighting of her room. She'd never seen them look more hypnotic or more piercing than they seemed this night.

"My God, they're beautiful." She sighed, not intending to give speech. Julia dropped her head to his chest in reaction to her err, hoping her words came no higher than a sigh, though she had no such luck in that.

"What is?" Michael asked, well curious of her slip. In its protracted length, she had never been willing to personalize anything between them, and he had promised himself to never push in that regard.

"Your eyes," She shrugged, finally lifting her head. "Of all your many attributes, and there are more than a few, I think they're my favorite." A slim shoulder lifted slowly with the insight as if suddenly unsure. "Or maybe it's in the way you look at me. I'm not sure."

"So you like being lusted at?" Michael muttered gently, gliding a hand over the soft skin of her back.

"Not the before, but…the after," she hummed, dropping her eyes to his chest. Her answer sailed startlingly low. "I like it. It's…nice." She purred. "You don't have to say it. I already know what your favorite on me is, so there's no need to elaborate on that." Julia groaned, turning quietly from his side, she rested her head on the adjoining pillow, and her smile was almost mocking in the radiance it grant.

"And you would be wrong." Michael smirked.

"Really?"

"Really,"

"So you're telling me that your favorite part of me is not my——"

"Nope!" he grunted, cutting off what he knew was certain to be her thought. "It's definitely high on my list—number two maybe." Michael frowned, looking overly contemplative, as if the decision was exceedingly hard. "Definitely no lower than three, but no, not my number one,"

"Really?"

"Really," he chirped, an affirmative smirk following his simple reply.

"What is it then?" she asked, her question piloted fully by skepticism. It reared bold in her tone.

"Do you really want to know?" Michael asked after a pause.

"Yes."

Rolling onto his side, he covered her body with his, lowering his head in the process. His mouth opened as if to speak, though his action stalled before the actual divulgence of words, brushing a kiss upon her lips instead, he smiled. "I'll tell you soon." He breathed in retort, his breath grazing the fleshy slopes of her mouth, lingering over the fullness of her lips. "I'm not much into talking anymore. You weren't really planning on getting any sleep now, were you?" he asked, dropping his thigh between hers.

"I guess I wasn't. If you're a good boy and stay put, I can give you tomorrow as well."

"I can do anything you want me to." Michael drawled, his warm breath caressing her skin as his kisses wandered down the side of her neck. Moving over her shoulders, they played on the peaks of her breasts. "All you have to do is ask, and I'm yours, Julia."

Chapter Thirty

With the propensity of a painter's hand, morning blossomed into a resplendent day, and blue, as varied as a welting bruise, papered a jocund sky. The descant of life erupted from every direction at once, like a serenade perfected with time. The enactment surged unrepressed, escorting the stunted body of a hectic week's end.

A small flock darted from the belly of a massive oak tree, heightening the tenor of their morning ballad, each song scraped roughly at the cusp of soprano. With wings friskily aflutter, their ceaseless motion explicated the flurry of a hunt. Julia's gaze followed their departure with admitted interest, relishing both the auditory and visual bliss, she smiled.

Still nested cozily in their place of respite and play, her expression imparted of her swelling content. And with no immediate intention of vacating her place, the possibilities were without end.

Almost soundless in its deed, the bathroom door swung open and stayed. Far from ambiguous in his effort, Michael promptly stepped from the room recently vacated by her. A large towel slung temptingly low on his hip. Behind him, the door to the spa-like elegance stuttered to a stop, and a mild creak mewed through the silence. Bright eyes, teeming with mischief, rushed to her face, giving more than a promise in their touch. Purposeful strides, dripped with arrogance and strength, carried him quickly across the room, a sure puddle lingering in his wake. Gently, his fingers moved across the snug knot on his hip, spilling the towel to the floor as he edged the bed. Julia smiled her appreciation of the chiseled display. With eyes keenly fixed to the body now traipsing towards her from the opposing side of the bed. Dark orbs belied the slow rock of her head. For certain, the man had an unfathomable way about him. Just his movements alone were immensely exciting to watch.

"What is it like to make love in front of the camera?" she asked with an almost child-like wonder to her voice, curious whether his effect only billowed that strongly in her.

"It's like…work." Michael shrugged as he slid across the bed. Reaching her side, he unmetered the full flask of his smile, tucking her body to his. His gaze then extracted its will in an ardent perusal of her physique.

"Yes, but…doesn't it ever…get to you?" Julia tentatively probed, smiling feistily with the question. Her eyes caressed the bold objectives of his face. The touch of his skin was as cool as it was warm, and the fresh smell of soap mingled, like spices in an exotic dish, with the fragrance of shampoo. It wafted pleasantly with the niceness of his own scent. "It always looks so heavy. So personal, it just seems hard not to be…affected."

"I believe that's the intention. It's supposed to look overtly intense." Michael shrugged, more intent was he on examining her, his lips brushed the rounding of a shoulder. "Or you wouldn't go to see it now, would you?" he smiled, focusing on the workings of his hand. A finger moved lazily around her breast, climbing the soft mound in a slow ascension to the chocolatey peak.

"Have you ever fallen for any of your love interests?" she continued inquisitively, unable to squash the unforeseen urge to know.

"No. I've dated a few of the women I've worked with, why?" he asked, turning his full attention on her face.

"Just wondering," She hummed, her brows lifting slowly, as did the slender width of her shoulders.

"Is there something you want to ask me?"

"I'm new at this, Michael, you're not. I was just wondering."

"Wondering what?" he asked, his question soaring calm, though he already felt the sting of her pending inference.

"I was just wondering if…this…" pausing, her palm opened as if to exhibit the distinction rutted in its lines. "Is just a continuation of your work habits?" she stated meekly, not desiring to offend, yet she blindly blundered down the troublesome path, ill-advised or not.

"Is it my affection you doubt, Julia, or is it just me?" Michael asked in an oddly flat tone, his eyes suddenly piercing. *Will anything ever be easy with her?* He frowned, though he clenched the pondering firmly in his head. "What if I met you while working in a bank? What of all my exes then? Or are bankers celibate now? Would my words hold more value then, or would you think me the same? Would I be meeker? A victim of my circumstance, or harasser in spite of the circumstances I have? One who creates only victims? What then, Julia?"

"I really meant no insult, Michael. It's just that…you—this, it confuses me, that's all."

"I guarantee it's no more than you do me. You block me at almost every turn, I—"

"Except this one," Julia enlightened swiftly, waving a hand inclusively between them in emphasis of her point.

Michael sighed, and almost reluctantly, his once ruched frown softened its pressed edge. "Except this one," he corrected. "My work in front of the camera is just that, Julia—work. Everything is done with angles and tricks to make it seem far more intimate than it really is. I'm not expected to really perform for her, just look as if I am, and as far as the women I've both worked with and dated, you can't give that any more credence than, you would, any other coworkers that got involved, and like so many relationships that fizzled, it didn't work out, so we moved on. I'm only a man, Julia. I never claimed to be a monk. We've talked extensively about my past."

"I know we have. I'm sorry. It wasn't said to offend you, I was just wondering out loud. Not about the numbers, just in the way they began."

"What about it?"

"Well, the reprisal of the act. It's well…" groaning in grievance of herself, she hurriedly stopped, throwing both hands in the air to mollify the sudden pull of his brows. "Don't worry about it. I shouldn't have brought it up. I really was just thinking out loud."

"So my attraction can only be conjoined with work? Is that your question?"

"No! That's not what I'm saying. And it's not that I think of you as a liar. I don't. I was more wondering if…well…me being so different made me the new must have for today. I'm just trying to understand why."

"How shallow do you really think I am?"

"I—"

"Don't answer that!" He barked, his arm jerking to a stop in midair. "Come to think of it, I don't think I want to know." He hissed, and his eyes rushed past her, in a mad dash, to gape placidly out the windows at her back. Taking a long, calming breath, an odd smile fitted his face. "You are different, that's for sure. I don't deny that. I like that about you, yes. I like you even though you make everything a grueling trek. Believe me, I've asked myself a million questions about us, including why you resist me at every turn. But, for whatever reasons, here I am, and here you are." Michael droned. "Lying in my bed as naked as the day you were born." He grunted, seeming unexpectedly aware of her nakedness, he smiled. "Looking sooo…decadent and desirable," murmuring thus, a groan wafted from the back of his throat.

"And that's my only worth?"

"Wasn't that the gist of your mandate? Isn't that the price you placed on me? Aren't I shunned in every place but your bed? Don't fault me for taking full advantage of what you give. I've been a lot of things, but with this, I don't intend on being a fool."

"You're angry?" she apprised blandly, hearing agitation further honed the edges of his voice.

His breath came in a soft whistle through the twin chutes of his nose, stilling abruptly before an answer came. "Not angry, Julia, call it…astonished."

"Can I make it up to you?" she asked in a thin voice, forgoing the usual sass, though the words came not fully without. A hand gently scrubbed the pleats now ironed on his brows, smoothing each, she warmly soothed him. Curiosity had impelled her inanely forward—perhaps further than it should. Once theorized a fling, her emotions now refused to stay veiled, and she badly needed enlightenment of this intensity they have. A category, perhaps, with which to place the madness in, needing awareness to brace for what she knew was sure to come.

"Oh, you most certainly can—and will." He warned dryly, and the quick flash of perfect teeth against a warm, olive complexion was enough to harvest his point.

"I'm sorry." She whispered with the tame offering of a smile, gliding her fingers through his hair, her voice titivated the air with its joules. "Now, roll over and I'll make it up to you." Nudging his shoulder with the heel of her hand, she urged him to comply with the sultry order. "Get on your stomach and relax." The gentle prodding now came as a coo, stroking him as ably as it did the room. With a gruff breath, Michael submitted to the demands of her hands, stretching out his long, powerful body. A smile dented his mouth, broadening with the second inciting caress.

As if to groom a beloved destrier, long, beguiling strokes quested the cliffs of his body with pride, pride, she knew, she had no right to have. Straddling his waist, Julia rested back on the vertex of his buttock. Slowly, the padded tips of her fingers inquisitively recced the muscles of his back. Wide muscular shoulders tapered to a well-defined waist, anchoring his body with long, stalwart legs, and the arc of his buttocks was sculpted solely for the purpose of art.

Lowering her body to his, she swayed until her breasts caressed the flexed muscles of his back. Dipping her head as she worked, she kissed his neck and the low angling of his cheek. Stopping at the pinched corner of his lips, she lingered in place, playing provocatively on the warm ewer of his mouth. Hair silky and wild draped forward like a shawl over newly bronzed skin, caressing his body like the fray of a feather. Lax kisses waltzed from the topmost to bottommost of his body and back. Michael groaned as her fingers walked along the inside of his thighs, and the excitement of her kisses quietly returned to the dented edge of his cheek, gifting him a tempting touch of her tongue.

Michael lunged in, what bred, no longer than, the time it took to finalize a blink, snaring her like a predator to prey. He pinned her under the rigid flex of his body. His mouth struck like an erotic flame, sinking deep. He altered the terms of their game, driving her further through the galleries of erogenous play. Julia sighed in compliance, turning her head to catch her breath; he leapt, without pause, to her breasts. His tongue seared each peak with ravenous focus, pulling each mound into the furnace of his mouth. He tempted her squalidly to let him do as he willed.

"Wait." She sighed, pressing a hand to his chest.

"Why?" he breathed back, showing little mindfulness to her plea, his mouth continued their torturous bent.

"Because I'm not finished with you as yet," murmuring this, in what came, as a whispery plea, her words were unheard by the hand now slogging along her thighs.

"This is beginning to feel more like a punishment than an imbursement to the cause." Michael teased, doing the same with the hand now pressed to the warm cavern of her body. His voice carried the same toning as hers, and had another stood sentry in the room, it was doubtful the exchange would be apprehended by any but the two.

"Let me finish." She begged almost breathlessly, enduring the willful stroke of hand. "I'm not through with…mmm…I'm not through with you. I promise."

Without offering a response, Michael reclaimed her mouth, kissing her passionately, he took his time. Setting the woods around them to a blaze, as her work bodes no less damnable on his body. Yet as quickly as he robbed her of control, he relinquished his hold, abruptly setting her free.

"You don't play fair, do you?"

"I promised you a punishment, didn't I?" He smiled, pushing her hair from where it fell on her face.

"Yes, you did. Now be a good boy and put your hands over your head." Climbing atop his impeccable physique, she dazzled him with the hypnotic vaunt of her smile. Michael's answer floated to her in the form of a raffish smirk, dispatching a dubious glare as he complied with her wish. Crossing both hands at the wrist, Julia touched them securely to the top of his head, returning unhindered to her previous provokes. Her mouth brought him anguish, and with her mouth she would bring delectation to their play. Michael's movements ripened firm. Soaring tempered towards each spiraling kiss, his virile exhales brushed the silence like odd notes taken from a primeval chant. Julia reveled in the body now under her command, delighted by the deep, reverberant echoes that came with ingesting his length. Cradled lovingly in warmth, he trembled as he summited her toils, fully sweetened by the ultimate kiss. The universe was again as it should be.

"You're forgiven." Michael advised through a rough breath. His head thrown far back as if the ceiling now warrants the inspection he gave, and even with clinched lids, the look on his face supplanted satisfaction.

Julia smiled, again scaling his body. She curled against his unbending physique, letting him feel the soft press of her breasts in her climb. "How's my debt now?" she murmured against his neck.

"Reduced," Michael panted, pressing a kiss to her temple. "By the time you leave here, I may just have gotten my dues." He grunted, pushing himself from the bed. He staggered drunkenly from the room.

Julia's gaze strode past the window to the action on the grounds. The symphony of the woods again drifted near, as was the romping in the yard. Squirrels trapeze the thin branches of trees, one most determined with a near invisible twig. He disappeared almost as quickly as he came. Slipping from the bed, Julia's eyes searched the trembling limbs of the tree, needing the distraction, as her body was well angst from the emphasis lynched to his earlier play. "Think trees, birds, bunnies, and baseball." She scolded through a frown. "Besides, he'll be out soon enough, take it out on him then." She smiled, happily resting the discussion with herself. Pulling the discarded sheet from the floor, she draped it haphazardly over her shoulders, peering expectantly at the trees as if waiting for a show. A robin pranced across scattered mulch in its hunt. The vibrancy of its colors seeming to blaze in the brilliance of the afternoon sun, dancing brusquely across a manicured lawn. His small body veered in constant motion. The sudden flutter of a dove's wings rent the silence, sending the small bird dashing in, what looked like, a vexing rush.

Cat-shaped eyes narrowed in concentration as Michael reentered the room, a smirk riding her exotic face. Stepping close, his arms encircled her waist, quietly gliding up her stomach to her breasts.

"Mm, you're back." Julia smiled, allowing her head to tumble to his chest.

"I had to come back." He growled. "I had some work I needed to finish." No temptingly draped towel was worn on his second exit of the room. A fact he promptly proved, pressing her to the girth of his body. He emulated the manner of a large cat.

"Maybe I should scamper off now."

"Not just yet." He purred, his voice falling like pure air against her skin. "It's my turn." He informed her then, kissing her cheek. He spun her until his chest cradled her breasts. "And I definitely intend to collect."

"Really?" Julia quipped, managing to summon a meager pitch to sound somewhat surprised.

"Really," He smiled, moving his hand to her shoulders. He returned the sheet to the floor.

"Give or get?" she shrewdly asked, yet already knowing the answer, she smiled.

"Give." He murmured against her throat, his voice coming in a gravelly drawl. "Definitely give." Lifting her head, he took her breath. Kissing her as if his objective was to devour, he lost himself in the potency of the act. Her skin felt like the silkiness of rain as he lifted her from the floor, resting her gently on the bed. His kisses leisurely travelled her body, tasting sugary wells. He feasted as ardently as she had fed.

Speculations, they knew, hove relentless intrigue. Thus it thrived as a teaser amidst the chaos. For almost a week, analysis ignited an ort of optimism in the hearts of residents, smearing amendments and views aptly across advertised slats. Now the forecast called, not only for rain, but for torrential relief. The projected drenching is expected to blow in by late afternoon, lasting them most of the night. The multi-cluster storm is imagined as a remedy for their now critical state, though it brought with it, the potential for further crisis. Flash floods waited on a paltry scale, with the capability to conform to something worse, mudslides lurked portentously at their backs.

Water, in whatever its basis, remains the topic on everyone's tongue. Simplified, supply no longer had the resource to equalize the extensive demand. Leaving all eyes anxiously trained to an ominous sky, with hopes and prayers ascending plentiful. The atmosphere seemed set to allot such results.

The balmy days of summer had been bounteous in more ways than just one, and rain—even in the slightest gather—had been absent from their visions for months. Reservoirs now teetered dangerously low, and already, mandated restrictions governed every resident's hand. California. Referred to as the golden state, possessive of wealth and beauty that's unsurpassed by most. Abducing smog, traffic and a string of disasters held strictly in reserve, the state rivaled none. Like the perfect sundae laden well with treats, the beauteous dessert was yet laced with periling concerns.

Michael pushed the much lessened dune from his reach with finality, dragging the stack of paper to the far edge of his desk. His elbows pillared the top. A grunt, melded with frustration and weary, gurgled low in his throat, needing a moment's cessation to preserve his waning sanity. He roughly raked the surface of his skull. Kneading the tension from his neck, long fingers cajoled the knots residing on the twin muscles of his shoulders, working long in their toils to set forth relief.

The week had extracted much from his usual calm, dominated with meetings, each more essential than the first. Enduringly, they shuffled between lawyers, agents and a brilliantly infuriating director, with those being but a mere few. The latter four days had grown remarkably strained, lent solely to the rigorous grind that came with a job that had no end. Twilight, for him, started a new ambit for the word "work". This, while others scampered home to rest, the dark was where many great deals brokered their start. With the unending celebratory bash to attend, he was obliged to appear at least at a few. Kisses and drinks were but one way with which to play the game. A game that, of all else, most certainly had to be played, if he expected to attain the perceived end.

Running into Camille Straus had been the most pleasant occurrence of his week, a surprise that offered a break from the tedium of work. Friends now for the middling of twenty years—since their junior year in high school—the two had once been very close.

Both he and Camille sprouted from comparable backgrounds, with parents waist deep in humanitarian rights, both found their own way of acting out. Retaliating against what, he'd yet to understand, both grew, within themselves, completely inane. She dabbled some with what soon hailed as his weakness, but alcohol and parties were where Camille's appetite bled. She could go strong for days on end, moving from one to the other with a stamina that surpassed even his. They soon got swallowed in a gloom that had no end.

Eventually, he was compelled to leave that world behind, which unfortunately, meant leaving Camille's friendship as well, though they vaguely stayed in touch over the years. Camille, it seemed, had done her own share of growing. Still, the two, as ever, rested at different spectrums of their lives. She still loves to party regardless; only now, she'd learned to lessen the scale as a result. Looking as beautiful as ever, her career, as always, was thriving, but then, that had never been the problem with Camille.

Schmoozing, for him, grew tedious after long. The effects now blossomed less potent than it once had, while the effort seemed overly large. That side of the business was no longer his life, the enjoyment the youth got from the continuous prate, in no way, thrilled the man. For him, most celebration came with a notation attached—work. Preferring to stay away from all the fizz and buzz that went with that part of his work, his axioms were but few. If it was at all avoidable, then he most certainly did just that.

He missed the quiet whispers of his house, and always had. But now, he missed her most of all. Something about her—about the rightness of them, had his mind fully entrapped in ways that were slow to make itself clear, thus making it impossible to free her from his thoughts.

"So are you planning on going to Simon's birthday bash?" Phillip questioned from the door, his voice slicing through the puttering in Michael's head. Folding his arms across the sturdy width of his chest, he wedged his back to the framed mouth of the room.

"Uh, oh, I'm still thinking on that." Michael shrugged, turning his chair towards the room, his eyes floated over the surface of his desk. "Really, what I want is to go home. I'm all partied out." He groaned.

"You doing okay?" Phillip droned, frowning slightly with the ask. His eyes skimmed for signs of weariness on his friend's face.

"I'm fine." He shrugged. "I just think this side of it is getting to me a little more than it used to." Michael grumbled, grabbing a pen from his desk, he toyed absently with its length. "Wouldn't you prefer to be going home to your family instead?"

"That would be nice. You know, we could always move back." He smiled. "This way we'd be home when all that schmoozing comes to a close."

"See, I always knew you didn't like me. I knew one day your true feelings would come out, and now we have it." Michael smirked, propping his feet reflectively on the edge of his desk. "Living here would be a superb idea for me. Can't you just see it now? All my old friends getting the buzz that I'm back. Boy, does that sound like fun!" He glared, rolling his eyes in a quick snap to the ceiling. He concluded with a tight grunt.

"Scared?"

"You better believe it."

"Good. Then we'll keep it that way." Phillip laughed, moving further inside the office, he seated himself across from the large desk. They almost never take a meeting in this place. Phillip reflected sagely, most in their field would consider this a small space. Though ample enough to house not only the large desk, but two winged back chairs that sat directly across. A plush leather sofa was stationed to his left, flanked by tall windows offering a spectacular view. An antique credenza stored various refreshments and snacks, as did the large unit boarding a television on the opposite wall. Two overstuffed arm chairs and a coffee table, burdened with the latest magazines, balanced that side of the room.

Their office was both similarly sized by design. Of course, the furnishings were where the resemblances ended between the two; having a wife certified that fact. Together, the two had spent much time working from everywhere else in the world except in the workspace that's paid to do just that. "I saw you and Camille getting cozy the other night, it almost looked like you two were an item. Well, it seemed the photographers thought so. They couldn't take their cameras off you two."

"Camille? Please. If she's anything, she'd be more like a sister or even a cousin than anything else. For as long as I've known Camille, if there was ever going to be something between us, it would have happened years ago. Not now." Michael groaned, frowning with the thought. "Besides, she's with your friend, what's his name?"

"Who?"

"You know. The one who did, 'Wide-Rules', Jeremy…Jeffery, um, Jo—"

"Him?" Phillip barked, deepening his frown, his voice sounded more incredulous than it should.

"Yes him. Why?"

"That overly eccentric buffoon?" he carped. "And you have the nerve to call him my friend? Now who doesn't like whom?" Phillip grumbled, chuckling to himself as he shifted in his seat. Drawing in a long breath, he turned his attention to the windows at his friend's back. "Sarah wants your opinion on something, but she's a little nervous to ask you herself."

"Sarah, nervous? This must be big." Michael teased, removing his feet from the desk. He straightened in his chair, giving full attention to his friend.

"It's about, Julia," Phillip announced in a mellowed tone, pausing in thought. He returned his gaze to the window, missing the near startled expression on Michael's face. "You know how much of a fan she is of Julia's books?"

"Yes." Spitting the guarded response, Michael swallowed to squelch the sudden pounding that rose in his chest.

"Well, she wanted…she'd really love to have lunch with Julia sometime—just the two of them, but she's afraid to ask. She's worried she'll come off looking like an annoying fan. So now she wants me to get your opinion on the whole thing first. You know, you being famous and all." He shrugged, his wide shoulders plunging as if relieved to unload the baggage from his chest. "Do you think Julia would be offended if Sarah asked her to lunch? Would you?" Phillip probed, eager to have the matter over and done, having had many conversations of the same persuasion with his wife. He needed a solution that negates further worrying from her.

"I told her I didn't think she would. Julia seemed genuinely sweet to me, but she's still deathly nervous to ask. I've been tempted to call and extend an invitation on her behalf, but she made me promise not to interfere."

"Well," Michael started in a brooding tone, picking each word carefully before uttering his thoughts. "We both worked with her, and we both thought the same thing, what you see seems to be what you get, so…no. I don't think Julia would be offended at all. But the only way you'll know for sure, is if you ask." He smiled, finishing with a prideful sigh. Michael shrugged, not wanting to make decisions on Julia's behalf.

"So you think she should call?"

"I think maybe *you* should call, but since you gave your promise then I guess you can't. The two of you got along so well, the whole thing would have probably been easier using that route."

"And you don't think that I'd be taking advantage of the relationship we built?"

"I don't know. It may, and then again it may not. Associates who later become more, isn't that how many friendships first sprout? I think the only way you can get your answer for sure is to take the first step. But I doubt anything but good would come from the whole thing. You've seen the two of them together. It didn't seem as if Julia was straining to be kind." Michael shrugged, pushing his chair again to recline. He smiled with a new sense of pride, knowing he supported his friend without bruising his lover's toes.

Phillip's once nervy expression slowly faded, and his customary smile returned to view in a flash. "I think I'm going to call Sarah and give her some advice." He exclaimed, throwing his body from the chair, he turned to exit the room. "She's been bugging me about this all week. I think it's time to return the ball to her court." He smirked. Halfway to the door, Phillip pointedly stopped, turning back to his friend, he offered a welcoming thought. "I'm thinking we skip the bash tonight and grab the next flight out. Let's load up with the stack most essential to finalize the Metzler contract. The hill almost seems manageable on that. Though while we're at it, another stack or two might just knock out a near essential need. That ought to help, you know, to abet the sudden case of stomach virus that one of us is about to come down with. Emails, fax and maybe a rather indulgent gift works just as well the last time I checked."

"Oh, I'm definitely going to have to ponder that for a while." Michael quipped, his feet slamming immediately to the floor, palming his phone before Phillip rounded the aperture of his door.

Chapter Thirty One

Bourgeons of white coasted across a milky-blue sky. Abetted by a stifling wind, soft combers wafted mutely through rippling limbs, thus veiling the radiant blast from its mordant intent. Duskiness swooped the terrains like the coveted signal of a recommencing show. Spurred slavishly to such by the endurance of vagabond clouds, their efforts brewed willful in a fleet confiscation of the sun.

Irrespective of the wind, the day was exceedingly hot. With no promise of relief in the forecaster's continuous depose, reprieve came only at the imagination's length.

Shielding her eyes from the glare, Julia gazed cheerily at the bulbous clouds, admiring the oddity of their shapes. The resemblance was immediate for some, as likened names dashed to her mind in accordance of their game. And although others proved more difficult to match, the task was no less fun.

Michael's lean fingers gently combed the wet strands of her hair, skiing the dome of her scalp in a sublime caress. He alleviated the furrowed thorns of her stress—had she had any such irritants left in her body. Long lashes fluttered slowly in answer to his touch, resting on the soft edge of each cheek. Julia's smile waded the full length of her body, basking gladly in the saccharine embrace of his massage. Pleasure sloshed roughly from her throat.

"Why aren't you married?" Julia passively purred. "Why hasn't some sassy, long-legged supermodel snatched you up as yet?"

Smiling quietly to himself, Michael shrugged, though his fingers tarried not in their work. Swirling across the slick pate like implements foisted for just that, they worked the fragrant scent of Jasmine through her hair. The afternoon now edged on the advent of evening, yet the punishing August heat remained inexorably ripe. Shaded by a cabana, the housing offered them little in the way of relief. Cool liquid poured from the belly of a jug, felt astonishingly good to his nigh desiccated sense, seeming sensual and playful while it streamed through his fingers to her hair.

"I don't know," Michael rasped, his voice like a groan in his throat. "Maybe I wasn't what they wanted."

"What about you? Were any of them what you wanted?" she asked sweetly, the words gliding from her lips like a lively chirp, now strangely curious by the thought. If the way he treats her was the only indication of a catch, then most would consider him a well coveted prize. Disregarding wealth, profession, the exquisiteness of both body and face, or the devotion of his prowess for everything else, all roads pointed aptly to perfection in every sense. Was he really that adamant to remain single?

"That's hard to tell; perhaps everything was too bright back then. I wasn't able to see things as clearly as I should. Perhaps…" Michael shrugged, his shoulders tight as he rinsed the conditioner from her hair. "Young eyes don't always make you see the things that you should. "*Ou peut-être, je viens t'attendais pour vous*. Or maybe, I was just waiting for you."

"What?"

"I said, maybe I was just too much of a fool back then." Michael smiled, calmly muttering the lie. His fingers sweetly persisted their circuitous strive, walking delicately over her scalp in a slow caress.

"What language was that?" she asked curiously, showing obvious by the deep pull of her finely arched brows, surprise was well palpable in her tone.

"French," he muttered elusively, shrugging behind the word.

"I didn't know you spoke French." She warbled, her lithe endorsing the magnitude of her stun, tilting her head back. She gazed up at his face.

"There are many doors yet to be opened, Julia." Michael whispered, brushing his lips along her ear. He trickled the last of the water over her head.

"Which further argues my question as to why?" she teased, matting a finger to a splatter near her eyes. "Now that your youthful armor has tarnished some with age, what now? No cream floats to the top of those milky memories you have?"

"Let's just say, the more closely I examine each day, the more sullen the past becomes. So I'm working now on taking things one day at a time. It's a work in progress but well worth it." He smiled, prideful of his expressive choice. His fingers deepened their task, adoring the coolness of the water as it dribbled from her hair to his legs. "Whatever comes…comes." He calmly vowed, lifting his shoulders in a haphazard shrug. Ten fingers fanned the hardened surface of her scalp, surfing the edge of her forehead to the nape of her long neck. "I'll deal with each diurnal event as they dawn."

"Mmmmm," Julia purred, her answer wading like a warm, panoptic hug, paddling deliciously through every cell in her body before spilling from her lips. "That feels very…good." She sighed, shifting her shoulders as he lifted her head from his lap. Strong fingers toiled persuasively down the entirety of her neck, soothing the muscles in their path with practiced skill. "You have great hands."

"It helps when your subject lets you do whatever you want." Michael teased, his voice sounding strangely like the grating warns tethered to a storm.

"Not…anything." She corrected sweetly, looking over the slope of her forehead, she smiled. "Almost, but…not everything…."

"What do you think is left for us to do that we haven't already done?" Michael growled, softening his voice. He thenceforth deepened the tincture matted to its rumbly vaunt.

"I'm sure there're still things that we haven't bothered to try." She crooned, acceding to his descending tone with the shrinking of her voice. "Things I doubt I share an interest in, I suppose."

"So everything *does* cover it then?" he smirked, his deep tone ruffling the wet strands of her hair.

"I suppose you could be right."

"I know I am. The adventures have been a rather decadent treat, so, too, the creative process. One does not forgo a drop of that."

"A rather revered course, to be exact." She smiled, though the baring of a sardonic frown extinguished such gesture from life. "Why, Mr. Dunhill, could it be we now verge a crossing? Is that the cease and desist flag I hear flapping in the wind?"

"No such luck, Ms. Berwick. You have my complete attention to do with as you will." He drawled. "Unless, of course, you're expecting me to be the director in this frenzied derby we share. Are you?" Michael asked, sounding almost incredulous.

"Why not, you're more experienced at this than I am." She chirped, her answer sounding like the flavored lyrics of a memorized song. A long silence followed without the usual witty retort, stretching startlingly taut before his fingers finally stopped.

Like shades being drawn tightly shut, so, too, the ambiance darkened, riddled, in a fleet trice, with the eerie substance of something else. Of a sudden, Michael's face grew blank. No longer showing the playfulness of the past, he gave no hint of the whimsical smile that rested there only moments before. "*You do?*" Julia asked starkly, and as like metal in its piercing of flesh, truth slashed through her muscles like a blade. A debilitating pain slammed through her stomach at once, sharpening like the kiss of asphalt to one's chest in a fall. Her body cringed in its dread of the answer to come. The fear of his reply had her stomach constricting in knots, surprising even her with the level of anxiety that burrowed home in her chest. She was not too foolish to realize she had grown exceedingly attached, and was even fonder yet of the times they shared, knowing she would miss whatever they had when the time came to do just that. She just never thought it would be this soon or this suddenly done.

"You need me to make that decision?" Michael asked in an oddly tight voice, sounding austere and reserved to the channels of her straining ears.

"I know we said that—" Julia started, feeling strangely weighted by the heat. It pushed dastardly down on her chest, scraping like claws over her flesh. The hulking mass held her almost fully compressed.

"We?" he barked through what seemed a hoarse breath.

"Okay. I-I guess...I..." stuttering the clumsy retort, she sighed, feeling her body ominously lock, as all thoughts promptly fell from their place, leaving but a single track. Her mind, in its resistance, screamed its own warning, imploring in its need for silence. *Just shut up!* It yelled. *Just shut your mouth and let this pass! Veer to something else.* It further advised. "I knew we would...well, I knew the day would come, Michael...but..." she moaned, irrespective of the riotous warning blasting through her head. Thus, she barreled forward despite the rankling in her contrary self. Shifting her body, her fingers fastened to the frame of her chair in their sought of new strength, while her brain, in its bewildered state, searched for corroborating words to jury the place in which they now stood, truly hating the twist their conversation took, and dreading even more the verdict at its end.

Fear, portentous and bold, grew to a lofty level. Sending small quakes through her slender limbs like the thudding pulse featured in one's mistake. The look on his face made the matter no less terrifying than the pictures now swirling in her head, for of a sudden, his body resembled the sculpting of a granite erection, looking roughly braced for an unexpected thrust. He stiffened as if expecting the impact of something hard, or for the next hammering shoe to sever the essentialness of his limbs. Julia's insides welded to a solid knot, and the piercing pain in her chest did not dim, as she thought it would, when she told herself to relax. "Well…is it really here? You—you want…to–to… take a break?" she asked, shaking her head as if to answer the query herself. She forced a small lilt of hope in her voice, praying then he would turn with his easy smile and put the matter swiftly to an end, gifting the answer she knew she desperately wanted. Yet he gave no such response. Staring, instead, in the distance, his expression was neither solemn nor joyed.

"Why don't *you* decide that?" he muttered dryly, promptly jumping to his feet. "I'm going inside to get something to drink, would you like some?" Michael asked without throwing her a glance, his voice sailing tightly graveled, almost tart. It propelled his legs well before the question's end. Ignoring the soft call of his name, he found himself stomping through his bedroom door before realizing his intent, or that his feet were, in actuality, still wet.

He was hurt. He could not deny the verity of that. But fear was what constricted the vicinity of his chest most. Suddenly, getting swamped with a prickling sense of horror, one guileless question that begot one less minimal than the first. What if she decides to press end? What of him then? With the passing of these months, he had waited patiently for her to change her mind. Waited for her to admit what they have, as well as the intensity imbedded in her feelings. What if she never does? What then?

Bewildered eyes scanned the house franticly in their search, calming the moment they settled on the man now sitting on the couch. Feeling fully angst, the room held its breath as she entered, plunging remarkably quiet as she closed the door at her back. The forest around them drew astoundingly near, bubbling through the stillness as she sat at his side. He granted no acknowledgement of her presence as she hove near, or of the proximity at which she rested. No words were spoken between them and no glances were exchanged. The two just sat aphasic, cloven together in the thatches of their fear, time neither furthered nor faded.

"Michael." Julia whispered softly at last, taking a quiet breath with the sound of his name.

"Yes." He grunted, the short, gruff answer sounding almost like a soft bark.

"Are we really out of time?" she asked softly, taking a long breath to calm the roiling of her nerves. "I was hoping…well, I had hoped we had…more time." She murmured timidly, her palms clasped tightly in her lap. "I wasn't ready…well. I wasn't ready for it to be…today." Forgetful of all the times she decried their venture a temporary fix, Julia's voice wilted, seeming almost a plea in the softness of its spill. She saw not that they had gone months past what she had presumed a logical fit in her head. Sitting this close, she saw only the dark precipice at which they rested. Feeling only the coldness of her loss, and at that moment, she sorely missed, above all else, the warmth of his smile. His personality had always been just that—warm and infectious. "If it's my decision, can I choose to say no? I don't think…I don't think I want to…stop. Is–is that okay?" she quickly asked, lifting saddened eyes to his face.

Michael's head turned slowly—daubed with what he hoped was a blank expression masking his face—his eyes plucked the details well ladened in hers. She looked deathly frightened, asking a worthless question of him as if she had or needed to ask, and he wondered then. How blind must she really be that she needed to edge that ledge?

"You're still unclear? That vision of yours is still unclear, isn't it?" Michael grumbled, grating the static silence with the resonance of his voice. He stared past her at the wall. Air burst roughly from his nostrils in what seemed a sudden squall, finishing the gusty swirl. A crude smile groomed the area surrounding his mouth before his eyes returned to hers.

"I'm sorry. I only know that right now…I. Can we hold off for a little while longer?" she asked, not taking the time to decipher the meaning of his words. Slipping her hand in his, she quietly caressed his palm. Desperate in her need for him to be okay, and at the moment, everything just felt wrong. "Did I hurt you somehow?" she asked, even as she wondered how. It was just their usual play with words, nothing more.

No answers came to enlighten that of her inquest, nothing that he was yet willing to give, though he wondered should he try. Should he tell her that his feelings sprout stronger each day? Or of the depths to which they root? Pondering greatly on such facts, Michael sighed. Sobering in a flash, he suspended the rumblings in his head. Confident she was not yet ready to hear any such confession. And after today, the truth of that was even more certain than it had been.

Before an integral answer came, she did, wrapping her arms around him, she offered him solitude in her. Her hair fell like a curtain around his face in aid of her deed, spilling moist fragrance in its wake. Michael left the clingy wisp as full evidence of his truth, while he pressed her close. And almost as effortlessly as it began, everything was again rectified for what it was. A oneness reminiscent of skin, not unlike stepping across a threshold to the esteem ardency of home. Its emission of warmth surged infinite. Humbling in its weight, its substance was both craved and revered with the same inhalation of a breath. This being their place of belonging. And each time they left, they were bound, by unseen or unspoken motives, to return to each other as they had before.

Savoring the feel of his arms around her, Julia sighed, acceding to the pleasure such action awarded, and to the fear it now vanquished from her mind. She had never seen him look more anguished, and she doubt she ever wanted to endure the terror of such mincing spurs again. Strangely, the feelings it erupted were unexplainable, seemingly too new to comprehend. They darkened more with each thought. "I'm sorry." She whispered against his cheek, pulling back from his chest. She gazed into eyes that were again soft. "I'm sorry if my words hurt you." she sighed, lightly touching his cheek. "I didn't mean to...I-I couldn't. I mean, I wouldn't hurt..." fumbling with the lyrical stilts now bobbing in uncharted course, she stuttered to a full stop, her eyes dropping with the death of her words. Gingerly, she pressed a kiss to his lips and felt his immediate response, accepting the palpable profess. Julia put all she could not express in the potency of her kiss, mining his mouth for all the elements and flavors it possessed.

"Say it." He growled against her mouth. "Say it, Julia."

Frightened eyes tumbled slowly from his, knowing, without asking, what he wanted from her. And though she desperately wanted to bequeath him the words to set his furrows flying—anything to calm the trepidation she now felt. Fear blanketed the moment instead. "I'm not ready to give you up." She breathed, her breath stroking the stubble edges of his cheeks. "I'm not ready for this to be over."

"Would you ever be?" he asked in a soft grunt, lifting a hand to her face, his thumb brushed the slight swell of her lips.

"I don't know." She cried, mouthing the vague utterance bleakly, even as her head wagged. Knowing the truth was more frightening than she had previously perceived. For the first time since their peculiar beginning, the reality of that day came to her clear, and it was not as she expected or plotted in her head. The gentle swing of her head said what she could not, giving him an answer that surprised even her. "*No*" had not ever been an answer sighted in any subset of her thoughts, since the word had not entered her consciousness once.

With a growling breath, Michael attacked, crushing her to his chest as he lengthened their bodies on the couch. Her body fell eagerly under his spell, and as with the wont of his mouth, she bent, bowed and curled to his every whim. He left no question unasked in the decadence of his drive, and no answers were left unspoken on her lips. A cauldron of ecstasy then verdict their discussion, answered truthfully with every ounce of their souls. It ruled the lengthy colloquy at an end, putting to bed a question or two that had long lingered between them.

———

For what tallied now the fifth time in as many minutes, Michael's shrewd glance discreetly noted the clock. Nerves and excitement tugged vengefully at the hammering in his chest, jangling wildly, whilst his mind preached caution to the odd demeanor balking on his face. To the many platens of his life, this day was infinitely symbolic. A weekend he was unlikely to forget. One, though willingly conceived, advanced only with the exorable tender of cautious steps. A foundation he had artfully laid to achieve a desired end.

Thus far, only one other, besides him, was cognizant of a plot. Betty's perceptive antlers again rearing their ugly head, though not because he chose to confess any part of his sins, but the sorceress that she is, she figured it out. Thankfully, she won't be around to witness the crumbling of his psyche, but he fully suspected, with good reason, that her usual means will be used to acquire every morsel of the remaining truth. Not that it would surprise him if she already guessed the precise sequence contrived in each phase of his plotting, which would surely explain why she hurriedly volunteered her leaving for the weekend.

"How's this?" Julia chanted as she pranced through the entrance of the kitchen, modishly twirling to a stop. She offered a giddy smile.

"You look beautiful—as always." Michael vowed, knowing it mattered not the style or trend of her garment, only needing her presence to achieve his goal. Wearing a simple white slack fitted to her body, the white tank and olive shirt complimented her curves well.

"Thank you." Julia chimed, taking a playful bow, she asked. "So, now that I'm all dressed up—as per your request—what are we having for this breakfast date?"

"Pancakes," Michael remarked tunefully, sending another tactful inquisition at the clock.

"And does this date leave me on the sidelines watching, or sweating in the line of fire with you?"

"Since when do you cleave to the outfields?" Michael inquired huskily, his hazel eyes growing roguish. "You're better at this than I am. So I expect the measurements on our fluid-loss to definitely sit the same." He smirked, winking as he turned towards the sink. The unexpected sonata of chimes froze his momentum in its track, drawing their attention from the other. Their gaze then winged in the direction of the door. The musical notice sliced the tranquil morning like the harrowing echo of a Browning M2, and for a moment, all things ceased its forward propulsion. "Who the heck could that be?" Michael frowned, looking bothered by the unforeseen interruption. He immediately edged the counter in protest of the call, tossing the cookbook with a perturbed flare as he inched from the room. "I'll be right back." He muttered in what seemed more like a snarl, taking a nervous breath as he hurried down the hall. "Mom!" Michael hailed, and his voice rushed back to the kitchen with sufficient confusion, marring the deep tone, to sound truly flummoxed by the visit, almost incommodious to any listening ears.

Frozen in the very spot he left her, Julia waited nervously for expounding comments to sail back through the house, though nothing floated to her clearly past the hysteric trills now pinging her ears. Her mind then travelled at warp speed as a result, survival rightly honing its cause, searching for a reason to be at ease, as there was none, quite plainly, but the obvious to be at his house. A stack of papers waited on a small desk off the kitchen, and whether pompous in their wave or jeering, they flew to her attention like the need for oxygen in the principal stage of a crash. Thawing in a flash, she hastily commandeered the pile as her own. Not needing to know what they were or their rank, since her interest rested not on the content but on the result they tendered. Her only need was to present a professional front. This, she recited to herself as she garnered a seat at the bar.

Their muffled voices seeped through the house in the guise of a mocking chant, steeping like sweat beneath the asylum of a woolen smock in their rattling of her nerves. Indistinguishable grumblings twisted menacingly at her bones. *What if she comes in?* Julia's mind worriedly probed, sounding to the woman like a child, and the answer was not to her liking should they have to endure such end. Having never had the slightest inter-ruption before now, she was unsure of the proper procedure to accommodate such irks.

Offering his mother a bright smile, Michael swung the door wide. "What a pleasant surprise, come on in." He called, letting his hand fall to the back of her shoulders.

"Well, a good morning to you, too, son!" Hyacinth smiled, her hazel eyes dancing into his. "Someone looks to be in a very good mood."

"Fine, I'll be an old sourpuss the next time you stop by then."

"No need to take it that far." Hyacinth quickly rejoined, waving her hand across her body as if yielding a plea. "I'm happy to have a son who still enjoys seeing his mother."

"Good." Michael grunted. Trying hard to keep his face blank, an eager arm tightened around her shoulders as he led her through the house. Nearing the kitchen, he asked. "So, what brings you here this morning?"

"Can't a mother just visit her son?" Hyacinth asked, gazing playfully at his face.

"Of course, you know you're welcome any time."

"But this time I'm here because you invited me for breakfast, remember?"

"No. Breakfast is next week, mom, not today." Michael smiled, looking almost apologetic as he stirred the lie with the thickness of honey and the deep basting of his voice. "I'm working today, mom." He beamed—all be it from inside. The syrupy reply rounded the door of the kitchen as they ventured near, bounding well ahead of the two in its granting of information. Michael's eyes rushed to the beauty now stationed at the bar, eyeing her warily, he smiled. Her head popped up the instant they stalled the impe-tus of their pace, a nervous glint flashing in her eyes. "Oh, mom, this is Julia Berwick. Do you remember me telling you about the writer Phillip and I have been working with? Julia, this is Hyacinth…my mother." Michael drawled, summoning every ounce of restraint to keep both his voice and expression vacant of what he felt.

"Oh, of course," Hyacinth chirped, moving quickly across the room. She gathered the other woman's hand. "It's nice to finally meet you. I've heard so much about you."

"Oh, my, I'm not sure I shouldn't be nervous now." Julia smiled, taking hold of the older woman's hand. She returned the warmth in her smile. Ascertaining the strong resemblance between the two, she now knew, with certainty, where Michael got his piercing gaze. A stronger stippling of green sparkled within her depths, though both gazes blazed just as sharp. Although, Michael's eyes were more striking in the way that they gleamed, drawing you in with their hypnotic glint, their gem-like glow kept you riveted to his face, or so it seemed to have transpired with her. "I hoped there was at least some morsel of good in their introduction."

"All very good things, I assure you. Including allied distinction on your talent."

"In that case, I'll honor their kind words with a profound 'thank you', and just go off and blend with the furniture while you visit with your son." Offering a pleasing smile with her chant, Julia's eyes slid in a sideways glance to Michael's face for clues. Needing a hint of what came next, though with his head cast downwards, not even the slightest inkling staggered forward to her aid. His eyes, instead, shifted slowly over the pages of the small cookbook in his hand.

"I doubt that would ever be a possibility, dear. Not with a face like that." Hyacinth smiled, turning her attention to her son. With his face interred deep into the pages of his book, he seemed to have lost interest in their exchange or for that matter—grown peculiarly mute. "Don't you agree, Michael?" she asked sweetly, her eyes tact keen to his face.

"Huh…what?" Michael queried calmly, pretending not to have heard the question asked, for the delay gave him the chance to pluck something serenely casual from his head.

"I was telling your guest that I thought she was too beautiful to be confused with your furniture, don't you agree, son?" Hyacinth challenged with a smile, the radiance hardly dimming in her wait. It flickered from one jewel depth to another.

"I guess I'd have to agree with you, since she is a beautiful woman." Michael rasped matter-of-factly, turning back to his book. Without the linger of doubt, he knew his mother now studied his face, and gaggles of questions should now funnel that halo of shrewdness she had. But he had not the power with which to appease her at that time.

"Then that should make me about even with the furniture around here."

"Wrong again, dear. That's not likely on any aspect." Hyacinth vowed, though a curiously, beguiling smile tottered on her face while she eyed her son. Thus, she declared a morsel of her thoughts with a simple probe. "Isn't that right, son?"

"She's right." Michael averred with what seemed a reluctant smile, instantly dropping his head. He thumbed through the stodgy pages without seeing a word.

"So…" Hyacinth spat coolly, veering her route. "My old brain caught up with me at last, I see?" she shrugged, moving closer to her son, she glanced at the page now displayed in his hand. "Next you'll probably need to hire me a nurse." Announcing the theory in a somber tone, thin fingers brushed the wide surface of his back, and a wan sign whispered its view of such thought. "Why don't I get out of your way so you two can get back to work?"

"But I'm—"

"You really don't have to do that on my account…." Rashly blurting her thoughts, she fumbled to a terse stop, and her eyes quietly hopped to Michael's face in repentance of such, feeling oddly uncomfortable with the idea of his mother having to leave. As a mother herself, she knew well the attachment she had to her kids, and of the times they shared together. It was a protected right. After driving all this way to garner a visit with her son, it just would not sit well to let the matter be, not with a mother. "Actually, Michael…I don't mind taking a break so you can have a visit with your mother." Julia tamely assured, gazing intently at the man in hopes of conveying her point. "Instead of a working breakfast, you could name it something else. I could just go off and busy myself with some work while the two of you visit." Looking nervous now that she gave voice to her thoughts, she stumbled to clarify her place. "That's…well, if you don't mind my… suggesting."

"That's a great idea!" Michael beamed, feeling more attracted to her in that moment than mere minutes before. With one single gesture, she made everything right, fixing the runnels without him having to spill his hand. "Why don't you stay and join us, mom? We're having pancakes." Michael broadcast then, displaying a large box of said mix. He offered her what seemed his most charming smile.

"You're making breakfast?" Hyacinth asked with disbelief well molded in her tone.

"Don't sound so surprised." Michael laughed. "I've been known to tool about the kitchen now and then." Twirling the whisk with an expert twist, he walked the wiry gadget through the rumpled dune. A billow of white scrabbled through the air like dust in a storm, coasting forward with no foreseen end. "I've come to like it." He finished with unmistaken pride tinting his speech.

"Really?" Hyacinth scowled, sweeping her eyes over her son and his surround-ings. She absorbed the area in a single fluid-like glance, and only one question rushed to the forefront without pause. "Where's Betty?" she asked, turning with simplicity. Unmeasured elegance metered her pace, while her eyes searched for sure signs of his devoted protector. Her love for him was surely an unconditional fact, but the kitchen had always been considered *her* exclusive domain. No one was exempted from her wrath if they dare to traverse her space. "I seem to recall that she hates to have the borders of her kitchen breached by anyone—especially you." She groaned, sarcasm tainting her words, though a light frown creased the angling of her brows. "You might burn a finger or something, and we wouldn't want that, now would we? Then again, she just might enjoy it. This way she'll get to play mother-hen to her precious little boy." She laughed, barreling forward before Michael had a chance to lend voice to any answer he might have had. "Do you think she knows you're no longer ten?"

"That's a very good question, mom. What do you think?" Michael asked, his own sarcasm heavy in the deep rumble of his tone, blaring obvious, even with the smile now broadening on his face.

"I was never that bad." Hyacinth grumbled, pointing short, perfectly manicured nails at his chest. A distinctive poise controlled the unfurling of her deed. "Besides," she sighed. "I've already accepted the fact that you're now a grown man, but you'll always be my little boy, no matter how old you get."

"Will we be going through the usual soliloquy today, mom?" Michael frowned. "I do have a guest this time, so it would be nice if you didn't leave her with the impression that I'm just a spoiled little boy."

With a loving smile directed at her son, Hyacinth ignored his jibe with a slow shrug, turning her attention on his guest. Curiosity again hurdled to the forefront, wishing to know more about the exotic beauty in the room. Something about the morning and her did not fully compute. There was nervousness below the surface for both, why is that? Business only—not a chance, Hyacinth sneered. Chortling at the folly of such thought, for she knew well the customs of her son, and a woman that gorgeous would never stand a chance without him making his play. "I'm sure she has her own speculation on such matters."

"Please," Julia snickered in response, pressing a hand staunchly to her mouth. She stifled the simmering rant in its track, as Michael's gaze captured hers, with a witty glint, from behind his mother's back.

"Betty went to Charleston." Michael rejoined in what whistled as a calm grunt. "She's meeting her sister for the weekend." Elaborating with a shrug, he stayed clear of the parts where he was partially involved. "She'll be back soon enough for me to still have a mother around." He droned, his eyes playful. "I'm not sure if it's a curse or simply fools luck having two mothers constantly fussing."

"I think you can definitely rule out the prospect of it being a curse. It certainly worked well in your favor as I recall. Do you have kids?" Hyacinth chirruped, whirling abruptly with the sweetened ask. She set her full attention on the younger of them.

"Yes I do. I have two." Julia smiled, well aware of her reason for asking.

"Sons?" Hyacinth probed curiously, surprised by the answer, though her expression showed no such verity on that.

"One of each, actually,"

"Good." She crooned, slanting her head as if to engage her son in their chat. She stopped mid-point of the task as if thinking better of the chore, throwing him a feigned look of perturbation. Hyacinth remarked glumly instead. "Then you'll have your daughter to ease the pain caused to you by your son."

"I'll try to remember that." Julia nodded with a gauged smile, her eyes travelling past the woman to rest quietly on the man. His only reaction to the banter was a sedated smile, seeming happier than not with the situation. She felt oddly gladdened to have offered the thought. Gladder still, for her mode of dress, or his mother would not have needed to hazard a guess as to why she was there. Yet the coolness of the tiles greatly mocked her predicament, leaving her longing to slip her toes in the soft bed of her slippers.

"Would you like some help? Or would that push me under the over-mothering banner?" Hyacinth humbly asked, seeming to glide past him as she waited his sardonic reply.

"No! You stay there." Michael exclaimed, throwing his hands up to stall further entry in the room. Water swished across the counter from his newly washed hands, while collective droplets leapt sedately from the limbs' elevated stance. "I told you, I've done this before. I can do it without help, thank you. You just have a seat and make yourself comfortable. Have a cup of coffee, why don't you?" he drawled, thoroughly drying his hands, he smiled. "How often do you get to meet one of our writers?" Michael rasped, his eyes holding what seemed a plea, locking his gaze to the curious sparkle of his mother's. He mentally sent her what could not be said. She was an intuitive woman, and he knew, with certainty, she would soon get the gist of his intention. But that's as far as he could go without fostering Julia's suspicion of the truth. *How else was he supposed to get the two of them to meet, if not this?* Michael griped, praising the cunning used to ensure the smooth progression of such end. For as smart as they both were, he'd had to work thrice as hard to stay on his toes.

Narrowing her gaze, inquisitiveness marred their hazel depths, and the start of a frown quickly vanished from its place of rest, though whether from acknowledgement or complaisance. He was irresolute on that. "Coffee?" Michael slowly growled, spitting the word as if the meaning was a distorted farce of what it was.

"Coffee sounds wonderful!" Hyacinth warbled with a smile, her tone bearing the seedlings of a syrupy fruit. Turning back to the bar, she confiscated a seat to Julia's right. "Miss Berwi—"

"Please, call me Julia."

"Julia," she nodded, and the thin lines of maturity folded with acceptance of the young beauty's name. "Tell me, how old are your children?" she probed in a soft, sugary tone. Her gaze comfortably settled on the other's face.

"Eleven and thirteen," Came the immediate response.

"Great age," Hyacinth crooned. "They're independent, but still young enough to share their affections with you." Rolling her eyes at his heckling glare, she flashed a playful smirk at her son. Yet no words came to broker a response, only a grin that took up the entirety of his face.

Michael whisked through the batter with an enormous swell of pride distending his chest. Pleased with his action, as neither woman knew the contriving it took to bring both to this place, or of the depths of his feelings for the moment and them, and the duplicity of the act made his body smile. His eyes then flickered with said bliss posing as their guide, catching hold of Julia's from across the room. They tarried as if to garner rest, stretching the moment longer than his original intent. That smile held him fully transfixed. So used to gazing was he, that it was not until her eyes dropped, that he was able to do the same.

"It seems good enough to eat, doesn't it, son?" Hyacinth voiced, gently breaking the pause, having caught the end of their exchange. She grew even more curious than she once was. *If there's something between them, why not just come out and say it? He'd never needed her permission or consent to do as he willed with his dates, so why the secret?* "The food," She smiled, noticing the look of confusion on his face. "It smells good enough to eat. Tell me, are you hungry, son?" she beamed, angling her head to the side as if to survey him from a new prospective.

"Never more ravenous, mom," Michael returned in a slow drawl, allowing her recognition. He acceded the affirmation of her instinct with the full extent of his gaze. "I think everything would be to your liking."

"You think so?"

"I know so."

"When do you suppose I'll get to have a sample on that?" Hyacinth inquired sweetly, and her hazel eyes twinkled with enough excitement to almost show. Is her son saying what she thinks he's saying?

"Once I get finished. However you do it, I guarantee you'll only have to sample the first to agree."

"Okay. Say I agree with the recipe you choose, what's next? Should I expect more invitations?"

"They say it never hurts to have hope." Michael rejoined in his rumbly tone, lifting a brow as if in challenge of that which hovered but was not said. "They also swear that at its best, it scoffed at impossibilities, bringing such cowering to its knees with a simple strike."

"Why, Michael." Hyacinth whined in what sounded like a giddy song, pressing a hand to her chest. She looked almost shocked. "Do you now feign being obtuse with your mother? Now that doesn't seem very fair, does it? I seem to recall being invited."

"Give me time, mother. I'm working at it as fast as these hands will let me." He droned, and his retort trailed the residue of an unperturbed sigh, raising his head in a mocking display. His gaze was somewhat earnest as was his smile.

"I could help you with that." Julia blurted blandly, ignorant that their lyrical sparring pertained solely to her. She bestowed both with a reedy grin. In truth, her manner was guileless. Not having attended what was being said, she remained heedless of the facts. Something about such crude deed felt more slithery than not, like being embraced by the lowest order of a voyeur's guild. She felt it best to leave such things untouched. The affection between them was obvious, not just in the way they greeted each other, but also in the way they conversed. Still, anything was better than sitting there twiddling her thumbs. She was never one patient in the art of leisure, and did not intend to start doing so now.

"What a wonderful idea!" Hyacinth chirped in response, her smile brightening to illuminate the entire house. "With you helping, the load would be so much lighter than it once was."

"But——" Michael putted in start, sounding like a dying engine. He stuttered to a stop, thinking it unwise to share the kitchen with her. Not when spotlights were already aimed at their heads. What if they abstractedly resort to the familiarity of the past? He was certain she would not want to be outed without giving her consent, especially not in front of his mother. "But…but you're my guest." He muttered at last, saving himself for the time being.

"I know, but…I'd like to help." She stiffly shrugged. "That's…if you don't mind."

Michael smiled, fully aware his mother now watched them fixedly. And while the encounter gave him no pause, he worried much on the repercussions for her. "As long as you're sure," He muttered with an accompanying smile, and saw eager sparks race through the dark pools of her eyes, and as quickly as the answer fled from his lips. She swooshed past him into the kitchen, ready to be of aid. In quick corollary of their new scenario, Michael used the introduction of her back to send his mother a disapproving smirk, shooting darts at her face, though his smile softened the penetration of their tips. Together they had carried the nondescript conversation longer than they should have. In his eagerness to award her information. They broke from the necessary chit-chat they should have had instead.

It was with a hint of pensive nerve that Michael strolled towards the sink, though it was not fear, nor was it worry, that seized his mind, but caution that held his body tense. He watched as Julia rinsed the last of the soap from her hands, turning fully towards him. His eyes rushed to archive a quick survey of her face, affirming things about her he already knew, but more still. He noted she wore no mask of apprehension for the job ahead, easing no small amount of weight from his chest.

Soft batter smeared on the spatula needed to be rinsed, a purposeful accomplishment he was quite proud of, at its start. That is—until she flashed him a smile. It was an easy, fresh, early sunrise type of smile from one lover to the next. Not unlike the ones she'd given him on so many mornings as this. Showing the intimacy between them, her eyes seemed warm with the rapture of friendship, and he could do naught but stare at the eminence they granted. He had seen those eyes, dauntless in their witchery, stalked the many corridors of his dreams. Sourced as his only form of authentic communication outside of her body, he could find no immediate urge to drag his gaze from the curving of her face. Michael offered then a light smile, and again his appreciation lingered longer than his intended aim. But for a moment, he could have sworn the morning's rays effloresced from the reverence of that smile.

Passing the island on his trek to the newly vacated sink, Michael brushed his fingers over hers in a bequest of assurance, though she disclosed no need of any such aid. He was suddenly uncertain if the venture was meant to mollify her or to placate his own angst, only knowing the certainty that he needed to touch her in some manner. He took what was available to him.

As if ready to float from the boundaries of her skin, Julia's body grew rapidly light with the miniscule act. And in such, odd though it seemed, one would think he shouted a proclamation from the highest summit, instead of offering the mere simplicity of a touch. The soft indent at the corner of her mouth lightly deepened, though she tried, unsuccessfully, to sate the stupid grin that now threatened to fly free.

Awaiting his mandate as to her next step, her eyes caressed the back of his head, moving low over his tall sinewy frame. Yet, without access to his eyes or his expression, she still knew, with certainty, a percentage of his thoughts. The touch was not just a greeting between lovers, but a promise, a reminder and an enlightenment in one. Yes, a declaration in every bit of the actual sense, and the inference had an elating effect.

Remembering the relevance of his mother, Julia shifted her attention to the clotted batter now unattended. Collecting the whisk slugged on its side, she stirred brusquely, assigning herself something else, besides the man, on which to dawdle upon. Raking the beater deep inside the ringed groves of the bowl, Julia smiled in satisfaction, disturbing the edges of a hardened lump while she worked. Grateful for the genuine distraction, she ground the tip of the whisk through the center of a small knoll, dislodging the lump, she whipped it smooth.

"What, you didn't like my work?" Michael asked as he drew near, drying the spatula. He quickly removed an assortment of brown pancakes from the griddle's bed, adjusting the heat. He sprayed the surface in preparation of the next batch.

"You missed a spot at the bottom."

"Oh, thanks." He hummed, handing the pancakes into an already warmed oven. "I always miss some."

"Try a butter knife next time." Julia offered with a casual shrug.

"What?"

"When you're finished mixing and you think you have everything all smooth." Stating this, Julia paused; affecting a soft shrug as if that was, in truth, all that needed to be said.

"Yes?" Michael huffed impatiently, though the word came spliced with a hefty smirk, eyeing her more intently than he should, while he awaited her response.

"Just scrape along the grooves with a butter knife," she crooned, affecting yet another shrug. "And, ta-dah! No more lumps." Teasing with the obviousness of her tone, she grabbed his eyes with her own, and her fiery taunt surged to him bold, laughing without offering a single sound. A million things flew to his lips in response, none of which, she assumed, was appropriate enough to announce, as he only offered her the docility of a smirk.

"Now why didn't I think of that?" he chimed, baffled by the truth in that fact. It held tight the harnesses on his tongue.

"In comparison to you, I've spent a lifetime in the kitchen." Julia warbled as she broadened her smile. "You're newly birthed." She proclaimed with credence, her eyes brightening with the challenge hidden in her words. "Mine is a passion, and I'm good at it, if I do say so myself."

"I know you are, but——" grateful he caught the words before they flew from his mouth, he immediately stalled. Dragging the spatula across the heated surface of the griddle, as if removing something hard, Michael regulated his thoughts. Mentally, he bit his tongue in reproach for the almost foolish slip. "You're mocking me again, I see. Be careful, sometimes the mouse wins." He smiled, commending himself silently for the agile quip.

"How exactly is that statement mocking? I stated a fact, did I not?" Chortling the question with a faint sting hoist within the humor it held, Julia pulled a small towel from the rack, tipping the vessel forward. She fitted the pleated towel under the wide-base of the bowl. The new angle offered him an easier access to the depleting batter, and both brows rose slowly in defiance as she awaited his wryly response.

"You know, I may have preferred it the other way." Michael smugly countered, jerking the ladle through the batter, his mouth twitched at the falsehood bowing that thought. The advantage of her adjustment was immediately clear, splaying the batter more aptly to his hand.

"I'm sorry. Let me rectify that." Julia rejoined sweetly, reaching past him. She took hold of the bowl.

"No, no!" Michael carped, waving a hand across hers. He quickly blocked her attempt to remedy the chore. "You already did the work, the least I could do is…try it." Throwing her a generous smile, he expounded. "After all, you're the guest."

"And as usual, you're too magnanimous for mere words." She laughed, her voice warm and syrupy, gliding over his skin in a slow fluid-like slide.

"To a fault," He growled. Flashing then, what was surely, a superlative smile. The radiance of which, should have rendered her speechless and ruled the matter over and done, thus awarding him top prize in their benignant squabble. However, things are never quite that simple when they involved the mad alchemy that was her. Not to be outdone, Julia smiled back in rejoinder of his charge. Her tongue flicked, like a terse addendum, over the plumpness of her lips and, as if to mask her intent, long lashes slowly dropped, and the exotic dance ended almost the moment it began. Had he blinked, he would have missed the intent, but he had not. Not only had he witnessed the exploit, but he understood the meaning just as well, if not more.

Julia moved back to the sink to wash naught from fingers that held nothing to warrant their cleansing. Feeling the heat of his gaze on her back, she smiled. Triumphant in the victory she was sure she held.

Realizing his expression now bordered on that of a pubertal cub, Michael dropped his gaze to the task at hand, for although her gesture lasted mere seconds, it was enough to steal the thunder he thought he had won. The deed was a modest thing to look at, or perhaps so for a scant few. A simple roll of her tongue, it moved like the underlying of a wave. But he knew well his response when she applied said action to her kisses. Just thinking about it set his body to drool, fetching a new meaning to the premise of breakfast. She's lucky his mothe—*mom!*

Yanked swiftly into awareness, Michael's head whipped forward in a flash, his eyes then searched the far corner of the bar. Finding his mother's gaze fixed raptly on his, he groaned. Both elbows were planted firmly on the stone surface in approbation of the show. Clasped tightly in the grotto of her hands, her cup wavered close to her lips, and a truly satisfied smile tugged ingeniously at her face. Her eyes then played mischievously with his, recognizing fully the circumstance related to the two, amusement dawned as boldly as the sun. "Mom, how is it going?" Michael questioned tightly, sensing more than seeing Julia's equally stunned response. With months of never having an audience, they simply forgot about his mother's quiet, but intrusive presence, purposefully done, on that he was sure.

"Wonderful." Hyacinth warbled, dropping her eyes to her cup, she smiled. "Great coffee, is it new?" she asked, gazing assiduously at her son.

"No. Not very," Michael smiled, knowing the coffee she drank had been a favorite of hers for the past five years. "I've had it now for months, and have grown quite attached, actually."

"Really!" one perfectly arched brow rose slowly over the dainty mouth of her cup, staying perched as Hyacinth savored another taste of said drink.

"I can honestly say it's become a favorite of mine." He murmured dryly, his eyes again lifting to acquire his mother's gaze, even as his hands fostered their work. The richness in his tone softened, carefully caressing each word, he magnified their importance. "The flavor is quite grand."

"I believe I can see why." Hyacinth muttered in response, taking another sip from her cup. Her eyes discreetly swept the young beauty now waiting by her son. There was a tempestuous lenience that lingered between them, more than just the familiarity of lovers. The air between them was mature, augmented with conjectures for now, though spiced like the flavor of a good wine. She did not seem to need to drape his person for him to be aware of her presence. A fact you don't always see with the women her son seemed predisposed to date. Could this be the dawning of change?

Breakfast pinched forward languidly, forever engraved on each participant's mind, though for each, the reasons were as diverse as the day itself. With the preparation completed, Michael progressed to the table sandwiched by the two women he had plotted against for weeks, working diligently to schedule the perfect time for them to meet. His mind was fired bright with thoughts of his toils. Sitting between them, pride again boiled in his chest, and he silently gave thanks for still being clothed in his skin. The nervy twinges alone should have, no doubt, seen to the opposite of that end.

On their own, Michael's eyes flitted to Julia's face, being so used to doing so, they stayed. He could feel his mother's gape drilling hard at his face, and knew, with certainty, they were not just to send him her love. Swarms of questions were now aimed at his head. He also knew he had no other way to give her the answers she sought. Not without fully betraying his promise and he had no intention of doing that. The morsels he sprinkled throughout would have to suffice for now, since no other cryptic infer jumped forward to offer aid.

Years of living in the public's eye had schooled them in the art of communicating on the sly. A nod or a simple stroke of one's ear, could all have layered meanings attached, and they used such skill as the primary language between them—mostly when in the company of others. In the world they inhabit, you learn little tricks necessary for survival, or you'll sink farther than you swim.

His mother, however, showed none of the struggles that now hampered his mind or body. Ever the expert, she looked well collected from her dazzling, platinum perch on his left. Shifting her focus at times, she concentrated on the offerings of her plate, showing more enthusiasm for her food than her small appetite would ever allow. You could see well she was lost somewhere in the wild paddock of her thoughts, and, in truth, only rearranged the food on her plate. Yet the pleasantness of her smile never wavered once. She was as gracious and supportive as he knew she would be. There was no better mother on the planet, a true nurturer through and through. She gave everything from the heart. Her mind was fast, and the crumbs he fed her took her exactly where he wanted her to go, faster than even he had expected.

Even now as he watched her, he could still hear the wheels turning in her head. See the smoke coasting from her ears with the gear's quickness. Yet what mother wouldn't be in such a state? Michael mused, a smile touching his lips in delight. Hoisting his cup as if to drink, Michael caught the gleam in his mother's eyes, stemming the small chalice to the air, it hovered between them for no more than a millisecond—if that. In sustained silence, he touched the mug to his lips, and a smile broadened behind the concealment with the paltry show.

Hyacinth inclined her head as if to start the beginning of a nod, stopping the effort before it attained its core. Her focus shifted to the refilling of her cup, seeming now for the third time, though in actuality she only topped the liquid off. The action and the cup offered her an advantageous point to observe the room. Being able to watch her son and his guest with great leisure from behind the task, it gave her an almost saturated air of disinterest.

This was a whole new side of her son that she never once thought she would see, though one she was most pleased with. A first for her in all her years as a mother, could she be deciphering right? His words were well shrouded, so any questions she had would sadly have to wait his discretion. As enjoyable as the morning was, the strangling anxiety between perception and truth was wearing thin on her self-control. He was all she had left of her children, so whatever he had going on in his life, she had a right to know—and damn it—fast! He'd better not be enjoying her bemusement, she groaned, or he'll find himself branded with a great big bruise on those well-defined arms. *Was that love she just glanced in his eyes?*

"Oh, Michael," Hyacinth chanted, taking matters into her own hands. "I'm just about finished with everything for your birthday party, so don't try to weasel your way out. I need you to leave that entire day clear." She warned, and her finger, in its yielding of judgment, loomed accusingly across the table at her son, though inside, she rightly beamed with pride. Noting in her peripherals, Julia's quick glance of surprise now aimed at that very one. No woman who cares about a man ignores his birthday, any loving wife or girlfriend can attest to that. "Julia!" she smiled sweetly, turning just as quickly to the young beauty, almost singing her name. "I'd love for you and your family to come."

Julia's mind froze in its search of an adequate retort for an occasion as this, looking like a deer caught in the high blaze of a beam. Her always sharpened mind struggled for the right words to make sense of things. "Th-thank you, but…I–I couldn't." She stuttered, throwing an unsteady look in Michael's direction as if to gather some aid. "That's…for family."

"And friends." Hyacinth added quickly, unwilling to have any answer but the one she wanted, she persisted in her goal. "There'll be friends and some acquaintances, too. It's a simple thing in the afternoon, nothing formal, just good food, good company and good conversations, that all." She chirruped, glancing quickly at her son. Michael's eyes skid sharply across the table, holding in the place she sat. They lingered as if in wait for an unspoken request. Hyacinth ignored all aspect of his presence, though she was willing to bet his body now seethed with undiluted excitement, even if it could not be said. If there was any truth in her decoding, then she was sure he reared ecstatic with her plan, and the sequencing of that had always piloted her objectives.

"But…" Julia paused, not willing to openly insult the kind invitation. She is, after all, Michael's mother. Someone he obviously loves. She deserved that respect if nothing else. But then…*she's his mother!*

"You wouldn't refuse an old woman her simple joys, now would you?" Hyacinth asked sweetly in a near feeble voice, again smiling with pure charm at the young beauty, seeming oblivious to the spike of her unease. "My son's life is far too busy to spend at any length with his aging mother. My only joy comes from my activities, their success and the people greeted along the way. Call it my elixir if you will. It's what keeps me going. So come on. Take a break from all the work my son has you under, and come and enjoy a piece of birthday cake. No presents necessary." She coaxed, and as if to halt the younger woman's mind, her hand flew like a limp fan to her face. "We stopped that a long time ago. Just you and your family is all that's required."

Methodically, Michael folded his napkin, making certain each seam was ironed stiff with the press of his fingers. He leveled the cup in front of his face as if to inspect the fragility of its rim. Surreptitiously, his eyes slipped over its edge, stealing a glance at his mother, amusement welled in the pit of his stomach. This was his mother at her best. She can be downright rabid when she wants something. Thankfully, he was in full agreement with her plan, and was more than content to sit back, with a look of indifference, while secretly urging her on.

"Well…" Julia sighed, her voice small as she struggled for a proper resolve. The fact that it was his birthday shackled her like a prisoner afield, feeling somewhat obligated to do something. Even while knowing she could celebrate with him in the privacy of his home. Yet a part of her wanted to be there, and she wondered how their secret would play around his family and friends.

"Good! Then it's settled." Hyacinth interrupted with a light chirp, her voice like the interchange of a note. "I won't take no for an answer." She announced with a pleasing smile. "It will give you and Michael something to talk about when I'm gone. He'll tell you what a pushy old woman I am. That I'm sure of." She groaned, though her eyes twinkled as she turned her gaze upon her son. "Don't try to deny it. I know some of the talks you have behind my back." She grumbled. Cutting across whatever had been Michael's intended response, deliberately silencing the man. Her gripes knew no end. "But I'm old and I'll be gone soon enough, and what will you say then?" Again directing her gaze to her son, Hyacinth's brows hovered, as if frozen in an elevated state of wonderment. She returned her attention, of a sudden, to Julia's face. "September tenth, at two, Michael will give you the address." Broadcasting thus in a sugary tone, she brightened, and one would not have guessed that that was, at all, a possibility. Yet her action proved the assumption wrong. Tilting her head a mere fraction towards her son, her smile gave of her thought.

"Thank you for inviting me." Julia nodded, smiling the acceptance, as there was not much else to be said. "I look forward to being there." Sharpening her nod as if to affirm the decision to herself, her eyes quickly sought out Michael's face, needing his approval. In-part, she lingered, not wanting him to feel intruded upon. His eyes held hers warmly for a trice, and the jewel-like depths screamed, rather than murmured, his choice, enveloping her in a full embrace. A sudden quiet descended on the room as a result, as if each, in their separate guild, adjourned with their own thought. Great attention was given to the remaining morsels residing on their plates.

"Well!" the intrusion came on the soft lilt of Hyacinth's voice. Tapping her fingers together, her wrist turned with an elegant flare, noting the time without seeing the answer for sure. "As wonderful as this breakfast has been," she sighed, her eyes sweetly sweeping both faces. "And it's been a treasure." She averred, and hazel eyes, in assurance of such truth, dueled playfully with its mirrored self. "I have a meeting of sorts that I need to be on my way to."

"Meeting?" Michael frowned. "On a Sunday, normal business hours still not enough for you?"

"It's more like two old friends catching up, with maybe a spot of business while we're at it, nothing more." Turning, she gave Julia her unwavering attention, stilling any further comment from her son. "It was truly wonderful to meet you, Julia." Hyacinth smiled. "And I look forward to seeing you in a few weeks. Remember now, or I may have to come fetch you myself." Mischief danced riotously in the sparkly beds of her hazel orbs, jumping to settle on her son. It chipped at the sweet smile she bore.

"It was very nice to meet you, too, and no, I won't forget." Julia pledged, returning the polite gesture with her own pleasant smile.

The boisterous bellow of her chair cut the pending silence, snarling across the floor, it howled rowdily through the room. Hyacinth moved around the table as Michael's chair sang the echoing chord, taking a position by her son; both smiles grew rich as their gazes dropped to her.

"Excuse me a minute while I walk her out." Michael droned, dropping his arm around his mother's shoulders. He tucked her against his side. Once honed a patterned drubbing, their footsteps dimmed as they weaved through the halls of the house, dying in the distance. A heavy thud announced their departure through the door.

Julia smiled at the house's sudden stillness, the excitement of the morning dying in the abrupt method it began. The deviation from their norm had not turned out as badly as she expected. Meeting his mother was definitely a terrifying affair, but that dread eventually eased to a more sedated numb. Gathering a glass container, she stacked the leftovers inside, delivering the small bowl to the refrigerator in her strive to be busy.

"Did you enjoy breakfast?" Michael murmured in an absent tone, gazing out at the lawn, as if her response mattered little to his ears.

"I did. You did a good job."

"I'm glad," he smiled, nodding in response. "It's a great day, isn't it?" Michael asked through what funneled like a deep groan, his smile widening.

"Will it be scrabble or do we now proceed to charades?" Hyacinth probed, wondering more on what she witnessed inside. She watched him keenly.

"What?"

"You heard me." She hissed, her retort flying back quickly. Prying eyes analyzed fully the mien of his face. "What can't or won't you tell me outright? Or better yet, why?"

"I have no idea what you talking about." Michael smirked, though the gesture ended in a soft chuckle.

"You don't?"

"I don't." He shrugged.

"Okay, my love." Hyacinth sang. "Then tell me, how have you been?" changing her tactics, she sweetened her voice. Whatever the reason, he's choosing vague as his only means of communication.

"I'm good. Things are very good."

"Good. Nothing new you'd like to share with your mother?

Michael's answer dashed forward as a shrug, even as his eyes danced damningly into hers. "No." The single word slipped from his lips without delay, though his eyes never faltered in their press. "We talk all the time. I've granted you updates over lunch, dinner and sometimes…even breakfast." He hummed, his shoulders lifting softly against her. "You know everything that goes on in my life."

"I see." As if collecting evidence only a mother could, vastly experienced eyes lingered on his face, and when she again spoke. Her voice held what seemed muted interest wedged tightly between each space. "And work, any new ventures you care to share with an old lady?"

"Stop playing coy, old woman." Michael laughed. "I've served you everything I can from the pantry."

"Did you, now?"

"You know I did."

"And no one new has turned that handsome head of yours?"

"There's no one new, mom." Michael vowed, his face broadening with a full smile, knowing it was not exactly a lie. Julia was no longer considered new to his life, if she ever had. Having been deeply enmeshed with her for the past six months, though at times, it felt like forever had somehow sailed by since their beginning. More essential than the rest, it was as if her face was etched in his memories from a time preceding him.

"So you wanted me to meet her, but you won't talk to me?"

"I have no idea what you're talking about," Michael laughed. "We just got our signals crossed, that's all."

"Why is that?"

"What?"

"Why can't you say?" at his shrug, she continued in her probe. "Will you?"

"I can tell you this," Michael smiled. "There's no place I'd rather be than where I am at this moment." He paused, squeezing her hands gently. "I can't give you what you want right now, mom, but when I have something to tell, you'll be the first, as always. Now stop pushing."

"Pushing? Can't a mother show some interest in her son's life without being called names?"

"No names, pushy woman, just a warning." Michael chuckled, turning his mother towards her car.

"You're in a hurry to get rid of me, eager to get back to…work?"

"Yes." Michael drawled, his smile slowly widening. "We have a lot to discuss before this day is through."

"How very productive of you," Hyacinth scoffed. "Your father would be very proud." The tame words hung weirdly above them as if needing a category with which to fall in. Slowly, they dissipated from mind with the aid of a tame wind. Taking a slow breath, she stared down the long stretch of his drive. "She's stunning." She whispered dryly as if to herself, dropping her purse on the passenger seat.

"Who?" Michael asked innocently, a wide grin gripping his face.

"You don't find features like hers with contrasting assemblage every day." She smiled, dipping like a graceful cat into her seat. Her ankles softly locked, hovering slightly before they touched the carpeted floor of her car, her body gliding quickly in-tow. "Smart, composed and looked to be strong. I like her. She seems quite genuine, too, that's almost an anomaly in our crowd." She announced then, ignoring his weak shrug, since the skin on his face was now stretched to its max. His head bobbed in answer as if its joints had gone suddenly loose, and she could not help but wonder if that was all he wanted of the two, an informal introduction, so to speak. Ecstatic with her response, he reached calmly for her door, pushing it shut as she started the car. His smile was ceaseless. "Okay, my darling, let me run." She sang softly. "I love you too much, you know that."

"I know. I love you, too, mom." Michael whispered, pressing a kiss to the cheek she leaned out the window.

"There's nothing like the first day of spring after a long, cold winter, is there?" she smiled, staring distractedly out the windshield as if suppressed fully in thought. "It changes everything, doesn't it, son?" She smiled, sounding retrospective in the body of her speech. She dragged her eyes from its mark to acquire his gaze, though she gave him no time to respond. "Goodbye, my would-be angel." Hyacinth chirped, rolling her car forward without pause, she waved with finality as her vehicle amassed some pace.

Almost trancelike, Michael watched as her car coasted down the long driveway, disappearing like a phantom in the brilliance of day. The brandish of his smile was unyielding. Turning, he strode towards the house, and quick strides, maneuvered by his mind's crusade, propelled him through the halls in a flash. Depositing him raptly in an empty kitchen, his eyes hastily scanned the room. Already, everything was revoked to a replica of its earlier self, even the griddle now stood tall inside the basin-like inlet of the sink.

"Julia?" Michael called from the threshold's edge, his voice faintly winging through the reticence space, straining gravely to abjure his excitement as he waited her reply. Drinking shallow breaths to stable the menacing swells, each gulp sailed like a trifling gust, sounding scantly lyrical in its whirring departure from his mouth. Her voice flitted to him from the bowels of the family-room. There she stood gaping out the window at the view, and his arms wasted no time with intent. Slipping around her waist, he pinned her body to his, manipulating the radius of her turn. His mouth hungrily plunged, ravaging her, in an instant, with his usual verve. "I've been dying to do that all morning." He informed hoarsely against her mouth. "Sorry about my mother." He smiled, and it was a sincere effort to keep the ruinous gloat from taking its rightful place on the placard of his face. Yet knowing he needed to attempt some form of rationalization on the morning's protagonist and her wont, if only to offer a placating theory to smooth the event—one favoring that of an explanation.

Julia chuckled under the onslaught of his mouth. "She doesn't like to take no for an answer, does she?"

"Nope," He rasped, brushing her lips with his. "She's used to getting her way, but she's harmless."

"I can see that. Do you mind that I'm coming?"

"Why would I?" he inquired bluntly, his head sharply reeling back, analyzing her expression with a near scowl.

"Well, you were less than happy at your own pool party, remember?"

"That wasn't because you were there; that was solely due to the outfit you wore… and my lack of nourishment leading up to that event." Breathing his answer in her mouth, he smiled. "Remember?"

"So no swimsuit, then?" Julia teased, leaning her head back as she gazed in his eyes.

"You can wear it if you want," he growled. "Just don't expect me to keep my hands to myself. I can't promise you I'll be a good-boy."

"When are you ever a good-boy?"

"I was good at the pool party, wasn't I?" Michael smirked, his voice thundering softly against her cheek. "I didn't even take your offer to pet kitty, and boy...did I ever want to play with kitty."

"You got your due."

"Not even close, woman." Michael growled, tightening his hand around her waist, he pressed her firmly to the bulges of his body. "I don't want to waste anymore of the few hours we have left in this day." Grumbling thus, he teased the side of her neck. "I won't see you again for another fourteen days, and with only hours left in this one, you need...to get out of these clothes."

"My worth just keeps getting lower and lower, doesn't it?"

"Oh, but on the contrary, it's because of the magnitude of your worth why I need to see these clothes off." He averred, offering a languidly structured smile, his voice danced warm and husky upon her throat. Quietly, his hands vanished beneath her shirt, assisting the garment over her ribs, his fingers glided in the guise of a leisured caress.

"You do know I'm quite capable of undressing myself, right?" she quipped, squinting curiously through an endearing smile.

"I know. But when I do it, I get to see...smell...taste and feel you as I go." He rejoined through a grumbly purr, his hands manipulative in the exploit of her body. Caressing the round mounds with infinite care before pulling the barrier over her head. "I'm patient enough to wait for the last of my senses to be appeased." He smiled, retreating a mere step from her body. His eyes ravished her renderings for what evolved like the miring of time. "God, what a sight you make." Michael roughly sighed. Pulling her back to his chest, he dove greedily for her mouth, and the passionate heat of her response, held him suspended as he molded her to him to supplicate his want of more.

Reminiscent of a fiery call to war in some distant time and land, his heart thence drummed in the forest of his chest, and swells of pimples colonized his skin in reaction of thus. A fervent tremor bore then full evidence of her work, quarrying through his body at will like the odd tempo of a dance. *Man, I could kiss you forever.* Michael whispered in his head, sighing this to her in the privacy of his skull, his entire body grew malignant with his awareness of her, and her throaty whimpers did not command his will to broker control. When at last Michael lifted his head, he stood as a well primed weapon, immaculate in its design, and masterfully efficient at its job. Cocked, and ready to do damage, it awaits only its master's hand to but emit the blow.

Silently, his fingers caressed the button on her pants, and, like a weakened maiden under a spell, it quickly fell from her waist. A hand strolled possessively inside the garment in an illustration of intent, while the other maneuvered the receding of her zipper. Soon, both hands worked inquisitively upon the warmth of her skin, one channeling deeper than that of the other. In succession, his breath refused to sail from his nostrils with ease, for with anticipation rearing its greedy head, it howled more from a tunnel than the quiet of his skull. Eager hands ardently rode the sensual lines of her body, pushing the garment from her hips. His eyes humbly grazed her slender thighs, thighs that marked the patent runway to his terminus of choice.

Sinking to his knees, Michael flattened the cottony raiment to the floor. Silent in his prodding as she stepped clear, and his eyes, in their spiraling yen, fed fervently upon the crevice of her body. In appreciation of the view, his lips skimmed the inside of her thighs, and an awkward smile crept slowly athwart his face, seeing then that she watched him as closely as he watched her. Eyes big and igneous in their exhibit, vaunted the sweetest connotation in their depths, stilling his heart between the boisterous drumming.

The corners of her mouth barely dented with her ensuing smile, lowering her hand to his face. She brushed lightly at his cheek. Her fingers swayed like the scuff of a gentle breeze, encouraging his rise with a slight tilt of her hand. Michael silently conceded the request, leaving light kisses in his slow ascension. His voice came like the distorted droning in the eye of a storm.

"A man could look at you forever and never grow weary of the view." He sighed, his voice slanting like a dark, husky drawl.

"And do I get to see what wares you harbor for dicker behind those barriers of yours?" she asked, cooing the ensnaring query while she caressed his chest.

"Seems only fair," Michael shrugged, pulling at the neck of his shirt, and as if by magic, it promptly dangled from his fingers before mutely touching the floor. His brow rose quizzically as he waited before her like a show piece, of sort, in wont of approval.

"Not bad." She smiled, tilting her head slightly, she sweetly asked. "Is there more?"

"Perhaps," he leered. "But it may help if you tell me what you're looking for. I may be able to save you some time in the drudgery of having to search." Dragging each word judiciously over his tongue, Michael's shoulders sheepishly vaulted the air, returning to its proud stance as if he discarded the decision in the middle of its pursuit.

"Thank you. But I think I'll best know it when I see it." She countered, gifting then a provocative smile. Her dark eyes glowed warmly in his.

A soft nod preceded Michael's answer of her goad, as lean fingers clambered to his waist to see the chore through, and with what seemed a mere twitch of his hand, his button rested undone, opening himself to the warm stroking of her gaze. Both thumbs flew inside the waistband of his boxers and pants, ready, by the blatancy clipped to the act, to eradicate them jointly in one sweep.

"Wait!" she sang, negating his intention with the gentle stilling of her hand, Julia again stepped close. "This part I claim as my own." She smiled, and the hardened muscles of his chest flexed under the inspection of her hands. Languidly falling to his waist, they aided the plummet of said clothing to the floor, while her eyes leisurely accompanied the garment's descent. Michael's hands quickly encircled her frame as she straightened, caressing her buttocks. The heat of his hands widely contrasted with the smooth coolness in her skin. "Mmmmm," she exclaimed through a protracted purr. "Exquisite, and not even at its full potential," declaring thus, her smile widened as she touched her body to his, feeling him throb with suspense against her.

Gently, Michael tugged at the barricading ornament at the back of her head, sending the mass of her curls tumbling to her shoulders in disarray. His fingers glided with care through the silken locks. Dipping his head, he filled his lungs with her scent.

"Am I allowed to carry out my own search on you?" he rasped, walking his lips down her neck.

"Are you, in any way, definitive as to what you want?" Julia tested coyly, simpering this amidst the kisses she now rested on his chest.

"Not particularly." He whispered atop her ear. "I usually need to forage my way through before I know for sure. It might take me a while to see the job done."

"I have some time." She breathed, giving life to her words. Her tongue stroked deliberate fire across the slopes of his chest.

"Explore, invade and conquer, that's my favorite sport." Michael growled, plucking her from her determined bent. He rummaged her mouth, and although she came to him soft as a morning in spring, she nourished him as wild as a tempest at sea. A deep moan funneled his throat as he swept her from the floor, and like an eroding sigh, her breath fell soft against his neck. Outside, the sun blazed its radiance across an aging day, and evening threatened from an ever dwindling distance. Goodbyes, they realized, would soon have to be said, but not for this moment, and not before a euphoric end.

Chapter Thirty Two

Splashed mordantly across the entire page, the picture postured like a galactic gonfalon for the world to see. Two people looking frighteningly intimate at a glance. The depiction splendidly painted the scene of a sizzling romance, though nothing could be farther from the truth. Yet the enigma of investigative reportage was of little credence in this display. Only speculative parallels were needed for things to be proclaimed as truth.

Michael gawked at the spectacle Sam puckishly left him on his desk. Ominously shrouded in shock, his once lively demeanor firmly fled with a glance, and a horrified expression now wrought the features of his face. Assuming he would find humor in the outrageous report, she left it as a centerpiece for the chaotic tailoring of his desk, sprawled bluntly atop a papery knoll. It bore the preemptive valor of an assailant's attack. Little did she know how wrong she would be with the implementing of said jest, for humor did not surface once in the throngs of reactions he had.

It was an innocent kiss between friends. But that was not what the interpretation inferred, nor what the story implied. And the conjecture, Michael wanly confirmed, would have indeed been hilarious had it come at any other junction in his life. But as it stood, he found no waggish spoof to ease the stinging effigy, not when it held the probability to impede with the succession of his plans.

He'd only seen Camille once in the last two years, and that was at "*Takoda*" of all places, where the night was a healthy mixture of business and cause. Benefiting needy kids, the silent auction had had both Phillip and Adam, their lawyer and a trusted friend, bidding heavily against each other in support of the foundation and their projected mission. The impromptu visit had added immensely to the drear of his azygous mood, though that, it seemed, bred more mental than not. Since the evening had left his, unusually restless demeanor, further tattered than the dull, gloomy way it began. *He didn't even bid, for Christ's sake!* Only donating a sum, they eventually just left, sighting fatigue as the cause. And that was eons before the evening's estimated close. How the *hell* did they come to such a ludicrous decision after all this time?

Suddenly, the air grew pungent. Reeked strongly with the persistent tang of agitation, worry pressed its hulking mass against his chest. Thus it syphoned the certitude of his strength. Michael groaned with unconcealed disgust, grounding his face deep into the palm of each hand. The treble of his breath sliced through the stark air like a blade, and he hoped, in his heart, that this would not exact some costly penance, in anyway, from his life. Will she believe him? Will she give credence to the verity of his words? Would she understand his innocence once he explained that the picture was nothing but a lie, a farce to interpret someone else's truth? His reputation for never being faithful was not exactly propaganda or hype. Would that past return to hurt him now? He'd never been this committed to anyone before in his life. An astonishing feat if dissected of its meaning, since they had yet to title what it was that they had. Yet regardless of the lapse, he'd never been this happy before in his life, and he did not intend to lose her over something as innocuous as that.

"Eleven, thirty-seven," Michael grumbled darkly, glowering at the clock as if he intended vengeance upon the inanimate piece, a decisive snort dashed forth in aid of his query. *She should have some free time to talk.* His inner voice croaked, sorting through the relentless whirring in his head, he wiped all thoughts from their place but the existence of one. The grumbly words leapt to his mind with an agile thrust, pushing his body in motion like the propellant in an aberrant gust. Raucously, Michael set his chair on a backwards sail, tipping the massive lounger in his haste. It grazed the shelves at his back before slowing to a halt. Grabbing what he candidly concurred with as "Rags" he stormed from the dispirited stench now crowding the room, acquiescent that the name had never been more fitting a title than it was now.

It may have been the galloping pace of his mind that gave the verdure of his action wings, or it may have just been that he sped. Whatever the cause, his truck now consumed the thoroughfares of her neighborhood like a vortex on the hunt. Soon to be conquering the linear of her street, Michael glanced at the cellphone solemnly roosted in the console, in near reach of his hand. Shifting almost anxiously with each turn, it rattled through the cab like the weird clink of a cow's bell, and whether taunting or inviting, he had yet to rule on that.

Now would be a good time to call and warn her of his impending visit, but this was not the kind of visit he ever envisioned they'd have. Not the kind of conversation he thought would ever dredge between them. Not now, and certainly not this soon in their start. What do you say to ease the puncture of that? And how does one broach a subject of its kind on the phone?

Turmoil held his body in agitated suspense, uncertain of the level to which his feelings mine. He knew only one logic to be true, that being the benefit of a face to face, needing to look her in the eyes when he tells her that it's all a notional tail. He needed that as much as he needed to witness her reaction when she hears such denial from his mouth, for he needed to see that she understood the true substance of what was being said. That confirmation was desired as desperately as he was now destined to give in his accounting of the facts.

Her house looked almost desolate standing at the end of the long driveway. Or was that just his own desolation sawing through his head? Taking a deep breath, Michael strolled squarely to the door, jamming a finger immediately to the protruding bell, as if afraid he would waver from his goal.

"Michael! Hi!" Julia exclaimed as she swung open the door, happy to see the recipient of her thoughts. Well cognizant their feisty repartee would now be an added feature to her hurrying day.

"We need to talk." Michael barked, spitting the gruff reply to the sweetness of her greeting. His expression abnormally blank, that being all he could manage through the constricted muscles in his jaw. For the moment, his witty badinage was lost, as was his usually large arsenal of small-talk.

"Sure. Uh…come in." She frowned, and the act aptly transmitted her fears to the bright outlet of her face. She'd never seen him look any dour than he did now, not since that unpleasant conversation of the previous month, one she prayed they were not about to repeat in any sense. His body brushed hers doggedly as she moved to let him in, and for the first time, since their fiery existence of two, there was no lingering embrace on which to harp on. No hello kiss sweetened the vaunt of her day, and no clever or lusty remarks were given to lighten her mood. *What could possibly have him so beside himself?* Julia tensely sighed, worry now transcending her mind. "Are you okay?" she timidly asked, finding she was suddenly more terrified than worried of the cause.

"Are you alone?" he asked gruffly, frowning back the question as she locked the door.

"Yes…." The soft sigh fell mawkishly at his feet, faltering as surely as her breath. It died as he furthered his progress in the house, and the air around them felt suddenly despondent, ruched well, with the sharpening of her fears.

"Good." Michael grunted after a trice, not knowing what better diction to interject. His eyes blanketed the living-room in thought, pondering where was best suited to launch his unpleasant explanation. Should he just stay his ground on this neutral site, or should he risk venturing further in the house?

"Michael, what's wrong?" Julia nervously asked, taking a step towards him. He quickly shunned her effort by springing precipitously back, furthering the distance between them in the guise of a bullet.

"Wait!" He warned in a rough breath, and his fingers moved, in succession of his croak, like clans of a reptile through the short bristles of his hair. Dropping roughly down his neck, he dragged it athwart his flesh as if to soothe a pestering ache. As if to use as a club, the so called "Rag" was rolled compactly in a cylindrical form, clutched firmly in his left hand. It now waited at his back. "You should sit." Michael murmured through a heavy breath, his hand shooting abruptly through the air, indicating just that. The formality of the living-room, it seemed, had assimilated his need, preferring the rigidness at the moment than the intimate setting of the other rooms. Slowly, she complied with his wish, lowering herself indignantly. She dropped controlled to a seat, an expectant mask veiling her eyes.

Julia's breathing immediately stopped, and had it not been for the loud, chaotic hammering in her chest, she would have likely faulted a trance. The intensifying anxiety had grown unexpectedly strong, and its spikes now shredded the fleshing in her chest.

Without further wording, Michael handed her the folded mess, the appearance looking true to its wildly known nickname. Warped, mangled pages curled tattily upwards upon itself, seeming like a disbanded tube than anything else.

"What's this?" Julia asked before uncoiling said chaos, wondering why he thought a tabloid magazine would be of importance to her. She gazed numbly at the mess in her hand. No words followed in answer to the question asked. Standing inert in rejoinder, he looked as tightly helical as the publication in her hand. Beautiful eyes gaped back at her coolly, void of hints or explanation. Jagged barbs heralded his demand with determination poisoning their depths, willing her effort until she opened the tattered mess to see for herself. Julia's fingers worked slowly over the rounder pages, carefully flattening each fold. Horror jumped from the waiting page to rest exposed to her eyes, stalling her momentum as surely as the foray of death.

"Oh." She managed through a sharp intake, as a sudden tightness surged possessively to her throat. The pain of which was like nothing she readily recognized or understood, for the thrashing in her chest bred ludicrous in its pace, setting her body to tremble. It would not grant her hands rest. The room grew deathly silent in its wait, while she absorbed, with a shudder, the couple plastered on the page.

Like the intricate phase of some horrific crash, there it sat before her eyes. The man she had been unquenchably intimate with, now stood with his arms around someone else, and she could not have torn her gaze away from the depiction of such, even had she dared try. Eagerly drinking in the details that laid bare to her gape, she studied them as if for a test.

Outside, the sound of a bird's song sharpened the tuning of her ears to a solemn appreciation. The rendition sounding to her sad, though it beautifully serenaded the moment in time, and it felt as if the song was meant to gall her further into feeling a fool.

"I swear to you. It's not real. At least, not in the way that it looks." Michael vowed, his words climbing through a rough whisper. "I promise you, I've kept my word. I haven't looked at anyone else."

"Who is she?" Julia acidly asked, her words coming undeniably dry.

"Camille Straus." He droned, still standing across from her like a stranger awaiting news from a crucial missive, one now caged by her hands. His voice drifted to her firm. Inversely, she needed to fully understand the importance of his words without any influence seeping through—least of all his. "The two of us have been friends for more than twenty years now; we were just catching up." At her tart-like gaze Michael quickly illuminated his point. "On what's going on in our own lives, that's it."

Julia's eyes again travelled the cozy scene depicted on the page, drawing on minute details that were there to find. Her mind was like a blank slate in the midst of a vital test. Their mouths loomed, in its intimate press, only inches from each other, her hand resting gently on his face, and it was not unlike what she must look like when she leaned to him for a kiss. "Were you two...are you two in—"

"No! Never!" Michael howled, his answer flying by her like a blur, grateful that the abettor in this was not a former lover. He almost sighed with relief. "Camille and I have never been anything more than just friends."

"Never, not even the type of friendship *we* have?" Julia intoned softly, gazing hard into his eyes. "And is that even the truth, Michael?"

I've never had what I have with you with anyone else. His mind screamed, yet knowing this was not the time to bridge that gap. He rearranged his thoughts. "Not even when we both partied together—never!"

"You two look awfully cozy, Michael." Julia groaned, her eyes again scanning the picture, dissecting whatever detail she could discern. Perhaps something missed in her previous scrutiny of the shot.

"I know it doesn't look like it, but I promise you, it was an innocent peck between friends, nothing more." Michael sighed, sitting by her side at last. His body dwarfed her wilted frame. "I told you I saw a few old friends while I was there last, and although I may not have mentioned her by name, I know I distinctly said 'she'. I have nothing to hide pertaining Camille or anyone else."

"And yet she's the only picture I see here, Michael. Unless there's more?" she inquired hastily, frowning as the thought raced through her head. "Is there?"

"I don't know! That's very hard to say." Michael shrugged, not knowing what answer to give to placate the point. There was no way for him to offer a guarantee on such issues as that, for he knew not how many pictures of him still floated in paparazzi-land, or on what speculative positions they held. The lights on their cameras are a near constant, any innocent embrace could be made to look like something else. "There are a lot of pictures being taken depending on where I am, or how desperate the photographer is. Anything can be made to look more than it is."

Julia's eyes grazed the sultry portrait yet again, wondering should she take him at his word. There was definite truth to the argument he gave—truth she could well understand. But a playboy is always just that, are they not? They never truly renounce their duplicitous ways. Was she foolish to have entered into a treaty with such a man? Ending it now would staunch any other surprises he may have down the road, saving her from the hazards of more pain. "I will give you—this...thing between us, an out. A chance for us to walk away as friends, or...maybe—"

"No!" he growled, slicing her words with grimness marking its depth.

"We could take some time apart, Michael." She advised tightly, continuing the arid spiel without lifting her head. "This way we can both clear our heads. Reassess as to how we feel about the road we're on. Maybe after...a while, I don't know. We could come back with fresh eyes and mind or just...fold here and now...Call the whole thing..." she droned, her voice trailing slowly to its death, finding the moment especially hard. Pain cruised as her most prominent comrade in her time of need.

"Not on your life!" Michael scowled, moving quickly. Large hands swallowed the smaller of hers. "Ask Phillip if you must! He was there. We went together and we both left at the same time. Camille and I sat in plain sight the entire time we were there. What reason would I have to seek out someone else? Camille of all people! What could she possibly do for me?"

"I would imagine the same thing I do for you." Julia hummed, and a quiet smile slowly clambered the raw depths of her chest, ebbing the dark hollowing of her pain. For the first time since he entered the house, she felt an inkling of hope, liking that Phillip was named chaperone for the offending night. Unsure if her reason for the uncertainty lied only within the pages of trust. Or was it just that they had no base or foundation on which to hedge this strange liaison they have? Nothing for her to use as a basis of judge, only tenets in an association established by her. Was she wrong?

"I doubt that with all sincerity." He droned, brushing his lips lightly against the skin of her wrist. His warm breath glided over her like a plumose caress. "I'm unbelievably well fed, there's no need for me to stray."

"Would you tell me if you wanted to?" she asked through a choppy whisper, hoping he would give her the truth. But in candor, she hoped he would make the matter right. Eradicate the harsh churning in her stomach and, too, the pain within her chest. With one definitive swipe, he could make her body whole once more.

"I'll tell you that I haven't thought, or looked at another woman since you. Nor have I wanted to. I'm too busy coming up with the things I want to do to you—to think—much less crawl into someone else's bed. Yours is the only bed I'm crawling in." Michael vouched hoarsely, dipping his head to hers, he clasped her face to his, and his eyes commanded naught but her full attention. "Julia, please—please believe me. There's no one else! I swear to you on everything that I am. On everything I've become, on who I am when I'm with you, on my life. There is no other."

On its own, a sniff escaped the pause, scratching the silence as tears blindly welled in her eyes. Her head simulated a faint nod, yet no words accompanied the action to title her intent. Was he telling her the truth? His words had tunneled through her as he spoke, and she felt the bolstering effect as her body absorbed them as food, while her mind blindly reasoned the declaration truth. Was she being naive to conclude the matter such? Something inside her chose to trust him, and she badly needed it to be so with every fiber of her being. Somewhere deep inside, she needed him. And she no longer wanted to ignore that truth, for she could no longer claim that as a factual account.

"Okay." Julia sighed, ending the strain of the silence she bred. She again nodded, and her voice propelled like air across his cheek.

"Okay." He affirmed with an absent nod, dragging the continuous bounce past acceptable as he crushed her to his chest. His eyes clambered to some distant place as he savored the moment and its meaning, and as if manipulated by a hand, the tight semblance of a smile slowly marketed a corner of his face, in what elapsed like eons. Michael held her like a new source of life, letting the slender press of her body grant him the comfort he desperately sought. As he needed to affirm that she fully belonged to him. His breath came then as a long, gladdened sigh. Grateful, a blatant lie did not hurt what he'd come to treasure most.

———————

September tenth blew into existence like the dispersing of an overcharged bullet. Menacingly aimed at some vital organ—if not all. Michael's birthday party now sits precipitously at hand. The occasion danced perilously on every emotion she had, kicking up dust of excitement and fear with every stomp, and as if to mock her tumultuous plight. The weather turned out one of its best creations in days, breaking from a week of wet or overcast days. It promised an auspicious occurrence—for him.

Only thirty minutes from her home, the gated community of Brentwood Estate was less intrusive on her family than she had hoped. Removing yet another reasonable excuse from a well diminished tray, while she yet struggled with decisions of old. Her mind had to be well tattered and bruised by now, having been tugged in opposite directions for weeks. It sat no better than it had on the day she accepted the lure, wanting, yet not wanting, to give an appearance.

The wrought-iron gate stood wide opened at the end of a long, cobblestone drive. A diverse collection of luxury showpieces crowded the wide thoroughfare in pairs, trickling deep along the shoulder of the street. They pranced like the luxuriant guests of an exotic show.

Julia slowed as she drove past the majestic apparition called a house, though the building she now assessed, in no way, came close to that miniscule name. Feeling strongly like running, her fingers tightened on the steering wheel of her car, and had she been alone in that instant, she most likely would have done just that. However, at the moment it meant perjuring herself with her kids. Should she, on a whim, defect so bluntly from a promise made, any explanation she gave would not bring enough satisfaction without furthering a lie. Almost begrudgingly, Julia parked in an opening on the street, making certain she left ample room for escape—should such an occasion arise. She needed a clear path with which to take her leave.

Music and chatter could be heard coming faintly from the house to the street, dousing the pleasantness of the day with a pledge of merriments to be had. A sudden cackle rung the eerie stillness surrounding the space, bursting atop the melodic hum as her feet crowned the first step. And even though it came, like a vociferous jangle, from the back, tiny demons warned that it was directed at her. A cringe surfaced as the thought swirled tauntingly through her head, confident everyone was about to know what it was she protected. She could not settle the roiling of her nerves. *What are you doing? You don't belong here,* the ridiculed tone hummed. Yet, irrespective of logic, the argument's bleat came low in start, it soon shrieked with conviction in her head.

It was not that she thought the occupants better than her, or that she believed they stood above her status, nor did she think of herself as less than the rest. But that sanity depicted its ascendency of the rest, she truly did not belong in this place. She was neither friend nor family to anyone already fenced within. Michael being her only link, and even that could hardly be easily defined, not enough so to be considered okay. The sound of Richard's continuous gawk set in stone what was already on her mind—*she really should not be here.* "What do you say guys, should we just turn around and make a run for the car? We could be gone before anyone suspects we were even here." Julia asked through a fixed smile, though inside she was deathly earnest, given the option, she would be gone.

"I want to go in!" Richard shrieked excitedly, his sister quickly following with her own elated squeal.

"Me too!" Rachel exclaimed in awe; her eyes wide as it strolled over the architectural wonder.

"Are you sure guys? I happen to still have my keys out." she laughed, yet the light titter sounded nervous and false to her ears, though to prove the validity of her offer. She let the keys hop jauntily to their faces. In some strange way, the sound was almost music to her ears, as if lending her a small source of its clout in her time of need. The door swung open even while she swayed in contemplation, and Michael's mother, of all people, proclaimed herself their greeter.

"Julia! Hello!" Hyacinth chirped from the wide arching of the entrance. The sweet florally scent of her perfume greeting them as conspicuously as she did. A pleasant bouquet, with meticulously designated spice, the aroma serenaded like a signature piece. "I'm so glad you made it!" She sang, and cool fingers clutched expressively to the younger woman's hand, as if to stall her wont of retreat. If on their first meeting she thought the young woman exotically stunning, then she just elevated the bar to unsurpassed. It's no wonder her son was so taken. She was literally breathtaking. "Did you find us okay?"

"Yes I did, thank you. The directions were very explicit." Julia answered calmly, though feeling anything but. A fish void of its rightful home effectively described her angst. Maybe it was the gnawing punctures of their fib that had her so on end. Perchance that was her reason for wanting to evaporate in the very place that she stood. "Mrs. Dunhill, this is m—"

"Please, call me Hyacinth."

"I'm sorry, Hyacinth." Stumbling over the name in her head, she righted herself. "Hyacinth, this is, Delia, my mother, and my children, Rachel and Richard."

"Hello." Delia muttered politely, well aware of whom Hyacinth was. Only a few years younger than the once famous actress, her loyalty as a fan had yet to dwindle from its height.

"Hello and welcome!" Hyacinth smiled, sweeping her view downwards to the children. Her hazel eyes sketched each face with warmth. "Oh, my, look at you!" She warbled, touching a finger to Richard's chin. "You're such a handsome young man!" The

smile that followed her lively relay stayed, though her eyes grew distant as if remembering another time. "And you," chirping thus, her gaze efficiently switched to the angling
of Rachel's face. "You're beautiful! My goodness, you're like an early image of your
mother!" She declared sunnily, straightening, Hyacinth smiled. "You're going to have
your hands full when she gets older. What a beauty!" Delia's snicker brought the comment further to life, garnering Hyacinth's attention in a flash. "I see you agree?"

"I've mentioned it once or twice." Delia laughed, knowing this was a topic her
daughter did not yet comprehend. But since she had raised one beauty herself, she knew
truly the madness that would come. The phone calls alone can be quite provoking, and
that was putting it mildly.

"Come in! Come in, guys! Why don't we join everyone?" she caroled as like the
lyrics of a song, sweeping the door shut, Hyacinth beamed as she turned. Guiding them
through a circular foyer that stood larger than an average room, eminent in stature, its
ceiling towered at least a dozen feet atop their heads. Wide halls, exquisitely furnished
with art, escorted them to a large verandah that sat high above three tiers of a massive
backyard.

Grayish-blue water enveloped the eyes as far as one could see, touching the horizon.
Its tides walked the wide edges of the yard. An artful staircase, made primarily of stone,
ushered guests to the landing of the second tier. Designed solely to appease the mind,
the assemblage of flowers was a showpiece within itself. Stretched past the width of the
massive structure, plants of varied spices walled the banks of stone, and natural wood
furnishing sat elegantly beneath the cover of trees. Choiring a large fireplace that sprout
chicly from the ground like a living piece of the yard, its purpose was well intended.
Assimilating a living-room housed in nature, with a beauty that was supreme.

Two waterfalls trickled from opposite ends of the garden, streaming from a cave of
rocks, as if the ocean dribbled a part of itself for the cause. Below the balcony, a kidney
shape pool dominated the next tier. And shimmering blue tiles gave the impression that
the heavens now rested within reach of one's hand.

Julia's eyes strode over the many faces flocking the balcony as she passed, ferreting
the gaggling group in search of one. Seemingly blank faces twitched politely as she
moved through the clustering crowds, with Hyacinth playing show-horse to the lagging
brew. Graciously smiling in response, yet she was somehow convinced she witnessed
curiosity in each gaze. So far, his face was absent from the quantity, and disappointment was but one of the emotions that materialized in her chest. Unsure of what she
expected, she groaned quietly to herself. Did she want him to claim her in some way?
Maybe it was just that she needed the comfort his presence always seemed to provide.

"Julia!" Phillip called, stepping from behind a small group of attendees. He altered
her path.

"Phillip!" Julia chirped, startled into a happy tither. Her face showed, in full, the
extent of her joy, and much like their association of the past. Her dependency on Phillip
was again renewed.

"Hyacinth said she asked Michael to invite you! I'm glad you made it!" He hummed, smiling happily in that usual way. "I'm glad she did. After all the bragging we did about you, your reputation precedes you, it seems. She insisted she had to meet you."

"That was very nice of you." Julia chuckled lightly, though her emotions were far from being sighted as that. Spitting the words in Phillip's direction, yet intended the import solely for the ducts of Hyacinth's ears, she turned her gaze slowly upon the older woman with a shrewd yet perceivably gracious smile. Under any other circumstance, she would have been grateful for the discretion her argument gave, had it not meant one thing—she knows. At the very least, suspicion now reared its grisly head, miming the arcanum that there's something going on between her and her son. *Great!* Now someone else knows about them. Soon everyone will, and then she'd be known as the biggest hussy that ever lived.

"It was my pleasure, really." Hyacinth avowed radiantly, as if answering the question now wavering on the other woman's mind. "The type of praises you received does not come along every day. This way, I can at least say I've met you." She laughed, her tone a soft, musical chortle that tickled one's mood like the tuning of a harp. The type expected from a rich socialite when swallowed in the company of friends. Touching her fingers lightly to her chest, she fingered a pyramid of diamonds in a likened shaped pendant around her neck. Her expression seeming pure, it gave naught of her thought.

"Thank you. That's quite a compliment. I think I'll need to practice more control to keep it from going to my head." Julia smirked, unsure of how she should feel about Hyacinth's knowledge of their fling. "Oh, Phillip…this is my mother, Delia. Mom, this is Phillip, one of the partners I wrote with."

"Hi! Nice to meet you," Phillip chirped, his hand shooting forward without delay. "Your daughter is very talented, but…I'm sure you already knew that." He laughed.

"I do. But I don't mind hearing it again. I'm very proud." Delia smiled, accepting the hand offered.

"And you remember Rachel and Richard." Julia chanted, her hands moving quietly to the children's backs.

"Of course; how are you, guys?" Phillip muttered, dipping his head low to their faces.

"Fine," they answered almost cohesively as one, leaning shyly into their mother's side.

"Mine should be around here somewhere." He announced gaily, peering through the many faces as he straightened. Phillip scanned the area for signs of his kids. "Well, I know for sure they came here with me, and I still have my keys. So they couldn't have left without me. Which means, they have to be around here somewhere, don't you think?" He inquired with an exaggerated frown, widening his eyes as he finished.

"They're probably downstairs." Hyacinth advised in a tweet, waving a hand in a subtle, yet flamboyant manner. She beckoned a server as she spoke.

"Probably," Phillip nodded in acceptance, seemingly assured that the answer was so.

"Why don't you get yourself something to drink, while I show the kids downstairs? Oh, good, there's Michael!—Michael!" Hyacinth chirruped, waving her hand like a placid lasso to the beat of her song.

At the mention of his name, Julia's heart did a quick summersault in her chest. She was almost unwilling to look in the direction of Hyacinth's call. But like a magnet, she was uncontrollably pulled.

Dressed in his usual attire of blue-jeans, a crisped white shirt conformed lovingly to the chiseled doming of his pecs, looking fitted, yet comfortable in its fit. The sun's rays tinted his olive skin to that of perfection, and had a painter administer each inerrant brushstroke himself. He could not have looked more striking. Already seated at the top of tall, dark and handsome, he was quickly adjusted to God—if he was not already seated there before. *Beautiful,* Julia purred, swirling the obvious assessment to herself. It was an unlikely description when the connotation was of a man, but she could find no better adjective to describe him in her head.

"Hello!" Michael greeted as he neared, his deep voice slicing through the rumblings in her head.

"Hello." Julia smiled, immediately forgetting the follow-through required with feeding her body air, seeming to forgo the essential procedure, in a dazed blink, with the stalling of said deed. Ultimately needing air, her body pushed the effort, forcing her to wheeze through a series of coughs. "Oh! I'm…um, I'm–I'm sorry." She coughed, clearing her throat. She turned her back to the small gathering.

"Are you okay?" Michael worriedly asked, bending as near as he could without raising suspicion. He lingered in wait.

"I'm fine." She whispered, taking the hand he discreetly offered. Julia squeezed the proffered limb, as if the very breath she needed waited inside. The contact being instantaneously fruitful, like a lifeline in mid-drowning. It gave her feet on which to stand, as if he knew exactly what she needed and made it so.

Delia watched her daughter through the subtle interaction like a hawk on the prowl, finding her curiosity strangely piqued. Julia was no fair maiden, and had never been. Nor was she, for that matter, a damsel in distress. Priding herself on her strength, she wielded it mercilessly to dissuade the pursuit of many. But this was a different daughter that stood at her side, one softer and more open than she had ever witnessed before. Could it be? Remembering him from his visits to the house, Delia recalled also that Julia's spirits had grown better on her return. It was also after that particular weekend that she started her habitual trips. Was he the man in her life, and if so, why would she hide that fact?

"Mom," Julia hummed, remembering her manners, as well as the eyes now focused on her. She gave the introduction as tamely as she could. "This is Michael…Hyacinth's son and Phillip's business partner. Michael…this is, Delia, my mother."

"It's very nice to see you, again." Michael gushed, offering his hand, his smile widened, and hazel eyes twinkled happily into the vital nadir of green.

"Yes it is. We've never really been formally introduced, have we?" Delia smiled, comprehending, with some certitude, the verity of their involvement. She would not be surprised to learn he also wore the title of covert admirer.

"Delia!" Hyacinth's voice rang sweetly through the slight pause, slicing effectively through whatever else would have been said. "Why don't I show you around?" She purred, winding her arms around the kid's backs, she smiled warmly at each. "And why don't I go find you some playmates. I'm sure Britney and Jason are still commandeering downstairs. If not, you can have the whole place to yourself, who knows. You may find it more fun that way." She laughed, turning to Michael. She finished her lyrical sermon with a dazzling inscription of a smile. "Michael, could you help Julia get settled please? Show her where everything is, and get her whatever she needs. Thanks, son," Hyacinth hummed, spurting the last of her directives over her shoulder as she turned. Not giving either the opening in which to answer her bid, she blazed a fiery trail with her smile. "I'll be back as soon as I get everyone all settled in." She called, flouncing down the path, she suddenly stopped. "Oh, Phillip," Hyacinth again chirruped, and like the venerated soloist in a choir, she commanded full attention. "Could you help me for a minute?" she asked, pausing deliberately in wait.

"Of course," Phillip chortled back, turning without delay or suspicion. "Excuse me." He mumbled as he hurried off.

Julia stood unmoved as she watched him go. Compelled by the expressive language of Hyacinth's body, it danced in communication as the two conversed. Skillfully, she turned and maneuvered her way to the house, cradling the kids' backs in each hand. All five disappeared through the entrance in, what was surely, a flash. It was an amazing sight to watch. The lady was certainly used to getting her way, but it was her proficiency at that fact that was most impressive; granules of sugar did not register nearly as sweet.

"Your mother knows." She whispered, returning her attention to the man at her side. "Or at least she suspects something."

"What? Why would you say that?" Michael frowned fretfully, wondering what could have happened to give her that impression.

"She told Phillip she asked you to invite me because she wanted to meet me. Why would she do that unless she knows something?"

"I'm sure a part of that is just from the fact that she suspects that I like you. That's not hard to see, is it?" he asked, hoping his point took hold.

Julia's smirk bloomed fully indicting, rolling her eyes. She let the answer drip from her lips. "Not the way you tend to leer at times." She teased. "I guess I can see how a mother could pick up on the nuances of a son." Acknowledging the idea as a satisfied conclusion, she followed his lead, moving comfortably past the cluster. The two strode to the far end of the verandah with a casualness they did not feel. There along its edge, they had no mass with which to contend with, no ears to perk with interest while they spoke, and scrutiny was but a fleeting glance. The cozy bay stood vacant, as if slotted by reservation just for them. It granted the privacy they needed—at least for a spell.

Michael leaned his hip against the balusters with a concentrated guise, as if admiring the view. His eyes slid past her to the water, absorbing the beauty before he spoke.

"You look truly like something to eat." He murmured, still gazing at the blue vastness sitting beyond.

"You look like something worthy of being devoured yourself. I certainly wouldn't mind taking my time. Playing with my food would be a definite prerequisite here." She challenged, though her eyes followed the small gathering by the pool.

"Would you eat everything to the last drop?" Michael smiled, his eyes dipping for a moment to hers.

"Maybe," Julia purred, tossing him a teasing glance from the corner of her eyes, she smiled. "It all depends on which way the mood swings. I may just get the urge to go riding instead."

His smile was slow in building, meticulously encrusted. Lust polished the synthesis of colors in his eyes, and nature's amalgamation of sunflower, barley and the mini stratums of walnut made their gradual descent, ravishing her body in full. Reluctantly, Michael dragged his gaze from her arresting physique, scanning the area coolly for intruding stares, he groaned. Satisfied there was none, he returned for seconds, lapping up her presence. Michael drew in a slow breath before renewing his curiosity in the orangey flecks of the horizon. The warm trace of his finger was his only means of communicating what he felt, curled slowly around the pinky on her left hand. It tightened in an unusual embrace.

"It's nice seeing you like this." He whispered, leaving his gaze on the water. "Out—during the day—with other people; I like it." Murmuring thus with a well restrained smile, his finger caressed its liken with pent cravings boiled within.

"I thought you hated not being able to look at me?" Julia quietly goaded, shifting her gaze from the water to the horizon, as if, that, being the topic of discussion, needed to be appraised.

"Only when you're wearing a certain suit," Michael shrugged. "Anything else and I'm fine. Besides, once I'm able to get you alone, I'll get to take my frustration out on you in spades." He apprised roguishly, his deep voice sounding more like a groan. "Later?"

"It's your birthday," Julia quietly shrugged. "I may be somewhat…obligated to give you a present. It is the…social thing to do."

Air whistled from his nostrils in a weighty sigh, skating through the silence. The hoisting of his shoulders was hardly visibly by a glance. "A dessert perfectly worthy of the wait," Michael growled. "I'm all a-drool with anticipation."

"Careful now, you'll want to save that appetite of yours."

"In case you haven't noticed, mine is of an ample size." Michael raptly assured, his lazy smile signifying more. "Appetite…" he clarified, as if the word came to him as an afterthought, lingering on his tongue. It waded like the grumble of a predator on the hunt. "I'm always famished with you."

"I've noticed. Am I ever going to feed you enough? Will you ever get filled up?" Julia asked, giving then a lazy smile of her own. She squeezed his finger in a sublime caress.

"I think yo—"

"Michael!"

Once mesmeric in it swathing, the high shrill of a female's voice ebulliently extinguished the amorous aura from its place. Startled, the clandestine couple turned to only distinguish the blur of a woman's physique, before she launched herself at Michael's chest.

"Happy birthday!" she exclaimed in a happy lilt, enveloping his body. She ironed her stilt form to his, lingering well past what's deemed an appropriate display.

"Jennifer! Hi." Michael exclaimed above the affliction on his chest, forced to take a step backwards to maintain balance, an awkward smile surfed his face. His hand then moved to rest gently on her back, while his gaze clambered her shoulders to quickly acquire those of Julia's eyes. Woven brows published confusion, though the hazel depths bellowed surprise, veering apologetic with his next blink. "How are you, what are you doing here? I haven't seen you in forever." He rambled confoundedly, his voice drifting through congregated strands of her hair.

"I know! But...it's your birthday, silly! Why would I miss that?" Jennifer chirped, slowly straightening her long body, though not without obtaining some aid.

Julia watched the interchange with a veiled frown, feeling a sudden pang without knowing why. It rocketed sharply with the appraisal of perfection standing mere inches from her feet. Supermodel—there was no doubt in that. The sound of Jennifer's bracelets rattled through her thought, bringing Julia's eyes to her hand, while she, in playful guile, deliberately licked the drink from her lips.

"So! Hello!" Jennifer panted, and perfectly manicured nails slid wickedly down the length of her glass. Her smile was intently coiffed. Showing just enough to dazzle with flawless, white teeth. Long, tan legs shifted easily as she turned, lodging her shoulders against his. She erected a beauteous wall, setting the other woman gaping at her back.

"Jennifer, allow me to introduce you to my guest." Michael interrupted calmly, irked by her intentional disregard. He sought to repair her slight. "This is Julia Berwick—the writer." He announced, sensing her nescience, Michael paused. Quickly recollecting her passion was never aligned with books. Not known for her analytical thoughts, incisive reading was never her forte, nor was she much into sociological conversations. Her voraciousness bore only one name. "Julia, this is Jennifer Haskell, a very old friend."

"Hello." Julia smiled, allowing her gaze to leisurely shimmy down the tall frame. Standing almost equal with his column-like stance, she was a vision of flawlessness from any angle that one gaped.

"Hi." Jennifer grunted, barely glimpsing to whom she spoke, her gaze swerved in a detour of Michael's face. "So, Michael, what have *you* been up to?" she resumed in a chirpy chant, turning her shoulders. She decisively dismissed Julia from the partaking of further exchange. But in most, she staked full dominion on the man himself, fencing him profoundly from view. "You look good!" She exclaimed, her eyes running the length of his body.

"Thank you. So do you." Michael nodded, motioning a hand towards her, yet the extent of his gaze tracked the woman at her back.

Clad in a small, summer dress kissed, subtly, with gold, the stylish frock halted a foot above the spry goddess's knees. Intricate strappings snaked smoothly around her long neck, leaving bare the exhibit of creamy shoulders and back. Her hips swayed provocatively with the cadence of her voice, shifting often, as if demonstrating some aspect of her work. Yet, impertinent or not, her aplomb was astoundingly clear, so, too, her objective. With an exaggerated flip of her hand, she swatted brown hair from her face, sending the silky mass in a cascading fall down her back. Icy blue eyes, highlighted in sunlight, sparkled with tacit words, though none who watched her was numbed to the blatancy of her action, for she chaperoned it pertly with the pursing of pink lips. Plainly evident was that she commanded attention. Being used to weaving her spell, she incessantly honed the incantation her body recites.

"I'll leave you two to catch up." Julia announced sternly, not wanting to witness another minute of the sad display, not without being tempted to flaunt a bit of her own.

"There's no need to leave," Michael averred earnestly, halting the process of her turn. "When your friendship is as old as Jennifer's and mine, there's really no need for secrecy, since everything that could possible form a shadow has already been put to light. Besides, I'd like to finish our conversation if you don't mind."

"I'll be around. We'll catch up then." Julia pledged, swerving abruptly. She slammed sharply into the body of her predestined savior. "Sarah!"

"Hi!" Sarah beamed brightly, wrapping her arms around Julia's taller frame. "Phillip told me you were here."

"Yes!" Julia chimed gaily, squeezing the chirpy blonde tighter than she ever had before, truly thrilled at having the friendly interruption. Her smile suddenly knew no bounds. "I saw him earlier, which reminds me. I need to go check on the kids."

"They're fine, there're fine." Sarah assured in a hurry. "They're with Jason and Britney downstairs. I'll take you down in a minute." She smiled, her easy Texan accent sounding like music to Julia's ears. "So tell me, how have you been?"

Jennifer turned curious gaze upon both women now chatting gaily at her back. Suddenly rocked with interest, she stood prurient for more on the stranger's identity. "Sarah, fancy meeting you here," She laughed, declaring her observation like the punchline to a skit.

"I know, right." Grafting her usual gleeful persona, Sarah smiled. "Usually I avoid these things but…" scooping her small shoulders as if that of itself was explanation enough, her eyes widened. "This time I just thought…why not."

"Oh." Jennifer droned with a newly affixed blankness to her gaze, unsure how to take the offhanded remark. Was there something going on between the inseparable trio?

"Jen, we'll catch you later. You know how it is, business first." Sarah caroled in a drawl, seizing the pause like water on a sandy shore. She swerved promptly, towing Julia by an arm. "Let's grab a seat. Have you had anything to eat?" She asked in the same melodic twang, ushering Julia to a table diagonally across from the two.

"No. I haven't had a chance."

"Then let's go get some food, the choices are out of this world." Sarah laughed, her hand still locked around the other woman's arm.

"Sounds delicious," Julia rejoined with a low chuckle, not bothering to wait on the release of her arm, being long used to the confiscation. Although at the moment, the gesture sprouted more in the guise of a crutch, a source of strength in her time of need. "Do you think Betty would take offense to that remark?"

"Knowing Betty, I guarantee she's responsible for at least a portion of this spread. She would never let Michael celebrate his birthday without putting her own stamp on things; she considers taking care of her baby, her primary job."

"Two mothers, both devoted, how special can one person get?" Murmuring the reflection, brown eyes darted surreptitiously backwards, snatching a peek at the recipient of their talk. His head bounced in response to something being said, and a vague look of interest carried his eyes to the grounds below. Lingering, his gaze remained tethered to whatever it held.

"Well, I'm not sure Michael sees it that way." Sarah countered with a shrug, looking playful. It came forward with a bouncy jerk.

"I guess there's always a downside with having too much nurturing. As with anything, it can affect one's health."

"If there is, Michael could give lessons on how to handle the strain. Granted, I haven't met a man who didn't like being catered to. *He* just happened to have it twice as much as most, though I wouldn't waste my pity on him for that." Sarah cackled, patting Julia's arm as her body slumped forward. "I think he loves it. He has to. Think of how long it's been."

Chatter between them remained effusively light and infectious, supplying a steady current of effervescent titter. Yet on their own, Julia's eyes frequently sauntered to the couple by the rail. The conversation between them seemed somewhat relaxed. Evidently, it was as he said—they were old friends, emphasized thusly by the familiar way her hands grazed him as she spoke. Though within minutes of watching, Julia found her attention stationed chiefly on the man instead of his companion. Only then did she recognize the rivulet of emotions that lies beneath.

There was a coolness to his mannerism that she hadn't noticed before, though hardly rigid. An underlying aloofness stalked his mien, shifting as if to find ease from some roiling discomfort. His gaze veered often to everything but her, though she could not say the same of his companion. Watching the comportment of the goddess herself, Julia could not help but wonder on the relationship between the two, as well as the reason behind their split. Clearly, the woman had not yet worked him out of her system, and had tried in earnest to tell him this.

"Julia." Sarah mouthed hoarsely, shifting nervously in her seat, her eyes sunk warily to the plate in her hand. Filling her lungs at last, she asked. "I've been meaning to ask you something and I hope you won't be offended."

"What is it?" Julia cautiously queried, hoping it had nothing to do with her wandering gaze.

"Well…" Sarah begun, pausing as her eyes nipped at the food on her plate. "I was wondering if the next time I'm in town, we could grab a cup of coffee—just the two us? Or maybe…grab something to eat…?"

"Of course, I would love to! Why would I be offended by that?"

"I didn't want you to think I was taking advantage of your working relationship with Phillip."

"Sarah, you've been nothing but wonderful to me. I'd love to have lunch with you."

"Really!?" Sarah chirped, quieting her expression from one of surprise, to one of casual interest. "I'm glad. It should be fun."

"I'm sure it will be." Julia smiled, unsure why such a question reared a difficult task for the queen of affability.

Once more, Michael straightened to his full height from peering below, assessing the circumstance for an opening to escape. He gave the tame resemblance of a smile. She stood so close that he felt like a caged meal under the scrutiny of her avaricious gaze. Turning, he folded his arms loosely across the width of his chest, and his nod was in acknowledgement of something useless being said. Inventing interest in the past two years of her life, as if her tales, thus far, had not been monotonous and droll. The drab resonance rang, to him, like the curb lyrics to a lullaby. Both elbows bowed heavily out as he again surveyed the action by the pool. Nodding faintly, his eyes returned to explore the length of the verandah, stopping only when they found what it was that they sought. They lingered in their chore, seeing that she watched him on the sly. A smile wafted, like magic, through the arena of his chest. Quickly stemming the reaction, he stalled all evidence of that, remembering where it was that he stood. Michael's head immediately dropped in response, brushing a hand determinedly across his shirt, as if to dislodge a stubborn ration of lint. Using the effort to steady his expression, he wondered on her thoughts. Did she suspect he and Jennifer once had a thing?

An explanation for that would be reasonably short, since there really was nothing concrete between them even back then, none besides the obvious as their guide. Mentally, they were both so young, and still until this day, he can find no name for what it was that they had. Neither friends nor affiliates, he learned a long time back to leave Jenny be. Since Jenny does only what Jenny thinks is beneficial to her. Squelched now for more than a decade in his past, he had long since outgrown her and any inklings that they had. There was nothing about her he would ever allow near him in that way—most especially, not now.

"So, Michael," Jennifer chirped, her lilt intruding sunnily on his thoughts "Are you seeing anyone...?" she asked softly, leaving the words to hang like the intro of a challenge.

"Why?" Michael asked, his hazel eyes narrowing.

Jennifer's pale shoulders rolled softly, sending a coy glance his way, she smiled. "I'm just...curious on what's going on in your life."

"Bedlam for sure, I can barely find room for sleep much less..." he shrugged. "It's just been that crazy with work. I have no space for anything that's not already on my plate."

"But a man—"

"Michael!" Hyacinth caroled, pruning Jennifer's words with precision. She stretched her hand to him in wait. "Can you come here? I need your help for a minute." She announced, and the practiced perfection of her smile, cooled any thought of irritation in the beauty at his side.

"Sure, mom!" Michael hummed with subdued relief, whisking by his companion as if his mother's summon had been the blare of a fire alarm.

"I won't dominate his attention for the entire day, Jenny, I promise." She laughed. "After all, there are other guests he'll probably find more desirable of his attention than just me."

Michael's eyes rolled softly as he hurried to her side, a smile growing wide on his face. Tucking her arm affectionately in his, an exasperated growl wafted from his chest.

"You're welcome." Hyacinth cooed, patting his arm with the other of hers. She led him through the sprawled cluster to the house. "Understanding only goes so far, son. After a while they become questions." She smiled. "A big, cartful of questions,"

"I know, mom, but I was stuck. I was trying to be polite for old times' sake, you know, our families?"

"And now you're not." She smiled, sweeping her hand affectionately up his arm. "Happy birthday, my darling, may you get whatever it is you seek." Hyacinth clucked, turning, she retraced her steps.

Michael watched as she stopped by Julia's chair, sweeping her hands with the usual flare as she talked. Her gestures were exquisite to watch, as they flaunt like the studied part of a scene. In mere minutes, she had both women out of their seats, and all three sauntered jovially towards him in full compliance.

"Right through here," Hyacinth sang sweetly as she passed, flouting the presence of her son. The three passed without much more than a glance in his direction, none that was obvious to any but him.

Elated screams immediately greeted their descent of the stairs, bringing Julia's mind readily back to the focus at hand. An attendant smiled as they entered the echoic space, though she returned her attention to the kids at once. The massive area was divided to accommodate several sports, with a bowling rink consuming almost half the room. The entire far wall posed like a hummock for the climbing, with a squash court anchoring the opposing end. Ping-Pong and a sizeable hockey table balanced the generous space. Rachel's shriek was near deafening as her ball slid into the gutter from her lane. Yet her body spoke only of fun. Jason's mellow laughter grumbled smoothly within the troughs of her shrill, though his body loomed like a hoary protector from some distant time.

"See, they're having a blast." Sarah laughed. "They can have it now. But later, it's the grownups' turn."

Upstairs, Delia observed Michael's action with acute interest from across the room. To the casual eye, he looked to be taking a breather from the many clusters on hand. But his intermediate patrol of the area hinted of something else. So tight was he wrung, that he looked ready to climb from his skin, though the exhibit was not fully obvious to all. She had witnessed their "so called" lack of exchange, and their pretense of denial simulated strongly of guilt, for the exception they took spoke greatly of more.

"Hello, Michael." Delia muttered sweetly with an auspicious smile, taking a chance to better understand him.

Michael spun with his brows already fashioned like a compressed accordion, unable to remember Julia's maiden name. He stumbled to a halt. "Mrs.—!"

"Delia is fine." She offered softly, watching the eager affection on his face. It swam jauntily through his eyes.

"Delia it is, then." He hummed, and his handsome smile was never more evident than then, flashing it deftly. He charmed the important figure now studying his face. "Are you enjoying yourself?" he asked, his eyes trained to hers.

"I am. Thank you."

"Good. My mother would be beside herself if you didn't." He laughed.

"How about you? Are you enjoying your birthday, so far?" Delia inquired in a gentle tone, as he did not seem to be enjoying the full merriment of the day.

"It's fine. My mother enjoys it more than I do really. Maybe my taste for parties has grown somewhat thin, because a quiet evening at home sounds really good right about now."

"I'm sure you'll be able to enjoy that later." Delia smiled, giving him points for revering his mother's wish, even when he didn't want to. *Good*.

"I certainly hope so." Michael drawled, replaying in his head, an earlier conversation with his person of choice.

"I have to say, Michael," Delia chirruped, choosing to hold true to what her instinct now suggested. "I admire your work."

"Really, which one?"

"Your work of late, that is. I'm truly infatuated with your technique." She smiled. "It's something a mother could definitely cherish. I admire that." Delia crooned, her smile sweetened as she paused shrewdly to procure a long drink from her glass.

"But—" Michael stalled, not knowing whether to deny or concede what he supposed she now referenced. What if his supposition bodes wrong? He'll have admitted to the ordnance of things he was not yet ready to disclose.

"Happy birthday," Delia sang, effectively smothering his thoughts. "You have a *great* rest of the day, now. And by the way, much success in your endeavors,"

"I—"

"Just keep up the good work." She chirped, her smiling voice advised him this over her shoulders as she turned towards the stairs. Not waiting for him to gather his wits, she left him looking stunned. His eyes were in full gawk as she threw back a lasting smile. A verbal confirmation was never a need in the circumstance at hand, for the secrecy clipped to their liaison was theirs to have regardless. But having garnered what she sought, she was surely ecstatic to say the least.

Julia's hurried pace came close to causing a head-on collision. The two having to stop short to avoid an eminent crash, though the noise of the arena proficiently smothered both women's gasps of relief.

"Hello, darling," Delia chirped happily, skirting around her daughter in glee. "Enjoying yourself?"

"Sure. How about you? Are you ready to go yet?"

"Nope, not quite," Delia chuckled, moving further into what felt more like a sport complex than the subordinate level of someone's home, she expounded. "I'm having too much fun."

"Okay. You can have a couple more hours, but see to it that you behave." Julia teased, widening her grin as her mother simulated the action of a grateful child. Laughing, she turned on her way. Hastily ascending the stairs, she slammed fully into the barrier of Michael's broad chest. The collision pushed her forcefully backwards, though half the effort was perpetrated by his hand. Half carried half dragged, Michael wedged her in the corner of a large curio piece hidden on the opposite side of the wall.

"Come here." He growled before his mouth plummet to hers, molding his body to that of hers in an erotic embrace. Together they tasted of a flavor that was neither new, nor archaic, but one that bred magical as if under a spell. Pulling sharply back, Michael groaned in concurrence of the exultant swells, resting his forehead to hers. His thumb glided over the edge of her chin. "Mmmm, you taste good." He breathed against her mouth.

"So do you."

"Jennifer, there's nothing—"

"I gathered that after a while." Julia assured softly. "You don't have to try so hard when it's already yours." She smiled.

"So that's the reason why you wait for me to come to you." Michael drawled, his eyes lingering intently on her face.

"Please, don't look at me like that." She breathed, feeling her resolve weaken under his gaze.

"Why not?"

"Because, I may just say yes,"

"I wish you hadn't said that." He groaned, taking another taste from her lips.

"We need to go before someone sees us." Julia announced with remorse streaking the hoarse pitch of her tone. "Later." She explained with a smile filled with promise.

As if they shared a quiet joke, a soft chuckle rose from the back of Michael's throat, though he tightened his embrace for a spell, stepping back from her body, he sighed. "Later." He whispered in affirmation as she turned. His fingers softly gathered around hers, squeezing firm in acquiescence of his thoughts. He delayed her departure. "Go." Michael drawled in the balmy silence that followed, nodding in assurance. A slow sigh sailed warmly between the two.

"To be continued." Julia avowed, ducking from the opposite side of the piece, grateful no one witnessed their exchange.

———

It was not until the clock's hands effectuated north and south at once that Julia pulled into the spacious garage. The long tail of her coat danced loosely about her legs as she stepped from her car. Except for a few spots, the house looked to be dressed fully in black, shadowing her movements as she turned. From his station at the door, Michael smiled broadly as she drifted close, noting immediately that slender fingers worked methodically over the tie to her belt.

"Happy birthday," Julia exclaimed lightly, granting him full view of the intricate lacing used as her only mode of dress, her eyes completed a sale that required no coaxing, barter or aid. His smile, in reply, grew wolfing, dragging his gaze with leisure over the warm glow of her skin. He took his time in the appeasement of his eyes.

"The perfect present. I can't wait to unwrap it." Michael growled, leaning in for a kiss. Her mouth was, to him, like welcomed sustenance to an unfed, and he lost his intent of going slow. Stumbling through the rooms, satiny lace littered the floor in streams of curling red, forming an indication as to their path. With her body wrapped compactly around his, a series of explosions sent them on a celestial climb. Reeling back, Michael released a guttural groan, pressing deeper still inside the fiery marsh. He further sweetened his strive.

The mollified sighs that followed further feathered the sudden silence of the room. Julia dropped her gaze to find Michael watching her. His eyes tender, though they seemed darker with the passion they showed.

"Hi." She breathed against his mouth, stroking his lips with her own.

"Hi." Michael breathed back. "I'm glad you came." He rasped, and lean fingers climbed her spine in a sensual caress.

"Me too,"

"Was I hungry enough?"

"Perfect." Julia sighed, again touching his lips. She softly rolled her tongue over his in assurance of such. "Just perfect,"

Deeply inquisitive, his eyes roamed her face, and something akin to ardor surfaced their depths. A heavy breath toppled the reticence of the room, scraping her cheeks like swatches of a squall in its descent. As if suddenly resolving a thought in the quiet of his head, Michael hugged her roughly to his chest, passing long moments together as such. He savored the rhythm of her breath. Lifting his head, he commanded her lips, and there was no rawness that stalked the new flavor of his kiss, nor did greed surface in its boil. The fire that it bred did not burn. It simply roared to a simmer, walling the two like a protected floret. It bore as beautiful as a rainbow's promise, sprouting as magnificent as stars on a soupy night. Two people giving all that they have to each other, giving each other their best. He kissed her as if she held the very fountain of life. The very thing he needed to survive.

"Mmmmm," Michael grunted from deep inside his chest.

"Happy birthday," Julia purred, feeling herself float further on the sweetness the moment lent.

"When I was twelve," Michael began in a whispery tone. "They came out with a new G.I. Joe action figure I couldn't stop rambling about. So for my birthday, my brother, with Betty's help, surprised me with a limited edition." He smiled, and his eyes grew distant, as if the story took him someplace other than where they now rested. "We spent the entire day—just the two of us—playing with our action figures, which was, in part, his gift to me. He was a great big brother. I would have followed him anywhere without question, on just his say so." Nodding, a tender smile swam pleasantly through the pause. "Up until this morning, I still think of that day as the best birthday I ever had." He finished, pausing to gaze into her eyes, Michael smiled. "This one is better."

"Then I wish you the happiness of many more." Julia offered through a serene smile.

Nodding in answer, Michael rolled with her pinned to his chest, furthering their position on the bed. He settled them comfortably atop a pillow. *That is my most sincere wish.* He groaned, and his eyes eagerly ravished her face at the thought, brushing a hand lightly upon her cheek, he asked.

"*Vous avez vu mon cœur ? Je crains que j'ai perdu-il.* Have you seen my heart? I fear I've lost it." Michael sighed, filling his lungs with her scent. At the bemused look on her face he explained—somewhat. "You look especially beautiful tonight."

"I could say the same to you." She smiled, stretching herself back onto the pillow.

"How long can you stay?"

"Until dawn or there about, will that do?"

"It will have to." Michael shrugged. "Sure. I can make do with that—for now."

Chapter Thirty Three

Morning ruptured much too fleetly to soothe the stun. In what blossomed like minutes, the room's resplendent silence was starkly rent. Ridiculed mildly by the low buzzing of her phone, it annulled a miniscule sum, and her doze, she acknowledged with a frail sigh, was at its end. Birds chirruped noisily with the dispersal of night, varying their ballads like apparatus in a symphony. They heralded the verdure of a new day.

Darkness colluded with the warmth of his body to inveigled defiance, encouraging ignorance of the persistent chime, though knowing she could not.

Reluctant to renounce the coziness of his bed, Julia languidly stretched, and a soft groan screamed mightily through the darkness, voicing her aversion of the hour and its niggling ask. Leaving him had always carted a small margin of tension in its fold, but the hour and the occasion seemed to have amplified that in her head, goading her more so than it had before.

Partial to the efficiency of her guileful efforts, Julia hastened her grogginess's demise. Preferring to endure the inconvenience sutured to such, than peddle the brazen act of a prevaricator in the eyes of her children, her goal was but one. Although the profit, mirrored with such feat, left her no room with which to negotiate a compromise, since all exploits, done in accedence with the farce, would thence forestall a chance experience with her children's questioning gape. Stalking home at sunrise left her little exegesis besides what the obvious suggested, and she was not yet willing to market the benefits of a blatant lie.

A sigh of resignation stretched weakened wings through a tranquil room. Julia pushed from the cottony dent of her pillow with a languid yawn, swabbing a hand across her brow. She awaited the cover of lethargy to loosen its hold. Clasped tightly in its rigor-mortis-like grip, a subsequent yawn stalled an already piteous resolve, thus it tapered her progress with a seismic stretch. Curls, tamed by the torrid heat of a flat-iron, tumbled wildly down her shoulders and back, swaying against her skin like the fabric of a coat. It, too, hovered betwixt slumber and wake.

Ten fingers sluggishly threaded her long mane in a leisured stroke, working their way down her neck in relief of the tenseness she held. Thus the gentle press hailed like a waking to her senses. With eyes quietly intent, Julia gawked admiringly at the man reposed at her side, wrestling tersely with the urge to curl against the infectious heat of his body. Her questing palm floated across the hard grading of his chest, intending to surf the ripples of his oblate stomach. She stalled her fulsome aim. Deciding, instead, to absolve such contact, her eyes reclaimed their duty of admiring the view. Tenderly, she transferred a kiss to the tips of her fingers, feathering her affection to the toasty skin of a rib. She sighed in reticence as she turned from the assuaging view, finding her objective promptly robbed and her scant momentum expunged. In what seemed no more than a quiver, though laced in the assonance of a tick, Julia froze, discovering herself locked in the stable grip of a presumed sleeping man.

"Wait." Michael murmured in what pierced the darkness like a broken sigh.

"I thought you were asleep."

"I was, well…until the weird twitter of someone's alarm penetrated my dose." He smiled. Pressing her hand to the basin of his navel, Michael softly recited his thought.

"What am I if not worthy of a touch? What then, if not to feel the fond stroke of a hand, soft and dainty upon my flesh? Touch me and tell me of your needs. Touch me and tell me I still breathe. Touch me, for it is with that that I know I still live."

"That's pretty. Did you write that?"

"No. But it's from a favorite author of mine, so that makes it pretty much the same in my eyes." He shrugged, his timbre scaling the quiet like a rumbly purr, and long fingers slid, like soft twines, around the slender reach of her hand.

"Is that so?"

"His…mine, here…there, what's the difference?"

"Not much beyond a doubling of pence for you. But there are those that may disagree with such liberal concept."

"I suppose." He drawled, humor lacing his words well. It rang obvious in his tone.

"You know, some say admiration can be as good as a touch, better even, in some instances."

"Yeah, right, not likely!" Michael scoffed. "Ask any of the maidens throughout time and they'd gladly expose the folly of that vision. Most, if not all, would happily resign themselves with less, if it but brought them the one thing they desired most. They learned well that adoration feeds you no warmth. But to be fair does hold a substantial price, and the penance, at times, can be monumental."

"If that's true, where do I fall in that plot? Which one am I?"

"What do you mean?"

"Am I the prince or the pauper here to feed you warmth?"

"I'd say you're more a combination of both."

"Wouldn't that then make you *my* maiden? My own fair maiden that has long been in need of her prince?" she inquired coyly, shifting under his gaze. She settled jauntily back on her heels.

"Me? Fair? Not a chance. My virtues are far too friable for that." He rebuffed with an earnest shake of his head, adjusting the glide of his fingers through hers. Michael shrugged. "Though the competition would be a landslide if it was only a matter of faults, I've spent virtually a lifetime collecting the credentials for that. To bolster the obloquy, I've wallowed soundly in dungeons that market themselves as palaces, where only their bellies gave full credence as to what they truly were. I've tasted things most people shouldn't, and in so doing, have branded myself with titles most wouldn't. I've built mansions, in my years, furnished with regrets. Took forever to grow a day, and rightly needed to be schooled on what most find a natural succession of life. No fair maiden can lay claim to that." Cleansing the darkness with his sigh, the sound meandered, not unlike, the shift of a hand, filling the gap between them with its corpulent weight. The room again fell still. "Am I your maiden?" he asked. "Yes." He announced in a soft hum, answering his own question without thought. "If you want me to be, I'm bruised, tattered and well used, but your maiden I am."

Julia smiled as she leaned forward, touching a kiss to the hard curve of his rib. Well cognizant of the pleasure she took from his words, more than she anticipated she would, as myriads of sensations now rappelled down her spine. "My very own maiden; I've never had one before." She sighed, fanning her breath upon his skin. She dropped a second kiss to the crest of his chest. "Hear ye! Hear ye! Hear ye! Let it be known through all the kingdom, and to all ears, that you are now claimed wholly as mine. For I have just branded you such, and that from this day forward. You're forever patented as my possession."

"You know, you'll need to press that brand harder to make it stick, try putting your whole body into it." Michael coaxed, choosing not to ruffle the sweetness of her words, yet liking the emblematic meaning behind them.

"And how do you suggest I do that?"

The slap of his hand, against his chest, was almost flouted into silence, as the intrusive sound merely disbanded in the place that it sprouted. "Step right up and stake your claim." Michael gallantly invited, a flash of white seeming like dawn's entry in the dimness of the space.

Julia candidly smirked in response, though she gamely obeyed the mischievous request. Climbing aboard his body, a glint of roguery sparkled in the brown depths. Calmly, she set her back to his chest, spitefully rocking her hips. She shimmied down his sculpted truck in a guise of comfort, nesting her head on his chest. She aligned shapely legs to balance on hard. Unruly strands, scented faintly of almond and mint, cascaded onto his shoulders and chest, and although amused, Michael's arms enfolded her like the pages of a book, wrapping her in a heated embrace. He relished the enticement of her taunts.

"Okay?" She goaded quizzically, as if seeking instruction for her next jest.

"Your scent is magnetic." Michael sighed, breaking the lengthy linger of a new pause.

"You probably just smell your own scent." Julia cooed, settling her hand atop his, both now comfortably roofed her navel.

"Hmm, I like the thought of that. That's one more thing I get to spread all over you."

"It figures you'd like that."

"But it's not me. It's your scent that I smell." He assured, affirming this with another stocking of his lungs, he smiled. "If I smelt anything like you, I'd bottle it." Michael vowed, his voice suddenly muffled as he again inhaled the fragrance from her hair.

Avidly, his words, simple though they were, templed her body like rooms in the bowel of a sanctuary, commanding an attentive response, they necessitated compliance with the surety they held. The comfort she felt with him was extraordinary, noting that even their bodies fit with rich precision. Julia purred. "I really like *your* smell." Her whispered voice came through the silence like a breeze, falling soft between them, the quiet grew provocatively sweet.

A gentle kiss grazed her hair in response. Quietly gliding over the slope of her breasts, his hand lingered warmly atop a taunt peak, while the other swept past her navel with intent.

"Haven't you had enough of me, yet?" Julia probed in a voice that mimicked the sonance of a contented feline, even as her lashes faltered with a silent sigh. His answer flew with the strength of a gust, swinging prompt. It came void of pretext or veils, catching her unprepared for the honesty in his response.

"I don't seem to have an end when it pertains to you." He rasped, his voice soaring like the grating of something hard. With an agile twist, Michael rolled from his place, pressing her beneath him. His lips stroked the outer edges of her ear, tenderly narrating lyrics as old as time. "My hunger for you doesn't seem to stop. I ever want to take you dining. Only it's you and only you that's splayed on the menu, and all my appetite craves." He vouched, calling each word from deep inside the grotto of his chest. Michael gave them life with the veracious heat of his mouth, igniting her. He proved the veracity of his hunger as he fed.

Dawn's shadows stood less robust by the time Julia backed her vehicle from the expansive garage. Michael gazed out at the darkness with a deep furrow plaguing his brows. A pensive sigh thence waded from the firm set of his lips, feeling strangely chary with her leaving, though the ominous hour worried him more. Logically, he knew it was morning, grasped, too, that her drive was less than the passing of an hour, yet knowing that facts did little to ease the angst in his mind.

"Drive safe, please." He cautioned through the gathered flap of a frown, leaning against the door of her car. He again stared at the sky.

"I will."

"Just so you know," he warned. "I'm claiming this weekend as mine."

"And which side of the skirmish do I fall on this time, getting or giving?" she quizzed, smiling from her seat behind the wheel.

"Give. So wear something especially pretty. I want my date."

"What kind of date?" Julia frowned.

"Something fancy, so you can wear whatever you think will accommodate that."

"Sounds intriguing, I look forward to the challenge." Julia chimed, resting her chin against the door. She smiled. "Now I'm really looking forward to seeing you on Friday."

"Please drive safe." Michael advised yet again, his eyes lifting from hers to the surrounding dark. "If you had your bluetooth with you, I'd have you stay on the phone. But then again, I'd rather your focus be on the road." He announced glumly. "I don't like this, just…"

"I promise. I'll be careful." She offered in a consoling voice, understanding what was not said. "Hardly anyone will be on the road."

"I know. But that's not always good. Say on the odd chance that a need comes up. Just…just be safe, okay."

"I will."

"Thank you for my birthday." Michael gushed, his forlorn expression quickly changing to a smile. "It was…unforgettable."

"It was…my pleasure." She countered, smiling impishly as she leaned out the window for a kiss. "I'll see you this weekend." She murmured as he drew near.

"I can't wait. Call me the minute you get home." Michael ordered hoarsely, his smile changing to a frown.

"I will." Came the soft response, seeming unbothered by the mandate.

Again puckering his brows, Michael scanned the waning blackness. Gradually resolving the issue in his head, he turned, at last, towards his truck, following her departure from his home. Two vehicles punctured the denseness of a graveled road, saying their goodbyes. He watched as she disappeared in a cloud of black. Night seeming to swallow her whole and he could not help but feel that a part of him followed her home.

Julia watched from her rearview mirror as the details of his vehicle grew faint, observing dual dots of lights until they merged with black. An ominous mood softly fell. Feeling suddenly solemn, she sighed, and an odd sense of sorrow shepherded the inroads of her leave.

———•——

Long, stringy hair drizzled down the collar of his heavy work vest. Stretched snug beneath the coarse fabric of the uniformed guise, a black crewneck shirt smeared atop his body like paste. Thus it fondly cuddled the ball of his gut. Stained bespattered jeans sat loosely across the mouth of his boots, both generously splattered with oil. Mangled laces draped their apron-like tongues. The padding to his girth was especially perfect, adding at least twenty pounds to his weight. It shrewdly affixed another ten to his age.

Michael patted the bushy mustache fostering the camouflage of his face. Tapping light fingers assuredly to its weld, he snatched what was certain to be the last vacant slot in an already congested lot. With a grungy hat yanked ineptly low on his brows, he effected what seemed a last minute change, straightening the bill of his hat as he settled on a pose. His order had been called in at least thirty minutes prior to his show, twenty of that was given for the estimated pick-up. The extra ten was slated as a precautionary tact.

Stepping listlessly from his truck, Michael allowed the largeness of his girth to dictate the method of his gait. A loud snort followed a none-too-subtle cough, hacking purposefully to assimilate that of his new self. He spat roughly upon the ground in his achievement of that, almost hitting the wheel of his truck before ambling inside to conclude the act.

The restaurant seemed abounding with patrons at every end. Chatter mingled actively with the chimes of utensils and the melody of a song overhead. A shrill, presumed as laughter, leapt free from the hum, though it in no way accomplished the acoustic pleasure associated with the descant of that act.

Well palpable to the eye, the dinner-rush was in full swing, and agitation soon partnered with the bustle of work, as waitresses finessed their way along chaotic isles. With cargos held high, patience thence became a test of titanic strength.

The chirpy, young blonde behind the counter hardly made eye contact as he moved forward to announce his wish. Glibly reciting the eatery's welcome monologue, her manner was polite but dismissive in the very same breath, and with that—as always, the exchange grew simple and quick. Concluding his business in minutes, he quickly reversed his steps, and his effort seemed, at times, like a dash.

Already, the sky flaunted the beautiful ruddiness of dusk, with streaks of bright orange holding true to its edge. The long, hot day slowly made ready its rest.

On return, Michael set to task on refurbishing the vaunt of his exterior self, switching quickly to the charismatic decadence of old in a series of steps. Time slowed as he laid bare the implements in his trap. Handsomely clad in the dark, elegance of a tuxedo, a quiet shimmer danced nimbly upon the crisped slickness of black, highlighting its assets like a diamond's dispersion of light. Urbanely, Michael checked the sleeves of his jacket, deftly adjusting each cuff. He smiled with satisfaction as the posh attire fluidly amended itself with the descent of his arms.

The mellow sound of a jazz pianist regaled his promenade through the house, enlivening an already lascivious mood. It flounced with a leisured wave of its balmy wand. Stashed intimately in the left corner of the verandah, a primly dressed table awaited its finishing touch. Lighting the lone candle, Michael eyed the simplicity of his work. Contrast of red swabbed crisped, white linen, spilling as delicate as it soared sweet. The rich tint of rose-petals delegated its prominence of the space, littering the surface of a table cozily sized for two. Adjusting the volume on the stereo, mellifluous music wooed the atmosphere serene, drifting as if from a distance. It instituted, further, the affable wallow of his mood. Pleased with his effort, Michael's grin widened as the instrumental rendition of "Brown Sugar" wafted from his jacket, knowing it was her with the pinging of the very first note.

Charged, like a maiden embark, amid the tolling of all prior events, he awaited her entry in a dim hall. Parked just outside the mouth of a near dark living-room, the niceness brewed as a fundamental variance from his usual frenzied loiters of the garage. Yet conscious that neither destination, nor his preference of place was of any consequence in the way that his body felt. Responding to her with a fever, such fervor needed only proximity as a rule, though the tangling it caused will surely braise his brain as a result, yet he could think of no sweeter way to deal himself death.

The large door opened sedately as if goaded by a transient brush, easing slowly to a stop. The soft, distinct spoors of her perfume swept through to him first, spreading wildly throughout an already roused body. It honed senses that needed neither rein-forcement nor aid. Or was that just his mind playing tricks? Was she that much in his head?

"Mmmm," Julia hummed, immediately stealing his thought with her chanting of the note. "You look...yummy." The lusty grunt rattling deep and the breadth of her smile summed her approval from the very depths of her soul.

"My turn, what do you have for me?" Michael rumbled back, stepping close. His eyes plucked impatiently at the concealment of her coat. Her smile grew almost fiend-ish in response, halting her steps; deliberate fingers touched the buttons on the long, tuxedo-style coat. Shrugging the covering from her shoulders, it fell to his waiting hand in a rush. "You can't wear that!" Michael exclaimed sharply, his notice sailing like a tight shriek. Seized well by the errant display, his eyes almost bulged.

"And why not?" Julia teased, expecting and attaining her imagined response, she beamed. "You said something nice, and this...is very nice, is it not?" she asked coyly, turning slowly. She sharpened the attack.

"That's not fair and you know it. You saw my reaction to that particular piece the first time you tried it on, didn't you?" He groaned, catching her firm against his chest. "That couldn't be the reason that's going through your head now, could it? That's a rather unfair advantage, don't you think?"

"I assure you, I have not the faintest idea of what you mean. But if the dress pleases you, then I must concede I'm quite thrilled by the thought." Professing her naivety of any crime wrought upon his nerve. She recited the oration with the decorum of a saint—almost—had it not been for the soft twitch affecting the indent of her mouth.

"Oh, I like. I definitely like." He grunted. "And so for that, you can be assured you'll pay. Make no mistake on that." Michael warned. His voice like the underlying throttle of a lion's roar, it eased down her body with the slow descent of his eyes.

"Whatever do you mean?" she asked with an overly sweet sigh.

"Isn't it funny how the wicked can always find innocence when they need the benefit of a shield?"

"Hmm, you seem extra fiery today. Do you also kiss with that mouth, Mr. Dunhill?"

"Oh, I do a lot more than just kiss with this mouth." He rumbled, his tongue flicking, as if in attestation, over her ear. "I also use it to sample my meals. Did you know the tongue has close to ten thousand taste buds embedded in its surface? Just perfect to ascertain and heighten the sensation of certain exotic fare. Care for an illustration?"

"Mmmm, I think—"

"Okay, stop." Michael growled, taking a steadying breath, his hand skidded down her body and back. "Damn, you're a bad influence." He announced through a grunt. "I think we took a wrong turn somewhere. Faulty directions I guess." He smiled, tightening his hold, his hands again surfed her curves. "You do know where we're headed right? And we're supposed to have a detour today."

"What? Do you think that suit bodes any easier for me? A superb packaging as that is not exactly conducive to a snowy disposition now, is it? So, fair is fair." Came the sunny reply, and her upturned face creased with lust brewing in her smile. Cut sharply with the vehemence of his mouth, he pressed her against the hardness of his body, slanting his mouth across hers. Michael tasted deeply of the flavors she possessed.

"Now look what you did." Michael grumbled with a roughish grin, shifting his body to better acquaint her with what now plagued his thought. "We're not supposed to navigate this way, remember? At least not to start with," he reminded with a groan, leisurely kneading his way up the smooth gradient of her buttocks.

"Haven't we already tried this enough times to know the result?" Julia purred. "It doesn't work." She informed, trailing her tongue temptingly down his ear. "Mm," she hummed, her shoulders dropping as if dragged. "You smell...good." Whispering thus from the base of his neck, her body draped his like the second layer to an already fitted coat, and the steel like enclosure of his arms well encouraged the stringent press.

"Maybe we should delay the game a bit. What do you think? Do you want to?" he asked, and in the silence, he became aware of the arduous thudding yet persevering in his chest. It drummed as if to a primitive song. Complemented well by the sensual clef of a saxophone, the notes sailed as if on the wings of a downy gust.

"No...." Julia panted, shaking her head. She inadvertently stroked his chin with her hair. "We're adults, aren't we?" voicing this like the start of a whine, she raised her head as if to seek confirmation on the status of her thoughts. Michael's eyes immediately held hers, poised with possibilities. A charismatic smile rejoined her question in full. Expertly fabricated from start to fruition, as if the performance was segmented to tutor one less endowed with such grace, it took its time spreading across the entirety of his face. Settling lastly in the magnificent flecking of his eyes, it waded like the visual facsimile of an idea taking shape. Or was the observance just a distorted resemblance of facts? Though irrespective of which, she yielded decisively to the warmth radiating from the devious rendition without pause. In that moment, not only did she know what mandated his thoughts, but she fully concurred with the perception as well.

"Oh, you look good." She purred, sending an explosive breath on the tail of her ardent announce. Her eyes then cruised his body as if on a tour. The fit of his tux screamed perfection. Giving nothing away, it but brandished a pledge, playing slyly with the conjuring in one's head. "Very, very...good; you shouldn't be allowed to wear a suit."

"I could say the same thing about you in that dress."

"It's meant as a treat for you. No one else will see it."

"Good. But the same still goes for some of those things you call underwear. Namely the one with the butterfly wings as a...cover. That's a laughable thought!"

"But who's going to see that?"

"That dress..."

"I believe we already covered the dress. Besides, your friend made it. Good eye, huh?"

"Good filling."

"You like?" she cooed, spreading her hands like wings. She perfected a scant depiction of a pirouette.

Roguish eyes crawled greedily athwart the small dress, leaving bare smooth shoulders and superbly defined legs to the invoking of his thoughts. The slinky fabric hugged fetchingly to every curve, advertising amply the beauty of her caramel skin. "Oh, yeah..." he smiled. A devilish twinkle entrenched in his eyes.

"What's my name?"

"What...?"

"My name?" repeating the inquest, Julia's smile supplanted the usual exquisite display, for victory seemed surely within her grasp, as it should be. "You know. The one I'm supposed to carry for tonight. What is it?" she crooned, mischief holding bold on her face.

"Oh." Hardly sanctioned by the blatancy of her chide, his eyes flickered down her body for a final intake before relenting his gaze. "Silvia."

"Silvia?"

Michael straightened as her skepticism sailed to him bold, gathering his full height, he lent her a satisfied smirk, one well befitting an over confident rat. "Somewhat sassy with a hint of dull, don't you think? Now, entice me."

"I could just back off this dress. That should help my cause some."

"Then you'll be breaking the rules now, wouldn't you."

"I seem to remember you doing just that the last time we played."

"Hey, I couldn't help the fact that Jonathon turned out to be a klutz. Besides, he spilled wine all over his shirt. He had to take it off, and who knew chilled wine could be so...uncomfortable once it drips down your pants. But he was nice enough to continue the date, even without his clothes on. I really don't understand what was wrong with that date. It turned out quite...judicious I think."

"I'm thinking...um, Silvia may turn out to be a nudist."

"What?"

"And an exercise enthusiast at that." She smiled, ignoring his frown.

"Julia."

"That's, Silvia, thank you very much. And you are?" Julia wittily asked, sending finely arched brows on a dash up her forehead. She clamped a hand stylishly to the alcove of her hips.

"Carl, Carl Levine." He promptly informed, loosening his possessive handle with the spry reply, Michael smiled. And much in the guise of a disreputable cat, he thrust his hand forward, completing the introduction with a puckish grin. "I'm very pleased to meet you."

Julia flavored her smile with all things sweet. Yet the nucleus of her expression was a collage of cunning, shrewdly arming her ammunition for the playfield. She cooed her reply. "Hello," taking aim for the first shot with full eye contact. "It's very nice to meet you." She murmured by way of a melodious chant, slowly subtracting her body from his. *So, the game has begun? Good. All the better to find the end. Now to get the actor to be the first to flinch,*

"It's very nice to meet you. I didn't think I'd be able to make it with this weather we're having, but..." he shrugged. "Here I am."

"I wondered the same myself." She sang. "How often in one's lifetime do you get to see the seasons converge?"

"I would imagine not much." Carl calmly replied, a smirk touching his lips. "I can honestly say I've yet to witness that phenomenon in my lifetime—that is, until now."

"The whole thing gets to be a little bit much, don't you think? The occurrences change so drastically from one minute to the next. You're just never sure how exactly to dress. Then again, I have no right to offer complaints. Since this, 'Phenomenon' as you call it, has been more like a miracle for me."

"Is that so?"

Silvia's eyes widened with a paltry illustration of innocence, nodding in affirmation. She watched raptly as his brows jumped in bewildered alert, his amusement building. "It is." She asserted with a sharp uplift to her words, each sailing like the jovial ping of a chime. Livening the bounce of her head as if to solidify her answer as true. "Just yesterday, a blizzard with hail the size of boulders flattened my wicked stepmother and both daughters in one shot. How lucky is that?" She warbled gaily.

"Oh, I'm sorry to hear that." Carl offered, sounding almost contrite in his response. His head waved in feigned disbelief. The corner of his mouth twisted meekly without effort or aid, as staying sharp easily ripened into work. Quite skillfully, she veered their game down a new road. A road she now biased in favor of herself.

"Oh, don't be." She chirped, smiling prettily behind her words. "They were wretched. They never let me have any visitors, and they constantly spewed this ridiculous necessity for chasteness. Of course, it was only in regards to mine, my step-sisters went out every night. How backwards is that? To experience anything I usually had to sneak. But..." she crooned, wiping the start of a giggle from her voice, Silvia smoothly persisted. "Here we are, and I didn't even have to take any of that weird stuff that annoying rabbit keeps insisting that I take." Leaning forward as she warbled, her breasts gently strummed his chest, and a small miasma of her scent nipped raucously at his senses. "Between you and me, it gets pretty weird down in that hole. With so many things growing and shrinking, you're just never sure what goes where, or, for that matter, if they're being used in the right way."

"Is that so?" Carl sang in a bassy hum, looking almost incredulous as he cleared his throat. "I had no idea things were so…conflicted where you're from."

"How could you?" she smirked, recognizing the spores of certified defeat as it swam to the surface of his eyes. As the sure sign of a noose being slowly constricted was now obvious in the magnificent depths. "Unless you've had to deal with the farce yourself, it would never have crossed your mind. But it was nice of you to say nonetheless."

Caught unprepared by her impracticable tale, Carl managed a discreet breath, glancing heedlessly about the room. He quietly realigned his face. Scratched cleverly to the frayed edges of his wit, the subtle jibes in her apologue proved almost resilient in its effort to squelch his restrain. More so, from the sassy look on her face, she expected as much. Well, he had no intention of conceding his grip—marginal that it was. He was not yet ready to fall sapless as her prey—not this time. This one was his to win.

Quietly, she shifted her stance, her attention now tethered to the effulgence of her physical self, and as if to gauge the sureness of its fit. Her gaze floated down the front of the alluring dress. A hand thence glided in follow, commencing its scrutiny atop the round peak of her breast. Her fingers slowly waltzed the slopes of her curves. *The witch*, Michael chastised in the silence, fighting his impulse to pervade her estate—one effectively denoted by her trail. "Shall we go?" Carl hummed, suddenly eager to dismiss the invoking in his head. "I made reservations."

"Oh, of course," She murmured in swift compliance, returning her attention to his face, she chirped. "I'm very excited. Where exactly did you make reservations?" setting forth the inquest, she accepted his elbow with a gracious smile.

"Café Soixante-Neuf," Carl coolly replied, his expression serene, as if the name had not been plucked from the grittiest branch of his mind—a passionate commission of his in actuality. *Oh, to be so involved*, he mused, sending a heated glance to his libidinous companion, he smiled.

Darkness drew forebodingly close, dowsing the existence of light. Scant illumination, at converse ends of a majestic garden, softened the thickening body of night. Feet void of wears, quickly vacated the smoothness of wood, traipsing upon the coolness of tiles. They acceded to the customary fashion of choice.

"This is beautiful." Julia remarked gaily, abandoning Silvia's capricious persona. Her eyes exhibited pleasure the instant they gathered his. "Very sweet,"

"Thank you." Michael returned with an equally balanced smile, confiscating his arm from her stingy grip. He immediately seated her, sauntering around the table to his chair, inverse characters seated themselves. Instantly, he saw to their drinks, pouring two glasses of wine, Michael quietly touched the crystal to her hand. "To new friends," he smiled, tapping his glass to hers.

"To new friends," reiterating his lyrical salute, the soft clangor of crystals rang like the starting bell at a fight. Yet it tolled almost serene in an ambiance sighted for two, sounding sweetly natural in the pending night. "So, Carl, what do you do?" Silvia began.

"This and that, nothing too special, I go wherever the work takes me."

"And what exactly is your line of work?"

"I'm more of an understudy, really. I work behind the artisans who adorn the bodies of playboy bunnies with oil." He shrugged. "It's actually quite intricate work, if you can get it."

"Sounds like a dream job for you." Julia blurted, unable to stop the offhanded remark, she kindly explained. "I mean…for a guy, wouldn't you agree?"

"I'm not sure about other men, but…I certainly enjoy the work. I'm told I have remarkable hands." He proclaimed at a near growl, seeming determined to transmit his meaning without the utterance of words. His eyes hotly perused her body.

"Really? Imagine that! Just days before, I was told the same thing."

"That's quite a fascinating parallelism." He drawled, seeming astounded by the rareness fastened to the reveal itself. "Maybe we should swap techniques. I could show you the hasher aspects of my work. It's a little consuming, but it's well worth the exertion to procure the finale. Recognizing how and when to apply your instrument can be an eddying grind. Take the glide of a finger for instance," he hummed, snaking the longest of such around the cool base of his glass, his eyes grew downright Machiavellian. "Something as miniscule in size as that, one might negate the proficiency warded in its use. Yet just a slide of said digit aloft a soft, propitious conduit, can sometimes cause tremendous sparks. It's astonishing, the effects it can have. Around and around it whisked you if you let it, regulating and assuaging the pressure while you work. It's an incessant climb. Do you gallop or do you trot, and if so, when? And should you bother to daub, savor or drink with your grind? Tasting the blend, at times, is a necessary need, for that, the process is continual. Back and forth you go until you literally explode. This from the relentless quarrying expected with this job. Financially, it's more pauperizing than not, but the joy of an artist lies not in the paltry munitions of monetary gains, but in the pleasures awarded with his work. At least…that's what I think." He smiled.

"Well…um…that's…" coughing, Julia hurriedly cleared the evolving picture from her thought, eager to move past his amatory description. She quickly shifted her tack. "It must be pretty special work for you to afford this place." She shrugged, pausing to offer him a coy smile. A sweetened essence that seeped over the rim of her glass, lingering in place as if posing for a photographer's shot. Slated by intent, the richness of the wine proficiently bathed her tongue, erupting with flavor in her mouth. It skied smoothly down her throat to further anchor her will, a dark gaze shuffled lightly down his face in a masterful show of omnipotence, convoying the tenacious mission with a lazy flick of her tongue. She boldly alluded that the parameters were not just set—but understood, and arousal was but one of her intent. "I've heard rumors that there's a rather exclusive waiting list to this place."

"I didn't think rumors carried to one so…sheltered."

"And there lies another of my many reasons to sneak." She crooned, smiling wickedly in answer as she dropped a hand to the arm of her chair. Working with deliberate bent, she stroked the rim of her glass, using naught but two fingers to affect her damage. "I'm sure a part of the reason you're here is because you've heard the stories attached to my name." Stating the words more so than inquired, a healthy show of pride swam boldly to her face, and it was no less pronounced had she done so to flaunt her invention of the wheel. "It's all very well-earned I assure you." She preened. "How else does a girl gather her knowledge?"

"And what exactly are the facts?" Carl immediately prodded, leaning forward. He propped both elbows on the table like the erection of columns, shelving his chin on the overlapping sill of his hands. He gave forth his rapt attention. "Refresh my memory." He asked curiously, his voice airing his smile. Seeing big, hypnotic eyes narrowed seductively with the inquest. His eyes grew keen as she leaned forward in her seat. Her fingers languorously folded around the slender stem of her glass, prolonging the slow, intimate perusal of its transparent stilt.

"Let's just say, an evening with me leaves your imagination spent and your appetite *well* sated."

That you do. Michael averred with a leer, steadying Carl's mien as he savored her sassy remark, though both characters gaped with anticipation as she further assaulted her glass. Like a flower at sunset, her fingers closed delicately around the cool crystal, moving with gentle precision from base to its extreme platinum tip. A finger softly skated its mouth, circling blissfully aloft the goblet with measured pace, only to impishly repeat each step.

She's too damn good at this. He groaned, not that he expected anything less. He'd yet to find a dislike much less garnered a complaint, as she had him truly enamored from cranium to tail, and a thousand times thus for all the places in-between. If her method of attack persisted much longer, he'll be forced to jump direction and swerve directly to dessert, and that would only give them the usual result. "I see." Carl managed in a rough whisper, trying to stem his grin from swallowing his face.

"A girl gets tired of emotionally challenged dwarfs, you know, even if every night is a party. After a while, something amply sized becomes a thirst, and before long, the word…'anything' no longer holds the stigma it once had." Taking her shoulders on a gradual incline, she sunk a finger in the rosy-hue now gullied in her glass. Bathing the svelte appendage in wine, she touched it to the bed of her tongue, as if granting him a glimpse of an alternate portal lined with the prospect of bliss. Succulent lips closed slowly around the base of said digit, marketing its function as, it would, the exhibited use of a lollipop. She thence stroked the surface from tip to base with deliberate bent. "Mm," She smiled. "What do you think?"

"I think we should eat—dinner—before it gets…cold." Stammering gruffly his response, Michael groaned in censure of himself. Resisting the urge to gape at her blatantly forward affront, as that would only grant her a wealth of ammunition she did not need. Thankful for the forgiving fit of his trousers, he disappeared inside the house in a flash, not bothering to wait on an answer. He reappeared moments later with identical sterling platters and their lids. Setting the first in front of her, Michael reclaimed his seat, flashing a wide, expectant smile. He asked. "Ready?" testing this in what sounded like a merry growl, his long fingers already primed on the round knob of his lid.

Julia answered in her own perfected display, sending a consensus smile, her head brusquely bobbed. "Go!" Michael howled, and his voice echoed like the signaling shot agnate to the start of a race, sending both hands on a frazzled dash to remove their lids.

"Hamburgers!" Julia laughed, finding humor in the contrary evening. The choice of food being as inversed to their clothing as it was to the starkness of their feet. "You're amazing." She whispered in a low breath, holding her eyes to her plate.

"Ostrich burgers, actually," Michael smiled. "And so are you." Whispering his answer in kind, he left no room to elaborate this as fiction or fact. Skirting the avowal the very moment it's said, neither eyes veered from their plate, for it seemed further dialogue held no place in whatever was said.

"Suddenly I'm starving." She exclaimed. Sniffing lightly at the new aroma filled air. "Me too,"

The meal permitted him reprieve from the onslaught of her attack. Acceding a break from their game, it sojourned their relentless molest, stilling their punctilious strikes. Combat loitered the air like the tolling of bells in a war-torn village. So, too, the adversaries held, understanding that battle resumed with the finish of said bells. Conversation, instead, sauntered with the leisure it always had, scaling familiar commentaries in its drive. One of which being their discerning palates on certain foods. The exchange vied on opinions and views on the many samplings they've had, grumbling harshly on the best places to eat. Some of which they shared as conjoint perception without a row, with new ones chronicled to memory for future review.

The smooth, velvety voice of Nancy Wilson, skimmed amiably through the balmy night air. Pleasantly fencing the evening's quixotic ambiance. Night digested their surroundings in full, leaving them cratered in an enchanted glow centered on two.

Julia's smile exhibited the enormity of her content, savoring the fondness of the view. She singed enamored eyes to the beauty of his face. *Damn, he looks good,* she hummed. Perchance as appetizing as a complexly designed feast, with eyes as vibrantly illuminated as rare, exotic gems. The view was mesmeric in every option it held. And the list, now tallied in her head, had already grown acutely long. The dark tint of his suit contrasted devilishly with the bronzy tinge of his skin, ringing home evidence as clear as an avalanche suppression of a knoll. When they allocated sex-appeal, the man was clearly a favorite of someone at the top.

"Would you like to dance?" Michael asked, his voice like a husky murmur, emceeing the evening well, while his gaze remained locked on hers. The awareness in her eyes

tickled him in places that had naught to do with his mind, for he knew well the traversing of her thoughts.

"I'd love to." She sang, her words sounding like the chorus to something uncannily
sweet.

Michael's chair gnawed emphatically at the rough tiles as he stood. His upturned
palm accepting the warmth of her hand. Lean fingers promptly closed around a smaller
liken of itself. In contemplative silence, he led her from the verandah to the house,
preferring the mute swill the seclusion of the kitchen provided instead.

Dressed almost fully in black, the room's only lighting came from the illumination
of a clock. Maudlin music wove seductively around them in accordance with the dark,
gliding to a stop the moment they faced each other, though the two gave no inkling of
hearing the tuneful stem. Hardly serving as deterrence to the man, persuasive hands
made known their will, pulling her firmly into the circumscribing of his arms. Long
fingers spread possessively across the arena of her back, pressing her soft form to the
harder of his. A new song started within seconds of the other, though the two, in acuity
of the mood, simply held. Swaying in time to the cadence, both bodies held like the dour
trunk of a tree. Slowly, his arms twined around her in an embrace as passionate as the
man himself, smearing her body to the wall he provided with his own. None was left to
the imagination of the other.

Anchoring her hands around his waist, Julia sweetened the texture of his embrace
with the fitting of their form, snuggling further as she listened to the cadence of his
pulse. Another song ended as time drifted without aim, weighting the darkness with its
substance. The lull grew astoundingly warm, yet the unorthodox dance neither started
nor stopped. A new song commenced as with a signal from his mouth, heightening in
flavor as his lips grazed her temple, walking deliciously down her cheek like the gestic
of a waltz. He encouraged the angling of her face. Tenderly, he tasted her lips, feathering the lush beds with a gentleness that was unnatural to his usual wont. Time again
lingered to a virtual stop. Her lips parted after long, like the hasp of an effective lure.
Avidly stroking his tongue with her own, she emboldened his feed. His mouth slanted in
answer while his tongue hungrily played chase, drinking as if from a jug. The passionate
vaunt of his kisses seemed an imprint spliced deeply in his genes, wading unmistakably
distinct as it would the color of his eyes. Another song ended before Michael at last lifted
his head, lust fully brazen in his eyes.

"From Michael," he rasped, his tone falling soft, though it blared with undisguised
danger rearing in its bed. "He needed to do that for a time when he didn't."

"As I recall, Michael was granted his due. It's rumored that Julia took the matter in
hand and instigated their kiss."

"She did." He grinned well pleased with himself. "She did kiss me first, didn't she?"

"That's a technicality I'll leave for another debate." She smirked, stretching
towards him for another kiss. At the moment, she was not in the mood to be entangled in that form of dispute. There were other things far more scrumptious ambling

through her mind. "But for now, I want more." She breathed, not having to wait for his response.

"What about our date?" he drawled, laced tightly from the distraction of her mouth. He savagely fed without awaiting her response.

"Here, let me help you with that." Julia retorted once given the chance, moving a hand along the left seam of her dress. She dragged her fingers slowly down its edge, taking the hidden slider with the descent of her hand. The front of her dress drooped forward like a decoy to something else, slipping without aid. It fell from her body in a silent blink.

Michael's expression teetered slyly between admiration and greed. With eyes fixed to the body unsheathed in the garment's descent. He hardly noticed the plunging of her dress, seeing only the ramification of its dive. Bare, except for the warm lighting on her skin, one shapely leg lifted slightly through the air, followed swiftly by the other. She stepped clear of her meager attire without shifting her gaze from his. "Do I get what I want now?" she asked.

"There's never a need to ask that." He pledged, and a quick step brought him back within contact of her stunning visage. "Just come to me so we can take the ride as one." And although soft, his answer seemed to rumble with the emotions of something not said. Already, his hands enumerated their demands on her body, partnered by his mouth; they succored the boisterous spunk of his intent.

"I could be wrong, but…your attire seems somewhat inappropriate to me." She crooned, dropping her head back as his tongue grazed the swell of a breast.

"I can fix that." He drawled, shifting the breadth of his stance. The jacket slid from his shoulders in a flash, falling before her insight had the time to correctly forecast its end. "Easily remedied," Michael hummed, sending his trousers and shirt fluttering in a rush to the floor. His smile grew rascally, verging on the likes of a sinister leer while he adjusted the waistband of his boxers. "Better?" he asked as he again pasted her to his chest.

"You're almost there."

"I thought I'd leave you something to play with." He teased, his hand moving softly over the hill of her breast. "Do you have a preference as to our destination today?"

"I have some partiality to be ensconced against something…soft; beyond that—no."

"I'll try to keep that detail in mind." Michael whispered as he nibbled her ear, caressing the soft skin with his tongue. His fingers walked through the heavy tress of her hair, exposing her throat. He scalded her skin with the incredible heat of his mouth, and teeth, tongue and lips worked concurrently in the relishing of her taste. "Mm, you taste good." He sighed, molding her body deeper into his.

"Wait until you taste my darker parts." Julia purred, holding him snug to her breasts. She dangled from his grasp like a bone under the tethered clasp of a dog's fang. "You know what they say, the darker the…mmm…" she moaned, answering as his tongue flicked in question over the dark peak of her breast. "The…sweeter the…oh, God…."

Washed with waves of sumptuous delights, her breath staggered forth in the sweetest form of distress.

"Let's see if that's true." Michael grunted, covering her mouth with his. He drained her of the very source he seemed to need, while a hand worked the smoothness of her thighs. Like a pianist broadcasting the aptitude of his instrument, his finger played her depth with skill, making her warm, dank and inviting with every touch.

Clamping her trembling body to his, she availed her sensory plains to whatever his delight and he hungrily abide whatever she gave, refusing to relinquish the ferocious-ness of his drive, or to squander the smallest drop. Softly, her hand moved over his skin, dipping inside the waist his shorts. She claimed the eager member inside, and fingers delicate, though firm, closed around him as if to stake perquisite on what's hers. Languorously, his body dispelled a dim shudder as she moved, and a groan rose from his chest in acquiescence of the rousing rhythm. Though had he been considered one gifted, she then rose to the venerated stature of a savant. He soon found himself teetering near a euphoric cliff, fighting for control of his body from the drudge of her hand. In a quick shift, Michael lifted her from the floor, setting her on the table. His mouth immediately covered her breast, consuming the swells in a ravening dive. Her sighs taunted the air with a lyrical tune that was well pleasing to his ears.

With her legs barred effectively at his back, she glued her body to his, pulling him closer in an open prodding for more, though he lengthened his fill, allowing his mouth, instead, the freedom to play as it will. Frolicking with purpose upon her skin, Michael's mouth plowed a heated trail down her body, resting, in time, upon a liken of itself. Warm, soft and moist mirrored its warmth and softness, one eliciting pleasure while the other collected, with both revered as masters of their trade. Her cries grew enticingly pronounced as his tongue hastened its tasting, caressing as profoundly as it demanded. Time drifted onward astoundingly sweet.

Now aptly imparted by his mouth, his argument broached little reproach, utterly convincing in its burrow. It sent shockwaves of pleasure through to her toes, while her legs trembled in response to the decadence of his drive. Perched sweetly for the fall, his name wafted softly from her lips, surging her hips in vehemence to the sensation of his mouth. The intensity suddenly stopped. Straightening, he kissed her breasts in an ardent climb, shifting his stance. His hands were almost rough as he pulled her from the table to the floor, setting her to her feet behind a chair. His maneuvers bred almost barbaric, singed with the assurance of intent inside the primal display. Instinctually, Julia leaned forward once his body convoyed her back.

Softly trembling hands moved again to her breast, gliding down her stomach. They fondled the warm fissure of her thighs, further stirring a fire that needed no bolster to stoke its flames. The well heated engorgement aptly aiding in his drive, stroking her beyond excitement. It elevated ravenous yearnings into vociferous need. Releasing her breath in a long, slow sigh, his possession of her was like the first swallow of a toddy to one well in need. Fiery, solid and thoroughly filling, heat pressed staunchly against heat. Seasoning the dip, his hand tightened on her waist with the ecstasy of the inclusion, holding her firm as he nibbled the soft skin of her shoulders. Rousing kisses then sanctioned the side of her neck, scalding her back. His movements thence garnered a full dissertation on the pleasure it gave.

Accepting the music of her aver, Michael answered with the rough resonance of his own, as her hips raged war on his body. Touch for touch, the two challenged each other. Skill for skill, they dredged through a fiery brush, with pace matching pace until there was but one.

Julia listened as his breathing grew gruff, straddling the room until it seemed to resonate from a dark place deep inside his chest. When at last it came from, what sounded truly like, the fringe of his toes, his body stiffened in acceptance of apogee, pressing deeper still in the height of their boisterous climb. Only then did he drag her over the edge, pulling her with him to a waiting chair. He pinned her to his lap, while he yet strained for sweeter depths.

Sanity's return to the two was slow in coming, ebbing the mad quivering in his body and hands. Michael pressed a kiss to the spread of her back, resting his forehead against the coolness of her skin. He honored the sumptuousness of their romp. "Mmmmm," he purred, lengthening the exclamation as a true interpretation of his content, and the note was well befitting the jargon of a large cat. Turning her head towards him, she smiled, and her gaze blissfully conveyed all the things yet hidden in his thoughts. And, as always, the sight was a wonderful averment to behold. Indulgently, he leaned towards her in a testament of such, kissing her soundly in answer, or was it that she kissed him? At the moment, he was somehow unsure on the accuracy of that fact, only knowing their kisses soon had no beginning or end. "I keep waiting for it happen." He hummed. "But it seems I still haven't gotten there as yet." Whispering the thought hoarsely against her mouth, a finger gently stroked the side of her face.

"Waiting for what?"

"For my reservoir to be filled,"

"It's strange, isn't it, us not being sated after all this time?" she droned, understanding fully what it was that he meant. "Maybe we were just too starved before, that it's taking a while longer for the void to get filled. I know I was."

"It's nice though," Michael averred tamely, his voice heavy with unspoken emotions yet to be said. "I don't think my legs will be working any time soon." He informed with an appreciative smile, letting a long, slow breath again highlight his content.

"That's okay. Your mouth seems to be working just fine."

"It would, since it especially enjoys your taste."

"Have I mentioned that I like its work? Call it by whatever name you will, but just the idea of being sampled…" she sighed, her voice rumbling between the nestlings of their lips. "Devoured or consumed…sprout doubly yum, for they all boil rather intriguing in however they're done. But I have to say, my favorite," she breathed, caressing him ambrosially with her tongue. "Is the ravishing, and you ravished very…very…well."

"With such succulence, my palate only grows hungrier each day."

"Still as smooth as silk I see." Julia smirked, slowly shaking her head in reproach of his words. She caressed the lines of his jaw, sketching his cheekbones and the soft edging of his lips. A frown slowly crossed his forehead as she neared his nose, demanding that she clarify her jibe. His brows tightened to expedite the refine. "Your tongue," She explained, lifting a stilted brow as if bemused by his curious gaze. "The bluff still cascade like a cask of silken grog, it placates and regenerates in one breath. What chance does a poor girl have?"

Mid-point of accepting a kiss, Michael paused, his frown returning promptly and with less playful gleam than it had before. Curious, his gaze found hers from under the tight furrow of his brows, as his mind scurried to assess the meaning of her words. Words that came amply laced with sugar and brush with much affection from beginning to its cloying end, that he was not at all surprised that he did not feel the sting from her affront. Her eyes held no vicious glint in the masking of their depths. In fact, they danced with zealous delight, though with any other woman, he would have surely felt the prick of that jab. Yet it was not so in any matter that pertained to her; for with her, truth was all that he had.

"I think of all people, you'd be able to decipher that truth if it was indeed so." He drawled, giving his reply in a calm, matter-of-fact tone. Knowing no other woman had ever piqued his interest, his desire, or his mind more adamantly than her, nor had any engaged it so decisively well. Since laying eyes on her, his thoughts had been of no one else, and he was certain he knew the truth of her affection regardless of the riddle, as it held the same veracity as his. She rose as the ultimate match in every aspect of their strive, decreeing such act as proof. Her eyes, her touch and her body discounted the vagueness of her words as lies, giving so much more in their dividend than any boisterous dispel could. "Had I not grown used to that magnificent tongue of yours, I might have thought your words an insult."

"But it's not and you know it." Julia smiled, pressing another kiss to the corner of his mouth. "I only offered to highlight your charm—which you have to admit—have served you well." She chirped. Her face brightening as her smile grew suddenly auspicious. With a gentle hand, she stroked the hard slope of his forehead, moving calmly through his hair in her hike. "You're a charmer, Michael, through and through. The fact that I'm now sitting naked on your lap attestes strongly to that." She intoned warmly, curling her shoulders. She settled both arms around his neck. "I gave you no's and enough reasons why, yet—"

"I can be stubborn, arrogant sometimes to a fault, but I'm not a liar, and I wouldn't be—not to you." Michael chimed, his eyes daring disbelief. "You asked me for honesty and I've given you that. I admit I've done a lot of…ill-advised things in my life." He frowned, and the stern set of his eyes dropped for a moment to the floor. "Call it charm if you feel you must, it doesn't make it any better than what it was. But…I'm growing." He sighed. "That was a long time ago, Julia. I've really been a good-boy for a good number of years now. I've learned." He vowed, refreshing his smile, he gazed deeply in her eyes. "I've done some maturing—a lot of maturing, actually." He reminded, softening his gaze. His fingers moved through her hair as he gave forth his plea. "I promised you before and I promise you now—if that is at all helpful. I won't lie to you. I couldn't even if I tried. I know where you stand and I know what it means if I do."

Gathering a handful of her hair, Michael gazed intently at the locks in his hand, reining his thoughts before uttering his next word. "So, surrender to me, Julia." He laughed, hiding his thoughts behind a humorous cloak. For the urge to tell her that each encounter latched him more profoundly to her side, rumbled strongly in his chest. But he knew such confession would not be taken fully as truth, not yet. No. With her, he would have to be smarter than he'd ever been in his life. Undoubtedly, he'll need to charm without the benefit of a single spoken word. Yes. Michael affirmed decisively. That, most certainly, was the plan. "Let my charm steal you away." He prodded, putting his brightest smile to the forefront in his spiel.

"You've already succeeded on that. Or am I so different with my clothes off? Then again, that's the only way I seem to be these days."

"I have no complaints." Michael smirked, giving her body his greatest regards. His eyes dropped to rest where the two yet shared each other, and his smile widened with true decadence at the thought. "None whatsoever," He averred, shrugging unapologetically, he answered the well-defined arching of her brow. "More wine?"

"Are you trying to get me drunk?"

"I don't know. What are you like drunk?"

"I don't know. I've never been drunk."

"You've never been drunk, really?"

"Never,"

"I don't know if I should be pleased, or get to work on rectifying that as a flaw." Cocking his head to the right of her body, he studied her face with a curious expression. "No. let's leave it as it is." Michael droned, calmly shaking his head. "I think its best we leave well enough alone. I don't think you'll be much fun drunk."

"Why not?"

Hesitating, Michael offered the placating gesture of a shrug, analyzing the circumstance, he smiled. Without the benefit of any additive, she evolved as the most fun he'd ever had. What could possibly be better than that? "I've had enough of everything to make me an authority, and I say it's definitely not for you. Let's just leave you unspoiled." Nodding as if to answer himself, he repeated his query. "So, how about it? Would you like some dessert?" He smiled. "We could feed each other chocolate cake."

"Chocolate cake, mm, that's sounds good." She cooed, easing from his lap. She collected their littered garments from the floor. Betty, she imagined, would not take kindly to such behavior in her kitchen, so all traces needed to be removed at once.

Michael flexed his legs lightly as he stood. Assessing the damage with a clumsy step, he steadied his stance with a firm hold on the chair. His legs felt uncannily weak, tingly and twitchy were also good descriptions as to how they felt. "Do you think I'll ever be the same?" Michael asked, looking strangely curious.

"Maybe a little less attention might do the trick, what do you think?" she smiled, missing the meaning of his query.

"Your guess is as good as mine." Michael shrugged, looking almost cautious as he turned. Gingerly retrieving his boxers from the edge of the chair, he again flexed his legs.

"Are you really feeling that bad?"

A loud sniff raced through the space between them, laughing at the worry in her voice before giving answer. He shrugged. "I feel fine, great, actually." He averred, his laughter laden with the usual smutty flare. "My legs on the other hand seem to need more time to recover from you."

"Me?"

"You,"

"What did I do?"

Michael's head popped up brusquely from his task, settling his boxers on his hips. He took his time arranging his words, knowing in his heart they had flown eons past the point of a casual fling. Their start alone had flung them well past such paltry beginning. "Everything," he mumbled hoarsely. "And so very…very…well…"

"Has the champion found fault with the rigorous stint of sporting, or has the habitual nature of the act worn thin?"

"That would be the day!" Michael snorted. "An experiment perhaps? A farthing in the charge, a mere mite if you will, something simple enough to prove this? It would grant you the authenticity needed in your quest." He hummed, his question coming in a slow drawl, while he mused on the possibility of growing tired of her. He would sooner grow a new part, and not one in a flattering place. "Let's see what it would take for you to tire me out. Are you up to the challenge?" Michael smirked, his hands trailing down her side to rest on the rounded curve of her hips. "What do you say? Are you willing? It would be appetite for appetite, hunger for hunger, I'm willing to try." He goaded, daring her with a wink.

"I bet you are." She groaned, and the lightness of her laughter teased the dark that, by now, had grown thin. It came to him playful and soft, almost echoing in the space. "Why don't I take some time to judge your worthiness with dessert before we decide how much sporting can be done? I think we both already know how, so weapons are all that remains to be of choice. What do you think? Then again, you can always use what you find…handy."

"Something for your thirst perhaps, anything I can offer you to cleanse your palate with?"

"The night is still young," she muttered behind a dim shrug. "Who knows, maybe both. Let's just play it by ear and see where the night takes us."

"Why don't you grab the cake? I'll get the bottle and lock up. I'm suddenly eager to ponder the possibilities."

"Done!" she giggled, turning from him as he hurried towards the door. All signs of his tentative steps now quickly forgotten, with the promise of entertainment sitting in wait. Twinges, aches and discomforts were of no profit. There was but one goal now waiting to take aim. The fun of their foreplay was surely without match. Not in either memory did the game flow more easily than between the two. Nor had it ever yielded such scrumptious fruits.

"By the way," Michael called friskily over his shoulder. "As conqueror of this round, I get the biggest take on dessert."

"Conqueror; how so?" she shrieked, sounding almost suspicious.

"Simple," Michael explained with a rakish grin, swaggering to a stop by the door. His arms leisurely closed across his chest. "I wasn't the first to change the game."

"I beg to differ."

"No, not officially," lengthening his words, Michael softly wagged his head.

"You certainly influence the—"

"All perfectly allowable, as per the agreed guidelines, in fact, I recall asking—"

"Yeah, yeah, yeah," Julia groaned, rolling her eyes at the arrogance dripping from his tone.

"Your answer to my dither, and I quote, 'Give me more'. How could I not—?" He hummed, ignoring her unrest.

"I'm aware of what I said." She carped, slicing through his reenactment of her speech. "I'm just not sure if you realize how bitter your desert can become."

"What? I merely accommodate an invitation." He rasped, touching a hand in innocence to his chest. "Oh, what was that saying…?" Michael paused, lifting his eyes to the ceiling in thought. "Something about impersonation being the greatest form of flattery?" returning his eyes to hers, the sneer of a tomcat widened the range of its trap. "Or something of that sort," he shrugged. "How far ahead are you in this game?"

"Light-years, at last count." Julia crooned, hammering forth her own screw to his pride.

"Indeed." He drawled, and dark brows rose slowly in challenge.

"Here's to round two then."

"To round two! I'll see you at the start-line." He droned, giving his answer in a near growl. Fire flew boldly from his gaze, walking over her skin like the douse of a propellant. The promise was not misjudged but proudly proclaimed, holding her fixed as he exited the door.

Chapter Thirty Four

Plucked roughly from the lush inlet of her vehicle, Julia felt the hard protrusion of the handle serrate the soft flesh of her hips. Accosted soundly by the sapid brute himself, Michael's body swathed her with the tenacity of scintillated skin, pressing her firm against the cool metal in an indurate hug. He conferred welcome in the most despotic display, bracketed well by the estimable gauge of a sigh.

"Hi." He growled greedily into the lair that was her mouth.

"Hi." Julia sighed, returning the torrid breath to his mouth. Her lips further parted with a smile.

"Mm, I think I may have forgotten what you taste like." Michael gruffly informed, thrusting his tongue, like a ladle, in the inferno of her mouth. He procured her exotic sapor, drawing forth a rewarding fill. "Two weeks is a long time to conserve the memory of one's food. I'm going to have to reacquaint myself with every inch of your body, and I pray something jogs my memory before this weekend gets through."

"Is that so?"

"Most indubitably," he groaned, surging his hips harder to hers. "I'll also need to forage deep. You know…for stowage. This way I can ward off the possibility of this ever happening again. My memory just doesn't seem to be working well these days. I guess I'll have to remember to go see someone about that."

"You are unsalvageable, you know that?" Julia blissfully advised, furthering the tilt of her head in offering, her hands clamped receptively at his back.

"I've been told something to that effect before."

"Really?"

"Mm-hmm,"

"And do you foresee slating any plans to work on that? You know…maybe taper a few of those compulsions that tends to plague that mind of yours?"

"Not one." He hummed cogently. "You know what they say about things not broken, and thus far, mine have served me well."

"Well…in that case" she sighed, looking almost despondent. She adjusted her fit against his chest. "I guess I'll just have to abide your assertive pursuits then. And since that seems to be the only selection obtainable, I brought a somewhat piddly token to the table."

"And what's that?" Michael warmly inquired, touching a kiss to the fullness of her lips. He eased the press of his body. Peeling them both from the vehicle, his hands rocked down her arms like the rhythmical tail of a cat, dropping lower to revere the curves of her hips.

"Patience," Julia advised sweetly, gifting him a sly smirk. The two negotiated their way through a dusky garage, strutting with the same alacrity as they always have. It bred no different since their enkindled commence. With months now authenticating their magnetic affair, the ardor had yet to diminish, as did the zest. As ever, the two flew to seclusion like birds at the onset of dusk. All cordial chit-chat was then attended to as a subsequent thought.

Thus far, Michael had yet to determine the exact fervency mangled within the riff of their rummage. Did such bedeviling sprout due to the evolution of his feelings? Or was it born of this mystique that sits between them? Whichever conjecture now bore the full argot of truth, it mattered not in the way of results, since veracity and perception now tottered on opposing fence. Well augmented past the astounding portent it once held, their act now budded to that of mesmeric. It was like residing in a new realm. The euphoric pull alone was enough to keep him well anchored to his knees.

Julia smiled as she pulled the small container from the pocket of her purse. Thwacking the brassy belly of the tin, a soft chorus ensued, as the content yelped like tiny pebbles trouncing the sides of a metal can.

Leveled promptly in the stead of an enigmatic smile, a light frown dented the edges of Michael's brows, shifting his eyes to hers. His voice sifted through the room like a mercuric hug. "Is there something you're trying to tell me?" he asked, mischief overtly braided in his tone, biting into the flesh of her arm as he tightened his squeeze.

"Not at all," Julia explained with a flirtatious laugh, her eyes climbing seductively to his face. "They're Altoids!" She chirped with an incredulous flip of her hand, confirming the obvious by indicating the name already visibly on the can.

"I know what they are." Michael nodded, looking thoroughly confused. Yet recognizing the latent clues of something enthralling to come, though this time he was at a loss in the aiding of their game.

Julia searched his manner for the slimmest speck of perception, holding his eyes. She awaited cognizance to summit the medley of colors that was starkly distinctive to his gaze. *Surely someone as well journeyed as he would know what it was she offered?* "I would have sworn you, of all people, would be astute to such simple delicacy."

"I'm sorry, but you have me at a loss this time." Michael shrugged, frowning perplexedly as he wagged his head. "I'm drawing a complete blank."

Brown eyes circumspectly dredged the befuddled flecking of hazel, finding no hint of familiarity with her lascivious plot. Her smile morphed to the swampy stature of an impious sneer.

"I know they're mints, but beyond that I don't know what you..." Noticing her expression, Michael paused, for the rendering was such that an ache mushroomed through his body. Her countenance spelt one thing and one thing only, and total compliance will, no doubt, be an emphatic demand. Not a problem, Michael grunted, as he had no trouble being the subservient slave. Not in any pursuits instigated by her.

"Would you care for a mint?" Julia asked in a slow, hypnotic tone, resting the small tin on the bed. She slowly worked the brown T-shirt atop the swell of her breasts, dropping the garment in a cluttered clump at her feet, she moved without pause to her skirt.

"I would *love* a mint." Michael retorted through a beastly purr, following her lead with a single exception attached. Though unlike her, his clothes vicariously hung, dangling eerily from various stations in rejoinder of her hands. While she meticulously peeled, he excitedly shredded, sending each piece on high sails through the air. They tottered oblivious of a beautiful wool covered floor waiting just beneath.

The small can rattled in a quiet that soared like a strong aegis around them, sounding louder in the large room than its stunt size would suggest. Julia pulled free the shallow lid from an equally shoal body, spilling a quartet of the tiny contents on the bed. She eyed them in contemplation. With a coy smile, Julia shifted her attention, leaving the mints behind. She sunk her knees to the thick matting of the bed. Much like an offer of debauchery, now plated in the center of her palm, so the small mint pageant between them, resembling that of an inconspicuous pill.

Catapulted in a flash to his past, the mint served as a strong catalyst to his then idiotic bent. Partaking of poisons he once considered treats, most often with much the same scenario attached. But this day was far from being that. The warmth of her smile set his pulse on a merry trot, watching her raptly as she touched the mint to her tongue, Michael smiled.

A mere tinge of hesitation surfaced not. No questions of how, what or why rushed past his lips. In its stead, Michael gave his most avid compliance. Coolly following her guide, he laid the mint on his tongue. Expectation brightened his features as he awaited her next maneuver, his mind ablaze with a whirlwind of thoughts, dipping sweetly into avenues they so often traverse.

Michael met her leisured advance in the middle of the bed, leaning delicately against the brush of her hands as they surfed the ridges of his chest. Her lips stroked both hillock and valley in her climb to his mouth, sharing the sweet fire of the mint. She twirled the flavored disc across his tongue, blazing a fervent trail in each place that she touched. Hungry hands readily roamed her body, staking claim to the places they love to tease, their kisses soon grew voracious the deeper they delved. Pushing the venture until they clung, their bodies forged in a melding caress.

Breaking the pull in their sumptuous climb, Julia pushed him backwards on the bed. Passion now eroded the employ of her smile, swilling her like a fruited drink. It flashed brashly in her eyes. Devotion, coupled well with greed, thrived profusely in the dark depths, urging her hands while she crawled astride his hips. Commandeering the carnality of his mouth, Julia peppered the furiousness of their feed, taking caution to stay his usual wont to ravish. Yet she lingered as she seared a trench down his muscular chest, her breath like a warm whisper atop the smooth head of his pecs.

Unfaltering in its intent, her tongue maneuvered the minty sweet with authority, twirling in place as if tethered to an unseen string. It grew relentless in its toil. Sliding over the peaks on his manly chest, she extracted the lengthy chorus of a moan, vibrating like an aftershock in the very place that she rest. Lean fingers manipulated the silky strands of her hair, cupping her head to his chest. His breath sailed in a protracted sigh.

The icy fire grew eccentrically rousing. Cool tingles seemed to almost burn from a fount of unremitting heat, and the momentum of her touch bloomed exquisitely tortuous the longer she drudged. Whisking with precision across his body, it robbed him of his breath. Gentle fingers, in dictate, softly worked the pulsing of his thighs, clasping him in the warm, assured fold of her hand. He rose to her claim with the sweetened twinge of anticipation stoking his action. A lean thigh moved between his with deliberate intent, pressing the essence of his manhood against the silken limb. Her caresses then tutored his ferocious need. With the skillful use of her body, she further heightened the exchange, as her attack thence grew riotous and wild.

Wickedly, Julia halted her torment. Her brown eyes skimming the darkened pool of his, and the most alluring smile washed her expression in concurrence with the sight. Though it was not quite so for the man, as he barely commanded the muscles required to replicate the exacting of such feat. His only fathom was of the creature perched devilishly aloft his chest, and he greatly ached to let her know of his need.

Stretching for another mint, Michael captured her breast, his hand easing over the swell in a calculated glide, while the other redirected her focus back to his mouth. His rummage then debilitated the efforts of her hands, sending a shiver through both bodies. Passion welded their bodies together like the fusing of steel, and their kisses, before long, vaulted the barriers between cultured and barbaric. The new mint trundled roughly with the demands of their tongue, swapped sweetly between them; it set a chilled draught with the release of their breath.

Astutely, Michael's leg rose between hers, pressing sturdily against the flower that resides on the receptive estate. He heightened the exigent fire of their drive with the soft stir of his leg. And the delicate paragon felt pleasingly as flowers are wont to do—after a misting of rain. Eager to nourish the bloom, Michael rolled, though she quickly nullified the effort with a caper of her own. Reaching between them, her fingers beguiled his body, again seizing his breath, and had it not felt so good, he would have reclaimed dominance with a sturdier press. But she effusively thwarted his every attempt, pressing him back onto the pillow. She instructed him in a near voiceless sigh.

"Not yet. I'm not finished giving you your present."

A gritty grunt vibrated through his entire chest, marveling at the length of her schooling, Michael grumbled his quest. *How much basting can one man take?*

Slipping yet another mint in her mouth, she smiled before dismounting his leg, touching a finger to his knee, Michael obliged the tacit command. Lowering his leg, he eagerly awaited the next dais of their climb. Knowing whatever her plan, it would be well worth the wait, irrespective of the length. Pushed wickedly to exceed the realms of his limits at times, she'd always taken him home; this regardless of the many torturous routes.

Her mouth wasted no time in narrating its mesmeric bent. Brushing him with her lips, her tongue scraped delectably over the smoothness of his most sensitive skin. Circling like a shark to its meal, she daubed him with the icy-zest of her sweets, dispensing the sensation of being doused in a frosty bath while in the middle of her heated strokes. The concoction tilled like chaos on his senses, wreaking havoc on every nerve while she deepened her plunge. Gruffly recited, Michael sent her his most avid esteem, calling it from the furthest depths of his throat, her kisses grew brusquely abyssal. The thrill of ecstasy drifted blithely within his grasp, raining assuredly from inside out before her kisses suddenly stop. Surprise was but one, if not the rarest, emotion he battled when he looked up in her eyes.

"Now," she sighed, her whispered breath rising like the ditty to an advertisement being aired. It called him fully without a tinge of subliminal elements hidden in its note.

No further diction was waited upon, and none came as a construal to what was said, rolling without resistance. Michael instantly brokered his reply, assaulting her with every part of his body. His hands, mouth, tongue and the beautifully primed projection, fervently worked her inside and out. A cavernous grunt escaped them as he drilled her body, hastening their gluttonous feed. The two clambered towards a revered ascension. Two together as one in more ways than just that, it was coupling at the very core and at its very best. Around them, the soft hue of darkness descended loftily upon the room, clothing the couple inside as apogee torrented their climb.

The raggedness of their breath in time eased, dulling the lusty squall. The room again fell silent. Michael slowly lifted himself to gape down at her face, balancing his body above hers. He drew his brows to their maximum height. "Mm, who knew a small mint could be so…robust." He smiled, his deep voice sounding hoarse. The words then rattled from his throat like the droning of bees.

A faint curl in her shoulders gave a non-committal reply. Yet an aura of satisfaction openly communicated her pleasure in the act, given aptly in the action itself.

Michael's gaze donned hers for what felt like a vastitude of minutes, and although the lapse seemed only a lengthy silence, the communication between them was an endless edict of their hearts. An exchange told as fervently with the bestowing of their hands, stroking each other in, what seemed surely, like the vestigal of an absent thought.

More than ever, he had come to treasure these moments as intensely as the amatory dance itself. When her eyes told everything she seemed so determined to suppress, and he'd often wondered if she knew what she relinquished in the emotive depths of her gaze. Amazed at how a look from her can say so much, and bequeathed so much more in the crux of their play, it was at these times that he was most grateful for his command of a second language. Almost spilling his hand at inopportune times, he appeased the urge to tell her how he felt under the cloak of such prettily dressed anonymity, choosing to employ the obscure confession as an armament instead.

Beholden to his grandfather—a Frenchman born to an English parent—his mother, Jacqueline, was a popular French model in her day. Blessed with a temperament as spirited as she was refine, she was, therefore, credited for his passionate side, so, too, his opinionated views. Roland was as tenacious with his grandkids as he was with his son, making certain French was a learned language between them. The dialect had since grown fairly comfortable on his tongue. And at those moments when she had him locked in a firestorm of passion, he has had to make full use of that fact.

Michael smiled as his long arm extended past her, plucking the tin from the edge of the bed. The tiny contents eagerly clattered in their metallic house, as if to signal their penchant to play. The chorus seemed endless in their petition for the next act. Thoughtfully, Michael stared at the can, a tepid smirk tucked to the corners of his mouth, lifting his eyes to hers, they instantly returned to the can.

"For later," Michael murmured then, rattling the quiet with the gentle twist of his hand. He tucked the small treat beneath the edge of his pillow. A spark instantly brightened in his eyes with the underlying inference, while his brows, in jocular aid, fluttered grandly in a dance that conveyed the full gamut of his lusty thought. "Refuel, refresh, but…a definite revisit." He hummed, kissing the corner of her mouth as if to assure her of his pledge. His smile spoke only of intent. Tucking her body to his, Michael swiftly rolled from his place, taking her with him to a vacant pillow. He planted her flat atop his chest. Her breasts spilled along the hard bedding of his ribs as she adjusted their fit, rounding their softness along his side in a not-so-insignificant caress. The two drank full of the gloriousness laced in the aura adjoining their zest. As with the onset of a zephyr, so, too, the workings of Michael's hands, skimming the soft curves of her body in a sensual climb. They flounced over the smooth curve of her buttock from the silky serpents of her thighs, sweeping the spill of her breasts. He stroked the smoothness made surely of silk, his hands, in time, falling to the upper curve of her back, and a long draught, yoked solely of contentment, sailed from his nostrils as his body relaxed.

"You like?" Julia asked in a lazy whisper.

"Oh…most…definitely," came the staggered reply, his head bobbing lax and incalculably slow. "I most definitely like." Again covering her mouth, he answered her query, leaving her little doubt on his view.

Though progressive in its unremitting bent, evening did not sail by on the wings of a mighty dragon. It floated, instead, on the soft basins of clouds. Moving only with a modest draught, its progress challenged the conviction of a sloth. Dimness converted to syrupy black before long, painting the atmosphere only that, gray, in time, revivify with the luster of a new day. The sun once again tarried not in its dominance, but lent all the entirety of an austerely smile.

The two watched the evolution of morning from the sanctuary of their bed. Their murmured voices cooed through the stillness like a soft melodic hum, for the onslaught of their chatter again varied with no seeming end.

"I like you, you know that?" Michael droned after a pause, his voice lifting in what sounded like a matter-of-fact hug. Hazel eyes dipped to affectionately fondle her feet. Coming from nowhere in particular but that it had to be said, it permeated the space with mute emotions that was yet unsaid. Spritzing softly from his roost at the foot of the bed, persuasive fingers continued their delicious focus, caressing the soles of her feet through the silence. His proclamation seemed then an immaterial quip.

"I know. I like you, too." Julia purred almost shyly, turning her head on the pillow to better assess his face.

"A lot," Michael breathed, pressing a kiss to the arch of each foot in a casual show. The room fell further silent—as with the abrupt holding of one's breath. He watched tamely as her eyes dropped contently to the bed, and a slow nod served as her response.

"I know." She retorted softly at last. *How could she not?* "Me too," spitting the words dryly through a whisper, it came like the ambling of an afterthought, as if the admission strained her somehow. Lasciviously, she'd been exceedingly flagrant in every way. Working his body as if the world was at its end, she poured her soul into every movement she granted, and can communicate her desires in nefarious ways. But beyond that, her mind was a stagnant bog. She did, however, like him a lot. As she would make herself a liar if she did not admit that he inhabits an important place in her world. She just could not fathom where or how. Being as different as they are, there was no simple answer to such quest.

Michael's hands eased over the padding of her calf, tenderly caressing each as he watched her, comforted, as always, by having her close. His smile was almost luminous in its dispense——all be it from inside. She was an amazing source of contentment to his senses, like being home. She seemed to be the foundation from which all gladness stemmed. "Hungry?" he asked, his voice casual, closing the curtain on his admission, Michael smiled.

"No, but maybe after my shower we can go scavenging. By the time we agree on something, I'm sure I'll be truly ravenous." She smiled, giving his toe a firm squeeze before removing her feet from his chest. Standing, Julia dragged her fingers along the length of his arm, continuing the climb over his chest. She brightened her smile. Lowering her face to his, she touched a kiss to the corner of his mouth, though her eyes remained transfixed to the brindled eminence stoking his own.

Watching her closely, Michael's smile grew perceptive, gliding a hand gently up her side. His mien warmed as if privy to her thoughts. No words were exchanged between, though their eyes dallied meritoriously long, staying the other from anything but the resolution of such deed. Still yet holding his gaze, Julia straightened, squeezing his hand. She sighed as if to finalize the consensus of a lengthy debate.

"Did I hear an invitation somewhere in that?" Michael chortled, turning his head to better appreciate her departure.

"I didn't think a man like you needed such things." Came the silky reply, thrown provocatively over her shoulders. The exaggerated swing of her hips was but a deliberate plus.

"Do I have one then?" Michael asked in what sounded like a growl. His eyes tethered to the movements of her shapely behind.

"You can have whatever you want." Julia taunted, turning then. She tendered her assets in a prolonged view, measuredly veiling the show. Her smile was the last to disappear behind the cover of the door.

Like a jolt of lighting, Michael leapt from the bed. Not needing time to ponder the decision, for the outcome was but one. His smile was almost supercilious as he sauntered through the door, taking a seat on the floor. His gaze followed her action as if they now watched a beautifully scripted show.

"I see you're enjoying the view." Julia teased, noting the grin on his face.

"It has all the components I like, what's not to enjoy?" Michael grinned, folding his arms like a pillow behind his head. His long body arched with a satisfied stretch.

"So will watching become your thing now?"

"It has its merits." Michael hummed, donating a lazy smile to his satyric cause. His scrutiny sprang blatant. This time, she *was* the show, and his eyes took full advantage of that. Walking up her body from the tip of her toes to the pouting of her lips, each seductive curve tweaked both mind and body. Twisted atop her head in a bun, rebellious strands clung madly to the slender lines of her neck, threatening defiance with each movement of her head. The bundled mass rocked jauntily as she lifted her head to the flow. "You're so...*damn* sexy." He panted gruffly, wagging his head as his gaze blazed a path across her thighs.

"Is that your expert opinion?" she laughed, not bothering to spare him a glance. She turned her face to the water instead. Well cognizant of the consequence of his approach, and what that meant.

"Do you need another?" Michael teased as he adjusted the position of his head.

With a twist of her wrist, the water's death granted the room the purity of silence. Turning, Julia pushed open the shower door in a well protracted show, pulling a towel from the rack. She smiled. "Should I get another?"

Silence quickly swallowed the vaporous room, preaching patience while it held the occupants close. Michael watched as she mopped the water from her face, leaving her question to hang like a flaccid whip. His expression morphed to that of serene. Quietly, without propounding an answer, he stood, taking the towel from her hand. He dabbed it across her body.

"I'm sure you've heard it all before, Julia, and you'll continue to hear it repeated without any foreseen end. The mirror does not lie." Michael rejoined then, turning her until he had full access to her back. He slowly mopped the droplets from her spine. "I, on the other hand, have an added codicil inked in each word I give you." He advised, easing the towel down her thighs. He promptly squatted on the floor, lifting her foot onto his lap.

"And what's that?" she asked, sensing he was less inclined to elaborate had she not pressed.

Lifting the other of her legs to his thigh, he touched the thirsty towel to her toes. Conscious of the abrading gaze now centered atop his head, though his enjoyment was such that he refused to relinquish his focus or his task. The answer did not fly to him in a hurry, nor did any remnants that could supply him truth, none that was not already discussed or known between them.

"It's what corporations sometimes refer to as a secret ingredient." Michael informed calmly, straightening from his bend. He solidified his answer with a beguiling smile. "Some even say it makes everything better." He shrugged. "That's what *they* say, though someday, when I'm in the mood to share, I'll give you my opinion on that." Draping the towel around her neck, he fashioned its ends like a bolo-tie. "I'll say this, though," he added matter-of-factly, reaching inside the enclosure, his hand swept the lever with calm, instantly adding rain to the sound of their voice. "I'm sure if you ever find the need to give all that chatter some thought, you're sure to iron out that perplexity in no time flat." He shrugged, stepping past her into the shower, Michael smiled, and only a sideway glance gave hints as to whom he spoke. "I think it's my turn to wash." Michael laughed, his deep tone lifting above the hissing of manmade rain.

"So then that would make it my turn to watch." Julia smirked, pulling the towel from her neck. She made herself a narrow bed. Mimicking his behavior past, she squirmed in her effort to find a comfortable position on the floor.

"Comfy?" Michael quizzed with a sharp lift of his brow, singing the gentle mocking as easily as her earlier tease.

"Enough." Julia shrugged, refusing to acknowledge her gnawing discomfort. She struggled to ignore the hard tiles quilting her back, cold and unbending beneath the protruding knots that were her bones. Most indubitably, her new bed was not pliant, rearing especially so against the knotty bulge of her tailbone and worse so, on the knobs of her wrist. But she'd happily endure, for the short spell of a shower, to return his ogling bent.

The dark hairs on his body grew proficiently bold, darkening below the clout of a full lather, the muscles of his chest flexed with the slightest reach of his hand. Clumps of suds slipped down his body to rest carefree at his feet, dragging the focus of her gaze on their giddy descent. The view was truly worth its price of admission. Smiling in agreement of such, she watched with satisfaction as the last slipped from his body to the drain, preferring the unhindered view of his physique, though either prospect was profoundly enticing to regard. With a slow sigh, her eyes eagerly retraced their tour of his body, pausing as they landed on his face. His gaze seemed patient as he waited to take hold, locking instantly. A twinkle sparred fiercely with the darker of hers.

"Do you see something you wish to make a purchase on?" he asked with friendly sarcasm, sentience already evident on his face.

The corner of Julia's mouth moved in a meager smile, unashamed of her open perusal, though mindful there was little option but, as she could not have claimed denial then. He'd seen her succumb too often to try. Though she never meant to linger that long. "Why? I'm sure your perverted mind has already made its summation on the grubby path my mind took."

"Then perhaps you'd like to come in so you can better argue that point. This way I can better assess the facts as they are."

Julia pondered the tempting request with genuine interest, a smile staying fresh on her face. "No." She groaned at last, giving a small shrug with her response, she wrinkled her nose in aid. "I'm not in the mood to get wet again." Sighing thus, she threw her eyes to the ceiling, cringing at the realization of her words, as she knew she just flung wide the gates to his darkly distorted mind.

"I like you all wet." Michael growled. His retort zipping back in a flash, yet the cadence in his voice was almost hypnotic. "It makes my entrance…enthralling, and my stay…mm, so…much more thrilling. Don't you agree?" he asked with a taunting smile.

"You are a pervert and a poet through and through, aren't you?"

"At your service and damn proud of it," he averred, and the room again grew happily still. The sound of water quieted to a meretricious drip, aiding the magnetic lull in the room. Michael stepped from the shower in all his mesmeric display, grabbing the last towel from the rack. He slung the hefty towel across his back. "Besides, there was nothing perverted about my words, I merely offered you my service. You know, there was a time they hailed a man a gentleman for that." He remarked spryly, flashing a devilish grin. "And, might I add," he further grumbled, leaning forward, he offered her his hand, towing her to her feet with a gentle tug, "You like my perversion."

"Is that so?"

"Mm-hmm, you've even told me so on numerous occasions."

"Now that I know I did not do. Why would I ever encourage you in such absurdity? That would be asinine, wouldn't it?"

"And yet I'm here to tell you that you have." Michael smiled, the decibels in his voice dipping softly. "Do you always forget the things you utter?"

"I wouldn't forget that?"

"Should I grant you a reminder then?"

"Evidently it's a need." Julia muttered, setting both hands on her hips with an air of defiance, certain he had no such proof to offer.

"You said." Michael started in a low rumble, leaning forward until her breasts pressed his chest. Cool air fired its icy breath across the surface of each peak, chilling them to a stance, but that was not what his body responded to. "And I quote, 'Oh… Michael, that feels so…good. Oh, God…don't stop.'"

"You…" Julia gaped, her eyes widening with a modicum of shock, and the look on her face was almost skeptical—had she not known the truth.

"As if I would," Michael drawled. "Why would I, when that particular song is a favorite of mine?"

"You…" she cringed, knowing he spoke the truth, but hearing it replayed seemed somehow abnormal to her ears. "You heard me?"

"It's hard not to, Julia, when you recite them so close to my ears." Pulling her against his chest, Michael smiled, his arms locking effusively at her back. Kissing each cheek, his mouth settled gently on the corner of her mouth. "I savor every word as they are the topping to my favorite dessert."

"You know I can hear you, too, right?" Julia announced coolly, though a mischievous smile was his only response, and his eyes glowed with the secret of a titillating thought.

"You're supposed to." He whispered through the soft rendering of a kiss.

Shorted appeasement by the quickness of his confession, Julia pondered the insight he gave, her mind retrieving charts of all the times he'd whispered in her ear. Things she had no understanding of, as they were always professed so sweetly in French. "Then why, French?"

"Isn't French the language for lovers?" Michael asked after a pause, his eyes softly caressing her face.

"That hardly seems fair. You understand my deepest cries, while I need a translator to understand yours. That's a somewhat fraudulent advantage, don't you think?"

"How exactly does one translate an appetite?" Michael droned. "If I request anymore of you, Julia, there won't be much left for either of us to enjoy. And I do…so…enjoy you, Julia." He breathed, stroking the side of her chin with his thumb. "I'm really not that hard to figure out, you already know more about me than you think. I'm a simple man, Julia. I'm just trying to satisfy the avarice you put in me. I'm just trying to get my fill." He proclaimed with a kiss, silencing any lingering in her head.

Lifting his head, Michael gazed at the fullness of her lips, moist from the slow flick of her tongue, and the look in her eyes made his heart flutter to a near stop.

"*Ah, mon ange, que peut faire un mauvais sève dire pour vous faire comprendre la profondeur?* Ah, angel, what can a poor sap say to make you understand the depth? *Je suis impressionné par votre beauté à chaque fois que je te vois*, I'm awed by your beauty each time I see you," Michael whispered, his hand brushing her skin like a gentle kiss. "*Pour vous tenir renforce aussi décidément car il affaiblit.* To hold you strengthens as decidedly as it weakens. *Une touche de vous envoie mon pouls en vrille. Vous me garder voulant vous, vouloir toujours plus.* A touch from you sends my pulse in a spin. For you keep me wanting you, wanting more still." He sighed, gliding his tongue over the swell her breast. He covered her nipple with the heat of his kiss, returning, in time, to her mouth hot and demanding. He again granted her a disguised potion of his thought. "*Viens avec moi et laissez-moi prendre ma dose. Permettez-moi de vous boire jusqu'à ce que mon cœur vous pousse encore.* Come away with me and let me take my fill. Let me drink from you until my heart grows still." He groaned, returning his kisses to her body, his fingers brushed the smoothness of her thighs. "*Reste avec moi jusqu'à ce que le temps s'assombrit. Rester avec moi jusqu'à ce que jamais, plus un jour. Dis-moi, dis que tu vas rester.* Stay with me until time goes dark. Stay with me until forever, plus a day. Say to me this, say you'll stay."

Her hands came to move over him as persuasive as her breath, and inside, Michael sighed. "Is that clear enough for you or do you wish to have it interpreted?"

"Maybe later," she purred, pressing against him as she kissed his chest. "Right now, I want to see if you can make me say your name—out loud that is." She invited in a husky sigh, staking claim to his body with the determined bent of her hand. A groan then vibrated from deep inside the silo of his chest, and his kisses grew almost primitive in counter. "Mm," she hummed as he swept her from the floor, strolling with her to the bed. He placed her at the edge.

Slowly, Michael reached for the small can, and the tiny contents again voiced their excitement with a vociferous cheer. "I have a debt I need to repay, remember? And I am nothing if not assiduous when I work." He smirked, sitting the small can in the middle of the bed. He gently lowered her to her back. "Suddenly, I'm famished." Michael growled, dropping his head. He teased the indent on her stomach.

Time again knew no haste in his work, returning to her all she gave him. He left no part on her body untouched. No savory nectar went unrealized in his determined drudge. He would know her as she knew him—complete, grasping a smidge more of her mystique with the passing of each day.

Chapter Thirty Five

October harbored little changes from the fervid days that had erstwhile preceded the month, for although the protracted body of the year neared its end, only miniscule shavings were wrought from the torrid heat. In stark contrast, the air soared with less rigidity than it once had, boxing the willowy limbs of trees. Leaves tinged with yellowy-orange frolicked in a soft squall, singing joyously while the orchestra swirled. They echoed the denizen's glee, abetting the chirrups of a polyphony melody to the sun.

A litany of adjectives was used when describing the magnificent extension of summer, soaring to an endless stock. The gift was truly a Carolina treasure, blessed with a truncated blast of the wintry months; warmth reigned officious in the gorgeous southern state. Sanctioned with a robust body, the harshness of summer easily dominated the waning year. Manipulating the days until autumn aptly stifled its reign, assuming its place as the incumbent sovereign for a phase. Darkness brought with it a stern promise of what was to come. Holding its own in faux variance, the once throttling heat of summer gave forth a softened chill with its rest.

Julia's eyes trolled wondrously across a stodgy night's sky. Awed by the impressive display. Velvety-black amiably canopied the miniscule arraying of their heads. Festooned by an endless sparkle of lights, darkness weakened with the spray of a silvery moon, pampering the night in, what favored, the backdrop of a diamond show.

Dinner started with the inception of the setting sun, enduring the oscillating pigments of dusk. The two stayed to watch night's resplendent display.

Throngs of aging oaks, maples and pines walled the slope they now lingered upon. Resting miles afar the imposing structure of the house, civilization seemed but a perception to come, as nothing but the natural blessing of night enveloped their camp. Preparation was reasoned the key to hindsight, or so it was inferred, soaring after long like a pledge. The two aligned themselves with all the illustrious comforts of home. An air mattress, countless blankets and pillows were but a few of the imperative musts. Each piece thoroughly deduced as a sound necessity, should a need arise.

Michael's breath sailed contently as he surveyed the night's overwhelming beauty. Ruched in a passive exhale, its tune wafted through the silence like the distended chord of a note, fanning the tranquil night in its rise. Horded haphazardly at his back, a growing stack of pillows balanced the mattress's wavy sway, stabling the lenience of their rest. Muscular legs stood stationed like guards adjacent each hip. Drawn to a virile stance, a knee tabled the elbow of a hand. Casually, his leg bowled the soft flesh of her hip, tapping her with the stalwart limb, he asked. "Care to join me?" inquiring this in a rumbly breath, playful fingers pestered the wildness of her hair, though its softness barely ruffled the serenity of the night. "Your spot's getting cold,"

Julia smiled in an impish response, scooting backwards to his chest. She laid her back snug against the broad span, planting a gentle kiss on his cheek like a bauble for her cause.

"Not so fast, you." Michael announced in a whispery breath, his hands obstructing retreat. "I'm not quite finished with you yet." He proclaimed mildly, leaning to her with a rakish grin. His thumb stroked the outline of her jaw. Avidly, he took his time relishing her mouth. And much like the air that swilled around them, the kiss was leisured and quiet, conflicting some with his usual wont to forage deep. Nonetheless, the grazing parked a patent flutter in their chest, and he knew she felt his as certain as he felt hers.

Julia shivered as he released her from the turbulence of his hold, snuggling further into his chest. He mistook the gesture as a sure indication of the night's chill, reaching for a blanket, Michael swaddled them both.

"Mm," he rumbled as he locked her to his chest. "You're even more delicious a treat to snack on than you are a feast for the eye, and that's saying a lot."

"Flatterer," Julia scoffed, dismissing his statement as bait. She curled her body further into the wall of his chest, seeking an additional boost of his warmth. The mattress grunted loudly with each movement she made, grumbling its discontent, though the two had long since flouted the disgruntled laments, snubbing the continuous descant of their night.

Michael smiled sagaciously at her gentle rebuff, knowing nothing would come of the compliment he gave. But the night's perfection demanded that something be said. "What a beautiful night." He muttered in a faint breath, gazing admiringly at the moon. He shelved the possibility of an imperative talk.

"Hmm," she hummed, giving the lazy sigh as a wholehearted reply. The strong push of her breath capped the docile answer as a culmination of facts, needing no further wording to make it so. Chatter caroled aloft the ensuing silence, wafting like music from a distant stereo. Small creatures gave rhythm to the night, voicing their squabbles and jollity like plaintiffs in a tribunal.

Betwixt the decorous cackles, water trickled softly from a distant creek, adding harmony to the eclectic mix. Its music further coddled the night. "This was a great idea." Julia sighed, rolling her head on his shoulders. She brandished a lethargic smile.

"I'm just trying to keep up with you." He grunted in response.

"Me? I wish I could take credit for this one." She smirked. "The idea was a solid ten. I have to give you the totality of that."

"Maybe yours bred a little differently in places, but you've certainly kept me on my toes. I've had to work twice as hard to make mine at least as exciting as yours. Especially since you're already ahead of me in that department"

"Who knew the stipulation for fun could be such a challenge." Julia laughed, and the sound was like the unskilled twang of an instrument not yet known, though it was no less beautiful to regard. "But where does it say a variant of pleasure could not be had while you're having…fun?"

"You're a tutor and a scholar for sure." Michael smiled, drawing the other of his leg to a stance. "Doth the work ever end?"

"You find it work?"

"Not nearly as much as I find it fun, my mind is in a constant pother with itself."

"Nothing quite that drastic here, a little imagination goes a long way with you," she hummed, dropping her hand atop his. She implemented an affectionate squeeze.

"I know. It's the gift that keeps on giving long after the package has been unwrapped. I like that."

"I've heard it said that it's always easier to plan a party when you know what the guest of honor wants. After that, it's just a matter of acquiring an appetizing outfit for the show." She shrugged, smiling overtly with the analogy. She surfed the protrusion of his knuckles with her thumb.

"As I've told you, I'm a simple man, Julia. No need to trouble yourself with such thought. Come as you are works just as well, maybe even better."

"I bet it would." She snickered, groaning behind the thought. "I may have a little trouble with the drive. But I'm sure that wouldn't bother you now, would it?"

"Now that hurt." He droned, frowning as if injured by her words. His voice sailed provokingly soft. "Far be it from me to wish you any ill, since I do so love our sparring, and have always looked forward to every ounce of the adventures we have."

"Shouldn't you be at the weaning stage by now? You've had me in every conceivable way. There can't possibly be anything left."

"You're a rare fire, Julia. One I just can't seem to put out." He shrugged, giving his answer in a whisper. Michael gazed out at the darkness as if prompted by a cue. "One I don't want to put out." He finished in a rough breath, holding his gaze to the distant woods.

More satisfied with his answer than she rightly dared, Julia smiled, brushing his cheek as if concurring. She kissed the hard edges of his jaw. As always, Michael was eager to rummage in his samplings of her, manipulating her placid attempt. He set flames to her body with the practiced drudgery of his mouth. Beneath them, the mattress quarreled incessantly, grousing its grievance through the quiet night, as each body quested a worthier fit. Michael altered their position until his body amiably swaddled hers. The heated stroke of his hand sat gently upon her breasts in his quest, plying her exquisitely. His labor grew arduous with his affluent knowledge of her body.

For a moment, Michael simmered the delicious ambling of his toils, gazing into the volcanic vat of her eyes. A smile touched the corner of his mouth. As if reading her darkest confession, his smile widened, for it seemed well scribed in the blackening depths. Returning to her indubitably more demanding than before, his kisses promptly scalded her skin, coercing the will of her body in his ardent drive. A less civilized consort swam forward with the benefit of his strive. Partnered well with an urgency of her own, desire surpassed the logical guide of reason, and she spoke boldly of this with the furious swing of her body, delighting him as he syphoned the sap of her sugary clefts. He answered her every summons with truth, imparting his thoughts commendably with his body. He replied by name, his voice raspy and soft in her ear.

The wild droning of their breath slowly abated with the descent of their summit. The night's blather, in time, drifted to their consciousness as if from a protracted distance. Michael smiled as he lifted his head from the cradle of her neck, his long fingers moving like thread through the needle of hers, bringing them to his lips. He tenderly kissed her hand, casually inspecting each digit. He asked. "Are you cold?"

"No." She purred, wagging her head in answer. Her beautifully contoured lips twisted in a beguiling smile. "I think it's safe to say you're an expert at seeing to the averting of that."

"What can I say? You bring out the worst in me." Michael groaned.

"If that's your worst, then I'm not sure I can survive your best."

"The flames were no doubt a mutual fix." He assured through a rough grunt. Kissing the side of her neck, Michael smiled. "My pulse has yet to slow." Uttering thus, he pressed her hand to his chest as an offering of proof. "I think each unearth a more mesmerized ending than the first." Winking slickly behind the announcement, well satisfied by his omission of the word, "day".

Brown eyes glowed warmly under nature's magnificent light, arching her body beneath him like a cat. Her voice assimilated the anciently revered beast. "Tell me, Mr. Dunhill, do you have to brew your own sugar, or does sorghum always flow that naturally from your tongue?" Touching his face to lighten the weight of her words, she glided her fingers through the short curls of his hair.

"I'd have to say that depends solely on the muse. Some, regardless of effort, make it a necessity to draw what's needed from storage. Or build the pith of your momentum like a locomotive gathering steam. But then…" Michael sighed, brushing his finger across the contour of her mouth, he smiled. "There are those times when everything just glides off the tongue, flowing without effort or urging. It just…" he paused, lifting his shoulders in a slow shrug, his eyes slid down her body as if in search of a visual aid. Lowering his head, his kisses strolled the column of her neck, climbing the soft crest of her breasts. He gently nibbled the already initiated peaks, taking each into the cavern of his mouth for a taste. "It just glides with ease—like magic." He hummed, and his kisses again painted the cording of her throat.

"What am I going to do with you?" she asked with a lame snort.

"I vote for punishment." He quickly advised.

"Really?"

"Punish me until I beg you to stop, make me say it over and over before you relent your pace." He counseled, his fingers slowly tracking the lines of her neck, stopping aloft her chest. They circled the smooth, erotic tors. "It's a suggestion." Michael shrugged

"You know..." Julia started in retort, flashing a faint smile as she eased his hand from her breast. Quietly, she feathered his finger across the warm spread of her lips, sinking the lean digit in her mouth. Her tongue worked cogently upon the slender limb. One by one, she kissed the consequential body parts, applying varied techniques. She heightened the thrill of their game. Watched fastidiously as she worked, his cocky grin all but vanished from his face, so, too, the once meritorious glint that blazed in his eyes. A dim scowl lodged aptly in its stead. Its focus set solely on the workings of her mouth. "That may not be such a bad idea." She hummed in finish.

"I'm like putty to you, aren't I?" Michael asked, giving then a low grunt. He eyed her warily as he shifted his body in preparation of retribution. His taunts came with added puncture to their bite, and the rivalry, again, commenced without warn, for, as always, the two worked diligently to outdo the other in their game.

"My turn," Julia whispered through the dark strands of his hair, burying her face there in answer to the toils of his mouth.

"Is it?"

"Oh, most definitely," she averred in a sweet tone, and the petulant moans from their rubbery bed, amplified well the truth of her claim. It blossomed beneath them like an escalating row, grumbling rowdily as she straddled his hips. Smiling, Julia ardently kissed his lips, her mouth paying homage to his body with the fortitude of her work. Travelling the length of his frame, she ruthlessly dragged him to the edge of delirium. Every part of her body worked to intensify his suffer, pushing and pulling him through an erotic kaleidoscope. She remanded the finale at bay.

His throaty exalt gave no warning of a threat, serenading the night with its warm cadence, Michael's muscles, in reply, precipitously flexed. Pouncing like the deadly strike of a Mamba at the point of attack, he sprang, in an agile thrust, to his feet, dragging her hard against the barrier of his chest. His effort was without flaw, and her retaliatory inklings stood stunned in the shadow of his feat. Awed by the authoritative elegance shown in his skill, Julia tasted the cool glibness of metal as he labored masterfully at her back. Setting to simmer a new perception, since the rich concept of being ensnared across the cab of a truck had never before surfaced in any region of her mind, nor had the notion whispered any of its decadent thrills. Yet, the encounter rose to be a most assuaging delight.

A gentle wind swept soothingly over the canine bend of their bodies, cooling the pesky heat of their brows in its wake. It strutted deliciously upon the nakedness of their skin. "Are you okay?" he inquired softly against her neck, peeling his face from her back.

"Never better," Julia cooed

"Come. Let me warm you up."

"Didn't you already do that?"

"This one is supposed to be a little different." He averred with a grin, towing her with him, the two resettled themselves on the bed. "Are you ready for some wine? It will help to lift this chill."

"Wine sounds fine."

"So you do rhyme?" Michael laughed, dropping the large blanket atop her body. His laughter worsened as she threw him a pitying glare. Jumping then from the bed of the truck, he opened the larger of two doors on the driver's side of the cab.

In counter, Julia rolled her eyes to the heaven with a quick follow of her head, flinging a jesting glower at his back; a groan trailed the placid display. Quietly, she tugged the blanket around her shoulders and neck, snuggling further into the vacillating surface of the bed. The loss of his heat was instantly felt. Gone was the sultriness that swath them only hours before, as the night, though bountiful in beauty, no longer held the warm residue sanctioned with day, and the lateness of the hour now breathed its frosted breath to solidify that truth.

Returning triumphant with a bottle of Chateau Calon-Segur—a new addition to a lengthy list—Michael proudly brandished the intoxicant in his hand. Tunneling through her cozy enclosure, he taunted her with the coolness of his skin, pressing chilled cutis to the steady vapors of warmth.

"Woo! You're cold!"

"Come on! Share some of that warmth with me." Michael waggishly implored, plastering the full weight of his body, like a moor, to hers. A snicker bounded the rear of his throat, sounding deeply sinister in its persistence amidst their struggle. Julia bucked wildly in her efforts, stiffening her body under his unremitting press, though she soon settled inside the starch paddock of his arms.

Mollified with his dominance, Michael pasted a sloppy kiss on her lips. Smiling roguishly as he tickled the warm pockets of her arms. Lean fingers curled spitefully in their taunt, scuttling across her flesh in attack. He sharply flinched, halting his assault as retaliation came in the form of a fictitious snack—or so it seemed when her teeth found its mark on the gradient flesh of his chest. "Hey!" Releasing her with a beggarly scowl, he clutched the abused site as he would a mortal wound.

"That's what you get. I hate to be the bearer of bad news, but…recompense sometimes carries its own tax."

"Okay, I supposed that's not to be confused with revenge, which still taunts with the promise of its own sweet fruit."

"Just name the place, Beelzebub."

"A true hellion no doubt?"

"Happy to make your acquaintance, we might have been neighbors for a spell." She purred, her smile sweetening the body of her affront. Michael rolled from her side then with a mocking grunt, retrieving the bottle from the corner where it rest, he set his fingers to task on their drinks.

The ruby red liquid rode the clear surface of their glass like the melted petals of a richly colored rose, bringing with it the subtle scents of mixed berries and spice. Steadily filling her nostrils, she savored the broad multifarious aroma before enmeshing her taste buds in the sundry ingredients it held.

"What do you think? Do you like it?" Michael softly inquired.

Julia gazed admiringly at the wading liquid in her glass before giving a response, placating her palate with another swallow, she smiled. "It's very good. But now I think I'm ready for dessert."

"Oh, I can appease your craving on that." He announced coolly, grinning indeterminably slow. He drove home his meaning with a decisive wink. "How about some dark chocolate to go with that?" Michael propounded sagely, giving his words as a statement of fact. He suppressed clarification on which "that" he intended to compliment his treat. Reaching a long arm across the breadth of the truck, Michael fished through the bamboo basket that once carried their meal. Retrieving a black box from inside, he showed off an assortment of dark indulgence.

"You do make the perfect date, don't you?" she teased, and her playful demeanor of old suddenly froze. "Well…" stammering this in start, she stopped, realizing then the ramification of what was said. She prayed there would be no offence taken from the dim meaning in her jest.

True, but it's just you that bring out this side of me. Michael countered inside, gazing at her in the silence that followed. His sigh was nigh the aural ping of a note. Rooted in place with the demeanor of a cornered prey. She gaped back with eyes widened with shock, looking almost wounded by the import of her slip. He could not help but wonder what she thought would come from the playful grumbling of an ineffectual jest. What they had was so much better than that, and he'd be damned if he'd let something that trivial affect the prominence of that, even if she hailed some truth to her speech.

"I'm sorry, I didn't mean to—"

"I am, aren't I? Now open." He prodded, not wanting or waiting for her finishing reply, Michael touched the thin wafer to her lips. Sinking the treat in her mouth as she complied. She offered then a rueful smile, looking truly timid as she chewed. "It's cooler than I thought it would be," Michael remarked blandly, his eyes vaulting for a quick tour of the sky. Resuming his aberrant pursuits with the careful emancipation of a wink. He immediately lightened the mood. "Why don't we go back to the house and take a long, hot shower?" he continued, his voice like a rumbly purr. "I could light a fire, turn the temperature down and love you by firelight all night long?" he rasped, and the bassy timbre pulsated, as like the gentle tapping of a drum, from the darkest depths of his chest. Licking his fingers in conclusion, his countenance was fully expectant as he awaited her reply.

"Didn't you just do that?"

"There's loving…and there's loving. Who's to say we can't do both."

"All…Night long?" Julia mused, and intrigue flew forward to flirt boldly with the pleasure of such thought. Yet, try as she may, she could not quell the contentment she felt.

"*All* night long." He affirmed in a soft, gravelly hum, lengthening the inclusive word.

"I'm glad I'm not food, or this wouldn't be pretty after a while."

"You should be extremely thankful you're not. With an appetite like mine, I'd have nothing left to crave, and I do so enjoy eating. Where else can I find a midnight snack that satisfies so well?"

"I think that's a given on certain street corners, really."

"Maybe, but every chef has a different approach. The same ingredient does not always harvest the same result. That's why people have things that are labeled…preferences."

"You're not trying to name me a favorite, are you?" Julia teased, though cognizant the idea was remarkably pleasing to every sense that she held, as she was well riveted to his pending reply. If asked, would her answer be the same as his? Is *he* a favorite of hers? She wondered, retracing their steps. She appraised the probability of that, assessing the ferocity of their beginning and everything since. Ironed well in the exquisite way he regards her, or in the way she regards him, and how their time together makes her feel. He had far exceeded every expectation she held, though she had yet to ascertain what was expected in the precinct of an interminable tryst.

One weekend, hadn't that been the extent of her well-laid plan? It seemed, now, a lifetime since the budding of their treaty, and it all stemmed from that one incredible weekend. Now instead of distance, they're woven even more soundly in each other's lives. Working their way from scattered conversations to the cherished weekly banters of old, altering, before long, to daily. Now they talk whenever and just because. Does that make him her favorite? Oh, yes. She acceded with a faint smile, it most certainly does. And strangely enough, irrespective of prior covenants governing their time, she already knew, with conviction, what his answer would be.

"Let's just say you're a rare delicacy whose taste is truly sublime. I assure you, you can't find that on just any street corner?"

"Mm…Sounds heavenly,"

"The title has come up once or twice." He assured with a raffish smile, biting a sliver from the chocolate in his hand, Michael slid the remaining half in her mouth. Caressing the fullness of her lips, he asked. "What do you say? My offer is still waiting on the table."

"Hmm, let's see. I see your offer…and…" she paused, frowning as she muttered in thought. "And I'll raise you with an assortment."

"Call," He commanded in a grumbly sigh, sinking another wafer in her mouth.

"Grapes, preferably red if you have them, snacks—good snacks—and all the treats you can find. I'll need something to sustain me if I'm to indulge you all night."

"Done!" Michael sang, pressing a kiss to the side of her neck, he swilled the last mouthful of his wine. Easing from her side, he alighted from the bed of his truck. The truck's engine roared almost the instant he left, shattering the night's reticence like the wail of an angry storm. It purred gruffly in an echoic distance.

Dense vegetation stood sentry around them like an imposing fence, tall and unwavering, like a legion foist in magnificence. Their sprawled limbs casted a haunting shadow thus fostered by night, thickening the seclusion they lent. Seemingly, there was nothing around them for miles. As if dropped in the middle of an uninhabited forest, the feeling that engulfed them was of unrelenting peace. A splendorous grace vaguely dimmed by the specter of night, and she loved that he brought her to this place.

"Come on. Let's get back to the house." Michael called from the side of the truck, his outstretched arms waiting to aid her descent.

Standing well erected in naught but his sandals, Julia's eyes were immediately drawn. For nothing around them could have captured her attention more raptly than the delicious vaunt he presented to her face. Brushed in silvery-black by the bold lighting of the moon, his sculpting rested like the shading of a beautiful sketch. Lifelike and magnanimous in its grace, it was a scrumptious sight. And at that, it relinquished its spores of inducement to the very last drop. A smile bloomed in approbation of his stalwart physique, spreading richly through her body. The man, and everything about him, was like a magnet she had yet to repel, commandeering her gaze in full, and everything she possessed beneath.

"Does the view delight you much, *Mon amour?*" Michael asked in a gravelly breath, setting her to her feet on the ground. He smiled.

"Oh, indeed." Julia chirped. Smiling as his hand slipped beneath the blanket to acquire her own. Hers curling hastily in response.

"Show me how much, later?" he asked in his customary rumbly tone, stroking her cheek with the warmth of his breath.

"Work, work, work, is there ever any rest?"

"Sure there is. I believe you get a mandated fourteen days to see to that. If you asked me, that's an outrageous amount of time to recuperate from a measly two nights, don't you think?" adding the confectionary lilt to his appraisal, Michael pulled open the passenger door, nudging her inside. His sedentary smirk broadened. Heat blasted the interior like the upsurge gust of a tornado, the velocity well evident by the rustling of her hair. Two blankets further aided their comfort, smoothly daubed across the surface of their seat. It averted the irksome cling of their skin to the sterile texture of leather. A dashing smile preceded his entrance of the truck, dropping the focus of his gaze on her, Michael asked. "Why so far?"

"Now I know what pasties in a bakery feel like." Julia griped, wobbling her head. A benign grunt rushed past her lips. Yet her eyes gleamed with the laughter she hid.

"Then you understand me when I say you grow more appetizing each day."

"But, do you truly see me, or do you only see my body?"

"Are the two not the same?" he asked pithily. "Would you prefer it more if I admire your face and refuse your body, or do I need to attack that in reverse?" Michael teased, tugging the opening of her blanket. He encouraged the cover's descent. "Perhaps I *should* only lust that luscious body of yours, and ignore the gorgeousness of your face, ditto for the personality. Such a combination had surely proven itself deadly throughout time. Man, I should be running for the hills, shouldn't I? Damn. Maybe I'm just a sucker for punishment." He groaned, looking utterly unconcerned, mirth chimed clear in his voice. "Forgive me for liking the whole package." He announced. So saying, broad shoulders casually curled, and although a smile was effectively pasted on his face, mischief was the dominant distinction forging his gaze.

In the cramped silence, Michael dropped his hand to the side of his seat, brushing a finger against the diminutive control. He compelled his leathered throne on a slow glide, expounding on his bawdy reasons with a grin. "Filling, shell and design, for the flavor is extraordinarily sweet. But feel free to lodge a grievance if you so need. I usually set aside the middle of the week for complaints, never on the weekends. So by all means please stop by. And if at first you don't succeed, be diligent, you know…tenacity. It's the only way to be certain you're heard. But until then, *ma jolie*, your seat awaits." Scraping his palms down the length of his thighs, Michael brandished a radiant smile. Instantly setting his directive to task, he hoisted her onto the proffered seat on his lap, adjusting their fit with skilled hands in a flash.

Julia amended herself to the warm, obdurate seat. Astounded by the ease with which she swallowed his inane narratives, irrespective of time. "Why do I keep listening to you?" she queried tamely against his cheek. "You're very good. That's what it is." Conceding the answer, she brusquely nodded as if to further affirm what was said. "Diplomacy, that's the problem. You've had a lifetime to practice at that, so it comes to you with ease. But it's slated to be my downfall, isn't it?"

"Diplomacy?" Michael scuffed, repeating the starched word in a grunt. Laughter filled the dark interior of the truck. "How does diplomacy explain one's attraction?"

"I could tell you that…" she slowly shrugged. "But it wouldn't be as much fun to be told, now would it?" smirking the stealth-like answer, she kissed the tight pull of his brow, nestling her shoulder to his chest for their drive back.

"Evader,"

"I'm bulletproof or didn't you know?"

"I don't doubt that." His quiet mutter falling to her ears tinged with humor.

The short trip home bred immensely leisured, crammed with pause for cosseting the palate. Sweet, ardent kisses that showed no beginning or end—dominated the length of their drive. Brashly inciting their wont on her body. His kisses skied her slopes with reverence and skill.

The evening brimmed with triumphs of such kind, though it was not the possessions that made the night inherently sweet, as those, for the most part, were already sated. Long ravenous kisses, coupled well with their sensual bestowing, made the night a treasured preference in every sense. It was the lengthy perusal his mouth took along the grotto of her body that made her mind truly melt. Embraces that had no conclusion, market their medicinal use. It was about him never saying or showing an end. Loving her from head to toe, he savored every inch of her body. He may not yet be able to declare the truth of his affection, but he could, most emphatically, demonstrate the enormity of his feelings. Laboring long into the wee hours of the morning, he did just that.

There were no words clearly reachable nor explanation for what she felt or why. Electing not to pester neither theory nor thought, Julia gave herself over to his hands.

Choosing instead, to cherish the night's perfection, as it truly was that. It flourished flavorsome, as it would, a favorite dessert.

Time drifted as if with a sigh, dragging with it scraps borrowed from another. The two, in time, slumbered as if they tottered on the edge of death, as exhaustion bled the very essence of their strength. Day strutted its eminence while the two yet slept. Coasting well past noon by the time Julia opened her eyes, a spry speck of sunlight streaked past what seemed a sliver in the drapes, giving voice to the vibrancy of a new day. Immediately turning, her eyes sought out the man pressed staunchly at her side. Splayed exhaustedly on his back, Michael laid with a hand nested on the low plane of his stomach. Suspended in a coma-like drowse, his breathing wafted aberrantly deep, coasting like one who toiled expansively through the night.

As if it, too, lolled stricken with fatigue, the house stood dreamily quiet. Birds warbled joyously in the distance, and the soft, continual swish from his nostrils was but the only sonance to be heard. Julia slipped gingerly from abbreviated podium of their bed, flung capriciously on the floor. The rumpled tick served as the night's memento, and in the purest form of esteem. Her gaze lazily caressed the masculine figure now vaguely ensconced beneath the covers. Tamely, she admired more than just the aptness of his physique, with feelings that rocketed farther than the simplicity of just lust, as there was something extraordinarily peaceful about watching him sleep. Every fiber of his being now lazed deeply reposed and the vanity foist upon her by the sight, intensified the longer she stayed.

Not unlike the deed of an errant child, Julia skulked from the room, submersing her body in the assuaging heat of a shower. She liquesced in what seemed the residue of a spell. Twenty minutes attributed much to the rejuvenation of her body. Needing only food to complete the reversal, Julia guardedly ducked from the room. The smell of freshly brewed coffee taunted her the moment she entered his office. Pummeling her senses, it watered her mouth. Betty—in her adept keenness—now makes preparation for two, and as usual, the clairvoyant woman was remarkably well clued.

Deliberately, Julia evaded the kitchen. And although the heady aroma wickedly beckoned with every breath, she refused, in her ambling, to be swayed. Lodged in her reasoning, there was something innately uncouth about waltzing in his kitchen with request, this especially, while he slept.

With morning already teetered past the infancy of noon, the day was already whipped to perfection. Yet, it seemed ripened with the potential of things yet to unfold. Julia curled languidly in a vintage wingback chair, stationed, like identical siblings, by a window in the furthest corner of the room. Her gaze was almost ethereal as she gaped out at fragments of a hurrying day, feeling more rested than she ought to have been. Considering how little they slept, it was expected that their toils would demand a resounding pound of flesh. Michael, being the most amorous of them, seemed barely able to stir from the extent of his productivity.

"Julia!" her name pulsed through the silence like the pattering of rain on a tin, ripping through the wittiness in her head. It simpered like the starting of a jest. "I almost missed you sitting there." Betty sang, her soft voice stroking the air like jubilant notes in a song, clutching a hand to her chest, she smiled. A round vase laden with flowers, stalled in the other of her hand, hovering above a squat table in the center of the room. Yellow tulips shifted impatiently as if to protest their precarious perch.

"I'm sorry. I didn't mean to startle you." Julia droned, sounding truly contrite, yet feeling at odd with being discovered in such insouciant attire. Typically clothed before encountering the older woman, a bathrobe was far from her standard mode of dress.

"Have you been here all this time?" Betty asked, setting the basin-like vase atop the table. She relaxed her stance.

"Not too long."

"Are you hungry, how about some breakfast while I'm here?" Betty inquired in a lively lilt, straightening a collection of references as she waited a reply.

"Um…" *Starved would actually be a more accurate description,* she grumbled. Caught off-guard by the intrinsic question, Julia struggled to pacify the lobbying of her stomach, preferring to wait than to indulge. This, since, be it in person or on the phone, they had yet to miss the sharing of their morning meals—once the practice veered as a ritual deed—and she did not intend to amend that practice now. Hopefully, any loss of consciousness, from her lack of nutritional intake, will not place her in a vegetated state. "Not quite yet." She lied.

Betty smiled her usual docile, unwearied response, awareness streaming instantly bold. Yet, her expression seemed one of a gifted bettor. Suspecting correctly the reason behind the younger woman's delay, she gave naught of her thought. Though the deed, she concluded with a smile, was a thrilling sign. "How about some coffee instead?" she chirped.

"Maybe a small cup—if you don't mind," she uttered dully, her answer seemingly unsure, though her eyes were eager as they skirted the older woman to again assess the door.

"One small cup of coffee coming right up," Betty smiled, looking almost ecstatic. She hastily spun, already skipping past the cough when she turned in response to her name.

"Betty." Julia called softly.

"Yes?" The older woman chirped, staggering her steps, she whirled as if the younger of them had summoned her with a rousing bellow.

"Just coffee is more than fine." She assured.

"Coming before you know it," Betty twittered, and the deep creases that warned well of knowledge, tore promptly across the entirety of her face as she seemingly skipped from the room.

Julia stared at the empty doorway long after Betty's retreat, a smile now seething in her chest, truly tickled by her interaction with the ageless nanny. She threw her attention gleefully out the window. The expansive yard was like the rendering of a painting. Beautifully still, everything waited as if in suspense. Layers of colors created an alluring landscape, feeding not just the eyes, but the heart as well as the essence of one's sense.

Betty whisked back as promptly as she vowed she would and, as always, Betty was true to the many compulsions ascribed to her name. Though in her defense, she was not nearly as emphatic as she could have been. As per Julia's request, the small tray yielded a single cup of coffee, flanked by a small platter, the arrangement was but one. Peeled, cored and meticulously sliced, a grapefruit waited dressed with sprinklings of sugar, looking more like a pineapple than it did itself. A squared bowl anchored the other side of her cup, loaded with an assortment of berries. The cream for her coffee seemed likely an afterthought.

"Betty, you really didn't need to do so much." She chirped, giving an appeasing smile, Julia noted the bland shrug that waded forward in response. "Thank you. This is very nice."

"It's no trouble, just a few pieces of fruit." Betty stated with a matter-of-fact smile, stepping away from the low table, known before then as a stool. She again affected a meager shrug.

"Still, thank you. It's really very nice. You know, if I'm not careful, I may just end up being spoiled by you."

"How exactly will a few pieces of fruit spoil you?" Betty eagerly asked, and all five of her thin fingers stamped her skeleton-like hip in wait of a reply.

"It's not the fruits but the service that will spoil me." Julia laughed, sending the older woman a comical expression from behind her cup. "I'm afraid when I get home, I'll forget that there's no one willing to do the fetching. At home, I'm the getter."

"Then you should take the time to enjoy it more while you're here." Betty informed in her usual timbre, her eyes locked to the other woman's face, ferreting as keenly as a spotlight in the pitch of night.

"I don't think I know how to do that, Betty." Julia answered with an absent shrug, taking a renewed sip from her cup. Her eyes drifted from the older woman to the floor, as the truth of her words rang clear in her head. It's only been of late that she'd afforded herself such luxury or such right. Was he teaching her, or hurting her cause? She wondered. "I don't think I have for a while." She murmured faintly, giving the older woman more honesty than she intended. She straightened her posture as if to retain composure of herself.

Betty watched as her expression shifted back to the sweet facade of old, looking up from her seat. She smiled before returning the cup to her lips. The small statement granted more insight than the younger woman planned, unwrapping a little more of her disposition to someone other than the man. Something that was inherently hard, since she spent her time avoiding the two of them. She did, however, know, with certainty, that the beauty was like a beacon her boy had long needed. Beyond that, her nuances were an irrelevant facet of who she was.

"There's a good reason why it takes as many as sixty ticks to give you one, and twenty-four more to give you another within that. Somewhere along the way, you will find something to catch your eye. Once you've noticed that, then the trick will be to remember how it felt. In time, you'll learn when and how to look up on your own." Betty smiled, straightening the pillow on the opposite chair, she continued with a soft smile. "Once you get the hang of that, it becomes like a simple stroll."

"So that's the trick?" Julia haphazardly probed, understanding fully the importance of the older woman's logic, though it was the uncertainty of "how" that held her in check. "I guess first I'll need to work on the task of looking up, then? Maybe, with growth, I can tackle the part on recognition." Julia groaned, giving a doleful smile with her words. Her eyes hastened to the door, scurrying beyond her companion's small frame as a movement snatched the full gauge of her interest.

Michael strolled through the entrance looking sinfully rejuvenated. Freshly washed, he looked as crisp as a sunrise in spring, and in an instant, her heart frisked from the smooth cadence of a persistent drum, to the chaotic rigor of madness. Of its own, a smile bloomed, as with the emergence of the sun, widening in radiance with naught but a coaxing. Her demeanor bade not of one schooled in the etiquette of nonchalance, but blazed with an amateurish vaunt. Subsequently, had she tried then, her eyes would have refused to budge from evoking their will.

"Now do you see? That wasn't so hard now, was it?" Betty whispered, giving then a slow smile. She turned to see what had, so obdurately, grabbed the other's attention, though certain she already knew.

"Good morning." Michael called, his deep voice breaking the soft crest of their feminine lilt, sending a warm, rugged rush over the room. Hazel eyes chose their target and held, and even had they needed, in their ruthless strive, to tunnel through the mass of Betty's thin body, they gave no hint of budging from their mark.

"Good morning." Julia whispered in answer, though her effort came more as a mouthing of words than those perceptible in an actual oration. A feeling of euphoria quickly flooded her body. The sensation being greater than anything she'd ever felt before, as the urge to harness their connection grew startlingly strong, needing to touch him in some way, irrespective of how. A slow dawning propelled forward through a caliginous cloud in the quietness of the room.

"Why don't I get you some coffee?" Betty muttered as she ducked from the room, not wanting to hinder the progression of what so plainly exuded from the two.

"I missed waking up with you this morning." He drawled as he neared, his hazel eyes brushing her skin like the flexing of sparks.

"You looked so tired. I didn't want to wake you." She purred, mesmerized by the beauty of his gaze. Seated in the companion chair to her left, he leaned his towering form onto the resilient arm of his chair, propping his head on the back edge of the seat. He smiled.

"I was, but I would have gotten up with you."

"I know, but——" not wanting to waste another moment on the peddling of words, she paused, only knowing a potent need to appease the vehemency of her feelings inside. In a flash, Julia bounded from her chair, perching her svelte form like a bird upon his lap. Her lips forgot to ask, or cajole the needfulness of their wants, but demanded their covets instead. Pressing his head back, she took her time, flooding his mind and hers with a montage of emotional epilogue that quickly dwindled to one. His arms became a sturdy wall at her back, and the softness of her breasts became the erection of a scintillating pillow wedged between them, each sprouting, as they should, without question or pause. And when she at last lifted her head, every limb on her body went limp. "If I wasn't starving, you'd be in some serious trouble right now." She advised in a rough breath. "Since I'd be drawing a feast on that."

"I don't mind putting off one meal, for another." He rasped, his ragged breath sauntering back in a flash. Brushing his hand under the fold of her robe, he smiled. "Especially when it means I get to start my day out dining on you."

"Let me at least take in some nourishment before we start, or you may find yourself being my snack, and I'd hate to blemish perfection."

"Party pooper," He grumbled rakishly, his voice wafting up the side of her throat, while his fingers worked the smoothness of her thighs. "Besides me, what do you think you'd like to eat?"

"Please stop that, you're not being fair, Michael."

"You can't kiss me like that and expect me to be fair. I know you can feel me, don't I deserve to feel you?" Michael asked, rumbling this through the placement of a kiss.

"And you can feel me all you…want, just…mmmm…." She moaned, dropping her forehead to his with the expulsion of her breath—hoping—yet not wanting him to stop. Thoroughly enjoying the undertakings of his hand, his mouth soon joined the roguish attack, pressing deliberate kisses along the side of her breasts. "You're being wicked."

"I know. I'm feeling wicked after that kiss. Care to retaliate?" he groaned, even as his tongue thrashed the darkened peaks already at a stance.

"Betty——?"

"She won't come in." He rasped, his warm breath lingering atop a sensitive crest. "I was all prepared to have a nice breakfast with you, but you changed that, now you can't go back."

"Fine, then I'll never kiss…oh, God…you again. Oh, my, God, Michael…stop… mm…Please."

"Really?" he growled, sounding sharply incredulous, a smirk reiterated his nonchalance to her erroneous oath. "Come on. Let's go discuss that over an additional hundred kisses—give or take a few, of course—though, in all fairness, I may have to feed you something before we're actually done." Dropping his hand from her robe, he immediately set her feet to the floor. "Let's go." He repeated through a raspy sigh, bounding from his own chair in a flash. Michael pressed close, and without pause his hands circled her waist like the closure of a lock, piloting their hassled exit from the room.

Two hours sailed past before the two dispersed themselves from the house, both parties now looking fully quelled. All discussions of meals and their purpose were fully capitulated for the wont of something else. Michael plucked a white tulip from the vast array, pressing the crisp bloom to her hair, he smiled. And it was she who gathered his hand as they continued the dreamy tincture of their stroll.

Chapter Thirty Six

With the tenth month scuttling to a hapless end, only a dusting of days separated a reputed attack. Hailed largely for its inordinate gaiety, the happenings throve esteemable for some, so evidenced by the festoons on their dwellings.

Slated thus by the mass, the apparition of Halloween threatened not compunction but fright. With this yet oath to an evening encrusted in black, the assurance of excitement and flavorful sugar, as a treat, dangled haughtily as their onliest marketing tool.

Astonishingly, preparations for its tarriance were launched weeks in advance, with some beginning promptly amid the focal of August's birth. Discourse on provisions drew near the realms of madness at times. Conferences were held on an almost diurnal cycle, and conversations pertaining key particulars grew to a constant feed. A vigilant search commenced in earnest for the perfect costume. Yet only those suitable, amongst the many, were chosen to adorn a fastidious princess and prince. The Berwicks' household knew no end to this enduring quest. As daily proceedings unfurled like the intricate acts of a play.

The subject knew no respite since its young inauguration, and with the revered jollity yet skulking near, none waited in the shadows. Thankfully, her contribution to the obsession had long since waned in strength, as the desired costumes had subsequently been tested, modeled and approved by the pernickety pair—this in more ways than just what was dictated as normal.

In the meantime, Scarowinds appeased the savagery smoldering in each beast. Unsheathing vestige of their fears, they return appetent to the harrowing grounds. And the mania was not unlike the witnessing of drunken moths being shepherded to a blaze. The harmony of their shrieks, affixed well with laughter, chorused the smoky night air like contingents in a band. Yet the sum, now credited to the repetitious venture, never bland the fervency of their thirst, nor the enthusiastic retelling, and with yet another visit expected in hours. The tales succeeding such outings will suffuse an endless dither for a wealth of days.

Evening barely conceded its eminence from an awed beginning, though signs of fraying grew evident with the simmering swank of day. Saturated in sunlight, shards of utopian rays gleamed rambunctious amid a vast ocean of blue. A gentle breeze ambled the atmosphere like the flourishing of a hand. Sweeping across the heads of trees, flowers swayed fro as if in delight.

Squinting, Julia gazed at the sky through the vacillating limbs of trees. Filled with an inexplicable aura of excitement, a sigh bracketed her fascination with the plot to a foreseeable thrill. Intrigue, as always, gauged her anomalous response, yet both mind and body now germinate as one, articulating their penchant, as a union, with the oddest appeal. In the throngs of many, none but one sailed forth to take its place. A single sport racing to the forefront to spell interest, for regardless of caution, their unusual tete-a-tete was not easily put to rest.

At David's behest, his weekend with the kids was expanded by a day. Gifting, with that, the freedom for her to venture whither at will, yet the thought unveiled as promptly as the decision was made. For no greater pleasure surfaced through the ramblings in her head, than the erogenous act itself, and had he not informed her of his scheduled obligations for that day, she would have likely darkened his entrance long before now. Hungry to do just that, she counted each second since the harshness of noon consumed morning's gentle breath.

The strange tenet lashed to their unusual affair, had somehow mushroomed centuries past the envisioned result. Though as of yet, she had not determined which, of their many indulgences, prejudiced her more. Was it in the company or the accompanied acts? And which of the two detained her, so potently, for its prey? With both bordering on the verge of an addiction, it was a futile verdict to discern.

Arrogance had named her dogmatic in their wild beginning. Confident her incisive control would have easily recouped the loss of its strength. She acceded to the aberrant remand of her senses. Yet to date, both mind and body showed no hint of abstaining from the man, for the niceties he awarded in their dalliance, seemed an inimitable snare. One revered in more ways than just one.

The graveled road was hardly the lengthy trek it once boasted to be, for it seemed, no more than, the lapsing of a blink before she gaped protectively at the ominous iron guard, and in what esteemed less than a thrice of that. The reason for her visit sauntered onto the spherical drive, looking like a matador approaching his bull, confidence fountained his sinewy physique with every step.

As always, a mere glimpse set her body to tingle with auxiliary excitement. Roping her further still, his smile grew decadent in its unhurried dispel. Slowing as she turned into the spacious garage, he fell in step with her car, and curious eyes rushed to the rearview mirror with their need to lengthen her view. Admiring the stealth beauty of his approach, the benefactor of her interest waded to a lazy stop. Tensed with anticipation, the air seemed riddled with unrelenting angst, and it was not fear that caused a tingle to race rashly through her core.

"Hi." Michael simpered in a gallant display, already swinging the ingress wide.

"Hi." Julia quietly mouthed in return, taking her fill of the appetizing view. Barbs of ravenous goading saw at her strength.

"Now that we have the usual familiarities out of the way, what do you say we—"

Striking with the lithe arc of a reptile, her preemptive attack came without decision or plan. Capturing him by surprise, her slender body slammed into the harder of his with an enacting force. There was no waiting in the way she kissed him, and no questions remained obscured in the way that she asked. She wanted as he wanted, and she wanted it at exactly the time that he did—now.

The force of his embrace fleetly winched her from the ground, kneading her avidly to his body. He drew from the entrancing vessel of her mouth. Their breaths melded in time as a singular tune, and the depth of their passion grew tempestuous in its work. The melody of which became a conversation of its own.

"Go close the door." Julia whispered through the imparting of a sigh, filling the immediate vacancy with a chill. He hastened to oblige as bid. Reaching a hand inside the neighboring car, Michael hammered the small control with a resounding thud, and a slow darkness quietly descended on the room. Returning to her side, he pulled her roughly to his chest. Dragging her, with little effort, to the waiting vehicle, a crudely executed thrust widened the entrance in a flash. Together the two stumbled inside, as if tripped by an unseen trap. Falling against the thick ply of leather, the dusky room aided the coziness of their hunt.

The undersized vehicle swallowed them like the inclusion of a warm embrace, echoing the voracity of their sighs. It amplified the rending of their clothes, so, too, the deepening twirls of their tongues. Long murmurs of pleasure rose beguilingly from their throats, soaring above them like the forgotten lyrics of an ancient mating cry. Used when the earth was still primitive, the music evolved no less sweet, with the last of which rocketed darkly primordial, thundering through the space as the ruckus combusted.

"Should I even bother saying hello?" Michael queried in a rumbly groan. "We just don't seem to be very good at it. Or is this hello?" he asked through a frown, dropping his head back, curiosity danced in the magnificent hazel depths. "If this is our way of saying hello, then I take it back." He smiled, kissing her cheek. His mouth trailed the hard lines of her chin, settling, at last, on her lips. Michael's smile slowly broadened. "We are definitely good at hello. Hello is very good."

"Then hello to you." Julia returned with her own sweet smile, loving the mellow brush of his hand on her skin.

"Hello." He retorted hoarsely, his raspy murmur falling against the slender arching of her throat, taunting the silky skin with a meager touch of his tongue.

"How are you?"

"Doing so much better than yesterday," he averred in what came as a rumble, his hand moving slowly down her back. "How are you?"

"I'm good. I'm very good."

"And it shows." He teased. "By the way, thanks for the fantasy. Now when I drive this car, I'll have more than just your face in my head."

"I thought you might like that."

"And you haven't been wrong yet." Michael smirked, brushing another kiss across her breasts. He played gently upon their tips.

"Mmm," Julia purred, arching her body in display of his wont. Contentment instructed her dazzling mien.

"God, you're gorgeous." Michael gushed in a deep, gravelly grunt. "I love...your skin."

"So is that why I get the odd sense of being pawed all the time?"

"That...and the fact that I think you're a rather ravishing creature to partake of."

"So I'm being used for my looks then?" she grumbled, feigning discontent with his words. She adjusted the cumbersome bend of her legs.

"You bet. So what am I being used for?"

"I'll have to ponder hard on that before I can get you an answer." She shrugged, spitting the lie softly from her lips; her eyes rappelled down his face to his chest. "Maybe it's your prowess. Would that be a satisfactory fit?"

"It could do—for now." Michael shrugged, adjusting his head on the high cushion of his seat. He reviewed the offerings of her face, and the sweetness of her smile launched a small erosion in his chest, drudging intently. It wreaked havoc on the already feral pace of his pulse. Seeking solace from the turbulence extant between mind and body, Michael brushed a hand across the damped dome of her forehead, pushing the wispy strands from her face. He mused on the astounding clarity of her gaze, for he knew, with certainty, that what he now witnessed in her eyes was no kin to the likes of indifference.

Daylight lengthened palely under the waning veil of dusk, and darkness soon loitered like a parasite waging its attack. Isolated inside the large manse, the couple thoroughly savored each other, and although the requiescence attributed much to the length of their stay, it was the enhancement of the frolic that truly heightened the indulgence of that. Conversation, in time, flounced as stimulating as their play, as did the vivacity of their laughter, swirling meekly amongst the descending shadows of dusk.

Amidst the toll of their rambunctious chatter, dinner remained leisured and light. With a solitary candle to scathe the ascendancy of night, the room's core flickered with the warmth of amber. Hand in hand they treasured dusk's enthralling display, awed by the colorful array. Its vibrancy soon vanished in a sea of black.

Darkness swept atop them as if by the stroke of a hand. Smothering day's fading battle with night. The air spoke softly through the impelling auger of the wind. Much like flames on a candle, the once vivid atmosphere bowed its gay head in rest. Evaporating like a breath, it left them wrapped in the cool, quiet of night.

In silence, the couple admired a variegate patch that yet cleaved to the far edge of the horizon. Swaddled jointly in a sweet, hypnotic embrace, unmarred by time, neither stirred nor spoke. Seeming unwilling to break the purity of a spell, the two luxuriated in the tranquility and each other, as amiably, as they did the dark. The house stood ominous in the remnant of a deadening day, looking almost sinister walling their backs. It reared like the runt clone of a Himalayan crest. Partially cloaked in the shadows, it gave the pair no heed.

Julia sighed in rapt appreciation of the view. So, too, the oasis at which she rested. Complimented well by the besieging lull, there was no better gift to be had. It was the perfect end to a most enraptured day, and in truth, there was no other consort better than he to be ensconced with. Smiling contently from thus, her eyes sought out his features through the thickening black, finding her bliss already waiting in the softness of his gaze.

Michael reciprocated the gesture with a telling smile of his own, his hazel eyes beautifully alert as he lowered his head to hers. A groan wafted from his throat as the gentle kiss' end, though he stayed to nibble the lush splendor of her lips, pulling her closer with each taste. His hands affectionately waltzed the sides of her body, pressing her firmly to his form. They thrived in earnest upon her skin. Quietly, her fingers skimmed the dark waves of his hair, now hardly visible in the engulfing mat of black. A gentle breeze feathered their bodies in its placid haste, adding a slow chill to their sizzle.

Breaths, sweetened with the fruity sapor of strawberries, mingled harmoniously with an inference of chocolate and red wine, fondled fondly the essence of each kiss. Heightening their forage, the two drank of the other as if parched, and in accordance with the wind's gentling stroke. Michael's hand deftly moved to the underside of her shirt, caressing the soft mound. His thumb teased the dark hillocks of her breasts, while his mouth persisted in the harshness of its rummage. Doyen fingers dropped to the inside of her thighs, and his resolve, then, grew astoundingly deliberate. Caressing her through the meager fabric of her shorts, his fingers soon ventured in search of warmth, dulcifying the game. The sweetest sound escaped her throat in credence of his play.

A gentle breeze lovingly kissed the nakedness of her skin, sweeping atop her as he detached her shorts. It fanned the intimate furnace of her body as she kicked the trapping free from her legs.

"Do you want to go inside?" Michael asked hoarsely, even as his hands continued to conjure their spell.

"No." Julia purred, her near soundless answer returning to him slow.

Piece by piece their discarded garments sought refuge on the floor, scattering this way and that, until at last, he seated her pertly on his lap. Pressed firm within the enclosure of his arms, her body trembled with the delight he gave, while his, enlivened and ablaze, pulsed with the rapture of her. His voice ambled soft with the workings of his body, whispering words he knew she did not understand, though words, he conceded, that needed surely to be said. Together, their breaths came and went as one, as did the frantic drumming in their chests. Slipping past an insanity well sought, they clung sharply to the promise of gratuitous content.

The night, in time, fell eerily still once the music stopped. Settling, as it once was, a quiet air swept their bodies in an ardent embrace. Seeming blissful in the deliverance, it held them keenly until, they, too, in time, grew still.

Morning waved its parting to the splendor of an aging day. Roused soundly from its once ghostly cover, the day flaunted its brilliance with the clever ejection of flaws. Mutely governed by what seemed a stealth hand, yellowing leaves gambol atop the dainty sway of gnarled limbs. Fanning the atmosphere with their continuous dance, the quiet symphony bred tranquil in the listen.

Serenely secluded amongst contrast vegetation, Michael plucked a toppled leaf from their makeshift bed, while a snicker notched the corner of his mouth. Twirling the dead foliage betwixt lean fingers, he drew his leg to a bend. Adjusting the shortened stance of his limb, he laughed, his interest directed gaily at the sky. With her odd verdict unearthing more humor than it should, his laughter trembled in his chest. Perhaps the action was just another valiant badge donned in proof of his growing gladness. Though with her, the agility of her wit was among his favorite things to partake of. But a cloud in the shape of a snickering ass seemed somewhat unlikely.

"What type of ass exactly are you referring to?" he muttered tightly, trying hard to keep a straight face.

"What kind of ass did that mind of yours conjure with a question like that?" Julia challenged, shaking her head in scolding, she sighed. "That mind of yours is like a rusted steel-trap, it needs to be cleaned before you find yourself infected with Tetanus."

"There's nothing wrong with my mind." Michael promptly professed, chuckling faintly behind the zealousness of his words. "So what? It's more…encompassing than most? I've always considered that a good thing. I get to ponder…things from many angles, instead of the usual one."

"So that's how you vindicate those infectious boils in your head?" she remarked dryly, though her jibe escorted a prettily contorted grin. Shifting her body, she adjusted the cozy fit of her head to the spread of his arm. "You pretend they're logic."

"What exactly is it you find that makes my thinking such an illogical fit? You wouldn't call a patron names for frequenting a fine restaurant, now would you? Is he perverted for exhibiting some reverence to the quality of the cuisine? I've told you before, my appetite has always been…sizable" Michael shrugged, his wide shoulders curling like a wave under the slump of her head. "You've somehow managed to heighten that fact. My taste buds are what they are. I can't be blamed for partaking of the opulence."

"Then God help me!" She spat effervescently, sweetening her jeer with the musical lilt of laughter. "Maybe it would be best if I discouraged you instead, don't you think? Perhaps in granting you that small deed, your stunted brain will have the chance it needs for growth. What do you think?" she asked spryly, turning her head to better witness the result of her taunts.

A gentle smile came first in answer to her impish quest, crossing the jewel of his eyes, the silence softly held. "You can take whatever action you wish." He announced sagely, though the thought of telling her that they had long since surpassed the paltry of such boundary, barreled through his head. Just thinking of her smile was equally as appetizing as everything else, and the significance of that weighed his tongue like rocks. "But know this, after your turn comes mine and I am nothing if not cohesive in my work."

"Is that so?"

"My ark has already been outfitted."

"You know, sometimes I wonder on the foolery that goes on in that head of yours." Proclaiming this quietly, as if to herself, she dislodged the silence with a sigh, knowing truly that her question masqueraded itself vaguely as a thought.

"To find out, all you have to do is ask, Julia." Michael remarked coolly, and a slow nod alluded to the answer of that, bouncing before the sentence's end. Her eyes fell sharply to the ground.

"But do I have the right?" She asked in a small, contemplative voice, gazing out at the enclosing woods, she again sighed. "Do I have the right to invade that privacy?" she clarified, sending him a tentative glance.

"Even in myths, Julia, the rules are still the same. If you enter with an invitation, then you most certainly belong. It can't be called an invasion, if you're holding an invite and your name is already on the list. After that, it's all between a host and his guest." He advised sedately, his voice curling in the refuge of a patterned hum, lifting his shoulders in a casual shrug, he posed his own test. "Perhaps there's something you need to know—or say? If so, you should set the gremlin free. Who knows, the answer may surprise you."

As if previously queued, the rustling of leaves languidly dulled, and the air around them grew almost oppressive. Silence thickened in successive swells, as if the universe itself paused in reaction to her pending response.

"I have one." Julia whispered timidly at last.

"Only one?"

"For now," She mumbled after some thought, nodding as if to affirm the idea to herself.

"Then ask me." He goaded almost brightly, his deep voice seeming like fingers upon her skin.

"Why do you look at me the way you do?" she asked, her eyes pressed hard to his.

"How exactly do I look at you?"

"I don't know," she shrugged, shifting almost nervously under his gaze. "Like... well...strange. I'm not sure, but it feels sometimes like, well...like you're looking at something...precious."

In the silence that followed, Michael's gaze encompassed the enormous body of the adjoining woods. Staring past the innumerable presence of trees, he intently pondered her inquest. Variance of answers swam to his head in response, yet none grew to the lofty stature of a suitable fix. "It's actually simpler than you think, Julia. The truth is nigh guileless since...I am." Michael droned, letting a long breath fly from his lips, he asked. "Why do you?"

"What?" though stunned, her voice wafted no higher than a whisper, yet surprise was plainly heard in the softness of her tone.

"Why do *you* look at me the way you do?"

"How do I look at you?" she asked with an obvious frown.

"You want me to give you a proper description?"

"Well, unless you know some other way to have me understand your meaning, then I imagine the answer is…yes."

"I don't know." He parried, giving his answer with a shrug. "I don't really have what you would consider a thorough description. At least not in this…particular spot, it's just an observation, that's all." He lightly soothed, shrugging the lie in a soft breath, his eyes moved from her gaze to her mouth. "I'm just saying…I like it." He informed. "It's… nice." He affirmed, broadening the confirmatory gestures with a nod. Michael tightened the reins on his hold, smiling as if to console the slimmest chance of a worry. His hand slowly rappelled down her arm in his strive to set her at ease.

"I didn't think I was that obvious." Julia grumbled perplexedly, wrinkling the slim arch of her brows. Her eyes clouded in thought. "But I guess I shouldn't be surprised, should I?" Shrugging this in answer as if to reassure the musings in her head, she gave sightless attention to their surroundings, yet her mind progressively heaved in eager response. "You were bound to notice at some point. So I guess I might as well admit the obvious. You're really quite…nice to look at." She hummed, stating the thought dimly as if to profess the intro to some fiendish sin. Seemingly neglectful of the countless labels he had long earned to fortify such datum as truth. "I like…looking," she shrugged.

So saying, silence strewn between them like a weighty spread, blanketing both bodies, it did naught to cease the whirring in their heads. Michael's gaze grew aching as he stared into the dark tarns of her eyes, desperate, in his cravings to tell her how he felt, even while sensing she still yet needed time. "Then that makes it synonymous." He muttered hoarsely, dropping a kiss to the top of her head, he tightened the lock of his arms, as if to verify that which could not be said, though the truth was most avidly felt.

With bodies steadily pressed in stark rejoinder to their encrypted dispel, the deep indent of her smile dismantled the focus of his thoughts, and a hand rocked lovingly across the softness of her cheek in reaction of that.

"I did remember to put clothes on this time, didn't I?" Julia jokingly asked, breaking the mellowness of the pause, though she recognized the intensity that came with his gaze and, as always, the witnessing fed a distinct sense. His smile nipped warmly at the quietude between them, ingesting the meagerness of the space. It sent an ardent shudder through her body. Questing eyes warily scanned the surrounding's edge, slowly returning to hers. His thought spilled forth in a whispered breath.

"Come back to the house with me. I have a matter of some importance to discuss."

"Back to the house, why? We're alone, are we not?" she asked, tracking the path of his eyes.

"We are. But I don't want to have my discussion here." He averred blandly, releasing the vice of his hand. He set her from his side. A smile, though crudely drawn, felt boyish in its gradual dispel, amended his expression as he pushed to his feet. "Besides, in case we're not, I definitely don't want to have to defend a movie, not this kind anyway." He droned, widening the leer of his smile. His eyes expounded his intent, fondling her assets as he pulled her to her feet.

"I'm not sure I have my appetite set to dine just yet."

"Oh, there's no need to worry on that. I'm sure I can provide the right seasoning to awaken that sense."

"My, aren't we cocky."

"But you may call it hopeful if you deem that a more fitting label." He growled, slotting his fingers warmly through hers, they turned in unison in their trek to the house. Her body was bolshily grafted to the hardness of his, while his own, of itself, grew stringent with the emphasis necessary to maintain his restrain. Yet he could think of no other assertion to make clear how he felt. None that clarified well the depths of his feelings.

Julia smiled sagely in observance of his wavering mien, perceiving, from his countenance, what appeared to be an ill-fated plight, ably told, by the vacillating set of his brow, though it was his devilishly sexy smile that towed her anxiously in its wake. Ahead, their desired destination mocked the treads of their steps, errantly wading further from reach. The distance seemed uncannily long the farther they trudged. In haste, the two dashed across the modish threshold, scuttling with intent to the privacy of his room. She immediately felt the familiar press of the hard door at her back.

The third quarter of an hour coasted before the first sprinkle of sanity returned to the occupants of the space. Sprawled atop the large bed, Michael rested blithely on his back. An arm, in its possessive trait, encompassed the narrow cut of her waist, encouraging the drape of her body aloft his. With the other of his hand now fashioned in aid of his pillow, contentment need not be a quest. Barred sedately by the thin skin of his lids, his eyes remained unseeing, a splendorous smile washing the entirety of his face, while his heart yet galloped under her head.

Julia shifted sluggishly against the inferno of his body, adjusting her leg across the muscular pillar of his. She snuggled serenely to his warmth. Applauding the wild rhythm beneath her breasts, for it drummed in reminiscence of her own, thenceforth, assuring their awareness of each other.

In reverence, her hand glided over the small furring on his chest, moving over his stomach. She luxuriated in the sculpted scarp of his masculinity. From the breadth of his chest to the large lankiness of his feet, he was incontestably man, and although his appearance could be considered superbly primed, there was naught about him that could be judged effeminate in the merest trace.

"I see now why you were so adamant to come back to the house. Conversations like that cannot be had in public." Julia purred, breaking the purity of the silence with her jest.

"I'm glad we understand each other." He rumbled lazily, displaying a lethargic smirk in aid. "We most certainly could not have conversed as freely if we stayed. Nor could I have attempted to explain some of the things that were said. It just would not have been quite as…eloquently put." Michael averred, his voice sounding distant, as if slumber now threatened to steal his waning focus. "But in any case, I don't think that's the kind of dialogue we want captured on film. Unless, of course, that suits your taste. If so, we can get right to starting on our own collection." He laughed, knowing full well the answer to his jibe.

Like a serpent preparing to launch the noxiousness of a deadly strike, so her action denoted as her head rose from his chest. Purposeful and leisured in its bent, gorgeous eyes narrowed suspiciously with controlled detest. And although her smile softened the blow intended, her perception on the topic was delivered with the exacting heat of her gaze, flowing swift from the dark depths of her eyes. There was no misconception as to how she felt.

Armed with mischief, his smile ward off the fever of a lasting lament, as both arms hastily ruptured the air above his head, showing surrender in the flat of his palms.

"It's a joke. I swear it. It's only a joke." Michael vowed calmly, laughing. He waved both hands drolly in acknowledgement of that. "A bad one, I know. But that's the only meaning it has."

"It better be." She grunted, returning her head to his chest.

"It is. I promise."

"Do you always fear you're being watched?" Julia asked in continuance of their earlier exchange, resuming this, as if no pause had been thrust in the middle of their chat.

"I don't fear it," Michael drawled, gathering a handful of her hair. He allowed the wavy strands to glide through his fingers in playful wonder. "But at the same time, I don't disregard the possibility. This is mine to protect," he added in a whisper as if to himself. "And I intend to do whatever it takes to see to that." Grumbling the advice matter-of-factly, he shrugged, seeming still on the verge of a doze. To the casual observer, his dispassionate demeanor could be perceived as a general reply, since his home, in their perception, could be thought of as the intended recipient of his oath. But he hoped she knew better of that. Veiled in a clandestine chamber not yet distinguished by man, the imperative organ roughly thudded its yearn. And he prayed her understanding of him, burrowed as deeply as he suspect, enough so, to know of what he preached.

Julia snuggled further into the delicious rigidity of his body, basking in the comfort of his arms. The glow on her face waded near the crest of resplendent. This, she sighed sedately, almost giving life then to her thought, is not at all what she expected of him when they met. Contentment was not what she envisaged would await them in their target beginning. Nor did she expect to be so intricately entangled with a man who—by his own admittance—had lived his entire life being a flirt. Yet the thought of not having him in her life or of him with someone else, was profoundly troubling to the very essence of her senses. A slow shiver journeyed the narrow length of her spine, spreading through her body as the picture evolved more lucid in her head.

"Are you cold?" Michael asked roughly, his voice vibrating under the nesting of her head, and the other of his arms descended immediately on her back.

"Just a little," she sighed, feeling almost mawkish with the impetuous reply, though she chose to use the simplicity of a lie. The ache that suddenly usurped the corroding crater in her chest, flourished like a negating breath, growing more innately with the focus of her thoughts. *Another woman—here—in her stead?* The possibility seemed suddenly a terrifying thought. Rearing remarkably like anguish in every angle that it held, even from her place on his chest. The energy spent on dissuading his efforts, now seemed, utterly inane, since regardless of her pains to stay properly detached, all ballast capsized with her so-call disdain. She was never able to deter his intended ambition of making her his own, and the notion of him supplanting her in that fact made her entire body numb.

Michael's eyes opened the minute she lifted her head from the platform of his chest. Appraising the posterns to her soul as if sensing the turmoil she held. Each pair remained locked in silence as they held; though each, haunted, for divergent cause and only the possessor was privy to the turbulent source mantled within.

A grimace intending to mirror the concoction of a smile, awkwardly worked forward in a docile siege of her mouth. Though the laborious procession tapered as swiftly as it was assembled in start. Its dashed effort forsaken, pre-finish, for the wont of something else. Lowering her head, Julia touched a kiss to the corner of his mouth, and he quickly rejoined her inquest with ponderings of his own, shifting what seemed the intent. He took as greedily as she gave. Whatever the question, the brush of their tongues competently debated it through; rendering avowals they dared not voice. Though, in truth, they gave more adamantly than mere words could explicate.

In riposte to the brewing, Michael's pulse wildly sped, his heart thrashing in counter within the flexed caging of his chest. Evinced so, by the strong coercing pen of his arms, they grew unyielding in the endeavors at hand. Searing her to his indurate form, his hands gave no let, as if his will was to assure the practice of osmosis.

Thin pages, now lined with inflicted fury, could not dim the sickening zest of pride that stomped wickedly through her chest. Pricked by the revolting thought in her head, she wondered on the likes of his new flame. Could she furnish him with the same response? In her, would his body sprout as fervently from a mere kiss, or, for that matter, would hers? His kisses were like no other, and she had long since lost herself in the ecstasy of what came only from him.

Jealousy goaded her feat further onward, wanting to wipe from him any possibility of another; Julia imparted her soul in the structuring of her kiss. Unspoken or not, she needed him to be rightly informed of that fact.

Michael implored her reaction as vehemently as he demanded the tasty grotto of her mouth. Needing to draw the flavored sap of her response, he ruthlessly probed the mellifluous depths. She, in all his recollection, was the only woman known to so easily put a tremor through his body with the slightest touch of her lips. He could feed ceaselessly from said vessel and never get filled, drink everything she offered, yet still find his thirst unquenched. It was a cycle he endeavored to remain on.

Replete with proof of his passion, his hazel orbs blazed magnificent, avidly fixed on her. They conversed well in silence. Julia gazed back at her lover with a bolstering sigh, her own eyes an echo of his gaze.

"You're so beautiful." Michael murmured against her mouth, his breath falling sinuous, as if to give life to his words. He dropped them inside the warm ingress of her body, and only he knew the full meaning behind the encomium comment. With a faint sigh, she stroked his cheek with the smooth roundness of her own, seeming to search out an answer amongst a bevy of disquiet thoughts. Reverting her eyes to his, turmoil grew less vibrant with the exquisiteness of their gaze, thus it expended in time to near nil.

"*Dans la fraction moindre, votre sourire enlève mon souffle.* In the merest fraction, your smile takes my breath away."

Warmed by the sweet decadence of his words, Julia smiled, though unwitting of what was said, and was yet uncertain if she really would. There was a sweetness to the emotions crushed within the rough timbre of his voice. Such cadence floated profoundly pleasing to her ears, and the fear of spoiling the harmony it gave, though nice, somehow troubled her more.

"You grow more sapid with each passing day." Michael rasped. "And it has you ever harder to resist." Clarifying—in part with a grumbly sigh, he took comfort in the fact that his words were in, no way, a lie.

"I see." Julia replied with a near infectious smile. "I think I may have become something of a muse for you. You seem to nicely outdo yourself the longer this goes."

"You like my words?" Michael asked with the tender cascade of his hands.

"As usual, they're beautiful, so how could I not?" she answered in a gentle voice, knowing the meaning was far more complex than what she showed. In answer, his hands travelled the silky trench of her back, mowing a light trail, sensual and soft, in the soothing of her nerves.

"I've yet to give you anything but the exactness of what I see." He hummed, allocating each word like an afterthought to himself. Michael smiled, careful in the appearance of a neutral resolve, neither participant knew of the inner turmoil the other held.

Taking a sedative breath, her forehead came to roost lightly on his. Wearily, with eyes steamed tightly shut, she rummaged for an answer in kind, for the urge to impart some semblance of truth, ambled strongly through her mind. Yet no brilliant insight swam to the surface of her head in defense, naught of where to begin the oddity of her confession. Disappointment thence drenched her through and through, and a long frustrated sigh kissed the silence in response to the void.

As if sensing the root of her despair, Michael gently raised her head from its perch, and the speckling brush of hazel, gently pierced the anxious doting of brown. A bestowing that offered him more than she seemed sentient of, for truth bloomed bold in the shadowy depths. Brushing a kiss across the plumpness of her lips, he softly smiled, alleviating the friction from the air with the tenderness shown.

In resignation, her elbow evolved as a sturdy footing for her head. With her face stationed above his, she returned the tenderness of his smile. A finger thence traced the trimmed furring of his brows, moving to the hard lines of his jaw. She sketched the rosy hue of his lips. The warmth of his tongue raked the outer edges of her finger, savoring its taste with a slow glide, as if it carried the residue of some sugary treat. Curiously, Julia sought out the wordings in his eyes, finding their bold utterance a transcending sight, for they ravished her as raptly as they always had. In the fleeing of an instant, her heart felt as if it would fly from her chest, like chaos trouncing her ribcage in a futile response. A shiver raced through the center of her body in counter to the delicious exhibit. The lowering of her head came without intent or remembrance of the act itself, for they came together like kindles caught in the surge of a sudden gust.

In a quick twist, Michael had their position swapped, and it was she who now peered into deeply enamored eyes. With each kiss growing more satisfying than the last, the zest bred like the extract of an intoxicating treat. As both, in a zealous hunt, willed the intensity of the forage still, eager to fulfill a need only the other can quell.

Time stopped while the two swayed in unity. And in adjunct, the choreograph frolic of trees grew intricate and wild with the aid of a ruckus-like wind. The universe, in its magnificence, lends the proficiency of its voice with a chorus of twitters to serenade the intenseness in their strive. It connected all things like the quick shift in a balletic bravura, as both hearts seemed honed to but a singular drum.

Sweet, fiery, yet serene in its dispersal, their mouths sang of a pure operatic cliff, pleasing to the touch. Writhing bodies conducted a symphony as old as time, and as maestros. Their artistic input and articulation was but a necessary toil, as were their melodic rise and their rhythmical involvements. Dredging with determinate resolve, their bodies communicated a nuance of gestures in an arduous quest, and in the throes of rapture. She divulged snippets of her soul with the whimpering of his name, as he, in return, poured his heart into her. His answers fell to her as a hoarse, rumbly sigh, and although barely coherent, it was not so for their hearts.

Time ceased its onward momentum like the arresting of one's breath, stilling all action but one. It sojourned the ambling of their thoughts. But for the thirst of garnering the next quaff of their breaths, the two remained inert. Awed by the intensity that yet swath their frolic, Julia lazily focused her gaze, for curiosity now burned bold in the brown depths, needing then to understand more. Somewhere, not-so-deep inside, she craved to acknowledge him—this—them, and the significance that skirted past on its tail, as all now scurried wildly through her head. But it was her need to confirm the magic as autonomous of everything, said or unsaid, that goaded her more.

Plated like an emotional epiphany packaged neatly with a vociferous bow, so the moment stood, feeling truly surreal in the way that it rested. Was his reaction forged with a similar reply? Did this odd lunacy burn as boldly in his blood as it did hers? This her inner voice probed dazedly, and wonder reared as a liable source. Buried aptly in the unruly locks of her hair, Michael's face remained hidden from view. His breath ragged as it sprayed across the skin of her neck, mimicking the summery exhaust of a car. Slow to regain composure, a tremor waded through the scant balance of her hand, exhibiting thus as she swiped the moisture from her brow.

As if to reset the sequence of time, Michael's body shifted to lessen his weight, turning his head on the pillow. His eyes glowed like irradiated gems. Quietly descending on hers, they screamed the thesis of his thoughts, and without the benefit of a single word. He knew she recognized the earnestness of their position, for no veil masked the honesty from the other's view. Understanding, in full, the implication of what now was the verity between two, as there could be no retreat nor farce with which to form a negating rely. Solidified in time, molten wax yet carried the indent of their crest. Stamped firmly in place with apperception, all barriers were eradicated with the ardent legation.

Fortifying his arms around her, Michael rolled with her locked to his side, settling her with his usual wont atop his chest. Silence cascaded warmly in reaction to their mimed confession, thus it aged like the body of a balanced wine. No words bloomed in exchange between them as they waited, though both sought the remedy of that. Desperate in their need of clarifying speech, yet neither knew just where or how to begin. Do they, on the apex of such poignant account, acknowledge or ignore what it was they construe? And should they ineptly venture past such trappings, what then? Of the two, neither knew what direction to veer. Nor of what, or how, such verbal spitting could meander their end.

Lacking the use of their usual banter, the two quietly held, clasping the other as if time dithered at its end. Sleep, in time, removed the uncertainty of their thoughts, wiping clean their slate with slumber. It granted them peace.

Day drifted into night unbothered by the disquiet that yet dallied beneath the sprawling roof. The dark suppression tamely tottered amidst a magnificent scene, rearing vibrant like the blossoming of a flower. Gone from the manse was the couple's usual verve for jesting. While the evening's evolution bred uncannily smooth, it lacked the finesse now customary to the two, though it was not so for each other. With long hours spent ensconced in the arms of the other, conversations for them stayed effusively light. Uncluttered and unbinding with the hesitance they felt, sleep once more extinguished the lethargic lull, reclaiming their bodies well earlier than their usual wont.

Julia woke abruptly from the peaceful nadir of sleep with a sigh on her tongue. Perplexingly tense, excitement plagued the pivotal regions of her body like the eroding of effervescent waves. The dark tips of her breasts already stood indomitably charged, and the erotic cadence of her pulse cantered without limit. Yet it was the crux of her womanly body that seemed the officious master to the outrageous display. With stanch certainty, the aching strongly beseeched to be quenched, and it took but a moment to realize the cause of her sensory fray. Sighing in resolve of the fact, Julia dragged a hand over the cool sloping of her brows, as if to soothe the distorted direction her thoughts now led. For even in slumber, she knew no freedom from his reach, nor did rest stem the vaunt of her desire for him.

Outside the lunacy that was her body, the room sat quiet. Wrapped in darkness, a sweet, enveloping calm embraced them as one. The occurrences of the hours prior, hastily refreshed the details in her yet befuddled head. Although no words were spoken to assuage the matter, both were pointedly aware of the grounds they now tread upon.

Bewildered by an assemblage of fear, elation, lust and indecision held her just as tightly as the first, thus she set sail a despondent sigh, hastening further the anxiety of her mind's pursuit. If only to challenge the uncertainty she felt, Julia craved the honesty of their lascivious act, this for the fond way it's hold near nothing in reserve. She'd shown naught of reservation in the lectures she held. None in her debating of factual essence, and was equally as open with her grasp of the roles she played. Conducted with the fiery wave of her hips, each gesture flowed without effort or thought. Yet words of a certain kind eluded her the very moment she willed them free.

Locked, as ever, to her body, Michael reposed tranquilly on his side, and the soft spill of his breath faintly pierced the stillness of a slumbering house. Vaguely visible in the dimness, the broad outline of his shoulders seemed a mere sketch, so, too, the inertness beholding his form. A strange sense of belonging inundated the shadowy space, bathing her fully in the very place that she rest. Its tincture was unlike any previous perception of appertaining. Knowing, without suspicion, she intrinsically belonged. Irrespective of time and events, she would be his and his alone. There could be, nor would there be, anyone else, as his was a prominence unsurpassed. His aura, the very essence of his moods, each granule now coursed through her body as aptly as her own blood, and the thought of waking him to confess such revelation, surfaced rapidly through her head. But fear of the unknown and the poor phrasing of her words, froze her dead in her tracks.

Gingerly, Julia rolled from the comfort of his bed. Slowly navigating the darkness to the adjoining room, she attempted to calm the frenzy of her body. Bathing her face repeatedly in the cooling liquid now gushing to her aid, her sigh wafted sharply through the quite air, as all the familiar venues heralded their need like the grumble of a tornadic riff. She could still feel, with certainty, the voracity of his body. Sweet and unyielding in its brewing, as if he yet taunted her vale and hillocks with unwavering bent. He had meandered well the fissure of her mouth, and his kisses were, as usual, volcanic. Splayed ardently against the skin of her thighs, his work bred unending. Whether awake or in dream, the variance mattered not, for the result was yet the same, rearing through her body as vivid as the pangs of a lengthened fast. They merged, wove and braided to the rankling of her thoughts.

Pensively, Julia paced the cool tiles in abject discontent, missing the warmth of his body. She contemplated the benefits of voiding his rest, asking just a smidgen more, in her prodding, than the constraint associated with a chat, though the decision unfurled itself more as a compulsory fix. Hurriedly, Julia brushed her teeth in answer to the unspoken decree. Staggering through the darkness, she slipped quietly back in bed.

The warmth of his body branded her the instant they touched, singeing her skin. His heat stroked her as superbly as she now stroked him. Warm kisses moved freely over the wide width of his back, ascending his neck. She touched her lips to his ear; there, she beguiled the sleep from his body with her song. "Come out, come out and play." She coaxed, scaling the hard ripplings of his body. Her tongue willfully stroked his lobe in command of such, murmuring the impish inquest. Her hands strove more determined in their bent. "Are you too tired to play, Michael?"

Drunk with sleep, Michael rolled sluggishly onto his back. His focus clogged with the vagueness of indecision, he could but gaped confusedly at the woman now perched sprightly atop his body. Darkness shielded her action, but not that of her intent. Remedying the haze before long, Michael paused amidst the vivacity of her attack, and it took but moments to recognize the decadence she tendered to his hand, and fewer still to show his awareness of her cause. Already, her hands were everywhere, and his body gave response long before his mind ascended the lethargic fog.

"Give me a minute." Michael rasped, detaching her with care from her roost. He slipped hastily from the bed, returning in what seemed less than a blink, smelling freshly of mint.

In the scant space that hovered between the dissolution of a ternary tick, she loped into the spread pen of his arms, scrambling aboard his body. Her mouth syphoned like a ravenous ware as she asserted her will. Zealous hands kindled a ferocious trail down the plateau of his chest, reiterating their goal. They laudably schooled the wont of his neurotic nerves, setting a blaze to his blood.

In his vie to wager control, Michael raised her slender form above his head, resting her beauteous assets within reach of his mouth. He touched his lips to her breasts, imbibing the taut peaks at leisure. His tongue bathed the delicate swells in adoration and warmth, and her sighs breached the chard encasing like a sweet, dramatic song, growing avidly more pronounced as he ventured down her stomach. Much in the way of a flower, he feverishly separated the petals from the trove, careful in his love of the dainty beauty that waited inside.

Time built, and the labor of his mouth, could not easily be rebuffed. Propelling her farther on an upwards slope, Julia stemmed the ascension with a shrewd shift of her body, as trembling hands brought him close. The aperture of her feminine form eagerly acceded the swallow like one with a protracted thirst, as her body drank him in like a desiccated sponge. Although hunger shouldered the lead in piloting his homecoming, greed fostered his stay an inescapable task, held so, by the firm clasp of her thighs.

The persuasive ardor of his kisses knew no end. Deepening their drive, they consumed all manner of her thoughts, and she soon lost herself to the movements of their bodies. Hence, it wielded like a well-rehearsed dance. Perfectly nurtured, it ripened to a scrumptious connotation of body and heart, each fostering an exhilarant verve, sweetening that of their thrust.

Together, the two slid from control to wildly indigenous. From real to the rim of madness, the gift of dialogue enhanced its stature to but a primitive hum. Though when at last the rumpus ferment to an ambrosial brew, and the blend readied its explosive salute, her body adeptly heralded thus in a splendorous relent. Closeted firmly in the arena of his arms, he stroked the interior of her body with virtuosic vim, dredging hard until his body followed suit with her own. Collapsed jointly in the spent effort of release, his breath sailed to her jagged and rough, effectively slicing through the darkness. They quietly awaited composure's return to the muddle in their heads.

"It seems you've evolved into quite a discerning alarm clock." Michael advised hoarsely, pressing a kiss atop her head. A chuckle rose in true sinister form from his throat. "Although I think you play a somewhat dangerous game."

"Why's that?" she panted.

"What if I develop dependencies?" he asked sedately, knowing he was long past any such developmental phase with her.

Julia paused in the hush denseness, as if suspended in thought. A frown frozen prettily on the set of her brow. Wanting greatly to give him something bosom of herself, she rifled her brain for the aiding of such. "Always a pleasure," She averred at last with a smile, though looking almost stern.

"That, I claim as my own on any given day." He returned in a husky breath, his voice drifting back in quick response.

In a slow, unhurried motion, Julia nested her hand aloft his left breast. Gingerly, she lowered her gaze to the podium of her hand, and her breath burst forth in a stirring gust. The gentle movement of her thumb assuaged the skin atop his chest, and as if she caressed the crucial organ itself, her strokes reared determined but light. Bending forward to his chest, she kissed the spot newly vacated by her hand. In reaction, his hand flew to her integrally soft, cradling the back of her head. He sequestered her stay.

"Julia." Michael sang, her appellation soaring through the glorious dispelling of his breath, and even in the darkness, her eyes hastily gave answer to the poignant weight of his call. Yet no words came in follow, and the silence that trailed quickly dulled his thoughts. Eroding all trace of his confession, apprehension held him strongly transfixed. Time drifted while he waited, for what, he was yet unsure, staring instead into eyes that gleamed back through the tensing dark. " *Je n'est plus le propriétaire.* I no longer own it." He informed her in a whisper. "*Il appartient désormais uniquement à vous.* It now belongs solely to you."

A quite smile seeped wondrously onto her face, as if understanding some morsel of his words. She showered him with the bestowing of her lips. Dismounting his body, Julia rested her head on his chest, snuggling close to his side. She hugged his warmth to her breasts. The emotions behind his words were again undeniably strong, though she dared not ask him to explain, even while she longed to know the full essence behind the emotive lyrics. Something about his whispers in French gave her an odd feeling of satisfaction. Balancing greatly the precipitous ledge on which she tottered upon, as it offered the shelter of ignorance to an otherwise blatant affair. For although her heart was already primed for further descent, she, however, was not. She was not fully ready to play show and tell with her feelings, as she still had trouble with the truth she needed to tell. Though that, in actuality, was the least of her trouble.

Shifting his head on the pillow, Michael sighed, noting that she did not seek translation of his words, and although he was greatly perplexed by her choice, he was also
grateful for the decision, as it meant he did not have to lie. He would not need to rummage for truth to placate the evidence of a fib.

"I have a thought." Julia whispered at last, needing to break the lingering silence.

"What's that?" Michael asked in a well leisured timbre, sounding like a cat being
appeased by the grazing of one's hand.

"How does a hot bath sound to you?"

"Now?"

"Why not now?"

"Well, it's—it's two o'clock in the morning for one." Michael smirked, twisting
his head on the pillow to confirm the accuracy of his guess. Though it was, however,
two-seventeen to be exact.

"Don't you think there's too little of that already?" she asked coolly. "I mean...time
between us."

The truth of her statement was irrefutable, and it left him no choice but to nod his
agreement of such. Conscious that the paired visits allotted each month was neither
sufficient nor good, not in his eyes. Not when each day held such commanding appeal.
Time, though closely acquainted, was definitely not a friend. "Would you like bubbles
with that?"

"That, as well as an overused stallion for sure,"

"What makes him so overused?"

"Don't you feel overused?"

"Did you know in preparing for winter a bear can eat almost his weight in food?"
Michael queried dryly, his deep voice almost melodic in the quiet of the room. "It's a
survival instinct." He clarified with a shrug.

"Do you foresee winter coming?"

"Every time you leave," He averred. "But you also bring other seasons as well."

"That's awfully damning, how can I be your winter, your summer and your user in
one?"

"My user?" Michael growled, laughing at the preposterous concept behind the unfit
word. "So now you're using me?" he asked through the deep rupture of his mirth.

"Isn't that in the headline every time I breach the gate? The purpose of my visits is
an obvious fact."

"I've been seduced in ways too numerous to say, and I'm sure along the way,
there was an elaborate amount of using on both sides. But let me assure you, if I
haven't already done so, they were nothing like this. So please, by all means, use
me however you like. You have my permission on that, and I'll do my best to be a
good sport and not complain." He laughed, his deep voice trolling the quietude like
the pulsing of rain, sobering quickly, he asked. "Why do you refer to yourself as
. summer?"

"If I'm being likened to seasons, one of which you proclaimed as winter, I just presumed the other side of that made me summer."

"But why choose summer over the others?"

"Well," Julia shrugged. "If my absence reared as winter, then my coming must be something arduous and harsh for you. It departs with you thoroughly drained, does it not?"

"I've always thought of you more like…spring."

"Spring, why spring?"

"Let's just say…everything grows whenever you're around." He hummed, brushing his hands over the smoothness of her buttocks as an added reply.

"Everything or just one thing in particular?"

You say…tomato…" Michael groaned, his shoulder climbing softly through the air. "I say…tomahto." Informing this with another pass of his hand, he sketched the roundness in a slow glide. His voice sailing playful and soft, and although there was much left to be said. He preferred, at that moment, to bask in the golden amber of silence, still yet holding some pride. "Why not come closer and study the result for yourself?"

"I'm practically using you as my bed, how much closer would you like me to get?"

"There are times when there's no such thing as too close, and there are people who make that construal uncannily so." He vouched, his voice seeming to hover in the back of his throat. "Ones you just can't get enough of."

In quiet retort of his pledge, Julia smiled, and it seemed her entire body shuddered with a sigh. At times, he had a way of addressing her that made her whole body hum.

Languorously, she obeyed his request. Climbing aboard his body, she laid atop him fully stretched. Her face now pressed firmly to the cording of his neck. Michael's fingers sauntered down her spine in rich tenure of the premises they patrolled, and her body gave a sated purr in concurrence of such. Inhaling the soft residue of his cologne, his manly essence wafted smoothly up her nose like the flavoring of food. The odd thought surfaced as with the strike of a match, as she could not help but wonder if a cat felt much the same when tested with their addictive treat.

Ambling his fingers through her wild curls, Michael held her snug. Yet no words sailed forth to further their usual jest. Since uttering the encrypted dedication, neither seemed inclined to speak, and although she had not yet given a verbal response, she hoped he would take much from her action.

Like the fall of a feather, her lips touched the side of his neck, as if to solidify intent. She rose to gaze raptly in his eyes, answering thusly with the flavor of her smile. "Surrender to me, Michael." She goaded through a kiss, explaining in muted effort the reluctant truth of her thought. "Come away with me for the freeing of a bath." She coaxed, stroking his lips with her own.

"You don't need to convince me. I'm already with you on that."

"Good. Then let's go." Sounding almost defiant, she shifted her balance in readiness to roll, finding herself fully ensnared by his arms instead. "Are we still considering?"

Julia asked guilelessly, smiling with girlish glee at the intensity of his watch, for even in the darkness, naught was hidden from her view. A soft glow danced through the brilliant tinting of his orbs, and it whispered the sweetest promise in return to her enduring gaze, seemingly filled with affiances yet to be said. The warmth it encouraged befell the totality of the room, submersing the space in a comma-like lull, as if, it, too, waited in anticipation of his words.

His thumb gently painted the outer crest of her lips, savoring the fullness. The thudding of his pulse further roused the organ under the spill of her breasts, and she found herself anxiously waiting in expectancy of his next breath. Craving with every fiber of her being to hear the words he wanted to tell, although certain she already knew.

In time, a deep sigh cut the protracted patience of the room, and its tautness was instantly felt, carried on a gust like currents in its drive. His mouth touched with the releasing of said sigh, yet it brew persuasively explanatory in its declaration. In arrogance, his finger wove through the thick strands of her hair, holding her to him in contrary defiance. His mouth imparted the very depths of his soul. The oration being an unmistakable datum, and she drowned in the level of intoxication it gave.

With every part of her body Julia clung, holding dearly to his strength, while the room awkwardly tilted and swerved. And she greatly suspected that, had she not already been reclined, she would not have had far to go to be similarly inclined, for he wickedly plucked the very air from her lungs, leaving her well pliable under his hands.

Pausing, Michael gazed into her eyes as if searching for the answer to a quest. Clasping her face firmly in his hands, his breath came persistent, like a soft breeze strolling the angling of her face. A deep sense of longing welled inside her chest, twisting mercilessly at her heart. As the passion in his eyes was overwhelming to regard. A verity of great proportion, the moment flounced like none she had ever had before, none more eternal and none more sublime.

Dropping her head to his, Julia savored the honesty of her body. His hands then grazed her skin like a predator devouring its prey, softening as he broached the junction of her thighs. He unleashed the full measure of his will. Relenting, as always, with wild abandon to his questing of her, she donated amply from the very depths of her being, for she needed him to understand the truth of her response. Equally roused in their awareness of the other, she needed him to know that his feelings were reciprocated with the very best that she had, and could find no better way to substantiate this, than to relinquish her body to the meanderings of his hands.

Outside, the gentle hoot of an owl twirled steadily through the pre-dawn blackness, barely stirring its calm. Though inside the storm of their passion howled like the gusting of a squall, and their chirrups in accedence of such, intensified the darkness. She was his and she told him this, as buoyant and as enlivened, as any woman could, leaving no premise unsaid. The dialogue between them grew compelling, as their bodies exquisitely grounded a soliloquy of everything that the two had yet to say.

Silence followed as two bodies reclined well spent. Julia lay with her back snug against the spread of his chest, an arm draped her navel like the swathing of cloth and, as always, the feel of their bodies collectively, set cool against the superbness of warmth. Together, they watched the tapering thickness of night. Growing uncannily weak, their lids slowly sank to a place of rest. Wrapped together in a deep hush, the two remained as still as the air on a breezeless night. The reticence being of mutual delight, for their bodies already paid their debts in full.

The drive home was, without qualms, her most strenuous undertaking, feeling as if her heart was being pulled from her chest. Though their voicing of goodbyes appeared to have done just that. Regardless of why, denial no longer seemed a plausible excuse. For the truth now howled it boisterous pitch without relent. It was not the sharp gnawing of a fantasy that had goaded her so, but the entrenching of emotions that now heralded within her like trumpets staged on a hill. Armored by the faux benefit of defiance, she barred what could have once been apparent long before now, had her mind not been otherwise detained. *It was not lust that pushed her ever onward, but love.* And at that, no manner of effort she summoned will continue to repress that truth from herself. She loves him. And the mockery of that averment was in its depth. For even in her denial of him and the mutiny he had, so easily, coaxed from her body, love controlled the propensity of her action, as he meant more to her than she ever thought anyone could.

Their launching saw her less than candid with herself, unwilling to accept the feelings he unfettered in her. She never allowed acceptance or even the honesty of what she felt, certain the madness would pass. How could it not? They were of different worlds, were they not? And hers did not wade well with the psychosis revolt that was his. The mix was like a tentative field laden with mines. How will he feel when the true aspect of family hit home? Would his affection for her linger or haze? Would he still feel the same if there're kids traipsing underfoot? Would he be as understanding when lazing naked can no longer be a frequent forte? Theirs was a time scored with illusory pits, built on the parody of a fantasy. Reality does not come anywhere close. When chaos surrounds them, would he still feel the same as his silent pledge contend?

With an appetite like his and the life he'd led, kids were a tough sell, and she just could not see this die because of that. How could she bear to watch him go on so foolish a cause? Would not silence be a more fitting response? If this should die, then let its death be of another than that, for she could not endure the rending of such a calamitous plight.

If she but left them as they are, would that not afford her some happiness to come? Having him at her side meant more than just the partnership of their act. If doing naught could grant her that wish, then she can and will, remain the happy mute.

Chapter Thirty Seven

Garbed vivaciously in the pomp of sunlight, the day in all its grandeur hailed itself flawless with an impeccable display. Tireless extol floated without prodding or prime, for none found bias in the veracity of such jubilant brag. Drizzled generously in consummate beauty, the surroundings seemed but the portrayed stroke of a hand. With temperature tottering blissfully at a moderate sixty-eight, yet dubious of the projected forecast of a garish seventy-five.

A blithe draught maneuvered the boughs with its barraging breath. Flaunting the panache of a puppeteer's skill; trees waved like characters bidden in an erratic scene. Perpetual of such, their splayed bodies cheerily bowed in response, enacting the rituals of a monotonous dance. They frolicked like jesters in a well-rehearsed skit. Thus, they enhanced the richness of the show. It was the perfect day to be of a wanderlust wont. Perfect for embarking on activities conducive to the beauteous display, had such laxity been afforded or easily had.

With subtle elegance and a mute show of tepid frustration, Julia swiped a soft pimpling of sweat. Dragging the back of a fist brusquely across the top of each brow, she shifted the stern breadth of her stance. Ripping free the lid from yet another portly bin, her lips twisted in thought, tightening with the potential at hand. Sequential claps barreled brashly through the dimly lit space, reluctantly negating the potency of its hold. Its plasticky strums grated sharply at the sultry attic air.

Time courted what wrought well as the master of malaise. Prospering wanly upon itself, though less than half the revolution of an hour had elapsed since she descended on the preordered chore. Yet, already, her body gave full protest of that, peeved with both errand and site. Perspiration speckled odd regions of her body, and in another few minutes, she'd most likely accede to her disfavor of both venue and cause.

Signs of the awaited advent now thrived everywhere. Sprawled in disarray across the squat bodies of shrubs, eerie garnishing marked the entranceways of homes, with some interiors faring no less odd. Now with the proposed haunting set to debark in less than two days, Halloween's sluggish progression postured much in the way of an arduous taunt, having had to perceive its auspicious arrival for months. Her three month inundation was, at last, nearing an end. Though that was not foretold in the proceedings of this day, for her hunt now hearkened that which is of the utmost importance. Today, her search rested perilously on the meager adjunct of a pair of gloves. One precisely specified in the sly details of its design, segregating itself from the needless plight of the rest.

There convened amongst the bundles of many, a purple accessory pageant itself. Strutting easily forward in its adornments of black—this gamely dotted the slim tips of each hand. Next came black with white veins streaming the full show of each hand, with lace curling against the soft skin of both wrists. Promptly trailing both finds, orange mottled a stingy canvas of black, all of which could now be labeled as found. But her instructions, with all certainty, were astoundingly clear. Thus far, she'd found stocks of unwarranted surplus that had naught to do with her need, and even less to do with her cause. Not one had anything to do with the lengthy tutorials she'd had. The last of which was given only that morning as a refresher to the ones before that.

"This is really not that funny, so you can quit your none-too-sly snickering. Have a heart, will you?" Julia scolded in an absent tone, giving a soft grunt as her eyes drew flushed with the bottom of yet another bin. "This is what I get for taking help? Nothing is where it's supposed to be!" She griped, reloading the bin gruffly in half that of its disburdening. The certified clack of its lock echoed with the slap of her hand. Balancing the bin between hands, she returned the tub to its designated station on the shelf. Aiding its settling with a hard shove, she pulled another from its place. "You know, if you don't quit with that warped humor of yours, I may be forced to seriously contemplate repayment with some strategic admonishing of my own."

"Is that a promise?" Michael challenged huskily, his deep voice rumbling in his throat.

"Jeez. Can I ever say anything to dissuade that distorted mind of yours?" she groaned, adjusting the earpiece on her ear. She hastened her finish of said bin. Swooping an attack on the last remaining three, her mood instantly lightened at the thought of departing the muggy attic air, even at the cost of negating her efforts for the so ordered gloves.

"I don't know. Why don't you try me? What juicy smut can that tongue of yours dish?"

"How exactly did this conversation turn to me soiling my tongue with filth?" she inquired pertly, pausing in her effort. Her hands dropped to nest on the notch of her hips, daring the validity of his response. Though the man was true to the rarity of a perfected knack, torquing, any and all, conversations into that of pure smut, which, evidently, was viewed haughtily as a gift in his eyes.

"Maybe I just wanted to see what sweet tidbits you'd bring to the table." He expounded in a husky breath, though a smirk stayed heavy in the dark cadence of his voice. "Come on. Play with me a little. I haven't seen you in five days."

"And how exactly will my dirty talk help you with that? Wouldn't that make it worse?"

"Maybe, but it certainly would be fun while it lasted now, wouldn't it?" He smirked. "Come on. Tell me where you want me to kiss you when I see you next."

"*I'm not doing that!*" Julia gasped, and the lightly toasted color of her skin showed then a strange tint, seeming suddenly like the start of a blush.

"Don't you want me to kiss you when I see?" Michael murmured in coaxing, his voice sounding suddenly warm.

"Of course, you know I do!"

"Then tell me how?"

"Got it!" Julia announced triumphantly, her fingers locking around the small gloves as if they hailed as a priceless find. Immediately stuffing the treasure inside the pocket of her shorts, she returned the discarded items at thrice the pace of her efforts before.

"Good! Congratulations! Now tell me how you want me to kiss and where."

In delight, Julia slammed the lid shut with a hard, decisive stamp of her hands, whirling without delay for the exit, an iridescent smile courted her face. "This is too weird, Michael, even with you." She grumbled, carefully charting her descent of the creaky steps.

"Do you have someone else in mind you want to tell how to kiss you?"

"There're few things in life you get to answer with absolute surety, this I assure you is one of those few. Since I'm confident when I say, you do not need instructions on how to kiss me. You supplant the mastery of that." She averred, and the softness of her tone swaddled his frame like a customized cloak.

"I didn't say I needed instruction," Michael assured with a darkening smile. "I just want to hear you say where you want me to kiss you and how."

"Okay, fine." Julia agreed with a stingy groan, pulling open the refrigerator door. She immersed herself fully in the dim boundaries of such iniquitous thought. "I want you to kiss me everywhere." She sighed, selecting a bottle of water. A smile crept forward in counter of her stern reply, still yet musing on the answer she gave.

"Should I be soft, slow or ravenous?"

"Hmm…I say all of the above." She muttered in a slow breath, rolling her eyes to the ceiling in thought. A once dim smile now flickered bright on her face. "Start with one and end with the others."

"Where would you like me to start?" Michael probed, his voice swaying through the phone like a sensual caress.

"Where you normally start is just perfect." She apprised excitedly, her memories falling to the avarice of their play, and the insight was an inspiring view.

"Anything else I should add?"

"Well…you can—" singing the tame lyrics in start, her directives hedged to a sharp stance, twisting her head in anxious reply, dark brows ruched at the sudden intrusion of a bell. "Hold on. There's someone at my door." Julia announced contritely, swallowing another mouthful. She turned cautiously in said direction, toting the water in her hand.

"Hurry up and come back, will you. I want to hear all the other places I'll need to kiss."

"I will." She pledged in what seemed a consoling breath, though still yet bearing her frown. Weary of unwanted solicitations, her steps grew gingered, cautiously staying all sounds within. She set the bottle to a table as she passed. In true pragmatic dictum, her gaze narrowed upon the thick portal, fitting her vision to the small opening, she froze.

"You?" she shrieked, swinging the ingress wide. Her eyes blazed with the immensity of her gladness.

"Special delivery for one Miss Berwick," Michael announced warmly, his smile deceptively slow, brandishing two large pizzas across the breadth of his chest. His eyes strolled leisurely down her body and back, settling at last on her mouth. He roughly laid bare his expectation. "I'm told payment is expected at time of delivery, by the way. And how often does one get to say they achieved that by compensating with a mere pittance? A kiss should suffice well in this instance."

"What are you doing here?" she asked with diminished breath, uncaring of motives or cause, but could find no words more fitting to add. Hence, she grappled to stem the preposterous sheen daubing her smile.

"I brought you lunch; pizza from another favorite of mine."

"Lunch? That's a mighty trip to see to such a miniscule task. Soon your armor will be downright blinding with the severity of its glare. Isn't that type of doting supposed to be more predominant in others?"

"What can I say?" Michael shrugged. "Perhaps these are newly emerged repercussions from my many years of addiction. For of late, they seem to dine profusely on my will. As it is, it's a niggling chore just to keep my thoughts straight these days. And it seems I'm ever on the verge of erring on things that stands without precedence."

"How unfortunate for you," she sang, her body seeming to glow with the verve of an unfettered smile.

"That would be the least of it." He hummed, stroking the reservoir for which his thirst perpetually lies with the heat of his gaze.

"You know," she countered mildly, her voice drifting playful like a sweet, melodious taunt, beaming in response to the badinage they trade. "Your earlier comment somehow implied that I've yet to dare a certain line, that is…with a delivery…person." Julia smiled, lifting a slow brow. She issued a large seedling of doubt. "Perhaps your certitude should be given with a little more reserve. I mean, who is to say what, or how far one's willing to progress in their need." She shrugged, lowering her lids coyly. Her voice thickened with the sugar she intentionally stirred. "I'm just saying. You never know what's what with anyone these days."

"True. But I'm definite when I assure you. It hasn't been done quite the way I had it pictured in my head."

"God, you're hopeless." She groaned, though her voice stoked the ambiance like a lascivious moan. Her head thence waved in ambiguous response. Ogling his peerless assets at will, the set of her smile slowly widened, brightening the delicate features of her face. "Why am I smiling like this?" she inquired dazedly, questioning this with a breathless sigh, the utterance flew forth intending for none but her ears, though her obvious gladness wielded transparent in the sweet brush she devoted in her gaze.

"Maybe it's because you know what I'm thinking." Michael droned, stealthily closing the gap between them in what passed no slower than a wink. "And what's even nicer, is that you're thinking it too." He hummed, pressing her body with his, a lazy smile grew bold. "I miss you." He announced huskily, cutting the languid pause. His gaze grew longing, plunging the dark, entrancing depths with his confession. "I can't seem to get your beautiful parts off my mind." Michael breathed, his breath sliding warmly in follow across the smoothness of her cheek, and without hesitance, her head turned for the capturing of his lips.

"Dare I ask what parts of mine have encumbered you so heavily? Though I'll admit, there are some specific that has held fast to my memory as well." She crooned, giving answer against his mouth, her words sprouted new life. Still clutched sternly within her grasp, the door's obdurate feature gave reminder of the spectacle they yielded, and in reparation, she let the burdensome portal fly. The heavy barring thudded resoundingly in place at the urging of her hand, sounding much like the warning thwack of a gavel. It rattled the windows with its gale. Summarily, Michael reached behind his back, abetting the deeds of her hands. He swiveled the locks in place with a faint twist of his wrist, though his mouth gave no ease in its delving.

"Are you in the mood for pizza right now?" Michael hummed, burying his words in her mouth. He flattened the firm ridges of his body, to slim. "Or can I interest you in something first?" he rasped, relieving his burden on the table adjacent their hips, long fingers spanned the back of her head. "How about we find out together what parts of yours rile me most effectively. Is it accessible from your back or your front, or could the location matter little in the sense of geography?" he growled, recapturing her mouth. His tongue grew insistent, hurling the thumping in her chest on a wild lope.

Gentle fingers blindly skied the round dunes of her breasts. Climbing upwards beneath the snug fit of her shirt, he thrust the cottony draping atop the soft swells, while his tongue labored and coiled in a circular caress.

"Mm...Wait! Let me take a quick shower first." She exclaimed through a raspy breath, straining greatly for the wont of control.

"Why?" groaning thus, his kisses lazily ascended the slender length of her throat.

"I'm really sweaty from being in the attic."

"Then that would make it the perfect start for what I have planned." He hummed. "Last time I checked, you can't summit Everest without building a good sweat, and it's my intent to see us do just that. I've yet to find one thought that is in anyway clean when it pertains to you. Every single one has you spread, draped or aloft a spirited steed. And just so you know, I'm not much for dirty dialogues, at least not on the phone. I've always preferred the rewards that came with the reality of that in opposed to its games." He droned. Pulling the top free from its perch, he asked. "How long do we have?"

"About two hours." She retorted through what seemed the start of a sigh, her hands systematically harried, eliminating the nuisance that was his shirt. "Mmm," Julia cooed, running her hands languidly over his chest. She savored the hard trenches under her hands, missing the intensity he repaid her in his gaze.

"Then I better get the most out of this that I can." Michael droned, pasting her body to the wall of his chest. His embrace was well telling of his yearns, and again his mouth bred almost brutal in its drive. A slow plummet saw his hand inside the waistband of her shorts, curling gently. He relished the warm softness as it engulfed the slender digit on his hand, pulsing madly in the swallow while he worked.

Roused by the delectable palpate of his fingers, a soft moan rose in avowal of his toils. "Why don't we make this a little more comfortable to start with?" Julia hummed, clasping his hand to her breast as she turned. She led him to the lush comfort of her bed.

In simmer, tranquility daubed the quiet radiance of the room. Sweetening the solace of the space to unparalleled height, it cloaked their sapped bodies in warmth. Michael's long bulk rested like a shroud at her back. Affixed snugly, his arm curled possessively around the indent of her waist, and perfection bred, too vague a descriptive, when labeling his feelings of content. Being with her seemed as natural as breathing, and contentment was no longer just an unachievable word.

"I'm glad you came." Julia purred, hardly breaking the slumbering peace in which they now rest.

"Me too," Michael smiled, lifting his head from the pillow. He cradled the weighty bonce in his hand while he studied her face. "However, this time you have me at a disadvantage," he informed her lazily, bringing her hand to his lips. He kissed her palm lightly, touching the limb to his chest, he smiled. "I miss having you in my bed." He vowed, gazing wistfully at the wiry fingers now nested in his hand, as if his words were intended solely for them.

"Then how does it suit you to be in mine?" she inquired with a solicitous smile, rolling fully onto her back. She gazed into his eyes, her adoration brimming in the dark pools.

"I like it just fine. But then, any place with you is always a treat." He advised her in a murmur, his voice rumbling against the skin of her wrist.

A gentle squeeze came forth in answer to the lightly given pledge, quietly lifting her head. She offered then a feathery kiss. "It's nice…you being in my bed." She tamely informed, though those were not the words blaring in her head. *I'm deliriously happy to have you here in my bed.* She caroled inside. *You make my heart go wild every time you're near.* Her inner voice further goaded, sailing to her like the persistent lyrics in an unforgettable song. Yet she chose only to exhibit the simplicity of her smile, staying the verity of her words in the very place they rest.

Smiling, Michael gathered her close as he rolled, settling her atop his chest. He adored her assets from every angle that he had—this being his favorite roost to have her rest. Her hair fell in loose torrents around her face as she lifted her head, brushing his chest like the gathering of silk in each sway. "God, you're breathtaking." He sighed, tucking the wayward strands behind her ears. He feasted on the arresting view laid to his gaze. Saying to himself more than his words indicated to her.

"Funny, I was thinking much the same thing about you." Julia smirked, laughing as a growl rattled the quietness between them. Almost indignant in its retort, her stomach rent the mellowness of the room, grumbling loudly as if in answer to a question asked.

"I think we better heed the warnings before your stomach starts telling secrets. How does pizza sound to you?"

"Pizza sounds great! And it just so happen that I had two delivered earlier for lunch." She chirped, rolling from his chest. She scurried from the bed to the shelter of her closet, returning to his view garbed in an oversized shirt. "Sexy enough for you?" she asked, spreading her hands wide in her effecting of a pirouette.

"On the contrary," Michael smiled, stepping roughly into his shorts. His eyes seized there fill. "I know what lies underneath the sly tenting, and that, on a whole, makes it… very sexy."

"Does your mind ever escape the gutter, a small furlough for something not truly understood, perhaps?" she probed, purposefully grazing his body with her own. Her astonished yelp pierced sharply through the room as he abruptly grabbed hold. Dragging her roughly to his chest, he clasped her firmly within the vice of his grasp.

"Never!" He vowed in a rumbly breath. "Why would I when I have such enticing treats to devour while I'm there?" he smirked, dropping his hand slowly to her navel. It locked like a bolt in place, preventing any chance of escape. "You bring out the monster in me." He confessed in a raspy breath, brushing a kiss across the soft indent of her neck. "I'm only doing as he bids."

"Will there ever be such a thing as enough with you?"

"Of you? Doubt it!" Michael rasped, his voice wafting from the barrel of his chest, and hazel eyes flashed their certainty of his words. Releasing his hold on her shirt, his hand slid possessively down her back, riding the curve of her buttock as they turned from the room.

Dressed sassily in the radiance of the midday sun, the kitchen's honey stained walls glowed warmly in an argot of welcome, generous in its dispelling of joy. Built amid a cluster of trees, rays yet streamed vibrant, drenching each window of the room in its lively hue. From sunrise to sunset, the house held a constant glow, an indisputable trait well distinctive of its mood.

Michael's eyes strode through his surroundings with wonder marking their depths. As if attaining insight into the rare crevice of a forbidden archive, his gaze drank of the contents it gave. Made predominantly of cork, a wall of exhibits—labeled "the hub"—revealed much of the house's happenings to his riveted view. Prominent in his perusal was a compendium of fine art—so titled by the artists themselves. Report-cards, pictures and ads publicizing the latest deals for a quick meal, all bolstered the eclectic compilation, as did a calendar marking every upcoming event for the next few months.

Obvious to any who ogle the details, the chronicles were a bold depiction of domestic life—hers. Faced with that reality, she wondered on his thoughts. Would the realism affect his judgment of her? Could that remand his value for the seductress in his bed? And would he, even with time, see her as anything but?

A soft thud nestled close the smaller of two ovens. Its spiky clunk groping the silence like a diktat willing it's due, towing Michael gruffly from his meandering thoughts. He sauntered in an instant across the room. "Can I help?" he asked, taking his place at her side. His hand descended the pocket of her navel with accustomed ease, branding her body with his heat.

"Why don't you get the drinks?" she advised with a tame smile.

"I can do that." Michael averred spryly, bobbling his head as he turned. His hand lingered in its rakish task, slowly slipping from her waist to gather the hem of her shirt.

Always prolonged in play, Julia simpered. Vouching such summary with her ego, for his appetite manifested much like a competitive sport, though a five year drought rendered her especially grateful for such deeds, having had no cause to find faults with the bevy of their jaunts. Had there been naught between them beyond the benefits of said games, their zenith would still yet derive a place that was almost as sweet, for she had yet to find a comparison with which she could assimilate the exquisiteness of its gift. "How about a picnic to go with that?" Julia asked in a stirred tone, noting by the impiety of his smile that he understood her meaning well. "Minus the fire, of course,"

"Though I'll ever work to put a fix to that,"

"Now how did I know to expect an answer like that?"

"Astounding insight I guess. I'm beginning to wonder if I should fear that you know me so well." Michael smirked, his words falling slow, yet they brew no less the caress he intended. "Only one?" he quizzed tamely from her back, noticing the set portion of their meal, though he already suspected why.

"Just trying to not be too lethargic," she chided, curling her shoulders in aid of the impish response. "How about you, does more seem fitting?" she probed, a stilt brow lifting in wait.

"One seems plenty." Michael assured raptly, his hazel eyes ablaze with the magnificent whirring of his thoughts, as visions of her promise raced through the trenches in his head. "May I bring anything…else to the table?"

"Hmm, how about a chair?" she offered matter-of-factly, knowing the intrigue was effectively set, as he watched her with ravening zeal.

"Your wish, mademoiselle, is surely my lead." With a spindle-back chair hoisted in one hand, Michael's smile broadened, and ripened excitement vapored the usual ardor in his eyes. "After you," he rasped, balancing their drinks within the other of his hands. He waved a path plotted for their departure.

The wildness of her hair now sat twisted in a disheveled bun. Roughly reclined at the back of her head, it bobbled jauntily like a trapezist with each feat. A dark smudge coasted her left temple, and the oversized shirt draped her like the exterior of a tent, cueing not of the exquisite physique waiting beneath the sly cloaking. But, to him, the evidence all bore nil. A stunning vision in any light, she transcends a league tailored for none but the dissident spirit in her. If given the chance, he would spend every waking hour devouring the many angles she had. No grand draping could be any more enthralling that the picture she presented then, having always been attuned to every side of that. None came close to the mania she untapped with just her presence, and the urge to scream "*I love you*" was almost too potent to resist. But a better time was needed to broach such topic as that, fearing the words would require more than just the simple discharging. He retained his cool. *Find a better time, Michael,* he coolly scolded.

Unless fabricated, there may never be a better place than the very grounds they tread upon. But the timing needed to be unspoiled and unrivalled by all, and he had yet to acquire a concept nearing his taste. He'd never confessed emotions of its kind to anyone before now, not in all the lengthy tenure of his roguish zeal. Never had his heart been so fully labyrinthine with anyone, or the very tincture of their deeds. Nor had the structure of his world ever been so dependent on the perceptive value of someone else. With each surfacing idea being quickly dashed as an inferior step, he was left wondering if the prospect had him more petrified than even he suspected of himself.

Her request was that their interaction remain effusively light, no relationship and no attachment beyond the spiritedness of their play. Yet no deviation was more significant than those when bearing your soul. How does he counteract the predisposed judgments she'd made? That, in part, was half the battle he now wrestled with, for the effort, it would seem, was more like the undertaking of a delicate crusade. Unsuited to be manhandled or rushed, the need was but one to see it through—assuaging, quietly extracting the coveted outcome well-fitting of a fray. What if such confession scared her enough to damper the very essence of what they had? What then?

They've yet to revisit the agreement once brokered between them, not once, not in all these long, ardent months. Why hasn't she asked to revise the laws in all this time? Surely his confidence in her affection was not a derisive trait. Nor was his perception of such taken from the visage of a maimed bat. Her feelings, he was certain, rivaled those of his own, and were as definite of that as he was of himself. Yet the significance towing between them had never gotten broached, not once. Isn't it said that women, of the two sexes, are the emotional beings? Why is there a galactic flip in the expressive verbiage between them? Will his effort be enough to change this thing that they have?

The air bend, curled and swayed in a nigh jubilant chant as he reentered her room, veering like the praxis of a massive kite. A plush blanket smothered the rug at the foot of her bed. Imperious, like the dispensing of a challenge, pillows scattered atop its surface like the preamble to some Arabian event. Purple marked the site readied for their anticipated regalement. Shunning the lone chair from their revelry, it looked almost dejected sitting lamely across the room. Sharing the pillows propped chaotically at their backs, the two sat unsparingly close. Conversation never slowing between them, it swerved this way and that without strain or a designated end.

"Are you still going to New York this weekend?"

"I am." Michael hummed, his head bowing in mid chew.

"How long will you be gone this time?" she inquired tamely, her voice echoing through the can now fastened to her mouth.

"Two weeks at the most." He retorted dryly, his eyes absorbing in their noting of her face. Tucked demurely beneath her body, her legs peeked daintily from the hem of her shirt, and the sight squealed rousingly of a dubious fact, as she was inimitably different than what her beauty projects. At first glance, she looks like a princess, and carried herself much in the way one would. But she lived as free and as wild as the help themselves. She can traipse through a wet thicket, roll through a bed of leaves, and still not show a bother on how or why. Plodding through a bank of mud in a friendly fray came without fuss. So does her dig to craft the perfect projection to set sail at his head, and she had yet to voice complaints on the care of her nails. Dainty came nowhere near to describing who she was. It held no meaning in the lengthy descriptions she held.

Waiting below the hem of her shirt, the smooth texture of her skin was an irresistible draw for his hand. Reaching forward, Michael traced a finger along the merged edges of both thighs, slowing at her knees, they returned to their preparatory beginning.

"But I'll be back between that to see you."

"I know." Julia proclaimed with a confident smile, taking a meager sip of her drink.

Michael's hand ceased its wandering midpoint of her thighs, intrigue dimpling the corner of his mouth as he lifted his gaze. "Is it the man you know so greatly, or does the man's action predict him that much?"

Slender shoulders slowly elevate from their roost, the upsweep dredging longer than a mere shrug in its dispelling. Swallowing the now masticated food, she washed it clear with a large sip of her drink. "I don't know." She remarked lamely at last, throwing him a waggish smile.

"That's your answer?" Michael questioned gruffly.

"It is." Sailed her none-committed response, taking a last bite of her food, she returned the crust to her plate. "Or…maybe not," she smiled, patting the napkin across her mouth.

"Is there a reason why the answer is held as a secret?" Michael inquired coolly, setting his empty plate aside, he smiled.

"No secret. Just…." Julia smirked, unfolding her body like a graceful cat. She rose to her feet, deliberate in her movements as she sashayed from the room. Impelled to wash her hands, she further splashed the cool liquid on her face, cognizant that she now harbored an audience of one.

With arms woven atop his chest, his eyes mauled the lithe features at her back, feasting well on the uppermost gradient of her thighs, as the mesmeric attributes, once hidden from view, now sat exposed beneath the raised hem of her shirt. Leisurely, his hands glided past her waist like a new belt, attaining its mark. Firm thighs stood like pillars granting aid to the shapely stilts of her legs, driving the hard press of his body. He connected the prominent elements of their parts.

Under the administering of his hands, water splattered gauchely across the counter, dousing the front of her shirt, this under the feeble guise of washing his hands. Time showed little substance or haste in its march, and his affectatious efforts grew more leisured the longer it held. Purposeful in the taunting of her breasts, his body shrewdly lingered aloft the caged softness of hers.

"Are you quite finished?" Julia queried tritely, grafting the slow hike of her brow to the bolstering of her quest. She turned leisurely in the diminutive circle of his arms. A covert smile daubed lightly to the concave junctions of her lips, seeming more the aiming of a rifle at his head. She pinpointed her sights fully on the target at hand. Assertively, an arm grazed the soft flesh of her waist in response, and the torrential hiss instantly halted its boisterous chanting. Straightening, Michael smirked as his hand towered above her head. Releasing his miniscule hold on the cargo he towed, he showered her with the spittling he carried in his hand. Raining silver droplets atop her head, water dappled the dark strands of her hair in a flash. It trickled in haste down her face, shoulders and back.

"Hey!"

"Did you know I would do that?" Michael queried softly, broadening the breadth of his smile.

Craftily constructed from the flash of a sugary beam, Julia's smile exhibited perfection in just the onset of its rendering, flouncing exquisite in its build, proemial to the havoc stitched to its inevitable kill. Judiciously, the oversized shirt climbed her body like the practice coup of a burlesque's fan, summiting her head. She mopped the wet tresses, dragging the garment down her face. She smeared the dampness over her neck in a plummet to her breasts.

"Did you know I would do that?" she inquired in return, lifting her eyes at last to his. She feigned surprise at being so perused by her audience of one.

"No." Michael grunted tamely, his eyes well appreciative of the view. "Though I'm always hopeful to gain such recherché sight," promising this through the aid of a lustful smile, his palms stamped the counter alongside her hips as he absorbed his fill, and a daft smile manipulated the features of his face. With the slight arching of her back, the dark peaks of her breasts were already inclined, their chocolatey tips seeming almost erect, and the pleasure he got just from watching her was beginning to show in the warm stroking of his gaze.

"Michael."

"Yes."

"Do you think you'll be finished anytime soon?"

"That's hard to say." Michael shrugged. Leaning in close, hazel eyes exhibited the budding of a wolfish smirk.

"Had I not already fed your appetites myself, I would have likely thought you somehow starved. It was you that I fed, was it not?"

"It was. Though neither of the two was nearly enough for a grown man to live on. I barely see you enough to triumph in that. Two servings per full moon can hardly be considered a full coarse meal." Shifting his balance, Michael reached behind her back in a sly stretch, undoing the loose tie from her hair, he smiled. "There." He sighed, watching in delight as the cascading mass clad the upper half of her back.

"I believe you have an odd perception of the number two. Surely there's some ineptness in the multiplication. But fine, here." She invited puckishly, settling back in her seat. She offered herself as a feast to the gluttonous wont of his gaze. Widening the closure of her legs, she further arched her back. Her head then reposed atop the mirror like a bed, and the smile she awarded him doubled nicely as a taunt. "Go ahead and satisfy that inquisitive mind of yours. Have your fill then."

"That could take a while, Julia." Michael rasped, swaying backwards on his heel. His gaze grew heated, harvesting the advantage they now had. "But we don't have the time for me to linger on that." He sighed, placing a feathery kiss on the side of her neck. "I don't want to merely admire the fruit. I want to partake of every flavor it has to offer." He informed hoarsely, brushing his lips along the spill of her breasts. "I intend to feast to the limit that I have left."

Thrusting the imbibed features further forward to his mouth, her head fell limply back, for her body gave swift reception to the slow bathing of his tongue. The ambrosial employing left her no recourse but to give compliance to his will. Time saw her hoisted roughly from the hard, coolness of marble. Thusly inclined, the two staggered across the threshold of her room, and a slow, baritonal growl accentuated his measured slide to inhabit home.

No longer discarded, the chair creaked timidly in protest of their jaunt, enlivening the sumptuous flavor of the ride. She gave forth validation from the shadowy chambers that have long since been untouched. Nurtured arduously to full apogee, a heavy groan doused the din of the room. It then billowed to a melodious sigh.

Determined to elongate the flawlessness of their frolic, Michael strode to the plush comfort of her bed, nestling her body against his like a porcelain treasure. They laid in silence.

Julia shifted after what bled like the incision of an hour, though, in truth, only minutes had elapsed since their spilling. Lifting her head slowly from his chest, he gave voice to her thoughts in what sifted as a rumbly sigh.

"I know." He assured glumly, opening his eyes to a half-mast stance. He propounded softly. "But I don't want to. I wish—"

"Shh…" hushing him weakly with the lengthy exhale, she barred further comment with the gentle press of her fingers across his lips. "I know." She vowed. "I wish it wasn't so…but, well…soon…. I'll see you soon." Murmuring the reminder, her head fell heavily to his chest. Bobbing lax like an untethered fruit aloft a submerse bin, cognizant there was so much more that needed to be said. So much more trimmings needed to accompany the sparse phrasings already said, though silence swallowed the engaging prospect instead.

"Something giving you worry?" Michael tamely quizzed, sensing she had more to say on the topic at hand.

"No. Well…" she groaned, exhaling the words with little strength, though the truth was boldly splayed on her face, discrediting the answer she gave. "It's just…" she moaned, sweeping her hand over his chest. Her eyes trailed intently. "I like…this."

"Me too," Michael retorted, his baritone spill wafting soft. "You are, by far, the best part of my day, Julia." He smiled. "The best part of any day,"

"And what of the days I don't see you, what then?" Julia probed, her voice sounding strangely diluted in its dispelling, almost wilted as if the words clambered from some hiding place in her chest. Fanning from her uncontrollably quick, the question soared forward without the benefit of consequence or thought. Leaving her no time to reflect on what answer he would give, or on the worthiness of knowing the results of that.

"Of *any* day," Michael reiterated firmly, folding his fingers over the smaller of her hand. He anchored the limb where it laid on his chest. The smile given in reply was truly a satisfying treat, as her eyes did not dip from his for, what bred, an extended spell. Nor did she stall any of the sweet renderings now given in their depths.

In measured pace, Michael's skull pulsed with the hammering taunts of a digital clock. For time, in its splendor, would not be stemmed irrespective of cause, speeding swiftly by. It took with it the beauty that was them, and the sweet tranquility he felt in his place of rest, did naught to bolster his cause. It seemed but minutes before the need arose for yet another adieu to sail forward in their midst. And he wished he could give voice to all the things that now pressured his heart, though knowing truly that goodbye still came with its telling.

"Do I have to go?" he enquired tensely, as if testing the torrid current of a pool.

"You don't have to," she advised tamely in reply. "But…*we* do." She clarified with the weak swing of a finger, stoking the air amidst their chest, the thin digit added aid to the translation she intended.

Michael's pale rejoinder showed in the faint bobbing of his head, for it was precisely as he assumed it would be. The wild seductress well known to bring him to his knees would now vanish from his sight, and the face celebrated in her everyday life would swiftly morph forward in its stead. "I know." He assured, affirming the answer to both her and himself.

"You've never wanted to do that before?" she quizzed palely, propping a hand under her chin. She pondered the duality of her speech.

"You've never asked or gave me the opportunity—nor the option, for that matter." Michael droned, elaborating further on the elusiveness of their affair in the quiet of his head. He almost grumbled the burdening of his thoughts. She felt more like a dastardly stashed mistress at times, than anything else, wading through his life without attachment or care. No questions or expectations were preserved as a must between them, none that required the regiment of a commitment. Yet there was one, most avidly, set in place. His allegiance to her stems like no other, and although she was said to be adamant on that directive, he'd gladly bestowed it with naught of reservation or care. A promise that now prevailed with every fiber of his soul. Between them, there were no lurking partners outside of who they were to each other. No lies or deceit stands as a fault on which to rest. It was purely her and no one else, for she concocts the sole proponent imperative to his world.

"I didn't know you wanted to."

"I know." He hummed. "But someday, I may just get the urge to enlighten those ears of yours." He warned, a stiff smile supplementing the factitious threat. Surprised by the simple play of words, and how much that lightened the feel. "If I am to be a saint, I'll need something to cart me through the adversity ahead. Something tasting like a treat for the road." Twisting his long body, he pinned her under the rigidness of his. Smoothing the wild strands from her face, he smiled, though his eyes hardly mirrored the musings now torquing his mind.

"I thought I just did that." She mewed in a soft, seductive pitch, arching her back. Her arms scored the air above her head in a stretch.

"Are you serious? Do you really want to tempt me now?"

"You find a measly stretch…tempting?" she cooed, carving her brow in an impish test, already astute to his riposte, though his smile served well to answer that. "Come take a shower with me." Julia invited in a whisper, brushing her hand across the ruff stubble of his cheek.

"Let's go." He rasped, pressing a kiss behind her ear, the two rolled in unison. Appointed for a thorough washing neither would likely forget.

———————

Clothed almost fully in black, the bedroom felt strangely sterile. Absent was the energetic chatter that came with her presence, so, too, the vivacity of laughter, or the vigor of them in itself. Leaning his shoulder against the door, Michael peered through the darkness inside, and as usual, the room was an immaculate display, Betty, being matriarch, made full certain of that. Everything remained forever in its place with her meandering about. But to him, the room felt uncharacteristically cold, more so now than ever before. It grew ever more algid with the vastness of his bed. Sleeping alone was becoming as abhorrent as a loathsome chore. For in her presence, the very essence of his home breathes only life, looming in her absence as if it rested in a trance. The very air stood rigid. *How did one woman's reach serpent so imposingly through the faceted tiers of his life?* He groaned, though only silence gave answer to his query of truth, knowing he had long since passed the point of caring. Michael shrugged.

Swirling the hay colored liquid in his hand, it sloshed in soundless play along the sides of the chalice set to totter in his grasp. Absently, Michael touched the stubby glass to his lips, swigging a hard swallow of his drink. He savored the sweet scorch of aged Brandy with the barring of his view. Torrents of fire stormed through the hollow in his chest, torching his stomach in reach. It warmed him from the inside out, encouraging his entrance in the room. Ambling inside, his every act seemed a methodical strive, setting the glass on the console by his bed. Michael ripped the shirt from his body, tossing it in a somber pile atop the bed. He dropped down gruffly beside it.

The day had grown into a long, bittersweet sham of itself from beginning to its almost end. It veered at a constant hike, and of late, the bitter seemed a lengthier repast than it once was. His intention had been set on them having *their* talk, with this coining the sole purpose of his visit, had the truth been told. But the mantra that keeps replaying in his head had him fully perplexed. Having her in scant doses was surely better than none, for he did not want to set loose the succulence that came fully with that. Yet knowing he wanted it all.

There was no doubt that he needed to articulate these feelings he had. No doubt they needed to confront what they so skillfully evaded in their well-rehearsed gambol. But the how had him tottering instead of seeing it through. Whatever the correct appellation for what needed to be done, *they* most certainly needed to address the underlining facts. Surprisingly, he was both dreading that result as much as he yearned having it said. What if she runs?

Why is she so *damn* contented to let the matter rest? In all his experiences, women have always found ways to steer the discussion to whatever was their wont. Why hasn't she? What the *hell* is that all about? Why couldn't she just be normal and rearrange the rules by now? Had she done that, this whole thing would be so much less work, and his turmoils would, most likely, be of a different source. Could it be that she was sent to drive him crazy? Michael groaned. Sounding almost sorrowed in the tense weightiness of his breath, since God knows, she'd already done that, he barked, musing lightly at the thought.

Had she been anything like the others, then conjectures of this variety would not be the variance running through his head. His eyes would have probably wandered by now; wouldn't they? With her, he seemed hardly a replica of his known self, but a clone of what makes him his best. The old him would have already bobbled the scenario by now, since patience, as it stands, was never a word associated with his name, not when it pertained to women. Now the one thing that dwelled as the hardest to uphold was the one most important to his life, since he was not about to let a little resin as forbearance deter him from his goal. Unwilling to let her out of his life, he was prepared to do whatever the requirement of that. If procuring such prize meant acquiring endurance, then that's just what he intended to do.

Chapter Thirty Eight

Thin fingers curled fluidly around the heated surface of a stoneware mug. Cradling the rotund posterior in the palm of her corresponding hand, Julia strode to the front windows and back. Pivoting artfully, her gaze swept the scenery in a lax flash, observing the sparseness of a tale told with the inclusion of a single pass.

The soft, aromatic fragrance of Jasmine wafted pleasantly to her nostrils as she retraced her steps. Flavoring the hull of the kitchen, it stalked the edges of adjacent rooms like vagrants posturing on a swing shift, soothing that which already slept. In mere minutes, the slumbering phantoms will bustle with renewed life. Rocked soundly by the blustering energy of her children, they waded like strobes flashing out warnings in the dead of night. The house will again be a titter with the giddiness they bring. A respite well greeted in the stead of a deafening silence. Sprouting prevalent the lengthier their absence, it gnawed at the structure's cavernous core.

With cup midway to her mouth, Julia glanced at the dark-blue duffle now bedded on the counter in lingered suspense, setting sail what could be mistaken as a protracted sigh. She slurped the scalding drink, her thoughts turning perceptively to the luggage already stationed by the door. Snacks, treats and various modes of entertainment, best suited for travel, were already laden inside, though she suspected there'd yet be requests for the addition of an elected few to enhance the stack.

The approaching weekend, as always, stood as a designated pillar in the plodding of their parental mandates. With its effervescent sparks belonging solely to David in the upcoming days, these set to surely unfetter a thrill. But work had him locked in a quandary for the hours preceding his time. Necessitating the obligatory trip, carting the kids as consorts was the only logical recourse left to be had. Eliminating a day of school from their extensive list, the single absence saved him the hassle of rushing back to retrieve what little would be left of his time.

In a fleet instance, the hissing of brakes kissed the mulish muteness of the ambience to full wake. Julia rid her hands of the steaming brew. Yielding a minimum pageant of zeal, she hurried to the window as the first bus coasted to a stop. Her smile grew intuitive, while her gaze feverishly marked the features of each face.

A handful of children departed the large, mustardy chariot, all seeming to brim with surfeit reservoirs of glee. Sprinkling merrily in every direction at once, their voices chirruped through the quietude like chicks squawking in portend to be fed. The last to skirt the front was none other than the anticipated attributes of Richard himself, though he was not the last to get to his terminus of choice. His feet pounded the stone driveway with haste umpiring his action, stuttering his pace as he neared the rise of an essential step, his eyes now lynched to the target at hand. Appreciative of his rush, the door, as if on its own, swung open in welcome. Widening its girth as his feet vacated the inaugural step, his momentum, in accordance, neither slowed nor stopped.

"Hi, mom!" Richard twittered as he passed. Dressed with ramped elation, the melodious notes sailed affably over his shoulders like a cheer. His hands thenceforth released their entire freight, and the sound of his heels flogging the floor equaled the hoist of a hammer in a man's hand. Skidding to a shuffle, the bathroom door slammed with a resounding thud, and the house again plummeted to a gentle lull.

Behind her, the second bus grunted and groaned its incensed approach. Sounding almost unwell, the engine sputtered as it slowed to a spasmodic stop. In tally, a copious count, twice exceeding the previous sum, descended the cumbersome steps. With most looking roughly vexed, they sauntered in differing routes. Rachel moved in the middle of a small cluster of girls, their heights looming closely exact, and the gist of their dialogue reared ostensibly private. Five heads pressed together as if one, snickered softly at something said, their faces vibrant with the resolving quest that conveyed clues to the secret of life. Stammering their pace, the murmuring throng slowed to a stop at the top of the long driveway. Whispering in a rapt display, their heads, in unison, rolled back with the musical drizzle of laughter. Dipping together in retreat, they closed like the sides on a square in a four-sided embrace.

"Hi, mom!" Rachel waved, turning from the prattle of her comedic gang. She skipped gaily down the driveway in a bubble of sunshiny cheer.

"Hi, sweetie!" Julia chirped as she neared. "How was your day?"

"Good." Rachel answered in her usual elusive lilt, stepping through the doorway. She paused in her dispensing of a hug, lingering in the refuge of her mother's warmth.

"Your dad will be here shortly to grab you and your brother for an early start on the weekend. He's taking you with him on his trip to Asheville."

"Really!" She squeaked, the exuberant twitter soaring high. "But…wait…" she frowned, recognizing the disparity in the school week's length.

"Yes. You'll be gone for the full weekend." Julia caroled sweetly, giving added rise to an already arched brow. She clarified the imminent question before being asked.

"Yes!" Rachel hissed in response, clutching the whistling air well past its expected doom. Her body gleamed with the inflicted vim of new life. Without waiting for further comment, Rachel readjusted the bag on her back, dashing to the stairs in a rhythmic huff. Her smile competed aptly with the blaze still yet central in the sky.

"I've already packed everything you need!" Julia informed in start, lifting her voice in reply to her daughter's disappearing back. She hastily rescinded her station at the door.

"Richard, we don't have to go to school tomorrow!" Rachel gladly advised, yelling this as she neared the small room. She doused the hum of her mother's apprising prattle.

"What?"

"No school! We don't have to go to school tomorrow!" Rachel shrieked, enhancing the volume of her speech, her feet trounced the center of each steps in her hasty ascent of the stairs.

"Cool!" came a resounding squeal.

In tiered progression, her bewilderment sharply grew. As all thought of their pending trip appeared to have fled, and she could not help but wonder if a jaunt to the dentist might have attained an identical rise, had the unpleasant procedure guaranteed them a day's absence from school. "Guys, not that it seems to matter, but your father *will* be here in a matter of minutes." She interjected in a matter-of-fact lilt, her voice winching upwards to their ears. "So let's force a little pep in our step—in regards to your dad's time that is. Now to save you some madness, a cinch with the little time that you have, I've already packed *all* your must-haves. Your suitcases are already waiting by the door. So be warned, anything that is not already packed, I'm definite in your survival without. Now, chop-chop!" she urged, signaling the importance of thus with synchronized claps, she smiled. "Maybe you can oblige the effort out of some courtesy for your dad, or on the understanding that he has a tight schedule to keep." She shrugged. "Now don't forget, any and all outstanding or expected assignments coming due *must* also partner this trip. Daddy will be seeing to that once you guys get settled, so see to the required materials first. I know you guys are well acquainted with the 'misplaced' or the 'I forgot rules', so I'll leave those choices to you, less now or more later. You decide."

"Okay, mom," they hummed, their answers drifting low from opposing levels of the house, and the timbre soared like the monotone droning of bees, sounding far less enthusiastic than only moments before. The bathroom door whipped opened with its own interior draught. Richard, in a dizzying blur, blew past her for the stairs, his feet notches ahead of their usual rudder-like gear. Julia held her tongue on the boisterous ascent, not bothering to admonish or curse his incessant haste, not after setting blaze to their feet with her speech.

Time waited at a standstill until the last goodbyes were said. Though its resurrection saw her racing for her closet like a cheetah locked in the throes of an essential hunt, scrambling in preparation of their next indulgence. Her elation was hardly contained. In the ten days since Michael's visit, their time had since tripled on the phone, both in frequency and length. Her affection for him, she'd since discovered, stretched well beyond that of an eternal abyss. No man had ever been more revered in her eyes than the glorious seraph himself. Not even David in the embryotic stage of their marriage. Not since the Godlike qualities of her dad.

Her father was the single most important person in her life. Theirs was a love incommensurable. Even more so than what remains precious between her and her mother. Always taking the time to make her feel special, his skill had no kin, making every day with him an unending thrill regardless of task. With limitless efforts irrespective of significance, or of the magnitude required in each, his reliability was a documented fact. Ascribed strongly for the idol he was, when at age seven she was stricken with the chicken pox, his decision to come home early from work was but a small tip to a legacy that grew even fonder with time. In that, the two spent hours celebrating her so-called emancipation from school with a coveted Barbie party in her bed.

Her dad loved to laugh. So silly became a rotund catalyst that stayed the seams of the friendship they had. Lasting well through the many cycles of adulthood, it was the foundation of who they were as people, outside the distinction of a father's love, and he was master of the title he held. The similarities in their humor were an astounding trait. More so when the two collided on a single perceived path, as they found laughter in the oddest of things. Some, her mother felt bound to quiz the solidity of their sanity on. Such jest saw much pranks within the walls of the Waltham-Berwick's households, with each striving to outwit the other and be first to acquire that task. His every effort, it would seem, was to make the women in his life feel cherished. And he accomplished that feat superbly, beyond everyone else, succeeding at the set task every day of his life. He voiced the full depths of his affection at every opening he had. His loss had been an unimaginable burden on every organ and limb, and there had not been a day, since his death, that she did not miss having him near. And in conformity of such, she had struggled enormously with the anguish of his loss, thus making it exceedingly hard to summon the courage or even the will to let anyone in.

In arrant retrospection, Michael seemed to have awakened in her, a side that had slumbered since the passing of her dad. Fond memories were not looked upon with quite the same shredding effect attached to their tumble. Though meager, their similarities had not gone unnoticed to her systematic brain. Nor had their astute knack to make one feel the reverence reserved for a deity. Although their methodology was not the same, their vivacity for life was uncannily close. His was a humor that waded shrewd. With an ascetic current trolling beneath its unwavering bed, its bite was a delicious treat to perceive. Yet, she greatly loved it, just the same, on him.

He made her feel the ultimate in adoration every day. Though that, on its own, was an astonishing feat for a self-proclaimed bachelor—a renowned bad-boy at that. The latter were not known for the deeds he tended to bestow. Where was it written that one so titled would draw a lover her bath in the morning; wash her hair, just because; or feed her her favorite food by candlelight, in addition to the rest? Yet those were but a few of the things Michael, in his wizardry, had imparted on her. Every exploit pilfered yet another piece of her for the alliance of him, and thus far, there was not much left that he did not already own.

Selecting the right attire soon bred as an incredible chore, for the array spanned boundless. Should she pursue the consequence of an audacious assault and rend his sanity with none but a stitch left to the imagination? Or would the provocation of a subtly demure affront be best? Stringing him leisurely to the dark dungeons through anticipation and yen does make for an exquisite retreat. Not that her choice of outfits had ever mattered before, since he made ferocity the attribute of a well-honed skill.

Small, black and silky with a bandwidth the size of spaghetti, frail straps matched its miniscule size, thus it reared as the decider in her arsenal of tools. The accompanying scarf was only in the case of an anomalous chill, though she foresaw zero probability of that. For the crucial trimmings underneath, the choice was surprisingly clear. If less grants the bearer more, then nothing was unquestionably better than that, and she was going for the absolute best. Electing to pull her hair back, Julia twisted the wavy strands into a loose ponytail that trickled down her back. This, so she could ensure him the option of letting it down, seeing no reason to interfere now with his preference. Generous in her application of moisturizer, her lips bared a light dab from a, nigh imperceptible, coppery shade, with faint attention paid to the emphasis of her eyes. Only the bare minimum was given in the care of her face. Already anticipating the ensconcing ahead, sweat was a prerequisite for what she proposed, and makeup was the last thing she wanted to see extruding from her skin.

With her overnight bag firmly in hand. Julia slid freshly pampered feet inside heeled sandals identical to that of her dress. Studying her reflection in the mirror, she assented to the result of her work with a brazened smile.

It evolved quite fortunate, for both, that Michael was able to wrap-up his venture earlier than the expected time, or all her finely astute preparation would have been to no advantage, and an extra day of fun would have been poorly missed. Hurriedly, Julia scribed a note to her mother, blaming her sudden departure on much needed research for her book. She set forth on her way.

The drive to his house was almost surreal in the way it unfolded, such was the grandeur of her excitement. Every jittery twist of her pulse only serves to amplify the jubilation she felt, having never seized the initiative to surprise him before, though he had had some practice at that.

Standing broad but quiet, the iron gate seemed almost rueful in its effort at thwarting her path. In its surroundings, the clatter associated with the city, or that of rural existence, faded effusively in the presence of an old, rustic gate. None but the merest breath was left audible in its stead. Overhead, a canopy of fading green rustled lightly, shifting like feathers caught in the underpass of a draught. Their song trilled of welcome, this as their heads softly bowed in abetment of the show. Lifting her phone in hand, Julia's fingers gently stroked the smooth glass of her screen, selecting the desired name. She swiped the green highlighted button now prominently displayed.

"Hi!" Michael exclaimed elatedly after what summed as only two rings. "I was just thinking about you."

"Good! Were you thinking about kissing me?"

"I'm always thinking about kissing you."

"That's good to know, since that ties quite nicely with my plan. So, I was wondering," she paused, needing to calm the pounding in her chest with a steady breath, "Would you care to meet me for a few samplings of that?"

"Where?"

"I'll need a little clarification to better answer that." She teased. "So which is it? Where do I want you to kiss me, or where would I like to meet?"

"Both."

"Both? Hmm, I guess then it's only fair that we share the assignment of that. How about I make you the deciding factor? I'll let you decide where on my body you'd like to kiss most, and I'll decide where we could meet to make it so."

"Deal,"

"Do you have a place already picked?"

"I don't need to think on that. I know exactly where I want to put my mouth."

"Good, since I have my place already set."

"And where's that?"

"Why don't you open the gate so I can tell you my choice in person?"

"You're here?" Michael queried with an obvious rise tilling his pitch, bounding excitedly from his seat. His smile waded discernible through the phone.

"Waiting patiently for you to let me in," she purred, swallowing the sprouting lump in her throat. Julia smiled, and both hands glided atop the steering as if pushed solely by air. "I thought I'd return the favor you seem to have acquired with much practice."

"Then come do your will. I'm open to whatever payback you have in mind."

"What if you don't like the plans I have set for recompense; what then?" she smirked, inching her car closer to the widening barricade. Julia adjusted the phone to her ear.

"I guess I'll just have to shut up and bare the pain of atonement now, won't I? What other choice do I have? It's either that, or I never show my face in certain circles again, and I'm rather attached to the niceties that are of benefit in such case." He remarked slyly, trotting onto the driveway with a furrow to his brow. His gaze spanned the encompassing grounds. Sunlight glistened across the body of a variant sea of green, brightening the lush fields. The atoll was a true coherence of peace, and fall, in its eccentric splendor, was faintly showing its hand with a gentle breath. Mere inches from his waiting hand, her car rolled to a leisured stop. Michael's smile broadened as he removed the phone from his ear, shoving the clever unit in his pocket. His eyes followed staunchly as she tastefully unfurled from her seat, looking more beautiful than a rare orchid in full flourish. Her outfit of choice was an inspiration of its own.

"So, have you decided?" Julia prodded, stalling within arm's reach of his body. Her eyes grazed the length of his unyielding frame.

"Decided on what?" Michael murmured in an absent tone, watching her as if she was but the eminence of his meal, and he, being the victim of malice, had not eaten for days.

He made no effort at being discreet, none in the averting of the sparks now dripping from his eyes, nor could he, had he tried. With great appreciation ambling their rich depths, his scrutiny grew deliberate.

"On which particular site you'd like to kiss most." She crooned, her voice profoundly sweet, so swathing his body as assuredly as the heat of her gaze. Thus descending his chest in a slow plunge, the vision was as it would be had he been freshly baked. Like newly baked bread sheath in the simplicity of black athletic shorts, his fragrance still wafted sweet across the space between them, sifting up her nostrils. Her body watered for its need of his taste.

"There's something to be said for starting at the top." Michael informed dryly, closing the gap between them, he smiled. "And working your way to the bottom," He hummed, cupping her face in the warmth of his hands.

"Where's Betty?" Julia whispered, breaking the sweetness of his pull.

"Out doing house stuff, she'll be gone for a few hours at least." Pausing, he took a slow breath before resuming his oral advance. "You look like a recurring fantasy I've had." Michael droned. "And smell as heavenly, too."

"Feel free to bury your face in whatever cavern there is of your choosing. Who knows, you might find that I taste even better than your nose predicts."

"Hmm, can you feel my curiosity already rising?"

"Is that the name for it? I could never retain the extensive litany accessible for that, and all coding the same thing."

"Names are of little importance in some things. All the vital dividends worth retaining comes with the urgency given in the welcome itself. The rest all falls by the wayside with time."

"Is that so?"

"I'm summarizing, of course."

"Is there possibly another side to that door?" she queried to his hovering face. "I've come a long way. Perhaps you have something that can quench my thirst."

"Do you have something particular in mind?"

"You've earned a modicum of trust. Is there a suggestion you can make that would give a fitting fulfillment?"

"I might be able to think of a few things."

"Good. Glad to hear it." She shrugged, offering a measured smile, she asked. "How about pressing engagements, do you have any looming?"

"None but one comes to mind. Everything else can be rescheduled." Michael pledged. His hazel eyes afire as his hand dropped to her waist, gathering her close. He turned towards the house.

"I'm glad to hear that. Have I covered all possible obstacles?"

"I think so."

"There may be some arduous riffs on this road, I'd hate for it to get…interfered with."

"That would be a most unfortunate shame." He averred, scanning the driveway over the top of her head. "Shall we get the details underway?"

"Lead the way." She sang in reply, and the zest given in the stricture of his embrace, further tightened as they entered the house. Securing the locks, they walked in a miasma of galvanized silence to the privacy of his room, though at the ensuing barring, he pulled her roughly to his chest, pasting her back to the wall. His mouth descended like an arc of light in trice that of a blink, leaving her no room to wonder on intent. He biased her will, and had she had a smidgen of defiance left, he further delved. The parading of which had haunted the very recess of her dreams. Dished unfiltered and noshed in caroused abundance, it's the sensation that flourished every time he traipsed through the luxuriant regions of her brain. It's, in part, the reason that guaranteed her incessant return. His passion was indisputably the most saporous entity she'd ever encountered. Insatiable in its rapacious bent, it amplified a greed she never once thought that she had. "It took you long enough." She panted when at last he lifted his head. "I think that's an actual first."

"I blame you." He murmured against her throat. "You drive me to do weird things."

"In that case," she smiled, her eyes a fiery haze. Pushing slowly from his chest, she kicked the sandals from her feet. In what unfolded like planned coercion, she guided the quiet zipper to its end, and silk shimmied softly upon the caramel warmth of silk itself, until the tiny garment found its home as a mat at her feet. "Come get me and extract your preference of revenge." She purred, flaunting the stunning aspects of her suit with an accompanying smile. She offered this as a template of the very best that there was, exhibiting the depiction of such with the lazy sway of her hips, and looking sublimely carved to famished eyes.

Tempted greatly to hasten in her steps, Michael slowly straightened from his lean. A smile spilling supremely across the handsome chiseling of his face, though he resisted the voracious urge to throw himself at her feet, staying his will. He watched the soft swing of her departure instead, and the view was an inspiring thrill. Mimicking the finale of a marathon race, he entered the bedroom in a hush of silence, finding her already spread. She rested like an exotic repast for his watering palate.

"My, aren't we slow today."

"No. Not slow, just…savoring." Michael vowed as he neared the bed, sinking a knee to the mattress, he queried in a whisper. "Now," grunting this in start, he dropped a hand to her leg, and five fingers moved in feathered unison up the length of her thigh. "What was it you said I could do?"

"Whatever you like still sits somewhere on the table last time I checked."

"Is that right?"

"Oh, a girl never jests about vacating such power as that. It tends to make weaklings mad."

"Come here." He ordered, his whispered words sounding closely like the grazing of a lion's roar. It penetrated all layers of her skin.

Julia smiled warmly as she obeyed the gruffly given command, covering the space between them. Her heart thudded wildly under the heat of his gaze.

"Hi." Michael breathed against her lips, his eyes dipping to swallow her whole.

"Hi." She mouthed back, caressing the broad span of his chest, she smiled. Though had she intended further comment, the opportunity was quickly snuffed, as his mouth descended on hers with unconcealed tenacity and zest, making her body scream with anticipated pleasure. She trembled with her need to have more. Drinking him in like rain on a dusty field, she held no opinion in reserve, spending herself on the consuming. She loved every inch of his indurate frame until his body quivered and gave.

"Mmm, definitely the best part of my day." Michael hummed, planting a feathery kiss to the corner of her mouth. He smiled. "Be careful, I may need to come begging for more."

"So you can grow tired faster, I bet?" Julia goaded, already knowing his answer.

"Do you fear that?" he groaned, showing then a frown. He dropped his gaze sharply to hers.

Lowering the long, dark shields of her lashes, Julia masked her thought, though her head waved slowly in response. "No." She shrugged softly, her voice at an almost whisper. "I guess not."

"Good. I got you a surprise—two actually, but you'll have to wait a little on the second prize. It comes with a rare inking to the print." Michael stealthily informed, hoping to break the weightiness in the room.

"Why?" Julia inquired impishly. "You didn't need to do that."

"I know. But this is for a cause. Besides," he shrugged, drawing his fingers over the soft skin of her navel as he spoke. "Even a mistress gets a present now and then."

"So now I'm your mistress? If that's the case, where's my apartment in Paris?"

"You never asked."

"Does that mean you'll give me an apartment if I but asked for a souvenir?"

"Why don't you ask me and find out the answer for yourself." Michael coaxed, almost hoping that she would, as the prospect felt amazingly good. Buying her the two trinkets unfolded as a matchless delight, perchance the purpose held some reason as to why. Since each gift held the certitude of an unsurpassed meaning whittled in its grain, but as a unit, they mark the ingress to an entirely new world.

"What's my surprise?" Julia groaned, not knowing what else to say, as she had no need, or the care, for a new abode. But would never risk insulting him by an outright refusal of his gift, he meant too much to her for that.

"Chicken,"

"Chicken? Why am I a chicken for not asking you to buy me things?"

"You're being a veritable chicken for not risking the question."

"Am I still being a chicken if I already know the answer?"

"You think you already know what my answer would be?" he grumbled, wrinkling his brows as he gazed curiously in her eyes.

"Maybe, maybe not," Julia shrugged, refusing to commit to a definitive response. She smirked in playful jest, for to answer would be to throw open reality's door. A door she could not bear to confront just yet, and, in truth, did not know if she ever would. How do you prepare yourself for the possibility, authentic or not, to lose the one person you love more than you do yourself? "Do I get to know what this surprise is, or will I have to wait for Christmas?"

"Fine, it's waiting for you in the closet." Michael advised dourly, lying back onto the pillow, he smiled. "Go see if you can find it."

"A treasure hunt?"

"Not quite that extreme, but it may be something of a chore to find." He warned, taking hold of her hand. He leapt sprightly from the bed. "Come on. Let's see if you can figure it out." Michael snickered, pulling her to his side. Ten fingers spanned the entirety of her waist as he aimed her, like the leg of an ill-design yoke, towards the closet.

Impeding their entrance of the sizable closet was the draped tail of a slinky, silver gown. Splayed almost fully in the threshold gap, the indiscernible sign "wear me" was hooked jauntily athwart the hanger's neck.

"You got me a dress!" Julia exclaimed hoarsely, shrieking the statement more so than asked. Her shock showed thusly in the force of her whirl. Not waiting his response, her eyes returned swiftly to the dazzling piece. The dress itself was a stunning model of sophistication. Flawless in its elegance, something she, most avidly, would have fawned over in a purchase for herself, and in that, it allotted yet another example that the man knew her too well.

"I thought we could have a dinner date this weekend." Michael clarified from behind. Knowing his plans included more than just the simplicity of a meal, for his plot involved the acutely unaccustomed course of a confession. Professing his feelings at dusk with the aid of a candlelight meal, this far away from the deeds of their bed, was the only solution his brain had since conjured as an infallible quest. Their liaison started with the perseverance of a single sense, and telling her the full verity of his affection should be trilled worlds outside of that, as he needed her to understand that it was more than just the intimacy that had him mesmerized. She needed to see that everything else was as true as the tenacity of the first.

"Another play-date?"

"Of sort, though not exactly. This time we go as ourselves."

"What's the second half of my dowry? Shoes?"

"No, not shoes. Better!" Michael assured with a diffident smile, wrapping his arms around her as he turned her from the room. "But you'll have to be a little patient on that. It comes as a bookend to something else." Explaining this, he kissed the side of her neck as he tightened his hold. "Can you stay for a little while longer?"

"Could you tolerate it if I can?" Julia asked, tendering then a decadent smile.

"I think I may be able to manage."

"And tonight, would you be able to manage then?"

"A few things do surge to mind with that prospect." Michael drawled, turning her in the circle of his arms, he asked. "Where are the kids?"

"On their way to Asheville as we speak," she warbled. "So, what will you do to me for ambushing your plans?"

"What would you like me to do to you?"

"Mm, I think maybe a little bit of everything fits quite nicely in this."

"Oh, the possibilities," he groaned, leveling his body as a topper to hers as they resettled themselves. Michael smiled. "I can't decide if you were always like this, or if there's some corruption from me?"

"Wouldn't you like to know?" she fired back with a smirk, adjusting their fit until her breasts lay as a smooth swell against his chest. "Does the how or why matter?"

"It doesn't." He lied, braiding the slight pause with the casualness of his shrug, Michael smiled. "Though I have to admit, the thought has surfaced from time to time. But I'm sure the answer to that would escape you even if I asked." He smirked, touching a finger to her nose.

"I can tell you this," she purred, scaling the short distance needed to touch his lips with her own. She nibbled the soft, sensual fissure before continuing her speech. "I've dreamt about doing nothing more than spending the rest of this day kissing you, and I'd like to get to that if you don't mind."

"Then by all means have your fill." He drawled, reciting, with verve, the substance of her own quote. Hazel eyes sparkled like jewels in their observance of her. In a lifetime before her, he could not remember being told anything that gladdened him more, or experienced anything that was more poignant. "A man can go a lifetime without hearing simplicity voice so sweet. I'm glad you're mine in that." Michael rasped, his voice seeming strongly held, and he hoped she'd hear the collective meaning behind his words than the words themselves.

Whether to stifle the continuance of a protracted speech, or be it to feed the crude cravings of desires newly rouse, Julia's mouth ascended the climb to his, feeling the uncertain intrigue of that. She sweetened the implement of her drive, putting forward what hails as her best. His arms encircled her body like doors on a cage, slamming shut on a trapped prey. He pinned her body to his. His hands then worked freely on the dictates of his will, and as with his customary wont, his mouth was insistent. Dredging wicked and unsavory notions through the captive regions of her brain. He drained the very essence of her strength. Slowing the decadence of his magnetic kiss, Julia sighed, resting her forehead to his. She pacified the moment with a calming breath.

Michael's hand gently skimmed the slope of her cheek, gliding fondly through her hair. He fidgeted with the tie that held the unruly strands in check. Undoing the rigidity of the clip, on his third try, he regarded the splay. His admiration well evident in his smile. Julia smiled with serene satisfaction at her prevision of that, feeling the long tresses fall free about her shoulders, and liking the envisioned result. Long fingers, in turn, pushed the crowding from her face in a leisured fall.

"Mmm…Boy have I missed you." She purred sincerely, her eyes communicating her words as fact. Michael smiled, and his mouth opened as if to offer a retaliatory confer, but she quickly silenced any probable discourse that lingered on his tongue. Chary of unfavorable truth lurking in his speech, she entombed both bodies and minds to the mission at hand, wanting only to feel the desired result, and needed it void of the bog weighting the seams of a convoluted dialogue.

Once given as an adumbrate thought, dinner was now officially scheduled for seven in the formal dining-room. Specified directives on the advisement of such topped her pillow on the morning of. Seeming to mimic the troughs of an authentic date, allocate proceedings, prior to the elected hour, were also attached. Their familiar bedroom was to be her prescribed domicile of dress, her escort, having made other arrangements, promised to be prompt in his arrival. Thankfully, the imposed severance would only be enforced in the latter part of the day. Though by the time seven befell them, she was well antsy from the unaccustomed division.

His gentle rap thrummed the entrance like the resonance of a preemptive ballad. The notes proclaiming not just his presence, but the assuredness of his compliance to what now bred like an indefatigable strive. Navigating the vice of his venture into what had little enraptured his taste. Yet, of late, such gnawing had barely yielded him rest. His heart strummed madly in concomitance of the truth, fear and excitement sparing for dominance in its place. Hastening the cadence once the notion was broached by his hand, the repetitive oaths of console did little to ease the gallop or the whirring of his mind. The door opened almost the instant his hand fell, ceding him admittance. It revealed a vision to the yen stalking his gape.

Clad appealingly in the shimmery vestment chosen by his hand, the long dress swept the floor as she swayed impishly in exhibition for his eyes. Soft fabric molded its compliance to the curves of the figure provocatively donned inside, and like the opulence of a full moon. Its rich, silvery pigment made the dark, caramel of her skin a radiant sight. The mute shimmer of pearl embellishments sparkled well in the dark depths of her eyes. Highlighting silver on silver, its luxurious luster dimmed beautifully on dark. Thin straps flaunted the slender square of her shoulders, augmenting a wealth of elegance. Intricate beadings adorned the spread of her bosom. Draped sparsely down her back, it dazzled the long edges of her hem. And she looked better than he ever imagined she would. This she dually stressed in her affecting of an added pirouette, thus annexing the full potency of his view.

"You look…amazing." Michael averred in a long exhaling breath, his eyes absorbing their feed.

"Why, thank you. So do you." Julia crooned, feeling her playful self. "I have to admit. You have incredible taste."

"I'm beginning to see that." Michael remarked slyly.

"Mm, yummy," she purred, turning her gaze upon the urbane length of his body. Julia smiled, taking her own fill. She ravished the physique so ably displayed. Attired in a dark suit favoring that of a tuxedo, his look was superbly classic. With a tinge less formality than the hindermost choice, he was no less appetizing in the bequeathing of his charm. "You look like something worthy of procuring a taste."

"Don't tempt me." Michael cautioned softly, dropping his hand forward. He signaled the start of their date with the attaining of her hand. Cognizant of the evening's importance, he steadied his focus. Needing desperately to get the essential objectives over and done, he steered her to his podium of choice. The two strolled then in silence, her slim form carved intimately into his, and although he held his body close, his mind, while active, was not.

Two places were set aloft the long table, one like a parallel brother to the other. Their seats were instantly assigned under his sly directives. A multi-tier candelabrum furnished the only light, swathing the room in a warm, entrancing glow. It set the stage for a romantic escapade for two.

The menu prevailed again as a simple offering, steamed vegetables and her favorite—an impressive display of a lobster's tail. For it was not the meal that concerned him so, but the conversation to be had, which, at the moment, was staying on an unusual bend, as it bred with far less verve than the customary vaunt. Broken, at times, by the persistent pause, awkward silence dragged without the benefit of a projected end, stilling the room to what seemed an aged papal with its persistent rent. How can it be this hard to tell someone they mean everything? Who knew he was this much of a coward? Still, the caveat soared brashly in his head, what if she was adamant about things remaining untroubled, misguided and fictitious though it was, could he? So the questions swirled endless in his head.

Julia slumped forward in recompense of a new pause. With head bowed languidly in wait, she allowed the niggling of yet another lengthy reticence to pass. Barely seeing the remnants of her food, though her gaze punctured the contents scattered on her plate, giving her mind further into the weight now anchored to their lull. The air around them ripened to a taut fullness, and the ease of their waggish banter trickled, instead of its habitual flow. Although she knew, for her, the indisputable cause, she could do naught but endure the persistent spurring. For it was her inherent need to skirt what seemed always on the tip of her tongue. *I love you. I love you. I love you.* There, I said it, she reasoned arrogantly, though it soared to no one but herself, *now let this end*. She grunted then.

With both dreading the consequence of fitting such thoughts with wings, the two held fast to the advantages offered in a fully debunked lie.

"Time out," Julia proclaimed dully, gifting then a long sigh, her eyes slashed downwards to her plate, and a playful smile came precipitously as she straightened in her chair. Still averting the astuteness of his gaze, her chair groaned loudly, rending the silence as she stood. "Would you turn around please?" she asked softly, and instantly heard the echoing chord of his chair in compliance to her request. Gathering the delicate fabric of her gown, she raised the hem high above her knees, procuring a seat, sidesaddle, on his lap. She smiled.

"Man, you're good to look at." She crooned, brushing her hand across his cheek. She enlivened the warmth of his response, silencing further comment with the dynamism of her mouth. It was not the pleasantness of his words that she needed then, but the feelings he steeped with the merest touch. She wanted, instead, to capture, savor and ravish every part of his body for posterity. All the parts she'd then miss in the two weeks to come. "Delicious." She sighed, resting her forehead to his.

"Delicious doesn't even come close, Julia," Michael vowed, his timbre seeming more graveled than its usual grate. "I could dine on you night and day." He groaned, coiling his arm like a snake behind her back. His fingers parted the loose strands of her hair.

"I'm sorry. I know, technically, that was cheating but…well. We needed to break whatever that was."

"Don't be. I'll concede to your wisdom on that. There may have been a small hint of constriction dotting the air." He smiled. "Stay here." He drawled, brushing a kiss below her ears, his breath drizzled like warm air down her spine.

"Okay." She replied without hesitance or pause, as there was no place else she would rather be than the place she now rested. Nor would she want to be with anyone else, outside the small stricture of her family, there was no one else, certainly no one treasured in this way.

"Now, where were we?" Michael inquired with a deepening smirk, his mind blank of everything but the kisses they shared and the notions they fed.

"I forgot, but then there wasn't much being said. Maybe we should just skip the small talk and start on the prospect of dessert." Emphasizing her words with the slow slanting of her hips, Julia smiled in acquiescence, feeling the hardness of his body almost joyous under hers. As he had not far to go on his journey to a very playful end.

"But…I need to, well, okay." Michael grunted, swinging her legs to the floor. He expounded upon the venue of her thought. "I have something I need you to try anyway." He droned, leaning forward, he extinguished the lower of three tiers, leaving a remnant of one to light the enrichment of their steps.

"And this is new?"

"Call it revamped if you will."

"Really! And how exactly is that done?"

"I'll be happy to illustrate the finer details at length. But for now, a verdict on our site is at hand. Should we try for the novelty of my place, or have you grown devoted to yours?"

"I believe mine to be more suited by way of vicinity." She quipped, and a low snicker escaped her with the nicety of the thought. In follow, a new mound of excitement rushed through the crux of her body, asking questions that had not been previously studied or conceived. Had she been crazy to think the attraction between them would simply mellow and die? Surely she had to have been, or, at the very least, benumbed, though it seemed such odd phenomenon lied only in the territory atop her shoulders. Had her eyes been open or unmarred by the contagion of madness, she would have seen the physique, or paid full heed to the ammunition that came with his face, hence perceive a correlation in her response. Why was she so certain that the repercussion was just lust? Her long abstinence, it seemed, had befuddled more than just the capacity of her appetite, for by now they should have long since tapered to a steadier rhythm for two—not still foraging. Yet more often than not, she seemed the instigator in what stirred much like an unquenchable yen. "I am like the deviant carbon of a rapacious brute. I must be. Did you put something in the water?"

"How dumb would I have to be to drink my own poison?" Michael droned, shrugging from the tailored skin of his jacket. He hooked it stealthily on the long tip of a finger, slinging the raiment in the direction of a chair. His eyes gave no heed to the garment's direction. The dark vestment fluttered through the air as if with wings, catching the outer arm of said chair. It slid fraily to the floor in conclusion of the act, the result of which was stanchly missed, as his eyes seemed tethered to the action of her hands.

Julia's smile grew wryly with the absurdity of her conjecture. Slipping the thin straps from her shoulders, her hips sluggishly swung, and like the tame sample given in a seductive dance, the slinky attire shimmied weakly to the floor as if under the guise of a spell. "Maybe it wasn't an intentional judgment to imbibe your own drugs. An accident perhaps, or some bizarre test to your immunity?" she probed, flouncing to the chair. She draped the garment across the width of both arms. Gathering his jacket from the floor, she bedded it on the seat.

"Then I should be immune to its effect by now, care to test my will?" Michael challenged, undoing the knot of his tie. He slung the silk strip to the floor, aiming at no particular target in the lob. With eyes fastened on the swatch parroting the roll of her underwear, Michael stepped close, and a growl bounded from the inner sanction of his skull, vibrating gruffly through his body until the remittance of its lazy dispel. It touched the air like the sweetened lyrics of a mating song. "My, what a vision you make for one's appetite."

"Some tiny morsel of my payment, I suppose?"

"You wish to be rewarded?"

"Shouldn't I be?" she queried in a sweetly, rebellious tone, winging both hands gently outwards from her body, as if to emphasize the magnificence warranted in the stamping of his prize.

"Yes. You most definitely should." He avowed, giving then a low bow. He waved a hand across his body in concurrence of such, tapping a finger to the edge of his bed.

Michael signaled the position of her seat. Quietly complying with his request, she sat looking demurely pedantic, seeming for a moment like a rare dove on a showcased perch.

Gently plunging to his knees, Michael lifted her feet from the floor, kissing each softly. He turned his attention to the inside of her legs. His mouth grew majestically deliberate the loftier the climb. Lingering along the upper curves of her thighs, he positioned his body more fitly amid her legs, nudging her further on the bed as he went.

Closing her eyes as a languid rejoinder to his quest, Julia sighed as scorching breath moved over the center of the small cover flanking her hips. Like a chill whipping beneath the hem of one's coat, his strive was relentless, but that this hailed as a fiery draught. Piquant in its dispersing, it bred remarkably rousing in the fiats it gave.

"How am I doing?" Michael asked, a nasty smirk polishing his face.

Julia's eyes rolled skyward in response, and disappointment lunged forward as a goad to his carefully gauged pause, though she quickly made the next play to counter his act. "Not bad. Do you do more?"

"I think maybe I do." He shrugged. "I'm definitely getting ideas as we speak. But what's in it for me? I need to know what kind of payment to anticipate for the value of my work. What do you have to offer me?"

Skillfully unhooking her bra, Julia slung the still warm garment aside his neck, securing its fit like a matchless key to unlock the offering she gave. She smiled. "Only soft hills, lush peaks and a wetland like no other."

"Do you expect me to just take you at word?" Michael probed, concurring with the factual riff in his head, he smiled.

"Absolutely not," she hummed. Her voice as sweet as the honey she stirred. "Please feel free to inspect or sample whichever acreage you like."

"I believe I'll do just that." He grumbled in oath, lowering his body to hers. Michael returned his attention to the leisured trek of his mouth, skating past the crevice of her navel. He nibbled the feeble edges of her coverlet. Using his teeth as a fastener, he wrenched the small string from its station on her hips, strumming his fingers on the soft flesh as he worked.

"Now what type of renderings do you have to barter with?" she purred, giving a near breathless sigh with the question, and felt the instant dilution of his work as a result. Hesitating as if in search of an answer, his frown was surely a picture worth the regard, though she knew full well what answer he would give.

"All I have is a sturdy bridge for your wetland. It's assured to last you a very long time." He hummed.

"If that's true, then it sounds like a must have. However, you really don't expect me to just take you at your word on that, do you?"

"I most certainly do not. I expect every facet of my goods to get tested. The most rigorous calisthenics you can find would be your best bet." He smiled.

"Are you done playing?"

"You started it."

"I guess I did do that, didn't I? So, then, have you had your fun?"

"I haven't even started on that."

"Here, let me help you out of these before you choke." she baited, tugging at the waist of his pants. She brazenly caressed the warmness of his skin as she unbuttoned and unzipped his free, smiling at her knowledge of him.

"*Souffle de ma respiration Permettez-moi de vous tenir à moi. Cœur de mon cœur, que je vous ai trouvé enfin. Peau d'or et de la poussière, aux yeux de feu, elle dévore et donne pouvoir à la douceur de son toucher. Détourner mon regard et me libérer. Dire que vous allez rester. Dites que vous allez rester avec moi, donc je peux respirer.* Breath of my breath let me hold you to me. Heart of my heart I found you at last. Skin of gold and of dust, with eyes of fire, she devours and empowers with the sweetness of her touch. Look my way and set me free. Say you'll stay. Say you'll stay with me so I can breathe."

"Do I even want to know what you just said?" she frowned, pausing over the last button on his shirt.

"Come, I'll show you instead." Michael pledged. His words falling in a low growl, covering her body with his, the workings of their tongues grew brusque. Her legs coiled promptly around his waist in answer of his amorous strive, hugging him with her entire body. She bathed him in emotions that were now as natural as air. Pausing in his toils to pull the shirt from his body, he tossed the crisped garment to the floor, gazing down at the spread she offered on his return. Michael smiled. "God, you're beautiful." He proclaimed almost breathlessly, pressing himself eagerly to her body. He resumed his earlier dredge. The evening had not evolved as he had hoped. But he could not nor would he offer complaint on its end, not when her body moves to him in the way that it does.

Sunday unfurled to a stultified existence in what felt like two blinks. Varying in its tint, piddling of gray faltered with the gentle spitting of rain. Though morning, in time, blossomed with a simpering sigh of blue. A gentle wind played chaise through the sparseness imparted on trees, soaring light atop their limbs as if to taunt the absence of what was. Julia reclined further in the torrid suds of her bath, consenting to her wonder on the days that will surely come, already feeling the niggling of that. Two weeks, in actuality, was a minimal span in one's life. She knew this, for they had suffered the disjunction endlessly over these long months. Fourteen days to be exact, each spent without feeling his breath upon her cheek, or the warmth he surrendered in his hug. Would that time not be judged as a miniscule duration in others? So why then had this gloom taken hold? Was it possible that she loved him from the start? And if so, why did it take her so long to recognize that fact? The probabilities of what could be and what was, made every axon in her brain hurt from the strain that such thinking provided. So much needed to be said, but would they?

In a rough ascension, Julia scrubbed her hands tartly over her face, as trepidation and truth sank uncannily deep. For in this, she needed to be certain before she ventured any place near the next step. She had to be sure he was first ready for all the factors she represents, as life for her was not just that of her own. Would he be at all receptive to broaden a relationship with readymade kids? A man whose only experience came from his sporadically extended flings—for there was no better name to label the temporary landings he'd had. With such few parboiled alliances under his belt—this does not a father make, and more definitely so, for one who had never wanted the adventures of that. An expedient family is a tough ask regardless of affection, yet she would not, nor could she, allow her children to be a guinea-pig for anyone's aim, not even that of her own. If she had to, she would undoubtedly rescind this hold that he had, if that result benefitted her children. But *she,* most emphatically, would never be the same. Life for her would take on a whole new meaning, one she most significantly dreaded.

With a resounding decision, Julia remanded the questions to the mute barrens in her head. Half drying herself, she wandered from the swelter of a misty room, finding her host lounging in the sitting-room, she smiled.

Michael's eyes twinkled with the start of a smile as she entered the room, broadening quickly to an outright leer as he studied the vision over the rim of his mug.

"What are you doing?" Julia smirked, knowing something under the heading of "smut" now galloped through his head.

"I'm committing you to memory, that's what." He announced in a gravelly hum, not bothering to accede awareness of her eyes, as the employment of his was well spent. "When I recall you in my memory, this is one of the pictures I want to leap forward instead."

"Of all the ways you could remember me. This is the one you choose?"

"You don't see yourself the way I see you, and you certainly can't think like a man. Which, by the way," Michael chuckled. "Are all very good things in my eyes."

"And how exactly do you see me?"

"I think I gave you a long hint of that last night, and again this morning." He teased. "Do you seek a reminder, or do you just need to hear me say it?" he asked in a slow, raspy purr, crossing the room in an equally slow saunter. He towed her body into his. "And if I asked, would you answer me that? If I asked you how you saw me, what would your answer be? What of me do you remember when you're no longer here?" Michael droned. A smile spread softly on his face in a casual sheen, though he wondered truly on the verity of that.

"It's your eyes." She sighed, looking past him as if her words were meant for someone else. Slowly, as if being pulled, she returned her eyes to his. "But it's your touch that haunts all aspects of my dreams. Your hands work with the familiarity of owned and owner, as if I belong to you somehow." Informing this in a muted breath, her voice cracked in finish. Dropping her eyes, an awkward smile crept to her face, and with the new silence, her nakedness became suddenly pronounced, rudely reminded of such by a cold blast from the vents. She flinched lightly in response. Michael's arms came about her with the first warning of a chill, swathing her in warmth the very minute she needed such aid, as if he felt the change in her body deep within himself. And she was once again stunned at the depth of his knowledge of her.

"Life is an awfully strange paradox, don't you think?" Michael grumbled in start, and for a moment the truth battered every nerve extant in his tongue, as he needed her to know how wrong her summation had been. He did not love her as he did because she belonged to him, but that he, with all his blighting, belonged to her. He'd never wanted, hungered, or needed anyone as much as he did her. For he craves the man she roused in him, and only the decadence of her touch seemed to set him free. Hence, he slumbered in her absence and avidly awaits her every return. "Since mine is almost of an equal offering, do I...please you...enough, Julia?" he muttered hoarsely, exhaling a jagged breath. This being an asinine query for sure, one his ego knew astoundingly well, but it was the closest he could get to asking if he made her happy.

Astounded by the question, Julia looked up with a slow frown, stunned into silence by the reality of his words. Nothing in her behavior could have possibly said otherwise than the veracity in her response. How could he ask her that? Where did she fly to once a moment could be spared? Was it not *his* name that she cried when darkness turn to pure light? Was that not him she cleaved to when the two shared but one heartbeat? How could he ask her that? If she submersed herself any deeper in the sweetness he gave, she'd likely forget decorum and just campout at his feet.

"Yes." She mumbled lightly, nodding slowly in aid of the word. She chose to give him simplicity with her truth. "Do I...you?" she blurted rashly in follow, the words seeming to cruise past her sensors in a wild dash, hailing thus before they had time to ready the gate.

Michael's fingers slid cautiously to her cheek, slowly slipping under the hard edge of her jaw. He adjusted the position of her head, lifting her face until he held full command of her gaze. "Can't you tell?" he asked hoarsely. "You are like no other. You have no equal in this venue or any before." He vowed, dipping his head. He affirmed his words, granting her then another piece of his truth.

Chapter Thirty Nine

"You're what?" Michael rumbled sharply in reply, the inquest crawling like a croak from his throat, though it soared lurid regardless of constraint.

"I'm late." She recited wanly, her words crawling through the intake of a jaded breath, dragging the weak gulp behind the horrifying speech. Death came the instant the stream stilled. Time slammed to a redoubtable stop, and even the merest speck bided neither will nor voice.

"How late?" Michael asked dazedly, shattering the inflicted pause in his pursuit of knowledge, as she did not seem keen on furthering his interest on that.

"About six days." She retorted blandly, moving further into the closet as she spoke. Her nerves roiled in response to the irksome words.

"But—but you're on the pill."

"*I know, and I've been vigilant!* I—I don't understand what went wrong." She groaned, shaking her head as if to gather some elusive thought. Her breath came as a gargle in her throat, smothering a voice that now tolled heavily pained. The knit of her brow spoke volumes as to the extent of her worry, corded stiff like the starch pleats on some tunic of old. They held. "I don't know. I don't know how." She moaned in finish, exhaling the dejected breath, death again swallowed the room.

This can't be happening. It just can't be. Her alternate mind counseled in, what rocketed like a schizophrenic haze, seething beneath the surface as if with heat. It dominated what little was left working of her mind. How, perchance, would she explain something like this? What bizarre rationalization could she sell her children that would make this okay? Her daughter most of all in this world, what clever logic could she possibly grant her on this? What kind of example would this be setting for her? How does a mommy—without the rituals expected in a relationship—ends up pregnant? A result, as that, only spells one thing, and that's all she would remember on those laborious teenage days.

"Did you miss any?" Michael asked strangely curious, again cutting the constricting pause, though still reeling from the blast of her initial shook.

"No! Well, I did miss one. But I doubled up the next day, and that was a week before I came over. God, I can't believe this is happening."

"Is six days bad? I mean…well, does it make your fear a more definite issue?"

"When you're on the pill? Probably, at least I would think so." Shrugging the woeful reply, Julia dropped to the floor of her closet, not bothering to wait on further comment as to his view. The sharpness of the silence ingratiated its will, as perception weaseled well inside the charged regions of their heads.

"What would you like to do?" Michael delicately asked, not knowing what other decorous thesis to add, having never been in this position before. Caution had always been a stubborn datum in every encounter he'd had, irrespective of whom, though the attributes was purely selfish on his part then. Today, however, his mind was apparently frozen, or, at the very least, well jarred from the trouncing hammer of shock, since he did not feel half the expected terror as he probably should.

"I don't know." She griped dejectedly. "I don't know." Reiterating the disgruntled reply as if to someone else, her tone instantly dimmed. "I can't think. I can't think about this right now. I don't want to think about what this could mean. It just can't be happening. It can't be. I thought I was being so cautious with this." She whispered in reproach of herself, scrubbing a nervous hand across her brows. Her back thumped the floor like the body of a drum. Stinging eyes, moist with agony and dread, trolled the ceiling in painful consternation. Taking no comfort from the resolutions that will have to come; another sigh flounced its escape of her throat.

"I'm sorry." Michael whispered then, his voice barely audible through the phone, as there was nothing he could think of to give her that could easily be said. He had no quick offerings that would set the moment right. None that would change what may have already been done.

"For what?"

"Well…for this. I'm sorry this happened. I'm sorry we had to confront something this massive on the phone. It wasn't a part of the plan, I know that." He assuaged in a meek breath, feeling strangely numb.

"This wasn't even in the same galaxy, Michael." Julia attested flatly, seeing only shame waiting as her consequence ahead. A sigh summed the discomfiture stalking her tale. How does one get pregnant without ever once mentioning a man? For so long now, she'd strived to keep both halves of her life quartered in their prospective sites. What now? What they had did not bring with it a title, nor would it an eager partner make. Kids, coupled with the strict demands of a relationship, tallied well with all the ruts that will thenceforth sit in-between, such purport cannot be compelled nor finessed with the harmony of speech. Is he even ready for the responsibility of that? Hitched heavily on her children, she had contemplated the many endings there could yet be in broadening the fictitious aspects between them, making it, in turn, real. Although three should definitely kill all possibility of that for sure. "I have to go. I can't talk about this anymore. Bye."

"Okay. We'll talk later, then?" Michael asked softly, feeling her anger soar obvious through the phone.

"Sure. Bye." Grunting this, Julia immediately pressed end, slamming shut the door on any placating utterance he might have had. Her hands shook as she swiped a drizzly trail beginning its rash descent, and the full ramification of what could soon be realized as fact, hit the sturdiness of home. She knew, with certainty, his affection for her was strong. But would that be enough for a man, such as him, to undertake the onus of a family he had no part in the planning of? More so, one with a status such as his—a confirmed bachelor no less. Her tears fell then of their own volition, as there was no holding them back, regardless of repeated attempts.

Almost listless in his actions, Michael strolled dazedly through the woods, his sub-conscious parked in an odd state of expectancy. Awaiting the crippling pangs of distress to descent, his mind sought refuge, confounded, surely, by the absence of a jittery panic. All day long he waited for the rending of the cataclysmic effects, yet none approached but the soft fringing of solace. Even with the continuous blather thumping through his skull, dread neither surfaced nor dwelled. Though he saw little of the things he tended, and heard even less of conversations being had, giving short grunts as a fitting reply. Shrugs, nods and the ever endearing silence conquered whatever was left to be had.

It was not panic that had him feeling edgy. Nor was it fear that made his mind gallop without end. When the woman that you love tells you she's pregnant, should terror be a natural side effect of that? The topic of children had never really been of relevance to him or his life before now, perhaps because he'd never pictured himself suited with the qualities best needed in a dad. Only recently did he start his adventure of living as a grown-up should, and only in recent years had he acquired the full handle on that. Past those miniscule steps, he just hadn't taken the time to ponder much on that. Chronologically, his age may broadcast one thriving at forty, but he was young when it came to the natural progression in an adult's life. Marriage and children was never scribed on the formative pages of his agenda, for in most, they had never been a factor that interested him in any way.

Her call came at exactly eight-fifteen on the dot. Startling the deep slumber of dusk, the musical tell pierced the enveloping blackness like a bullet. This, nine hours and twenty-six minutes since the onset of their dilemma. It jarred the room to full wake, and everything seemed suddenly at a stance. It was not their usual time for lingering on the phone. Not the time to attempt a heartfelt tête-à-tête, or to express, in anyway, the depths to which his feelings ran.

"Hi!" Michael saluted softly, arranging his thoughts by way of importance as he awaited her reply.

"False alarm!" she blurted in place of the usual address, and her whispered voice tumbled through like the residue of a croak. Holding fast to her restraint, her excite-ment squealed forward like the pelting of a horn.

"What?" Michael asked limply, already mindful of what was said, but needed to hear it repeated for reasons he could not comprehend.

"It was a false alarm. I just got my period!" She whispered ecstatically to the phone, and her lips, in their eagerness, brushed the smooth surface as she spoke. Having only just confirmed the abhorred visit as true, she hastened to disclose her news. Confident he would be as relieved of the outcome as she. She wasted no time in the divulging of said facts. "I can't talk now. I have to go." She added hurriedly, her words darting as her voice further dipped. "We'll talk later, bye." She chimed, ending without granting him the option to offer a reply.

"But——" Michael started in quick rejoinder of her lyrical notes, realizing in an instant that she was already gone. He stared blankly at the numbers advertising the length of her call. Thirty-six seconds—double zero point three six—was all that she required to again set him straight. "Okay." He muttered in response, staring at the now darkened screen. "Okay." He repeated to the quiet, as if to someone listening near, relieving his hand of the phone with an almost peevish thrust.

The cool blanket of night felt strangely satisfying on his skin. November, in the early stage of its birth, seemed scarcely that. Hardly anything moved in the stillness of this night, not even the colorful palette now flaunted on the dwindling crowds of leaves. Everything seemed locked at a standstill as if stunned.

Michael jogged the length of the long driveway and back. Turning, he repeated the process more times than he dared to tally in his head. Quite oddly, the burdensome threads laced in a couturier's cloak of melancholy, now swathed him with the sure fit of a neoprene suit, and its weight offered him no rest in the hours since their talk. The crisis had ended as abruptly as it began. So, in truth, he should be back to his old cheerful self by now. Why then, is he feeling so much like an inherited reject of himself? Why is it so difficult deciding what that self should really be? Could this be disappointment brewing? Or was there sadness cleaving to his inexplicable mood, and if so—why? What the *hell* was he feeling, and why? It had nothing to do with the way he felt about her, that much he was at least definite of, so what then?

Weaning his pace, Michael gazed expectantly at the house, seeming to search the broad exterior for an answer to the lucidity of his quest, though none flew forward in response. Nor did he find the urge forming to set foot inside. Not yet ready to brave the starkness plaguing the space, he gaped wearily instead. Something about the cool night eased the tautness of his senses, as he just did not feel like listening to the usual soundless drivel that seeped from the walls itself, not this evening, most especially, not now.

Settled in his truck before realizing his decision, he parked in a tight, diagonal display long before having made successive blinks, or reasoned the cause of his flight. As always, the outside of his mother's house was splendidly lit, looking, at that hour, as if the occupant expected a long list of guests. Though the inside drooped in contrast of that, almost in full darkness, only a soft glow peeked past the shutters as a signal of life. Out of reverence for the hour and her space, Michael announced his presence with two quick depressions of the bell. With one coming immediately after the other, he ignored the keys still harnessed in his hand. A long minute passed before the soft residue of light skimmed the front entrance. Heralding her approach with her musical lilt, Michael watched the billowing of her robe. Flapping like a kite at her back, she hastened her progression through the foyer in observance of her guest. A smile stapled on her face.

"Michael!" Hyacinth beamed, spitting the name from her lips with gladness, concern trickled past as she beckoned him in.

"Hi, mom," Michael hailed back softly, faring a concerted effort to place his best smile forward. He stepped close for the usual greeting they share. Though tonight, above all others, her hug felt especially comforting, branding him with the warmth he seemed to need. He hesitated in place longer than he normally would.

"What's wrong, are you okay?" Hyacinth questioned, her voice muffled by his shirt.

Not having an answer, Michael's shoulders moved slowly to the ceiling and back, and even the sharpness of his wit, seemed then, to be of little avail, for he knew not what entity to blame for the cause of his discontent.

"Michael, you're scaring me. Did something happen?" She inquired sharply, spilling each question in a soft shrill. She strained to garner a look at his face. "Are you sick?" Hyacinth probed impatiently, stepping back swiftly. Hazel eyes, heavy with worry, tunneled the likeness of themselves.

"No! God, no, Mom! Nothing is wrong, really. I promise." Michael pledged, offering then a renewed smile as he eased the door from her hand, his effort methodical as he secured the entry. "It's nothing, mom. I'm fine, I swear." He assured in a positive tone, moving past the self-depicted statue she instated, still feeling the heat of her gaze. "I'm just a little off this evening, that's all. I'm…tired I guess…" he reasoned, though more so to himself, stalling his thoughts with a lazy shrug. "I don't know what I am." He groaned in finish.

Relieved on one hand by his assurance, Hyacinth's answering smile grew guarded, for concern now brewed in the other of her hand. Gliding forward, she forced an auspicious smile, scattering its sweetness with practiced effort. She led him to the only lit corner of an exquisite family-room. "Tell me everything." She hummed, inviting him to take a seat at her side with the gentle pat of her hand.

"There's really nothing to tell, mom. Maybe my age has finally caught up with me after all this time, or maybe I'm just lonely because of that. Who knows?" Michael groaned, affecting the start of a smile, though the result seemed the dejected effort of a sneer.

"And don't you tell me it's nothing. It's written all over your face, Michael." She warned, ignoring his rambling as anything but that. "Now, everything, and don't leave anything out. Everything can be fixed, Michael. Everything can be made better." She smiled, squeezing his hand in assurance of that.

Desperately needing answers, Michael took a deep breath, allowing the gist of her words to sink in. He threw his head backwards to the pillows now cradling his spine, and a light squall sailed from his body in the issuing of a sigh. "It's Julia," he started, the words rumbling slowly from his throat.

"I figured as much." Hyacinth smiled, liking the conversation thus far, though dreading it just the same. These past months with the young beauty seemed almost sacred, having witness a series of changes in her son. Changes that had been quite splendid to perceive as a mother, an adjunct to the rest, since he had already managed a wide proportion of those on his own, the others solidified the man from the lad he once was. With her, he seemed happy, more so than she'd ever seen him in his entire adult life. A mother can't ask for anything more precious than that. Any woman responsible for such profits was more than just okay in her book. "How long have you two been seeing each other?"

"Since April," Michael rasped, running his fingers slowly through his hair.

"That long?" Hyacinth asked coolly, though the urge to pounce with an added chapter of questions was immeasurably strong. But she stayed the calmness she held.

"I'm sorry I wasn't more open with you, but she made me promise to keep everything truly private between us." Michael groaned. "It's a little complicated, mom, trust me."

"And now you're in love with her?" she asked, her voice wafting again like a warm breeze. Not bothering to push for clarification on what the "complications" meant, she waited patiently while he mulled the question over in his head. Eager for information on the where, what, why and the possibilities linked with the furtherance of that. She bit back the urge to interrogate instead of aid.

"I think probably from the start." He sighed, hearing his truth for the first time out-loud. The purity felt somehow relieving to his ears.

"I see." Hyacinth hummed, suddenly worried for what could be his next words. "Is there someone else?" she whispered, aware of her son's tendencies to stray.

"No!" he rasped, turning stunned eyes upon his mother, his brows gnarled in their show of ire. Remembering the lengthy scroll attesting to his earlier indiscretions, Michael slowly relaxed. "No." He reiterated, given dimly with a soft wag. "We had something of a…scare." He announced glumly in a gravelly breath, dropping his head again to the pillows. His breath sailed like the hissing of steam.

"A scare, what kind of scare?" she pressed gently, her brows tacked tightly as if the two now rested as one. In answer, her son's head rolled slothfully atop the creased indent of the pillows now cradling his head. As if to bore a hole through her head, hazel eyes narrowed, stating his answer in full without the use of a single word. "Ohhhh!" Hyacinth sang, extending the lone word on the full intake of a breath. She acceded her understanding of his mood. "And she—you, don't…want this?" she asked, hesitating in her query, for she knew his continuous rejection of any such prospect in the past.

"She's not, mom." He droned, still not understanding the oddness of his mood. His tone almost mimicked that of a petulant child. He should be giddy with happiness at missing so close a call, shouldn't he?

"That's good then, isn't it? You look as if she was! Why aren't you out celebrating instead of—?" with the words hovering in her throat, Hyacinth paused, her eyes widening as recognition slammed home like a brick to her head. "That's not the answer you wanted? *You* wanted her to be? Michael are you saying you—?" she queried in a strained voice, stalling as she tried hard not to scream the finish of her inquest in his ears, or show a speck of her beginning delight. "Are you thinking you want to be a father now, Michael?" she asked tightly, showing more control than she felt.

"That's just it, I don't know. I don't understand what's going on with me. I don't know what I'm feeling or even why. Everything just feels…off." Michael groaned, scrubbing both hands roughly across his face. "I just can't get over it. I can't get it out of my head, and I can't get myself to be happy in accordance with such news. Why am I not ecstatic?" he asked, turning his gaze expectantly on his mother, he again sighed.

"Maybe the scare brought something to light that was already in the back of your mind." She murmured slowly, biting back the multitude of questions that jumped forward in her head. Could this be? Could her son really be contemplating the prospect of a next step? A grandmother, is that probability in her future after all this time? "How does she feel about the whole thing when you told her how you felt?"

"She doesn't know. Besides, how could I tell her what I'm feeling when I don't even know what that is?" Michael grumbled, propping his feet up on a waiting ottoman, his shoulders slumped further in the cushions padding the couch.

"Then the best suggestion I can give you, son, is to advise you to make preparation for a heartfelt talk. It sounds as if the two of you have a lot to discuss."

"That's not even the half of it." Michael groaned, taking a deep breath. He flinched at the sudden blaring of his phone, a pianist's reminder of his nightly talk. Knowing he could not, at that instant, bear the upkeep of a playful discussion, Michael froze. What could he say to stall her questions without giving himself away, when he can't even find his own humor? "Damn, it's her." He groaned softly. "She'll know something is wrong. I can't talk to her right now. Quick, help me! What do I do?" he asked, leaning forward, his expression broadcasted a smidgen of the panic he felt. With fingers hovered atop the green button, he waited in a state of suspense.

"Answer it!" Hyacinth quipped, fanning her hands brusquely as a visual indication of the suggestion she gave.

"Hi!" Michael sang loudly, his timbre drifting brasher than was necessary to the phone.

"Hi!" Julia chirped spryly, adjusting the covers on her bed as she settled in its folds, now rejuvenated by the anecdote extolled in a lengthy shower. Searing steam pummeled free the stress she once held, and her excitement was again verified in tens. "Are you getting ready to go to bed?"

"No. I'm actually at my mother's house right now." He shrugged, a pleading grimace now stationed on his face. Subtly, his mouth formed a single word, and it needed no sound for understanding to be had—"help".

"Michael, could you get me something to drink? I can't seem to stop myself from shaking." Hyacinth called in a high voice. "Are the police gone?" she shrugged, as if in defiance of his frown.

"Ah…sure, mom, I'll be right there." Turning his voice to the ceiling, his answer came short. "She thought she saw someone hiding in the back yard, but everything is fine now." He mumbled dourly, rolling his eyes at the lie. He offered a silent groan, feeling shame for his part in deceiving the one person he swore never to lie to. "I should go," he sighed dishearteningly.

"Michael! Michael, are you coming?" Hyacinth called.

"Yes, mom! I'll be right there." He answered with a small grunt. "I should go. I'll talk to you soon."

"Okay. Bye." Julia sighed, already missing their lengthy repartee that habitually preceded sleep.

"Bye." Michael replied in what seemed a groan, ending the call abruptly. He dropped the phone on the arm of his seat. "Jesus, I can't believe I just lied to her." He grunted, staring at the phone with a strong taste of disgust daubing his tongue. "I make it a strong point to never do that to her."

Hyacinth smiled brightly in acceptance of his words, acknowledging the information for more than it was intended. When it pertains to women, slick was a likely name most suited for her son. Lying, for him, was like a second language, it's the way he kept things going with the throngs he had. If he was not lying to her, then this just became so much more enlightening than it once was. "Then call her back and tell her the truth." She whispered sprightly, patting his thigh in soft consolation.

"I can't. I need some time to think."

"Then take the time you need, so you can fix it with the truth."

"How do you know when you're ready?"

"Ready for which part of it, son?"

"Well…all of it I guess."

"There's no uniform method to it, son. It comes in different formats for everyone." Hyacinth puffed tamely, the jewel of her gaze slipping past her son. A distant smile floated to her face, wading still as she resettled her view, as if a picture, obscured to all, but her, wheeled to her vision. "Traditionally, it starts when you meet someone that, in time, becomes exceedingly special to you in every way. Life before them, or the paucity of some moments, is just not the same. You find you want them with you always. Or that they enhance you regardless of how small an aspect they add. They set the world apart from everyone else, that's the true simplicity of it all, and that's usually how two becomes one in the foundation of a family. After that, it's more like turning on a light switch, really. For some, it may feel like something is missing. For others, they just know, finding a connection so strong that they know this person will bring to life another aspect of themselves. And then there are those that require something a little more profound to set the process in tow, like an encounter or a sighting of these miraculously tiny humans." She smiled. "Or perhaps it's a phone call that gives you a small taste of what you never thought you wanted, but surely needed."

"Do you think I'm ready for all that?" Michael asked in a near muted voice.

"I don't know, sweetie. Only you can answer that. But the fact that we're having this conversation says more than a few things to me. It tells me that if you're not now, then you will be somewhere down the road. If the answer was no, then these feelings would not have surfaced as strongly. They came to you for a reason, son."

"You think I've grown up enough to become someone's dad?" Michael asked in a fretting tone, his voice cracking as if with fear.

"They don't come out knowing all your sins, sweetie. They don't care who you were; where you've been or what iniquities you've committed in the empty stage of your life. They only care about who you are; what you're about now and how you treat them. They come into this world fresh, and as clean as a newly minted coin, looking to you to teach them what they need. Think of all the things you've learned, son. Think of the wealth of knowledge you'd be able to pass on and how wonderful it would feel to impart that to them. You'd be able to add aspects that your father and I knew so little about. They don't care about your mistakes, son. They love you regardless, and in spite of them. Their love is unconditional in every way, no matter what. You give them your love and they return it to you in spades."

"No matter what?" he asked, as if unsure of the solidity of such accounting as that.

"No matter what, sweetie, their judgment is only on the dispelling of your love. Money, fame, past indiscretions or sins does not get weighed into any portion of that. It's a gift that is augmented more rightly once you've notched out the framework of the man you want most to be, and in turn stay true to that." She crooned in confirmation. "And for the record, I think you would make a wonderful father. Look at how you are with Jason and Britney; it's a million times more divine when they're sired by you." Hyacinth smiled, brushing her hand soothingly down his back.

"Really, you think so?"

"With every fiber of my being." She smiled.

Nodding, Michael offered a scant smile in return, his eyes skidding from her face to an imperceptible target on the floor, seeming to take comfort in her answer and what that meant. "This is really strange, us having this conversation. I bet you never thought that this would be the topic of discussion when you answered the door?"

"Not even if it was hinted beforehand in the middle of the day."

"Thanks, mom, I know this has been a niggling for you."

"Whatever gave you that idea? Could it be because I've been waiting forever to have grandkids of my own? I was cool though, wasn't I?"

"Yes you were. You were very cool; you are, by far, the coolest cat I've ever seen." He chanted, a soft chuckle twirling from his throat. His first, since experiencing the strange angst allied to her call, and the release felt astoundingly good on the tautness of his nerves.

"Are you hungry? Hey, I just thought of a great idea! Why don't we stay up and watch some of the classics like we use to?" Hyacinth warbled stealthily, wishing to witness more of his smiles, though also knowing she was too excited to sleep. She'd never allowed herself the freedom to ponder the prospect of grandkids before now, not with how adamant he'd been about averting the probability of that. A prerequisite when coupled with the cavalier praxis trenched in the way that he lived his life. Now he's actually with someone who seems the very essence of the word "sweet". Someone who seems amazing in every sense, though the verdict stemmed more from a speculative notion garnered from the little she'd been able to ascertain for herself. His demeanor was light. Blissful even, and now he's hinting that his adamancy on such topic may have changed. Why would she sleep, how could she?

"Why not?" Michael shrugged, feeling his mood lighten and shift, the company was an added incentive to stay. "Do you have anything I like?" he teased.

"I should backhand you just for asking me that." Hyacinth warned, a deep scowl pleating her brows as she delivered a glare. "You've been around Betty too long, son. I think you forget which one of us is your *real* mother. Of course I have the things you like." Hyacinth groaned. "Just in case you need a reminder, *son*, I'm your real mother, and I believe I have the scars to prove it." Sending him a stern but playful glare, she stood and glided from the room. "Come on. Let's go see what tweaks your fancy."

Michael's gaze dropped to the fluttering hem of his mother's shimmery robe. Waving jauntily about her ankle in a breeze spawned by the brusqueness of her steps, it thrust forth the memory of a time gone by, and a smile leapt sharply to his face as recollection of his awed reaction came flooding back. For at a time, the witnessing of her skittering tail had had a boy properly impressed.

In its quest for restoration, the evening labored to right itself, as trace of under-standing scuttled beneath a turbulent tide. Did he want kids? And if so, was there more hidden beneath this deceptive blow? Or is this all about her? Is it that he wanted this evolutionary sequence with her? A son perhaps, Michael questioned with a smile, feel-ing warmed by the picture that promptly barreled through his head. Or would his preference be more vested in a little girl? One baring the most beautiful complexion there ever was and, too, the darkness of her mother's eyes. Would her hair be as wild, and would they share the same heart wrenching smile that had captured him so fully? *My God, is this for real? Did he really want this?* Michael debated softly, feeling his pulse quickened as the pictures unfolded in his head. *A baby! Kids! Not just what already was, but the furtherance of that? Could it be?*

His happiness had been well magnified these elapsing months, and with her being the sole proprietor of that cause. He would move mountains to be certain of the same for her. Hence, his reasons for taking things as slow as he had, though that, it seemed, was now nearing its end. More than just witticism, the gentle teasing of his mother was the first sign in his reanimation of self. It builds like a gesture of marvel in the subsistence that was sure to come.

———— • ————

With the scare of new motherhood behind her, Julia was more diligent than ever with the regiment of taking her pills. Although the anxiety had nothing to do with the effi-ciency of the chore itself, it became an additional step to brushing her teeth, fearful of such possibility proving itself true. A baby is never best when gifted as a surprise, and she was in no position to yet call them a couple, much less poised, in any way, to offer a baby as an unwarranted reward.

Yet, as harrowing as the notion seemed, the incongruity of the matter was in knowing that she'd always wanted the rumpus that came with having a large family. Being an only child, she supposed, fostered her need in that. Four or five kids had always been her goal in start. But that was two lifetimes before now, long before she learned the many lessons life had to give. She'd since learned to abandon the burden of some dreams by the wayside, those, undoubtedly, that went hand in hand with marriage. Though should she ever remarry, would she even want to after all this time? So many years had already flown between the two she now had, would the prospect even be wise? All this only necessitated the creeds and prerequisites to let sleeping dogs lie, since it's never wise, as a rule, to dwell on things that may never be.

In the six days since, the two have discussed everything under the sun, conversations veering with the usual fervor as it always had, except that which could have possibly been an objectionable fact. Although, knowing her, she would not have allowed their natter to take fully that bend. She—they, did not seem effectual when discussing their feelings, and the scare did not sway that manner much from the usual path.

Julia arched her body like a taut bow aloft the cozy comfort of her couch. Unsure of what to do with herself, she gaped blindly at the flickering pictures on the television screen, and each movement grew more listless than the one before that. Silence sprang forward like the eerie lyrics to an unrelenting chant, grounding its presence further distinct. The house quivered like a desolate being, augmented thus, by the kids' departure. The irregularity of her wait had her locked in a state of suspense. With Michael concluding the buttoning of last minute business, her usual verve was somehow lost, as two days now swiftly dwindled to one. Their weekend was not due to begin until early Saturday morning—if that, leaving them little time to enjoy the fruits that came freely with so little of said feature. In accordance, the anxiety of the wait had her virtually climbing the walls.

Unable to curb a surfeit of pent energy now bubbling in store, gaunt fingers blindly depressed the buttons on a sleek remote, sending vibrant pictures fleeing in a momentary slide, though none dashed forward as a slayer to the storm now brewing in her head. The soft, classical stirring of her phone, tersely routed the monotony of her fingers. Thinking it to be Michael, Julia pounced, barely allowing the sequence to middle its melodic chimes.

"Hey! Are you free?" Vanessa chirped sprightly, her voice like a lyrical hum. "Carol and I were going to get a bite to eat, want to meet us?"

"Actually, I *am* free." Julia remarked gaily, springing forward in her seat. She beamed brightly at the phone, elated to have a distraction for her mind and its habitual bent. "Why don't we meet here instead? What are you guys in the mood for?"

"Why, are you cooking?"

"With this little notice, are you kidding me? I was thinking more along the lines of letting our fingers do the walking. Or you can stop along the way and get us all something."

"And what goodies are you bringing to the table if I took the time to do all that?" Vanessa fired back dryly.

"Mine is the beautiful ambiance, of course." Julia quipped, throwing her feet up on the soft edge of a stool, she lounged further back. "But I'm sure you were only asking me what I wanted, weren't you?"

"Who said our restaurant would be stuffy? For all you know we could be going to some new posh spot that's definitely the place to be."

"Unless it comes with a kitchen, dining, a swank living-room vibe and me, it's stuffy."

"Stop hogging all the good points and let me win an argument for once, will you?"

"I didn't know we were having an argument." Julia smirked, flipping through a series of channels. "Next time give me more of a heads up so I can be better prepared."

"Smartass," Vanessa groaned.

"Whatever; where are you?"

"On my way to you, what do you think? I know a good deal when I hear one, so which one of us is the smart one now, missy?"

"I guess that would be you. Since you have some paper claiming you're a doctor of some sort."

"You better believe it, baby, and don't you dare forget it. Let me call Carol and tell her where we're going. I'll see you in a few minutes. Bye, cutie."

"Bye, smarty." Julia chirruped, bounding from the couch in closure. She hurried to the kitchen to start the preparation needed in the assembly of their snacks. With a smile plastered on her face, she traipsed through the pantry door with an added sachet of vim, and a new sunniness radiated from her body as she worked. So focus was she on the compiling of snacks, she heard naught of Delia's entry in the room. Nor did she notice her mother's keen study of her face.

"Aren't you supposed to be going on your spa getaway?" Delia asked, breaking the silence at last.

Startled by the sudden intrusion, Julia gasped, almost spilling the newly retrieved bottle of salsa from her hand. "Mom!" she panted, catching herself. She clutched the jar safely to her chest.

"I'm sorry, dear. I didn't mean to startle you."

"I was thinking maybe I'd go tomorrow." She remarked coolly, promptly returning to the casual procession of her chore. "Carol and Vanessa are on their way as we speak for a little girls get together." Julia informed calmly, and had the lines been intoned from the orator of a skit, they could not have sailed any smoother than they had.

Delia smiled slyly at her daughter's back, finding it curious that they both continue to lie. "Have you seen your new delivery today?" she asked shrewdly, moving further into the kitchen. She settled herself primly in a seat at the bar.

Julia's eyes barely wavered from the pinpoint precision they held, seized thusly by the small bowl in her hand, though the language of her body gabbed loudly of her ire regarding such theme. "I really hope this stop soon." She grumbled in a voice unlike her own, placing the bowl in the center of the tray, she shrugged. "This has gone way past the point of being ridiculous. Who has that kind of money to waste?"

"Evidently he does, dear." Delia smiled, taking a chip from the tray. She severed its gnarled body with a raucous bite. "Apparently, he thinks you're worth it." She shrugged, her smile growing almost mocking. "So why not just enjoy it?"

"Don't start, mom. That wishing nose of yours is already showing. I'd hate to see it grow to the point of spoiling your gorgeous face." Julia smirked, placing a large chip within reach of her mother's hand. "I'm not going to marry the guy."

"Never say never, dear, since you never know now, do you?" Delia sang, accepting the offering, she roughly snapped it between her teeth. "Who is to say what really is, in this weird paradox called life." She crooned. "Life has a strange way of dealing with us, my darling. Don't give away what you don't know, for you never know what benefit it may bring."

"For all you know, mom, he's some old man who happens to be rich. He probably has nothing better to do with his time than to try and lure women by calling his actions romantic. Would you still want me to marry him then?"

"Somehow I doubt that very much, and I never said anything about marriage." She smirked, putting the last of the chip in her mouth, she smiled. "I only told you to keep an open mind. I just want you to be open to whatever the universe has planned, that's all." Delia chirped. "I'd hate to see you close all of your options down before first assessing their worth."

"You're being a romantic again, mom." Julia laughed, setting the finished platter aside. "You were very lucky with daddy, that's all."

"Yes I was. And I'm extremely mindful of that. But everyone has their own luck waiting in store. This world is a busy place, Julia. We seem, most times, to run more so than we actually walk. So more often than not, we miss the things that are right under our noses. I'd just prefer that not be you."

"Okay, mom, I'll try not to be so closed-minded." Julia groaned, ready for the conversation to end, sarcasm pinched lightly at her tone. With their shared intensity of the past few months, she was more assured than ever that this guy, regardless of whom, or any other man, for that matter, did not stand a chance. Not in this lifetime.

In only an hour, the once gorged platter laid sparse. Riotous chatter clattered through the rooms like droves of carillon soaring as one. Sailing endless in their haggle, war was near predicted on the preferred ethnicity of their meal. It took the group another fifteen minutes before pizza became the harmonized choice, though the where, thankfully, grew less grinding.

"Okay, since we're all here and we've finally gotten our choices out of the way at long last, now let the ruckus discussions begin." Vanessa proclaimed spryly, clearing her throat at the advice, she smiled. "So, who wants to start first? Does anyone have anything new they wish to add to our minutes?" she asked in her usual lively lilt, glancing tamely around the room at two vacant faces. She slowly raised her hand.

"You're pregnant!" Julia shrieked, making her words more a statement of fact.

"Stop that, will you! What did I tell you?" Vanessa groaned, looking stunned by the accuracy of her friend's guess. "You need to let me win sometimes. How do you do that?" she asked with a broadening smile, giving confirmation through its luster.

"You are?!" Carol asked dazedly, her eyes like inflated circles with the full facet of surprise, astounded that a baby had been Julia's first guess.

"I got the result of my blood test today." Vanessa smiled, looking completely happy with herself. "And as usual—smarty-pants over here—is the first to know."

"Oh, my God! I'm going to be an auntie?" Julia cried, ignoring the feigned tartness of Vanessa's words. She sniffed loudly in response, feeling herself almost in tears. "I can't believe it."

"I know!" Carol sniffed in reply, already searching for a tissue in her purse. "Now all our kids are going to grow up to be best friends like us!"

"How do you feel, any sickness?" Julia chirped, draping Vanessa's body with her own. Her arms tightened in an infectious squeeze, with Carol closing the bracket on the opposite end.

"I feel fine. Well, I did." Vanessa groaned, crimping her shoulders stiffly in response. She shrugged coarsely, trying, without success, to dislodge their weight. "After the two of you finish suffocating me. I'll have to reassess that."

"What did you expect?" Carol jeered, again sniffing loudly, she dabbed at her eyes. "You had to know we'd be all over you. So toughen up and take your lumps, missy. Besides, you love it just as much as you love us." She laughed, swiveling her head sharply as the doorbell howled its interruption of their bonding.

"Food!" Vanessa grunted, shrugging her shoulders free as all three heads snapped in the direction of the door.

Drunk with giddiness, Julia detached herself from the two women with a hearty shove. Darting over the arm of the couch, she ran to the portal with the gaiety of a teen-age girl, complete with the terse protrusion of her tongue. Satisfied with her escape, her smile was near majestic as she swung open the door.

"Michael!" she gasped, voicing this in a half whisper. Her hand stalled midair on its descent. The rumpled edges of two twenty dollar bills sat visible at opposing ends of her grasp, seeming to gnarl further in the tightening of her fist. "I thought—"

"Hi." Michael hailed softly, his hazel eyes immediately locked to the brown basins of hers. "We finished early so I thought I'd come to you for a change."

"Oh." Julia mouthed in lieu of a characteristic reply, feeling her heart launch an urgent revolt with just the mere gift of his presence. Drubbing like a sleeping dog at the sound of an intruder, it simply would not rest. Looking again better than the picture she kept in her head, his smile grew decadent in the soft, slow way it dispersed athwart his face, wading forward like a hand. Feeling suddenly weak with excitement and shock, Julia wedged her shoulder to the hard frame of the door, a gay, inviting smile softly splayed on her face.

Slowly advancing through the threshold, like a predator on the hunt, Michael smiled, his eyes dipping greedily to her mouth, and the warm, masculine scent of his cologne embraced her long before their bodies touched. Muscular thighs brushed hers as his body pressed closer yet, mouthing his earlier greetings. His head lowered to hers in an inkling of his wants, and their lips met in an introduction, more so, than the voracity of a replete kiss. Leaning her body firmly into his, her hands eagerly twain his body in the sameness of a vine, parting her lips in response, she soared upwards, on her toes, to better savor his taste.

"So is that the pizza or not?" Vanessa griped, her voice coming like a shot at their backs. Sailing playful from the mouth of the other room, it boomed no less the equivalent of lightening being struck at their feet. Their heads came apart with a resounding jolt, yet both bodies lingered as if afraid to relinquish all the sweetness at once. Michael's hands descended her arms in a long continuous caress, reaching her fingers, they closed.

"N-no," Julia stammered weakly in response, coughing deliberately to clear the bog from her throat, as she badly needed the time to collect herself.

"There's a starving, pregnant woman in here—" Vanessa chided, her words grinding to a stop, stemming her steps. She stalled in the middle of the room. "Oh, I'm sorry." She muttered tamely, yet holding her ground as if in wait for the complexity of a stunt to unfold.

"I'm just—this is, I…" stammering faintly, she stuttered to an abrupt halt, unsure of the exactness of what invention to use. She gaped weakly at the undaunted trespasser, as her mind refused to return to its quick-witted self.

"I'm sorry." Michael smiled, quickly taking the cue from her hand. "I'm interrupting, aren't I?" he asked, remorse strongly sweetening the body of his words. His head rounded the door still standing as an ineffectual guard at her back. "Why didn't you say you were entertaining?" Michael smiled, squeezing the fingers still clasped in his hand. He lent her the forte of his support.

"I–I'm sorry. I—"

"Please, forgive the intrusion." Michael drawled, stirring his charismatic timbre to warm. His gaze shifted upon the woman now gaping at the two. "I'll just be on my way." He smiled, glancing at the woman whose hand he still cradled in his. He again effectuated a comforting squeeze. "We'll do this another time." He vowed softly.

"But—" Julia panted in what seemed a sorrowed breath, greatly hesitant to see him go. Her fingers tightened their hold.

"No, please! Come in. You're not interrupting at all, really!" Vanessa averred with a widening smile, stepping forward to beckon him further inside, well prepared to physically assure such end should the need arise. Ever on the prowl for her friend, she was not about to let one, looking this good, out of her sight without first verifying suitability. Not without a struggle, or whichever best fit. "I'm Vanessa, by the way. And you are…?"

"James, James Dunn." Michael announced spryly, trudging forward with his hand outstretched. The two met in the middle of the foyer, like would-be adversaries feeling their way, bearing the full magnitude of their charm.

"Come on in and make yourself comfortable, James." Vanessa invited in a musical lilt, refusing the release of his hand. She smiled back curiously at her friend. "Yes. Come in, please." She repeated sweetly as if to herself. "We were just getting ready to eat. You like pizza don't you, James?"

"Sure. Pizza has always been a favorite of mine." He vowed, equaling his pace to the smaller of hers. "Are you sure I'm not interrupting an important meeting? I should have called first, I know, but I was in the neighborhood." Michael informed meekly, throwing the words over his shoulders. He glanced discreetly back, noting the nervous frown on Julia's face.

With relief and apprehension coupled strongly as one, Julia returned her attention to the broad opening, noticing the small car pulling onto her drive, she smiled. "Pizza is here!" she called, announcing this to an already empty room.

"So, James," Vanessa started in a spry voice. "Tell us, what do you do? You look a little familiar to me. Have we met before?" She smiled, fearless, as always, in her ventures. She vaulted head first into whatever had her piqued, and at the moment, nothing held her interest better than him.

Julia walked in in time to hear the fullness of the question asked, her eyes seeming, for a moment, ready to pop from her skull with the significance of the truth. "Pizza!" she chanted quickly, hoping to steer their interest from the question at once.

"Actually, I'm an aspirant writer." Michael replied calmly, ignoring her mutterings. He smiled. "Julia has been helping me put my ideas more rightly in order."

"Really?" Carol squawked, gaping at her friend in disbelief. She wondered on the reason why someone as handsome as he would remain an unmentioned topic between them, especially since her friend now seemed suddenly disinterested and mute.

"That's our Julia, always helpful." Vanessa smiled, also eyeing her friend. "Are you married, James?"

"Vanessa!" Carol screeched in protest, her voice like a mother scolding her child. From her seat at the far end of the couch, Julia's eyes again bulged, and a tame couch touched the unexpected pause like the preface of a tocsin. Struggling to retain her control, she fought to choke back the mouthful she now had trouble swallowing.

"What?" Vanessa barked, shrugging unapologetically, her eyes scraped Carol's face. The other of who gaped back truly stunned. "You know you were also wondering the same thing." She grunted.

"I'm sorry." Julia muttered in a hushed voice, finally swallowing her food. "My ex-friend thinks being subtle is a waste of time." She informed tartly, paying full homage to her statement with a well-defined glare. Neither frightened nor cowed, Vanessa's expression stood resistant to such deed, as her manner hardly differed from the moment the question blew past her lips. "I keep trying to tell her it doesn't work like that in the real world, but she doesn't get out much."

"You found your tongue again, I see." Vanessa smirked.

"It's fine, really. And no, I'm not married." Michael smiled, adjusting the brim of his hat like the adapting of a shield.

"Julia is single." Carol mumbled shyly.

"Carol!" her name burst through the room with the spiked equivalence of squawking hens, as both women gasped loudly in shock.

"What? Well…she is!" Carol exclaimed in a light grunt, straightening her shoulders. She threw a stubborn glare to the braver of her friends, one resembling that of a defiant child.

"Yes. I've heard that." Michael droned, enjoying the rebellious interaction between the three, and the genuineness of the affection they showed for each other. Their names were like an unremitting ode in conversations they've had, and it was now nice to match both names and personalities to a face. "I was extremely surprised on the discovery of that bit of news." He rasped, widening his smile, his eyes flicked softly over said beneficiary's face. "Extremely surprised."

Stoic as a judge, Julia's gaze remained tethered to her plate, afraid of what her friends would read on her face. She held fast to her expression, though anxiety had her wavering very near the edge of an abyss. Plagued with no such bother, Michael sat coolly in his seat, looking like the encounter was the prelude to a job. The three warbled sprightly. Yet every time his voice rumbled through the room, it brought forth a reminder of what would surely be her preference at that time.

"What about you, James?" Vanessa persisted, veering back to her question of old. "Are you available?"

"No, actually I'm not." Michael hummed, grating the room with his gravelly timbre. The words rumbled like a willful graze from the back of his throat. Almost in play, his eyes again searched out Julia's face, and the beginning of a leer simmered quietly in its usual place of rest. "I've made a promise to someone else, and a man is nothing if not true to his word." He advised warmly, and hazel eyes, in their scrutiny, lingered well past the time that they should. Dwindling long, they offered Vanessa a glimpse at the passion he tendered in his gaze, and not unlike some covert language coded between friends. A barely distinguishable smirk alerted Carol of her thought.

Clearing her throat as she stood, Vanessa moved slowly towards the small table housing the oversized pizza-box. Purposely scraping her friend's body as she passed, she knocked her clear from her seat on the arm of the couch. "He likes you." She whispered over Julia's bent head, pretending assistance in the regaining of her balance.

"What?" Julia queried under her breath, looking stunned. She pretended not to have heard what was said.

"He likes you. You should go after him." Vanessa coaxed softly. "Did you see the body on him? You couldn't find a better specimen if you put the specifications in yourself." She announced. Furthering the sell at her friend's befuddled frown. "Come on, Julia. Live a little, will you?" She smiled. "Eat something off that stomach of his, for Christ's sake."

Julia's cough broke the continuance of her friend's inveigling pitch, the congestion now being very real. Vanessa's words having hit home more exact than one would think, as her memory was instantly vivid from already doing just that. Semblance of tears skidded down her face as if on a sprint. Slapping her hand to her throat, she wheezed loudly as if in preparation to evacuate a lung. Taking a healthy portion of her drink, Julia rushed off to the kitchen to soothe the irritant from her throat.

"James, could you help her please?" Vanessa asked sweetly, showing off the large crust in her hand. "Your hands seem to be the only one free at the moment." She smiled.

"Sure." Michael retorted quickly, though he took his time getting to his feet. Collecting his plate and hers, he turned to follow. "Can I get you ladies anything while I'm there?" he asked calmly, taking a long step as he waited their reply.

"No. We're fine. Just help our friend." Vanessa cooed, raising her drink to her head, she smiled.

With her hip wedged firmly against the hard edge of the counter. Julia cleared her throat to ease the continuous sting, taking another lengthy gulp from her glass. Residue of the mock-tears, once pooled in her eyes, again glided freely down her face. Wiping the galloping moisture, she blew her nose and again took a swallow of the cool liquid. Michael smiled with pure satisfaction as he entered the room, happy to have a moment alone. He hurried to her side.

"Are you alright?" he whispered, resting the plates on the counter. His chest grazed the back of her arm.

"I'm fine." She sighed, looking up with adoration written in her eyes. "I guess I just swallowed too fast." She smiled, removing the plates from the counter. She place them in the deep belly of the sink. "Sorry about the interrogation."

"Don't be. It's nothing I can't handle. Besides, I'm having fun."

That's a lucky thing for you. She grumbled in her head, unable to say the same for herself. "I guess that's good."

Michael gifted a non-committal response with the implementing of a lame shrug, glancing curiously around the kitchen in reticence as he waited. His ears tuned to the sound of the water as it strummed the occupants of the sink. The women's voices carried easily to the kitchen, though it came mostly as an unclear hum, twilling the space before laughter fractured the otherwise quiet room. Leisurely, his eyes returned to rest quietly on her face, caressing the uniqueness of her profile from his place at her side.

Outside, the sun preened in preparation for the onset of its rest. A beautiful show of bright orange sat in the far corner of the sky. In the other, a soft tinting of blue grew gently dull. The room blushed with the warm hue of auburn straddled lightly with gold, for the sky seemed almost blooded in color. Streaks of the dimming fire rusted her hair, and her skin shone like rich honey in the etiolate sunlight, sweetening her features from perfection to something else. The appellation of goddess swept immediately through his head, and much like a shard of light in the arcing of a storm, dark crevices grew bright. Instantly highlighting the blackness, it dispelled manias once dreaded as nothing more than an eerie shadow of itself. Suddenly, Michael found himself stifling the urge to give forth a gasp, as actual words breezed past his lips with the quick expulsion of a breath.

"I love you." He rasped through a faltering sigh, and the rumbling of his breath was much in the likeness of a thief snatching the air from the room. *Uh, oh damn.*

Chapter Forty

As with the unearthing of an inimitable marvel, so, too, another now gape, his countenance ostensibly brindled with variants of shock. Michael's gaze tore anxiously at her face as the noise of the clattering stopped. Soaring distinctive to the four corners of the room, the buffeting stream distended swiftly through a paralyzed space. Slashing the tranquilness of their moods, it roared rowdily against the pooling surface of a stainless steel sink.

The droning of persistent chatter faded instantaneous to his confession. Like the wilting sustenance of life, it, too, deadened with time as if for a virtuous cause. Void of the exuberance once held, the room grew weighty from the silence he caused, stilling the very air that rushed past his lips, as if, it, too, hungered for the nourishment in her answer to come. Seconds toppled atop seconds, yet nothing came of the whispered declaration he gave. Soaring to a lengthy foray, silence thickened to suspense to further widen the gap.

She offered not the smallest hint of acknowledgement to ease the tension while he waited. Nor did her action indicate awareness beyond that of her stance. Gaping, instead, abstractedly out the small, un-curtained space of the window, she denied him the merest glimpse of her face. As beautifully lit orbs stared at naught but the distance ahead.

Her eyes had always been a shrewd source for gauging the cryptic thralls of her emotions, and inside he longed for their capture to better garner an appraisal as to her thoughts. But there was no such providence to be had, and even less to appease his grumbling censure or the velocious whirring of his thoughts. He had not anticipated the words exploding so freely from him then. Not in the impetuous way that it had, certainly not while hampered by the buoyant energy of a house still yet buzzing with her guests. Of all the metered hours lodged in his meticulous plotting, this was, by far, the most imperfect, of any, to beguile one so crucial with his words.

Swallowing the lump slowly asphyxiating the air from his body, Michael abetted the jolt of shock to seep weakly from his benumbed frame. Marveling at the indigence of his timing, since it was evident that wisdom could not have been more inadequately sown, and in reproach, he might have given effort to effectuate a laugh at the oddity of that—had he remembered how. Yet the terror once paired with his disclaiming of such, he asudden realized, no longer strangled his tongue. "I love you." He repeated in an airy whisper, though the words echoed boldly through the room. He made no move to further advance from her back, and she, in return, made none towards him. Not the smallest flick of her eyes did she sway from their focus ahead.

He did not need to touch her to express the full breadth of his love. Conscious he already did that every chance that he had. *This,* for him, was outside of all that. Past the realms of everything they already allotted each other, he needed her to understand the ferocious depth to which his affections dwelled. "I love you." He murmured once more, a new strength boosting the tumbling of his words. Amazed by the ease in which the once worrying words now glided off his tongue, a soft smile smeared the corner of his mouth in abject reply, for the lyrics now dripped like heated fudge, in a laggard sprint, on his favorite dessert.

In silence, the hypnotic miasma of the room unexpectedly stirred. Though the occupants held no known knowledge of the turbulence or the cause, welcoming another to the pother, as behind them Delia stumbled noiselessly to a stop. Crowning the doorway like a specter of naught but light, her eyes jumped to the starch back of her daughter as if impelling her reply. Stroking the like feature on the confessor himself, shock, brazen and bright, wallowed through her body to then explode on her face. Stalled in the uncertainty of what was to be next, she waited through the pause, as if, she, too, petitioned an answer to mince the tautness in the air. Suddenly collecting herself, she curtailed her invasion of their space, hastily retracing her steps. She fled as magically as she appeared.

"God, it feels good to finally say that!" Michael droned in continuance, not needing a response to further the structure of his avowal. His words bled then without tourniquet or gauze. "I love you. I love the fragrance that is only you. I love touching you and the way you respond to me when I do." He smiled, taking a long, slow breath; he swallowed the tenseness that yet fenced them in a grotto of confused angst. His eyes still tethered to her back.

"I love you." He further rumbled. "I love the way you taste and how you kiss me. And your lips, mmm," Michael slowly sighed, the long drawl crawling steadily from his throat, wrapping itself around them with astounding care. It left no doubt as to the intensity he meant. "I could spend an eternity just on your mouth. I could kiss you forever and never grow tired. Taste you every day for rest of my life and it would never be enough. I love you with every breath of air that I breathe. I love you. I love you. I love you. More than everything that I am and could possibly be, past, present and future combined. I love you." He vowed, his voice like the distant drubbing of a squall, softening with a lazy expulsion, he smiled. "I know you already know this, since I've told you in every which way that I could, but one. But although I've wanted to tell you this for some time, it was important, to me, the how. Independent of the rest, I needed to say these words far away from everything else that we are. I love you, Julia, more than I ever thought I could anyone."

The room plunged further quiet, as he, like the melody of a song, ended in a soft lull. In the short dotting of seconds, eons soared to the scopes of forever, dragging the room near the brink of a trance, when at last the water ceased its contentious hum. Julia spun slowly on her axis in the guise of a living dreidel, though one well stabled by a hand. Her movements, through scrutiny, wade like the noiseless feature of a cat, hardly stirring the haze still pressed around them. Her eyes stalled their worried ascension mid-point of his thighs, fear clasping her sharply within its talons. Wrapping her snugly in its frigid embrace, it hindered all actions, including those of her mind.

From the rigidity apparent in his stance, he awaited her reply, and she desperately wanted to give him the simplicity coded in the reaction he now sought. Though she knew it was not to be as simple as that. The trepidation bracketing a confession had always frightened her more than the revelation itself. Now with things hoisted so gallant in the forecourt between them, it was no less terrifying than the previously imagined sting. He had boldly stated, for all ears, all the things she kept hidden in herself, reciting them beautifully. He gave life, in a calm breath, to both fantasy and fright. But what of the rest, did he give thought to—?

The shrill of laughter cracked the pregnancy weighting the pause like the wallop of a whip. Soaring like the flipside of a record, mellow was immediately amended to rough, bringing with it reality. It cut through the sweet serenity of his words. Shocked, Julia's head jerked upwards in response, the rowdy chortle snapping her reaction like the riotous flap of a sail. Thankful for the intrusion, her gape shot gratefully towards the commotion. Sighing, Julia's gaze drifted softly back to his, an excuse already prepared on her tongue.

"Yes." He nodded, as if answering a question of himself. "I know. You have to go." He countered instinctively, seeming to read the miniscule lines of her thoughts.

"Ladies," Delia warbled as she entered the family-room, clasping the handle of a small, overnight bag in the pit of her elbow. Her smile grew majestic the further she ambled inside, clapping her hands lightly. She leaned forward with authority in her stance. "I'm afraid I'm going to have to insist we end this evening on a premature note." She announced in a whisper.

"What! Why?" the women whined in unison as if by practice.

"You guys have been friends for a very long time. Through thick or thin you guys have been there for each other. This, however, is not one of those times. You just need to trust me when I say. We need to go, and we need to all go, now."

"You saw something, didn't you?" Vanessa asked excitedly, her head swiveling in an instant with intrigue now dotting her eyes.

"What did you see?" Carol eagerly inquired, excitement spiking her lilt. She leaned her shoulders hard against Vanessa's back.

"What did you see? Come on, tell us! What is it?" Vanessa pleaded, taking hold of the older woman's hand, their eyes jumped in the presumed direction of the two.

"Did he kiss her? I hope he kissed her." Carol chirped, her eyes devilish with the enthralling zest of what that meant.

"Did he kiss her?" Vanessa probed like a zealous echo of her friend, sounding ecstatic at the thought. She leaned forward as if aiming to peer through the denseness of walls.

Delia smiled, straightening her shoulders. She glanced back in the direction of the two now being discussed, and a wish rushed forward still weighted with a tinge of hope. "God, I hope he does more than just kiss her." She muttered in a shallow breath, calling firmly to the others. She steered their attention to the task at hand. "Ladies, let's get going. We do this fast and without the slightest sound, if you get my drift."

"I told you he liked her." Vanessa announced as she stood, retrieving her purse. She lengthened the depths of her conjecture. "Though he may need to use some heavy persuasion to get that girl to veer on the right path,"

"Yeah, but he looks like he's up to the job." Carol laughed, edging close. She draped a hand confidently across the other woman's back.

"He does, doesn't he?" Vanessa snickered in returned, creeping stealthily to the door, both women now pressed at her back.

"Too bad we can't lock them in the kitchen for the weekend." Carol proclaimed in a twittery tone. "That would surely make it easier on him. It would be a sure fire way to seduce her then." She chirped, giggling at the girlish thought. "You know…grant her a little something to take the edge off."

"With her, I'm thinking more cobwebs and dust." Vanessa declared dryly, and hurrying feet stammered to an instant stop. Their voices rang through the silence in a thunderous chorus of laughter, abruptly shattering the once protected quiet. Each woman's hand flew instantaneously to their mouths, hoping to still the boisterous cackle. A chorale of shushes hissed back from the door.

In that—Julia moved tamely from the safety of the sink, sputtering her steps as if to leave. She paused reluctantly at his side; feeling obligated in some sense ergo the deed, though she found no lead on where to hitch her start.

"I already know, Julia." Michael uttered in a whisper, dropping his eyes to hers. His tone held no allusion of doubt. "I already know you love me. I also know it flourished, in every way, as deeply as mine." Professing this in a soft drawl, his head lightly bounced, as if relating a statement of fact on the date or the time. His demeanor waded forth with surety as its thread.

Julia's nod came slow in reaction to the diagnosis coolly given as a verdict of fact. Stepping lamely from his side, she gave no further indication as to her thoughts, or of an answer on which he could rest. "*Of course he knows*," she grumbled, spiting this the instant her strides cleared the archway of the kitchen. Her brows knotted with the pertinence of the thought. *It's hard to hide that truth when you're being kissed in such a torturous manner.* She groaned, a peevish note slicing her tone. Had she been able, she would have held tight to the imparting of such tale. But there was no acceding to that creed. Not with the wont of his hands, and not when she's likely to respond in the way that she had. She had no way of rescinding that fact from what it was, having long since learned that morsel of truth. If this was already a palpable distinction of fact, why then does she tremble so?

And why is it she so desperately wanted to cry? Could retribution fray what was, though imperfect, already sublime?

"Hey, guys," she cooed, freshening her expression as well as her thoughts, Julia beamed in preparation of a show, abandoning all else. She breezed into the room already asserting her excuse. "I'm sorry I took so—" Finding the room empty, the luster of her smile flipped instantly to confusion. "Guys, where—?" she halted, rushing to the front entrance at what sounded faintly like the slam of a door. Swinging the ingress open with rushed determination, she caught view of Carol's unheralded finale, stupefied; she gaped as the other's arm danced in a flutter outside the window of her fleeing car. Vanessa honked in response to her wave from the edge of the long driveway, her hand vaulting eagerly out the window in riposte of her approach. It slashed through the air as if in practice of a duel.

"Bye, sweetie, I need to go, Roger called." She chirped. Furthering their distance at a snail's pace as she spoke. "He's anxious about the test," she smiled, a shrug elaborating on the significance of her tell. "I'll give you the juicy details after the weekend. I'm going to be swamped for the next few days, love you!" Vanessa professed sweetly as she straightened her car, honking twice in affirmation. She waved in conclusion as she disappeared down the street.

"But—"

"Hi, sweetie," Delia hailed, backing her car from the garage at a less hurrying pace. She smiled pleasantly in her bequeathing of an explanation.

"Mom! What's going—"

"Iris called," Delia sang without pause. "Gail is having another one of her crisis again, so we're taking her out for a late dinner, and then watch some of the classics to try and divert her attention. It should be late by the time things whine down, so don't wait up. I'll see you tomorrow, bags, sags, circles and all. Love you." She smiled, reversing quickly down the driveway. She gave no pause, nor did she await a reply.

"What? When? But—mom! Wait!" stammering in confusion, she gazed blankly at the empty driveway. Her countenance now hiked well beyond stunned. In mere minutes, everything had somehow spiraled from giddiness to shock. What happened? Could they have overheard Michael's confession? She questioned in the reticence of her head. They couldn't have, could they? If they had, then she'd be swamped with questions instead of excuses. Groaning her bewilderment on the way things now rest, she swerved slowly through the threshold, hearing the locks click in assurance with each turn of her hand. A sigh sailed forward in follow of the anemic deed, as her once lively house felt suddenly quiet and cold, resting now as a contradiction of itself. All signs of life appeared to have wilted from view, and the worry of what was to come had her insides already shredded to mush.

Cossetted snugly in the restive arms of elusiveness, Michael watched quietly, from his seat, as she reentered the kitchen. With interlocking hands firmly cradled atop the table's dark surface, his eyes took keen note of her face, and her expression wavered sadly between apprehension and panic, with naught showing of her usual spunk. Like a convict awaiting the verdict of some odious crime, his eyes followed the details gifted with each step. Stuttering to a stop as she rounded the table, she stalled warily in what seemed a fog. Clasping the back of a chair in one hand, the other floated nervously at her side.

Dark eyes quietly marked their position on the table and stayed, refusing to rescind their hold. She gaped in silence at the intricate graining of wood. Minutes drifted with the two remanded as such, silence fully ingesting the body of their unused time, and although they stood muted on the outside, inside the sonorous bellows of cannons foretold of the battle ahead.

"Where's everyone?" Michael rasped, realizing then that a lingering hush now billowed through the house, for no murmurs of gaiety had wafted to his ears for some time.

"Gone," She muttered with a slow shrug, lifting her eyes for a fraction to his.

"Everyone?" he frowned.

A gentle nod came as his reply, dipping tamely in its dispel. Words followed as an afterthought to what was already said. "Everyone," she sighed, and again the arduous silence restored itself master of the room.

"We should talk." He suggested in a hushed tone, his voice floating as an audible rumble through the quiet, stroking the stillness like the tickle of a feather with its faltering brush. Her hair slowly slipped forward in retort of what was said, bouncing as her head bobbed in concurrence of his words.

"Would you like to go somewhere more comfortable?" she asked, acceding to his gaze for the first time.

"Sure." Offering this in a soft hum, Michael's gaze roamed laxly upon her face, and he could not help the analogy that leapt to his mind, for it paired her demeanor to a wary bird. Ever frightened of a predatory hunt, its restive body takes flight at the first rustling of leaves, and he hoped that that would not be a foretelling of things to come. A light frown creased her brows as she turned from his view, heading sharply to the exit. No words of warning lent itself to her intent.

As if to vent a complaint of its own, his chair growled foully in ire as he stood. Sliding gruffly across the floor, it feasted aptly on the quiet they created. Long strides quickly slashed the gap between them, though she tentatively paused at the entrance until he shadowed her back. Darkness plunged through the kitchen the moment he stabled her side, and the smell of her perfume wafted forward like a soft zephyr in the newness of night. It fostered his senses, touching him as boldly as the dampening of rain.

Irrespective of his certitude regarding her affection, his mind was not without dread. Cognizant her earlier refusal still stood strongly at hand, as does the added few she hinted upon. Could this be the reason for the dejected mien she so tightly disposed? Had the clock chimed its final tune, so severing them? Well, not without a cumbrous fight, Michael vowed, firming this in the whirring of his head, and even not then, he groaned. Ambiguity at its best, impeded his mindset before now, yet she still flowered as the woman of his dreams. The woman he bled his soul to, placing his heart, without a shield, at her feet. Exposed, he now sat as helpless as a newborn left derelict in the woods. This, most surely was not done to seed the verdure of their end, but to enrich the scribing of who they were.

Her stance was such that he could easily stretch forth and snatch her to his chest, and he wondered on her reaction had he broke his restraints and done just that. Would it be the way it's always been between them, or would she set the template in play for their decline?

As if prepping the house for an impending battle, Julia's hand stroked each switch with delicate haste. Forsaking the prospect of those rooms passed as a suitable venue for their approaching unrest. She moved to the next without bother or thought. The family-room stood bold in its dress of night, spotlighted by a portly chandelier, sinuous metal protruded like svelte arms espousing twelve globes of sunlight. Yet her steps never slackened the momentum they had, trudging onwards as if led by something greater than herself. Her hand, like a feather, grazed said switch, bringing forth darkness in an instant, hesitation had no part in the veer to her room.

Entering her bedroom, Julia clasped the cool metal of the handle as she turned, her eyes immediately falling to a target, not pictured, on the floor. Michael's feet thwarted the entrance at a sedated pace, stalked directly at her back. He hesitated further entry of the space. His feet seeming unsure of what direction to take, and as confident a man as he'd always been, she thought it a peculiar picture to see him so openly flummoxed. Yet, she knew no way to ease what it was that he felt. A lone lamp on a far console already brightened the room, biding them welcome in its unspoiled glow, though neither showed awareness in the regarding of its effort.

"Would you like to sit?" she asked dully, frowning at the absurdity of the question. *Come on brain, don't fail me now.* She pleaded, waving a hand towards the sofa as she turned. Columned by two windows at its back, darkness thickened upon the transparent panes, as night descended further upon a despondent hush.

Michael nodded as he stalked towards the proffered seat, lowering his tall frame. He allowed the plush cushions to coddle the tenseness clutching his body.

Closing the blinds at his back, Julia tacked herself to the corner of a vaguely imperceptible striped couch. Feeling the hard bite of its frame nipping at her flesh. She gave no heed to the discomfort it served.

Two sets of eyes, marred with anxiety and dread, stared directly ahead. With no theory of a proper opening or where to begin, the two waited in silence. Taut and unrelenting, the quietude soared as just that, for it reared no different than the behest of peace-talk amidst a barrage customary to those on a battlefield. Their angst grew paralyzing, as the fear, for them, was no less real. Julia's heart raced frantically in the twitchy cavern of her chest, her body in full juddered with the force of each thud. Clenching both hands in a tight fist, she dropped them stoically to her lap, subduing their quiver with the sturdy joints of her knees.

Why does she look so panicked? Michael groaned. He had not expected her to look this petrified from him spilling the lyrics of a song they already knew. Just where did she think this thing between them would end up? She had to know they would need to confront the obvious one day. *So what if one day turns out to be now?* He griped. Stalling the process of thus as the wail of a horn rent the quiet, a quiet that had lingered well past the length that it should. Rupturing the stodgy air, it startled them both from the deep fissures in which their minds dwelt. A sequence of boisterous bellows followed the obtrusive noise. Pinched transiently with a healthy round of cacophonous laughter, silence again saw well to its death.

"Say something, please." He asked, his words hanging loosely between a question and a plea. On any other woman, he would have indubitably reaped the rewards of his confession by now. Instead, he sits in fear of a threatening doom, and the terror bathing such prospect would not let him loose.

As if jarred from an intent task, she turned sharply towards him in reaction, seeming surprised by his words. "I'm sorry." She sighed, surfing her palms roughly atop her thighs. They persisted in their drudge as if her effort was to ward off the impact of a chill. In her own tangled mind, she had not thought much on his feelings, or on the turmoil that might also be his. In an ode as timeless as time itself, he had laid his heart out at her feet. Bequeathing her words in an eloquent recital of what many only hear in their dreams. Yet she had yielded no answer to the beauty that he gave. "I didn't mean to seem callous." She murmured, holding her eyes to the floor. "I just can't find…" dimming her voice, she stalled. "I don't know where to start." Stuttering this, Julia stopped. "I don't know what to say, Michael." She whispered in a gentling breath, and her eyes touched his face with care swimming boldly in their depths.

"Why don't you start by telling me how you feel, 'I love you, too' is always a good start." Michael counseled blandly, shifting his body on the sofa to better view her face. Her eyes shimmered down his face to rest gently on her hands, gazing at the folded limbs now bedded on her lap. Her head rocked in a slow, indiscernible nod, and he was unsure if her action came in acknowledgement of the truth or from what was said.

"We came so much farther than I imagined we would, Michael." She mumbled in start, sounding truly glum. "This—us, I never once foresaw us swerving on this road."

"I know. You said as much from the start." Michael drawled, concurring this with a slow nod, his voice drifted forward sounding almost cool.

"So many times I urged you to look elsewhere. I wanted you gone, but you stayed." She recounted dryly, pausing as if to ponder her efforts. She locked her fingers to steady the quiver of her hands. Swallowing the boulder now growing in her throat, her voice weakened with the immensity of a question that had to be asked. "How long do you think you will continue to stay, Michael? How long do you think you will endure in your love before you grow tired of the reality that is my life?" she croaked, her voice dimming as she fought to stem the tenacity of her tears.

"How can you ask me that?" he inquired in a rush, moving to her side at the speed of light. His hands swallowed the smaller of hers. Both limbs wobbled nervously inside the warm safeness of his grip. Tightening his grasp, Michael steadied her trembling with the gift of his strength. "Why would you ask me something like that?" he smiled, and even though she did not see the genuineness in its unfolding, he hoped that she heard it in his voice. "You can't have forgotten what a declaration means." He stated calmly, gazing at her face, though she offered him no smile in response. Hardly seeming to hear the words being said, her gaze remained focused on her hands.

"But everything about me and what I stand for is what you spent your life avoiding." She droned, informing him this without shifting her gaze. A tear spilled, as if on cue, to the rough clasp of their hands. Dragging her hands free of his, she raked them coarsely across her face in a hard swipe. "Isn't it only a matter of time, Michael, before—"

"Julia, my love is not meant to be dismissive of anything in your life. It's inclusive of everything that you are. I knew you had children when I asked you out, and I guarantee you, it's because of all that you are why I'm here." Michael sagely advised, his demeanor favoring that of a parent in the counsel of a child. "I love you." He whispered. "If I didn't go in the beginning, Julia, ten mammoths couldn't drag me away from you now."

Julia lifted sad eyes to his as if hearing his voice for the first time, and her demeanor seemed vaguely of one well spent. "But a woman with children, Michael, you hate that?"

"I never once said that. I never said I hated it. I just never thought it was something for me."

"And now?"

"And now, with you, I only see the possibilities you bring."

"But I don't come alone, Michael." She reminded in a whisper, again brushing a tear as it spilled down her cheeks. "And because of that, probabilities and conjectures are never applicable here. Here validity reigns as the master of fate. Your possibilities only come to mean in time—we'll see, and I can't do that. I can't do that to them. I won't."

"I spoke, did I not?" Michael inquired tamely, a frown deepening his already ruched brow. "I was sure that I did. Words actually came out of my mouth, did they not? You could hear them, couldn't you? You must have heard the things that were said? I could have sworn I made certain of that. Since nowhere in the body of my fervid speech did I offer you a guess. I know for sure I was definitive in every word that was said."

Julia's head bounced with a healthy show of despondency, lowering her eyes to her hands, she replied in a weak breath. "I heard your words, Michael." She griped, staring hard at her hands. "And they were as beautiful as the man himself. But you spoke of me—to me—what, though, of the baggage I come with? We're not talking about sampling a new flavor to some treat. Or tasting some exotic food you've never tried. We're talking work, hard, sometimes maddening work. Work you know not the first thing about, mostly because you never wanted to. I don't want you to think you have to change that aspect of yourself because of me. It has to be infected in your blood." She counseled glumly, her breath sailing hollow in its maudlin release. "I know this may be hard for you to hear, but it's only going to get harder if we stay on this road." Cautioning thus, she squeezed her eyes firmly shut, pausing as if to bar a fetid thought from her brain. "Maybe we should just nip this now before we go any further? Cut our—"

"*Don't!*" Michael barked cogently, his voice slashing through her words like a blazing sword through flesh. Determined and harsh, it left little room to lend mercy. "Don't you *dare* say it!" He warned, his hand stalling in the space between them. A finger stood erect mere inches from her chest. There was no anger in the manner he dispelled, only a strangled anxiousness that bled bold on his face. His tone commanded the full reach of her attention and nothing less. "Don't you say what I know you don't want. *Don't*. Don't you do this." He advised while shaking his head, as if to eradicate the thought from his mind, he sighed. "Don't do this." He repeated, softening his voice. He touched his forehead to hers. Broad shoulders fell softly as if to relax, and a long draught flew from his nostrils to further aid its result. "Don't. Don't slay me with your own hands." He pleaded in a husky breath, and almost instantaneously her head bobbled under his in response, and he was yet unclear of what meaning that took. Whether in agreement or understanding of his plea, he was unable to discern.

"Do you understand what you're asking, Michael?" she whispered at last, breaking the silence that followed. A soft sniff climbed roughly through the air. "Do you under-stand the ramification of what you want, or how such things work?"

"How can you expect me to speak on what you never gave me the chance to learn? I've waited all these months for you to let me into your world. I've waited patiently to be included. To see what comes with the other side of your life, but, outside of conversations, you've yet to waiver on that. You breeze into my life every fourteen days, and, God, you make me happy. Every part of my life is better when you're in it than those when you're not. Even the modest sleep I get feels better with you, than without. You are the warmth that draws me ever forward. You grant me sustenance and life. Nothing that springs forward after that is of any importance to me." He vowed. His broad shoulders lifting slowly as he tilted his head to better examine her face. "Do I know what it is I'm saying? Emphatically! Do I know the inference of what it means? Unequivocally, yes! I'm asking for you, Julia. Not you and your baggage, just you." Michael smiled. Lifting her chin, he brushed his thumb across her cheek. "To me, everything that is a part of you makes you who you are, and yes, Julia, I want you. My life has not been the same since you entered, and I'm not going back. For it would not be much without you in it."

"But what about your life—your lifestyle?"

"What about?"

"How would this even work? We're so different, Michael. Our worlds are not even on the same planet." Julia shrugged, wiping the remaining moisture from her cheek. "The terrains from here would be unmapped for you, and the roads are, many times, lined with deeply pitted traps. Are you even certain you're ready for the responsibility of that?"

"Why am I so different than any other man? Why do you keep insisting that this is something I would hate?"

"Because most men followed the natural process of growing up, and even you your-self have stated that growing up is a new venture for you. In estimation, most men, even the ones who consider themselves mature, don't want to get deeply involved with a woman who already has kids, not in the true sense of the word. It's a tough sell caring for another man's child. You're not just getting the woman, Michael. You also get the kids, the man and every other problem that could stem from that."

"I know I'm new to this concept of family, but that does not diminish my vigilance. Nor, would it, my alacrity for the work."

"My kids are used to stability, how does that even figure in your world?"

"Which world is this you keep mentioning, Julia? I'm a man who's in love with a woman, what comes beyond that?"

"Everything! I don't fit anywhere into that world, Michael. How could you think that we would? I'm not Madison Avenue or Rodeo Drive bound. The red carpet does not hold any fascination for me. I have no urge to jet set the world. Or have my face, or the faces of my children, plastered on the pages of magazines. I'm a girl who prefers to settle at home with her kids. I like snuggling in bed to watch television with my children, or have a tickle fest now and then just to have something different on the plate. Your life does not call for that."

"And who is to say what my life requires? Who can tell me what I want better than me?"

"Your affection for the writer clouds your judgment on the story itself. But if you took some time to assess the facts further, you'll see that the protagonists don't belong, their worlds have far too many disparities to make it work."

"And yet here we are together." He commented in a soft lilt. "Which world would you prefer I stand in to tell you of my love? And which world do you think would make my anguish of not having you, hurt that much less? There is no difference in our worlds, Julia, only the actual branding of the residences we reside in. People are people. We're each just muddling through the ventures in our lives. I'm still a man regardless of wealth. Happy to find the girl of my dreams, and I'm even happier to know that she noticed me, too. A lifestyle smothered in wealth can't give me any better than that. One world, Julia, one world with more than a billion people and we still manage to find each other. I won't give that up." He informed sternly. "I won't. Five kids, ten dogs and a herd of sheep couldn't do that trick. How could you expect that it would?" Michael asked coolly, drawing in a long, unhurried breath, his shoulders sagged with the weight of its release.

Julia quietly searched his eyes for the dissemination of truth, needing to be certain, as she had to be sure that he knew what it was that he asked. She needed to be sure he understood the enormity of his wants. "Are you thinking you're ready to be a parent to my kids, Michael?"

"I don't need to be a parent to the kids. They already have two very good ones. Their father is extraordinary at his job—so stated by your own mouth. I wouldn't dare trample on that. But I would love to be whatever else that I can."

"Do you really want to do this? You really want to change the premise of what we have?"

"More than I ever wanted anything before in my life." He averred in a rumble, softly touching her face.

"We could bury all of this now and go back to the safety of what we had, should you so wish, and I would still be happy to stay yours for as long as forever. It would be okay, really it would. I'm happy, in every aspect of the word, just to have you in my life."

"As nice as that is, and the journey has been that, I already gave you a full summary of my vision. I want the next step. I want more, Julia. I want it all. I want what comes with the rest of all that."

"I'm sorry." She droned. Nodding with the words as if they meant something else, a long breath sailed past her lips. "I didn't mean to add to your anxiety, but the questions really had to be asked."

"I know that." He assured in what came as a protracted hum, dropping his forehead to the slope of her brow. His hand moved gently to the back of her head. "Just tell me what you know I long to hear and all will be forgiven."

"I love you." She proclaimed without pause, her voice like a long breath, giving life to that which was said. Each syllable cascaded, with new life through his body, gushing forth from the very cheek she rested near. "I love you." She breathed, reinforcing the potency of her words and feeling suddenly free.

A slow smile prowled tireless in its issue, spreading, like a hypnotic gonfalon across the low slope of his face. It reared without end. Closing his eyes, Michael absorbed the very essence of her words, sipping the meaning inside the crux of his soul. It crawled, like a luscious cloak, over the length of his frame. From the crown of his head to the souls of his feet, he felt it shifted through him like the channeling of a tide. Yes, he knew, with certainty, of her love, but it was pure decadence to hear it recited from her beautiful mouth. "Mmm, words that gives me life." He sighed.

"So what now, what does this make us?" Julia smiled, finding humor once more. "Does this mean we're going steady?" she chuckled, breaking the ecstasy of the silence between them, as the thought flitted through her head. "Am I your girlfriend, Michael?"

"What do you think we've been doing all these months? We've been going steady since the day we began, Julia. There's been no one else."

"So this now gives me a title?" she chirped, leaning back slowly in his arms, a soft giggle flirted with her throat at the peculiar place they now rest. Is she really to be girlfriend to Michael Dunhill? "Is that it? Now I'm the girlfriend?"

"No, that's too simple a term."

"So what am I, then?" she teased.

"Didn't you hear me? You're everything, Julia." He breathed, brushing her lips with his. He stirred the tender caress like air across the susceptible follicles of her skin, reclaiming her mouth on the climb. His kisses soon built to a torturous blaze. Cogent hands reached for her then and she hastily complied, assenting to his will without falter or lag. His arms engulfed her and she melted gladly in the closure of his embrace. He asked, and she in return surrendered to his every request. Soaring higher with the intensity of their passion, a new sweetness wrapped them in its ferocious depth.

Climbing astride his lap, Julia ground her body to his in a deep, lascivious stroke, and he throbbed with the delight of her touch. In haste, her hands moved over the fastener yet clasping his pants, working intently upon the barring. He lay free, in but moments, to the wont of her hands. Michaels's breath came as a distended groan, rising from the cavern of his chest. Its rough octave blanketed the room in warmth.

Eager hands snatched the hiked hem of her dress in retort to her work, slipping it easily over her head. Her bra promptly trailed the apparel's flight. His mouth wasted no time sampling the flavors hidden on the once masked peaks, trailing heat on the silky slopes. He left no savory taste untouched. Her hands again became their willful self, lighting a fire within him he'd known with no one else. She set things to a familiar tune in his head. Hoisting her roughly from his lap, Michael stood, discarding his clothes in a fiery haste, each piece fell without the spoilt of ineptness marring his skill. Gray boxers were the last addition to the mounting tally now erected on the floor, though it made it the furthest of the dissident crew. Turning, she retreated before the garment left his hand.

Enthralled, as ever, by the swing of her hips, Michael stalked her progression towards the bed, and like always, her underwear hugged the pertness of her backside like a paradigm suited to mock one's will. Coining a stunning view, it held his attention transfixed. Grabbing hold of the comforter in one hand, she ripped it almost clear from its place, sending pillows scattering to the floor like a failed trick. She turned to gather his attention once more. Already pasted to her back, he pulled her hard against his chest, and his kisses quickly blurred the lines of gluttony and greed. Quietly, his knee broke the plush surface of the bed. Taking her with him on the fall, he pressed her body to the lushness of the tick in continuance of his drive. Long fingers skillfully worked along the edges of her underwear and, it, too, in a trice, lay free with its companions on the floor.

"I love you." Julia murmured as his kisses explored her body.

"I love you." He breathed in rejoinder as he made them one. Rasping thus as if the words titled his action, and in so doing, now made the action his words. Trembling softly from the intensity of his passion, his words moved through her with exquisite artistry and skill. Caressing her senses from deep within, she moaned under the relentless attack of his words. His lyrics taunted her until she gasped from the onslaught of their demands. "I love you." He repeated, driving his words deeper still. He hammered home his meaning until they both cried in sweet agony from the deliriousness that it gave. His words were his weapon and his weapon was used well.

Dawn came quickly, or so perception stated through the groggy veil of her brows. Julia peered drowsily through the darkness still blanketing her room, her lids hovering like the lazy drape of a mask. Blinking awkwardly, she scraped the sleep from the narrow portals in a gruff swipe, her fingers stirring to give aid to her plight.

An arm reposed across her, as if as deterrent to any who entered. Carved protectively under the spill of her breasts, it held her fixed to his chest. Firm thighs rested as a chair at the back of her legs, honing the enclosure she now laid within. The warmth of his breath glided slowly down the side of her neck, fanning her body, it dissuaded an imminent chill. With blanket pulled high, the heavy coverlet barred from fall's plunging nightly frost. But it was the man, at her back, that truly added comfort to her rest, for he granted her refuge that was equal to none.

His sleep seemed deep, as well it should. For between the lateness of their respite and the dispersed energy spent, recouping should expand his slumber to that of late morning—if not the day.

Never once did she fathom that the passion between them could proclaim itself better than the alp on which it stood. Or that she could enjoy him anymore than she had. But last night, again, proved her theories an erroneous dud. Perchance it was the freedom of no longer being guarded. A benefit of not having to skirt the things her mind wanted desperately to allude upon. Could it be that that freedom made her senses acutely attuned?

Julia smiled as her fingers curled devotedly around his, donating a gentle squeeze. She touched the warm limb to her breast. Michael stirred faintly in reply to her ardent embrace. Shifting his shoulders, his breath torrent heavily against the soft skin of her neck. Curious, her head rolled on the pillow with caution, turning her face to his. Spirally, madness spilled athwart the entirety of his face, spreading indiscriminately in every direction at once. It rest like a shroud where there should be none.

Michael flinched sharply from the soft, odorous attack. His lids flickered brusquely as an odd contortion marked the features of his face. Growing impeccably still, Julia quickly held her breath, as if intending her gesture to will him back to sleep. She made not the tiniest sound from the onset of his wince, awaiting the moment's end with the slowing of her breathing. Time lagged within the compact furrows of seconds. The intake of a long, lazy breath mimicked the breezy chime of a broken whistle, dawdling as his chest climbed erstwhile its release.

In a stretch, muscular legs slowly straightened. Stiffening behind the gangly elongation, his body softly twitched with the force of his yawn. Hazel eyes then moved confoundedly from one corner to the other in the room, and she was sure she read plainly what it was that encumbered his mind, for his head rolled slowly to better garner that result. The hand on her breast slowly familiarized itself with her body, and in a flash, he visibly relaxed. Drawing in a long breath of her scent, he buried his nose in the wild strands of her hair, pressing himself firm against the rounded curves of her buttocks as he took his fill.

"What other woman's bed do you expect to be waking up in?" she asked in a soft grumble, her voice like a tickle in the dark.

Michael's smile widened as if as a joke to himself, though his hand gave answer before words were given the chance. Curling his fingers to secure the soft swell, his thumb moved leisurely over the warm, dark flesh, mimicking the slow puff of his own breath. "I never slept over before. Not like this anyway." He murmured warmly, his voice rumbling coarsely in his throat.

"For the bed, yes, but you seemed confused on the body as well."

"My hands take great offense to that suggestion. I only sought to acquire confirmation, that's all." He whispered, his deep timbre drifting like a lazy hum in the quiet of the room.

"Why the necessity, have I suddenly grown similar to another?" Julia teased.

In answer, Michael pressed her until she lay fully on her back, propping himself onto an elbow. He threw a muscular thigh firmly across hers, securing her body under his, he smiled. "I had the weirdest dream about you last night." He announced in a gravelly tone, ignoring the implication in her quest. "I dreamt you told me you loved me. And the things you did drove my body to a state of being almost obsolescent. You made me do things…um." He groaned, shaking his head. His voice dipped roughly like a purr, and the speckled gems of his eyes twinkled lightly in the dimness as he gave then a wordless reply. "Horrible things, things I could never be prolific enough to repeat. Dirty, impious things that made me sit up and beg for mercy at your feet."

"Really? That must have been some dream." Julia stated in a somber tone, feigning a show of concern. "Either that or you must have a very vivid imagination."

"I've been told that." Michael smiled, arching the fullness of his brow. "But in my dream, yours was better. That's how you persuade me to do such unspeakable things. The strange thing is, if you can belief it, I kept going back for more. For it seemed no other held a candle to your likeness or in any sense. Weird dream, huh?" he warbled, his brows jutting quizzically with the ask. "How about you, how was your evening?"

"Pitiable in comparison to yours, mine was…uneventful." She shrugged. "I had a few friends over and by the time they left. I was beat. I slept like a rock until now. My night was definitely unlike yours. Nothing even nearly as exciting happened in mine."

"Pity," Michael droned. "I like the intricacy of my dream better, for it was oh…so… very intense."

"Oh, I forgot, I did watch a little television before I went to sleep. Some old movie was on. It wasn't that bad, really. Everything about it stands to reason." Julia aired calmly, rolling her eyes in exaggeration. She crimped the slender square of her shoulders in a callous show, bringing Michael's eyes to her barely covered breasts.

"What was it about?"

"Nothing much, just some guy—the actor seems familiar but I can't place his face—vowing to some woman the profundity of his love. It was kind of nice if you like that sappy stuff." She grunted, touching his chest. Her fingers labored meekly across the protruding muscles. "Very, actually,"

"What did he say?"

"I don't know. Something about her having the sexiest mouth he's ever seen. How he could spend a lifetime dedicated just to potency of that feature, and that everything about her makes him that much better than before." She smiled, lifting her eyes to his. Her voice softened to a whispery chant. "Or was it that a look from him weakens her strongest defense? Or that his touch ruptured every barrier she'd ever set? His kisses harbored no equal in this realm or the next, as they demanded that nothing be left in reserve. Driving the depths of her hunger, it harvested every speck of her breath. Hence, she craves the intensity of each day and what he brings with it, and wishes to stay forever locked in the paddock of his embrace. Or something of the sort. I can never keep these things straight." Closing with a slow sigh, her gaze lingered on his, silently communicating the repressed layers of her heart.

Leaning forward, Michael brushed his lips across hers, moving to her cheek in a slow ascent. He touched the lids of her eyes. "Interesting words, I have to admit they do sound somewhat...nice. I can see why some people would like that." He rasped, kissing the delicate lobes before continuing his taunt. "Who did you say the actor was?"

"I can't remember. I don't think he's well known, though. He must be new to the profession."

"Maybe so, but apparently he's done his job well. Your memory of his words, being immaterial as it is, is astounding." He smiled, dropping a final kiss to her shoulder. His body fell backwards as if abruptly dragged, slamming heavily onto the adjacent pillow. He tucked her neatly to his side. In what reared like a leisured stroll, his eyes slowly ambled the room, scanning the chamber with appreciation well obvious in their depths. The weaning darkness showed much of the discarded collection bedecking the floor. Clothes, pillows and the comforter from their bed, all lurked aberrantly in every direction, seeming like the result of a wild fray.

"Too strange for you?" she asked, quietly inspecting the path of his eyes. "Waking up like this in my bed?" she clarified to his frown.

"It's different." Michael quipped, adjusting his head on the pillow. He folded a hand behind the back of his head. "I'm used to waking up with you in my bed," he declared tamely, turning his head slowly. He offered her a wide smile. "But then, waking up with you is the objective here. Where could never be as important as the when."

"Be careful you. Your bad-boy aura seems to have taken a spill. If you look closely, you'll see that it's all mucked up, while the other now shines. It tarnished greatly even as we speak. I'm not sure you want that tidbit to get out."

"I know. You're really bad for my reputation." Michael groaned, pulling her closer still. He kissed the top of her head. "But you'll keep my secret, won't you?"

"Why not, I can always do with some leverage of my own." She laughed, pushing herself from the cradle of his arms. Her feet touched the floor in a silent thud, and a smirk dented the soft exterior of her face. "Your deep pockets might not even be deep enough to keep that little secret from getting out." She warned.

"I have other ways to make you keep my secret. Don't make me bring out my little bag of tricks, now. You might not like the result."

"I wouldn't mind having a look at those tricks." She warbled. "Maybe we could test a few against mine. Let's see how they stack up then." Julia purred, easing the bathroom door shut, she left him with an evocative grin.

Michael gazed at the closed portal with a broad smile grafting his face. His rapturous state well obvious in his rich demeanor, attest thusly by the path recently ventured upon. And although he knew there was more yet to say, the unveiling was nonetheless transcending. For it now gave wings to the once ponderous weight of his worry.

If the past months had tutored him any, it's in knowing when to speak and when to bite your tongue. One Everest's summit per confession is enough of a strain. His plan rested on him eventually getting to them all. Wipe the differences from their slate, fully clean, with time, since to do so in one sitting would then make him the lunatic of the day. And he definitely had no intention of being that—not with her.

The slight squeak of hinges pulled his plotting mind back to the door. Creeping open, light raced eagerly across the knotting of wood.

"I thought you might like one of these." She hummed, holding the small package up to be haloed in light. Her smile widened.

"You read my mind." Michael chortled as he sprang from the bed.

"That's not hard to do when you only have one thought." Julia snickered back, releasing the toothbrush to his hand.

"It's a good thing then I never claimed to be a complicated man." He smiled, waving the brush close to her nose. "Mmm, you smell good." Humming this as he retreated from sight.

Julia laughed cheekily in mocking response, amazed at how well he transmitted a singular thought. Never stopping, the man was an insatiable drone.

A light breeze rustled betwixt the sprawled limbs of shrubs. Whipping across the stark branches of trees, their rigid bow seemed to near the point of a snap. Milky blue already dilute twilight's softening gray. With wisp of black holding faint to the milieu of the horizon's west, it dawdled as if in wait for an astonishing event. The moon, though lacking its luster from the thickness of night, still yet hovered on its throne. It shimmered in muted silver like a distant reflection of light.

Julia turned from the window as a chill thudded through her body, accentuating the season's difference; summer now seized its well-deserved rest. The bathroom door opened like a soft mewing and, in a trice, Michael made his presence immediately known, greeting her with a broad smile. It seemed only two steps before he was there at her side, wrapping his long arms around her, he asked.

"Aren't you cold?" he frowned, feeling the coolness of her skin.

"A little," Julia muttered, not bothering to suppress a new shiver. Her body drank of his warmth.

"Come on. Let's go back to bed." He urged, turning her from the window with a smile. She offered him no resistance in the effort he showed, though she made known her opinion with a strong, skeptical smirk. "What can I say?" Michael shrugged, beaming as he held back the covers in aid of just that, moving in immediately behind her. He pulled her close. "I have a small mind." He vowed with a low chuckle. "I'm only capable of carrying one thought. Better?" he asked, daubing her body further with his. His breath came lax amidst the strands of her hair.

"Uh-huh."

"I have to tell you something." Michael proclaimed tamely, his voice like a gentle sigh.

"What's that?"

No answer came for a prolonged minute while she waited his reply, drifting profoundly quiet. His hand, at last, quietly touched her cheek. Cradling her features, he guided her face to his. His eyes grew soft as his gaze descended on hers, lingering for what felt like eons. He slowly brushed his lips across hers. There was no longing in the way he kissed her. Tasting of her in an intimate feast, he swathed her with the intensity of a promise, cherishing the very essence of who she was. He imparted a sundry of possibilities to come. Gathering her close as he lifted his head, Michael pressed her with the firmness of his body, smiling as he further adjusted their fit.

"In case I wasn't clear just then. I love you, very much." He rasped.

"That's it? You're done?" she inquired then, showing the start of a frown. "That's hardly enough for an appetizer."

"Aren't you cold?"

"And warming quite nicely, I might add." Turning her body fully into his, she smiled. "Just think. A few more of those and I'll be burning up." Purring this as she lifted her face to his. She stroked his lips gently with her own, making clear her intention. "Now, earn your keep, slave. Make your mistress happy, she wants to purr under you."

The blanket stirred roughly as Michael's hand found the full curve of her buttocks, lifting her from her place. He tucked her hips snugly to his. His body then moved in a deliberately measured caress, rejoining that which needed no words. His hungry mouth found hers with definitive purpose, drinking long and hard the deeper he delved. "Whatever your command, *mon amour*," He murmured in the curve of her throat. And in the lowly lit room, conversation between them thence sprouted dynamic. Energetic and robust in its lively oration, it soon soared pronounced. No words were spoken beyond that which was already said. None that required the employment of their ears, yet he pealed openly of his love, and with her body, she gave answer with a convincing warble of her own.

—•—

To elude a necessary explanation to her mother, the two thought it best to relocate the venue of their romp to that of his estate. Sparse roads saw the short journey over in less than a flash, deducting little time from the diminutive few they had left.

The graveled road welcomed them like a longtime family friend. Yet the house seemed almost solemn in the brightening of day. Bathed in the freshness of morning, the manse appeared newly awakened from an imposed slumber. Aloft its crown, a chorus of mist billowed indignantly. Patches of fog hovered as if to keep watch over the spread, holding like clouds under the sprawled limbs of trees. Michael flew to her door the instant the engine stopped, a smile raring without provocation. It blossomed the closer he got.

"Insurance money came through?"

"What?"

"You seem more spry than usual this morning." She teased, shrugging pithily with the taunt. "I was just wondering."

"Do I?" Michael sang, his masculine voice rumbling softly from his throat, and full brows jutted skywards in a pale show of innocence. "My dream did leave me with a plethora of memories." He informed with a brash smirk. "It may be that I'm having trouble simmering my thoughts."

"You do keep yourself warm now, don't you?"

"It's become a sort of hobby with you." He averred, glancing up at the house. He smiled, feeling more welcomed than he had in a long time. "Come on. Let's go inside before Betty comes out." Pulling her to his side, he allowed the door to slam shut, as if the thud now stated what was fully his. His hands gave further certainty of that, wrapped tightly around her as they turned. He asked. "What should we do with ourselves today?"

"Eat."

"Eat what exactly?" he grumbled. "Do you take suggestions? Perhaps I could interest you in something sweet. Or, do you have your mind already set?"

"*And, we're back*. Shouldn't you be tired?"

"Come on. You're fun to play with, even when the only thing I can use is my words. The spark is quite igniting." He smiled, tightening his grip on her shoulders as they ascended the steps.

"I'm beginning to get that inkling." Julia simpered back. "Now, wouldn't some food come in handy just about now?"

"Sorry," Michael drawled, his breath stroking her ear. "What can I say? I'm caught thinking with the wrong head again."

"You do know if you keep looking at me like that you'll eventually grow tired of the view?"

"I'll take my chances on that." He replied hoarsely, kissing her temple as he held open the door. "Come on, play with me." He grumbled sweetly. "I'll feed you. But will you feed me?"

"I'd say you were kidding, but then, I've been around you long enough to know that you're not."

"Have you already grown tired of my attention, Ms. Berwick?"

"I could answer that, but the proof is always going to be there, isn't it?"

"You know, I've alluded to this before, but, there's a danger about you." He growled. "You seem to go right to my head."

"Should I even ask which one?" she teased, lifting her face to his.

"Both, of course," he assured with a lazy smile. "I know you know what you do to me. You're like an addiction. I can't seem to get enough."

"Shouldn't that be a worry?"

Although his lower half remained compressed, Michael slowly straightened, and hazel eyes were unwavering in their intent. Deeply giving, they tarried not in relaying his heart. "Are you worried you'll eventually get consumed?" he smirked, raising her hand to his lips. He tugged gently on the back of said limb, his teeth nipping, as if exploring her taste. "Could it be you're trying to tell me I'm overwhelming you already?" he queried, tilting his head slightly, he tallied the worth of her inquest with his eyes. "You forget, Julia." Michael drawled, gifting then a warm smirk. He loosened his hold on her hand. In a slow dive, a finger brushed the side of her breast, and her eyes, as if on a hunt, dropped in leisured pursuit of his hand. "I know a few things about...you..."

Julia's eyes smiled coyly with the ascent of his hand, and not unlike the swing of a welcome plaque. Her smile swam warmly across the fullness of her face. "What exactly is it you think you know about me?"

"I know you have a sizable appetite." He hummed, his thumb falling to again feather the erogenous peaks. "A sweetly desirous one, at that; one almost as ravenous as mine." He vowed, donating a self-assured smile to his cause. Her lids fell softly as her gaze again targeted the work of his hand, smiling in response. She gave him naught of her thoughts. "It certainly keeps me panting. So, even though you'd like to put the sole blame at my feet, I know...." Michael rasped, his eyes seeming to twinkle with the merriment of his gaze. "You fulfill everything, Julia." He pledged in a soft breath. "No drugs ever came close to that."

"That's actually a new discovery, thanks to you very much. So irrespective of all that, the title still falls strongly at your feet. You hold the deed and all propensities on that." Julia remarked sweetly, recollecting with clarity their enthusiastic endeavors. The enjoyment was more so than it had been with any other partner she'd ever had. Not that three could be considered a myriad in that fact.

"Then I'm quite happy to oblige you in the aiding of that." Michael smiled, enjoying the new openness in their discussion, and he ardently looked forward to furthering their knowledge of each other. "Are you still hungry—for food?"

"Yes."

"Then let's go eat before this day is done. Before you know it, it'll be time for you to leave, and I'd like to get my fill before the clock signals that end."

"Speaking of that," Julia interjected in a rush, growing immediately cautious, she asked. "Would you like to spend some time with us this weekend? I mean…it won't be us, but…well. We'll be together with the kids. We can claim the whole thing as work related while you're there. I figured if the kids start spending more time around you, it would be easier to transition into a…relationship. That's if you want to." She inquired with a hesitant sigh. "Do you want to…?" she asked, eyeing him nervously as if expecting the certitude of a decline.

"Of course I want to! How many ways will it take for you to understand that? How many 'I love you's will you need, Julia?" Michael questioned gently, noticing her nerves. "Tell me now and I'll get them all out of the way. Understand this," he muttered, leaning close. "I love you. I want you. I want you in my life. And if that's not clear enough for you, then yes, Julia, that includes the kids."

"Okay." She hummed, nodding tamely in response. She brushed at the misting in her eyes.

"Now," Michael announced in a near grumble, taking a deep breath. His arm again encircled her frame. "Why don't you bring them here? We could make a day of it, and Betty could go out of her mind preparing for them."

"Are you—"

"Don't!" Michael interrupted then, giving the gentle warn. He pressed a finger to her lips. "I've wanted to have more with you for months, Julia. Now, for God's sake, give me what I want, will you? Don't you think I'm old enough to know what that is?"

"It's not fully that. It's just that the anxiety that comes with the commitment of family can be an overwhelming task. I'm trying to save you from being fully engulfed."

"I've also never loved anybody before. Not with the same intensity that I do you. What of the anxiety of that? Whatever we have between us, I've never come close to feeling that with anyone else. Yet, you don't seem to be questioning that. Why is that?"

"I don't know." Julia shrugged, marveling on his question, and realizing the facts stapled to his words. She'd never once questioned the validity of his love or its depth, just his readiness for the work attached. Was the incongruity of that odd? Somehow, she just knew. Felt it as plainly as she harbored her own and, too, in the harmonious way they interacted with each other. How he looked at her, and the way he touched her, each deed gave more proof than not, for the emphasis minced between each act said just that. "I don't know." She whispered, not knowing what reasoning to add. "It just seems…I just—"

"—Knew?" Michael asked, finishing her sentence with his own splice on her word. "You knew, just as I knew the same with you, without ever voicing our feelings. We knew. Not wondered, Julia, but knew. Trust that. Trust that feeling as true, and know, without a single doubt, that this is real."

"Okay." She muttered with a strong nod, her voice sailing with renewed strength, feeling for the first time completely at ease with his words. She'd never introduced a man to her children before, and although technically this was not to be an introduction. The intent was still entrenched in the tilling. "Now you'll just have to remember to keep your hands to yourself."

"I'll be on my best behavior." He vowed. "But you have to promise to find a way to give me a treat. And if we go swimming, you are not allowed to wear that white swimsuit of yours."

"Got it, but I'll grant you a deal. If you stay on your best behavior all day, I'll show you a mountain of fun that night."

"Then you'd better eat well that day and stack up on your rest, since your night will have no end. All frustrations will be taken out on you at length."

"Is the white swimsuit still off limits?"

"Yes." He hissed. "Have you seen what you look like in that thing?"

"Yes."

"You need to see what I see."

"What exactly do you see?"

"Temptation at its best, and not the kind I'd like to have when kids are about." Michael groaned, breathing life into his words. He gave them the strength to tear down the forest at their backs. Thus, he moved the mightiest mountain with just the spilling of his words, and made two beautiful, brown eyes glow with the decadence they brought. He gave it the life it was meant to have and his eyes made certain she not only knew this, but that she understood his meaning well.

Chapter Forty One

Like clandestine whirrs in the warning of a tempest, so, too, the atmosphere shifted, stirring the air with a newness that maimed like the wallop of a mallet. It severed what once sat as the aspiration of a few. Thanksgiving befell the Carolinas etched as a probable assault. Dragging winter numbly in its palm, temperatures hustled on a spiraling decline, setting fireplaces ramped.

Plunging nights crudely quarried below an icy brink, and the twenties, in retrospection, were soon heralded as a torrid wave. Thermostats ascended as the focus of continuous tweaks. Yearning to sever the tart grasp of an incessant chill. They dredged ever onward with a grumbly hum.

Frost sheet wilted lawns now static from the bath of an icy spill, smearing granules of white across a plane of tawny-brown. They caroled loudly underfoot with so mere a stride, harping, their diatribe, like alternates in a symphony that was winter itself. Radiance once judged a predictable sight, dimmed with the dark tinting of day, for the sun, in idleness, seemed to have petitioned respite for itself, as gray now looked to have settled in well.

Characteristic of everything else in their lives, the holidays bred harmoniously communal for the Berwicks' households alike, thus granting their children the best of both worlds, each devoid of conflicts or fuss.

Tradition topped the menu on this, a conventional day, though only in the way of their view. For, as per the family's request, the same entrees had steadied their table for almost five years. Chicken strips, biscuits, eggs and a large herd of sides, which, collectively, could dent the populous of hunger in a family of ten, now waited to be feasted upon. Forsaking the expected turkey repast, it evolved as their favorite celebratory spread. Reserved specifically for occasions as this, it was a carte du jour that thenceforth relieved them from having to again partake of the standard trimmings in a ritual meal with their father and his clan.

Absent from the gathering was the ever affable Michael Dunhill. Now a regular at the house, his presence is ever felt. Ambling by at least once on weekly intervals, work was still yet burdened as the motive for his show and, as always, his attendance garnered an impromptu invitation to join the family for their meals.

Whether through ignorance or through the genuine gift of trust, the kids hardly seemed sentient of the patterned intrusion. With Richard seeming to relish his visitations most, his offering of insights and opinions stretched on a vast array. Most of which, however, resides on the latest bulletins for his video games.

Condensed drizzling of the kids' weekends was spent within the confines of Michael's estate. With her pretense unfurling no different than his, the need to appear busy grew, at times, to a tedious task. There, an assortment of activities was tooled to bond adult to kids. Furthering their ploy, it helped the grownups with the layering of their act. Although of late, per the kids' request, their tarriance had lengthened in time, past that of perceived nuisance to solicit.

Their fascination with Betty continued thus without complication or slack. The older woman remained the first to get their attention, and the last to do so afore their final adieus, this, inevitably, was sure to be an added subsidy to the adult's cause. Snickering this in supposition to herself, Julia championed their interest. Though as a mother, she greatly appreciated the care attributed by the gifted nanny.

December breezed in a frostier fiend than that of its algid predecessor. Establishing a supposed fluke as fact, winter had undeniably clasped the southern state in a throe of ice. Arriving earlier than that of the customary appulse, a proposed attestation of its clout was through a thorough illustration, thus dragging temperatures with it down a rutted, dreary knoll.

Today, however, bloomed propitious in its dispel, granting, through its luster, a generous picture of its earlier self. Three imperative errands marked the calendar on this day. With two being prescheduled long so in advance, Julia's morning was but a continuous buzz. A lengthy wait at the eye doctor saw to her annual requisite of a suggested mandate. Backed, next, by an oral visitation, a thorough cleaning was expertly preformed, and in no time flat. A litter of miniscule missions were checked off a memorized list, labeling them achieved before tackling the next. She hastened her way through each proceeding, preserving the last stop as, she would, the relishing of a treat.

Slowing her vehicle to a gingered stop, the stylish carrier quietly purred its presence outside the old, unassuming barrier obstructing her path. Like all preceding visits, the formula remained unchanged—except one. Anxious to try out her newly revealed present, Julia reached excitedly for her own remote. Tucked nicely under the body of her seat, it sat in the very spot Michael legated for weeks. Hidden suitably from sight, he awaited the opportunity to grant her his revelation as to where they now rest, gifting her the freedom of access as a part of his commitment to them. The small device thus flipped effortlessly in her hand, clearing her path effectively like the blaring warns of a conveyance in haste.

Michael's truck postured before her like the Titan namesake that it was. Carved directly in front of convex steps, it posed salient in a globular drive. Betty's white Arcadia sat reticent, looking serene, like the owner herself. It rested tamely at the truck's back, seeming like the eerie contrast of a mastiff to the ethos of a mole.

Julia parked haphazardly behind the two in her hurry. Excited by the prospect of her first true surprise, jubilant feet raced up a gaggle of steps. Not bothering to apprise him of her spontaneous show, she leaned softly on the bell.

Gazing back at the weathered foliage incasing the broad manse, a sigh trickled from her body in acquiescence of the electrified jitters yet romping through her core, as brown eyes, almost unseeing, walked the arresting islet. The forest-like hemming stood looking like a sparse replica of its once beautiful self, ravaged well by the harshness of winter's frosted breath. What once stood corpulent and lush now seemed a mere skeleton of itself. Yet the magnificent statue of pines appeared purposely untouched by its icy embrace, looking almost as fresh this day as they had in the middling of spring.

The handle on the door clicked like tensing pins in the cylinder of a mechanical box. Julia whirled in a broadcast of true effervescence, swerving towards the sound. A wide grin stretched taut in its broadening on her face, suddenly stilling its momentum. She froze in the midst of her turn, swallowing a chant that had already started its spill. "I thought that I'd—"

"Yes?" the woman asked in a stern, ill-fitted voice. With brows pinched tightly, her light-brown eyes flittered over the visitor's frame with a nasty show of suspicion blatantly marring their depths. Jumping past her to the new lodger on the drive itself, anger burned bold in their toasted depths. "How did you get on this property?" she asked acidly, not waiting for an answer, she furrowed on. "Do you know you're trespassing on private property?"

"Hi…." Julia uttered nervously as an opening, unsure of where to begin. Her own suspicion steeped to a definite high, though her nerves were not fully due to the woman herself, but from the questions she asked. Hence, she remained hesitant of what answers to give.

At her own insistence, their relationship had been shrouded in secrecy, ethereal to others these many months. An occurrence known only to them, which now left her no option but one—that of being furtive. "May I speak with, Mr. Dunhill, please?" she bid politely, revamping the working of her brain once the shock of her interrogator dimmed. Forsaking the rest, she chose the cloak of formality, which, in turn, left her no explanation on how she managed to maneuver her vehicle through the doubly secured iron gates.

"You have the wrong establishment. No one by that name works here." The woman frowned, looking more annoyed now than she was in start. Her tart words whistled like the thrust of an expert's whip. "You need to leave this property immediately, or I'll be forced to call the police."

"My name is Julia, Julia Ber—" as if smothered by a hand, Julia's voice suddenly wilted and died. The error, she realized, would be to give over her name. The name of her children, the name she used in her professional life. If things ended badly, that was not the name she wanted to get dragged through a gutter of sludge. "Look," Julia grunted, showing her impatience for the insolent sentry as well as the incident itself. Her expression grew almost ominous. "If you'll just give Mr. Dunhill my name, I'm sure he'll see me."

"I told you before, no such person works at this establishment!" she announced in an incessant tone, her voice taking on a high roar, echoing brashly behind their backs.

"Excuse me? And you are...?"

"Who I am is of no concern to you! Your best bet is to turn around and get off this property now! Or this will not end well for you." She barked, each word like a repulsive epithet in a play, as if somehow stung by the audacity of the question itself. Her glare grew rosy, brightening to a fiery bed.

Narrowing eyes singed the woman's face in response. Moving in slow assessment, they descended the tall, slender wall blocking her path, dispersing their annoyance on a leisured ascent. They burrowed their blatancy with little masking their depths. Perplexity and resentment was but two of the emotions that now churned gruffly through her body, wondering, at the very least, who the woman was. Her mind became a firestorm of thoughts.

To the numerous tiers now wavering like a bold tag in Julia's view, there was nothing particularly frightening about the caustic persona the woman affected as her own. Neither was the clamor she spilled. She was just uncertain which course of action better fit the position she now found herself in. Though who the woman was may be of another matter for sure, and the position was not a place she relished being in. "That's very interesting," Julia began almost as tart. "Since I've had meetings with him at this very address, how do you suppose he got here? Perchance he morphed himself somehow?"

"That is an unlikely story!" The woman shot back in what surpassed the anthem of a shrill, edged nicely with disgust, undiluted scorn seemed braided tightly to every word. "You need to get back in your vehicle and vacate this premise now! Or find yourself vacating in handcuffs." She again warned.

"Then you're going to have to call the police, because I'm not leaving without seeing Mic—Mr. Dunhill." Julia returned acidly, her voice equally as stern, having had her fill of the woman's tartness. Her arms folded across her chest in a stubborn show of defiance, and she was almost tempted to clear the offal from the door with her very own hands.

A flash of movement in the long foyer caught Julia's attention, but the narrow opening left her no chance of confirming what—or had it been a who? Of this, there was no ready answer on which to latch upon. Should she call him now in-front of the virulent woman, or just pretend defeat and call him in private? She wondered, and was stunned by how difficult a decision the cumulative choices were.

"Why don't you guys get a life?" the woman continued in her acrid tone. "Find a man, settle down and have some kids, will you. Stop chasing after a fantasy you cannot have, and find something real." She spat mordantly, and her eyes drudged down Julia's face as if assessing something discarded, marred fully in filth. It hampered any worthiness of use. "You look sane enough to hear my advice. So listen up. You guys are all like little—"

"Sam!" Michael's voice rang soft from the foyer she guarded so deftly. "I'm ready to get started. What's keeping you? We need to——Julia!"

"Hi!" Julia answered with the start of a sensational smile. Looking past the startled woman into beautifully stunned hazel eyes, and feeling suddenly timorous as to what the correct response was. She had chosen to use the decorum of acquaintance, thinking it best at the time. So any show of emotions now would be quite telling to any who watched.

Michael stood frozen at the tail end of three. With doubling gaze now locked sharply on his——his sealed aptly on the face of one. Blinking brusquely, he made what seemed no more than three steps, storming past the now befuddled obstruction. His body slammed into the other with enough urgency to knock her fully back.

His mouth then crushed hers in an assertion of will, granting her little chance to refuse. The pressure was unmistakably schooled, relentless in its bestowing. He kissed her as a lover should, would and could, unashamed and unaffected, regardless of who watched.

"Hi." Michael tenderly rasped, as if to give aid to the life it already had, he breathed the soft salutation in her mouth. Easing the intensity as he opened his eyes, he gazed at her lovingly and smiled.

With jaw sagging low in shock, Sam gazed at the two from her employer's back, realizing in a swift, reminiscent tone, the truth of the other woman's words. Quietly, she moved nervously back. *Evidently, she was someone close.* Sam reasoned dimly in head, the kiss had stated that in more than explicit term. Would they now recognize that she was only doing her job?

She had not the faintest clue that he was seeing someone new, on the prowl, maybe, but not this. She had assumed all the rearranging she did to accommodate his weekends, just meant he was on the hunt. His ways with women seemed more a lifestyle than a need, so looking had always been his most fervent thing. Waltzing from one to the other like connecting pathways in a maze, there never seemed to be an end. Not that that had been, at all, a one-sided venture in his case, for she had witnessed the literal length some women would go to, to vie, not only for his eye. Being industrious in their inventive approach, his hotel rooms had been breached on more occasion than one. She was only trying to ward off one such attack. How was she supposed to know different in this case if not told?

Turning in silence from the corner that she stood, Betty smiled with satisfaction, and a gay tune vibrated low in the doming of her head. Utterly ecstatic with the couple now entrenched by the door, she retreated her steps, finding her place again in the kitchen. She happily resumed her chores.

"Sam, would you excuse us please." Michael bade rigidly, each word thrown over his shoulder in a soft authoritative tone. He spared her not the merest glance. No answer came forward in the way of a response. Neither did he hear an indication of her perceived departure, turning then. He addressed her once more. "Sam! Sam!" He summoned now sternly, watching the countenances on his longtime assistant sway. A distant smile nipped faintly at his eyes, and he could only imagine the things that now trounced, with the mirific vision, through her head. But he had not the time, nor was he in the mood to deal with her then. "Please excuse us." Michael calmly ordered, stating such once her eyes gave acknowledgement to his.

"Y-Yes Mister Dunhill," Sam stammered in a low breath. "I'm sorry, Mi—Mr. Dunhill," she mumbled in start, straightening tensely. She caught hold of herself. The informal address had always been an adequate mode of acknowledgment between worker and boss. But the moment felt too alien to have so personal a greeting slide from her tongue. "I'll be in the office." She muttered at last, hesitating, her gaze flew again to his back. Recognizing that something else needed to be said, for she needed to offer him—her, an explanation, or, at the very least, an apology for the transpiring before. However, his attention was already reverted fully on his guest, gently brushing the loose strands of her hair from her face. She did not need to see his eyes to know he was beaming at the woman he now held.

"Thanks for the surprise." Michael whispered warmly.

"I thought I could say welcome back and maybe we could have…lunch, but you're busy. I'm sorry. I shouldn't have come. I was trying to surprise you."

"Stop, will you." He commanded in a sigh. "I like surprises, you know that. Feel free to surprise me at any time. I wouldn't have given you a way to do that if I didn't think it was okay. Now, about lunch, I could definitely eat…lunch." He smiled. "Come on in. Let's go see what we have on tap."

"Michael, we can't. If I come in now, then everyone will know that we're having… lunch." She cooed. Acceding to the work of his lips, for they now played devilishly upon hers. "Maybe we can have a picnic instead…?"

"A picnic? Hmm, that's an intriguing thought. Just let me grab my jacket." He returned in a slow growl. "Come on. Walk with me."

"Why? Just meet me back here."

Firm hands skied slowly down her back, rounding the taut slopes of her buttocks. Michael steamed her firmly to his body, acquainting her with the protrusion now wedged low astride her stomach. "I'm already thinking of what to eat." Michael roguishly smiled.

"I don't mind the view."

"Then it's yours to have, though it hardly seems fair." He teased. "Where's my view? I don't get to enjoy the same divulging results on you."

"I think maybe I can arrange an equally accommodating picturesque."

"Have I mentioned yet how much I've missed you?" he growled, accentuating this with a gentle squeeze.

"Then let's see if you're worth the price of my ticket." She smirked, her voice as warm as a desert breeze. "How much life can you breathe into your words, and can you make the audience feel all the things that you say, thus making them real?"

"Let's take the truck." He dryly informed, his answer climbing through a soft chuckle. Still savoring the thrill of her words, Michael turned, pinning her around the waist. He pulled her eagerly through the entrance, catching the door deftly with his foot, the barring snapped soundly in place with an obvious thud.

"Michael! Where are we going?"

"Don't worry. You'll have your picnic." He assured with an added measure of pleasure in his tone, his words tumbling slowly from the spirally tress. "With the kind of challenges you tend to dish out, who, in their right mind, would want witnesses?" Michael shrugged, his fingers closing on the indent of her waist in a soft caress. "Let's go get my keys so I can see what other lyrical snippets you have to add. You know, I'm always eager to hear your voice."

"As I am to watch you roar." Julia smiled, tipping her head gently back. She gazed into the fire of his eyes. "It's a very appetizing sight." Another chuckle vibrated from the well of his chest, soaring almost sinister in its dispel. Silence, in time, enveloped what was left of the journey they had.

Although the drive to their terminus of choice was conventionally short, the journey for the ardent errand felt strangely a protracted one. Planted firmly at his side, Michael's arm kept her blissfully fixed, while the other of his hand sat equally as adamant on the steering wheel of his truck. An eerie smile articulated much on the avenues his thoughts now trekked. Daubed liberally across his face, the two dared endeavored small-talk to pass the time of their jaunt. Julia's hand rested as a stamp on the taut ridges of his stomach, her thumb swaying like an absentminded tail, taunting the thin furring where it rest. All trace of his smile was lost the instant her hand veered from its place, skating past his navel. The chuckle that hovered in his throat was then smothered with the sharpening of his breath.

Only the second in a long list of dearth, the day beamed radiant, knowing its return a welcomed sight. The sun bragged of its brilliance in an auspicious display. Yet its bold allowance gave naught in reprieve from winter's continuous gnaw.

The truck's engine throttled its full arrogance in the tranquil aura of the woods. Yet like a faint backdrop, its grumbles wilted brusquely from mind, so, too, the persistent whine that now chorus the blare of a fan. Happily quenched, Michael's back sat staunched against the passenger door, his sturdy chest firmly cradling the thin press of her back. Lifting her hair from her shoulders, he draped it atop her breasts, kissing her temple in his ascent of her throat. He smiled contently as she traced a finger along the protuberances of his hand.

"I'm sorry I came," she smiled, throwing a quick smirk over her shoulder to his chest. She further expounded on that thought. "I mean…well, I'm not sorry I came…." She clarified with a shrug, her palms turned now wide. "I'm sorry I outed you. I outed us."

"The privacy was your call, remember? Sam's been my assistant for a long time. She was bound to find out one day." Came the relaxed reply, filling a hand with her hair. He let the wildness ease slowly through his fingers on said hand, repeating the process as she spoke.

"So *that's* who she is?" Julia groaned, rolling her head on his chest in understanding. "She's tough. Mean, actually."

"She's good." Michael hummed. "Did she say something to you?" he asked, showing then a small frown. His head tilted to better assess her face.

"Well," Julia started, feeling now some sympathy for the woman's plight. "She was about to call the police." She informed him then, deliberately leaving off the intensity of her tone. "She wanted to know how I came to be on the property."

"So that's why Betty came to get me." Michael smiled, realizing now what the older woman wouldn't say then. "She wouldn't say why. She just said I needed to get to the door immediately."

"I couldn't give her the truth or an explanation of how. So I chose to go formal—"

"Why not?" Michael probed, cutting through the lyrics of her voice.

"What?"

"Why couldn't you tell her the truth?"

"Well…" Julia shrugged, recollecting the thoughts that had smoldered to a blaze in her head, and knew her assumption was not an irrational one. At least a thousand women, on any given day, would have thought the same. "I…" she sighed, remembering his acute insight into her, she asked. "You knew what I was thinking, didn't you?"

"I knew."

"I'm sorry." She murmured with a benevolent sigh. "Although you didn't have to be quite so emphatic about us," she grumbled, hiding the sudden pleasure that spread to her face.

"Yes I did." He proclaimed in a sure voice. "I love you. But before that I told you I wouldn't lie to you. What you thought was worst."

"I'm sorry. It just looked…" she droned, her shoulders crimping softly with the pause. "Assistant didn't even pop in my head."

"I can imagine what it must have looked like. I probably would have thought the same thing had the shoe been on the other foot." He remarked with a tamped groan, knowing, with all certainty, that had it been him, restraints would not have been foremost in any region of his head. For just the thought of her with someone else, put a sharp twinge in his chest. Leaning forward, Michael kissed her to pluck the bitter thought from his head.

"Mmmm," Julia purred against his mouth. "This is such a good place to have a picnic. We should come here more often." She smiled, taking a picture from the memories in her head.

"I need you to go somewhere with me." Michael asked hurriedly, brushing their earlier discussion aside in a flash.

"What? Where?" she quizzed, though not at all with her usual calm, turning quickly in her seat on his lap, she waited for the sparks of mischief to surface in its place. Certain such rascally deed would soon burn bright in his eyes.

"Chicago."

"Chicago! But...why?"

"I'm going to be a guest on the Oprah Winfrey show, and I'd like you to come with me." He rasped, his eyes racing almost nervously over her face.

"I can't come with you," she frowned, her eyes shifting from his face as if in search of a suitable decline. "It's...I can't."

"Why not?" he probed in his bassy timbre, yet his words flew to her soft. "This weekend is supposed to be our time together. I don't want to miss out on that. I have to go to Chicago and I want to have you with me. You don't have to announce we're together. You don't even have to be yourself while we're there. We could play dress up. You could look and be someone else the whole time we're there."

"Really?" Julia asked in a befitting drawl, her eyes scurrying out the window in follow of her thought, as the thought of playing dress up did nip at a highly intrigued nerve.

Michael plowed forward the very instant she gave pause, recognizing the cause of her delay. "Just think. You could be anyone you want—except a celebrity, of course." He teased, jumping ahead of the toiling in her mind. "A wig, some glasses and a different wardrobe, and you won't even recognize yourself. It's a lot of fun."

"How long would we be gone?" she asked, further piqued by the sell.

"Just the day," Michael smiled. "We'll be back in our own bed that night or by morning at the most."

"Just the day?"

"Just one day." He affirmed with a low growl, tightening the force of his embrace.

"Well...okay." Julia smiled, though inside it brandished itself as a snicker, fascinated by the prospect of being out on their first public venture. Yet none would be wise as to their private affair.

"Great!" Michael shot back in piercing haste, pulling her again snug. He wrapped her tight against the wall of his chest, mentally noting the hurdle he just crossed. "We have to leave really early on Friday, so how will you work out Richard and Rachel getting to school?"

"I guess I could ask my mother to see to it that they get on the bus. Then have David get them from school instead of waiting to pick them up at the house." She frowned, mulling the idea over further in her head. Her mind zipped through the myriads of things she would first need to complete before the designated day. But with near seven days with which to tackle them all, she could hardly worry on that.

"What time do you have to leave by?" Michael drawled, his breath stroking her ear.

"By one, one-thirty or there about,"

Tossing a glance in the direction of the dashboard, he smiled. "Good, that gives me some time to work on my appetite."

"Always famished will soon be your middle name."

"I'll just put the blame on the cook in that." He grumbled darkly, nibbling the soft edge of her lobe.

"Then I'll have to have a stern talk with that cook." She giggled.

"Please don't. I'd hate for the sequence of the menu to change. Everything is so good. I wouldn't want to lose even one thing." Lifting her with casual ease, he settled her higher on his thighs, turning her legs until she faced him fully. His eyes lapped hungrily at the shadowed junction of her thighs, roasting every pore with their casual ascent. "Everything else just seems bland in comparison." He hummed, his eyes lifting softly to her face. "And just so you know, just in case I haven't already told you this before now, this steed *loves* the way you ride."

"Would you like me to take you riding more often?" Julia smiled, knowing the feeling was truly of mutual esteem.

"No, the balance seems fair. Every man vies for himself here, how can you beat a deal like that?" He droned, a snicker seeping lightly into the rumbly cadence of his tone. "Conquer the scuffle, or pay dearly by being conquered yourself. It's always Dog-Eat-Dog with you."

"I could always make it easier by developing some docile traits, if you'd like."

"Not on your life!" he declared in what seemed the underside of a roar, his voice drifting like the throttle of an engine from the burrow of his throat. "I believe I just gave my compliments to the chef. I also implored that nothing on the menu be changed. Every drop remains too sweet to relinquish any, call me greedy if you will. I'll keep up… somehow." He sighed, and the faint sound of a snicker hummed tamely from the silo of his chest, even as his lips played on the softness of hers. Consuming, then, the nectar on which he had grown to rely.

———

The halls of the massive manse stood deathly quiet, more so than usual. Silence rasped from every wall in the house. Almost two hours had skulked languidly at her back. Stupefied by the earlier occurrence, it had taken every morsel of that before Sam marshaled enough courage to extract herself from the isolation of his office.

With eyes fixed aptly to the floor, her steps waded excessively light, strolling guardedly towards the kitchen as if in forbearance of her last rites. Not wanting to further invade upon the privacy of her boss, her gingered movements told much of the awkwardness she felt. But her dread rested mostly on the woman she so rudely insulted before. What would she tell him on the encounter they had?

As if of their own volition, her feet stammered to a gauche stop. Seeming unsure, she surveyed the lay of the land. *Empty,* her mind interpreted mildly, reciting the acumen as if to hammer an affront to her eyes. Hence, it ignored the grousing of the mixer in Betty's hand, blotting the subtle noise that now filled an otherwise calm room. Relaxed by the result of her search, she busied herself in the undertaking of zilch, confiscating a bottle of water from the door of a massive refrigerator. Her eyes scanned the shelves as if in pursuit of a demented gnat. Like a nebbish child in fear of the chastisement to come, Sam's steps stalled before reaching her destination at the counter. Once there, she waited warily for the whipping to stop.

Thin shoulders almost heaved as a result, indignant at the intrusion, Betty preserved the whirring longer than the need presented itself. Confident she already knew what was about to befall her ears. She gave full heed to the toiling of her hands.

"So, who is she?" Sam queried the instant the whirring stopped.

"Who's who?" Betty asked with a tight frown, spearing the younger woman a mere glance.

"The woman that was at the door,"

"What woman? What door?" Betty grunted, confusion deepening her frown. Moving her hands slowly to her hips, her expression wavered not in its balance of vague curiosity and fuss. "What are you talking about?"

"You didn't see her? They didn't come this way?" Sam probed, showing the fullness of her surprise, curiosity stirred anew.

"Who?"

"Michael and Ju-Julia, yes." She nodded, pleased with her memory of the name. "He called her Julia." Sam smiled, her eyes pasted to Betty's face. Yet the older woman offered her no enlightenment for her trouble, only gifting then a shrug. Her expression remained unchanged.

"Never heard of a…Julia," Betty grumpily informed, dragging a wet towel across the counter, she again shrugged. "But then, I'm not introduced to all his friends. I'm only the help."

"She must be new then. I haven't come across anything about a Julia. Not even for flowers, so she must be new." Sam droned, affirming this with a brusque nod. She gave answer to herself, reasoning the surmise with her ego as if expecting a reply. Held protectively in the role of a confidant, if Betty knew not the least bit about her, then how could she be expected to do better? "How long do you think this one will last?" she asked in a rejuvenated tone, gazing at the older woman's back.

"Who, knows." Betty grunted, chucking a nonchalant shrug. She pushed a finger over the smooth slide of the mixer in her hand, and dark eyes punctually dropped to censor the task. The raised hum promptly drowned out whatever else that was said, absolving her from the need to voice a reply. When again her eyes lifted from their task, the room sat afresh, exactly as she intended—bereft of prattling pest.

———

The oversized dress sagged copiously on her body like loose cloth on a stick. Donning her no better than the first was the coordinating shell—a black knit blazer of the same design, it thrived fruitful in the completion of the clever but inhibitive ensemble of choice. Like her dress, the maladroit wrapper rested slack across her shoulders—front and back. The buttoned enclosure locked in a steep ascension, clambering gaily all the way to the underbelly her chin. Short, graying hair floated tensely atop her shoulders, brushing the thick knit of her collar. It held fast as if compelled so by command. The extravagance of her makeup showed well in the richness of its shading. With copper brushed softly on blue, the vibrancy of both marred the lids of dark eyes. Each gifting a slim tale of the woman they so adorned, as did the reddish rouge of her lips.

Julia smiled as she ambled slowly to her seat, noting, with an odd sense of pride, that she sat only three rows back from a sacrosanct viewing of the stage. Lens, tinted softly of gray, barred full excess to her eyes, skidding tediously down the bridge of her nose. The oversized glasses prompted a low, exasperated sigh, as she again set the useless accessory in place.

At present, the simplicity of being garbed in her own clothes was sorely yearned, although the heat congregating on her scalp was but one reminder of why. Her fellow spectators sprang forth as an amalgamation of the rest. The dress code, it would seem, fell comfortably to stylish. Every outfit looked to have been meticulously nominated by a panel of their peers, and again her mind wandered through her closet as if on a guided tour, slowly building a new outfit in her head.

The spright atmosphere seemed hived with opulent entertainment. Bent on keeping glee endearingly high, the hilarities were not at a loss. For a moment, Oprah stood but a few feet away from her seat, looking professional in a conversation with a member of her staff, mutual affection and respect flowed forward at the end of whatever was said. Scanning the studio measuredly, she flashed a pleasing smile, building in exuberance at an audience member's eager wave. Her soft gaze thence toured the many faces locked aptly on her. Looking like a king assessing his tribe, fondness and pride wafted from her aura before she moved to her seat on the stage.

Michael strode out after long looking as beautiful as ever. Better than he had on what was supposed, at length, as their first date. The sight and circumstance grew no less foreign to her view, than the sluggish scenes in one's dream. Garnering her first tangible glimpse of his public persona, the surreal occurrence played, like the trailer of a movie, for none but an audience of one. Dressed, as usual, in jeans, its dark tinting looked almost black, partnering his jacket that bore similarities to those of a tuxedo. The wrapping, from shoulders to toes, was superbly done. The crisped white of his shirt reflected the lights back to his eyes, making the color further blaze in adjunct of the usual sheen. Or was that just a mirage directed at her? Scrumptious really did not come close when describing his looks, and the provoking vision left her salivating from more places than one. Shouldn't that have dimmed by now?

Thunderous applause vaulted their heads to loiter the dark ceiling like a plume. It vibrated like the trebly claps of cymbals in a vociferous band. Dragging nearly ceaseless in its yielding, she had to concede the moment and the extol for what it was, since, of all people, she fathomed, quite profoundly at that, the cause of their discernment and its relentless depth. The quickening of her pulse promptly elucidated that, pounding madly in her ears in response to the view. With naught but her skin to offer resistance, the frantic gallop knew no end, once the rhythm gave start. And already, she wished the interview was near its end. Deliberately, Julia cast her eyes over the energetic crowd, trying to wane the intensity of her focus, as pride, distended and fierce, now threatened to swallow her whole. Is that normal? She groaned in reproach of herself, reasoning the meaning as less than it should be. Does she even have a right to harbor such boast?

Torturous monologues barricaded themselves in her head, pondering the significance of such plague and, too, the usefulness of her pride in that a lover should. Though before long, the roving of her eyes needed to be stationed to her hands, missing, almost fully, its start or where the interview now bowed. Her probing gaze, she soon found, did not focus merely on the pleasantness of his face, but crawled, instead, over the etching of his person. Dredging ideas and memories rampant in her head, her recollection drew forth from the ribald things they partook of in the past. Things of only hours before, and the antagonistic essence of that, of its own, felt wickedly sinful atop the hillock of everything else. Knowing his every intimate details, preference and likes, flounced sweetly rousing in her head. And gazing at him while she feasted on the knowledge of that did naught to dislodge the pride that she felt.

"Every time I see you, it seems as if another project of yours has aligned you with additional acclaim. Do you get the time to enjoy your success as individuals, or are you usually off to the next thing?" Oprah probed in her soft proficient lilt.

"I think I do." Michael retorted with a slow nod. "I'm not sure if there's an exact science to getting it right, but I do try to incorporate the things and people I enjoy most in my life. That in itself has helped me with attaining some peace. After that, time is just a matter of knowing when to say when."

"So you find balance more a matter of recognition?"

"Mostly that's all life is, really. Recognizing the signs and being able, if you're lucky, to decipher the connotations attached. But if you're fortunate enough to get invited to the smart people's party, you learn factors of their tricks. If you live it, it becomes a habit you'll not soon forget."

"Be the list then?"

"Or something like that. It tends to make things easier once the focus is honed." He rasped, granting then an assured smile.

"With all the success you've had in the stretch of your career, are there still projects out there that grab you as a definite must? Something you consider a subsequent step?" Oprah smiled, adjusting her back to the fit of her chair.

"I'm sure there has to be at least one." He rumbled in a lazy reply. "I don't have a definite list to pluck from, and off the top of my head, none jump directly to mind." Expressing this with a swift moment of thought, Michael shrugged. "Though I don't think I come by my projects by actively plotting the next step. To me, it feels more like rightful selection than anything else. I think it's more likely that they select me." He droned, shifting his lower body. He pulled one leg aloft the other to then rest it on his knee. "Usually, if I come across something that elicits interest, we'll get together and see how the pieces fit, and what, if any, we can bring to the project itself. But other than that, I...I don't really...sweat the process, at least not these days. But I'll admit I'm tenacious once a decision is set." Lifting his broad shoulders in finish, a finger stroked the soft leather of his shoe. "I may not put the expected strain into strategizing what's next, but I'm pretty happy with the way I go about what I do once that selection is made."

"Some say that's a good indication of true love."

"True love?" Michael tested nervously, his shoulders tensing as if a sudden weight was thrown forward in an eerie game called catch.

"Being able to sort through your projects without conceding to the lunacy of work itself," she smiled, clarifying her point before scuttling forward. A new question already waited on her tongue. "I would imagine that enables you to differ the level of care. Would you say then that that's a strategy you weave throughout the many planes of your life? Does that solace also includes Michael or do you separate the two halves fully?"

"Me?" he asked, looking almost stunned.

"Yes." She hummed, her head bouncing as if in assurance of such. "Does your sense of contentment with one carry over into other parts of your life? And if not, what would you consider a constructive step towards acquiring that goal?" Oprah chimed, and trimmed, unpainted nails glided expressively through the air as she spoke, looking mute against the dark of her skin. She adjusted her elbow on the arm of the chair as she awaited his reply.

"Jeez," Michael groaned, shifting his body subtly in his seat. His head waved in wonder. "I keep forgetting you ask the tough questions and I didn't study for this one." A snicker tailed his grumble as the lyric's end, and the audience's, like a single voice, followed in quick pursuit. "I'm really not sure if it does. I've yet to take stock or notice a variance outside the regiment of work. A career of this kind takes many prisoners and oddly, it's quite stingy with the endowments it offers in the span of one's life. I think I've garnered some clues in the process, if you want to survive, then retain only what you need." He shrugged, his eyes suddenly distant. "But I've evolved into a more laid-back guy these days. I kind of just take whatever is being offered and try to be grateful for that."

"Laid-back, huh? Is it to be understood then that you use the universe as your guide?"

"It's a conceivable thought." Michael smiled, his eyes jumping to the audience without registering the details of their faces.

"And not a bad one to adhere to if you can. What are you most proud of? Of all your achievements, which one do you find touches you more or grants you the most fulfillments?

"Africa, hands down." He rasped.

"Really?" she asked while affecting a nod, as if already privy to his thought, and understood his reasons well.

"Without a doubt," he reiterated firmly. "It doesn't flourish or flash with the same pizazz as the other things in my resume. But for those small marvels I get to witness, it's so much better than the rest."

"It truly humbles you, doesn't it?"

"It really does."

"Are you working on anything in particular right now?"

"It seems there's always something in the works, Oprah." Michael griped, shifting again in his seat. "You know Phillip is conscienceless when it comes to me. I think it entertains him to see me jostled to the brink of madness, or perched somewhere between insanity and death. Maybe he thinks that's the best way to keep me out of trouble, I'm not sure. Though you can all hazard your own guess on that. Hi, Phillip," Michael chimed, giving full attention to the camera, he shrugged.

"So of the two of you, Phillip is considered the slave driver?"

"You got it. The man never stops."

"I can see that being so." She chortled, offering then a faintly condescending nod. "Do the two of you still play dirty with the intricacies notched in your practical jokes?"

"What? I hate to tell you this, Oprah, but your staff did not do their homework very well. You have the wrong guest on that. I've never played a practical joke in my life. I think they're quite childish, actually." He insisted in a rumble, fronting his most dissident frown. A noble grandeur affected his lilt.

"Is that right?" Oprah chirruped sweetly, her face beaming full with the beauty of the explosion itself. "I heard somewhere you switched his schedule once with his wife's and that it wasn't until he flew all the way to Paris, for a supposed meeting, that it finally dawned. Is that true?"

Michael's shoulders shook faintly in his vie for control, aided thus with the brush of his hand across the arching of his brows. He straightened the start of a smile. Her words flooded forward like intones of a limerick added in a prosecutor's pitch, and he could not help but respond to the taunt with a semblance of pride, pleased with the sharpness of his skill. It had cost him a pretty penny to ascertain the full reverence of that. But it was well worth every cent to watch Phillip sweat. Hastily crafting a speech to circumvent what, he thought, would tarnish the voluminous body of his wife's career. Though there had been no real need for that, meticulous in his scheming, he had spent hours forging a deal that would insure no mishap in such department as that. Careers are an unspoken rule in this war that they have. Like an ancient relic, it remains forever untouched.

"I'm not sure where your people get their information, Oprah, but that, unequivocally, is pure propaganda at work." He grumbled, while his shoulders yet shook. "Could you imagine the expense to do something like that? Who has that much time on their— ahem, who has that much time on their hands?" Michael shrugged, wiping a hand across his face as if to straighten its falter. He again cleared his throat.

"Rumor has it he got you back…good." Oprah mused, leaning forward in her seat. The familiarity of their friendship showed aptly on her face, for her eyes said she already knew the answer of that. "Your meticulous cunnings are infamous, I'm told. No wonder your projects are as successful as—"

"Yes, the projects! That's it." He preened, feigning confusion even as a grin broadened on his face. "Now I got you, Oprah." Michael warbled, again shifting in his seat. He straightened his back, as like the depicting of a pose. "You lost me there for a while but I got you now. Why, yes, Oprah, Phillip and I work very—ahem, we work very hard to accomplish the projects we have."

"Tell me about that?" she asked, playing his game, though knowing the question enabled her some traction on control.

"There's not much to tell, really." Michael retorted tamely, wobbling his head. His mien slowly softened with the finishing of a shrug. "Just two guys, who became friends, and later, business partners. One with brains and the other a sidekick in training pants." A gust of giggles waded from the audience to the stage, as his gabble ended, and all, he assumed, thought the reference an affront as to the aptitude of his friend, though the truth would be an indubitable shock. With eyes still casted downwards, his utterance came in a soft, evocative pitch, and a faint smile was all that remained from his earlier jest. "There's one project that I'm working on right now that does mean a lot to me." He informed in a matter-of-fact tone.

"Really, what's the premise about?"

"It's about life, really—a love story, actually." Michael droned, shifting nervously in his seat. He adjusted the position of his leg. "Something we've been working on now for almost a year. Usually I don't like to talk about the things I'm working on while in the middle of fine-tuning, but…" Michael shrugged. "We just redid a scene that I thought was so pivotal to the body of the story itself that…well…."

"Now you have me really intrigued. Can you at least give us a hint on what the scene was about?"

"It was about two people connecting. Actually, it would probably be easier to understand if I just showed you. This way you can see for yourself why I was so blown away, and why I think your audience will be as well." He expounded calmly, nodding as if to himself. He eased his body slowly from the chair.

"You brought a clip?"

"Not quite." He droned, and a hypnotic smile dipped to the known expectancy on Oprah's face. Amplifying the vaunt of said smile before he turned, he then stunned the audience with his request. "Maybe it would be easier if I got one of your audience members to help me explain." He muttered friskily, prowling towards the audience with an animalistic bark to his strides. The room exploded from none but the swagger that he showed.

With lance-like effort, fields of hands slashed wildly through a freshly shrilled air, vying for his attention or choice. Hazel eyes danced from one merry face to another in their search, squinting further. Michael peered patiently through the crowd, a sweet, playful smile positioned on his face. Elated eyes landed their choice after what seemed a lengthy sparing with hands, and a finger quickly made its assertion known with the precision of a spear. "You," He announced in an almost arrogant tone, pointing carefully to his choice. He made certain the selection was understood. "The young woman in the black dress, can someone get her attention, please?"

The audience's ruckus reared as a fascinating phenomenon to watch, as the chaos seemed more like a three dimensional movie being played. Julia's gaze roamed inquisitively across the faces of an electrified flock, ferreting for who was to be his lady of choice, unsure why the option should be of any matter to her. A hand brusquely tapped her back as she strained through the process of her own apropos selection. Leisurely in her resolving turn, another came before long to tug sternly on the sleeve of her oversized jacket. Hastening the radius of her turn, she saw that Michael's eyes were now lit to her face, as well as those in the entire studio.

"Could you come up here please?" Michael asked softly. "This will only take a minute."

Julia tapped her chest lightly in disbelief, four fingers pointing shakily to the caging of her breasts, questioning the lucidness of the request itself. Her body flooded with a pulverizing thwack of fear. The gnaw seeming to hover gravely in a semblance of shock.

"Come on up here!" Oprah encouraged with a soft chuckle, looking quickly back at her guest. She noted the ease in which he successfully riled the audience's actions.

Julia stood slowly in anxious reply, moving timidly around the legs of the spectators in her row. She turned numbly towards the stage, finding her fingers swiftly clasped in Michael's hand as he rushed to meet her half way.

"Hi!" Michael smiled as he led her to the stage.

"Hi!" Julia smiled back, giving her answer stiffly. The ferocious stomping in her chest instantly sent her body into a nervous tremble. Of a sudden, the room bred blisteringly bright, almost blinding in its sheen, and she had never wished more, in her life, for darkness to answer to its name.

"Here," Michael smiled, swerving from his stance, he sauntered until his body stood only inches from her own. "I know you're not miked, but you can use mine. It's okay, I won't bite." He announced with a wink, looking out at the audience, a mischievous grin dashed across his face. A soft murmur rose high in answer. Building, like the body of a squall, it rushed forward to the stage. "What's your name?" he asked enduringly calm.

"Gwen." She croaked. The lie tumbling easily from her tongue without hesitance or thought, and she was eternally grateful she remembered the name given to the character she now played.

"Gwen, are you married?"

"No."

"Is there someone special in your life?" Michael asked, leaning close yet again.

"Uh…well, kind of. Yes."

"You don't sound too sure, Gwen, but that's okay. You can tell him for me, when you get home, that he's a very lucky man."

"Okay." Julia sighed; feeling relieved at what she thought was to be the end.

"Now, Gwen, just relax and we'll brew magic together, you and I." Michael advised in a whisper, restraining himself from brushing her cheek, as he wanted desperately to soothe the tense look she now held, as desperately as he needed it himself. "I just have a question I need you to ruminate upon." He announced with a nervous smile, searching her eyes expectantly. He dropped to his knees. The audience's roar rattled his head as it jumped upwards to the roof. Mushrooming around them, it took every ounce of his strength to hold to the focus he had.

"What? N—no——" Julia started, though she quickly stopped her ramble, remembering then that his microphone sat near.

"Gwen, Gwen." He called softly, holding her eyes. His fingers tightened around her hands. "I promise you, this will be painless." He sighed. Reaching in his pocket, he brandished a small diamond ring, raising it to her gaze; he let the luster sit between them like an exclamation to something not said. Icy nuggets caught an abundance of light, sparkling like high beams on a dark, country road. His hand quietly trembled as he again offered her a smile. Taking a long, calming breath, he asked.

"If I told you, you own my heart, and that it beats only in your presence, and slumbers fully in your leave, would you say yes then? If I said your smile feeds my soul, and brightened every aspect of my day, would you say yes then? If I told you I loved you beyond this life and the next, would you say yes then? If I said I wanted more, more picnics, more slow drives home, and more nights by the fire? If I said you're everything I never knew I wanted, yet everything I cannot live without, would you say yes then? If I said I wanted a thousand forevers? A lifetime of untils, and an eternity to savor the pleasure of your jest, would you say yes then? You are my home, my world, and who I choose to be a part of. You're everything that is of dreams, yet your beauty is ever more so in the consciousness of my wake. If I told you all this, would you say yes, then?" he asked, his voice trailing, and the last of his words came as a dying whisper.

The heavy texture of his breath bounced off the pressure now rearing in his skull, sounding loud above the hush that ingested the studio. Michael's eyes anxiously searched her face, seeing shock spilled from the frozen stance she held. His mouth slowly opened, intending to soothe her. Her name formed on the tip his tongue—the name given to her at birth. The very name he's called her by for nigh that of a year.

As if to gift him a warning, someone coughed, and Michael's mouth slammed instantly shut, grateful for the reminder. He resumed his address. "You don't need to say anything," he advised softly. "I don't need an answer. I just…needed you to know." He whispered, standing slowly, his eyes unwavering from her face. Pressing the ring in the palm of her hand, he folded her fingers around the small, diamond encrusted band, covering her tense fist with his hands. He gave her knuckles a gentle squeeze.

"Thank you." Michael muttered through a lethargic breath, reluctantly releasing her hand. He leaned further forward. Affecting, what could only be titled as, an inelegant hug, the stiff gesture further anointed them strangers than the lovers that they are.

The audience stood then, coining their appreciation of the act. Their roars soared superlatively majestic. "Thank you. Thank you." Michael smiled, bringing forth the best of his brood, he watched her from the corner of his eyes. "How about a special hand for…Gwen?" he urged with a polite wave of his hand. "A hand for, Gwen, everyone," he smiled, pointing the way from the stage. "Thank you, Gwen."

"You're welcome." Julia whispered in a tight voice, trying hard to curtail the emotions that now had her firmly in a spin. A tear trickled down her cheek as she nodded her assent, and, in horror, her hand openly shook as she reached to swipe it from its place, bringing forth a nervous laugh as she hurried from the stage. Half the audience reached for their tissues, while the other dabbed at the corner of their eyes, leaving the gesture as inconspicuous as the rest.

A tissue flew to her hand, as if by magic, as she retook her seat. Julia accepted the small towelette graciously, giving her thanks through yet another soft, hysterical laugh. She dabbed the facet of her eyes.

"Now how's that for a proposal?" Oprah asked, her voice shattering the sniffling silence in which they now sat, and again the audience thundered their acquiescence of that fact. "If that's your next project, Michael, you have to come back and grant us first view." She laughed, looking over the audience. She adjusted her posture to again resume the full cusp of control. "I believe I can speak for most of the women here when I say, we definitely want to see the project." She advised with yet another stately laugh, prompting the audience to again erupt in a boisterous billow of applause.

Threadbare, ragged and etched within the creases of time, the universe righted itself, and the niggling of something contradictory to that of a banal sight, rested on a soft murmur for the wont of something else. With the studio settled anew, the interview again retook its professional bend. Michael pushed his best smile forward in a facade between director and self, flashing both audience and host with what he hoped yielded strongly of his creative pride. His eyes bounced aimlessly over their heads, trying his best to stay aloof of the rest.

Needing the moment to be just right, he had spent weeks plotting the intricate qualities of each scenario in his head. From the how to the complexity of his words, the place and every morsel in-between, were all meticulously prearranged like a storyboard for his work—all without parting with a single clue. With the severity of her disguise, he expects the tabloids to run with the already glib view, since no one would believe his proposal carried the legitimacy of a valid stunt. Not with her age, or, for that matter, her presumed pedigree.

Coughing lightly, Michael shifted in his chair on the shadow of a vague reply, giving answer to yet another probe on the secluded sphere of his life, and feeling anything but the cordiality of that. Pretending the need was not as it seemed, as his eyes, almost of their own will, searched out her face. *She's crying! Damn! Could that be good tears or bad tears?* He gasped, almost muttering the question out loud. He fought the urge to rush to see why. Taking a breath to settle the roiling in his head, he missed the next question asked.

"Michael?" Oprah called softly. "Are you okay?" she asked as his attention again swerved.

"I'm...I'm sorry." He sighed, sounding more casual than he felt.

"Are you alright?" she asked, her voice professional. Yet concern was well evident in her eyes.

"I don't..." Michael gulped, twisting calmly in his seat. He fumbled in search of the perfect words that would rightly fit his cause, something—anything—to excuse himself without furnishing suspicion. "I think skipping that nuisance called eating has finally made a statement of its own. My stomach seems suddenly in the mood to dish out its punishment for such deeds." He rasped, giving the half-truth with a meager smile.

"Would you like to take a break, perhaps get something to eat?"

"How much longer?" he asked, shifting again in his seat. Hope rushed forward on the silent wing of a plea. While a break would be well appreciated, being done sounded more like an exalting treat. For there were pressing matters he needed to attend.

"Just two more questions." She smiled, throwing a faint look of apprehension in the direction of her producer. She quickly scanned the card in her hand.

"No, I'll finish." He murmured coolly through the practiced perfection of his smile.

"Are you sure? I don't mind taking a break if you think it would help."

"I'm sure." Michael averred with yet another charismatic show, reaching for his drink. He took a tentative sip. The water was exactly as he liked it, chilled to near freezing, though the untainted hydrant did not rear favorable on this day. Poisoned with his fears, the taste was almost as harsh as the rusted bite of metal itself, stinging the rawness of his senses in its race to a hollow destination. The tell, in this paucity, flourished in the flinch that flashed openly on his face. "Let's just finish." He nodded, taking a deep breath as he straightened in his chair. Giving, then, what he hoped were plausible answers to her concluding queries, though he could not say with certitude what the questions were that he gave answer to.

Only knowing one need, he pondered the relevance of her response, hoping she'd concede with the answer he desperately sought. A simple word so freely given, yet, most times, flew with the merest of thought. Until that time with which it's used to transform the impetus of someone's life.

Three little letters, bound in a body of one, sprout ubiquitous in the way of its use. Given blithely in an answer to a friend, perchance to affirm a selection or assent to the heralding of one's name. Whispered in a ceaseless breath throughout the carcass of a day, the importance was usually thin, except on this—his most exigent day. When three little letters held him mercilessly as its hostage, that is, at least until she speaks.

Though it closed with a haughty outburst, the hotel-room door gusted open with controlled vigor holding it taut. Julia sprang promptly to her feet in stunned reply, shifting red, puffy eyes apprehensively upon the new inhabitant now crowding the entry. She braced herself instinctively for what would have to come, though what that was she was yet unsure. In silence, both bodies stood startlingly lifeless, yet a bevy of emotions plagued the dark crevices in their heads, some waltzing as vivid as the afternoon sky.

"I'm sorry." Michael whispered at last, taking a single step towards her, he stopped. His eyes dispensed then the full province of his love, holding her with tenderness in their depths, adoration spread wide across his face. "But only for any discomfort my actions may have brought you. I want to marry you. I won't apologize for that." He proclaimed softly, his voice trembling from the far edge of his throat.

His words lanced aptly through the carapace of her menial defense. Seeming astute to his pained restraints, Julia quietly dropped her eyes. Her head followed as a tear skidded down the soft ridge of her cheek. "I don't know why I keep crying like this." She shrugged, attempting a halfhearted laugh. She quickly turned from his gaze.

"It's because of the same reason it hurts me to see you like this. You love me, as deeply as I love you."

"Is this your answer or your hope, Michael?" she quizzed, offering him the full fencing of her back as he stepped close.

"I know this for a fact. I'm as certain of that as the breath I rely on. You grant me that every time you touch me, or when I look in your eyes. I know you like I know myself." Asserting this without hesitation or pause, his voice flowed to her unaltered, as if none but truth fell from his lips.

"Okay. So there's no doubt." Julia attested weakly, sounding almost lost as she wobbled her head. Her stance looked somehow guarded in the way that it's held, eyeing him from the corner of her eye as if suspicious of his next act. His chest calmly penned the drooping of her back.

"Then wouldn't this be the next step?"

"And I would say yes, yesterday if I didn't have my children's wellbeing to think of. This can't be just about—"

"But you do have the children. I know that. So what does that make it now?"

"Now..." Julia sighed, her voice wilting like the finish in a forlorn tale. "Now I just don't know." She shrugged, wanting desperately not to cause him pain, though her heart seemed oblivious of none but that. "Now we have a lot to discuss."

"I know why you can't look at me." He rasped, threading his fingers through hers. He filled his lungs to their maximum fill, releasing the air in a rush. His entire trunk followed the torrent's descent. "It's the same reason I know why you cry. I wish there was a simple way to have you experience the things you make me feel. I come alive when I'm with you, Julia. You're my first, did you know that?" He smiled. "You're my first in every sense of the word. You're my first love. I've never loved anyone before, not in the same way I feel for you. I've never wanted, needed or liked anyone this much in my life. I can't imagine my life without you. I would sooner hurt myself than see you hurt.

"Without trying, you've given me everything I've needed, and so much more that I never once thought that I would. My time with you has given me more happiness than my entire life devoid of any knowledge of you. Am I being selfish for wanting more of that? Am I selfish for wanting you to be mine in every way? I love you. I'm yours, body and soul, regardless of time. There's no one else for me, Julia. I just want you."

"Michael…" Julia pleaded, brushing back a tear. "I don't want to be difficult, I just—"

"I know." He assured sagely, turning her shoulders until she faced him fully. "I don't just love you, Julia. I adore everything about you. The kids are a part of that."

"But you have no experience with that."

"I also had no experience with someone like you, or these types of feelings, but I've held my own. Haven't I? I'll protect the kids as fiercely as I would protect you."

"But…a father, Michael? You hardly had time to get use to the whole…relationship…thing."

"I never wanted a wife either. Yet here I am begging you to be mine. I'm begging that you not let another day pass without you agreeing to be mine in every way."

"I love you, and I would love to marry you, but—"

"Are you that afraid?"

"I'm not afraid. I'm just worried about the adjustment for the kids as well as for you."

"Okay." Michael smiled, warmth surging forward discreetly, satisfied with her answer. Hope suddenly spread forth its wings.

"I saw that."

"What?" came the elusive return, an innocent glint burning bright in his eyes.

"You know what." Julia shrugged, trimming the edges of a pained expression, her face softened at last. "What should I do with you?" she sighed, a half smile creasing the corners of her mouth. How do you say no to the person that matters to you most? Outside of her children, no one surpassed the level he held. She'd never been happier, not at any other point in her life. And the man she loves is asking her to take a stance at his side, build a life together under the title of one.

"Marry me." Michael whispered hoarsely. "Then I'll tell you the rest."

"Do you see our future, too?"

"Nothing past silver hairs, brittle bones and hearing lost."

"That's it?"

"That's it."

"Wouldn't you like to wait a little longer, Michael?" Julia queried softly.

"What for?"

"So you can get better acquainted with the idea of jumping from one to three. Why not wait, why would you want to so soon?"

"Because I want to," he shrugged. "I want to so that when I say wife, it's you that will answer, and when you say husband, I want to be the one whose face you seek. Whose arms you come home to, and whose bed you're always in. I want to because you are the air that I breathe. Yours is the first face that I see when I open my eyes, and the last at the end of each day. I want to because life has an end and my end is with you. I want to because you are you, and just because. I want to. I want to. I want to. I just want to." Michael coaxed, stretching a hand to her, he resumed his appeal.

"Give me your hand, Julia, become my consort in every way. Take my name and let me spend the rest of my life loving you. Take my name and we can spend however long you want making it comfortable for the kids. Take my hand. We can do this. I promise you, we can. I just want to start my life with you, now. I don't want to wait any longer. Give me your hand and say you'll marry me." He prodded in a raspy breath, his hazel eyes, beautifully soft, fixed tenderly to hers.

"You knew, didn't you?" she asked in a low murmur, staring hard at his reaching palm. "You knew what my answer would be?" she quizzed, placing her palm gently in his hand.

Long, lean fingers closed slowly, wrapping itself snug around the slenderness of her hand, he gave an affectionate squeeze. "I had faith." Michael rasped, with eyes fixed softly on the firm enclosure of his hand. He allowed the first manifestation of a smile to churn softly on his face.

"Was it faith in me, faith in you, or faith in my love for you?"

"All of the above." He smiled, pulling her into his body. He fused her to his frame. "I trusted everything that is beautiful between us to wear you thin."

"How is it you get me to do these things so outside of my personality?" Julia groaned, her query sounding like a smothered grumble from her place against his chest. Lodged there firmly by the prominence of his embrace, his arms fitted her body like a tailored vest. Quietly, in answer, Michael lifted her chin, angling her face to his, his eyes probed the brown orbs before his head lowered to hers, and a sweet, gentle fire grew within her the further he delved. Built by the passionate foray that paid aid to his kisses, it set both bodies ablaze.

"Because you can kiss me like that," Michael assured huskily, his voice combing the air like freshly kindled wood.

"That's it?"

"That's all it took. You had me the moment my eyes had its first look at those lips and since this is not the time to talk about my samplings of the past, you'll just have to take my word for it when I say, you're the best at everything you do." He averred, his eyes brimming with mischief, and a fiendish leer played havoc with the wont of his brows. Lifting the trim bushes to their extreme height, he asked. "Where's the ring?"

Quietly uncoiling her fingers, she revealed the small sphere still yet buried beneath the tissues in her hand. Unwilling to dislodge it from the precise place chosen by his hand, the tiny object had fully dominated her thoughts.

Promptly taking the small ring from her hand, Michael smiled, dropping the gold band in the outer pocket of his jacket. He reached inside to the garment's breast, bringing forth a second ring, day flaunt its eminence of night. With a glare that flounced larger than the first, its beauty gushed from a galaxy unlike any before now, for worlds separated the crafting of the two.

Holding the ring high between them, his eyes travelled slowly to hers, smiling fondly. Their brilliance sparkled like the gems on the jewel in his hand, and for the second time in one day. Michael lowered himself to a knee before the woman that he loves. Taking a deep breath, he again recited the resolve of his pledge, using the strongest resonance he had, though it came to her like the sweet lyrics of a song.

"I want to spend nights just kissing you. I want to slate time to taste every inch of your body. I want to fall asleep with you locked in my arms. Feel you next to me in the dark, and wake with you as my sunrise. I want to be there on the days when you're sad. Dance with you on those that your happiness surfeits the opulent rims of its reservoirs, and play with you on those when your giddiness boils without end.

"I want to be there when your hair goes gray and your sight dwindles and dims, still loving you even more then than I do now. I want to get lost in the woods with you. Sleep under the stars with you at my side, and grant you all the magnificence that money could never buy. You're my Juliet. My Mona Lisa, my princess and my queen. And I vow to take the rest of my life savoring that, savoring us, so savoring you. I love you more than I ever thought I possibly could, and it would be, to me, a peerless marvel if you would grant me the honor of procuring the heart I have long missed." He pledged. His voice dimming to a soft tremor in the back of his throat, as his words, in finale, gradually stilled. Nervously sliding the ring onto her finger, his hands worked like an unsteady clasp in sealing its end. Moist eyes then slowly lifted to the equally dank visage of hers, and a strained, clumsy smile jumped forth as the last of his offering. He had no words left with which to ply her, as his heart was now fully spent.

"How much more of this do you expect to get out of me?" Julia asked with a nervous laugh, forsaking the spill down her cheek, trembling fingers matted the doused corners of her eyes.

"Maybe just a little bit more," Michael answered in a husky breath, straightening before her, he smiled. "As long as they're not from sadness I don't mind one bit." He vowed, his eyes dropping quietly to her hand, gazing long at the ring now prominently posed against the almond tint of her skin.

"I love you." She hummed as four fingers moved smoothly across the slopes of her cheeks, removing the translucent tracks in a slow glide down the gradient path.

"I know." He hummed through the embarking of a kiss, caressing her mouth with his warmth. His words fell as tender as his breath.

A satisfied sigh climbed lusciously from the dark depths of her throat. Sweeping the muteness from the room, it spiraled through them like librettos of an ancient hymn.

Julia adjusted her body against the hardened expanse of his, assuredly, she asserted her will. In slow measure, she enticed the intensifying passion in their kiss. Rousing him rapidly to a smolder, she pasted their bodies as if they were but one.

"Okay. Let me stop now before I'm reaching for seconds." Michael grumbled hoarsely, straightening from the press of her body. He took a long, cleansing breath.

"How can you already skip to seconds if you haven't yet sampled the main course?" she asked coyly, a petulant knit to her brow.

"Actually, I was hoping to have that particular meal as your husband." Michael professed tamely, his words drizzling in, what sailed as, a croaky breath, seeming somewhat hesitant as he dropped his gaze to hers.

His voice drifted to her low and husky, and like a poet narrating the blues. The harmony curved, dipped and swaddled with the author's intent. Yet, it lent a provocative sting to her senses. Training her eyes sharply to the details of his face, Julia smiled. Certain there was more to come that he hadn't yet told. "As my husband?" she repeated slyly. "Do you mean to tell me that I now can't show you my new mole until we're married?"

"You have a new mole?"

"Do you want see it?"

"Where is it?"

"I don't have one. But I *could*. Where would you like me to put it?" Julia goaded, stepping forward, she leaned hard against his hip.

Michael smiled, appreciating her test of the boundaries he created for himself. Grateful he had a sound method to the perceived madness he now dealt, as his decision was not meant to make this a more difficult task than it was. "Let me make it up to you." He invited in a whisper, his voice warm against her cheek. "Even if I have to stay up all night to see the deed done, you can punish me in any way you see fit."

"Is that so?"

"What do you say?" Michael continued in a murmur. "I do have a plan. I'm not as crazy as you might think."

"And what part am I expected to play in this...so-call plan of yours?"

"Not much really." He shrugged. "Just a simple '*I do*' should take care of that."

"But I already agreed to do that."

"*Now...*"

"Now! Now? What do you mean...'now'?"

"Well, technically it would be in a few hours, but..." Michael shrugged. "It could definitely be perceived as...now."

"Are you trying to tell me you're asking me to marry you now, Michael? Today...'now'?" she bayed, her finger stabbing forcefully towards the floor with the emphasis of each word.

"I told you, I didn't want another day to go by without you being my wife."

"Do you even know what you're asking, Michael?"

"I know this may feel a little strange, but it's not to me. I've been thinking about this for some time now. I know what I want, and I don't want to wait. Why should I? Why should we?"

"Because there are things worth considering, that's why."

"Like what?"

"Like…well. Like the church, a dress, family, schedules and a whole long list of do's which seem to have escaped my mind right now."

"We can deal with all of that after. All we need now is each other and a minister. That's all I need. After that, we can make plans to include others. Marry me a second or third time if you want. Whatever it takes to make you happy, I'll do it. Just this time let's do it for us."

"Michael." Julia called in a soft exasperating breath, feeling the grasp on her logical battle slipping sharp.

"Julia." Michael bade in his own gentle breath. "Can you just give me one thing without a fight?" he asked, giving her a tender kiss. He persisted with his sell. "It will be okay, I promise. Take as much time as you need to draft things with Rachel and Richard, or with your family and friends. I'll defer to your wisdom on every part of that as long as you do it as my wife." Reasoning thus, a chuckle burst from his lips. "Funny isn't it?" he groaned.

"What is?"

"That the man who swore he'd remain a bachelor for life is the one now doing the pleading. Nor can he wait to recite or live the true substance of his vows."

"Why do you think that is?" she asked in a low voice, already knowing his answer. But having it confirmed or explained could go a long way to rid her of this sense of flippancy she felt with herself, knowing how deeply she wanted to accept. Can a mother run off and marry a man after so short a time? A man her children haven't even had the chance to fully befriend? Wouldn't that be irresponsible of her?

"I have nothing definitive to give you beyond the generic remedy of faith. I can't provide you with concise details on the ins and outs or how the variation works. I'm not even certain of the what, whys or how. It just feels as if I've loved you forever, and I don't want to waste a drop of what we have.

"Life is short, Julia, and I've done a lot of stupid things in mine that I should have resisted. Wasted a lot of time on mistakes—most of which have harvested me none but regrets come the light of day. This, however, will never be one. You are the first to come forth baring answers—more so than concern. Answers that is as plainly appointed as the explosive imminence of dawn itself, and as sure as I am that that emergence grant over a new day, I know truly that we are but one."

"Can you tell me then I'm not being selfish for wanting this?" she asked, sounding utterly confused. "Can you tell me I'm not being foolish for wanting a life with you?" she sighed, and fear hissed back sharply from the belly of her words. She needed him to affirm that her feelings were not born of madness. For she needed to know that this was not the fruit of some childish illusion she'd somehow overdosed on. As she wanted desperately to accept everything now offered in his pitch.

"Are you ever frightened of me, Julia?" Michael gently probed, his eyes dropping to the ring now fingered on her hand.

"No, never!"

"I am. I am of us sometimes." He confessed in his gravelly timbre, his eyes still locked on her hand. "I'm afraid we'll progress to a point where I'll lose myself in these feelings that I have, though not enough so that I would change one thing about us. Every fear that I've had about this—these very steps—all have settled and tilted in place with you, for in you everything just feels right, as natural a step as hunger needing to feed."

A tame smile surfaced in finish as silence fell. Michael wagged his head as he lifted her hand to sit, like a podium, between them. His gaze still yet tethered to the sparkle atop her finger. Quietly, his thumb moved like a pendulum across the luster of its face. "Julia, we're not two people who just met. We're not caught up in some new surge of lust or in the splendor of the moment. I love you as certain as you love me. It's not selfish or foolish to want something more for yourself. We started backwards, I know that, and the marriage will put us even more in the rear. But we'll put it right. Together we'll fix that. It's really not that hard to do. There's nothing here that a little time won't take care of or set straight. I'm still here, Julia. It's been almost a year and I'm still here. And I'm going to still be here for many more to come. So you need to plan on that.

"I'm here to tell you, this is not the movies nor the scuffed lines sketched in some freaky off Broadway show. This is real life. Yours. Mine. You're not going to give me a reason good enough for me to storm out or walk away. My life is just not the same without you in it, and I don't intend to find out how. I don't want to go back to where I've been. I want you in my life and I'm prepared to do whatever it takes. So you'd better understand that." He warned, his shoulders scaling the cool air as he took a protracted breath, bringing her hand softly to his chest. He held it in place with the other of his hand. "For once, Julia, say it because you want to. For once, tell me what you truly feel. For once, Julia, take it because it's offered and you know truly that that's what you want. Take it, because you know it's the right thing."

Julia stared at the hand curled strongly around the slighter of hers, his words now drubbing through her head, echoing those of her own. They sailed prominent as if he had tooled through her mind and garnered a clue as to her simmering wish. "I do want you, Michael. I want everything you've given me thus far and more. I want to watch the sunset with you until the sky goes black, yet never having to police the clock as a supplement of that. I want you next to me always without having to count the days until when. I want to talk to you, play with you, without ever having to press end. I want everything and the more to come. I want you." She smiled. "I always did and always will. But…"

"Then let me give that to you."

"Do you even understand how much you'll be giving up?" she asked. "Things like spending the weekend naked in bed, or openly fondling each other. The same goes for smutty conversations, and there'll be nights when you're lying in bed without…."

"I'll learn to whisper, or we can develop our own sign language. We'll go to bed naked instead of taking the whole weekend for that, and I have a plethora of closets in which to fondle you in, anything else?"

"So you're sure? You're sure this is what you want? You're sure this will not veer, for you, as some nightmare you'll wish to wake up from after a spell?"

"The only nightmare I see, Julia, is if I let you walk out of my life."

"Okay. Not that there was ever any chance of that, but I get it." Straightening her posture with a long, lazy breath, Julia nodded, gaining a new sense of purpose from the sureness of his words. "Do you still want me?"

"This and every moment until you say yes. After that we'll talk."

"Then…yes. Yes. I will marry you—today." She declared in a near whisper, her eyes suddenly bright with the glistening spill of her tears. "Yes." She repeated as if affirming the decision with herself, though her voice dwindled to a soundless brush.

Time halted amidst the scant chasm that loitered inside the position they held. It tarried much between the sloth-like beats of his heart. Hovering betwixt the flutter of a mockingbird's wings, it lingered thusly between a man and the woman he loves. The answer was his and time again moved anew. "Yes?" he asked in a strained breath, looking on the verge of a happy burst, yet he remained somehow unsure, his eyes wide as if searching for the meaning to something else. Would she never once troubled his mind, only the matter of—when—soared forward as a bother to his nerves. How long would it take him to convince her to take that chance was his only concern. Without waiting a reply, his mouth crushed hers in a devilishly peppered kiss.

"Mmm, God, I love the way you kiss me." She sighed in pause.

"It's my most favorite thing to do." Michael rumbled back.

"I remember hearing that somewhere." She purred.

"You know, you're making this very hard." Michael growled. Pressing his hips firmly to hers, his hand strolled leisurely down her back. Even while he struggled to stem the progression his body sought.

"And here I am thinking I was being easy." Leaning her breasts further into his chest, she offered then a provocative smile.

"I like what comes after as much as I like the beginning." He informed then, offering a roguish smile. "If we start, I'll want to take my time, and…" Michael shrugged, his voice sounding hoarse. "I like our playtime. But we have a flight to catch and a schedule to keep.

"Just so I know I have this scenario correctly, you're turning me down, right?" Julia quizzed, a hand moving slowly to the protruding knot on her hip, and perfect brows arched in the wonderment of that.

"No, I'm only delaying, and since you know I'm putty in your hands, I give you leave to take your frustrations out on me at length."

"Now that I think about it, I think I feel a headache coming on."

"You wouldn't deny a husband all the merits adorning his wedding night now, would you?" he hummed, kissing the side of her neck. Michael's hands rolled down the soft flesh of her buttocks in a slow caress, pressing her staunchly to the expression of his body. "I promise you, if it takes me a lifetime of nights to make this up to you, I'll put the work in." He smiled, dropping an assemblage of kisses along the thin curving of her shoulders.

"Smooth. But it doesn't feel quite like putty to me." She cooed. Her hand sutured to the engorged member while her fingers yet played.

"And it wouldn't, not in the hands of its master."

"How can I be the master when the one who wheels it wheels it so well?"

"He's only a soldier trying to please his commander with the aptitude of his work, that's all."

"Smooth and sly, what does a girl do with one like you?" Julia smirked, taking a breath as she straightened.

"I'm sure I could come up with a few ideas on that."

"I bet you could. But you have a schedule to keep, remember?"

"This conversation will be revisited after, you can guarantee that." He assured in a grumble, his eyes bounding from hers. Glancing around the virtually lifeless living-room, as there was hardly any sign of their stay in, this, the second in a trio of suites, an old precautionary habit he will not soon forsake of.

"Am I leaving as Gwen or as someone else?" she called as he turned for the adjoining suite.

"No. Gwen will be taking a well needed vacation. Just in case there's some chatter about a certain event, it works better this way. Why don't you try being a man, or maybe just a masculine woman? That might be fun."

"And what if you get caught discretely grabbing some guy's backside?"

"Then they wouldn't be looking for Gwen now, would they?"

"But the rumors may not be very pretty after that."

"But you'll know the truth there, won't you?" Michael smirked, folding his arms casually across his chest. "Besides, we won't be able to keep this quiet forever, but it's been very nice having that. So I vote we keep it for as long as we can."

"I don't have anything to help me in the process of becoming a man."

"Just do the best you can. As long as you don't look anything like yourself, you should be fine."

"Is Sam flying back with us?"

"No. She'll be otherwise occupied. I sent her on a task that should take up the rest of the day, and probably most of the weekend, if we're lucky. We shouldn't be interrupted at least through the ceremony." Michael smiled, his eyes flashing with glee. "Did you hear? I'm getting married today."

"I don't have a dress! What am I supposed to wear?" Julia frowned, suddenly startled with the realization of that.

"Already in the works," Michael assured with an arrogant smile. "I told you, there's a definite method to my madness. Now, there's still a few details left to attend, but a few phone calls will see to that." He warbled. "Just sit tight and it'll be done before you know it.

"So, y—you…bought me a dress? A wedding dress?" she asked with reservation pairing her tone. Uncertain of what emotion she should let to the surface in, this, a plainly unorthodox case, knowing the groom was responsible for the bride's dress.

"Don't look so worried. I think you'll be pleased. My eye is not as bad as all that. Didn't I do a good job on your dress?"

"True." Julia nodded, remembering the elegant gift and her fondness for the style. "You did do very well on that." She agreed with a soft shrug, replacing her frown with an accepting smile.

"Then relax your worry; trust me. I have everything fully in the works." Michael smiled, waving the phone in his hand. He turned again towards their shared suite. "Give me a few minutes to get the ball rolling and we'll be out of here before long. Now, just sit back, relax, and make yourself look not, at all, like you. Go as opposite or as weird as you can, and I'll be right back."

Without waiting a reply, he left her standing alone in the large suite. Julia stared after him from her own befuddled cloud, wondering further on the many things said this day. *Was this really to be her wedding day?* She asked wondrously, turning her gaze out the window. *And in that, shouldn't the bride know something of the preparations regarding such end?* She smiled, showing the vagueness of her worry on that. Outside, the afternoon sun seemed a contradiction to the weighty jackets spread across the pedestrian's backs. Looking intense, it bathed the day radiantly in its majestic glow. That is, until you step fully under its waning heat.

Chapter Forty Two

"Mom, what kind of wedding do you think you can put together in four hours?"

"Well, that depends greatly on whose wedding we're talking about, son. Some visions can go a long way."

"How about for your son, would that do well as incentive?"

"What? You asked?"

"And she said yes." Michael intoned gently, his deep voice sailing back as an almost sigh.

"Are you serious?"

"Never more so, mom. Can you believe it?"

"Michael, that's wonderful! That's so fantastic! Congratulations, son!" Hyacinth squawked, her manner seeming barely lucid through the earpiece of the phone. "Wait! When? Son, are you trying to tell me you're getting married? Not just that, but…you're getting married…today?"

"But I need your help to fully pull it off."

"Don't take this the wrong way, son, but…why the rush, why not next week or next month, or…?"

"I want to marry her, mom, and I want to marry her now. I don't know what else to tell you beyond what's obvious. Maybe it's due to the limits that has hounded our time together; from the very beginning, our adventures has been inexorably crimped. I don't know. I don't know what drives this beyond any of that. I just know I don't want to wait any longer to claim her as mine. I want to take that next step to start our lives together, right here, right now. It's been basically a year and yet it feels as if I've been waiting forever. I don't want to waste another minute of that. So," he droned, taking a renewed breath. "Will you do it? Can you help me iron out the rest?"

"I see bliss has neglected to remind you who you're talking to, son." She preened, a light melody already dressing the significance of each word. "There's no one better than your mother at putting what seems the impossible together or in as little time. Now, tell me what you have so far." Hyacinth crooned, satisfied with the answer he supplied. Her excitement crept to a mountainous high. How could it not? She reasoned with a sly smile, when she now had her own son's wedding to plan.

Michael trundled off a short list of already completed tasks. His raspy voice drenched with excitement as he dispatched, to her, all that he had yet to attend.

Hyacinth listened fixedly to the details he gave, quietly assembling a docket of her own—thick with the things she judged, should be, of the utmost importance for a juncture as this. Affectionately, she set aside a vast sum of his bland ideas, dropping them coolly by the wayside. She assimilated concepts of her own, using her feminine aptitude to remind him of the prominence linked with such day, and what that stood for, for a bride. In prudence, he acceded to the wisdom she advocated in spades, leaving all remaining plans to the sole authority of her hands, just as she had envisioned the process from the start.

The caller's name had not the time to dispel from the small screen yet girdled in her hand, lingering as if to watch, it loitered as her voice scaled the air like the sweetened tune of a harp. Hyacinth dashed towards the once mute refuge of her office. Her voice soaring as she bellowed, with exuberant beauty, for her own help. Dropping her body hard into a stylish leather chair, her fingers raced over the buttons of her phone, pouncing on the first from a long list of contacts, some that will definitely be recruited as aid.

"Sarah! How fast can you get your hands on a few wedding gowns and have them delivered to my house?" Hyacinth opened, not bothering with her usual lengthy greeting.

"Ah…what size?" Sarah asked, her frown communicated flawlessly through the phone.

"Um…four or there about, yes. I think size four should be good."

"Why? Who's getting married?" Sarah probed, letting her own curiosity best the intention she had.

"Um, try, Michael!" Hyacinth hastily supplied, and the jollity in her tone was hardly subdued.

"Yeah, right, that would likely be on the next side of never!" She exclaimed, half laughing at the absurdity of the jest. "Michael? Please. No one is going to fall for that." Groaning this, her hand flew to her hip in defiance as well as disbelief. Thinking the older woman only teased, she goaded the farce further to a head. "Who exactly do you plan to say he's marrying—Julia? Oh, my God! That's it, isn't it? He's marrying her?"

"You got it. The one and only," Hyacinth smiled, pulling a notepad from the top draw of her desk.

"Oh. My. God! I knew there was something between them!" Sarah chirped, showing fully her excitement at the thought. "He was never truly himself whenever she was around. That's so romantic! Oh, my God! This is awesome!" she continued without the relevance of an added breath, rambling through her applause faster than what's considered normal, even for her. "God, that face of hers got him, didn't it? But Phillip said she turned him down. Well…never mind, all that doesn't matter now, does it?" Sarah professed swiftly, sobering her mind in a flash, she took an audible breath. "So, when is the big day? I want to design the dress."

"How does today work for you?" Hyacinth teased, setting her back firm as if to amplify her words.

"What do you mean 'today'? Do you mean today—today?" Sarah queried, her already chirpy voice growing high.

"I mean to say, today—today." Hyacinth replied calmly, calmer than the bales of excited nerves she willfully kept anchored at bay. "Or if you'd prefer, it could be simplified to that of mere hours—that today."

"That's so romantic!" Sarah squealed in a strained tone.

"It does hold a certain...*je ne sais quoi* to the whole feel, doesn't it?" Hyacinth chirped, pride galloping forward in the many tiers of her voice.

"Unquestionably so! Who knew?" she huffed, slapping her palms together as if to signal their start. "What can I do? I want a job."

"The dress is the most important part."

"I know that. But that's easy enough for me. I'm the reason why they met, remember? I'm the one who recommended and then pushed for them to check out her book. I want to be in involved. I want a job."

"Fine. Flowers. Get your hands on as many flowers as you can, once you get here."

"You got it!"

"Good! Then I'll see you and Phillip in a few hours."

"I wouldn't miss it for the world!"

"That goes without saying." Hyacinth beamed in reply, severing the call as perfectly manicured nails slid promptly over the button to indicate just that. Without bother or hesitancy marring her efforts, she again scrolled through a lengthy itinerary of names, selecting another. Hyacinth's fingers wasted no time, drubbing anxiously on the surface of her desk as she waited for the call to connect. Deeming three rings an eternity, she almost groaned in exasperation before Betty's small voice came in pleasant greeting on the other end.

"Betty! Guess what our boy did?" Hyacinth queried, again barreling forward without her usual playful address.

"He popped the question!" Betty shrieked, her small voice heaving at least five octaves beyond what was considered her customary chants.

"Damn! You're never any fun to talk to." Hyacinth griped, slapping her hand piercingly to the surface of her desk.

"He did? I knew it! I knew he was getting ready to do something." Betty cheered, happiness wafting through every cell in her body.

"Fine! Since you're so smart, why don't you tell me the rest?" Hyacinth grumbled almost sternly.

"What else can there be? He asked and she said 'yes'." Betty shrugged. "Now we'll get to have that wedding we've always wanted."

"Yes, we will. But did that crystal ball of yours give you any inkling that it would be today?" Hyacinth smirked. Happy to finally have some news that the other woman hadn't already guessed, or just outright knew before her.

"Today?" Betty frowned, her voice again coming high. "Where?" she barked, hoping the voice on the other end would not say what came to her mind.

"You're standing in it." Hyacinth answered coolly, knowing full well what the other woman feared, and understood the depths to which such lapse would sting. Since an oversight as that would hurt her just as deeply as it would the other. Elopement would surely be an acrid word for them both.

"Okay, how many people?" Betty hastily asked. Her mind already racing to the mission she assigned herself.

"Well, there's you, me, them, Sarah and Phillip and the minister which would make it seven—seven. Oh, Michael was going to call her mother, so make that eight. But I was thinking of just calling a few caterers to see what we could put together from that. You know, since the notice is so short. It'll be less work."

"If we're only having eight people, then nobody is touching the food besides me. Do you know how long I've been waiting to have one of these?"

"Yes. I believe I do, since I was right there waiting alongside you all this time." Hyacinth grumbled, scribbling another addition to her now extensive list. She surveyed the result with attentive care.

"I knew she was good for him. I just knew it!" Betty laughed, ignoring the other woman's rant. She swung opened the refrigerator door.

"Yes; now you spill it! Even though you wouldn't share your information with me before, I didn't hold it against you now, did I? See how nice I am? I called you so I could share."

Betty pulled open a large tray of mixed fruits in an effort that seemed distant. Checking her supplies, she mentally plunged through both recipes and ingredients for the upcoming event. "You know I can't tell you what's not mine to tell."

"I know. But it doesn't make it any easier when the actual mother is always left in the dark. But I'll forgive you that wicked folly, especially now, since I get to plan the wedding. God, I'm so excited!" Hyacinth chirped. "Don't kill yourself going overboard now. Remember, it's only eight people, and no one will really be eating. Do you hear me, woman?"

"Sure. And I guess I should take a moment to also remind you that, it is, after all, just the eight of us, and that means everything does not need to be perfect. You did hear that, right?"

"I heard you. Did you hear me?" Hyacinth asked sedately, adding a few scribbles to her list.

"I heard you." Betty shrugged, skirting the island on her way to the pantry. Her movements intensified as she unloaded ingredients from a shelf.

"Do you want me to send Margaret to help in the house?"

"Help is good. I won't turn it down." Betty rejoined, seeming suddenly frigid and aloof.

"So you have your end under control then?"

"Do you?"

"I guess we'll just have to wait and see then, won't we?" Hyacinth shrugged, her eyes busy in the scanning of her notes.

"I guess we will."

"I'll be there in about two or three hours to set up my side."

"I'll be here working on mine." Betty grumbled back, already rushing back to her quarters to grab what she needed to leave.

"So I'll see you then."

"Hey!" Betty called softly. "Congratulations!" she murmured, pausing in her hurry.

"Thanks, same to you."

"Thanks. Some journey, huh?"

"That's for sure." Hyacinth sighed, and heard a long push of the same from the other end. The small pause grew pleasantly long, as both women basked in the nicety that came with the pending event.

"Later." Betty whispered sternly, breaking the lengthy pause.

"Much later," Hyacinth sanctioned quickly, knowing fully the meaning behind the single word. With so much to do and so little time to do it in, now was not the time to ruminate on the past.

In the silence that followed the perplexing call, Hyacinth consulted her now elongated list. Feeling satisfied that nothing had escaped her in the planning; her laboring became as eternal as a perpetual cog. Solving every prospective problem with yet another call, determination grew to a maddening fault.

In mere hours, everything she needed was near completion or waited to be branded as such, displayed, in one way or another, to her face. It was at these times that she treasured the merits of her position the most, for it was utterly amazing how a few well-placed friends, can make the difficult appear astonishingly mundane.

***

Within six hours of proposing, Michael watched the large posterns to his estate close solidly at his back, sealing him in and the world out. A sigh of relief dropped coarsely from his lips. Feeling suddenly anxious and elated all at once, he smiled warmly at the passenger at his side, acknowledging the moment for what it was.

Julia shook her head in wonderment of what now sits strongly as a precipice of change. Looking moderately effeminate in baggy sweats and an oversized Bears jacket, she peeled back the hood of her shirt to reveal short, choppy, reddish-brown hair. With colors that looked more sprayed than natural, the ends teased the edge of her matching hat. "Are we really doing this, Michael?"

"Running the whole way," he smiled, slowly rounding the curve on the long driveway. He gently warned. "And just so you know. I have a lot of socks, sure in their competence to cure cold feet. So don't even think about it." Wrapping his fingers around hers, he kissed the back of each member on her hand. "You're not getting out of this."

"I wasn't thinking of me, Michael. I was trying to give you the option of an out."

"Why?"

"So you can have some time to really think about what you're getting into."

"Do you think I did this on impulse?"

"No. I don't think that. I just worry that you're going to find this harder than you thought."

"Which side of it?"

"All of it. For instance, our playtime, it can't and won't stay the same."

"I'm aware of that." Michael assured, slowing the pace of his truck. He smiled as if to ward off the worthiness of another complaint. "I have had the chance to observe this rare phenomenon you speak of, in others, once or twice. Give me a little credit, will you. I'm not fully as dense as my past suggests. Besides, if there's one thing that describes us to a tee, it's creative. We'll work around the tweaking of that."

"Okay. So then you know that this time you can't move on to the next supermodel, should there be a temporary drought." She scolded, narrowing her gaze until they were but piercing darts jabbing at his flesh.

"Damn! You mean I can't have you and some fresh, tight, twenty-two year old at the same time?"

Launching herself like a missile, she slapped his shoulder as repayment for his jest. "They do have male models, too, you know. So I might just find me a fresh, hard, twenty-two year old to take my woes out on."

"But *you're* not their type." He laughed, edging the vehicle to an immediate stop. Michael turned in his seat, though still nursing more than half the distance on the long journey down the driveway to his house.

"Not all of them. I'm sure I could find one or two to do the job well."

"Nobody does that job but me. You got that?" Michael grunted as he pulled her close. "Nothing, and, especially *no one,* touches this body but these hands…and…Well, whatever else I deem a necessary fit." He smiled.

"Do you think you can recite those rules to yourself?" Julia asked as he settled her on his lap.

"Why would I want anyone else to do that job? They don't know how I like my kisses. You do, and God…do you do it well. Now, kiss me before we go inside, since we'll both be swamped once we walk through those doors. I want something that will last me until tonight."

"So you're still going through with it? You're still going to marry that woman and her kids?"

"You bet." Michael drawled, pushing both hat and wig from its place.

"Don't say I didn't warn you." She counseled in a whisper, granting him a tender kiss. She pressed her body to his. "Don't say I didn't give you the directions on how to wheedle yourself out of the skein."

"So noted. The court has already logged your judicious exhorts in triplicates; now kiss me. Give me a good one. No, wait, scratch that! Not too good, my mother is inside. I'd hate to shock her when I walk in. Just kiss me." He encouraged with a broadening smile, his hazel eyes playful as his fingers slowly spanned the back of her head. Pulling her closer, he sipped of the nectar that was hers and hers alone, feeling the soft form of her body pressed his in mellifluous reply. "Mm, I love you."

"I love you." Julia purred, her eyes caressing his face. "Were you always sure?"

"No." He hummed, knowing without review what her question demanded. "It took me a little time to recognize the signs and what they meant. But once I did, there was no turning back."

"How did you know? How is it you were so sure?"

Michael's gaze shifted oddly upon hers for, what felt like, a brief trice, before opting a reply. Taking a soft breath, he gave voice to another piece of himself. "I knew I loved you because after the vehemence of our climb, when the intensity ended, when the fury of the hunt wears itself thin and the moment furnished its grandest serenity, after the blaze, when I was finished loving you, I loved you still. That sensation has never once dimmed. It only seems to grow stronger with you."

"Mm, I like that." She crooned. "Okay. I think we'd better go inside and get this over and done with. You just earned big for giving an answer like that, and the driveway is no place to get raped, at least not today."

"Will I be allowed to use my hands at such time?"

"Oh, but it's expected." She purred, easing her body from his lap.

"Later then?" Michael beamed in promise, starting the vehicle as a new thought swirled through his head.

"Count on it."

In the eyes of those who entered, the house sat astoundingly serene. For none would have guessed the furor it retained in the erstwhile hours of said day, or of the turbulence it brought the occupants waiting inside. Madness swam from its belly without mercy or pause. While each, in their endeavor, made fit the adornments pertinent to a bride and groom.

The heavy door opened meekly without grievance or sound, clicking as soundless at their backs. Michael guided his bride-to-be through the entrance without deferment edging his steps, holding her firmly at his side. Long fingers wove warmly around the shakier of her hand, offering a gentle squeeze. He smiled as his lips brushed the back of her hand, and his eyes gave assurance for this, another first, in a series of next steps. Now opening their relationship to the vision of family and friends, for after this, there would be no more hiding. Explanations would, without doubt, be an expected task, since all parts of their relationship would then lay open on the floor. And although this was a process he was well ready to confront, he worried a bit for her.

Together the two turned towards the kitchen in silence, stopping to drop their bags at the entrance of his suite. Large bouquets of red roses crowded the space with the vibrancy of their blooms, lining the floor of the hall like a hedge. They sat on nigh every viable surface to be seen, looking well elegant in their poise. The soft lilting of classical music swept pleasingly through the house, as if granting aid to the affluence of the vibrant florets.

Sarah, being the first to spy the awaited couple, burst to an instant bloom, and like a night-watchman in the throes of a heist, she sounded the alarm.

"Hey! Hey! They're here! They're here!" Sarah squealed, running across the room like the president of a welcome party of one. She launched herself in Michael's arms. "Look at you! Oh, my God! I can't believe it! Congratulations!"

"Michael!" Hyacinth sang as she burst into the room, her arms already outstretched. "You were just testing your mother, right?" she mumbled, giving him a strong hug with her jest. "Congratulations! You owe me details." She muttered lightly before turning to her soon-to-be daughter-in-law. "How are you doing, dear?" Hyacinth asked softly, wrapping both hands around that of Julia's free hand.

"A bit nervous, actually." Julia smiled, looking completely swallowed in fright.

"You'll have to get used to that," Hyacinth advised sweetly. "He has a way of playing havoc on your emotions. But you look like you can keep him in line. So from now on, I'm expecting you to use that whip well. Don't ever let him forget who's boss." She laughed, throwing her son a light glare.

"Mom, I'm your baby, remember? You're supposed to be on my side, no matter what." Michael grumbled in feigned shock, his thumb stroking the soft skin on the back of his expected bride's hand.

"And I am, son. But that does not prevent me from giving a small touch of advice now, does it?" Still holding Julia's hand, she turned towards her son with an adoring smile. "Okay, love. Time is ticking, and the sun will be setting shortly. We probably only have a little over an hour or so, to go. So you'll need to release her, my darling." Hyacinth counseled, giving the informative warn. Her smile widened, loving the exhibit of this protective and affectionate side of her son.

"I promise, Sarah and I will take the absolute best care of her, but she has some decisions to make. Besides, you have someone you need to go talk to before she drops dead." She informed with a light shrug, leaning affectionately into her son. "Everything you need is already waiting for you in the second suite upstairs, so don't bother going to your bedroom. It's off limits to the groom for the next hour or so. Now chop-chop! We have a wedding to get done."

Gently, Sarah's hand slid forward like a sheet in its cover of Michael's hand, tendering her usual sunny disposition. Her smile almost mirrored the angst of innocence on Christmas Eve. On his gingered release, the bride-to-be was then whisked promptly from the room. Escorted with determinate haste to the sanctuary of the master-suite, the two turned to her and smiled.

"Okay. First and foremost, you need to pick your dress." Sarah hurriedly apprised, rushing ahead to gather the first of such. She held it serenely across her arm.

"Dresses, I thought Michael bought me *one?*" Julia queried with a fattening frown, gaping in wonder at the mound of white populating the entire surface of the bed.

"He did. But we wanted you to have a choice, every bride should have choices." Hyacinth smirked, picking up a dress with what looked like diamonds melded within its design.

"That's beautiful." Julia sighed, moving sharply towards the dress in Hyacinth's hand. "How many are there?"

"Ten."

"*Ten?*" Julia bayed, whirling from her aim while uttering the soft bark, her eyes large with her show of surprise. "You gathered up ten wedding dresses within just the space of an afternoon?"

"Why, that's not enough?" Sarah laughed, placing the first gown in Julia's hand. "You forget what business I work in. It's not as hard as you think once you know where to look."

"Okay then." Hyacinth interjected, alerting the room with a gentle clap, she smiled. "Time is ticking. So let's start trying on these dresses so we can have ourselves a wedding." Advising them this, she turned as a soft knock trundled through the room. Without pause, Hyacinth's quick steps saw her giving answer to the door, opening the ingress. She revealed Delia's offering of a resplendent smile, blurring the vision. It flared from the archway in which she stood.

"Mom!"

"Hi, sweetie!" Delia chirped, rushing forward with her arms outstretched. She wrapped her daughter in the security of a loving embrace.

"I'm sorry." Julia whispered against her cheek.

"Don't be." Delia whispered back. "Later. We'll talk then." She smiled, looking down at the gown in Julia's hand, her eyes slowly swept over the others obscuring the bed. "It looks as if I got here just in time. Go on, sweetie. Let's see you pretty-up these gowns." She smiled, affecting a finishing squeeze. She retreated as she dabbed at the corners of her eyes.

"Wait? How...?" Julia frowned, looking suddenly confused. "How did you know where I was or that I was getting married?"

"Michael called me."

"So that's why he wanted to borrow my phone," Julia chuckled, gazing blindly at the floor in thought.

The room stilled instantly as if in observance of the news, granting her a moment of peace as she consulted the crux of her memory. Julia smiled openly with the torrent of her thoughts, sighing in resolute. She turned her attention to the task at hand.

First in the assemblage was a short strapless gown, covered in exquisite lacing, an intricately design floret gilded the left side of its waist. Collectively, it wheedled only the coolest smiles and nods from the panel on a whole. Likeable, Julia noted, though that would hardly be acceptable terms when it came to the merits of one's wedding dress. Of the next six, Julia liked the fit and the designs of two, though her audience could never fully agree on which tendered itself best. Always seeming to like or dislike sparse portions of each, the one before always reared better than the one usually on her back. Nevertheless, the eighth dress received warm reviews, with all assenting to it being the best. Julia beamed her agreement of such, slipping carefully from the gown. She placed it with the miniscule pile of maybes.

The dress Hyacinth held was handed to her next, a beautiful ivory silk with beadings of crystals, afire with light, augmenting the lace of the bolero style casing attached. Julia's jaw fell in amazement as she gazed at her reflection. Brushing her fingers lightly across the slick smoothness of silk, a short train swept the floor as she turned.

"This—this is my dress." She breathed, requesting neither opinion nor views, but glowed her love for the garment as she reentered the room. "This is my choice." Julia repeated in affirmation, her expression gentle, though set.

"Oh, Julia," Sarah murmured, her hands pressed tightly to her cheeks. "You look stunning. That's it. You're right. That's the dress."

"I agree. That's definitely your dress, sweetie." Delia added softly, pressing a finger to the corner of her eye.

Without adding her view, Hyacinth moved forward as Julia turned to gaze at her reflection. Placed in the room for just that, she smiled fervidly, in the mirror, at the replication of herself, her eyes distant as if in thought. The older woman stopped quietly at her back, her hazel eyes sparkled warmly as they moved over the gown's reflection. "Perfect. My son has beautiful taste." She whispered, her expression seeming strained. "It's perfect, just perfect. I'm even more certain now why he made that choice." She smiled, intending her words as an inclusive memorandum to the evening's cause, for she spoke not only of the dress but of the woman inside.

"This is the gown Michael bought?"

"The very one," Hyacinth assured then, touching a hand to her cheek, her head softly wagged. And inside she quietly acknowledged the intricacy of her son's insight, realizing now that he had put more thought into the day and the woman than she had once feared. Of all the dresses, she thought it strange that his was the one they all agreed upon. The only dress they all cheered without pause.

Hyacinth watched as the impending bride's eyes further lit the crevices in the room, sparkling like stars out with the fullness of the moon, their reflection glistened with the reverence they held. Smiling, her hands brushed the fabric with resounding care, earnest in their dispersal, as if suddenly afraid the garment would bruise, or that the fabric was somehow a duplicate of the man himself.

"Okay." Hyacinth called, directing the wakening tone more to herself than to anyone else. She again dabbed at her eyes. *This is not the time to have your emotions rule,* Hyacinth reminded herself sternly. There'll be plenty of time for that later, she smiled. With a last glance at the dress, she touched a finger to the pearl-like buttons showcased, as a beautiful seam, down the entire back. The gown's design was in the wont of a princess, and a princess they most certainly had. "Now that we have the dress, let's get this wedding on the way before we all lose it."

"Here, let me help you get out of that." Delia offered as she jumped forward, her expression veering near that of an over anxious child.

"Now, I want you to take a few minutes for yourself and get the lag of your flight out of your system. Have a nice, long, relaxing shower while we all get into our dresses." Hyacinth coaxed, gathering the first gown, she laid it across her arm.

"We'll be back to help you with your hair and the rest." Sarah called, hurrying to the door, her arms now laden with blooming midriffs of silk. Together the three cleared the room without offering further adage, giving naught but an awed smile as they leave. The door slammed soundly behind them in significance of that, and silence swept through like the breaking of a dam.

Julia stared pridefully at her reflection, the loosened gown now hanging in a wide droop around her bodice. Yet it took nothing from the beauty that it showed. And a smile rushed forward as she stroked the delicate beading on the lace itself, wondering then, how was it that the man knew her so well? "I'm getting married." Julia whispered to the reflection of herself. "Can you believe it?" she crooned, curving her shoulders. She allowed the dress to fall from her breasts, guiding it down the length of her body. She cautiously extracted herself.

How fitting, Julia thought as she laid the gown upon a now empty bed. By far, it was the most beautiful gown she had ever seen. Picked for her, by the most beautiful man, with a love she had never before perceived. How does one explain that? "Perfect." She acceded in the quiet, dragging the tips of her fingers over the fabric. "You're almost as beautiful as he." She whispered to the elegant gown, spoken without a cloud of humility masking the realization. Confident they were of accurate accord, irrespective of opinions contradicting such canto, her satisfaction rested on whose acuity counted most, and none other flew to the audaciousness of her view but those of her own.

Chapter Forty Three

✦

In what flounced like awed distinction, the evening sky beckoned like a resplendent paradigm of art. Smirched with an array of colors, orange brushed its perfect strokes across a richly yellowed crown. Breaths of rose played boldly aloft a fading tint of blue, once prominent athwart a vast ceiling, it thickened to a billow of heathery gray in differing spots.

Michael's gaze walked pensively across the lurid pigments now staining earth's plafond. Beautifully poised on, this, its final gradient, the sun heralded all eyes for its inevitable bow, and the occasion, munificent in beauty, drew forth a slow sigh from his lips. Standing lordly at his side was his best friend and partner, Phillip, the ever fidgeting best-man, looking, now, more nervous than the groom himself.

Smiling mildly at the eccentric paradox they now stood in, Michael gave the room an appreciative sweep, and was again awestruck by the fruits of his mother's toils. Considering the measly hours in which she had to do things, she artfully crafted an impressive escape. Perfect for two to amend to one.

The pool's surface stood veiled with an assortment of roses. Notched deftly between the soft, delicate buds, small, orangey-red globes floated like the shed feathers from a colorful dove, casting a warm, reflective glow to the water barely visible beneath. Sketched, as if by design, on some mystic stratum, the resemblance was of a vibrant field, set adrift on a bed of gold by some sorcerer's hand; it imprisoned one's eyes as well as their mood.

Tall, potted trees fashioned the canopied archway environing his head. With each of the six behemoth saplings generously showered in white, fragile buds appeared intricately woven amongst a heavy showering of leaves. Each splayed gracefully like fully bloomed blossoms awaken only for the day.

Candles glowed throughout the immense space illimitably, and the scent of roses wrapped them in an aromatic haze, sweetening the ambience's flare. Plush, red carpet lined the path designated for his bride, starting well beyond the entrance. It ended cozily under the spread of his feet, and the vista that lay before him was no less the beholding of an oasis, outstandingly done as a gift suited for a tsar.

Bach's Ave Maria, climbed through the atmosphere like soft vapors from kindling logs. Gifting the room its gentle warmth, the melody came in prelude of her walk to him. Michael's stomach soared skyward with the soft, melodic flow. Clambering towards the thunderous cavern in his chest, it roiled like a capsized vessel in rough waters at sea.

Hence it amplified the tremor that arose in his body, with each now showing no end in their synchronized blitz. Neither did the fact that his heart now knew only wild.

"This is it." Phillip whispered, leaning his similarly tall frame close. He tapped his shoulder to the other of his friend. Behind them, Sarah and Hyacinth hurried forward from the entrance, taking their places just wide of each of the men.

The warning, though clearly given, was abstractedly heard, and had he not lost the workings of his tongue, an agile answer would have surely been had. But all thoughts vanished once his eyes rushed the opening of the door, cemented there by the tense tendons mastering the movements of his head. Michael waited with all focus targeted to his expectancy of a face.

Toted like an angel on her mother's arm, his bride cleared the entrance at last, and had he had eyes for anyone but her, he would have noted the similarities they shared. He would have seen that their faces were shaped much the same. Or that the slope of their foreheads was an exact match. And their eyes, though different in color, still exhibited much the same exotic shape. Yet all this escaped him without note or acknowledgement, for his bride, looked, to him, more beautiful than any fantasy he'd ever had, more so, than any vision or any dream he had yet to discern in his head.

Done in a simple upsweep, the wild strands of her hair were roped tightly from her face, with braids intricately woven in a neat bun atop her head. Her only ornament came in the form of a small, tear-drop pearl, each dangled playfully from her lobes as she turned bright eyes upon him. Yet the word perfection did little justice to the picture she presented then.

Her smile was frenetically sweet. Brightening the room beyond the sizzle it already held, its warmth took roots where once sat barren. With astounding care, her mother placed her hand gently in his, and his fingers became an instantaneous cage. Yet the small pressure she bestowed in her gentle squeeze of said limb, were like boulders from her hand to his, lending him support on which he could lean.

Betty hovered somberly in the penumbra scraping the edges of the door. Her eyes already moist from the spurting of her tears, feeling pride as abounding as any birth mother would.

In scrutiny, Hyacinth's gaze snapped like an arrow from a well taut bow, shooting towards the entry of the room. A frown spliced harsh within the lines of her brows, seeming as if on a quest. Her eyes patrolled the dim corners with prodigious care, though they quickly found their target in the sorrowed creases of Betty's face.

With quick steps, Hyacinth alleviated the small space between them, taking the petite woman by her hand. She gruffly apprised her of her place. "What are you doing standing in the shadows?" she frowned. "You've more than earned the right to be here. You know you belong here as much as anyone else." Setting the elfin woman in the center of their small group, she held tight to her hand.

"Dearly beloved," the minister began, and his quiet tone seemed the equivalent of sirens going off in Michael's head. For the drowsy cadence instantly thrust his heart further up the incline of his esophagus. It then promptly lined the back of his throat, drumming like mad. The pace caused an echoic deafness to the arguments in his head, silencing all that existed around him. The room stood awkwardly still, and naught but a single monotone voice slid forward to dominate the space. Although in retrospection, in regards to such prate, neither bride nor groom lifted theirs voices any higher than his in the answering of their vows. And in what felt more like a trice, their oath of commitment, forbearance and love, were tenderly exchanged, dropping the two sweetly at the end.

The low, masculine hum remained astoundingly light, and before he expected the attainment to be fully that, the minister's murmured chant came to him with a smile. "I now pronounce you husband and wife. You may kiss the bride." He announced grandly, his bland expression breaking from that to delight.

Michael gazed at the cleric's face for a fleet moment. His mind locked, as if in a euphoric fog, feeling suddenly stunned by the clergyman's words. Understanding was slow to push through the murky swamp. Finally turning to his now wife, his arms slithered across her back as he pulled her close. Unlike his breath, his lips came to her soft, brushing her cheek in start. His kiss grew slowly more sensual and sweet, stopping of a sudden, once the trill of cheers rose softly from their backs. Rain of petals came in a drizzle from atop their heads, scattering about them in waves like a delicate squall.

Lifting his head, Michael gazed into the misty gems of her eyes, his smile thence widened before his attention dropped to her hand. Thin fingers rested as a soft mat near the center of his palm, seeming like a rare feather in his hand. He studied the prominence of the diamond hoop now swaddling her finger. An encrusted eternity band sat bold, as his own stamp, on her hand, and its shimmer was no less prominent than the lamp flaring in a lighthouse while bound in the thickness of night. Venerated by the lost, it blazed benevolent in its guidance of an adrift ship to the sanctity of home, his home.

Quietly bringing her hand to his lips, Michael pressed a noisy kiss to the cool metal that now labeled her his. Turning anew to his guests, he lengthened the display for all to see, and in a swift companioned act, Michael dragged his hand jadedly across the flat of his brows. Expelling with it a long breath, he elucidated the stint of an exhaustive journey, offering them a rich synopsis of his voyage to this end.

"Congratulations, son," Hyacinth crooned, throwing her body gently into his. She worked to harness the flow of her tears, quickly turning her attention to the newest member of her family. "Congratulations, dear. Welcome to our family." She murmured, matting her eyes as she pulled the younger woman close.

"Thank you." Julia mouthed more so than spoke, wiping her own tears. Her words came barely at a whisper.

"Congratulations!" The women sang in unison, launching forward with individual hugs. A soft hiss kissed the air amidst the congratulatory chirrups, each eagerly dished between them. They daintily matted the moisture from their eyes.

Phillip watched the exchange with incredulity matted in his own expression, frowning. He made no effort to contain his shock. "I know I'm the only guy here, and guys supposedly don't dig…but…I'm sorry. I have to know. When? How? And what the hell happened to never?"

Slowly threading his fingers through the warmth of his wife's hand, Michael laughed before giving answer to the eager faces all waiting his response. Aware he could expect no less from his friends. "Since… April." He quietly shrugged, stroking her fingers with his thumb.

"April! But you said she turned you down!"

"Technically, she did." Michael informed with a chuckle. "More than once, I might add." He groaned, throwing a sarcastic glance in the direction of his wife's head.

"So you've been seeing her since April, and *you* didn't mention a word?" Phillip asked in a hoarse shrill, and the purity of his stagger was without limit. In the entire time the two had been friends, he'd never known Michael to be that secretive with anything. Usually there's at least a hint. Here all everyone had were mere speculations on which to muse.

"I know, shocking isn't it?" he conceded, branding each with the perfected lure of his boyish smile. "I'm sorry, guys but…well, she countered my offer and I just couldn't refuse." Michael pledged, squeezing her hand. He tendered reassurance as he clarified but a vague tip of their game. "If I agreed to keep things just between us, then she'd agree to the specified simplicity of an unspoiled date. How could I pass that up?" He inquired as he pulled her close. "I had to agree. And if I wanted to see her again, I had to keep the whole secrecy going, and I…definitely wanted to see her again. So…I'm sorry, guys, but…then again, I'm not sorry. She had me really intrigued."

"Come on everyone. Let's move this party up to the family room so we can all toast the new couple." Hyacinth invited, her hands spread in a sure directive of the way.

"When did you propose?" Sarah asked in her usual melodious drawl, stalling everyone's feet, as all heads turned to them at once.

"This morning," Michael retorted calmly, giving a simple shrug with his reply. Knowing the evening would be filled with much of the same, and was in full understanding of why.

The questions finally dwindled enough that a collection of toasts were made, followed promptly by the couple's reluctant cutting of the cake. Strikingly done, the artistry itself was an astounding treat, as scattering of white petals spilled playfully down the sides of a large single tier cake.

To his new bride, Michael fed only a bite of the decadent dessert, not wanting to soil the perfection of her gown, though he smeared it willfully across her mouth. Taking his time, he tenderly kissed her clean.

"You look spectacular!" He rumbled softly as she took her seat at his side. "More perfect than any dream I could have visualized in my head."

"So do you." Julia whispered back, feeling unexpectedly awkward, as all eyes became suddenly glued to them. With her mother sternly leading the untiring charge, it soon grew obvious. Not only were they the spectacle donated for exhibit, but the entertainment as well. "I'll be right back." She advised tamely, feeling guilt rip mordantly through the pit of her stomach.

"Hi, sweetie. Congratulations again. You look truly beautiful in that gown." Delia beamed, and the effervescence of her smile was profoundly catching, for her eyes looked more like reflective pools in the green swallow of their depths.

"I'm sorry I didn't tell you I was seeing someone." Julia began dimly, her voice like a forlorn cry. "It kind of started out strange and I didn't think you would understand."

Taking her daughter's hand, Delia gave the limb a gentle squeeze, her eyes dimming lightly from the bold luster once offered with their zest. Patting said limb with the other of her hand, the essence of her smile further softened before she spoke. "You know, I was twenty-two when I met your father, just six weeks after I started my internship with Sterling, Jensen and Ross." She smiled, pausing as if to savor the picture that swam through her mind. "At the time, we were both engaged to someone else. Aubrey St. John, now there's a flash from the past." Delia crooned, giving the name with a short, throaty laugh. "God, I thought I was so in love with that man. And then I met George, and my world, and everything in it, just erupted from the pleasantness of a familiar path.

"When he stood next to me, I thought my heart would burst. He made me so nervous. I just couldn't stop myself from shaking. Whenever he looked at me, I had to remind myself to breath. Oh, how I loved that man!" Delia professed in a raspy whisper, pressing a hand gently to her cheek as tears pooled in her eyes.

"We got married in the short span of three months, which, in truth, could not have come soon enough for me." She sniffed, giving voice to a heavy sigh. "Your father was a gentleman, but I swear when I was with him, I wanted to throw everything about being proper out the window. I would kiss his feet if he asked me to." Delia laughed, quietly shaking her head. "And have," she announced, nodding almost as slow. "He never asked, but I did. Everything I learned about being a proper woman was flushed away with his presence, and together we created new rules based on our own expectations and wants. Just on the essential basis of what we learned from each other and from ourselves, he could make me do anything. Try anything. I wanted to please him just as much as he pleased me. And I'll have you know that there is, for me, not one ounce of shame in owning that." She averred haughtily, and without looking, she could feel the sudden sizzle of her daughter's gaze. And she suspected, bewilderment was but one of the many entities now burning bright in her eyes. "What? Your generation did not invent lust, you know." She remarked dryly, frowning softly as she refreshed her tale.

"Not just any kind, but what sits, in the aftermath, as the very best. The kind that rightly makes you its slave. Taking you back, like an infant, in its arms to reminisce the blaze, long after the fire ends." She smiled, straightening as she took a long breath. Her eyes grew suddenly distant. "Well," she hummed in conclusion, her eyes again bright. "I'll spare you the details of that. But I'll have you know, there are a few ways with which one could become a mother. I chose to take the road that was *most* fun." She sang. Shrugging lightly as her eyes quietly clambered to her daughter's face. "I know you know the details to some of this already, but I told you the rest so you can remember an important fact. There's always another side to every mother.

"Every mother started as a woman first. Don't ask me to forgive you for remembering you're a woman, for throwing out the things you thought you knew and putting new ones in place. You're only young once, my angel, and it passes by so quickly. Grab it! Hold on to it for dear life. You give so much of yourself to all of us. Good for you for holding something back for yourself! Good for you! I wish you could see your eyes and the light that now blaze inside them. They haven't sparkled like that in years. Not many people get to have that, sweetie. I had forty-one years of bliss with your father. Forty-one very, very happy years. That man did everything he could to make me happy, and I am grateful every day to have been blessed with that time I had with him. Grateful for the strength to look beyond our many differences, and to take that first step into what was not the norm back then. Not one moment do I look back and gather a moment of regret, not one.

"How many people can truly say they married the man of their dreams, their soulmate? I can. I can sing that from the highest peak, for the rest of my life, without a moment's doubt, and I truly suspect you can, too. No forgiveness needed here, sweetie, just high praise for stepping outside of your norm." Taking a long breath, an encompassing smile donned her face as she gently tightened her grip. "If I could add anything to what you've already done, it would be to remind you to make every day full. Experience it all, my angel, and love it as you do, even the bad ones. By the time you get to my age, you'll learn it wasn't as bad as you once thought. So take your time and fully enjoy that bliss. No explanations needed, just…*live*."

"I think daddy would have loved him. They would have been dangerous together, but the excitement would have been triple fold, don't you think?" Julia uttered with a quiet smile, her eyes rushing to her husband's face.

"I wouldn't be surprised if he hand picked him himself." Delia laughed. "Everything about this reeks of your father's personality. And wouldn't it be just like him to pull something like this off."

"Wouldn't that be something?" Julia laughed, her eyes again drawn to the man now watching her.

"She's beautiful, isn't she?" Hyacinth asked, seeing where her son's eyes now flickered.

"More than any words," he hummed. "Even more so than the outer vision itself,"

"Are you as happy as you seem, son?"

"And more," he smiled. "I have no words beyond that to give it the proper justice it deserves. Just know that I am."

"I don't know her very well, son, only by the small observations I've had. But I do know a classic when I see one. There's only one way to treat a classic, son, you treasure it. From the bottom up, you nurture, spoil and protect it from the hazards of this world, and with that, it will last you a lifetime." Hyacinth counseled, squeezing the hand that held hers. She quietly returned his affection, her own adoration evident in her eyes. With a generous smile directed towards his new bride, she further voiced her pride. "You did well, son." She assured then in a whisper. "You did very well. I'm very proud of how you went about this. You saw what you wanted and you went after it. But you did it like a gentleman. You protected it, and you recognized the rest when you needed to."

"Actually, that was mostly because of her. My only wish through all that was to have her near."

"That may have been how it started, but you kept it true. You knew you found something special, and you grabbed it and held on, with both hands, for dear life. You didn't let it go, nor did you squander a single ort of the beauty it had. Savoring, instead, the rareness of the treasure you unearthed. You didn't let anyone or anything hamper your progress in any way. She seems so unlike all the others and I think that's a very good thing for you."

"She's a continent all on her own, mom."

"You remember that description every day and you'll do just fine." She smiled. "Your eyes betray you, son, and that makes my heart truly full."

"I know you've been worried about me, at least on this front, and I'm sorry it took me so long to get it. But I guess you could say I was being very selective."

"I'm your mother, and you're the only one I have left. What other choice did I have?" Hyacinth grumbled, trying her best to affect a casual shrug.

Michael smiled, pulling her into his body. He pressed a kiss to her cheek. "I love you." He rumbled near her ears.

"You're my heart, my soul, my everything. What more is left to say beyond that? There's none more special than you, son." She sighed. "Now go. I know where you'd rather be, and it's certainly not here with your mother."

Michael needed no further encouragement for his feet to take heed, as long strides had him across the room in a flash. Julia stood in acquiescence of just that, noticing his direction. She met him halfway. "Hi." Michael whispered as he took her hand.

"Hi." The softness of her greeting was avidly given in her smile, leaning her body into his. She whispered the cryptic scribing of her heart.

Michael straightened slowly as her whispered voice clambered to his ears, his gaze faintly favoring shock. Devoid of dialogue, he promptly dragged her to the privacy of his room. "Tell me that again." He ordered in a gruff breath, setting her squarely to his face.

"I said," she smiled, resuming the soft hum of her proclamation. "I love you. And have loved you long before today, past that of my childish dreams and beyond those of my swaddling. Before we were yet bodies or spirits, but souls amongst the stars. I've loved you from the beginning and will love you past the end. For you have surpassed all my hopes and dreams for both this life and the next, as all those of my womanly tendencies have thusly been met. You have made my world infinitely better just because, and have since soared as the pillar at which I will forever stand. I did not recognize you when you came, and I thank you for not giving up. I promise to spend the rest of my life honoring you, for I will love you without boundaries, without barriers and without limits. I will love you endlessly, for we are truly endless as one." His grunt of acknowledgement became her finishing word, pulling her snug against his chest. Michael stole her concluding breath.

"That is the second thing you've done this day to solidify my dream. It's a beautiful aura to sit in."

"I just wanted you to know." Julia murmured back, smiling as his lips walked softly across hers.

"And I'm a luckier man for knowing." He rasped. "Mm, man, you smell good. Suddenly I can't decide which I like best, taste, scent, sight or feel. You're going to have to help me resolve that. You know, I'm really dying to see what's under that dress." Michael growled. "You look so damn proper, like a princess. A part of me can't wait to rip this off, just to see your wild side come out."

"Don't you dare!" she warned, stifling the soft flutter of a gasp, brown gaze looked him over with sure shock marking their beds, though a quiet smile remained observable on her lips. "This dress is very special! My husband bought it for me!" She explained as her hand glided over the fabric with reverence, dropping her gaze adoringly down the skirt with the venture of her hand.

"Your husband can afford to buy you another." Michael informed, watching her behavior with interest, he smiled.

"It wouldn't be the same. I love *this* dress. I love that my husband put such thought into his selection. So nothing touches this dress, nothing."

"Got it, I'll do my best to remember that." He droned.

"You do know that by raising the skirt, you can still see what's under the dress, right?"

"I'll raise your skirt alright! But so you know, my sole objective would be to take it off." Murmuring thus, he pulled her back to his chest, dropping his head lightly to hers. His mouth grew fervent in its devouring, igniting a passion that had already simmered close. "God, your mouth makes me insatiable." He charged breathlessly, gliding his hands firmly over the soft roundness of her buttock. He molded her to the firm weaponry of his frame.

Intuitive as ever, Julia knew his thought before he dared to utter a word. "Michael! We can't! Everyone will know."

"True, but—"

"Besides, leisure is always better than a dash. All night brand of leisure is especially good on one's wedding night. I would think." She cooed.

"Fine," Michael growled, heaving a heavy sigh. "Just give me a minute to…relax."

"However, I would be quite happy to undertake the rigor of my first wifely duty in this case." She apprised sagely, corroborating the infer with a slow lift of her brow.

"Oh?" Michael hummed, a cheeky smile following the desolate word, for he could think of naught more to add in acquiescence of her invitation, and the purity of his expressive anticipation was a priceless fine.

Without further adage, Julia lowered her eyes from his, lowering her body with the coercive bent of her hands. Tensing muscles flexed as she gave focus to her toil, acceding her effort. His breath grew ragged and rushed, as if he now exerted himself on the low gradient of a tor.

Compressing the determined effort in her exerts, her kisses made certain there would be but one result. Thus she anchored him in a torrent of sensations to accede such end. She kissed him until his sighs caressed the air that so softly swathed, the rare entities, that was them. She kissed him until his breath sailed jagged from his chest. Until his fingers tightened in the coiffed sculpting of her hair, and the stalwart limbs of his body twitched with the joyance of her mouth. She kissed him until his voice shook with the cadence of her name, falling to her in a tense guttural whisper. His surges mined as primitive as the threat spliced to a caustic wind. She kissed him until his hums grew savory and his body caroled itself quenched, dripping from his lips like a warm caress. She kissed him until he grew still.

"Jesus, woman! That mouth of yours should be illegal!" Michael panted as consciousness resumed.

"Better?" she asked in a languid breath, her eyes filled warmly with the tacit profess of her love, charted so by a conspicuous smile. A quiet breath scratched her cheek as Michael pulled her gruffly to his chest, locking his arms at her back. They bolstered like newly erected walls, tightening as they crushed the air from her body. Yet the soft twinge delighted her with the passion it vowed.

In the quiet that followed, she felt the thundering in his chest tilt as it differed its pace, heard, too, the howling of his breath as it barreled forward. Yet the two, in peaceful oneness, remained locked in the silence that fell, for the moment drifted not unlike the ending of a ballad, as their minds seemed seated as one. The storm that once raged inside him, slowly dissipated with the gentling of his breath, and in its stead, a beautiful stillness loitered. It was in that calm that his voice, hardly a whisper, addressed her at last.

"I love you."

"I love you."

"And, yes. I'm feeling *much* better." He smiled.

"Good. Now button up. You have gues—"

"We…remember that." He corrected, nudging her with a gentle squeeze.

"*We* have guests." Julia assented, smiling at the strangeness of what the acknowledgement meant.

"I know that, but…" Michael paused, adjusting the buckle of his belt. "What about you?"

"Just let me simmer. I'll come to a boil for you later." She smiled, her eyes twinkling softly. "Now, you go ahead, and I'll be out shortly."

"But—"

"I promise. But we need to go before we raise more suspicion than we already have."

"I hate to break this to you, wife, but they already suspect."

"Then out. Out with you, now!" she griped, turning him towards the door. "At least with a short absence, the implication it leached is not as bad. Now go!"

"Is this how you plan to treat your husband? Just tease him and then push him aside with the rags?"

"Tease?" she asked at an almost bark, her hands punctuating the lone word and its bite, notching them tightly on her hips. "Sir, I believe your descriptive well lacking, for I, most certainly did not tease. I effectively sated!"

"You may call it as you see fit, Madame, but such words change little, if not naught. For here I am, as proof, being hastened, like a plaything, out your door with a rather astounding shove. However, I'm a generous man, and I'm willing, AWOL all pretense or malice, to forget such comportment as this. So it would behoove you, Madame, to pounce upon what's surely an enfeebled state. Hence, you may procure my return to be thusly treated once more."

"Once again, sir, you speak with little sentience honing that drab tone of yours. For it is I, who should and will be treated as such, this I do troth. Now begone, serf, before you earn your mistress' wrath. Out!"

"I'm going. I'm going. Man, you're bossy." He grumbled as he pulled open the door. "Just know this, the revival promises to have teeth, tongue, hands and…Well, I'll let you wait for the late night screening on that." Michael smiled, pressing a quick kiss to her brow. "Don't linger too long or I'll come looking, and I can't promise you I'll be good."

"I won't." She vowed, elated with the oeuvre of their time together. Julia turned cheerfully towards the inner walls of the suite, smiling as the sitting-room door clicked closed at her husband's back. Intriguingly, her eyes grazed the elegant gown's reflection. Refreshing herself, she admired the intricate details as she worked. "The man does have good taste." She muttered to her mirrored physique, turning sharply as a soft knock hailed her attention to the door.

Polished to its truest custom, its luster bequeathed full warmth upon the recipient it held. Hyacinth's smile sailed in greeting as the bathroom door swung open without pace, and its progression seemed reminiscent of a torn page being wistfully turned. With hazel eyes locked to the younger woman's face, she noted that the inception of her smile fell slightly to reserve with recognition. "How are you doing, dear?" she asked as the young beauty advanced further through the ingress.

"I'm doing fine. Better." Julia smiled, brushing a hand nervously on the slim skirt of her gown.

"I can imagine. It's been a hectic day, of sort, for you."

"Just a bit, though more so for you and Betty I'm sure." Julia attested softly. "Everything was beautiful. Thank you so much for doing that."

"No thanks needed. It really was our pleasure to see it done. Look what we gained with the effort." She chirped. "The enjoyment was all ours, I assure you. We've hardly gotten the chance to know each other." Hyacinth chanted, trudging further forward, she shifted almost nervously with the change. "A fact I definitely plan on rectifying, of course." She smiled. "Today has been a wonderful treat for me, and I'd like to take this moment to thank you for that. You know, it takes quite a hike to get to my age, and even with the bumps, I've lived a very good life. I've been just about everywhere in the world, and I'm not want for anything in a material sense. But above all that, my family sits as my sole possession of worth.

"Unfortunately," Hyacinth paused, her shoulders falling with a weak sigh. "That family has dwindled vastly with years, now it seems to consist of just basically Michael and myself, barring a plethora of distant relatives, of course." Closing the gap between them, Hyacinth again smiled. "That is, until you." Opening her purse, she removed a small, richly polished wooden box. "This is the second most priceless thing I own in my view. Michael, of course, is my first."

"But you don't—" Julia started, stopping abruptly as Hyacinth hand pressed lightly at the air.

"Hear me out," she pleaded. Uncoiling the red bow from its perch atop an oblong shaped box, she again gave a distant smile. "This piece belonged to my mother." She declared meekly, pulling the lid open, she revealed a pear-shaped diamond pendant. Pronounced in its clarity, the glittery rock sat primly on a small, dark velvety bed. "It's one of the many things I gave her throughout the years. But this, for some reason, this was her favorite." Removing the pendant from its place, she gazed lovingly at the lemon-like sparkle, her eyes tender as if to reflect. "And now it's yours," She smiled, taking Julia's hand. She placed the icy perfection in her palm.

"It's beautiful." Julia attested in a near soundless breath, her gaze captured fully by the overly expensive gift. "I'm sorry, but…you didn't need to…" stammering to an abrupt stop, she gazed in wonder at the piece in her hand, not wanting to offend her new mother-in-law with the wrong placement of her words, not after all she'd done to see them to this end and, most certainly above all else, not on this day.

"You've given me something I never thought I'd have. That alone makes you deserving. But you have it because you're solely responsible for the light in my son's eyes, and for that, I truly thank you. It would seem, dear, today is your day for being branded." Hyacinth proclaimed in her warm lilt, folding the younger woman's fingers around the stone. "My son branded you on this day, his wife, and today I brand you daughter." She sighed, closing her fingers around the gently closed hand. "Thank you for breathing new life into this family. You're the heart my son has long needed." Hyacinth smiled, and her eyes flickered, as if in assurance, to their joined hands. "I thought we could go together to pick out a suitable chain for you to hang it from."

"Thank you. That's really so nice of you." Julia smiled, gazing down at their hands. "This is so beautiful. How can you bear to part with it, especially with who it belonged to?"

"My mother was not one to retain things just for the mere pleasure of a glance, she assigned them purpose. It's an object that holds a certain cost, Julia, no less, no more. Though it's not the monetary value that counts an item expensive, but what it gives the recipient erstwhile its end. Some may come with a certain meaning already attached, as this does, but their true value comes from the stories they tell. That's when they truly become treasures in the beholder's eyes, never before that. Now, as in the bequeathing of tradition, one old treasure will enhance a new, widening its tale like a sequel to something grand." She smiled, touching Julia's cheek in finish. "Now, so we understand each other, it's not important to me that you call me mom. You may call me whatever name you find that fits. But know you will be daughter to me from this day on. Any woman who can put that look of happiness in my son's eyes, is nothing but."

"I'm really very touched—honored, that you would accept things—me, so quickly, especially with how secretive we were. Topped now with a rushed wedding, this whole thing could not have been an easy venture for you. But you've managed to make this day so much more special than I could've hoped, and I thank you most avidly for that." Taking a quiet breath, Julia smiled. "I love your son." She whispered through a coarse pant, nodding as if to bolster the certainty of that. Sensing the need for an explanation, she dabbed calmly at the corner of an eye. "And I promise you, I'll always do my best to make him as happy as he makes me."

"Oh, I had no doubts there." Hyacinth assured firmly, turning her new daughter towards the door, a motherly smile planted on her face. "The answer to that churns throughout your entire body, dear. The harder you try to hide it, the greater the velocity of the turn. We can all feel it when the two of you are in a room. We could all feel it tonight."

"Am I that obvious?"

"Only to those with cherishing eyes,"

"Jeez!" she groaned, brushing a hand across her brow. "Your son does not believe in taking no for an answer. I guess that helps some with the why."

"I'm not sure where he gets that from." Hyacinth smirked.

"I'm glad he didn't."

"You mean to tell me there's still more I'll be beholden to my son for? With you alone, he may start insisting on tallying a list." She warbled, placing a hand dramatically across her chest in accordance with the show.

"I'll try to keep a rein on him for you." Julia snickered, dropping a hand on the other woman's arm.

"See, I knew there was a reason why I like you." Hyacinth laughed, wrapping her arms around the other in welcome as she voiced her wish. "I expect lunch, often." She informed in finish, releasing the younger woman with a lasting squeeze.

"That's a promise." Julia pledged as the two exited the room, returning as comrades to the rambunctious chatter of the house.

Upon spotting her reentrance, Michael immediately requested her hand, stretching his own forward like a quiet flag. He watched keenly as she crossed the room, accepting his proffered hand. She again took her seat at his side. Phillip and Sarah's joyous conveying of their barmy adventures to their wedding, slowly dimmed with her approach. Intrigue simmering fondly in their eyes, as both now watched him almost as acutely as he watched her. And although he knew this, he showed little inkling or care. This being an inaugurated voyage in an unaccustomed beginning. He openly admired the woman now labeled his wife, and his love of having that right, shone bold in his eyes, uncaring or undaunted by anyone who watched.

Delia watched her new son-in-law with pride and mounting affection swelling in her chest. From her suspicion to moderate confirmation, she never once predicted such end, sprouting this soon, though she was truly gratified to have witness the blissful result.

"Mind if I join you?" Hyacinth asked. "I recognize another beaming heart when I see one. I thought perhaps we could put them together and warm the whole house for free." Smiling, her open hand stuttered to a discreet stop towards the couple.

"Please!" Delia chuckled, her eyes indicating the space at her side, not minding conversation. Yet none came once her companion took the proffered seat. Both women's eyes followed an identical path, parking at the same destination. Neither woman broke the lyrics given in their silence, but their eyes spoke much of the sentiments they felt. Almost as if planned, a soft sigh floated simultaneously from their lips, and the two smiled with serene satisfaction at that. "They look exquisite together, don't they?" Delia remarked softly.

"She's so beautiful, how could they not?" Hyacinth retorted with, what sailed lightly as, an absentminded shrug, falling silent anew. The shuffling of feet broke the instilled quiet they brewed, dragging their attention from the object of their musing. "Betty!" Hyacinth frowned. "Betty, don't you start." She scolded, waving the other woman to her side. "Come. Come, sit down. Sit, and mind those tears." She warned, softly patting the old nanny's back. "If you start, then I'll start, and…Well, we're not going to do that, are we? We're not going to start." Gifting the authoritative warn, she tapped a hand to that of Betty's reedy show. Wadded with tissue, multiple tails of the soft paper flapped from the clenched fist of Betty's hand.

"I can't believe it. I never thought I'd live to see this day." Betty sniffed, dabbing again at her eyes.

"Betty, stop!" Hyacinth scuffed in a low whisper, and a finger jutted forward as if in silent challenge. "Just stop!" She cautioned with a slow frown. "Wait? What? What do you mean you?" she asked sternly, deepening the set of her frown. "What am I, putrefied cabbage? I made myself stop dreaming a long time ago." Hyacinth argued, her tone falling almost harsh, and manicured fingers made a wide stroke around the edges of her eyes, finishing in time to witness Betty's glare. "What?" she shrugged. "I told you not to start. Besides, I *am* his mother. I did give birth to him, did I not? If anyone is going to wash this night out, it should be me." She informed, looking innately defiant. She feigned the need to straighten the collar of her elegant, coppery-cream gown, throwing Betty a dignified smirk in finish. "And of course you, dear." She smiled, touching a slender hand to Delia's shoulder.

"I raised him." Betty announced proudly.

"You mean you spoiled him." Hyacinth retorted coolly.

"So did you." Betty groaned, and her dark skin wrinkled into what looked like a vexed frown.

"I mothered him, there's a difference." She declared with confidence.

"So what? Besides, he was such a charmer. I couldn't help but spoil him." Betty carped, and her eyes again rushed to the couple.

"He *was* a charmer, wasn't he? That boy was blessed with a silver tongue for sure." Hyacinth warbled, glancing at her son. "He had a way about him that just made you happy to be in his company, regardless of how."

"He must have. For him to get my daughter to this end, there's no doubt in that." Delia apprised tamely. "Julia is a tough one, or was. She wouldn't even consider other possibilities much less…."

"I don't think he charmed her, though. I think it was the other way around. I think she charmed every cell in his body until there was nothing left." Hyacinth smiled, and a look of thorough contentment swam slowly to her eyes.

"I watched them in the beginning when they first started working together. He couldn't take his eyes off her. I used to tease him by reminding him to close his mouth." Betty smirked. "She didn't seem to notice him much at the time."

"Now she dishes." Hyacinth grumbled, rolling her eyes to the ceiling in emphasis of her meaning. "I had breakfast with them a few months past, and you could just feel it. Even before he hinted, you could feel it. My son was long gone. She owns him."

"Think of what their babies would look like." Betty bleated proudly.

"Betty!" Hyacinth screeched in a near soundless cry. "Stop! Don't you put my mind on that path."

"But it's true. Look at them." Betty further prodded, showing not the vaguest hint of being daunted by the other woman's words. "Just look at them."

"I know it's true. But let me enjoy one fantasy coming true before you throw water on the seeds of another, will you?" Hyacinth groaned. "I've never pushed my wishes on him and I won't start now. Especially after he gave me something I've always wanted."

"That's my job." Betty chimed. "I can ask all the things you can't and not have to worry about him being mad." Smiling then at her old boss, she showed off her own brand of parental pride. "It's the same with speaking my mind." She slyly informed, nudging Hyacinth's shoulder with her own.

"You're wicked." Hyacinth cooed, squeezing the brown fingers affectionately, she smiled. "I know you already have grandchildren, Delia, so it's not the same for you. I thought…" she paused. "Well…we thought," she added with a smirk, swinging an inclusive finger between the old nanny and herself. She clarified her meaning. "Since she seems to think she's more his mother than I am. But in any case, we thought we would have, at the very least, two by now.

"It's funny, isn't it? How life has a strange way of going in the opposite direction of your plans?" She droned, her voice deeply reflective. "Anyway," she sniffed, dabbing at her eyes, while Betty's small hand devotedly patted her back in understanding. "Here we are, and I'm grateful for every morsel I get." She smiled, nodding then as if to affirm her statement as true, she again dabbed at her eyes. "I feel I must warn you, Delia, since I hope you won't mind sharing. I want you to know I'm too old to care how they come into my life. By marriage or by birth, I'm just happy to have children around. For I'm not too ancient, nor am I too stupid to know a fraction of anything is better than none. So I intend to cherish every bit of the pieces I have. Do you think you would mind me sharing my love, or claiming your grandchildren as my own?" she asked, seeming suddenly nervous.

Not having had the time to give much thought to such circumstance, Delia smiled, as she was, frankly, glad that the topic was broached. Here, it seemed, her grandkids will be treated well. If one side is willing to claim Julia's children as their own, wouldn't it then be equally fitting for the other to share?

"They say it takes a village to raise one child, but they never once said how many grandparents were needed in the fostering of such." Delia intoned sweetly, offering her own welcoming smile to the sorrowed eyes of the woman at her side. With absolute certainty, her grandchildren were the light that brightened her life. Sharing that light would hardly diminish the brilliance they bestowed, especially with someone who seemed to genuinely need that blessing. "A child's love, when given freely, there's no better medicine, is there?"

"Not even if you search the world a dozen times over from zone to zone. Garner the best medicine, and filter through each like a stream, the attainment bares no likeness." Hyacinth retorted palely, dropping her eyes. The two women fell silent, and the solidarity of motherhood and grief, bonded them in an understanding that went miles past just what was said.

"Then we should pray for rain to reach fertile ground." Delia muttered tamely, shrugging as two pairs of eyes stared back with shock lining their depths. "What? I'd certainly like to see what they would look like." She smirked. "Besides, I've always wanted more. It would surely grant us more hugs to go around."

"That's true." Betty agreed with a zealous nod.

"You guys are not helping. You're putting my mind where it shouldn't go." Hyacinth groaned, taking a renewed breath. "As wonderful as it would be, and boy…would it be wonderful if…. Oh forget it. Who am I kidding? You guys pray for rain, I'll weep for the potency of a monsoon." Chuckling at the surreptitious thought, their heads dipped in whispered affirmation. A long moment passed before each gaze again drifted to their prospective spawn, pride again shining boldly in their eyes.

Chatter soared limitless through the spry living-room space, and the crackle of a fire yielded its own serenading warmth to the eclectic buzz. The relaxing melody of music floated like a meek companion to the merriment they shared, preaching splendidly of a celebration at hand. Three sets of eyes tracked the couple as discreetly as they could, with conversation sharply following suit.

"Do you think we look as pitiful as I think we do?" Hyacinth scoffed. "Come on ladies, we can do better than this." She caroled sternly, straightening with obvious effort in her seat. "We're smart, intelligent beings outside of our children, aren't we? Let's just stop this. Come on. Let's find another topic to gnaw on." She coaxed, her voice like a newly vivified melodic hum, and in rejoinder, all eyes sank softly to the floor. Silence coiled slowly around the group in full dominance of the break, holding tight above their heads, a new topic imprisoned the fullness of their rummage. In preference, a discussion not having to do with the radiant couple beaming across the room, but try as they may, nothing but the joy of the day and its anomaly came dashing to their heads. That happiness dominated their every thought and discussion. Not unlike bobbers affixed to a lax fishing rod, their eyes again floated back to the couple, and there they stayed.

Chapter Forty Four

At long last, the spirited whirrs of engines slowly dimmed, smothered sweetly in the blackness of night. The long driveway swallowed the acrid gleam of their receding lights. Distance extinguished the grind of their mulish thrumming. Assuaging the atmosphere shrouding the secluded islet, night again gifted its silencing breath.

Promptly securing the majestic glass door, Michael turned to smile adoringly at his wife. Curling his arm possessively around the slim width of her shoulders, he latched her firmly to his side. Quietly, the two strolled in-tune to the mesmeric tickling of a jazz pianist, fanned amiably throughout the house. The mood was undeniably sweet.

Darkness stalked the train of their pomp procession. Favoring an unexpected eclipse, ebony shading interred the rooms now sited at their backs, as zealous fingers stroked the switches they happened upon. Time, in an expeditious show, slipped forward like the finale of a clause, and the master-suite, in a livelily flash, portrayed itself an inimitable haven for the couple's delight.

"We never did have our dance." Michael apprised then, turning her fully in his arms.

Julia smiled at the inference of his words and what that meant, cording her arms around his neck. She felt the instant warmth of his body as he pressed her close. "Do you remember our first dance?"

"Are you kidding me? How could I forget? I remember everything about that day. You kissed *me*, remember?"

"Yes, I do believe I remember that." She chanted. Casting then a pretty smile, she cautioned him in an equally syrupy tone. "And I could always cease the rite in that option."

"No, you can't." Michael countered swiftly, his heavy timbre vibrating roughly in his throat. It stirred like a sensuous purr through her body as he spoke. "I've got papers on that mouth of yours." He enlightened with a pompous smile. "I get to savor those pretty babies endlessly, anytime—anywhere I want."

"Is that so?" Julia queried with a slow hike to her brow, gifting him a sweetened smile. Her hands slid down the wide span of his chest, eloping leisurely to the warm enclosure of his jacket. She pushed the dark, elegant confinement from its place.

"Mm-hmm,"

"And what exactly do I have papers on?"

"As far as I know, it's free range. You'll need to stake your claim on that special piece of property you want."

"But what if I'm greedy, can I pick more than one?" she hummed in tamped deliberation, narrowing her eyes on the purposeful focus of her hands, bent, now, on the task of undocking his shirt.

"Since there's no one else here, I believe I could make an exception on that." He droned, his fingers stirring the small buttons on the back of her gown.

"Where do you suggest I start my assessment?" she quizzed in a placid tone, slipping her hands beneath the bivouac of his shirt, they roved the hard terrains of his chest. Stirring his cologne deliciously, he drifted up her nostrils like redolent vapors in a strive to captivate her sense.

"I like this dance." Michael vowed in a light breath, ignoring the question. His focus now stanch on the drudgeries of seeing her undress.

"It's very exhilarating." She smirked, sinking her hands inside the loosened waist of his pants.

"That it is." He smiled, pulling the shoulders of her gown forward. He awaited her arms to push clear of each sleeve.

"Such help. Thank you." Julia crooned, tugging her hands free of the delicate enclosure. She sent his trousers on a quick descent, and the dark garment, as if trained at such, settled promptly below his knees.

"I have a surprise for you." Michael whispered as he stepped clear, creating a scattered sphere with their discarded garments. The small mound entrenched the sway of their feet. "Are you ready?" he asked, surging her swiftly to his tall, sinewy frame. He touched his lips to the plumpness of hers and, as with tasting something exotic, his kisses lingered soft. Not yet ready to effusively partake, his eyes openly expressed the unending capacities of his love.

"Another one?" she asked jokingly. "It's a good thing I like surprises or you'd fray me thin."

"Good to know." Michael warbled in response, stooping like a lithe coil. He swept her swiftly off the floor. "Let's go see yours then." He grunted, showing off a refulgent model of his featured smile. Long strides ate up the unused portion of the rooms, depositing them in seconds in front of a barred bathroom door. He offered then the gentle command. "Open it." He whispered, jerking his head in the direction of the door.

Promptly obeying the soft directive, she threw open the door, and was immediately greeted with an aromatic zephyr. The smell of lavender mingled well with the light scent of rose. Drifting across the threshold like invisible clouds, it lingered about them like a new cloak. Flames flickered idly as if to mimic a coercive dance. Illuminating the room with the warm glint of candles, three dozen, if not more, hailed their dominance of space, as gold frolicked aloft an entire counter and shelf. Dancing friskily upon shadows yet hugging the walls, thus it waved from the bellies of miniature glasses. Underfoot, rose-petals littered the floor in clusters, scattered in multiples of orange, white, yellow and peach, red crested the shimmer of a half-filled tub.

"When did you have time to do this?" Julia asked in a strangely excited voice.

"I had my helpers to abet me with the task." He advised proudly, setting her feet to the floor. Michael guided the door shut without shifting either balance or glance, sequestering the dancing warmth to an already balmy room.

"You mean to say your mothers, of course." She teased.

"Partners, helpers, mothers, there's really not that much of a difference. Is there?" He laughed.

"We definitely need to come up with something very special to say thank you for all this." She advised, waving a hand inclusively about the room. She again surveyed the cumulative result of their work. Tossing him an affirmative glance, Julia leaned carefully over the side of the tub, swirling her fingers through the delicate petals. She checked the water's temperature beneath.

"As far as they're concerned, you already did that once you said 'yes'." He assured in a soft breath, while a finger traced the skeletal knots on her spine.

"As nice as that is, we still have to do something to acknowledge all this work."

"We will." Michael vowed, watching excitedly as she swirled her hand through the tepid water in a second test, looking almost like a child at play. "The bath only needs a little warming and…Well, you." He rasped, his words hovering loosely as if waiting to sprout wings, and he knew, with certainty, he would not have to say the rest. His eyes then mauled the draping of her naked body. Ignoring him in her enthusiastic ration, she, in time, threw him the start of a perceptive smirk, giving her own answer to what need not be said. She busied herself adjusting the velocity of the stream, steadying such from the faucet she now tinkered with.

Slow, careful steps brought him snug against the wall obfuscating her back. Folded easily about the middling of his waist, his left arm served as a footing to the elbow of his right. Said limb thence cradled the slow sag of his jaw. Hazel eyes narrowed as they watched her lean further across the opening of the tub, stirring the shallow pooling. She blended cool with the nicety of hot. Retreating slightly, she added caps of scented bubbles to the pool, mixing the gathering water. She stabled her body with a hand pressed to the opposite wall. Her hips swung then with the staunch motion of her hand, looking, to the observer, like an absentminded riff slotted in the throes of an eccentric dance. Lounging after almost fully on her stomach, she worked from crown to tail, blending the scented suds. She closely watched the progression of their bath, forgetful of the view she now tendered to her husband's eyes.

The smile he exhibited swept forward like the blazon of dawn. Growing to a lusty sneer, it deepened the dents now stapled in the corners of his mouth, as thoughts of kisses trailing her parts grew prominent in his head. He could almost taste her, so flagrant were his thoughts. For every essential part laid open to his errant imaginings, and his eyes and body battled for their own rights on the features she gave. Both equally ferocious in their ventures, even as his body, on its own, staked full claim to its wants, and the repast was definitely to his liking. Though it was hard to decide which method of feasting appeased his mind more—gazing or grazing?

As if suddenly sensing his thoughts, his wife slowly straightened. Glancing at his erect posture yet holding at her back, she smiled warmly in his eyes, seeing gluttony sit bold in their beautiful depths. Her gaze rappelled with awareness down his body. Michael unlocked his arms slowly from their stanchion set, his handsome face creasing with the start of a wary smile. Quietly, his shoulders lifted, in an unyielding gesture, towards the ceiling. Unapologetic, he found himself reluctant to give up his auspicious view or the favors they provided.

"You've been busy." She teased, her eyes fastened to the protruding limb that so gallantly stalked her, seeming set to pounce as he crossed the room.

"What can I say, a man is all about being visual, and you offered a devilishly good feast to appease the eyes. How could I resist?" he goaded, pressing the heated bough against her thigh as he adjusted their fit.

"Are you really that easily captured, Mr. Dunhill?"

"With you? Absolutely!" he drawled.

"Something tells me you were an extremely naughty boy. I bet you looked up little girls' skirts every chance you got." Julia teased, throwing him a pretty smile. She skimmed her arms around his waist, staring inquisitively in the jeweled depths for the answers she sought.

"Yeah, but they never gave me half as much pleasure as I get from watching you." He hummed, his deep voice cracking with humor. From atop her head, prurient eyes darted to the tub, noting that the once cornucopia of petals looked vaguely wilted and sparse, delicate blooms floated across a heavy cover of suds. "Your bath is ready." He rasped, unlocking her hands immediately from his back. He kept them ensconced in his while he led her to the opposite edge, eager now to enjoy her at length. The room fell promptly silent as long fingers twisted the knobs to a doze, and the last defying droplets toppled a floating petal as it drifted near, dipping its edge sharply beneath the sudsy surface with its force.

Sampling the brimming suds, Michael winced as torturous heat lapped wickedly at his legs, and he was again confounded by the scalding temperature of her bath. Wondering then, how the delicate skin and features on a woman could fare so well, while enduring such hazards. "Allow me to provide you with a most desired comfort," he smiled, turning his palms to the ceiling. He secured her grip, providing a stable anchor for her alighted toes. "The use of a cozy chair for my beloved's bath." Rumbling this with bold admiration in his tone, his eyes raked the toasted figure at the end of his arm.

With her hair still pinned tightly to her head, Michael smiled at his apparent foible in regards to that, for had it not been for their planned bath, he would have already searched out the source of her curls' captivity. Wagging her head, she smiled back fondly with acceptance in her eyes, though she sent him a simmering shot of awareness in response. Certain of his depraved plotting and the road they now veered upon, it pleased him, with unending satisfaction, to affirm her knowledge of him. Outside the perceptive tolerance of his mothers, he could think of no-one more attuned to every nuance of his thoughts. For, in truth, there sat a thoroughly decadent understanding between them.

"It seems of late my chair turns out quite often to be you. I wonder why?" Julia quipped. Setting her feet in the sudsy liquid, heat instantaneously engulfed the svelteness of her form, hastening through her body. It smothered all remaining chills.

"What can I say," he grunted, a feigned heaviness wafting with the whorl of his sigh. Lowering himself in the sauna-like seat, his protruding parts roiled greatly before calming under the intenseness of such heat. "I'm a selfless man."

"Is that what they're calling it these days?" she sang, her tone wafting sweetly, though it scraped like an incredulous taunt. "Mmmmm,"The soft moan came with the slackening of her head, falling to his shoulder. Her lids instantly fell as she settled between his thighs.

"Feel good?"

"Mm-hmm," sailed the throaty reply, adjusting her back against the hardness of his chest. Wet hands gently cupped his face where it rest, voicing her answer even through the sparseness of words. "This was a nice surprise, thank you."

"I thought you might like it."

"Especially since you seem to be a fixture in my baths of late,"

"Well…"

"Yes…."

"What can I say?" he smiled, shrugging in feigned innocence as he adjusted his arms atop the spill of her breasts.

"Not much I believe." She teased.

"I love you." Michael murmured with infinite care, his eyes warm as they stoked her face.

"Mm, though that, I'll concede, is a really good start." She purred, her lips soft as he turned her head to his. Tightening his arms around her, the corpulent dunes on her chest spread, tingling in response to his gentle ply, their peaks perked under the delicious offering of his hands. Strong fingers moved to span the width of her head, affixing her face to his. His kisses avidly deepened, warming both bodies to the sought of a rapturous end.

Beneath the water, his body raptly caressed hers, firm strokes aiding the drive of his intent, and she soon shifted to better accommodate the friend that beckoned. His hands trudged her body like a truculent doyen, strolling the depths of her sensitive cleft. It was not long before he maneuvered her will, inveigling her mind until she faced him in full.

Offering that which he already tenured as his, she surged forward as he brushed the clinging suds from her breasts, and time held no value once he drank of the chocolatey tips. Sighs of pleasure came muffled in the dark strands of his hair, carving her body to his, he worked with fervent zest, and it seemed an eternity before he, at last, lifted his head. Setting her to his lap, his kisses then ravished her senses as he recaptured her mouth.

Spurring her body onward with his voracious delve, she soon ached for the apogee that came in oath of an eminent invasion. Quietly, her hand moved between them, touching and teasing as his kisses rutted wild, thus urging the moil of her hand. Each stroke granted of a greater sweetness to come, and his tongue conveyed, in its adeptness, the pleasure of her work, as did the bassy glide of his grunt. Slowly, his hand descended on hers, steadying the competent bent of svelte fingers, the depth of his kisses quietly eased to ensure a pause. His breath howled like spurts in a tropical storm, as he gave then a pleasuring sigh.

"Your touch wreaks havoc on this poor body." Michael rasped, his tone seeming breathless as he nibbled the soft edge of her lips. His breath again drifted like a faint howl from the narrow passages of his nose. Lifting his head from hers, he turned her on his lap, caressing her back with the bulk of his chest. He settled her onto him, and a slow, rough, grunt rattled sweetly in his throat. Openly rejoicing in the exquisite verve of his homecoming, she enveloped him with the efficacy of a decadent embrace, wrapping the fiery shaft in her honeyed inferno. Heat meshed sweetly with that of venerated heat. As always, she had a scrumptious way of caressing him from the sweetest chasm there was, and she did so, then, without pause, drawing with ease, a shallow breath from his chest.

His hands moved over her breasts as he hugged her close, allowing her the right to pick the alacrity of their pace. For the moment, he would savor the ecstasy of them being one. In commencement, her toes slid beneath his thighs as she rose above him, and a long caress ensued with the climb. And he required no further encouragement to enlist in the surge of their dance. Their movements became a rapturous story in reply, each stroke the flounce of a purposeful tale, as one work to illuminate the beauty of the other in both tenacity and vim.

His hands taunted her maliciously in the enacting of their arduous drudge, and the music of her cries was like strings on the influence of his mind, stroking the very essence of his ego while he worked. The choreographed trot between them grew swift and untamed; surging until, it seemed, the vehemence of their effort sprouted wings. Hoisting them farther up a raucous climb, it threw them, with exuberance, beyond themselves, well past that of the desired end.

Sated, Michael buried his face in the moist beadings on her back, and the primitive argot of bliss tilled the air from the far edge of his throat. It sailed as a residual distribute of his unwavering ardor. Clasping her body to his, he reclined his back against the wall of the tub, as tiny waves of dimming pleasure cascaded throughout his frame, thus giving a slight tremor to his hands. Her head fell in a lax manner atop the ledge of his shoulder, and he immediately claimed her mouth. For the love in her eyes was unmistakably distinct, and he hoped she recognized well everything he felt in his.

The avarice stalking their breath, in time, slowed. He could feel the galloping pace of her heart wane to a soft trot, as it did his. And as like an autumn breeze over a flowering field, Michael's mouth lingered but yet returned.

"Mmmm," he rumbled in reverence against her mouth.

"Mm-mm," sailed her concurring reply, closing her eyes. She rested as if to seek slumber for the moments' past.

With lids fluttering close from contentment, words were an unwarranted need, and time drifted as if perched on laden logs. It simply coasted without end, as each now basked in the essence of the other.

"It's strange to say, but I never thought I would see this day." Michael rasped, breaking the serenity of the room.

"And what kind is that, one where you're a married man?" Julia warbled back, sending him a playful smirk. She locked her fingers through the eager caging of his.

"That, too," Michael acceded with a nod, widening his grin as if in thought. He grew silent, his expression becoming almost stern. "One where my heart would be this full. I never thought I'd find someone like you. I didn't dare dream."

"But look at you now." She smiled, touching his face with a long stroke that matched the swill of her breath. "And you did it so very adamantly, too." She laughed, sobering before giving voice to her thought. "This is something rare, isn't it? Us. This bond that we have between us—the connection, it's...it's really unique isn't it? I mean...I know it is. It has to be, since..." she groaned, and her breath sliced through the quiet like the blunt end of a rapier, though it marred little but the ears finely tuned in wait. "Well, I never had that with David. I can't explain how, but it was different between us. It's very different with you."

"It is. I'm almost certain of that. I can't explain the particulars since I know nothing of how they work. I just sense that it truly is. How you make me feel is beyond everything, beyond any expectation. And I'm very glad to know that this whole thing is as new for you as it is for me."

"It's strange, isn't it?" she asked, showing then a tender smile. "This whole development between us, how it started, how you convinced a very stubborn girl to let herself live, acknowledge and feel. Did I ever thank you for that?"

"I'm the one who should be thanking you. Even in your defiance, you gave me so much more than I was used to in a lot of ways. Being with you was an enlightening treat, which, in truth, only made me hunger for more." Curling his fingers around hers, he brought her hand to his chest, resting it upon the place that encaged his heart. He surrendered then another piece of himself. "It beats only for you, Julia." He pledged hoarsely. "Without you it would cease, for there would be no purpose for its incessant toil."

"As mine would without you. I'm not going anywhere, Michael." She vowed in return, her eyes growing almost limpid. "You have me body and soul. I'm here to stay. Not just because of you, but because of me. You've changed my life from the monotony that it once was. You've changed me. I could never go back to the ignorance that clouded my every step. This is my life now, the sustenance of you and me. From this day forward, this is who I am, your lover, your wife and your friend. All of whom simply adores you. My heart could not have realized happiness with any other but you. It simply would not."

"It's hard to believe I could love you anymore this day than I did yesterday, but I do. I love the fact that I can now call you my wife. I love the warmth that I'm surrounded by whenever I'm with you. I crave that." At her derisive glare, Michael smirked. "Well… that craving is on a whole different stratosphere. It deserves a separate introduction to give it the credence it has." Michael smiled. Gazing past her without truly seeing what laid to his face, his memory revamped the minutes only just lapsed. "Mrs. Dunhill," he sang, of a sudden, as if to hail her attention for some important task, unaware her eyes were already pinned to his face.

"Mr. Dunhill." She smirked in answer, keenly aware of where his mind wandered. Julia added her reminder in a whisper. "My…warmth…"

"What?"

"You were telling me how much you liked my…warmth." Propounding this, her eyes twinkled with mischievous intent.

Michael smiled as he watched her in silence, all arranged thoughts now mislaid and adrift. For with a simple elevation of her brows, she sent his mind scampering to places it should not have been, and there was no veering back to the homage he had once planned. "Have I told you how much I love you this night, Mrs. Dunhill?" he smiled, recouping a meager piece of his loss.

"Maybe, although Mrs. Dunhill does not mind hearing it again."

"In that case," he began, smothering the start of a smirk. "I love you more this night than there are trees that rises to touch the sun. And I will love you tomorrow, more than the earth loves the rain. I will treasure, love and honor you from this day forward with the tenacity of a bee. Relish you with the gentle strength of its wings. I'll toast you with the perseverance of duty and guard you with the swiftness of its sting."

"A bee, really?" she moaned, sarcasm drenching her tone, and a frown dragged hard on the angling of her brows. "That agile tongue of yours must have slipped some if you're grabbing at poor bees."

"A small bug, yes. But…one who's rather important, don't you think? If lost, it could change life as we know it." He assured shrewdly, shrugging off his clumsy word-ings with knowledge.

"Ah, I see." She hummed, her lips parting softly in acquiescence of that, though her eyes widened with a hint of mirth. "Very well then, I stand corrected. You're as astute as you are prolific." She pledged, waving a hand gently though the air. She extended her tease. "Throw in ferocious virility and I may just have myself a good catch."

Sliding his hand down her stomach, his fingers dawdled not, skiing past her navel. They rested gently along the curve of her thighs. "I'm ever like a blanket, you have but to reach for me and I'll be there with an inflamed ego to cover you every time." He advised. "Now my services whenever water is involved, are of legendary feat, my resume comes with full demonstrations. Want to see?"

"Is that so?"

"Mm-hmm," His muffled answer canted forward from the back of his throat, reaching her ears from the soft indent on the side of her neck. His hand intently admired the round placation on his lap.

"I'll have to think on that before I can give you a reply."

"Mm, I love your scent." He growled. "You remind me of a flower I came across in the Island. I really should look up that damn name, since every time I smell you, the memory pops in my head, just not the name. It gave off the most amazing perfume come nightfall. Once you smell it, you never forget that scent." He apprised through, what sounded roughly like a groan, closing his eyes as he swallowed the sweetness of her scent. "It's the second thing I think I noticed about you. Well…outside of appearance that is."

"Really, I'd like to smell that some time."

"I'll take you."

"Though I think this time you're just smelling sweat." She laughed.

"I smell my wife, beautiful and intoxicating as ever." Michael droned, burying his face in her hair. He pulled forth another breath, filling his lungs with the true essence of her. "Wife, hey, did you know I have a wife?" He smirked, looking almost stunned.

"I see news travels fast around here."

"You mock me? You would mock a man weakened by the emotional strain of his wedding?" Michael frowned, throwing his head at an angle, the furrows on his brows trenched immediately deep. "You're a mean one for a wife." He grumbled, shaking his head, he sighed. "You know," he announced hastily, softening the set of his frown. "There's something strangely nice about saying that. I think I found a new favorite—wife."

"How many more of those do you think you have left in you?"

"A few," He smirked, brushing his hand over what looked like an intricate tie in her hair, resisting the urge to let it down. "Why?"

"Oh, no reason," She shrugged tamely. "I was just wondering if I needed to set my tolerance gauge lower. That's all."

"You know—wife." He grunted, deepening the intensity of his scowl. He adjusted the spread of his legs. "If you insist on showing me this slight, I may be forced to insist that this marriage be dropped to that of a titular nature."

"Titular!" she gasped, the word flying forward in a forceful screech. It spewed from her lungs in haste. Twisting sharply in her seat on his lap, her eyes laid claim to his face. "Titular?" Julia asked at a near bark, a slow tremor building in her body. She shook with the swift expulsion of laughter. "How exactly are you planning to claim that?" she cackled.

Michael's expression seemed one of serene calm. Hardly a flinch showed on the chiseled features of his face, and although his own tremor begged in earnest to erupt. He did his best to quash the exhibiting of that.

"What interesting farce your eyes tell, Michael." She vowed, matting the corner of an eye. "Titular. Yes. I see it now, quite plainly, actually." And the riff of her laughter again soared high. "I see it as plainly as I do the nose on my face."

"Maybe I interpret the word differently than you do." He shrugged.

"I'll say!" she chirped, her eyes thrown mockingly towards the ceiling in emphasis of that.

"Potatoes—po-tah-toes, synonyms or antonyms, it's really all to one's perception, in truth." Advising this, his shoulders lifted in a casual shrug, while a hand glided sensually over her breast. "Such a provocative sounding word needed some provocation. Don't you think? I thought I'd give it a good try." He professed wanly, his deep voice drifting like the faint rumble of a warn. Primed and positioned to charm, a leer marred the perfection of the smile he then dealt. "Come, wife." He beckoned against her cheek, pressing a feathery kiss to said place. "It's our wedding night, and I'm anxious to drive all the sub-terrains you offer."

"No titular marriage for you?"

"A hungry man has to eat, does he not? And you make me very hungry, tonight more so than ever."

"Are we going to put the mattress by the fire?"

"You want to?"

"Wasn't that on your list of mores?"

"You were listening I see."

"To every word, why wouldn't I?"

"Because you looked so panicked, I figured only some of my words would actually get through. But as long as you got my meaning, I could live with that."

"I *was* nervous. I couldn't believe what I was hearing. I wasn't even sure it was real, not until you personalized it with some of the things we've done. That's when the whole thing hit home."

"I decided to do it there, but I wanted to be certain only you knew who I was talking to and what exactly that meant."

"Why there? Why so public?"

"It was the best place to catch you off-guard. And yeah...I love you that much. I wanted to share it with the world, even if they didn't know it was real. It still felt good."

"Won't there be repercussions? I mean...when expectations are not met?"

"Projects get shelved all the time." He shrugged, looking truly undaunted by the thought. "Phillip promised to help me work through the various possibilities. Worst case scenario, we give Oprah an exclusive."

"Oh boy," she sighed, seeming to wilt with the news.

"Don't worry, we're protected. I promise. We hold all the peremptory cards here. Besides, the full truth is so much better than the lie. Trust me, we're good."

"Okay." Tweeting this with a faint sigh, fortitude dashed forward with the scoffing of her next breath. "Regardless," she chirped in a soft rejuvenated tone, expelling the nonsensical worry from her mind. Neither illegal nor malicious, the explosion fixed to whatever the finale, however gauged, will remain a separate entity from the commitment they shared. A fabrication separate of them. "Fantasy or factual, it was definitely memorable. That's not something I'll likely forget. So…thank you." Tilting her head back, she kissed him thoroughly, taking the time to express her feelings without the tangling of words. The momentous night still yet hovered in its youthful stage, and the two were of one mind in their aim, wanting only to make every second count. It was of that thought that they drew from, as the two floated from the room. Like water cascading across a flat rock, their meanderings were soundless in every venue but one.

Eagerly, the two settled in the comfort of their bed. Yet, it was not rest that came in rejoinder when she straddled his hips. Nor was his action motivated by sleep once the two redeployed to the floor. Rest did not come until they exhausted an amalgam of situations, for loci and piquancy were of stanch importance to the fervency of their drive.

Hours, as a svelte body, drifted by languorously, and morning flounced majestically close to the ignition of a fiery birth. With consciousness roused, Michael woke from his slumber for reasons he could not understand. The room steeped of subtle desolation, drawing a mute breath, his wife's breathing trailed like a soft whisper in the silence of the house. Pressed tight to the warmth of her naked body, darkness feted like the baiting of a dream.

As if sensing his wakefulness, she stirred, shifting the silky warmth of her body against his. Essence of her attar raptly filled his nostrils with the meager arc, compelling his innate awareness to swill full of the flavor she granted. Lifting his head, he peered at her through the dark. Draped pleasantly in the blanket they shared, a folded corner sat loosely atop her breasts, with both hands clasped as added cushion under her cheek. A faint smile sat temptingly on her lips. Gentle in their pursing, as if in want of a lover's kiss, they summoned well even while engaged in dreams. Kissing her shoulder, Michael folded his body around hers, his arm falling soft across the breadth of her waist, and a sigh, in retort of his touch, escaped her as he again settled at her back. It was with that vision that Michael drifted back to sleep. Allowing the faint swish of her breath to be the source of his lullaby, he smiled as pictures of the night past welled as the maestro of his dream.

Morning, for the two, came some distance from then. In attestation of its verve, the faint spark of daylight tinged the quiet room while they rest. Julia opened her eyes and drowsily surveyed her surroundings. Nestled warmly at her back, Michael's body gently pressed hers, his arm racked, like a stern vice, across the hard knotting of her hip. Bathing her in warmth, the air from his nostrils rolled softly over the back of her head, soothing and warming in the crash of its quiet spills. Petals of mixed roses littered the floor circumventing their bed, and remembrance of their night flooded her mind in an instantaneous flash. A husband! The man at her back could now emphatically be called that. The very one who had so deftly swept her off her feet, doing so with unrelenting end; it was an outcome she could not be more thrilled to preserve.

With soft, timid movements, her action bought her a full glimpse at his face. Suddenly stirring, Michael rolled onto his back. An arm fell wide of his body as he again settled himself, while the other glistened with a platinum band, now nicely publicized, on his left hand. Julia beamed in reaction of the sight, giving a dazzled stare aimed at both their hands. She studied the remarkable radiance gleaming from said finger on her own hand. Sitting boldly alongside a platinum eternity band, was Michael's second offering of an engagement ring. Asscher cut, the center stone appeared flawless, like a well steamed glass. It bore no residuum or cloud, as was the smaller baguettes festooning its sides, equaling two. They looked vaguely like stars dappling her hand. Placing her ringed finger over his, she smiled at the contrast in their skin, knowing it was not unlike the contrast in their personality. Michael's eyes opened slowly in reaction. Seeing her, the sweetest smile leapt forward on his face.

"Hi!"

"Hi." He hailed back, his voice a raspy hum. Locking his fingers around hers, he brought them to his lips. "Good morning, wife. Well, afternoon is more like it, I'm sure." Michael shrugged, glancing then in the direction of fully obscured windows.

"Good morning-slash-afternoon, husband." She purred, squeezing the hand harboring hers.

"How do you feel?"

"Happy." Came the uninhibited reply. The single word, though small, came forward in truth, for she could think of none else to say that would elaborate more eloquently on that.

"That seems to be the special of the day." He smiled. "I love you."

"I love you."

"Will you wake me like this from now on?" he asked amid a long stretch.

"I'm sure I can come up with more creative ways of waking you."

"Yes, I'm sure you can. But it's like I've told you, for a man, the view is half the journey, and the view this morning is, well…" Michael shrugged, lifting his head. He propped his arm, like a pillow, under the dark tousle on his pate. His eyes then roamed her naked form at leisure, walking from cranium past that of her tail. "It's truly inspiring." He smiled.

"I'd have to agree with you on that."

"You like your morning view?"

"Afternoon, evening and night,"

"Nice. I like that. Why don't you come down here and show me how much. I'll gladly return the favor. After all, a husband has duties he must see to."

"You are, by far, the greediest man I have ever come across."

"I told you, I could dine on you forever. And man…do I intend to do that." He drawled, bringing her hand to his lips. He pressed a soft kiss to the rings now salient on her finger. "Even if that means just spending time on your mouth. Come here, so I can better explain."

"As usual, my aberrant darling, you tempt me sorely, though you'll have to wait on that. But I'll be glad to have you thoroughly school me after this very soft pause." Julia chirped, slipping quickly from the bed. Her hips swayed as if to flaunt the intro of a dance routine.

Michael watched the rhythmic taunting until it disappeared behind the refuge of the bathroom door, shifting his gaze then to the ceiling, he smiled.

"Unless, of course, you'd like an invitation to wash my back?" she asked, her offer sailing, with mirth, from behind the newly barred door. A low chuckle quickly accompanied the unnecessary pitch. Swinging the door open, she chortled with satisfaction as he hurried, without answer, to her side. The residue of sleep still sat bold across his face, twisting slight, while he affected a predacious stretch. It marred the usual freshness of his features, though not so, for the radiance quilting his smile. But from any angle, and at any hour, he was still extraordinarily beautiful to her.

What will being married now entail for them? She wondered, though the answer would have to wait until all slates have been rendered fully clean. Ahead, the road shows unending newness for both, so many firsts they'll need to adjust to. Not the least of which being who the man is, and what was sure to come with the magnitude of that.

Standing prominent were the thorny nigglings of his world, a bizarre contrast to the methodic meekness that environed hers, and no matter how hard they shielded themselves from the realism of that, those factors are certain to cross at some point in their lives. There'd be no getting around the importance of that, even if they had wanted to try, and that, of its own, was almost a frightening truth. Her worry on that wrung mostly for her children, neither of which had ever lived a life of secrecy before the indemnity of that to come. That, she suspected, would be the hardest nuisance to endure. But, a small price to pay for what she now had.

Thus far, the camaraderie he had since established with the children soared as a beacon in the concocted thicket they now rest, offering them a comfortable billet in which to set start. One, she sincerely hoped, once nurtured with time, would only continue to sprout further roots, since the three already seemed to enjoy their time together as it was. Now to work on the announcement of their relationship, Julia groaned. Decreeing it best to call their liaison dating at first, how long that continued depended solely on how well such commentary was received.

"So, where would you like to go on your honeymoon?" Michael asked in a gravelly drawl, adjusting a hill of pillows at his back, he smiled. With remnants of a late lunch scattered about them, the two cheerfully lazed by the fire. Without Betty in house, their meals were designated to the unusual territory of leftovers. Thankfully, with Betty's dominance of anything such, leftovers meant planed meals, which she had left them for every occasion of the day.

Julia's eyes drifted past him to the window as she gave his question full thought. "That depends," she smiled, giving answer in a sweet, deliberate tone. "What would *you* like to do on your honeymoon?"

"I don't know, what's the standard? What do couples really do on their honeymoons?" he groaned lazily, stretching the length of his body across the bed, he shrugged, a twinkle already sparring with his hazel flex. "We could go to Paris, see the Eiffel Tower as our backdrop every morning when we wake. Or we could go someplace warm. Whatever you want is fine, really."

"Do you want the body or person in this pictorial setting?"

"Is there a difference?"

"Well, let me ask you this. How much of our usual encounters do you see us encountering while we're away?"

"As many as possible, of course."

"So then it's my body you're after?"

"Can you blame me?"

"I guess not, since I'm not above using you for *yours*." She averred, tossing then a sweet smile. "We don't need to go someplace new for you to ravish me. You do that very well already. Here, we can at least do whatever we want, with more space in which to do it in."

"But every wife should have a honeymoon. Every wife needs one."

"Not this wife." She hummed, throwing him the chide of a sagacious glare. "Besides, the real reason for a honeymoon we already have. People do honeymoons to get away from the norm. This place is already like a getaway itself, it's far from the norm. None of their stiff rules applies to us here. Here, no one bothers us, we're always alone and always naked. What more could you ask for?"

"I guess not much." He smirked. "You'll be a hard one to please, won't you?"

"And yet you seemed to have mastered that skill. I don't want to go someplace else, Michael. Call it belligerent if you will, since the week my mother offered us will be gone in a flash. And with a small chink of that time spent on getting to and fro, I'll have to turn right around and leave the minute we get back. I'd rather just stay here and enjoy my time with you at leisure. We can fit in an extended trip some other time when the schedule is more lax. Now if that's being difficult then too bad for you, you're stuck with me."

"Then I guess that only leaves me one thing to do."

"And what, pray-tell, would that be?"

"The doling of the will, of course, what else?" He asked, reaching under the edge of the mattress at his head. He brought forward a small blue box, stabling the exquisite show in the palm of his hand. He tendered it to her, mindful of the small card attached.

"Michael?" she shrieked, her eyes growing wide, revealing the enormity of her surprise.

"You had to know I would get you a wedding present?"

"You shouldn't have, Michael. You can't give the bride a wedding present after throwing her a surprise wedding."

"Of course I can. Now open it up before I hold back my husbandly favors from you."

"Oh, really, now I'm almost tempted not to, just to accept a chivalrous challenge as that."

"Think you, woman, that you're stronger than me?"

"Perhaps we can put that to a test at another time?"

"My, how the gauntlet thunder in its fall."

"To the death, it decried, I do believe."

"Or was it such that the weaklings thought the chant of their own making?" he drawled, a brow lifting in obvious taunt.

"One can only be diligent in the weeding of such truth." Julia droned, though her smile gave fully her answer on that, lending her attention to the opening of her gift. She offered him no further counter on his jest. Only noting the treasure now prominent in her hand, a pair of princess-cut diamond studs gazed back intently from their bed. "Michael, you shouldn't have." She whispered tightly, her fingers gliding over the cool surface of, what looked surely like, chips of ice. "You didn't need to. You've already done so much."

"Do you like them?"

"How could I not, they're perfect. I love them!" She pledged. Her eyes staying on the sparkle entrenched in their cushiony bed.

"Put them on!" he pressed eagerly.

"But I haven't had the time to get you anything! Everything happened so fast, I don't have anything for you." She announced bleakly, looking almost apologetic.

"But I already got my gift when you married me, everything else pales in comparison."

"Really?" came the soft, incredulous cry, her eyes thrown like a whip to his face. Julia laid the small box between them as she turned, moving like an errant cat towards her husband, she purred. "How about me, do I pale in comparison?"

"I think you're the standard from which all things get measured."

"You're just a wealth of smooth, aren't you, Mr. Dunhill?" she crooned, perching above him like a domesticated dove. She scraped her body over his with the smooth-ness of silk. "Now, you just lie still and close your eyes and I'll make this quick." The whispered directive fell soft upon his cheek with the promise of something else, though, irrespective of the innuendo, he complied promptly without hesitation or doubt, smil-ing to himself as he felt her slip from the bed. Julia smoothed her hands jaggedly over the messy tangles of her hair, dressing her ears in the radiance of her new gift. She raked her fingers through the wild wisp before voicing a new command. "Open." She directed then. "How do I look?"

Michael's eyes bounded open with a single intent, set to ravish, they stroked her features at will. She wore no makeup in the aftermath of their day, and the curls in her hair seemed to splay in every direction at once. No fancy garments draped her in the accruing hours of what was, and no exterior aid came forward to dazzle with pizzazz other than what already was. Only the sparkle that brightened an already radiant smile jumped forward to his gaze, and still his eyes showed him the most perfect woman that ever lived. "Like the perfect dawn." He smiled.

"Great answer." She crooned, pouncing on the bed, she settled herself comfortably on his chest, kissing the very spot she rest before moving to his lips. "Since I'm without a present for you, I'm going to have to come up with a very creative way to say thank you."

"Open your card first." He rasped, brushing a wayward strand, amid the wildness, from her face.

"Oh! Okay." She chirped, gathering the card still dangling from her hand. She resettled on his chest. The hand written card was no different than what she'd come to expect, filled with beautiful words that stroked her at will.

Softly she smiled and morning waxed. A dryad clad in the favor of another. Woven in fables long battered with time, darkness frothed its dominance of such tale. Saplings whispered of such within the gathering rush, ere radiance called forth a name. Thus, an answer was had. She smiled and dawn bellowed its' affiance of truth. She smiles and the sun blooms. Like an oath once wedged in the crevice of lore, morning unfurled with the sweetness grafted in a simple smile.

"That's very pretty. How sweet! I love it! You really do know how to get your girl, don't you?"

"Did you think they were pretty before?"

"What?"

"Turn the card over." He drawled, pointing to the small stationary still clasped in her hand, he simply smiled. Complying with his dictate, she read the inscription aloud.

From your infatuated admirer, now husband.

Love, Michael.

"What! *You? You're my admirer?*" she shrieked, springing from his chest. Her slender form seemed coiled to launch the thrust of a deadly attack, as brown eyes widen with the incredulity of that truth.

"Guilty." Michael shrugged.

"*You!*" she yelled, slapping his shoulder with the expulsion. "Do you know how frustrating this whole thing has been? I kept thinking that some poor lovesick woman was missing out on the beautiful compilation of both flowers and words. I just knew they couldn't possibly be for me. *You!*" she groaned, and the sound of her slap echoed like the reverberated sting of a whip as it soared through a quiet room.

"I don't know why you're so surprised. I told you I was coming after you." Michael remarked dryly, flinching as her hand again drew back in preparation to strike.

"But…you never gave a hint. I even carped to you about the whole thing and you never…You!" she groaned, a shrilly spike hugging her tone as her hand again parrot the resonance of a whip. "Besides, who would suspect that? It continued for so long. You were already wreaking havoc on my body in more ways than one. The concept, then, seemed utterly needless. Oh, my God! My mother was right!" Julia exclaimed abruptly, touching both hands to her cheeks. "She kept telling me to keep an open mind. Wait until she finds out!"

"She already knows. Well, at least I think so."

"She does, how?!"

"I don't know exactly how she found out, but she hinted of her knowledge at my birthday party."

"You're kidding?! Oh, jeez! Now I'm going to have to revisit every conversation we had just to see how much she knew back then. And you!" Julia squawked, returning her attention to the man. "Now I'm going to have to go back and read all those cards all over again. Man, I'm glad I didn't throw them out." She groaned. "I bet you just think you're pretty slick now, don't you?"

"Not slick, just stalwart in my effort. I wanted to cover all my bases to ensure me the coveted result. That's all." Michael shrugged. "I wanted you, and you wouldn't play by regular rules. So I had to pull little tricks here and there to help me with the struggle."

"What am I going to do with you? You keep knocking me off my feet at every turn. I'll give it to you, that was pretty slick. I'm officially stunned" She crooned, wagging her head slowly in resolution of the cunning he showed. "The words were very beautiful, did you write them?"

"No, that was P. S. Campbell in the flesh, well, not so much the flesh now, since he's been dead for over a hundred years. But he's always been a favorite of mine, though I did add my own touches to a few." Michael rasped, curling his arm around her shoulders. He pulled her close.

"It felt too strange to fully enjoy them before, especially since I was sure they weren't mine, but I'll definitely go back and enjoy them now. Thank you."

"That's all I wanted, really."

"Why? Why would you go through all that? If I didn't even know who you were, what difference would all that effort make? How could that have helped you, whether I enjoyed them or not?"

"If you remember, I started it on Valentine's Day. I wanted you to know you had an admirer. But you complicate the whole thing by refusing to be swayed. I had to do something. I couldn't just give up. This was the perfect way to talk to you. I could tell you whatever hopes I had. Utter whatever feelings I held inside, plus whisper aloud all the things I was thinking as it pertains to you. And I could have you hear all that without me having to open my mouth. You may not have known who the sender was or even cared. But every time you read those words you were listening to me." Turning his head on the pillow, Michael smiled. "I was kind of wooing you—in an old fashioned sort of way."

"That's what my mother said!" Julia chimed, shaking her head at her obvious folly. "At least I truly enjoyed the flowers. I thought they were beautiful, by the way. Now I'll go back and enjoy the words as they were meant to." She promised. "I thought they were beautiful before, but I didn't take the time to enjoy them quite the way they deserve. Now I'll enjoy them as the words my husband used to court me. Who knew you were that much of a romantic."

"Certainly not me, that's for sure."

"What? You're kidding, right?"

"You were a whole new world for me, Julia. I've never been this patient, this quiet or this smart with a woman in my life." He growled. "Never,"

"I find that very hard to believe." She teased, frowning in disbelief. "You've always handled yourself so well with me."

"Oh, I can handle myself alright. I've never had a problem with that. It's just that, with you, everything felt so different, so heightened. I wanted to do more, give more and have more of everything at the same time."

"Then I'm grateful for the way you handled yourself. It all worked out very well in your favor and mine, of course. Because now, I'm inclined to think my husband is a genius."

"Oh, you do, huh?"

"You bet I do. I can't think of one thing that would have worked better than those choices that were actually made. Can you?"

"I did use my brain well, didn't I?" Michael smirked, pulling her close. He dropped a kiss atop her head.

"Along with a few other things, of course."

"Of course. No heat, no singeing flames to relish the essence tangled with dessert."

"Now there's a definite truth. The choir concurs fully with a plangent amen." She purred, amending the fit of her head on his chest. "So, is there...anything *more* you wish to add while we're on the topic of surprises?" she inquired palely, draping her leg across his thighs. "Is there anything else you wish to share while you have the floor, any other secrets to give?"

"I can tell you one. But the other will have to ferment a little longer before I can give you that."

"Why can't you tell me now?"

"I'm just getting acclimated to the openness we now have. I guess I need a little more time to dismantle all the partitions erected to protect."

"Is this something you're afraid to tell me?" Julia asked in a small voice, lifting her head from his chest. Her eyes jumped sharply to his, and a frown surged taut at the absurdity of that.

"Not fully, maybe more so for what your answer will be."

"So it's a question?"

"More or less," Michael shrugged, gathering a few strands of her hair. He studied the dark tress before he spoke. "Less because of what it says, but more because of what it means."

"Is this something that will affect us—our lives?"

"Yes. But not in a negative way. It's not bad, really. It's actually good—very good, actually." He assured, toying with her hair, he smiled.

"And you don't want to say what *this* is—yet?" Julia probed, recognizing, somehow, that although not said, the matter meant a lot to him nonetheless.

"Right. I'll spill it, just not this minute. Give me a few days to get comfortable with the idea first. Can you give me that?"

"If you want me to, sure. I have to respect that. But you do know you can share anything with me?"

"I know that." He assured without pause.

"And that I'll always do my best not to judge."

"I'm not worried about your judgment, Julia, just what comes with your choice."

"Would you feel better if I gave you a blanketed, yes?"

"That would definitely help...some." He nodded, and the resemblance of a smile showed then in his eyes. "That would be like opening your presents on Christmas already knowing what's inside."

"Sounds like fun." Julia shrugged, moving back to her place on his chest.

"Are you saying 'yes'?"

"I love you, Michael, but I can't say 'yes' without knowing what I'm saying 'yes' to. Especially when you tell me the decision will affect our lives. How about I meet you halfway? I'll say it's a definite maybe. How is that?" she asked, giving the question as her hand roamed soothingly atop his chest. "Does that help?"

"It does." Michael smiled, his eyes tender yet assertive of such truth. Wanting, greatly, to tell her of his wish, though he worried some on the magnitude of her reaction. How do you spring a topic so substantial this immediate in a marriage?

"Then will you tell me now?"

"Maybe tomorrow," he shrugged.

Julia eyed him curiously as a gruff sigh sailed forward from her nose, lengthening in value as it glided across the room. "Okay, tomorrow then." She agreed in a soft breath, and again smoothed her hand over the ridges of his chest, as if, in turn, to soothe him. "What's the other secret, the one you don't mind sharing?"

Silence fell for a quick trice before he gave answer, shrugging tamely with the start of his words. "It's no big deal, really. It's just an observation."

"Will I want to know this?" she teased, affirming to herself the workings of his mind. Sensing there was always more lurking behind that easy smile of his. Now, as if like a flower, he unfolded himself to her in gradual steps.

"Maybe," Michael mumbled low as he rolled, pinning her almost fully under him, he smiled.

"Tell me then." She purred, suppressing a giggle from the suddenness of the act itself. His eyes took full possession of hers in the settling of their wont, and mischief danced boldly in their jeweled depths as they worked.

"I love the way you look at me." He rumbled in start. "I wish you could see it through my eyes. Or drink of how it feels to have you gaze at me the way that you do. Without the use of words, you tell me you love me every time you're near. Every time I look at you, your eyes mirrored mine. I looked in them and I knew. I knew you loved me as much as I loved you. I've known the truth for a while."

"I was *that* obvious?"

"Wasn't I?"

"That's different. I'm the girl. I'm supposed to be demure and prim, remember? Maybe even a bit priggish when you think of it, and I wasn't. Instead, I literally acted the part of a paramour, serving myself up on a platter like a snack. I pretty much raped you every time I saw you."

"Did I happen to miss out on that fun? I thought I would have complained more if faced with the prospect of such peril." He chuckled, sobering almost as quick. "Have you ever wondered why I happily took whatever you gave and never once asked for more? Well, until later, of course."

"No. Not fully."

"I took it all, Julia, because you gave me so much more than just the heated fragments of lust. What you gave, you gave fully, and you asked for nothing in return. I was not want for anything in your presence. Whether through talk, play or the physical attributes attached to our sport, I could feed on every morsel you grant. There was no reserve when you touched me and none in the way you kissed me, and I could not help but beg for more of that. I wanted you the second I saw you, though I didn't realize just how much until later in the game." He professed, touching her face lightly, his smile looked almost pained. "I wanted to tell you this, Julia, in the hopes that you never stop looking at me in that way. It's truly a beautiful thing to be a part of, and I hope the flavor you give never dims from your gaze."

"I thought you stood, then, the most beautiful man." She murmured tamely, forging the abstracted sentence as a suitable response. Her eyes cinched to a target on his chin. "Your eyes alone are, by far, your most exquisite feature. They drew me to you like a magnet to steel. Every time I look in them, I lose all handle on my will. That's my secret when it comes to you. It's a part of why I look at you the way that I do, and why every time I see you my only thought is to fully consume."

"Mmm, like minds. Can you read mine now?" he droned.

"It's not your mind that's doing the talking, dear." She smiled, aware of the sudden intrusion along her thigh.

"Only a gentle reminder to say I'm still here."

"You mean a rather firm reminder, don't you? Almost adamant in fact."

"What can I say," Michael growled, his brows twitching lightly. "He likes you, very, very much I might add, and the thought of being consumed excites him."

"Yours has got to be a disease." She goaded, rolling her eyes in the assumption of that. "So now you know one of my secrets." She chimed, running her fingers through his hair.

"One? You mean to say there's more?" he asked, flashing her the start of a roguish smirk.

"There maybe a few others rolling around somewhere."

"Am I going to have to ask to hear them?"

"I'll dish them out to you, slowly, over the years." She smirked.

"Years?"

"It'll keep you interested now, won't it?"

"There're too many ways to keep me interested for you to propound doling. You really don't need to add another to an already preposterous list." Michael growled, brushing a kiss along the side of her neck, he smiled. "Attach anymore power and you'll have me walking on my knees before long. That hardly seems fair. So what do I get out of this monopoly? Shouldn't I at least have something to even the field? It seems to me you're holding all the cards." He hummed, trailing his kisses further down her throat to her breasts. His hand softly glided across her skin.

"Mmm, what would you like?" she purred, lifting her chest to better afford him access.

"What's on the table?" he inquired tamely, his lips caressing her as he spoke. Featherlike kisses glided across her abdomen as he awaited her response, his hand brushing each area as if in preparation for the sweetness to come.

"Could you perhaps throw me some hints?" she purred. Closing her eyes in concomitance of his work, for the warm sensation yielded by his mouth now roused her like the sting of one being thawed. Gently lifting her leg, his kisses moved along the inner smoothness of her thighs, surfing one. He imprinted the same on the other with equal zeal. His hands further worked her body as if as a persistent guide, encouraging a slow spin onto her stomach. His kisses softly surfed the trench of her back. Rappelling down the smooth slopes of her buttocks, they fell, again, to the valley of her thighs. His mouth worked upon the soft flesh without worry or haste, falling to her like the wisp of a feather. His kisses grew incredibly sweet. Returning at last to her ears, Michael whispered in a slow, gravelly pitch.

"Now I've kissed every inch of your body. That's a promise I intend to work on often."

"Mm, and done so very nicely, at that." Julia purred, turning her head, she brushed a kiss upon the corner of his mouth. "I'll have to come up with my own set of kisses for you." She warned, and the artful answer dragged like a purr against his mouth.

"Just so you know, I like my kisses in very discreet places." Michael counseled, his hand moving devotedly over her skin. "You wanted ideas...." He shrugged. "So I'm just letting you know." Pulling her up to sit fully on his lap, his kisses moved again over her back. Pushing the hair from her shoulders, they travelled farther up her neck to feed gluttonously on her mouth. Her hands worked leisurely upon the plains of his body, growing willful in her endeavor, until, at last, she piloted him home.

Assigning itself a new tone, Michael's breath grew staggered, fanning from his chest like a territorial ballad, it howled down the slope of her back as her body swallowed him whole. Slowly wrapping herself around the throbbing flesh, she sipped until there was nothing left. Soft, warm, dank and luscious drank him in in full. Holding him firm, her embrace made his warrior-like body tremble with the sweetness she gave. The heat of her back was almost as maddening as the drive itself, pressing her hard against his chest, his hands skated the mountainous lines of her body in a long, hungry caress. The pounding of his heart echoed roughly in his head, as her hips moved with the sweetened cadence of a well familiar dance. Eliciting an appreciative grunt, the resonance of which formed like lumps in his throat. His body tingled greatly with the intensity of their work, taking everything and giving the same in return. His oration came truly of his soul. "Good…God, you feel…good…." he averred in a low, airy growl. His proclamation sailing as his hips grew apt.

"Mmmm…." she cried back in a gruff breath, dropping her head back onto his shoulder. The wildness of her hair spilled madly down the flexing of his arm. Her breath whirled intensely from the recess of her throat in acquiescence of their dance, for his ravenous feed now gnawed relentlessly at her core and there looked to be no deterrence in the thoroughness he intended upon. His mouth and body grew obdurate in their strive. Arduous in feat, he stretched deep until she had no higher heights to climb. "I love you." She cried as the soaring ecstasy burst inside her, exploding on both almost at once.

Michael grunted as if attempting a response, cognizant of her pinnacling cry. His breath, hands and mouth grew astoundingly rough in their reply. For discernible words seemed, then, to have escaped his grasp. The room grew stagnant in reaction of thus, patient in its wait, as if in expectancy of their next act. The enormity of their affections conducted the fervor of each touch, abetting the drive of each sapping kiss, two satiated bodies collapsed back in quiet exhaustion at its end.

Chapter Forty Five

Soft, tinkling bells yowled merrily from dithering doors and lawns statuettes. Fixtures loomed majestic on adherent's steps, publishing the placards of an imminent approach. Spoils of the season grew ghastly fastidious. Bolstering an inspired drive, bustle ripened well into the orbit of madness, and preparation, at times, seemed rightly suited for some eccentric spurring, that, or in the stark contemplation of war, as strife amongst the masses neared the hilt of an extraordinary climax.

Daylight routed indubitably less, and nights grappled with its own plummeting chill in significance of such, nipping callously at the vivacity of the faithful throngs. Winter mocked the smiles yet fastened on the breadth of each face, though irrespective of such ominous cost, the jollity of the season sustained them well.

Already scant from a significant collage of days doffed, the ponderous year now pranced to an abstemious dissolution regardless of effort. Yielding Christmas its grandeur in less than two weeks, and the kids their avidly awaited winter-break in even less.

A week-long honeymoon—classified such by the technicalities it upheld, though only in the philosophy of a few—topped the schedule for the commencing break, rescheduled to then for the convenience it propounded. The delay coincided seamlessly with David's allotted share of said pause.

Thinking it best, the two acceded to postpone her conversation with the children, permitting the merriness of the season to remain just that. They agreed to resume said conference afresh with the New Year's commence, fully primed, as ever, to give forth a lie in the fortification of a complex truth, and to proceed thus to the necessary end.

The ebullient weekend left as dynamic as it began. Departing with little difference sheared from the couple's daily lives. Night came to find them again swathed in their prospective beds, with their phones poised, as ever, as their only companion. Mornings came with much the same pursuits as the months prior to that, and the Waltham-Berwick-Dunhill household, knew no variation from what had already established itself as routine. Julia trudged through the house fully suppressed in the throes of her most distinctive job, clucking incessantly behind the sloth-like actions of her bairns. Her efforts scathed, at times, like the shilly cackles of an overbearing hen. As her voice, in the middling of all that, neared its peak ascension, scaling ever upwards in her endearing hustle to herd them out the door.

Breakfast came as usual with a phone call. Adhering well to the customary habit they had since sanctioned a must, sharing their first repast of the day was as natural a practice as the provision was for some. Though today's collation held, for them, an added refrain—gossip, with much of the blather now directed at them.

Evidently, talks were now prevalent on the details of one supposed movie scene, named as the source for the dialogue used in a mock proposal. Compliments, of sort, went out to the lucky audience member who got to be proposed to by none other than the confirmed bachelor himself, one, Mr. Michael Dunhill. No one could be reached for comments or information on the tight lipped production that the scene was taken from, but speculation on the romantic incident had audience well primed for the finished product's release.

Of course, there was the theorist who speculated on the realisms that the whole thing had, and those who wondered why he just happened to carry a ring, inferring their views on the principal cause. Hypotheses flew rampant, though the countenance and the age of the woman herself had everyone stopping short of naming the scenario real. Thinking it more likely a publicity ploy, a teaser, in some way, of the creation to come, so priming their market for a desired result. This, since all trace of said woman had since gone cold, it's projected that a clip of the emotive scene would now make a staunch focal in the public's eye, at least, one can only hope, until the squawk of chatter expire from its high. Though, that, too, is expected to dim once the taping gets aired, which, some now surmised would only be a matter of weeks. And for the hundredth time since, Julia found herself thankful for the solidarity of her disguise. Though the apparent humor in Michael's voice, as he related the hypothetical drivel, did naught to steady the palpitations she now had.

With their weekly family dinner set for six on this day, the expectations ascribed to her jitters were a faultless right. Conscious of the addendum now attached to their previous lie, her nerves jangled as an endless twitter. In affirmation of her angsts, the doorbell rang at three, post meridiem, on the dot, half-an-hour before the kids expected departure from the bus.

"Hello!" He chanted as she swung open the door, his eyes already asserting their will. "Have we met?" Michael rasped. His deep voice sounding rich in the afternoon's chill. Coiffed with a lazy breeze and drenched in sunlight, his was a form surely sculpted to be revered.

"Met? Why, no. I don't believe we have. I pride myself on such things as that. I never forget a face."

"Neither do I, yet you, somehow, look familiar to me." He hummed. "I'm, Michael, by the way. Michael Dunhill." He announced sprightly, moving forward with his hand outstretched. He stopped a mere inch from her person.

"Julia, Julia Dunhill."

"Nice to meet you, Julia Dunhill," he rumbled, and a mocking twitch rushed the corner of his mouth, lacing the fringe of his smile.

"Nice to meet you," Julia smirked, her eyes tunneling his.

"So tell me, Ms——?" he paused, lifting a full brow as if to mock the duplicity of his ask.

"Mrs." Julia corrected quickly. "Mrs. Dunhill."

"I stand corrected." He warbled, nodding then. He brought forth a regaling smile. "My apologies on that,"The confession came in a soft, reverberant tone, as did the gentle press his body now injected in the cause. "Mrs. Dunhill, my team and I are conducting interviews with people we suspect are newlyweds. As researchers, we're wondering how these couples feel about the decadence of life now that they're married. Have their views changed any, with time wearing on the edges of such shock?" He droned, proceeding leisurely around her. His voice rumbled low like the distant brewing of a storm. Quietly, he shifted his stance, drifting forward like a breeze until his chest aptly walled the meager stature of her back. "So, Mrs. Dunhill, what exactly are your views; how do you feel about being married?" he asked, pushing the door shut with a subtle twist of his hand.

"Actually, I like it. I like it…very much. How about you, are you married?"

"I am." He drawled, his breath falling soft against her ear.

"And…?" she hummed, holding tight to her next breath. "What view do you have to share with the rest of us? What is married life like for you? And do you like the challenges it offers?"

"Prodigiously," he swore, and the word came sounding like a lyrical note.

"Wow! Really? You don't get that too often these days." Julia warbled in response, turning then, she slipped an arm slyly through his.

"What can I say?" Michael shrugged. "That's how I feel. Are you here alone?"

"No, I'm with my husband, actually."

"Oh."

"We're supposed to be on our honeymoon." She sang, shaking her head at the sudden show of a smile.

"Me too! That's quite a coincidence, don't you think?"

"I suppose. Your wife is not with you?"

"She's about somewhere; and your husband?"

"He's about. He's conducting interviews, I think." She smirked.

"Don't you think that's a little risky for a husband?" he asked, stroking her fondly with the slow rappel of his hand.

"What is?"

"Leaving a wife like you alone, and on your honeymoon, no less. To work? I would have expected such a man to be draped all over you."

"I had the same thought. Now I'm beginning to think he doesn't appreciate me. What do you think?"

"I'd have to agree. Why else would one leave your side and, on such an occasion?" he posed cockily, and broad shoulders shifted gently against her in concurrence of such. Much like the decoy in a sneak attack, his once hidden arm slowly came forward from its place, displaying, to her view, a small straggling of wild flowers once hidden at his back. "If I were your husband, I would give you flowers every day." He announced. "I would tell you I love you with every breath, just so you could fathom the range. If I were your husband, I would kiss you until you gasped for air, never giving an inkling as to beginning or end. I would savor every inch of your body until you trembled and begged. I would love you until your body wept from the ecstasy of having it thoroughly dredged: and when it was over, I would start the process all over again. That's…if…I were your husband." He finished, gifting her a gentle smile. He touched the flowers to her hand. "These were for my wife, but I don't think she would mind if I gave them to you."

"Thank you. That's so very nice of you. You know, I was thinking, since our spouses seem to be missing, perchance you could show me how a husband should treat a wife? Purely for the demonstrational purpose, of course," she pledged. "Do you think you could remind me how it's supposed to be?"

"I'd be glad to." Michael growled, pulling her snug into his body. His head fell without delay, pressing her eagerly while his tongue darted with fierce resolve. Strong arms tightened the deeper his kisses dove, taking minutes to give testament of what he felt before he lifted his head.

"Hi." Julia smiled, gazing weakly into beautifully roused hazel eyes.

"Hi."

"You're early."

"I wanted a little time to do *that* before the kids got home. I've missed you in my bed." He rasped, the warmth of his breath dappling her skin. Sliding down her throat no different than a subtle stroke, it sent, what felt like, a warm chill through her body.

"I've missed being in your bed." She hummed. "But I'll definitely give you the chance to stay in mine tonight." confessing this with a slow smile, Julia snuggled deeper into the hardness of his flesh.

"Is that an invitation?"

"Think of it more as a promise. That's if you don't mind hiding out in my closet for a while." She crooned, adjusting her arms around his neck. "I could make your night," she coaxed. "And since the kids have another day of school, you won't have to rush off before morning. Breakfast could be…on…me. What do you think?"

"Let's see, a little inconvenience for a night with my wife? Um, I think you already know my answer on that." Michael droned, his hands gliding over the roundness of her buttock, lingering there before stapling her close. "Just give me a pillow and your laptop, then lock me in and I'll be all set."

"You got it."

"How much time do we have before the bus?"

"Just about…fifteen minutes or so," she chirped, turning her wrist to affirm her guess. "Not nearly enough time." She counseled, already knowing his thought.

"Ten minutes to pet you then?" Michael smirked. "I could make that work. Let's go set the timer. We'll use ten minutes of what we have to cram in a full week of longing. What's so difficult in that?"

Forced to adhere to the grueling travail of such, the couple adjourned to an applicable venue that would concede them that. Ten minutes to kiss the one you love. Ten minutes to tell them all the things you couldn't before and cannot after. Ten minutes to show how much you missed them, and how much more so you will at its designated end. It was their ten minutes to use, and they used it rightly to the fullest extent, giving each other the best that they had. Ten minutes reared with the bliss of an ethereal daze.

At nineteen minutes exactly, the first bus steered noisily away from their quiet street. Rachel veered onto the long driveway with the grouse of the engine faintly serenading her strides, marching at her usual pace. She mixed in a hurried skip now and then to vary her pace. In a flash, brown eyes lit like a newly stoked fire, noting the freshly unbarred door, her feet jumped immediately to a prance.

"Hi, mom," she chirped, slipping thin arms around her mother. Hers was a gentle torrent in the love she bestowed.

"Hi, sweetie," Julia chirruped in return, placing a kiss on the wavy mass of her hair. "How was school?"

"Good." She panted, granting the familiar answer that had grown infamous as a reply. With sluggish steps, she moved past her mother, each tread exaggerated by the deep rounding of her shoulders, carved, now, to a flagrant "C". The backpack staggered down her arm like a reluctant child. Falling to her fingers, it jerked to a tense stop. Dangling from her hand as if weighted with rocks, it climbed backwards with a windup now aided by said hand. Awarding the pack thence an enthused swing, she flung her bag, like a bothersome sack, towards the stairs, releasing a heavy sigh as it skidded to a stop.

"Long day?" Julia solicited softly, her brows drawn fully, as if to voice some small tinge of surprise. Her answer came wrapped in a low grunt, needless of words to clarify such a reply. Rachel shuffled to the kitchen in her drone-like gait.

Richard's bus screeched loudly before its usual stammered stop, and in distinction, his entrance in the house was as opposite of his sister's as night was to the gruff breaking of day. Racing down the driveway, he took the four steps in two bounding climbs, almost stumbling as he crossed the threshold in his own gust.

"Hi, mom!" he bellowed as he blew past her, and as customary, the house winced with the force he honed in his small hands, rattling the walls before they again fell still.

Julia smiled at the clear variance in the two, shaking her head at the marvel of such. She followed her daughter's enervated progression to the kitchen. Michael's laughter rang forceful as her feet verged the vibrant space, as if privy to the punch-line of a good joke. His hazel eyes sparkled as he turned them on her.

"Rachel wanted me to know, I kind of look like one of her teachers." Michael explained.

"Really?" Julia smirked, heavily doubting that fact.

"Uh-huh." Rachel nodded, her glass anchored to her face. "Except he's older, and shorter, and his hair is a different color." She finished, giving then another nod.

"Which teacher is that?" Julia asked, already cognizant of the answer, since Rachel only had one male teacher this entire school year.

"Mr. Raeford." Rachel chimed, and great certainty tilled the fine edges of her voice. Taking another long drink from her glass, she missed the slow roll of her mother's eyes. So, too, the skeptical look that flashed across her face in remedy of that, or the tight smirk she threw, in counter, at her husband's head.

"Maybe one of these days I'll go steal a peek at this, Mr. Raeford, see what the competition is like." Michael smirked, waiting for Rachel to turn to the sink before looking at his wife.

"Michael!" Richard called with full excitement from the doorway of the kitchen.

"Richard!" Michael returned with mimicking excitement, matching that of his new son. "How's it going, Richard?" he queried, raising his hand in salutation, he awaited the thwack of concurrence from the smaller hand.

"Good!" Richard assured in his usual jubilant tone, slapping his palm with force to the other, he smiled. "Are you going to still be here after I'm done with my homework? It's really short."

"I think I could manage that." Michael smirked.

"Cool!" Richard chirped, rushing then to the refrigerator. He pulled opened the door. "We could finish that game we started."

"Don't you think you've beaten me enough on that game?" Michael groaned, grinning impishly at a new thought. Compared to him, Richard was in the alliance of a guru when it came to most video games. "On all the games for that matter,"

"You're not *that* bad." Richard chuckled, lifting his own glass to his head, his choice baring the rich brassy hue of masticated apples.

"Yeah, right! So, how was school?" Michael asked jauntily, waiting for the glass in his hand to descend.

"It was fine." Richard shrugged.

"That good, huh?" Michael droned, grinning as a sudden vision of himself, spurting said answer, flew to his mind. *Evidently, such sentiments grew timeless.* "Are we still set to go RVing after Christmas?"

"Yeah, I can't wait!"

"Mom, can I go, too?" Rachel asked in a small voice, suddenly interested in the conversation being had.

"You want to go RVing?" Julia asked with obvious skepticism now swilling in her tone.

"I want to try it." Rachel nodded. "Richard says it's a lot of fun."

"It is!" Richard verified eagerly over the rim of his glass, swallowing the last of his juice. He endured in his sell. "It's kind of like a rollercoaster, except you're on the ground." He enlightened, conviction now searing his tone.

"And I love rollercoasters. Remember?" Rachel prompted keenly, turning anxiously to her mother. Big eyes grew even wider with the anticipation she felt.

"Do you have room for her?" Julia asked through a tame frown, already knowing that he did.

Michael chuckled slyly in the quiet of his head, appreciating the anxious expression on Rachel's face while she awaited a reply. Seeing her mother boldly vented in every feature on her face, he could not help but wonder if their own daughter would carry the same keen resemblance of her mother. Wouldn't that be wild? He quietly hummed, snickering this to no one but himself. "We could just take the one that seats four." He reasoned, glancing from his new daughter to her mother. Who would have thought this a possibility before now—him—a family man? Not possible. But how does one deny the candor or the evidence at hand? A fidelity that plainly branded him thus.

Night descended in full before he distinguished the substance of time spent, and a trip to the closet became a necessary pretense to uphold the rectitude of their game. Though time, in truth, never sat still. It flew swiftly even while he waited. Still, the humor of his predicament did not escape his assessment as to where the two now rest, for it illustrated not the deeds of one already married. But those on the other side of that, and he was positive that none, not privy to the truth, would believe such scenario without proof.

Slipping into bed, at long last, with his wife, Michael whispered all the things he promised he would, following each with astounding demonstration. He took the minute details of his work to heart, carrying out each task equally as proficient as those requiring his every thought. Bequeathing such for the next pair of nights, he made true his oath. Arriving well late, he tramped, without notice, to her bed, resting like a husband should with his wife.

Their seven-day honeymoon began with no less fervor than their encounters of the past. Spending the first two days locked away from the world, only the need for replenishment saw the two vacating their haven. Though the trill of merriment heard wafting, at intervals, from their sanctuary were not always as they seemed.

"So, what would you like to do about Christmas?" Michael asked lazily, looking well sated in his stretch as he settled back on the couch.

"Christmas, why?"

"Well. I don't know if you've noticed this...but...Christmas is in a few days." He smirked, snuggling her further into him. He shifted his body to acquire a better fit. "I'm asking my wife, what would she like for Christmas."

"But...but your wife doesn't need anything." Julia stated assuredly, already wearing a frown. "She thinks her husband has been more than generous already."

"You're asking me to spend my first Christmas, as a husband, without a present for my wife?" he quizzed, his voice seeming but a whisper, though the look he shot her was one of incredulity.

"Well..." she grumbled fraily, understanding the influence behind his look. "When you put it that way it sounds bad. But..." tilting her head back with the granting of a sigh, she garnered his befuddled gaze. "I really don't need anything, Michael, and I just don't want you to think you have to keep buying me things. I'm fine without all the things, really."

"Then I take it you're not getting me anything?" he asked in an erudite tone.

"Well—"

"I thought so." He grunted, twisting a finger towards her nose. He stalled all further reply. "Never mind, I'll pick out my own gift for you." He countered, looking proud of the victory he gained.

"I had to get you something. I'm in the rear here, Michael." She grumbled.

"Likely story, Mrs. Dunhill; but you've been busted. Now, what should I get the kids?"

"Well, something very simple, I think that's your best bet. You don't want it to seem as if you're trying to buy them." She advised then, knowing she could not have denied him that right. "If you get Richard a video game or something athletic, he'll probably be your friend for life. And Rachel is into fashion, so something pretty—or shoes! She loves shoes. You can never go wrong with shoes. But don't…well. I could help you with that. Maybe I should just buy something and we could put your name on it. That would probably be easier."

"Okay." Assenting to this with a faint sigh, Michael smiled, well happy he would not have to remember the precision laced to her none-too-simple advice. Not with the approaching day being this close. "But I'd like to be a part of the process, okay. It's their first gift from me. I'll feel a lot better knowing, at least what it is."

"Duly noted," she chirped, feeling pleasantly amazed with his level of involvement in their family.

"We could have dinner here while we exchange gifts, or do you think it's better for me to come to you?"

"Dinner here sounds like a very good idea. It would be like having a doubly wild Christmas revelry for them. They seem to love it here." She shrugged, though her answer came with a serenely confident smile. "They think this place is a lot of fun, and they seem to like you a lot. Thank you for that." Pushing herself onto an elbow, Julia smiled. "Thank you for putting the work in."

"They're great kids. I'm very fond of them myself."

"I can see that. But I still thank you for consistently doing the work."

"Do you think the kids will always think that about this place?" Michael asked, skipping his usual clever return. "Or will this place lose its appeal after a while?"

"Basketball, tennis, RVing, swimming and that's just to name a few." She crowed, flicking a finger forward to indicate each. "Speak nothing of the trails, fishing or the other multitude of activities that could basically swallow you in the short spacing of a day. Are you kidding? I'm sure this place stays cool no matter what. After all, a big kid built it." She teased, missing the true meaning behind his query. "Why? Are you now eager to settle on the many hassles of family life?"

"Well…actually, yes. I am. Probably as eager as I am, the strain of…fatherhood," he intoned, his voice dipping astoundingly low, brandishing a cunning lilt with each word.

"Fatherhood!" Julia laughed. "Wasn't it you who reminded me that Rachel and Richard already have a father? I believe that was the selling rouse you used on me." Nodding as if to confirm her own answer as true. She threw him a soft glare, rolling her eyes playfully to the ceiling at its end.

"I did say that, didn't I?" he drawled. "But William and Stephanie wouldn't."

"William and Stephanie, who are they?"

"The other kids who may also someday…think this place…cool. The ones who may or…may not provide us with…grandkids—should they choose." He droned, shrugging lightly behind the last of his words. His expression grew hesitant in, what reared as, a quick trice, for with the matter now disclosed. His was a countenance that relied solely on her reaction.

Julia leaned forward slowly from her place of rest, sitting pin-straight, in counter to the spawning of a notion. She stalled as if a javelin had been sutured, as an anchor, to her spine. Her exotic features dithered rightly between skepticism and doubt with the filching of her next breath, almost surging like a gasp as it rushed forward. Thus, the tautness in her body lingered further unmoved. Brown eyes shot to his face in question, screaming words she dared not put to tune, not fully sure she hearkened what she thought she heard. Was he really posing what her senses now insisted he was posing? "Michael, are you saying…are you saying what I think you're saying?"

"What do you think I'm saying?" he asked in a nervous hum.

"You tell me!" She advised in a tight voice. "Who would know better than the person that's…well, the person asking the question…uh, I mean…speaking, right?" she probed nervously, her eyes as wide as the ocean at night.

"I'd like to audit the subject of our family dynamic." He started, his argument sounding to all ears logical. "I want a baby!" Michael blurted in a husky grunt, a heavy breath following the hasty reveal. "God, I never thought I'd be saying that, but I do. I want a baby." He smiled. "I want a little girl with big, brown eyes and skin the color of dark caramel." He sighed, his voice laced with emotions. "I want a little girl that looks every bit like you the way Rachel does. I just want her to be mine."

"But-but you never wanted kids, Michael." She stated almost blandly, her voice checked in a strained whisper.

"Or a wife," he reminded then, taking her hands in his. He caressed the raised tendons on the back of her hands, before he again spoke. "Not any of those things until you, Julia. I want what comes with giving a part of ourselves to each other. I want the fortune of it, something of you and of me with a personality all of their own."

"But…" she paused, brushing at a tear as it welled in her eye. "I'm…" a nervous laugh came in riposte to naught but the constricted pause, sounding like a choked hyena. It did nothing to obstruct the silence that had since mushroomed with the stall. "Michael, I–I don't know what to say." She whispered in follow.

"Are you mad that I sprang this on you so soon?" he asked softly.

"No. I'm, I'm...surprised." She mumbled, pulling her hands free, she roughly swiped them across her cheek.

"Pleasantly?" Michael asked, his eyes already searching out an answer in the dark depths.

"I don't know." She retorted blandly, lifting her shoulders slowly in time with the words. "It's...it's a little astonishing. I never..." gathering his eyes, she waited for the words.

"You never thought about it, even after all this time?"

"I wouldn't allow myself to." She droned. Her tone hushed as she studied the mystic gems of his eyes. "It was better to protect myself that way, you know."

"And now—now that your husband is asking for sure?"

"When did you start thinking like this?"

"I'm not sure, really. It popped in my head a few times here and there, I guess. But when you called me to say that you might be, it took on a whole new life." He moaned, pausing. He pushed a pillow firmly behind his back, taking the time to draw in a long breath, as if the recollection still troubled him some. "You were so nervous—and I understood why. I really did." He added quickly. "But all I felt was calm. I should have been nervous—I know that, and I thought I would be. But all I saw was a little girl with your eyes and your skin, looking like you with maybe a little bit of me, and...Truthfully, the picture only made me happy. I just couldn't find the fear. I wanted her as much as I wanted you." Squeezing her hand gently, Michael smiled. "But then, you weren't...." He shrugged, as if to emphasize the words he could not say. "I can't even explain to you the emotions that came with that, since I barely understood it myself. I just know what I felt and that it wasn't sweet. It felt as if I lost something, you know? And even though I never had it, I wanted it back." He sighed, wagging his head as if to purge his thought. His voice grew husky as he gathered her eyes. "Not having it, Julia, didn't change what I felt inside."

"But you never said anything to me."

"I knew how much you wanted not to be. What was there to say? I'm sorry you're not pregnant. Or, that I feel as if I'm mourning the loss of a child that never was. That probably would have scared you half to death. God, I couldn't even tell you I love you without the fear of losing you. How could I have told you that?" he groaned, and the gentle pressure of his hands tightened to a solid embrace, this, as if to reassure her, as well as himself. "I had to learn the art of saying things differently with you, Julia. So I did. I got the woman of my dreams to marry me, and I want everything that comes with that."

"I'm sorry. I didn't mean to be so blind to your feelings. I really didn't. I just wanted to protect myself from what I thought was the inevitable. There was just no way these feelings I had would last. I kept repeating that mantra to myself. The nucleus of who you are, your lifestyle and your reported views on such things were all enough to magnify my opinion on that. It was important that I kept you at bay. I needed to keep you at a safe distance to protect myself…but, God, you just wouldn't stay there, and you wouldn't go away. I thought everything I felt was due to my years of fasting. I didn't understand the root of my attraction or where its potency would lead." She croaked, curling her fingers gently. She returned the support he gave, though she was sure he knew her heart better than she did herself. "I can't ask you if you're sure this time, can I?"

"No, you can't."

"Once we gave voice to our feelings, everything happened so fast. I suppose I expected that with time, we would eventually cross that bridge, or, at least lay bare our views on such possibility. But…here we are…" she sighed, taking an afresh breath. "As an only child, I always wanted to have a big family." She shrugged, pausing again as if hampered by a thought. A tear skidded softly down the slope of her cheek. "I would have to go in for a new physical," came the contemplative remark, her tone seeming distant as she gazed past him out the windows at his back. She thence continued her wordings as if reading a pre-authored list. "Be off the pill for at least three months, and we would probably have to change some of our play habits, as in less at a certain time of the month." She proceeded, muttering the provisos almost absently; she ignored the look of joy on her husband's face. This would be her gift to him. A gift without the usual hesitance or obstructions defacing the beauty that it bade, knowing the outcome was also something she'd wanted her whole life. The pairing of their love was an exquisite reward, in its nurture, to bring forth new life. "You do realize that we can't do any of this for, at the very least, six months?"

"I know." Michael rejoined hurriedly, nodding his head with more vigor than there was need; he smiled. "We need to let the kids get use to us as a couple, tell your friends, and then have another wedding before we can do this. Six months! Yes!" Michael gushed, nodding quietly to himself.

"At the least, Michael." She reminded.

"Yes, I get it! Six months!" He affirmed in a hoarse whisper, ignoring the soft reminder as he leaned to her for a kiss. "I can't wait!" he chanted roughly, lingering in his place, he sighed. "I love you."

"Yeah, I hear that a lot." She grumbled. Resting her fingers pleasantly along the lean, lines of his jaw, she smiled.

"Don't I also show you?"

"Every opportunity you have." She purred, raising her face in the offering of a kiss.

"We get to make a baby together, wow!" Michael exclaimed, his breath sailing warmly against her mouth, and hazel eyes sparkled with the sublimity of what that meant.

"Yes we do." She purred, and dark eyes skimmed his features, as if to memorize the details of some secret scribing. "Man, do I look forward to that." She crooned, her own breath like a warm feather upon his skin, braising his senses before he led the tincture of his own malicious attack. Although her smile was immediately set adrift, the mauling was definitely to her liking.

Chapter Forty Six

The holiday sidled raptly to a canorous fruition. Drifting lazily in focus, it percolated like the blunt tail of a draught in the Sahara desert, yet vanished with the explosive jet of an exhale. Long before the second breath properly dissipated, January readied its dull valediction, rocketing past the squally gradient of its third week.

February already authenticated its ascendancy, as white dusting garnished the earth like the topping on a bun, with much promise streaking the forecast of more to come. Winter proudly stated itself unresolved.

Julia's birthday passed quietly without pomp or ruckus. Choosing the subtleness of a meager celebration, she savored the usual outings with her friends, relishing, more stoutly, a splendidly leisured night with her husband at its end.

Talks with the children went forward as planned, and although the experience left her grateful to have conquered a problematic hill, the occasion left her truly perplexed as to the effect. Since the conversation furnished on the spoils of her now dating and, most significantly, who, dropped like a colossal waste, with both kids looking sincerely disinterested and spent.

The small soliloquy she conspired in her head was even shorter when said. Their lax mien pinching the very verve from her drive. Given the newness of the circumstance, even an optimistic friar could not have predicted the result that she had. A brusque nod was Richard's only response, not bothering to give words in answer. He offered none in question of the news. Rachel was, as usual, her quiet reserved self, smiling with a sense of awareness. She, too, gave a quiet nod. "Okay." Was her only reaction to that, as if the topic was already a known one, like a book she had already read, therefore was fully cognizant of the tale. She gave no notion as to her thoughts. Without notice or further adage, the two raced from the room, and play became an immediate resumption. For, it would seem, the matter bore no further discussion nor needed no further end.

Now that the ferment of the holidays sat tenuously at their backs, the New Year foisted its tractions for the long path ahead. Work, in its abundance, toppled the couple's agenda anew. Julia's writing again dominated the hours of her day. Mindful that her customary three-month adjournment had ballooned, quite avidly, into six. But, she could find no regrets in extending her splendorous break.

A glitch in procedure had Michael fully suppressed in rectifying the cause. Continued commotion over a bitterly permitted film-site—an historic cemetery adjacent to an architecturally odd church, both said to be built in three hundred and eighty A.D.——had production now standing fully at a halt. With what parallels as a renegotiation of their procedural intent——staged oddly in the eccentric guise of a town meeting—— fostering such deferral beyond the trifling of three weeks, their phones became a necessary indulgence as it always had. Serving as their only means of contact for the better part of a month, conversations stayed, as usual, aberrant. For it was outrageous to fathom, just how much she missed the man, and to say she was ecstatic at his pending return, such piddling descriptive, would be a gross understatement of fact.

Petals fell from her hands like soft, red, velvety rain. Sprinkled artfully over the pillows on her bed, she affably established the mood of what was to come. All blinds and drapes were fastened tight, leaving the vicinity of her room in pitch blackness, fit, in truth, for but two things. One of which had no part in any of the forage she had planned, at least not until morning takes its waking breath. Julia smiled as she surveyed the result of her work, moving through the dim space with a concentrative flare. She lit a collection of candles dotted about her room.

In goading, her heart jumped as the sharp, musical chirrup bayed its warning through the house, twisting in the cavern that it rest. The organ juddered crudely before settling in a gallop, thus halting the sluggishness of her treads. Excitement rattled every nerve in her body as she hastened from the room, shaking her statue as she pulled open the door. With jubilance plastered on her face, her mind raced with the identity of the places she intended to exploit in her attack. Swinging the door wide as designated parts sped through her head, her breath came to a sudden halt. Not unlike the congruence of pictures with forgotten resolve, each scene flashed in her head like those in a forced collision, and the jolly of her jubilance died in the space a blink.

"Vanessa!" she crowed, her jaw almost locking on the dispelling. A nervy smile jumped forward in wait, and adoration, in an instant, flashed its limit. Loved dearly through the infinite eon coded in time, best friends are welcomed innumerable times in the coiffed refuge of one's home. Irrespective of hour or circumstance, the tincture of that love was unconditional, for such symbiosis is needless of invitation or key. Though today just could not be one of those times.

"Oh, thank God! You're home! Good. I've been driving around forever trying to make sense of this whole thing. But I just can't...I can't seem to get past it!" Vanessa rambled tartly in lieu of a greeting, traipsing past her startled friend like the sudden rearing of a gust. Her hands waved as if to silence some unheard noise in her head.

Julia gaped out at the street as if to survey the scene of a horror flick. Her legs now bonded in place with the gum of anxiety and shock, and a shriek of laughter chose its moment well to amplify her stun, callously rending the air. It stung the skin on her cheeks with its piercing force. A yellow sports car cruised by slowly, and inside the cheery young couple's head reared back as an obvious sign of their mirth, and although the cackle did not come from them. She could not help but feel that the lark was meant for her. Closing the door with a heavy thud that seeped outwards from her chest, she gave a heavy sigh, turning from the, now, stark entrance to her friend. Julia plastered on what, she hoped, would be mistaken as a smile.

"I know I'm the doctor and I shouldn't let this bother me, but it does!" Vanessa started in a rush, looking as nervous as she sounded. She twisted the cap free from a bottle of water she now clasped in a strangle, taking a small sip before slamming the refrigerator door. Oddly, the gentle thud soared through the quiet as like the slamming of a mallet.

"What's wrong?" Julia asked hurriedly, her own frustration immediately defunct, seeing fear now whitened the dark skin on her friend's face. All thoughts of inconvenience laid slaughtered in their tracks.

"I'm cramping! A lot!" Vanessa vented hastily, sighing heavily behind the candid announcement. She swallowed, as if to subdue the bile of her rising fears. "I know it doesn't always mean something bad will happen, but then again…it does or can. What do you think?" she asked again in a hurry.

"I think you need to sit down. Come on. Let's just relax. All this fretting doesn't help you any. It does the body more harm than good. You taught me that, remember?" Julia chirped, her demeanor calm and reassuring, knowing her reaction was as important as that of her friend's. Gathering Vanessa's hand, she led her to the couch, making certain she was fully comfortable, before bidding clarification with thus. "Now tell me what the problem is."

"I've been cramping," Vanessa groaned. "Since about midnight, and it hasn't slowed any nor does it seem to want to stop."

"Do you have any spotting at all?" Julia asked calmly, easily reversing their profession.

"No, none!" Vanessa chanted, with eyes already wide, her head waved in follow of her worried response. "I know what the facts are, and I know what those in my profession would tell me. But it doesn't seem to matter. I just can't shake this fear." She groaned, finishing again with a heavy sigh. "Did you have cramps? I can't remember."

"I did. It felt as if my period was about to start any minute."

"That's it! That's what I have!" Vanessa screeched. "What do you think? You're the best thinker out of all of us, if you tell me you think it's okay, then its most likely that. Do you think it's okay?" she asked almost childlike, her big eyes looking well swollen with fear.

"And you don't have any other problem, except the cramping?"

"No! Nothing!"

"Did you do anything different the past few days, anything strenuous?" Julia continued, not wanting to give an answer until she first had all the facts.

"I haven't done anything new. If anything, I'm being more careful now than ever."

"How about fun, did the cramping start after that?"

"No. It's been a week. You know how crazy our schedules get, it's feast or famine sometimes."

"No back pain, heavy discharge or etceteras like that? Nothing; even in the slightest outside of your cramping? Has it varied or gotten worse?"

"Nothing, nada, none, not even in the very least! I've been feeling great! Well, until now."

"Then I think you're probably okay. I can't find anything that would make it any different than that." She shrugged, happy with her conclusion. Julia offered then a smile, pleased with not having to give her best friend sour news. "But you'll need to call your doctor, just to be on the safe side. Okay? Go in and get yourself examined."

"Oh, thank God!" Vanessa grunted in reply, her sigh sailing like a billowing gust, sagging her shoulders heavily on its swift descent. "Thank you! Thank you! Thank you!" She chimed softly, tightening her grasp around the bottle in her hand. Her head bobbed with the momentous expulsion of each word.

"I think you need to calm down, though, Vanessa. All this stress can't be any good for you or the baby. In another couple of weeks, you'll be over the iffy stage, and you'll feel more at ease with the changes in your body. But until then, you really have to keep the stress to a minimum. God, your job is stressful enough. You don't need to add more to that worry!"

"Yes, mother." Vanessa hummed, displaying the start of a smile. "I knew if anyone could help put my mind at ease, it would be you. With your gift, you can talk a dead horse to get up and beg."

"Just wait until you get my bill; you won't be able to afford this kid after that. Are you kidding me, house call on a weekend? This visit alone should get me the down payment for that new beach estate I've been eyeing." She laughed.

"So that's how you afford your expensive trinkets? You swindle poor people like me out of their life savings." Vanessa warbled back, taking a long drink from her bottle. Her eyes grazed the features of her friend with feign displeasure.

"That water, by the way, is imported. It, too, will be added to your bill, and last time I checked, I didn't send for you, you came to me, remember?"

"Some good it did me! All I'm left with now is my hunger and a hefty bill. What do you have to eat around here anyway?"

"What do you feel for?"

"I don't know. Suddenly I'm famished." Vanessa shrugged, returning to the kitchen, she eyed the inside of the refrigerator intently. Looking much like a child in her pondering. She, at last, turned to the counter with her arms fully laden with the ingredients for a sandwich. The package of roast beef was barely opened before her wild snacking commenced. With few slices making it onto the bread before another was tossed in her mouth. "Mmm," she mumbled after the third slice. "That's good."

"Are you sure you can taste it? You seem to be going a bit fast." Julia teased. Moving into the kitchen, she poured her friend a glass of orange juice.

"Always the smartass, aren't you?"

"So now you have insults?"

"Why? Did you think you were the only one who knew what wittiness was?"

"Is that what you thought that drab was?" she chimed, setting the glass within reach of her friend's hand. "That's almost shameful to know. Are those the pitiful things they teach people like you in medical school?"

"Along with a few other things; want to see?"

"No thanks. I've already established the quality of my schooling for today, maybe next time, though." Julia chuckled, taking a seat opposite her friend at the bar. She pilfered a slice of beef from the mountainous sandwich. "Feeling better?" she asked, kicking her toes in taunting against Vanessa's shin.

"Much! Thanks."

"Anytime," she hummed, tensing of a sudden, she virtually bolted from her seat with the blasting of the first note, as the doorbell again caroled, like a young choir through the house. "Um, excuse me." She mumbled as nonchalant as she could, whirling eagerly from the room. Hurrying feet gradually changed their pace to publicize a skip, though she tried her best to look unaffected in her hurry. Julia swung open the door with unrestrained haste, her pulse dancing like mad. Shooting a sumptuous spark in every area of her body at once, her husband's tall physique adorned the arching of her door like a rare artifact newly exhibited. Looking tempting, like something deserving of a good thrashing with one's tongue, a purr wafted like silk from her throat to settle on said feature in agreement of such.

Michael's smile barely said hello before he lunged, smearing her back against the wall. He slammed the door with a quick swipe of his hand. Kissing her with all the pent up passion that fermented with the lapsing of a month, he drank himself into a ravenous fiend.

"Wait! Wait!" Julia whispered through a shallow breath. "Vanessa is here."

"Now?!" Michael howled, his hazel eyes flying open in shock. At her brusque nod, he drew in a slow, calming breath before straightening from his toil. "Damn! I was hoping that was your mother's car. To be continued, then." He growled, brushing his lips across hers.

"Oh, you can…definitely count on that." She purred, sweeping her hands over his chest. Her palms moved in a fluid caress down his sides.

"A little lower and to the left," Michael smirked.

"You tempt me."

"Not nearly as much as I'm tempted to drag you off to your room right now,"

"Don't be so sure on that." She crooned, moving her hand to the designated site he directed, a light caress ensued. "Anytime you're ready, husband." She teased, smiling wickedly, while her hand made-do of the same.

"You do realize that that's not playing fair, right? Not when you have my hands tied, well…you know what I mean." He droned, his eyes slowly soaking her in, sipping from her head to her toes.

"Then kiss me quick before we have to go in. Let your tongue do all that work it does so well. Heaven knows it's been missed." She coaxed, giving the gentle suggestion with the truest intent, as she could sense no fear, then, of being caught. No worries surfaced her mind of what if. Only knowing the sensations she felt, having not seen her husband in over a month.

Michael smiled roguishly at her seditious request, leaning forward to give response. Mischief shone bold in his eyes, pressing her body firmly with his, he slid smoothly down the full length of her statue in his quest. Confident hands throve on the long hem of her dress, folding it like a retracting step. His labor reared like the fermenting of a good wine, drudging, until the garment sat in a puddle atop her hips. The ardor of his tasting started along the warm silkiness of her thighs, staying close to the dank warmth of her body. He kissed the cherished cleft with leisured strokes, his tongue soft and velvety wet against her.

"You never specified where I should kiss." Michael whispered as he straightened, and mischief was the least of what showed in his eyes.

"Well played." Julia applauded breathlessly, feeling her body soar rapidly from hunger to outright greed in the maddening space of a flash. "Stay here and cool your heels for a minute." She advised him then, taking a breath of her own. She coaxed her body into doing the same. "I'll see you in the kitchen when you're done." Her remark cruised almost stern as she turned, sending a last glance over her shoulder. She edged towards the confronting of her friend.

Entering the kitchen, indecision boiled in the pit of her stomach, realizing then that this would be no easy task. Not with these friends. A friendship that saw them through everything worth withstanding and some that did not. An alliance well devoted and revered, as the three shared every factor of their lives with each other, knowing every secret breath that the other wrought—except this. That is, until now, for this was a secret that would be no more.

"There you are!" Vanessa chuckled, looking up from her newly prepared salad. "If I wasn't so hungry I would have sent out a search party to go looking for you."

"We need to talk." Julia spat determinedly, leaving herself no option but one.

"What's wrong?" Vanessa asked, and humor, like the flip of a switch, was instantaneously replaced with concern.

"N-nothing...nothing is wrong. I'm...I'm good, actually." She nodded, pausing as if to consider whether the statement was, in truth, a factual claim, her eyes darted to the floor. "I'm actually very good." She smiled, gathering her friend's eyes for the first time since entering the room. Strangled footsteps grabbed their attention, like the slow release of the safety on a gun, stalling the start of her explanation. Michael graced the doorway like the perfected vision of Rodin's Walking Man, dragging their stunned gaze over his person, as he offered them a smile.

"James!" Vanessa called in greeting, a high note of surprise ringing through his name.

"Hello, Vanessa, it's good to see you again." Michael answered calmly, his deep voice floating low across the room.

Julia smiled openly in welcome, holding his gaze with a promise quietly given before turning back to her friend.

Vanessa watched the exchange with intrigue turning swiftly to interest. Thus it fostered until a small splash of pride marred its jagged edge. *She did put her two cents in about them, did she not?* So in some small way, this was her right. The intensity in the room thickened to a boil the moment he walked in, and from the way he looked at her, there was no guessing on what he felt.

"Oh, my God! The two of you?" she screamed, and the elation in her voice blasted through the room like the blare of an intercom fully maxed. "You got her to bend?" Vanessa inquired loudly, slinging the anxious question at the man now leaning against the wall. "I was hoping you would give her a reminder of what it feels like with a man."

"Vanessa!" Julia shrieked, and a hint of embarrassment shone then in her eyes.

"What?" Vanessa queried firmly, glancing back at her friend without batting an eye. "We're all adults here. Besides," she shrugged, leaning into Julia's side, her voice immediately dropped, and only they were privy to the rest of what needed to be said. "You know there's nothing like it if the ride is good."

Julia's eyes dropped with her head quickly in-tow, and had it not been for the warm tones staining her skin, her face would have likely been as vivid as the petals on her bed. Although, she agreed whole heartedly with the edict, she refused to acknowledge the statement as fact to her friend.

"When?" Vanessa continued at a high pitch, shaking her head in confusion. "How? How did you get her to agree?" again directing her questions to the man. Although his body exhibited the purest essence of arrogance and pride, his expression, however guarded, veered not from the distinction of both. Yet he eyed his wife for clues on how to answer the questions being asked of him.

"Persistence," Michael vowed, making eye contact with his inquisitor, he smiled. His choice was a deliberate fact, unsure of how much he was allowed to tell. He gave her a small truth and nothing else. "I wouldn't take no for an answer." Michael finished, topping the avowal with a warm smile before again looking at his wife.

"Vanessa," Julia began softly, turning slowly in her seat, she ignored the look of pleasure now notched on her husband's face. Not wanting to create more questions than the answers she was willing to give, knowing he'll, in turn, draw the very same from her. Her gaze remained fully averted from his, for she was not yet ready to give all at this time. "Vanessa, Mic—I mean…James, just flew back from France," she paused, sending a nervous smile to her friend. "I–I didn't know you were coming. I…" she sighed, leaving the missing words to hang heavily in wait. She inserted yet another pause.

"Say no more! Are you kidding me?" Vanessa chirped, springing spryly from her seat. She snatched up her purse with fluidity as she turned. "If you needed it, I would stand guard at the door for that." She assured in her rush, slowing at the entrance, she offered the man a smile. "Thank you." She whispered before breezing by, slipping out the front door with Julia trotting high on her tail. "You owe me big time." She informed in a rough whisper. "I want details, dates and a chart laden with evidence. You hear me? All of that in minute specks. You do know how big this is, right?"

"I know." Julia assured dully, already apprehensive in the telling of the rest. "Give me a week, okay. One week, and you'll have all the details you need, I promise."

"One week." Vanessa warned softly. "Or I might be forced to resort to drastic measures, like—like going through your garbage or something like that."

"You won't have to resort to that, I promise. And if you tell Carol, tell her the same thing, okay. One week."

"You got it." Vanessa chirped. Opening the door of her car, she affected a sultry mien. "Now go have some fun."

"Call your doctor, please. And in the meantime, you need to stay on your side, and keep your feet up, okay?"

"Keep your feet up works just as well for you." She laughed, dropping her body behind the wheel. She tossed her purse on the floor at her feet.

Julia rolled her eyes tolerantly at the comment and smiled, knowing that that was just a trivial part of what would befall her in the next week. "Do you want me to come with you to the doctor?"

"No. I'm sure I can get him to see me somewhere in the middle of rounds. I'll call you if I need you." She smiled, knowing, with all certainty, that she would not, not on an important weekend as this.

"Okay."

"Julia." Vanessa called softly. "Don't kill him, okay?" She teased, winking impishly behind the jest. "Save some for another day." She giggled as her car rolled in retreat, waving one last time before she fled.

Julia offered a brooding smile as she pondered the next segments to come, setting aside the sudden pang she felt about voicing the truth. She closed the door with a gentle turn of her hand. Conscious that the two women were the only sisters she had, she wondered if that, in-turn, would make the matter harder in the telling. Or would it glide as sweet as a breeze?

Michael smiled as she reentered the room, still draping the entrance. He folded his arms boastfully across his chest. "So…? Now, what was all that talk earlier?"

"You know, I am…sooo…crazy in love with you." She purred, smiling brightly as she leaned her back against the cool surface of the wall.

"Prove it." Michael challenged gruffly.

"I seem to recall someone started a certain kiss that never got finished."

"You remember that, huh?" Michael drawled, unfolding his arms as she neared.

"Oh, a girl never forgets a treat like that." Julia smirked, leaning into his chest. "Not when it comes to that."

"That's a good thing to know."

"I hope you've already eaten because you have a lot of work ahead of you." She droned, brushing a kiss against the corner of his mouth.

"I came straight here." He hummed, flaunting a lazy smile. "Straight to you. This way we address one appetite at a time. The one that's more needing that is. We'll pick our way through the other as we go."

"Man, have I missed you." She purred, blowing such news in the aperture of his mouth, as if to give them and the man the life from her very own lungs. Although, such bulletin, in truth, needed not be said, as *she*, in a blink, became the prey to the predator in him. The joy of being absorbed in his arms engorged her every sense, as home, for her, had never felt that good before now, not before him. In attestation of her view, Michael swung her from the floor in a silent flash, hastening in a trice to the comfort of their bed.

Thoroughly appeased with the pinnacle of their romp, the two reposed in the middle of the bed. Fully sated, Julia's head now rested as a topping on his chest, and her eyes, though seeing, were unfocused. Michael drew his head back and smiled, grounding out the taunting remark. His hand moved over her buttock in a slow glide. "So, tell me again how crazy you are about me?"

"Always greedy, aren't you?" she whispered, kissing the side of his neck.

"Guilty as ever," Michael assured proudly, his hand moving slowly up the soft trenching of her back. "Fine, then I'll tell you. I'm crazy about you." He growled. "I love how fragile you look in my arms, yet knowing that you're not."

"How can you see me, when you seem so…busy?"

"I don't need my eyes to know what's going on. I see you with my hands and my mouth, and your taste is addicting by the way." He grunted, his words seeming to grate the back of his throat. "I see you through your sounds, wild and sinful that they are. Having tasted you with my entire body, my eyes are just a bonus to the show. A great gateway of appreciation, that's all." He informed then, his hands roaming her body inquisitively, as if to reacquaint himself with something forgotten.

"Here, why don't I help you with that?" Julia carped, rolling from his chest. She pressed a pillow under her head as she stretched out on her back. "Go ahead, enjoy your view." Sliding her legs slowly apart, she trapped both hands behind the press of her head. "You do know there are no new parts, right? Nothing new has grown since you saw me last."

"It doesn't make the sight any less than what it is. It's beautiful." Michael vowed sprightly, his hands and eyes slowly tracing her body.

"But you've seen a lot of beautiful women naked, shouldn't you be used to it by now?"

"I don't think a guy ever gets inure to seeing a woman's body. Or that would eventually trounce any use of the necessary equipment needed for what we just did. Plus, they're all so different. So sweet, it's like candy. One species but…mm," He growled, looking up for a moment from his lustful scrutiny, he smiled. "And you…my…God, are by far the fairest I've ever seen."

"Nice words from the one whose only goal is to molest me."

"What can I say," Michael smiled, his eyes dropping to her stomach. A hand skied the hard carving of her hip in reply, aiding the vaunt of his fingers. Each digit orbited her navel on their quiet descent, working like the skilled tip of a feather upon her skin. "You bring out the devil at his best in me."

"Why, Mr. Dunhill, are you trying to persuade my thinking?" she crooned, liking the path his hand now travelled.

"But of course, is that not my job, Mrs. Dunhill?" Michael droned, frowning before turning his gaze on her. "Come to think about it, that's my only job, the only one you'll have me do."

"What else would you like me to have you do?"

"You tell me." He frowned, seeming suddenly troubled by the thought. "Life is strange, isn't it?" Michael muttered faintly, grumbling this to himself as if a question had not been asked. His gaze drifted slowly from her face, resting lightly in the distance, he smiled. "I spent my life running away from everything, being stupid and irresponsible and everything in-between. Even after I grew up, I still shunned every idea of commitment there was." He laughed, returning his gaze to hers. "Until I met a woman who didn't need me," He droned. "You made me want all the things I shied away from. But, now that we're here, do...I really have a job with you?"

"Michael...." Whispering his name softly, she waited with her eyes pasted to his face, waiting to be certain that he truly understood the meaning of her words. "I may not need all the things you're capable of giving me, but I certainly do need the man. I love you outside of everything that is purportedly defining: money, name or estate. You know that. And yes, I do love your body—maybe a little too much—but that's your own darn fault." She smiled, not fully intending humor. "If you lost your money tomorrow, would you want me to be with you then? I hope you know that I would. I don't care about your money, because I have my own. Granted mine is not anywhere near the same vicinity as yours, but I'm very comfortable with what I have, and I know you know just how much I care about the man himself. Besides, I never said you couldn't take care of me, I only said I didn't need to be."

"Then what's my job as your husband if that's true? What am I allowed to do?"

"Those are all the things we can fine tune in an agreement. We haven't had that discussion because you wanted to wait. Are we having it now?"

"I guess we are."

"Okay, what's your first worry?"

"I'm new to this role as a husband, and I don't want to use some of the marriages I've seen as an example. I need to know, what else am I supposed to be doing? What does a husband that's considered a good husband do?"

"Truthfully, there really isn't much more to it than what you're already doing. A husband loves and supports his wife. He's her friend, her lover and her confidant. Financially, he supports her, but they can also share that particular job."

"And that's it?" Michael asked tamely, his countenance seeming somehow confused. "I already know those parts. It just seems there would be more."

"Tell me what you want, because I'm with you. I want whatever you want."

"I don't know. I just want to be sure I don't mess this up."

"You won't. Not if you continue to put us above everything, the way you already do. You make us the most important facet above all else. How can anyone mess up doing that?"

"You don't find anything missing from what I'm doing? You don't want me to do anything else?"

"Michael, you can't be any more perfect as a husband. You are a dream come true, you really are. You make me feel loved just with the way you look at me. That alone gives you top mark as a husband."

"Are you sure? Would you tell me if I'm missing my target? Promise me you'll always tell me what you want. Tell me if I'm not getting it and that you won't scold me when I buy you something expensive." He smirked.

"I promise. As long as you can remember that you don't need to put yourself in hack, emotionally or financially, trying to please me. I already love you. I love all the things you did getting me here. I don't need a lot after that, just having the man is fine with me."

"You already have the man. He just wants to make sure the woman stays happy."

"She is. She is very happy. And once school is out, she'll be even happier once their living together as man and wife, so will you. Your husbandly roles should come more easily to you then. Especially once we fine-tune all the details of who does what and when."

"It better," Michael smirked, rolling his head on the pillow. He offered her a playful glare. "If I recall correctly—and I know that I do, since I wouldn't forget something as important as that—we will be trying for a baby then. I wouldn't want to forget that. I may miss out on all the fun."

"Are we fighting?"

"No! Wouldn't we need some anger to intermingle with that? We're just sharing the other side of our opinions, that's all." He chuckled. "Why? Does that bother you?"

"Why would it? Your feelings are just as important as mine. How would our marriage work unless that's a rule?"

"I promise not to go overboard, okay?" He pledged. "And to be open minded when you tell me that I have."

"And I'll try to be more open to changes, to fight the process a bit less."

"A bit?" Michael laughed. "That should be very interesting. I don't think I would know what to do with myself if all of a sudden things got easy."

"Hey! Watch it! I've been nice. I've given in—in time." Julia reminded sternly, slapping his arm in warning. Her eyes threw darts at his flesh.

"Yes. Yes you have. Okay, promise accepted then." Michael grinned, throwing back a playful smirk.

"Since we're here, what about a prenup, or an agreement of that sort, don't you want one of those? It's a little late now I guess, but...I'm sure something can be arranged."

"Not particularly." He shrugged, looking truly complacent with his thought.

"We should put that on our list to discuss." She in-toned, nudging him with her hip.

"You don't mind that?" he asked, looking almost hesitant with the discussion being had.

"Of course not! I don't want you getting your grubby hands on my money. So what if you're worth upwards of tens—as in times—more than me? That's beside the point. I've worked too hard for my money to have some stranger off the street take half. Wouldn't you agree? I have to protect my kids."

"I see your point." He smiled, brushing back the strayed strands of her hair. He gave heed to her urging with an artful rumble. "I'll look more closely into ways of securing my assets."

"Good. I'm glad to hear that. So, are we done? Because I'd really like to get back to my job as head of this welcome party,"

"Right..." he drawled, his smile broadening. "My welcome, mm, you know me like a book."

"Enough talking, I have a much better use for your mouth right now." Julia crooned, straddling his hip in a slow climb. She seasoned her kisses with all the emotions she had welling inside. "Let me take you riding so we can loosen your kinks. A month is a long time to stay immotile." She purred, and his body in return saluted the persuasive diligence of her hands.

"I already have the reins in hand." Michael growled caressingly, his hands gliding slowly down her back. Smiling with amorous glee as said limbs settled promptly on her hips. His wife's body thence quietly straightened, assuming an equestrian carriage, she dragged her fingers over his chest. Her eyes closed as she quietly arched her back, lifting her hair high off her shoulders. She dropped the heavy mass down her back. His hands moved in a firm glide over the silkiness of her skin, teasing her body as their passion grew. Like a horse being pushed to its limits, his movements under her bred with alacrity, as rider and beast moved as one to attain a perceived destination. Michael's fingers greedily thread the wildness of her curls, pulling her down to him. His mouth singed her skin with its heat, taking the very breath from her body as they soared.

"Did you like the view?" Julia panted, once given the chance.

"Breathtaking." Michael assured hoarsely. "Now do you see why I always have a certain topic on my mind?"

"Would you like me to stop?"

"When hell freezes over, or when I've taken my last breath, that's for damn sure! Why would I want that, did you see me? I don't think my expression was one of complaint." He chuckled. "I'm staying right here in the gutter with you."

"What gutter?" she barked, drawing herself back. Julia stared down at him with horror tweaking her mien. "You can't be serious! You can't lump me in the same basket with someone as yourself?"

"I seem to remember, on many occasions, not being able to keep up with your creative mind." Michael droned. His condescending tone whipping back with skill, dark brows shot hurriedly to the ceiling in aid of his jest. "Or not being the instigator to a lot of our fun."

"But...but that doesn't make me as bad as you. It only makes me...playful." She cooed, touching her forehead to his, she purred. "You like playful don't you?"

"Ask me again in thirty years."

"That's your goal for our marriage, thirty years?"

"No. But reassessment can come at any time." He assured, lifting her hair from her shoulders. He removed a broken petal from her curls. The dim room grew suddenly quiet, as each occupant, in their musing, slipped slowly inside the peacefulness of their moods. Contentment, smothered in the guise of an ambient cloak, swallowed the simmering of a chuckle from the edge of their throats, leaving the space tranquil in the aftermath of their romp.

Chapter Forty Seven

"So where exactly is this place we're going?" Vanessa probed in a dry, skeptical tone. Her thin brows crimping at the perpetually verdant view. Absent was the welcome milieu of a city. Swapped with an ambiance of calm, trees painted the panoramic scenery instead. As each turn, it would seem, took them further from civilization than it should. "What kind of place is this supposed to be, anyway; a retreat?" she smirked, scowling as the next turn set them on a warped, pockety road.

"Something like that. Now stop asking questions. I'm taking you guys someplace special for lunch. I believe that's all you need to know." Julia replied coolly, ignoring the gauged expression that was sent hurling at her face—fingered much like the pricking of a sword. Carol's head swung curiously in almost a full revolution, orbiting near three-hundred-and-sixty-degrees. She craned her neck to assess the full gamut of their surroundings, her scrutiny setting the backseat to a constant flutter. Always her quiet, inquisitive self, she added her usual hums to whatever adage Vanessa spilled. Sounding, at times, like a soft resonance churning in the wind, her gentle nature affected that of a sheep being bookended by the formidable mettle of wolves.

"What kind of special place would be around here?" Carol whined, and her timbre sounded much like the riff of a belligerent child. Her eyes again scanned the wooded scenery inquisitively, their icy tint ablaze with the depths of her wonder. "You know," she began in an absentminded hum, leaning forward from the comfort of her seat. "I've seen the movies." She warned in a soft voice, a stark contrast to the inference her words now implied. "This is the kind of place two friends take their self-labeled third wheel when they decide they've had enough of her annoying questions. This is the dumpsite, isn't it? This is where you'll ditch the body after doing despicable things to your supposed longtime friend."

"Who says it's going to be you?" Vanessa chimed back quickly, adding fuel to flames and looking almost disgruntled at the thought. "You two are the nice ones, remember? For all I know, *you two* decided to gang up on *me*."

"Look!" Carol interrupted then, her hand jutting forward between their seats. "Now we can't go any further, there's a gate blocking the road." She apprised perplexedly, gazing almost timidly out the rear-window, she sighed. "Jeez, how are we going to turn around now?"

"We're not turning around, Carol, we're going through." Julia announced firmly, smiling faintly to herself, amused by their childlike ramblings.

"Through? Where is this place? And how the hell do you plan to go through a metal gate?" Vanessa prodded, again sounding incredulous. She peered tentatively out her window, seeing only the denseness of the woods, uncertainty wafted like a draught over her body. "We've been driving for a while, Julia, and now all we get is some damn gate blocking our way? Are you sure you know where you're going? I think it's about time you admit that you're lost."

"I know where I'm going just fine." Julia groaned, her voice almost scolding. Slowing to a stop in-front of the ancient iron gate, she asked. "Do you guys want to have lunch with me or not?"

"We do." The women chirped eagerly.

"Then all back seat driving stops right here and now, or I swear I will turn this car around." She smirked, eyeing both women in playful challenge.

"Listen to her." Vanessa grumbled, habitually the first to sound the signal with her bark. Though reality was more divergent than what it seemed, as she was more an overly affectionate brat than not. "She's loving all this power, isn't she?" she asked, directing her argument to the backseat. "She knows we're both dying to know what's going on, so she's dragging this out on purpose. I bet it's all to see how long we'll suffer through this torture she devised, as if holding out for almost two weeks was not enough of that. Maybe she thinks we'll give up." Vanessa grunted sulkily, rolling her eyes towards the sky. She folded her arms stiffly across her chest. "Maybe somebody needs to tell her that we won't." She sneered, dropping back in her seat. She pinched her lips tight as a finale to her rant.

"I'll be good." Carol whispered in follow, settling herself against the soft leather seat. She emulated the manner of an appeasing child. "I'm always good." She averred, and the interior of the car fell still as if to assent to the truth in her reply.

"Are we done now?" Julia smirked.

"We're done." Vanessa assured then in a gruff mumble.

"Then I guess we're ready then?"

"Ready for what?" Carol chirruped promptly from the back, forgetful of her promise in the trifling of a blink.

"For lunch, what else?" she declared calmly with an accompanying shrug, reaching under her seat. Her fingers moved lightly upon the remote, unbarring the blockade in their way.

"Okay, what the hell kind of place is this? And how come you know about it?" Vanessa scowled, biting out each word. She swiveled her body with potency in her seat. "I want to know that."

"It's no big deal, guys. I'll explain it later, really. Right now just know we're some-one's guest for lunch, that's all." Julia smiled, slowing the vehicle in anticipation of the herculean gate that drew ever near.

"More gates, who are these people, paranoids?" Vanessa crowed as the distant gate cleared to their focus. "And what's this, their secret chapter?"

Stopping, Julia repeated identical measures as before, her attention tethered to the wrought guard as she spoke. "Your fangs are showing again, Vanessa." She commented blandly, smiling out the windshield before throwing her friend a smirk.

The iron gate opened like the weighted pages of a book, widening until it granted them entry. In subservience of such, it jerked tamely to a stop. The car fell silent as she furthered their drive in the woods. Leisurely rounding a deep curve, the rough lane suddenly grew smooth, unveiling the long cobblestone driveway ahead. Scraps of the vast estate paraded in the new openness that sat before them, bringing their attention to the mansion at once.

"Nice!" Vanessa attested sprightly, gaping as a small piece of the specular sight came to their view.

"Ho, ho, ho, I know this one!" Carol proclaimed eagerly, pointing a finger elatedly towards the roof. Her eyes strongly favored her uniformly sound feathered friend. "She's a member of some secret society, and we're here as part of the initiation."

"If I'm already a member, why would I need the initiation?" Julia queried tamely, eyeing her friend in the rearview mirror.

"Oh…right." Carol huffed, seeming confused. She slammed her back roughly to the seat.

"This is why you don't get to pick the movies when we go, Carol. You're terrible at it!" Vanessa laughed. "You had me there for a second, though."

"Oh, I know." Carol chirped, unaffected by the assertion of her friend's words.

"Is this a private club?" Vanessa probed, her eyes swollen with awe. "It looks like it would be." Giving the answer quickly to herself, her gaze scanned the surrounding woods.

"Are you coming ladies? It's the best way to find out." Julia goaded, showing off the full weight of her smirk as she parked the vehicle within treads of the front entrance.

"Are you sure we're supposed to be here?" Carol asked in a soft, timid voice. "This place is really nice, but…I don't see anyone else around." She frowned, glancing hesitantly at the grounds. She again turned to her friend. "That may not be a good thing, Julia."

"Would I take you someplace where there's even a remote possibility you'd get hurt?"

"No."

"Then get your asses out here now." Julia exclaimed gruffly, exiting the car. She hurried up the steps to the door. The curved metal handle swung free with the gentlest touch, and both women rushed forward, in an instant, to be at her side. Hovering like a split cloak at her back each looked both daunted and awed at the same time. "Hello!" she called as their feet drummed noisily across the hardwood floor. "We're here!"

"Who are you calling?" Vanessa whispered, leaning to her friend's ear.

"Our host," Julia retorted almost as soft, looking back at her friends. She smiled, seeing that they now gaped with the vigilance of children perusing their first haunted house. So intent was she on the comical traits of their expressions, that she almost knocked Betty flat on her back. Turning the corner, the two came face to face within a wan hair of inflicting harm. "Betty! Oh my goodness, I'm so sorry. Are you okay?"

"I'm fine." Betty smiled, squeezing her hand affectionately in reassurance of such.

"Betty, I'd like you to meet my truest and dearest friends in the world—sisters in fact. This is Carol, and Vanessa." She smiled, bouncing her hand blithely in-front of each. "Guys, this is Betty." Julia hummed, making the introduction light and to the point.

"Hello." Both women sang in response, nodding their heads in foster. They smiled reservedly at the petite woman's soft gaze.

"Nice to meet you," Betty smiled.

"Betty is the one solely responsible for the decadence of our food. You'll be in love with her at first bite, I promise." Julia chuckled. Returning her attention to the older woman, she asked. "Where's our host?"

"Waiting for you in the family-room," Betty informed softly, offering her hand in acceptance of Julia's coat. She turned her attention upon the women intending to tender the same, receiving, instead, a tentative stare in reply.

"Give her your coats, ladies! It's fine." Julia smirked, straightening a wrinkle in her shirt. She affected the posture of a parent placating her children. "You do want to be comfortable, don't you?"

Michael stood as the three women entered the room like a soft flutter though the air, offering them a wide grin. He moved coolly towards the entrance, intercepting their progress halfway.

"James!" Vanessa called with high exuberance, feeling the levels of her apprehension drop with the sight of a familiar face.

Dressed in dark slacks and a silvery-gray shirt, his attire spoke boldly of wealth. Unreserved, for the first time under their clear perusal, he wore no hat to obscure his face. "Hello, Vanessa, Carol." Michael hummed, offering both women his hand. "It's nice to see you again." Michael chuckled, taking a stance next to his wife.

"You're the host? This is your place?" Vanessa probed, looking confusedly at her friend.

"I am and yes." Michael assured in a soft hum.

"But…why didn't you just say we were having lunch with James?" Vanessa grumbled, glaring now at her friend. "It would have saved us all the anxiousness and wonder."

"Actually, it's…Michael." Julia advised weakly, barely glancing in the direction of her friends.

"What?"

"Well…we're having lunch with…Michael."

"Michael? Michael who? I thought your name was James?" Vanessa asked worriedly, her frown deepening to resemble a scowl.

"It is. James is my middle name, my name is—"

"Oh, my God! It's him! It's you!" Carol cried haughtily, stilling the rest of his words. Her eyes flew wide as she turned stunned gaze upon her friends. "It's him!"

"Him? Him who?" Vanessa quizzed with a soft irritant attached to her voice. "Who're you ta—" clambering to a sudden stop, her voice dropped to a freshly deadened space that sprang between them. A hand, in benevolence, flew protectively to her mouth, shielding the aperture, as if to stop some parasite from seeping in. Both women spun, as one, to their friend in shock. Bewilderment and a reservoir of emotions, yet to be discerned in either likeness or vaunt, followed sharply in pursuit of realization. "That's not...?"

"Yes it is!" Carol confirmed with certainty, her eyes swerving back in assessment of Michael's face.

"You're sleeping with Michael Dunhill? *The, Michael Dunhill?*"

"Yes." Julia flinched in attestation, her voice lifting like a soft breath through the quiet room. Seeming more like a child affirming the truth of some naughty deed, in silence, she allowed the first shock to sink in. Gifting them time before throwing in the additional perks.

"You're sleeping with *Michael Dunhill, the, Michael Dunhill* and you didn't tell us? You didn't think that that little bit of news was jaw dropping enough to share with your best friends?" Vanessa asked in a tight whisper.

"Well...it's kind of a long story."

Sealed like a trap detecting its prey, Vanessa's mouth clamped shut in an instant. Her only rejoinder came in the abruptness of her turn, pulling Carol along as she slumped to the nearest seat. She encouraged their hosts to follow suit.

"How long?" Carol asked shyly.

Julia glanced at her husband before giving her reply, understanding their reaction, though fretful of the ones to come. "Since... April." She blurted in what seemed a single breath, her face contorting to an odd set as she braced herself for the consequence to come.

"April!!!" both women screamed, ignoring the sharpness of her cringe.

"April, of last year?" Carol asked calmly, though the question was, in truth, an unnecessary one.

"Yes."

"So when we met him at your house, you two were already...?"

"Yes."

"But you told us you were arguing about work!" Carol chimed, sounding almost skeptical at the realization of her friend's lie.

"I'm sorry. I shouldn't have said that. It wasn't quite true. Well...actually, it wasn't at all true. It was a lot more frightening than that. I'm sorry, guys. By the time I realized what was going on, there was just no short, easy way to give you the truth."

"Why didn't you say something? Anything? Why would you hide that?" Carol asked tunefully, her voice, as always, sweet.

Michael folded his arms arrogantly across the broad width of his chest. Reclining further in his seat, a heavy smirk graced the features on his face, seeming then the clever fox. He awaited the intricacy of her response.

"Don't even start." Julia warned him softly, judging that the question gave her husband far too much pleasure to be fair. "Well…you see, I'm…I, I wasn't exactly…dating him." She informed in a whisper, her gaze lengthening the statement like visual cues on a plaque.

"No! You? No-way!" Vanessa exclaimed in a flash, her body jutting forward in disbelief. "You don't—" she started, halting once her friend's head bobbed in assurance of the truth.

"What? What?" Carol queried as the conversation progressed to wordless communication between the two.

"She was having fun with him." Vanessa explained hurriedly, her gaze staying constant on the other of her friend, as insight dawned on the situation at hand.

"Oh." Carol sighed. "Wait. What? You? No!"

"So now, do you understand why I wasn't exactly in a hurry to tell my best friends I was being a plaything for one, Mr. Dunhill?"

"Eh," Vanessa shrugged. "I guess."

"Plaything?" Michael howled, his deep voice breaking the women's melodic hum. "Don't make me out to be the bad guy here. I asked you out on several occasions."

"He asked you out?" Carol probed, sounding dubious in her query, her eyes again wide.

"Thanks, dear." Julia moaned, tapping her hand firmly on his thigh. She stayed the chance of further comment.

"You're welcome." Michael smirked, seeming happy with himself. "Why would you want them to make me out as the bad guy, if I recall yo—"

Julia's hand instantaneously became a lid for his mouth, sealing the cavernous gap. She forcefully barred any telling of his side or his truth. "As I was saying," she smiled, looking casually at her friends.

"So are you guys dating now? Is that why you're telling us the truth?" Carol smiled, liking the playfulness between them.

"Not…exactly," Julia grunted, her expression quickly sobering from the lightness it once held, and her hand pointedly dropped as she straightened in her seat.

"What does 'not exactly' mean?" Vanessa asked in a rush, her voice low, though somewhat stern.

"Well…" Julia groaned, and her face again became the prodigy for some contortionist's hand. Rummaging anew through the recess of her mind, she hunted for a truly painless way to tell her best friends she got married without as much as a word.

"Have you seen anything about me in the news lately?" Michael asked, swiftly coming to his wife's rescue. "Well, the tabloid news mostly,"

"Just tidbits about the scene you did with some audience member on the Oprah show." Carol chimed. "Pretty slick by the way. What better way to get everyone buzzing about your new movie? Are you almost finished? I want to see it."

"No." Michael spat coolly. "There's no movie. It was just staged to look as if there was."

"So you just went through all that for publicity?" Carol groaned.

"No. He went through it for me." Julia punctured softly. "The whole thing was all a rouse for me."

"What? Why? Was he trying to get an answer from you?"

"Yes…in a roundabout way."

"He wanted you to see him propose to someone else to get an answer from you?" Carol asked spiritedly, sensing a quick flutter in her chest.

"No." She sighed, taking a deep breath. She gave the truth in a whisper. "He proposed to me. That person they keep talking about…is me." Sounding again like a confessor on his death bed, she gave over her darkest crime.

"You!" Vanessa roared, her voice of a sudden like a blanket in the room, smothering everyone in the spill. "Are you two getting married?"

"More like…got…"

"What?"

"We…*got*… married." Julia stuttered faintly in reply, slamming both hands immediately to her ears. She squeezed her eyes shut as if to bar all orifices from an impending blast. Both women gazed at each other in silence, and their mien, instead of the expected shock, exhibited disbelief.

"So…you're…married?" Carol asked in her soft tone.

"Yes."

"To *him*?" Vanessa added calmly.

"Yes."

"You're married to *Michael Dunhill*? *The, Michael Dunhill? Him*?"

"Yes." She retorted in a fine whisper, dropping her eyes to the floor in wait. Gently, Michael's hand covered hers, lending his support. He offered then a tender squeeze. "Aren't you going to say anything?" she asked without looking up.

Carol casted stunned, questioning eyes to the woman at her side, unwitting of where to start. Her mouth hung open as if to await some new torrent of words. In return, Vanessa gaped back dazedly with no clue as to a response.

"Are you mad?" Julia asked wearily, casting a worried glance in the direction of her husband. Her gaze again scouted those of her friends. Michael pulled her roughly to his side, kissing the top of her head. He nestled her face against his chest.

"You guys are really married?" Vanessa queried at last, waking from her stupor. She monitored the interaction between the two.

"I'm sorry I didn't tell you, guys. Everything just happened so fast." Julia shrugged. "I just…well—"

"Yeah, yeah, yeah, whatever!" Vanessa barked, waving both hands dismissively in a wide arch. She further propounded her view. "It's already done, we'll get over it." She grunted, deepening the set of her frown. "Give me the juicy details. That's what I want, like where, how, time and place. I want to know all of that. I want to know everything."

Julia's look was one of great relief, her beautiful face cracking with a smile, though her eyes showed a small streak of surprise.

"What?" Vanessa shrugged grouchily. "You're my best friend! What am I supposed to do, stop talking to you because of *this*?" she hissed. "You've earned the right to be impulsive at least once. Even Carol has been more impulsive than you."

In a flash, Julia erased the space between them, pulling her friend in a bear-like embrace. She planted a loud kiss on her cheek. "Thank you. Thank you. Thank you." She murmured softly to the back of her head, squeezing her tighter as she pulled Carol into her side.

"Whatever. Don't even think to jip me out of my story with that." Vanessa warned.

"So everything he said in that proposal was real, and that was you he was talking to?" Carol asked.

"Yes, it was."

"He proposed to you in public?"

"Yeah," she beamed, glancing up at her husband then.

"When did you guys get married?"

"A few weeks before Christmas. The same day he asked, actually."

"The same day?!" Vanessa howled dubiously, her voice again swallowing the room. "Okay, here's the deal, and I don't give this lightly, but I have to admit. I have a newfound respect for you and the tactics you opted in this case. Even more so than I gave to James when I thought he got her to bend." She chirped, turning her attention on the man. She smiled. "The fact that you got our girl to break out of that strict regimen she had, would have been enough to garner my attention. But you got her to take a step and do something impulsive, and that makes you more than okay in my book."

"Thank you. I appreciate that." Michael smiled, gathering the scowling mien of his wife, he asked. "Am I being kicked out now?" he rasped, sensing she wanted the time together with her friends.

"Thank you." Julia chanted in reply, smiling pleasantly at his insight.

"You're welcome." Michael hummed as he stood. His eyes lingering on her face before he sauntered from their view.

"Julia! Oh, my, God! He looks even better in person!" Vanessa chirped.

"He is yummy, isn't he? God, I keep thinking my appreciation for that will dim, but, so far, it hasn't happened yet."

"He asked you out and you said no?" Carol asked with unabashed dismay.

"I thought he was looking for his next conquest." She shrugged, sounding humorous.

"So?" Vanessa groaned, showing her own dismay. "It would be worth it just to touch that damn body of his."

"So what made you change your mind?"

"He tricked me."

"What? How?"

"After having his partner send me an email saying there was a problem with my script. He had me over under the pretense of work." Julia smiled, easily remembering the day and her reaction. "Instead, he had a romantic lunch planned. He went all out, too. It was beautiful. Three-quarters of the way through, I was the one asking to kiss him."

"*You* kissed him?" Carol murmured sharply, her eyes wide with wonder.

"Good for you."

"Well...he kept trying to kiss me before, but I wouldn't let him. So this time he waited for me to make the first move, and man, did I almost get swallowed."

"You're kidding?"

"Nope, and I probably should have just let him have his way, because that's kind of how the whole thing got so muddled between us."

"What do you mean 'kind of'?"

"Jesus, you guys are going to have me give you all the embarrassing parts, aren't you?"

"Consider it penance." Vanessa grunted. "Now, what do you mean 'kind of'?"

"Well, I...kind of...came back...in the middle of the night."

"That good, huh?"

"Oh, if ever there was an understatement, it would be that. We're talking toe curling." She crooned, leaning back against her friends as the three huddled close.

"Good!"

"Where'd you get married?" Carol chirped then, leaning in tighter against the two.

"Right here. Michael and his mother did everything. He even bought me the dress. Can you believe that?"

"You're kidding." They sang, both voices sounding like a sigh.

"Oh, it's so...beautiful! You want to see it?" she asked, her face brightening with the exuberance of her smile.

"Yeah! Where is it?" Carol asked eagerly.

"Come on. It's this way!" Julia gushed, hurrying to her feet. She interlocked her arms with the women now flanking her sides, and the three seemed to skip, more so than walk, from the room.

Michael looked up from his desk and smiled as she entered, a grin brimming on her face. "Hi." She sang as she drew near, her eyes bright with girlish excitement.

"Hi." Michael murmured back.

"Hi." Vanessa hummed, looking as cheerful as she was content.

"Ladies," Michael droned.

"Hi." Carol chimed lastly, brandishing a gentle wave. The three disappeared from view as the door closed quietly at their backs, and a burst of laughter broke through the silence like the thudding of a gong. It signaled then a celebration at hand. The quiet returned but only in spurts, for laughter continued to dominate the full eminence of the space. And he could not help but savor the pleasantness of that.

———

March bowed its wobbly head to the joyance of April, and winter, at last, died with the perseverance of spring. Days warmed majestically, and the sightings of vibrant buds grew prevalent at every turn, as plants prepared to welcome the season that bestowed them life. Inside two households, elaborate changes stirred the rafters of both. Eclipsing the season with the escalation of thus, already underway, movers were now scheduled to compress two into one.

Invitations for their upcoming wedding went forward without hitch. Informing only those who were already cognizant of a reprisal date, gratified no rumor swirled in pertinence of that. The kids and their father being the only exception in the weaving of that truth. Although, her ex-husband's appraisal-packet was less invitational than it was enlightening, affirming an earlier conversation that the two already had. The venue for their nuptials remained exactly the same, with his mother again vaguely aiding—or so the matter appeared to her skewed vision—since she fully undertook the responsibility of seeing it all done.

By the time May rolled into June, one school's dismissal saw the kids enrolled in a new, eliciting excitement as well as apprehension from both. Rachel took her time getting use to the impending address change, troubled mostly by the depleted contact with her best friend. Yet the house, their secret society with Betty, and the handy proximity of her fretted destination, soon took care of that.

The mock wedding was almost as beautiful as the first, duplicating much from the other. It went off without fanfare or flourish. With a small gathering of guests at dusk, the two, again, exchanged their vows by the pool. Julia wore an elegant, yet simple summer gown, beautifully designed as a wedding present, by none other than Sarah herself. Her gown bore similarities to her first in meager spots.

With a second ceremony witnessed anew by God, fully attested to by kids, family and friends, it officially registered her as a married woman, free to live with the man of her dreams as husband and wife. Compensating such event, there would be no more scant weekend visits from this day on. After this, there would be no arduous goodbyes lining their path. No more wishing the person you wanted most was already by your side. The sequential wedding night marked the first in a true beginning. The start of a life primed with endless possibilities now danced before them. Tonight, the two furthered the sequence with the commencement of family.

"Okay. I'm ready." Michael murmured hoarsely.

"I can see that." Julia purred in answer, looking him over and seeing he was most certainly that.

"I love you." He whispered, touching his lips lightly to hers.

"I love you." She sighed back, pressing herself close. "You're shaking."

"I know." He groaned. "I'm nervous and excited at the same time. This is a huge step. I can't believe we're finally here." He hummed, brushing his hand down her body. "I know what we need to do. But…is there…anything you need me to do…differently?"

Julia smiled sweetly in answer, understanding the importance of what he asked. She slowly gathered his hand, bringing it to her breast. She rested it atop the soft dome of flesh. "Do you know how you devour me every time?" she crooned, smiling as awareness shone bold in his eyes. "I want it just like that. I want to lose myself in you. Bathe in the love you give me, and float away with the beauty of what I see in your eyes. Just continue to love me like that every time. Don't you dare change one thing."

"Thank you."

"For what?"

"For coming into my life, for teaching me how to love, for saying yes, for this, for everything, but most of all for making me so damn happy."

"In that case, I thank you for not giving up on me." She purred, wrapping her arms around his neck, she kissed him soundly, stroking him with the warmth of her breath as she validated their intent. "Let's make a baby."

"Mmm, lets."

———

With the year again dwindling at its end, the house buzzed raucously with the bliss of holiday cheers. Betty floated about the rooms happily outdoing herself at every turn, and there was no stopping her exuberance or her drive.

Christmas morning saw the children eagerly slashing at a small mountain of gifts, with Hyacinth, Betty and her mother happily cheering them on. It grew almost arduous, even with an in-depth evaluation of the scene, to discern who was more ecstatic of the group, as the older women's excitement saw them up well earlier than the newly conjoined household itself.

Morning left to see the children dashing off to their dad's, leaving the adults behind. The afternoon drifted deliciously on a euphoric cloud. Filled with the hums of garrulous grownups, laughter and music did well to take its place. The day held itself at a standstill while the adults slashed through the vibrant decoupage masking their own presents, a meager task, considering the sparseness of the fare, as traditional gifts were not usually exchanged by the Dunhills. An exception made on her behalf, viewed an induction, if you will, to the newly formed family unit she was now a part of.

"Okay guys," Julia began in a soft, cascading voice. "This is not much, but when I saw them, I thought only of you." She smiled, handing each identically wrapped boxes, none of which was any bigger than the snack-pack of a raisin. "You have to open them at the same time, okay. So…" informing them this, she paused, awaiting an indication of their readiness, Julia smiled. "One, two, three, go!" she yelled with full excitement, and her eyes twinkled with glee as she watched their fingers work with full diligence, each now hurrying to unmask the tiny gift.

Michael was the first to complete the miniscule task, frowning curiously. He stared at the small metal "A" in his hand. Betty's nibble fingers followed him quickly in that race. Her small face was almost expressionless as she studied the convoying "B" though the skin on her brow soon returned much the same look that Michael's held. Hyacinth's hazel eyes gazed confusedly at the "Y" she now held, while Delia rested the final "B" like a delicate quill across her fingers.

Each, in their wonder, turned curious gaze upon the other in the room, a silent question streaking from their eyes in a, not so, silent petition for clues. Turning their eyes, before long, on her, they awaited her explanation to make clear the game.

Julia sat back slowly with a silent sigh, her arms folded serenely on her lap, and brown eyes, in careful leisure, gaped back at their watchers with curiosity tinging their depths. A soft smile played with the corners of her mouth while she waited, watching to see who would be the first to solve the puzzle she gave.

"What exactly are we supposed to do with them?" Michael asked with an amused frown, gazing at his wife for the scant trace of a clue.

"What exactly do you think you're supposed to do with them?" She asked tamely, smiling softly. She shifted awkwardly in her seat.

"Well…" Michael's eyes rushed anxiously to each face, searching for a hint of recognition, though they all wore the same befuddled expression as he, for each now displayed their letter with a muddled stare. Slowly, the sparks fired in his head, and the answer came, like a bolt of lightning, slashing through his skull. "No! No-way! Really?"

"What? What?" Hyacinth asked excitedly, ignorant of what bulletin her son just figured out.

Betty studied Michael's face with meticulous care, turning in time to gauge Julia's response. Her eyes plucked the details they gave, and it took her only an extended glance to recognize the reason for his excitement, for the answer was now inscribed boldly on their faces. Jumping from her seat, Betty cackled in glee, launching herself across the room. She almost settled on Hyacinth lap in her rush to share the news. "Yes! We go it! We got it! I can't believe it! We got it!"

"What?" Hyacinth grumbled, still blinded with confusion.

"Baby! We're having a baby!" Betty answered in a tight, almost breathless sigh.

"Baby! Baby? You're going to have a baby? You're pregnant? I'm going to be a grand-mother?" Hyacinth reeled, each question flying sharply behind the other. She looked as frightened as she was ecstatic.

"Yes." Julia confirmed in a muffled cry, her voice drifting from deep against her husband's chest, stationed there in a strangled-like hug.

"I'm going to be a grandmother?" Hyacinth asked yet again, turning her gaze on her son, who, by now, had his wife locked in an embrace that was sure to steal her breath. "I can't believe it! Yes! Yes! I'm going be a grandmother!"

Michael sat back finally and smiled, wiping the moisture from his eyes. He gazed intently at his wife—soon to be the mother of his child. "I can't believe it. I'm going to be a dad." He rasped.

"Congratulations you two," Delia murmured, wiping the corners of her eyes.

"Yes! Congratulations! Yes, of course, congratulations!" Hyacinth added in a frazzled haste. With all signs of her elegance lost, she stumbled gauchely over each word, and could do naught to stem the flow of her tears. "You guys keep going grander each time." She crooned. "This is the second Christmas you've made exceptionally special. What do you guys have planned for next year?" she asked through the streaming.

"We'll just have to let the baby take care of that, mom." Michael answered hoarsely, pulling his wife into his chest. He kissed the top of her head.

"How does it feel, son? Knowing you're about to become a father?"

"Like nothing I thought it would. It feels…wonderful." He sighed, gazing down at his wife, love illuminated in his eyes like fulgent rays of light. "I love you." He whispered near her ear. "More than everything,"

Epilogue

The hospital room grew precipitously quiet, holding itself suspended in the rupture of cacophonous cries. Julia's yelps of pain lessened to the soft mewing of a whimper. Hence, it twirled through the room like the brewing of a wail, sifting roughly from the back of her throat. In an angst trice, her dewy body slumped graciously back, accepting the meager respite for what it was. Her breath sailed through the quiet like the flutter of a kite.

Michael wrapped her fingers snugly in the anxious grip of both hands. Loosening the grasp of one, he wiped the beading sweat again gathered on her brow. Beneath the tender employ of his hand, her chest heaved with the weight of each pant, as her body, fastened in a feverish fight, labored wildly in its sough of cessation. Regenerating the energy already spent, it ferreted the precious commodity of a simple breath. Stocking the necessity before the next contraction commanded, not only her will, but the waning volume of her strength.

Tired lids fell, as if to seek solace from the occurrence at hand, and her head swayed as if to settle some issue now running through her mind. Michael sighed glumly to himself, pressing her fingers to his lips. He covered the seemingly delicate digits with the other of his hand, feeling the anxiety of her agony writhe potently through the stratums of his body.

"Aaaaaggghh!" Julia howled in acquiescence of the pain, though mere seconds was all that passed before the splendor was again rent, and its clout almost levitated her body from the bed.

"Good! Good! Okay, here comes the head." The doctor announced softly, although ample excitement smeared the professional harmony of his tone.

Michael tightened his grip in support of her quavering body. Hunched forward in the summoning of energy she so zealously dispelled. He peered anxiously towards the doctor's hand. A small show of, what could be, dark wet hair was all the detail he discerned, realizing a sudden desperation for more. He lengthened the determined reach of his neck.

"Michael." Julia called raspingly between pants, seeing the eagerness in his eyes. She recognized the full enormity of his wish. "Go. Go so you can see your prophesied daughter take her first breath."

"Are you sure?" he asked, sounding in part ecstatic.

"You only get to see your first child being born once, Michael. Go."

Filched in a flash, there was no time to acknowledge the offer once made, or even to aid his accordance with a smile. Stopped short in his response, the next contraction took commanding hold, wrenching her body, a long cry rumbled croakily from her throat. Julia pulled her hand free from the support he lent, amplifying the contraction with every ounce of her strength. She waved off his hesitation with a small flick of her hand.

Michael reached her legs in time to see wet, matted hair become a head with a face attached. Looking limp in the doctor's astonishingly rough hands, nimble fingers worked on the cleansing of the nose and face. Julia bayed in consensus of her next step, and her body again shook under the pressure she applied, promptly dispelling their child in the doctor's ready hand. A muffled cry enveloped the room as a result, and he could neither draw breath nor laughter to offer as an aid of such sight.

"Congratulations, it's a boy!" Dr. Parker announced cheerfully, partnering the nurse's soft bellow of applause.

Julia sighed in approbation of her burden spent. Dropping her body laggardly back to the softness of the bed, she looked set to expire with the slightest swirl engendered in a whistle. Yet she smiled brightly in acknowledgement of the doctor's gleeful account, happy the ordeal was now done.

"Would you care to do the honor?" the doctor warbled, his thick brows jutting in a hurry to the ceiling, applying what looked like a clamp on the umbilical cord. He offered Michael the handle of a scissor already attached.

Nervously, Michael took hold of the proffered handle, set almost flush with a similar kind in the doctor's hand; he worried on the chance of hurting his son. Warily, his hand trembled as he applied a tender press, finding the cord more durable than it looked. He gave forth a second effort to see the job done.

"We have a son!" He whispered hoarsely as they carted the baby to the other side of the room. "I have a son!" Michael informed yet again, eyeing his wife with a soft glimmer of astonishment concerning that fact, tears doused the dark fringes of his eyes.

"So that's what that darn tickle was." She sighed, too tired to smirk.

A halfhearted smile leapt to Michael's face in rejoinder of her jest. Escorting the frail fall of silvery streams, liquid grazed the top of his cheeks in reply. "I love you." He whispered as he shadowed her side, resting his forehead on the pillow now cradling her head. He draped an arm gently across her shoulders. Julia's eyes opened slowly in response, and her smile showed its full concurrence in the dispersal of his love. Across the room, the sound of their son's wails played like the refrain of a resplendent sonata to both ears, swapped, like a new riff in an old song. One died joyfully while the other played anew.

"Say hello to your son," the nurse muttered as she drew near, carrying the new born close to her breast, she smiled drolly at the pout on his face. "He's a healthy six-pound, seven-ounce tiger who's in some hurry to meet his mom and dad."

Gently folding the baby in her arms, Julia's once depleted body instantly rebooted itself alive, and beautiful eyes grew magnificent as she gazed lovingly at her new son. "Hi." Julia whispered to the stirring form resting by her breast, feeling Michael's face pressing immediately close, hazel eyes grew jubilant with the emotions he felt. Caressing the pinken baby, now quiet in the crook of her arm, he beamed with assiduous pride. "Would you like to hold him?" Julia asked softly, and watched as his expression wavered through the sentiments that furrowed astoundingly near. Happiness and fear mingled promptly as one, though happiness, sturdy in its might, won in a flash, and at thus, he folded his arms in preparation of holding his son.

Julia placed the baby against his chest as he leaned his body close. Swallowing the infant in the powerful fold of his arms, he gently lowered himself to a seat by her bed. Myriads of emotions poured forward in a flash, playing on the handsome features of his face. It flounced in the scuttle of a single tear.

The tiny rivulet did not rush down the sloped channels of his face as is probable, but walked boldly with the grace of a swan. Like a stream afloat with shards of crystals, it sparkled with the brilliance of flawless diamonds. Set in the darkness of a million midnights, and reared in the blackest wilderness ever made. Voiced in great volumes, it bellowed in octaves past the limits of ears, and warmed like the sun at the edge of its reach.

Thus, it proclaimed itself valiant in echoes that waded like an ancient chant. It preached endless in a gaze trimmed, now, with moisture, and eyes that never wavered from the treasure in his hand. Falling light in a long, soft breath, it sits in a glance that prickled the skin and embraced the chambers of one's heart. It was a father freshly abreast of his new self. A replica of his own image now resting warmly in his arms, and there was no parallel to the reverence he felt. As it spoke with the resonance of a hundred orators all lifting their voices at once, though it came to two small ears in a whisper.

"Hi." Michael croaked softly, his voice as soundless as a stealth gust in the heat of a mortar jungle. Long fingers stroked the tightly balled fist in his hand, too fragile for anything but. He brought the tiny limb to his lips for its first in a series of kisses. "It's daddy," he announced hoarsely. "I've been looking forward to this meeting for a longtime. I love you." Michael sighed, again kissing the tiny fist. "He's so tiny—so soft! He's beautiful!" He whispered in a strained, excited voice, finally looking over at his wife. "He's perfect. You're perfect." Michael sighed, returning his attention to his son. "Do you hear that William? Daddy thinks you're just perfect." He smiled, brushing away a tear that spilled quietly to his cheek.

"He looks like a William, I think." Julia whispered in acquiescence of such, feeling beautifully thrilled with the sight before her, as it warmed her entire being to witness the richness of his love.

"William. Paul. Dunhill." Chanting the name without lifting his eyes, he smiled. "It does seem to fit better now that I can look at him." Michael averred with a broadening smile, his eyes drifting for but a moment from his son. "You're named after my father and my brother. It's a fitting name for a son, it suits you." He declared in a whispery tone, giving full attention to his son.

The last of the bustling stopped before long, and all personnel drifted, at long last, from the room, leaving the family the privacy they needed to bond. Michael held the tiny body of his new son close, refusing to relinquish the possession in his hand. He watched serenely as the infant slept, his eyes hardly veering from the features of the baby's face.

"I thought for sure we would have had a girl. Even after they hinted otherwise, I still held out hope." Offering an endearing smile, Michael's gaze again dropped to his son.

"I know. But I'm glad we had a boy first." Julia informed wearily, shifting her weakened body on the bed. "This way your family's name will endure for at least another generation to come. We'll try for the girl next time."

"Next time?" Michael asked in a musical hum, his eyes finding its mark on her face. And a smile broadened with the telling of his thoughts.

"The next time," she nodded, smiling sweetly as if to land the lure of a new game.

"And how many…next times are we talking here?" Michael droned, his deep timbre given in the way of a caress.

"How many would you like?" she asked tiredly, though her voice still held the same granules of sugar as before. "Within reason, of course,"

"My heart is already set on a little girl. A house full of those would be nice. I'm not picky." He shrugged.

"A house full, huh?"

"Or two, like I said. I'm not picky."

"Two sounds doable. But what if you get more boys, what then?

"Then I'm sorry for you, because I want my princess."

"A princess, really?"

"You bet." He smiled, looking down at his son. "I already have my queen."

"How close to the heir are you looking for this princess? I mean, some recovery time might be nice." She yawned, settling her hand as an added cushion under her cheek.

"I'm recovered, aren't you?"

"Just about, in another two hours I'll be rearing to go." She assured, carefully straightening her body on the bed.

"Is that so?"

"Absolutely, don't believe all that hype. Child birth, please, what a drag."

"So should I just climb up and get to work then? Think of the stories we'll be able to tell about the conception of this one."

"Well, we do have the room for…what? another hour perhaps? And while you're at it, we'll see if they can stir the pot and maybe hurry the process along."

"Hey, it has been almost two weeks, so I may just take you up on that."

"Not so, you perv," she groaned, knitting her brows in disbelief. "I believe I was quite generous only this Thursday past."

"Generous? Oh, yeah," Michael drawled, his eyes growing distant. "That you were, I almost forgot. But then...so was I."

"True." She smiled, assenting to his point. "How many people do you suppose have this type of conversation in a delivery room? Not much I bet."

"What's wrong with this conversation?" he asked innocently, brandishing a beautiful smile.

"Nothing, dear, nothing at all," she chimed, yawning with the lyrical reply. She adjusted her head on the pillow with a smile. "Do you think you'll put our son down now? I'm sure he'd like to rest. You do know the nursery will be coming to get him shortly, right?"

"He *is* resting."

"Yes, but a little less hand wouldn't hurt."

"Me? Have you met my mother? You'll be lucky if his feet touch the floor for the first two years of his life, and then there's Betty. Jesus, maybe we should move. You do realize the kids have three grandmothers, right? Two that's downright desperate, I might add. You know," he smirked, gazing down at his son. "We could say we're going on vacation and not come back. Get a little chateau in the countryside of France, just us and the kids."

"And what about *my* mother?"

"She can come, too. She's not as overbearing as mine."

"Let's do it. Oh, wait!"

"What?"

"I promised your mother lunch—often. Remember?"

"You could fly back for that. What do you say, every other month?"

"If that," She groaned.

"Twice a year would be good enough for her to have a visit with the kids, don't you think?"

"Sounds fair to me."

"I'll start on the plans."

"How long do you think it would take them to find us?"

"With Betty and my mother working as a team, two days max." He smiled, gazing again at his son. "I guess I should let everyone know then. Are you up to it? You look tuckered out."

"Maybe only for a short visit, suddenly I feel as if I'm fading fast."

"Close your eyes. I'll do the entertaining this time. I'll just send my mom a quick text so they can all have a peek." He assured, setting his fingers to the task.

"Okay. If I fall asleep and you need help ask Vanessa, okay. Not that you would, not with Betty and our mothers around. But I can guarantee you that Vanessa has everyone already scrubbed and wearing masks by now. Since Taylor's birth, she's become something of a germophobe."

"Some...?"

"Okay, a lot."Yawning, Julia rolled onto her back, pulling the blanket over her shoulders, her lids slowly lowered.

"Thank you for my son." Michael smiled, gathering her hand, he offered a gentle squeeze.

"Just leave the money on the table when you go."

"I hope I have enough."

"I'm sure you don't, but we can come to some agreement; installments, perhaps."

"Good. I'm glad to hear that. I'd hate to rock the boat so soon, not with Stephanie waiting in the wings."

"Stephanie?" she queried in a gruff tone, her lids fluttering open with what looked like surprise.

"What, too old?"

"We'll talk."

"As well as other things I'm sure."

"And, as always, you're blessed with a one track mind."

"What? I meant…lunch. What did you think I was talking about?"

"Just that…lunch."

"Cerebral dominance, that's why I married you, you know. That tight ass and your voluptuous lips had nothing to do with that cause. Give me the drear of arithmetic any day over one's riding habits and I'm gone." He growled, brushing her fingers with his thumb.

"I do remember you saying something to that effect in your second proposal. Something to the fact, I think, of you needing me to solve puzzles and read you bedtime stories until you fall asleep." She purred, taking hold of his hand. "It's what pushed me over the edge, you know. It's the very reason why we're here today."

"See, good memory. I'm glad there's no misconception between us. You do your job and I'll keep doing mine."

"Hey, do you realize with William's birth, it assures that Richard got his wish after all? There'll be no taming his glee."

"I'll make it up to Rachel."

"Got some grasp on the future, do you?"

"Why not? It worked before. I see no reason why my princess should not be a foretelling."

"Oh, poor man, a besotted fool, I presume?" she teased, tilting a single brow to accentuate the mark of a sweetly given jeer.

"To the very dregs of his being, was there even a doubt?" he hummed. "I should think, that, too, was already etched in the prognostic."

"But no less a pitying sight."

"Recoup your vigor with all due haste and I'll show you the real stench of pity." He growled, his eyes lending some assistant to the roughly spoken words.

"Sir, I'm afraid I must warn you that such blatant pledge will have my husband set to lay you low."

"That fool? The poor dolt is ten times as bewitched as I am, he'll never see it coming."

"Ever the cocky one, aren't you, Mr. Dunhill?"

"But as I've told you, Mrs. Dunhill, you may title it hopeful if you so wish. Oh, here they come. I love you."

"I love you."